MR MURDOCH IS DEAD

MAMIE PHILP

Publishing in the UK by

Rothiemay Publishing

For Margaret

CONTENTS

Friday 14th October 2022

THERE'S BEEN A MURDER

CHAPTER 1

Mr Raymond Murdoch was found dead in the history cupboard at the end of the corridor next to the stairs, face down on the concrete floor surrounded by shelves stacked floor to ceiling with books and clutter. It was Friday morning, the last day of term before the October holidays.

At about quarter to nine, his boss, the Head of Department, Mrs Caldwell, had gone to the cupboard to make space on the shelves so that she could tidy away some textbooks. When she opened the door, she found Mr Murdoch, lying face down, taking up all the floor space. At first, she thought he must have collapsed and hit his head. Her first aid training automatically kicked in. Without moving him, she had done some basic checks, establishing that there was no pulse at the wrist or the neck and no signs of breathing. Furthermore, he was already cold.

She shouted to the other history teacher, twenty-four-year-old Ellen Shaw, to get help and shooed away the cluster of students that appeared in the corridor outside the cupboard, firmly closing the door. She was careful not to move Mr Murdoch. After what seemed like hours, Ellen flung the door open again with paramedics following closely behind. They confirmed that Mr Murdoch was dead and called the police.

.oOo.

At the time of the discovery, I was sitting at the breakfast bar in my open-plan lounge/kitchen/diner drinking a double espresso, contemplating my last weekend before starting my new job on Monday. Lost in thought I barely noticed the aroma of fresh coffee that filled the room. Staring through the glass door into the garden shared with the flat upstairs, towards the houses in the next street, the greyness of the sky seemed to match my mood. I was wondering if I had done the right thing, coming back to Ayrshire, the county where I'd spent my teenage years.

When I left, I'd vowed to never come back. And yet, here I was at thirty-eight, newly promoted to Detective Inspector and ready for a challenge. It had taken time to get to this level and I'd worked hard for it. However, I was in no doubt I would have to prove myself up to the job. I had to hope that leaving the city would be worth it.

Everything here would be different to the life Patrick and I had in Glasgow. No more stepping outside the tenement flat in the West End to the sounds and buzz of the city; bars and restaurants on the doorstep. Now it was this traditional ground floor flat in a sandstone terrace in the small town of Troon, which hadn't been part of the initial plan.

We were supposed to have moved to Troon together. We'd chosen it because it was only forty-five minutes on the train back to Glasgow and decided we wanted a change of scene. For me, that meant living near the sea, minutes from views to Arran with its dramatic peaks that were ever-changing with the light and weather. Patrick had agreed, had even appeared keen and we'd had an offer in on a modern detached house on an estate a couple of miles away from here. However, in the end, he had chosen not to come and I cancelled the new house, forfeiting the deposit and found this place.

Two months ago, sitting at the dining table by the sash window in our second floor flat, he had suddenly stopped talking, glass of wine halfway to his lips and looked at me before telling me he wouldn't be moving with me. Apparently, he'd had enough of my irregular hours and the disruption to our plans which would only get worse with my promotion. That was it. No preamble, no prior indication that anything was wrong. For a moment I had sat there, open-mouthed in shock, before a surge of anger had taken over. I'd upended my plate, tipping my meal across the table. Not my finest hour. Only equalled, perhaps surpassed, by what happened when I left last week.

I'd planned to leave while he was at work but he'd turned up at the flat unexpectedly. My suitcases were in the hall and I was standing by the sash window in the kitchen, espresso in hand, waiting for my taxi. I hadn't expected to be waved off given that he'd stayed out of my way, moving into the spare room the night I'd thrown the spaghetti at him. It turned out he'd wanted to tell me he'd met someone else. When the taxi arrived, he'd had the audacity to pick up one of my suitcases and that had pushed my anger over the edge. I'd grabbed the nearest object and hurled it with force towards the opposite wall, smashing it to smithereens. It was an antique vase, our favourite wedding present. I didn't feel guilty about it; betrayal doesn't sit well with me. And in that moment, I had decided that our marriage was over.

Sipping my coffee, I reckoned that in a few days, I would know whether I was right to make the move. When I left Ayrshire, I was eighteen, a recruit taking up a police officer's post in Glasgow. I served my two years' probation, applied for, and got, my traineeship. Being a detective was what I had wanted, I think because I needed to play my part in getting justice for victims. I refuse to think I might have had more personal motivations but can't rule that out. I didn't want to accept that's maybe why I came back. I passed the exam easily, made sergeant after eight years and ten years later here I am, about to head up a team, the boss, knowing the job inside out. I was confident about that. So, what was it that unsettled me so much? Inside I knew the answer, but didn't want to acknowledge it. I got down from the stool to stand by the door leading into the garden. It was bare, a patch of grass surrounded by wooden fencing and a clothes line slung across the middle. It needed cheering up. I regarded my small patio and resolved to give it some colour, fill it with pots of flowers in the spring.

My thoughts were interrupted by the ringing of my mobile, amplified by the granite countertop. I was surprised to see that it was Detective Chief Inspector Lewis, my soon-to-be boss. The last time I had spoken to him was across the table when he interviewed me three months ago. I put my phone on speaker and his voice reverberated around the room. 'Good morning DI Berry. Kim. We've a dead body at one of the schools in Ayr. Thought you might want to start early.' He outlined what he knew so far and I felt my stomach clench, hoping that he wasn't about to confirm my fears. Unfortunately, he did. The room suddenly felt cold and I was glad he couldn't see the slight shake in my hands. I forced myself to listen, suppressing my apprehension.

Lewis wasn't really asking whether I wanted to go in to work. This would be my first investigation in charge of the team and he knew I would want to, probably should, establish myself as soon as possible, rather than play catchup. 'This is what I'm here to do,' I told myself. Pushing the nerves aside, I began to feel excited at the prospect of taking charge of the case, that my years of hard work were paying off. Assuring Lewis I was on my way, I gulped the rest of my coffee and hurried through to the bedroom to get changed.

Forty-five minutes later I stepped out of my car, looked up at the 1960s building and took a deep breath. A swathe of unexpected emotions that I thought were well buried confronted me. The uneasiness I had felt earlier hit me harder now that I was here and I had to blink several times to rid myself of the images crowding into my mind. I shook my head as if to shoo them away, determined to focus on the job ahead.

The DCI's call had brought me back to Riverwood Academy, the first time since leaving twenty years ago. The building on the outside hadn't changed much. Mainly concrete, red wine-coloured panels and windows. It sat in parkland next to the university, not far from the river. Glancing towards the woods, beyond the playing fields, I shuddered and quickly turned away. Doubts went through my mind again. Had I done the right thing coming back? Standing here, surrounded by bad memories, I wasn't so sure. 'Get a grip, Kim,' I muttered under my breath.

Turning towards the entrance, I smoothed down my trousers and adjusted my jacket. Running a hand through my hair, I tucked a loose strand behind my ear, briefly regretting having it cut into a chin length layered bob last week. The hairdresser had said it would suit my square shaped face. But it was too short to tie it up out of the way. I shook my head, emptying my head of such thoughts. 'Focus on the job, Kim,' I thought, 'and you'll be fine.'

Taking a deep breath and pulling back my shoulders, I brought myself out of my reverie and took in the scene in front of me. An ambulance and two police cars, blue lights flashing, were parked up close to the front entrance. Lined up on the concrete playground to the side, as if on a fire drill, were what I assumed to be all the students and staff. Someone had obviously already taken charge of the situation and decanted everyone until deciding what to do next. Thankfully, it wasn't raining and it all looked well organised.

There was a strange sense of calm. The fire alarm had been stopped and the students stood in their lines whispering to each other while staff strode up and down ticking off names. There was no shouting and jostling, instead a subdued atmosphere suggesting that everyone suspected something bad had happened. I needed to find out exactly what was going on.

I crossed the rough tarmac to the front doors, all the time pushing back that wave of memories. I showed my badge to the uniformed officer who nodded in acknowledgement and opened the door for me to step through. Inside, the foyer looked as I remembered it, from the tiled floor to the wood panelling on the walls, the trophy cabinet and war memorial. There was also that peculiar smell. The collective body odours of about a thousand students on the move that no amount of cleaning fluid could mask. A glance through the open double doors to my left provided evidence of the morning's assembly. Chairs were out of alignment and papers strewn over the floor. The beginning of what they expected to be a normal day.

A short man wearing a pinstripe suit approached, obviously waiting for my arrival, and moved a little too close into my personal space. He introduced himself as the headteacher, Andy McGregor. He'd already spoken to Detective Sergeant Fletcher and arranged for the evacuation of the building apart from himself and the office staff who might be needed to gather information. I looked at the man regarding me expectantly, glad that I didn't recognise him, and thinking here was someone with an acute sense of their own importance.

Keen to get to the scene of the incident, find out what was going on and take charge, I nodded and turned towards the stairs. At the second floor, a uniformed officer had been stationed at the double doors that led to the history department. I flashed my badge and he handed me a set of barrier clothing. I quickly donned the suit and shoes; the last thing I wanted to do was contaminate the crime scene. Making my way along the history corridor, I wondered if all I had to do was agree with forensics on-site that foul-play was unlikely and wrap things up. It would have been a wasted trip but at least I had shown willing. Ahead of me, I spotted a familiar figure, DS Peter Fletcher, taking notes in his flip book. From what I could see, Pete hadn't changed much at all. His brown hair was speckled with grey, but he still looked good for his fifty-three years.

I couldn't help feeling pleased to see my erstwhile boss. Pete had been the Detective Sergeant I worked with in Glasgow when I was a Detective Constable. I'd learned a lot from him. In fact, when Pete had taken a sideways move to Ayrshire, his job had become vacant and I got that promotion. I have a lot to thank him for. However, it had been years since we had seen each other, even though we'd always said we'd keep in touch. I hadn't spoken to Pete since getting the job and wondered how he felt about it. In the meantime, the main thing was that his approach to crime solving was as reliable as ever. If he was the Pete I remembered, no detail would be missed and, right now, he seemed to be on top of the situation.

I tapped him on the shoulder. 'What's the story so far, Pete?'

He swung round to face me and smiled, but not too much. Knowing Pete, he would think it inappropriate in the circumstances. 'Thought you weren't starting until Monday.'

I returned his half-smile. 'Lewis called. He said there had been an incident reported at the school. A dead body. He asked if I wanted to start early in case there was something to it. You know Lewis - not a request. And you know me of old, Pete. Even as a rookie, I never liked to be on the backfoot.' I paused and nodded in the direction of the history cupboard. 'Looks like it might be serious.'

I looked around me, taking in the familiar yellow walls, the long corridor with classrooms off and the stairs either end, avoiding the nook next to the stair well where I knew there was a toilet. Bringing myself back to the task in hand, my gaze finally rested on the body, lying face down, about four metres away. There was a fair amount of blood and I was aware of that metallic taste, like iron, on my tongue.

I wondered who it was and, as if reading my thoughts, Pete filled me in on what appeared to have happened. 'Victim is Mr Raymond Murdoch. At first, we thought he might have fallen and struck his head on a shelf but the head injury's too severe for that. And the wrong angle. I'd say at least one blow to the back of the head.'

'Mr Murdoch, you said?' I asked.

'Yes, Ma'am,' he replied.

I caught Pete's eye. It felt strange for him to call me 'Ma'am' but I would have to get used to that now I was his boss. I shrugged, turning my attention to the job in hand, and forced myself to look back towards Mr Murdoch's body.

'You alright?' Pete's voice broke into my thoughts.

He'd obviously noticed the fleeting look of shock that had crossed my face when he'd mentioned the teacher's name. Pete wasn't to know that in my mind I saw one of the younger teachers with curly dark hair flitting about the corridors of the school, always smiling. I looked at him and nodded. 'I'm fine, Pete.'

I turned back to the crime scene. From what I could see, the cupboard was dusty and untidy, piled high with books and stationery. An old metal filing cabinet was tucked into one corner. The available floor space was taken up by Mr Murdoch's six-foot frame. I took a deep breath. 'Any sign of a weapon?'

Pete responded, 'No. Furthermore, Mrs Caldwell, the teacher who found the body, also Head of Department, was clear that she had to unlock the door to get in.'

'Have you found any keys?' I asked.

Pete had already checked that out. 'Not so far, and there's no evidence to suggest that he would've locked himself in there. The cupboard is sometimes used for changing but there were no clothes to suggest that. Nor any other reason he would lock the door, no secret stash of alcohol, for instance. Whoever did this must have locked the door.'

It was clear to me that this was, indeed, a case of murder, manslaughter at best. I felt torn. On the one hand it was just my luck that my first big case since being promoted and starting a new job was at my old school and a teacher I had known. Not that I was going to tell anyone that. At least not yet. If DCI Lewis knew there was a personal connection, he might take me off the case and I didn't want that. I would have to keep my emotions in check. On the other hand, I was excited to have the opportunity to prove myself and take charge of the team.

CHAPTER 2

Nodding at the mortuary crew waiting for permission to remove Mr Murdoch's body, I approached the familiar figure of Duncan Cain, the forensic pathologist who was crouched over Mr Murdoch's body. I had known Duncan for a long time, as did Pete. Duncan was a leading authority in the field who, in addition to his own cases, was often called to be a second opinion if needed. I'd worked with him a few times and was glad to see him on his home patch, working on my case. I knew the search, recovery, and analysis of evidence from the crime scene was in safe hands. 'Initial thoughts, Duncan?'

Duncan stood up and smiled broadly at me, exuding an air of confidence that goes with the experience of the job. He had one of those smiles that lit up his eyes, genuinely pleased to see me. In his late forties, I couldn't help but notice that the years had been kind to him; no signs of grey in his dark hair and only a hint of crinkling around his eyes. 'Good morning, Inspector Berry. Or may I still call you Kim? Nice to see you again. And congratulations, of course.'

I felt my face go a bit red, realising I should at least have said hello. 'Thanks, Duncan. Sorry. I've never been one for small talk.'

He gave me that smile again and carried on. 'There's nothing wrong with being focused on the job.' He paused, rubbing his chin. 'I would say Pete's assessment is right; a blow to the back of the head resulting in a depressed skull fracture is the likely cause of death. And one blow could have done it.'

I stepped closer to Mr Murdoch's body. 'Any idea on timing?'

'I would estimate he's been dead since sometime yesterday afternoon or early evening. Full rigor mortis has set in which takes about fifteen hours. His body temperature is consistent with those timings, although I will have to wait on toxicology to see if anything like alcohol in his system interfered with that. And given he was teaching yesterday afternoon' - Duncan paused to think – 'maybe sometime around the end of the school day would be my guess. I'll be able to confirm things when I've had a proper look.'

I nodded. 'OK, thanks, Duncan. Let me know if you find anything interesting during the post-mortem. Especially relating to a likely murder weapon. Give us an idea what we're looking for.'

Duncan nodded and got back to work. I turned to Pete who had been watching and listening, making sure everything was properly recorded. 'What are you thinking?'

Pete looked at me. 'I don't think he would have seen it coming. No sign of a struggle. No disturbance to shelves, books, or anything else. No sign of anything that might be the murder weapon.'

I took a minute to think. This was huge. A school with almost a thousand students and over a hundred staff. Forensics would scour the crime scene for fingerprints, but loads of folk would have been in and out of the cupboard over the years. All the staff would have to be interviewed, starting with Mr Murdoch's colleagues in the Department, followed by his friends, everyone else and some of the students too. On the other hand, I'd be in the firing line if evidence was allowed to slip away.

Pete was waiting for my directions and I had to get it right. 'Who've we got assigned to the team?'

He was quick to respond, having already started to organise things. 'DCs Purves and Sutton are on their way. Bill Purves is a local and has lots of experience. Steady and reliable but, you need to know, he was very loyal to the old DI. Gary Sutton has been with us a couple of years. Very keen, wants promotion. Some uniformed officers are to be put at our disposal too. Oh, and there's also a new DC, Carmel Ilunga, recently finished her probation stint working on the drugs team. For the time being, I've asked her to stay at King Street to look up anything we need. Of course, that's now up to you.'

Pete assured me I could rely on Bill and Gary to do a good job. Having worked with Bill for a few years, Pete said he was a plodder with good attention to detail and the capacity to sift through mountains of evidence needed to get the conviction. I hoped we wouldn't clash because I tended to be more reliant on ideas and gut instinct to make progress, later backed up with evidence, of course. To get where I was, I'd had to prove I could be good at the detail as well as the ideas. If Gary was keen for promotion, likely he would gladly take on whatever was needed. I decided to leave Bill and

Gary to lead the interviewing of most staff and Mr Murdoch's students with uniformed help.

As Acting DI Pete had been thorough in preparing the ground for the investigation and so far, it looked like he was fine working for me. I knew he hadn't applied for the promotion himself but it was one thing to not want the job permanently and another to find yourself working for a previous subordinate. Only time would tell how it would work out.

Leaving Pete to put things in place, I walked along the corridor to Mr Murdoch's classroom. Coming to a halt in the doorway, I was caught by a feeling of being transported back in time, an image of myself as a teenager coming to mind. For some reason, I felt relieved that Mr Murdoch hadn't been killed in this room. Maybe that was because this had been his domain and my safe place. I blinked and forced myself to step inside.

It looked like it hadn't changed much in the last twenty or so years. The walls were a bright, almost garish, yellow like I remembered. I wondered if Mr Murdoch had ever been given the choice to keep it that colour and reckoned probably not. Somehow, I didn't think it was one he would have chosen for himself. The art work of the students on the white pin boards provided some welcome relief, even if it was carelessly displayed. The posters looked like they had been there a long time, drawing pins missing, curling at the edges.

The classroom was neither organised nor tidy. Rows of desks paired together all facing the front were out of alignment and there were books piled up on the window sills. Mr Murdoch's large wooden desk was covered in papers, closer inspection revealing a backlog of schoolwork waiting to be marked. Both desk drawers were locked. I tried a few times in case their age made them stiff but they wouldn't budge. I rifled through the papers on the desk to see if I could find his keys but, as Pete had already indicated, they were nowhere to be seen.

I paused, deciding that I could come back to the classroom later when I might have a better idea of what to look for and where to look. Closing the door, I spoke briefly to the uniformed PC in the corridor, confirming that no-one was allowed to go in there. Forensics were still busy in the cupboard looking for blood spatters, finger prints and any other evidence that might help us catch the killer. Taking in the scene, I felt my inner resolve tighten; I will find out who did this. I felt I at least owed Mr Murdoch that.

CHAPTER 3

Pete joined me at the entrance to Mrs Caldwell's classroom, the one next door to Mr Murdoch's. It was time to find out what the person who had discovered Mr Murdoch's body had to say.

I hoped that Mrs Caldwell wouldn't recognise me. In my school days I had favoured wearing copious amounts of make-up featuring heavy black eyeliner and mascara. My hair changed colour almost every week, the brighter the better to hide my natural mousey hair. Back then I wasn't Berry either, having opted to change to Patrick's surname when we got married. Not because I was traditional in any way, more that I liked the sound of 'Kim Berry' and I thought it suited me. I told myself that if she did recognise me, I would have to deal with it.

We removed our barrier clothing, Pete opened the door, held it open for me to pass through and followed me in. Mrs Caldwell was sitting at her desk staring at a document on the computer screen in front of her, her hands gripping a full cup of coffee. The room was a complete contrast to Mr Murdoch's, everything in its place, and the bright yellow walls barely visible behind posters depicting famous art and advertising museum exhibitions. A diffuser on her desk gave out the faint smell of lavender.

She didn't appear to hear us enter; she didn't turn round as we approached. Not surprising, given that she had discovered the body of her colleague a short time ago. She looked up when we pulled up chairs, startled at the scraping noise over the tiled floor, and sat down opposite her. I introduced us and, for a split second I thought she had recognised me. Thankfully, she looked away and, with a slight shake of her head, turned her attention to Pete, distracted by him opening his notebook.

Mrs Caldwell hadn't changed much at all, apart from her trademark jet black hair being streaked with grey. It was still cut in the same short bob with a fringe. She had always had a certain gravitas, with her tailored trousers and skirts, cashmere sweaters and sensible court shoes. When I was at school she had been regarded as efficient, thorough, yet fun.

I watched her intently as we prepared to begin the interview. She looked sad, her mouth turned down at the corners, eyes downcast, hands in her lap. My gut told me that she couldn't have had anything to do with Mr Murdoch's murder but nothing could be ruled out yet. I had to consider that she might be a good actress. She glanced at me and our eyes met again for a second before she began to stare at the mug of coffee cooling in front of her.

I gave it a minute or two before I started to speak. 'Mrs Caldwell?' I paused. 'Could you take us through what happened this morning?'

She raised her head and turned towards me, placing her hands on the desk, and interlocking them as if she was trying to gain some strength.

I continued. 'I know this must be difficult for you. But could you take us through what happened when you arrived in school?' A seagull screeched outside the window and flew off.

She blinked rapidly, glancing towards Pete before letting her gaze rest on her hands and speaking so quietly I struggled to hear her at first.

She had left her house about seven, a similar routine every school day. It was only ten minutes or so in the car so she was usually here by quarter past seven, depending on traffic. Today had been no different. A shadow crossed her face. 'Yet it had turned out so differently...' I couldn't help thinking.

When she arrived, she'd thought it odd that Mr Murdoch wasn't in his classroom because he was almost always in before her and it wasn't like him to be off. Furthermore, his car was parked in its usual spot near the door from the back playground. She had parked next to it.

When she reached the Department and saw he wasn't there, she had checked with the school office but he hadn't phoned in. She thought he might have left his car at school because he'd gone for a drink after work the day before. If he had got the bus, it took a lot longer to get in, possibly up to an hour stopping at the villages on the way from Cumnock.

On the other hand, she thought maybe he was too sick to phone anyone and no-one would know that he was ill; like her, he lived alone. It had never occurred to her that something might be seriously wrong. She had arranged for his classes to be covered and gone through to his classroom to organise his first class, all the while hoping he would turn up late and she wouldn't have to think about the rest of the day's lessons.

The room fell into silence as she paused, accentuated by the sound of the forensics team moving about at the end of the corridor on the other side of the door. She was obviously struggling to maintain her composure. It was clear to me from the way she spoke that the colleagues got on well, having worked together for more than thirty years. She took a sip of her coffee, which must have been stone cold, then carefully placed the mug on the table. She put her hands in her lap and took a deep breath before looking up to meet my gaze.

I kept my voice soft. 'Take your time. Remember as much detail as you can.'

She was still in Mr Murdoch's classroom when Ellen had arrived about quarter past eight. She remembered looking at the clock and thinking there was still time for him to turn up if he had got the bus. Ellen was as much in the dark as her in terms of what might have happened. They'd had a brief chat about looking forward to the holidays and Ellen had gone to her own classroom. Mrs Caldwell had left the materials with a note of what to do on Mr Murdoch's desk and returned to her own room.

She stopped talking, turning her gaze to the window, to the sky outside which remained a dark shade of grey. It looked like it might rain. I felt for her as what was to come would be the hardest part to describe. The whole thing had a sense of unreality about it, the only sound the scratching of Pete's pencil in his notebook. After what seemed an age, I prompted her to continue. 'What happened next?'

There was the usual commotion as the school bell rang and students made their way to registration. She had stood in the corridor as they jostled past her, laughing, and shouting as they caught up with their friends. When the bell rang again ten minutes later, she went to Mr Murdoch's classroom to wait for the class and cover teacher to arrive. Once everyone was there and knew what to do, that would be about quarter to nine, she came back to her room with the intention of getting on with some marking but the momentum was lost.

Having looked at the pile of papers on her desk she decided to clear away some textbooks instead. She had gone to the cupboard to make space on the shelves. When she opened the door, she discovered Mr Murdoch lying there, a pool of blood around his head. She stopped abruptly and shuddered.

I continued to watch her carefully, deducing as much as I could from her body language and facial expressions. She was obviously distressed, gripping the mug of coffee and staring at the contents as if looking for something. Her eyes remained downcast. Shoulders hunched; she bit her lip. Aside from what she had seen, it looked like something else was bothering her. When she at last spoke again, I could barely hear her.

She said, 'I feel so guilty; I did feel irritated that Raymond hadn't called in, that I'd have to sort out his classes. I shouldn't have misjudged him.'

I could see that she was trying her best to not break down, blinking rapidly and taking deep breaths. All I felt I could do was encourage her to continue. 'I know it's difficult, but try to give us as much information as you can remember.'

She met my gaze and said, this time louder and steadier. 'I want to remember everything for Raymond's sake. To help catch whoever did this.' She rolled her shoulders and sat upright. She described shouting to Ellen Shaw to get help, the paramedics arriving followed by the police. Despite feeling so distraught, she had to help clear the Department of students while waiting for the police to arrive.

I could only imagine how she must have felt, finding the body of her colleague, perhaps even her friend, like that and having to be involved in the aftermath. However, I had a job to do and ruling Mrs Caldwell in or out of any involvement in this crime was crucial. I looked across the room, not seeing the posters on the wall, instead picturing Mr Murdoch being taken away in a body bag in the corridor on the other side. I took a deep breath. 'I need to ask you... where were you yesterday afternoon and evening? When was the last time you saw Mr Murdoch?' I paused. 'I mean, the last time you saw him alive.'

She gasped. Yesterday she had been out of school all day for a meeting and in the evening, she had been at home alone. She had made a couple of calls from her landline which we should be able to check. The day before she had left for a dental appointment about quarter past three and had popped her head round the door of Mr Murdoch's classroom, waving goodbye because he had a class. That would have been the last time she'd seen him. She bowed her head.

I paused and looked out of the window, contemplating my next question, yet thinking I already knew the answer. The clouds moved quickly across the sky. Eventually turning towards her, I asked, 'Can you think of anyone who might want to harm Mr Murdoch?'

She stared at me; her eyes wide with shock. 'Of course not,' she whispered. There was no-one she could think of who did not like Mr Murdoch. No-one who might want to hurt him in any way. As far as she was concerned, he was the nicest man anyone could ever hope to meet. She thought he might have gone in to get some books and collapsed, hitting his head. That's why he hadn't been in his classroom first thing as usual.

She paused as if something had occurred to her and bit her bottom lip. If that were the case, the cupboard door would have been open and it had been closed when she arrived. She had unlocked it when she went to put the books away and found his body. Even so, she couldn't contemplate we would consider the idea that anyone would want to harm him. I turned away, finding a crack on the wall above the door. From my point of view, it was obvious why we would think someone would want to hurt him.

We looked at each other. 'Mrs Caldwell.' I paused, preparing for her reaction. 'Mr Murdoch was murdered.'

She could not conceal her shock. I had to tell her we would need evidence of her whereabouts the previous afternoon and evening. A routine part of the investigation, no-one could be ruled out at this stage. I followed her gaze to where the coffee mug had left a ring on her desk. All I could do was give her my details and ask her to get in touch if she thought of anything else. Pete and I left her sitting staring into space, grasping my card.

CHAPTER 4

We crossed the corridor to Ellen Shaw's classroom, which was located opposite Mr Murdoch's. Through the glass panel in the door, I could see the young teacher sitting at her desk, hands in her lap, evidently waiting for us to arrive to interview her. She had requested that Mrs Caldwell be with her but I'd made it clear that the interviews had to be conducted separately. On first sight she looked like she was in some kind of trance, most likely the shock of what was happening around her.

Ellen turned round when Pete opened the door and I preceded him into the room, making the introductions. I was surprised how young she was; she looked like she could not be that much older than some of the senior students. She looked ashen, emphasised by her hair being pulled back in a tight ponytail tied at the nape of her neck. Her dark eyes glittered against the paleness of her face as she turned to look at me.

Seeing that her desk was piled high with books and papers, Pete and I pulled up two chairs at the pair of tables immediately in front of it, indicating that she should get a chair and sit opposite. There was some hesitation, as if she didn't understand the instruction, before doing as she had been asked. Once she sat down, I could see how nervous she was, lips trembling, clenching, and unclenching her fists. I resolved to put her at ease, help her to remember the details.

Pete opened his notebook before asking her to confirm her name and status as a history teacher in her second year at the school. All the while I was weighing her up until eventually, I spoke. 'Miss Shaw, Ellen, could you take us through what happened this morning?' I felt no uneasiness using her first name. Mrs Caldwell was a different matter. Like Mr Murdoch, she was one of the teachers from my time at the school. It wouldn't be appropriate for me to call her Marina. I wondered if Pete noticed. If he had, no doubt he would let me know.

Ellen ran her hands over her hair as if checking that no strands had escaped from the ponytail. Her voice had a maturity that belied her years, taking me by surprise when she began to speak. She said she usually arrived in school about eight o'clock, always the last one in the Department. Mrs Caldwell and Mr Murdoch were early birds, but she always liked to run for at least half an hour every morning and that made her later than the others in getting to work.

She always stopped by the staff room to check her pigeonhole and pick up her register, often chatting to colleagues as she did so. She came upstairs about ten or quarter past eight and was surprised to find Mr Murdoch was not there. She spoke to Mrs Caldwell about it then left her boss organising his classes and went to prepare for registration. She was looking forward to being free after that to tidy up in preparation for the holidays.

So far, I hadn't taken my eyes off Ellen's face. Her jaw was set and her eyes wide, staring into space. I gathered she was reaching the most difficult part to remember. In the corridor outside, I was aware that Duncan was talking to the forensics team. Breaking the silence in the room, I urged Ellen to continue. 'What happened?'

She'd heard Mrs Caldwell call her name. She had been gathering books into the piles that sat on her desk, ready to find space for them in the cupboard. She liked to put away anything she wouldn't need next term and leave the classroom tidy. Throwing her arms wide to sweep the room, she gave a small smile. 'Seems so insignificant now,' she said. It struck me that Mrs Caldwell had said something similar, about being tidy. I looked around. Apart from the desk, there was no clutter and, rather than the posters adorning Mrs Caldwell's walls, these were filled with students' drawings.

Ellen followed my gaze before our eyes locked once more. She looked away. It had taken a few seconds or so to realise that Mrs Caldwell was calling her and when she went into the corridor, she couldn't believe what she was seeing. Mrs Caldwell was crouched over Mr Murdoch's body and shouted to Ellen to get an ambulance. She had immediately run down to the office which was quicker than waiting for someone to answer the phone from the classroom. She had called the emergency services and waited in the foyer for the paramedics to arrive.

Andy MacGregor had spoken to her and she had explained that it looked like Mr Murdoch had collapsed but that the ambulance was on its way. He had told her he had a meeting with a parent and trusted her and Mrs Caldwell to take care of it but keep him informed. When the ambulance arrived, she had directed the paramedics to the history cupboard and retreated to Mrs Caldwell's classroom to keep out of the way. Mrs Caldwell had joined her there once we had arrived.

She glanced at me, aware that I was still watching her intently. She lowered her eyes, and I followed her gaze to the graffiti carved into the desk. Probably a student carrying a penknife. A seemingly harmless object that could be used as a weapon. 'Why do I always think the worst?' I thought before pressing on with my questions. 'Ellen, I understand it would have been a shock. I must ask you, though. Can you think of anyone who might want to harm Mr Murdoch?'

As expected, Ellen responded that of course no-one would want to harm him, that everyone liked him. However, like Mrs Caldwell, I couldn't rule her out as a suspect. 'Where were you yesterday afternoon and evening?'

She had last seen Mr Murdoch at the end of the previous school day taking some books to the cupboard. She remembered thinking how unusual that was. It wasn't like him to tidy things away. She had called to him, making some comment about him turning over a new leaf, or something like that. He had laughed and waved at her. After she had spoken to him, she got ready to leave. She needed to get to the garage on Prestwick Road to pick up her car which was in for a service. There was no courtesy car available so she had used the bus which took about forty minutes, including about twenty-five minutes to walk to the bus station. She had left by the side stairs and crossed the playground rather than go by the main entrance. Once she had collected her car, she had gone home, eaten, then met friends in the Red Lion for a drink.

I waited, aware of the sounds of footsteps in the tiled corridor as the mortuary staff removed Mr Murdoch's body and the muffled sounds of Duncan and his team gathering every minute piece of evidence. Outside the chatter of students in the grounds waiting to give interviews or heading home, perhaps up town. Ellen continued to stare at the desk. There was nothing more to gain here. I'd ask Bill to take detailed statements from both women. I looked across at Pete who nodded; we had enough to go on for the moment. I explained to her that, as a matter of routine, we would be checking her movements. She didn't respond so, in unison, we pushed back our chairs and stood up. I handed Ellen my card and told her we would be in touch. We left her open-mouthed, staring into space.

CHAPTER 5

Back in the corridor, I felt my throat begin to itch. An occupational hazard, the cupboard having been sprayed with ninhydrin for fingerprinting, which always irritated my sinuses. I wanted to get outside and on the way have a chat with the headteacher to get some background information about Mr Murdoch, teacher, a body, a victim, a case to be solved. After saying our goodbyes to Duncan, Pete and I headed downstairs.

Andy MacGregor's office was lined with bookshelves stuffed with folders and box files. It smelled of cheap aftershave. The headteacher peered at me over a pile of papers on his desk, clearly perturbed to find Riverwood embroiled in drama. 'I don't understand. This sort of thing doesn't happen at our school.'

'Well, it has now.' I wasn't in the mood to pander to his concerns of what this might look like to parents and the media. My aim was to solve the crime as quickly as possible and part of that was to find out what information this man had that might help. I wasn't feeling optimistic.

As expected, Andy MacGregor confirmed that Mr Murdoch was a well-liked member of staff who had been at the school for thirty-five years. One of the stalwarts of the staff room, ready to dole out advice and jokes in equal good measure. He was considered a friend to other long-serving teachers and eccentric advice-giver to the younger ones. He consistently did a good job and was an amiable man, most of the time. Not that it made him a pushover; he would always make his voice heard if he felt something was wrong or unfair. Andy MacGregor couldn't think of any fallings-out nor anyone that might bear Mr Murdoch a grudge. Even most of the students liked him.

There were no surprises in what he said. I remembered Mr Murdoch as a popular teacher, amusing but strict. Although I would have to investigate every angle, I found it hard to contemplate that he would be anything but an innocent victim in all of...all of what? My job was to find out. I thanked the headteacher for his time, adding that a colleague would be along shortly to take his formal statement.

In the hallway, I turned to Pete. 'Let's get to the station. First day on the job and I've not even unpacked my stuff at King Street yet.'

Pete smiled at me. 'Nothing like being thrown in at the deep end. Just like old times. I'll see you back there.'

The quickest route to the police station was along Craigie Way, past the university campus, and on to John Street which followed the path of the river. The drive took less than five minutes. Pete was waiting for me in the car park, waiting to show me the way, considerate as always. I was reminded that Pete is a thoroughly nice bloke, and it felt good to be working with him again. We got out of the lift and headed along the corridor to the CID suite.

Allowing Pete to go ahead of me, I paused in the doorway of the incident room, taking it all in. Straight ahead were three pairs of desks facing each other with the DI's glass fronted office at the end. I caught my breath, remembering it was my office. To the right was a corridor leading to what looked like a small kitchen at the back, with a meeting room off to one side. My little empire, I thought and couldn't help feeling a bit excited. I walked slowly along the aisle, passing on my left what must be Pete's desk, obvious from the photos of Yvonne and the boys.

At the desk opposite sat a young black woman with immaculately braided hair tied into a ponytail, wearing a sleek navy jacket over a white blouse. This must be Carmel. She looked up as I approached, smiled, and got to her feet, introducing herself. We shook hands as I did the same. I took to her immediately. Her smile was warm and genuine. By all accounts she was a rising star and my first impression was a positive one. She had an air of professionalism and efficiency. It was good that she was new to the team too; she wouldn't be comparing me to my predecessor.

On the other side of the aisle was a set of desks facing each other, evidently belonging to Bill and Gary. Like Pete, Bill's could be identified by family photos whereas Gary displayed a photo of himself looking much younger, winning a medal for some sport or other. I had no qualms about Gary but got the feeling Bill would have to be handled carefully.

Reaching the office, my excitement rose as I pushed the door open. A large desk dominated the small room; two chairs in front of it and the big chair behind it facing back out into the incident room. There were a couple of filing cabinets against the wall to my left and that was it. I opened a couple of drawers and noted the place was empty apart from the furniture. All my predecessor's personal effects had gone, as well as all official documents. Everything in that office had been considered potential evidence because the previous DI had been suspended, then dismissed, after being convicted of taking backhanders to turn a blind eye to some serious drug dealings. I was happy to start from scratch anyhow; create my own space without having to clear out someone else's belongings.

Across from the door the window was almost the width of the room. I walked around the desk and stood looking out at the river towards the town. People would be out there, working, going to school, drinking, eating, taking drugs, sleeping. And everything else in between, good, and bad. I sat down in my chair and watched the comings and goings in the incident room. The team had loved working for the previous DI and been shocked at what had happened. I would have to prove myself the right person to replace him and that I would do the job with no margin for error or suspicion.

'Ma'am?' Pete's voice brought me out of my reverie. He was standing in the doorway, watching me curiously. I looked up and caught his eye, noticing again how little he had changed. He was wearing his familiar uniform of light brown chinos with a toning tweed jacket.

As far as working with Pete again, this morning was proving a case of so far so good. It was almost as if we were picking up where we left off, yet he also respected my new rank. He had treated me graciously and wasn't the type to feign his emotions. I would have to wait and see what happened when he disagreed with me, though. I took a deep breath, reminding myself that I had this. I know I'm not just a good detective; I'm an excellent detective, the reason I got the job. Shaking away the notion of creeping doubts, I turned my attention back to the task in hand. 'Sorry, I was miles away.' Pete nodded, handed me some paperwork, and returned to his desk.

Forensics and the post-mortem would take a few days, so all we had were witness statements and there might not be much to go on in those. The headteacher had given me a copy of the last school yearbook. Mr Murdoch had clearly been popular with his senior students as indicated by the many testimonials they had recorded there. I wondered again why such a lovely man could have his life cut short so brutally. Sometimes, a crime would get to you and this one already ticked the box. Not only because I had recognised Mr Murdoch but also, because it seemed he hadn't changed, remained one of the good ones.

I resolved to keep my prior knowledge of him quiet for now. Even though I didn't believe there was enough of a connection to get me taken off the case, I didn't want anyone to think it might cloud my judgement. My gut told me this was a senseless crime and I was determined to be the one who found the perpetrator.

My reverie was interrupted by Pete reappearing at the door, explaining that a neighbour had reported Mr Murdoch missing. He hadn't been seen since leaving for work on Thursday and the neighbour was concerned that he hadn't come home the previous evening, nor gone out again that morning. And his car wasn't on the drive. The neighbour had gone into the house to check he hadn't collapsed or something but it looked like he had simply vanished. They had keys to Mr Murdoch's house in case of deliveries and suchlike while he was at work. Deciding there was no time like the present, Pete and I set off to investigate.

I asked Pete to drive so that I could take in our surroundings and reacquaint myself with the area. The route took us along Holmston Road. Passing the cemetery on the right, glancing left I could make out Riverwood through the trees, the other side of the river in Craigie Park. I felt an involuntary shiver down my spine and had to make an effort to remain focussed on why I was here. Within a few minutes we were on the open road.

This was a landscape I remembered well, the bus route home. How I had hated those trips, shrinking into the seat, trying to ignore everyone else. Within minutes we arrived in Coylton where I had lived from the age of twelve. We passed the primary school on the main road. I never went there and maybe it would have been better if I had; as it was, I never made friends with other teenagers in the village. We had moved here after my dad took early retirement from the oil rigs. It was Mum's idea. She'd had lots of family holidays here as a kid and wanted to give living here a go. I'd been upset about leaving behind my life and friends in Aberdeen and never felt I'd fitted in.

It took only half an hour or so to get to Cumnock where Mr Murdoch lived in his family home, on Oakbank Drive. After university in Stirling, he had lived in Ayr for a few years when he first got the job at Riverwood but moved back in with his parents when their health deteriorated. That probably explained why he had never sought promotion nor moved to another school elsewhere.

Pulling up outside Mr Murdoch's house, a bungalow that looked like it could do with a bit of maintenance, we were ambushed by a sprightly woman brandishing a set of keys. She'd obviously assumed we were police and we pulled out our badges to confirm it.

She appeared excited at being caught up in some drama. Her voice was shrill. 'I've been wondering what's happened. I didn't see him go out this morning. You can set your clock by Mr Murdoch, you know.' The woman looked at me expectantly, arms crossed, legs apart. I didn't respond, waiting for her to continue, 'When I didn't see him this morning, I thought I should check, you know, because he lives on his own. Since his parents passed away...' She looked from me to Pete.

'Can you confirm the last time you saw Mr Murdoch, Mrs...?' asked Pete.

'Brown. Rita. That'd be yesterday morning, just before six thirty. I was looking out the window and saw him get into his car. I didn't see him come back after school, though, and his car hasn't been parked on the drive either. When I didn't see him this morning... That's why I phoned.' Rita suddenly stopped talking. I felt like I could hear the thoughts turning over in her mind. Somewhere close by, a car backfired. A look of disquiet crossed her face. The eagerness gone from her voice, she asked, 'Is he alright?'

I looked at Rita, thinking that for once it was good to have nosey neighbours. Whether she genuinely cared about him, or was more interested in having a role to play in the investigation, was hard to tell. Maybe a bit of both. Looking at her standing there in her tartan slippers, I wondered if I was being too harsh. However, there was no way to sugar coat the news, so I came straight to the point. 'I'm sorry to tell you that Mr Murdoch is dead. He was found at school this morning.'

Rita's mouth fell open in shock and, for a moment, it looked like she might faint. Pete stepped forward, putting a hand on her arm to steady her. She smiled at him, before gathering herself and stepping away. Pete walked away, taking out his phone.

'Are you up to a couple more questions?' I asked. She nodded. 'Is there anything you can tell us that might help us find out what happened to him? If there's anyone you think might want to harm Mr Murdoch?'

She shook her head. 'Raymond was a lovely man. A good neighbour, always polite, friendly. He kept himself to himself. Wouldn't come round for a meal even though we asked often enough. I knew his parents better. But he used to chat with Bert, that's my husband, over the garden fence. I used to take in parcels for him, that sort of thing, because he couldn't take time off. Surely, he collapsed or something? You don't think...' She stared at me, hands covering her mouth. 'If there's anything I can do to help...'

We both turned as a patrol car pulled up. Pete had called Cumnock police and waited for the uniformed officer to get out of the car. Rita watched intently, taking in the whole scene. I got the impression she was committing it to memory. It would be a story to tell her friends later.

'The officer over there will take your statement.' At the sound of my voice, she turned back to face me. 'And we know where you are if we have any further questions.' She nodded, but didn't reply. 'Are you alright?' I asked. 'We can call a friend to come round and the officer here will wait until they arrive.'

She shook her head but didn't move. Pete came over with the officer from Cumnock and made the introductions. Thanking Rita, I took the keys to Mr Murdoch's house from her outstretched hand and turned away, while she was propelled towards her own house.

CHAPTER 6

At the entrance to the bungalow, we put on our gloves and overshoes before Pete put the key in the lock. The door opened easily inwards. I went ahead and Pete followed.

We entered a small vestibule with enough space for a shoe rack with coat hooks above. Beyond that was a good-sized L-shaped hall which looked like it hadn't been decorated since the 70s or 80s. The floral carpet clashed with the striped wallpaper. The air was stale. Pete and I decided to get our bearings before taking a proper look around. The first room on the right was a large bedroom and opposite was a room which may once have been a dining room but looked like it was used as a study. The table was piled high with papers and books. Opening the door had caused a cloud of dust which caught the back of my throat.

'Murdoch obviously didn't spend a lot of time in there!' Pete remarked.

I felt a spark of indignance. 'I think we should refer to him as Mr Murdoch, Pete.'

'Mr Murdoch?' Pete was looking at me, a quizzical look on his face.

'He was a teacher, after all. It doesn't feel right not using his title. We should be respectful.' I tried to keep the note of defensiveness from my voice.

'Whatever you say.' Pete shrugged and turned away.

It occurred to me that he might have noted I had insisted on the same courtesy for Mrs Caldwell, but not Ellen Shaw. If he had noticed, it would re-emerge later so no point in worrying about it for the time being. That Riverwood was my old school is something I would be unlikely to hide from Pete for long. In silence we carried on our walk through the house.

Next to the dining room/study, there was a second bedroom which appeared to be Mr Murdoch's, given that the bed was unmade and several personal items were piled up on the bedside table. At the back of the house there was a living room and a kitchen with the bathroom tucked away to the right. The kitchen had a large window overlooking the garden at the back, dominated by a pine table in the middle and unfitted pine furniture against two walls. I could see the bits of dried cornflakes stuck to the bottom of a cereal bowl at the side of the sink which hadn't been left to soak. This would have been Mr Murdoch's final breakfast although he wouldn't have known it. I couldn't help but feel a twinge of sadness at the sight of that lonely piece of crockery.

The living room was large with intricate cornicing and a 1950s marble fireplace. This looked like the place Mr Murdoch spent most of his time. A massive television took up a whole corner of the room with a recliner armchair strategically placed for the best view. A sofa under the window looked neglected, used as a storage space for books and magazines rather than somewhere for guests to sit. Atop the small table within reach of the armchair was a half full bottle of whisky and a used glass, likely evidence of Mr Murdoch's regular nightcaps. The post-mortem should indicate if that were a problem or just a tipple.

Standing in the doorway, I pictured a bachelor sitting on his own each evening, watching TV and having a glass of whisky. At first, I felt a pang of sympathy for him but, who was I to judge if that was his choice? I'm no stranger to a glass of wine at the end of the day. How was I to know whether he'd been happy or not? From what I'd gathered already, Mr Murdoch had appeared content with his lot. What I did know was here was a life which on the surface harmed no-one and I needed to find out why someone would want to end it.

The bathroom had an avocado suite which went out of fashion years ago. Mum and Dad had replaced the one in our house as soon as they could afford it. It appeared that Mr Murdoch didn't much care for home décor and hadn't changed anything put in by his parents. The musty smell suggesting that he didn't open the window for fresh air either.

So far, the house appeared unremarkable and, on first glance, I reckoned Pete and I could do a quick search and leave it to the forensics team. Even that may be a dead end, but we had to make sure we didn't miss anything. After we had both checked the living room, I asked Pete to inspect the bathroom while I decided to take a more thorough look around Mr Murdoch's bedroom. We would leave the dining room as all the paperwork in there could be parcelled up and taken back to the station to be sifted through later.

In the bedroom, there was a double bed with side tables against one wall and a large wardrobe on the adjacent wall, behind the door. On the back of the door hung a striped cotton towelling dressing gown, the only thing in the pockets a used tissue. The shelves in the wardrobe were full of clothes, divided into types and neatly folded. The hanging rail contained one suit and a jacket; apparel likely kept for formal events. Clearly, Mr Murdoch preferred clothes that were smart-casual and comfortable.

I stood at the end of the bed and looked around the room. My instincts were telling me that something was off and I tried to place it. There was an odour, subtle, not perfume, a sourness maybe. And something else; the feeling that Mr Murdoch had recently not been alone in this room. I couldn't explain it, but it was there. Moving closer to the bed, I looked carefully at the rumpled sheets, pulling them back to get a closer look. It felt uncomfortable, intruding on the most intimate aspect of my former teacher's life. But needs must. I had a killer to find.

Leaning closer, I almost missed it but, there it was, a yellowish stain on the bedding. It looked like Mr Murdoch may have had sex since last washing his bed linen. If so, that meant someone had been in the house. Yet there appeared to be no other evidence of that; only the one glass on the table in the living room. The alternative was masturbation, which I found even worse to think about. Neither were things I wanted to know about my ex-teacher. Forensics would test the sheets for DNA and, in the meantime, I'd have to consider the possibility that Mr Murdoch had been intimate with someone. But not likely someone who lived here or even spent enough time to leave clothes or other personal items. A 'friends with benefits' arrangement perhaps. I would have to check again with the neighbour; she hadn't mentioned seeing anyone go in or out.

I looked up as Pete appeared from the bathroom, an evidence bag in his hand. 'Towels from the laundry basket. Two of them, a bit damp as if recently used.'

We could not know if Mr Murdoch had used both towels but there was no reason we could think of as to why he would, unless he liked to shower morning and night, using a clean towel each time. However, nothing we had seen so far would suggest he was that fastidious in his hygiene habits. I told Pete about the stain. 'Looks like he had a visitor.'

Pete nodded. 'And...' He paused, held up a second, much smaller, evidence bag. 'This is intriguing. Strands of auburn hair caught in the trap of the shower.'

We both knew those could not belong to Mr Murdoch whose dark hair had turned grey. Apart from that, like the bedroom, there was nothing in the bathroom to suggest someone else lived here, or had even been here. No products other than those that likely belonged to Mr Murdoch himself. If someone regularly stayed, we would at least expect a toothbrush. So, there was no evidence to back up the possibility that he had a partner.

I smiled at Pete. 'Checking the shower trap. That's impressive.'

He returned my smile. 'Keeping my eye on the details. Just like you.'

Heading for the front door, I thought it felt good to be working with Pete again.

We decided to talk to Rita straight away to see if she could shed light on the possibility that Mr Murdoch had a partner. If he did, she would surely know given her ability to describe his movements. The patrol car had gone so presumably she was on her own.

She smiled at us when she answered the door and invited us in. I politely refused, keen to get the information we needed and get back to Ayr. She was certain that Mr Murdoch did not have a partner. In her opinion, his life was about his job and, until they passed away several years ago, his parents. By the time they had died he had seemed set in his ways and, as she'd said before, kept himself to himself. I thanked her for her help and started to walk down the path. I was almost at the car when she called after me. I turned back to face her and waited.

'Although someone did come to visit him the other night,' she said, sounding pleased with herself.

I tried not to show my annoyance that she hadn't already shared this information with us. She was certain that it was the night before last, on Wednesday. It was late and dark so she couldn't even tell whether it was a man or a woman. However, to her mind, the build of the person suggested a woman. They were wearing a long coat with the hood up although it wasn't raining. Rita had been in her kitchen making a cup of tea and had happened to glance out of the window when she spotted the figure approaching Mr Murdoch's house. She reckoned they had arrived about nine o'clock on foot; there had been no sign of a car. They had left about eleven o'clock when she was putting her cat out.

I suspected she'd been watching the house but decided not to say so; howsoever she came about this information, it was useful. Mr Murdoch had had a visitor the night before he was murdered and that was significant. We could work on the theory that he'd had sex with the mystery person but they hadn't stayed the night. With nothing else to go on for the moment, we would have to wait for forensics and ask Cumnock police to conduct house to house enquiries. I wanted to know if anyone else in the area had seen someone around at those times or noticed anything suspicious.

After thanking Rita once again for her help, Pete and I got in the car and headed back to Ayr.

CHAPTER 7

The incident room was quiet when Pete and I got back, mainly the sound of Carmel tapping away on her keyboard. On hearing me approach, she rose from her chair. ‘Ma’am,’ she said. Our eyes met, I signalled for her to remain seated, and waited to hear what she had to say. ‘The headteacher from Riverwood called…’ She hesitated.

I nodded. ‘Go on.’

Carmel looked from Pete to me. ‘That stabbing yesterday… The headteacher said the victim was a student of Mr Murdoch’s. I was wondering if there might be a connection.’

I turned towards Pete, unable to hide my annoyance. This was the first I’d heard about a stabbing and I didn’t like being kept in the dark.

Pete could see I wasn’t happy. ‘Ah, yes… Sorry, Ma’am.’ He paused to catch my eye, making sure I recognised the use of my title. ‘A Riverwood student was stabbed by the river not far from the school, discovered by a jogger yesterday evening. I’ve left uniform at the scene, having to pull Bill and Gary in to the murder case. Of course, I should have said…’

‘Yes, you should.’ Turning back to Carmel, I asked, ‘What’s the name?’

‘Shannon Birch,’ she replied.

‘I don’t believe in coincidences. A murder at the school, a stabbing close by. There must be a connection. We’ll look out for Shannon Birch. Could you get me what we have so far on the stabbing?’

Carmel nodded and went back to work.

Out of earshot, I said to Pete. ‘Carmel seems like a bright girl.’

‘One of the Detective Degree Holder Entry Programme students.’

‘Great. Someone I can mould to my way of thinking.’

Pete gently tapped my arm. ‘Sorry about not keeping you up to date…’

I nodded and smiled, acknowledging the apology before walking over to Bill and Gary who were going through the notes from the interviews at the school. ‘Bill,’ I said. Bill turned and looked up at me. At fifty-five, he wasn’t much older than Pete. However, in contrast to Pete retaining his slim build and thick hair, Bill had a paunch and was thinning on top.

As our eyes met, I sensed a coolness in his manner. Pete had already told me that Bill had got on well with my predecessor and they had socialised outside of work. So much so that Bill had also been investigated. Although exonerated, it had left scars. Apparently, he'd wanted Pete to apply for my job and the fact that a younger person, and a woman to boot, had got it, didn't sit well with him. Maybe it exacerbated the chip on his shoulder that promotion had passed him by because he had never completed the paperwork following the exams. According to Pete, he felt he never had the time while his family was growing up. Pete had made a similar decision, albeit after achieving his sergeant's badge, not wanting more responsibility so that he could focus on family life whenever the job let him.

If Bill did resent having to work for me, I told myself that was his problem. The main thing for me was not letting his personal feelings affect the investigation. I held out my hand. 'DI Kim Berry. Pleased to meet you, Bill.'

His handshake was perfunctory, reflecting no warmth. Glancing at me, he gave a curt nod of acknowledgement, 'Ma'am,' and went back to the files in front of him.

In this situation, the easiest thing to do was get on with the job. Stick to the common ground. 'Any news on Mrs Caldwell's alibi or the CCTV footage for Ellen Shaw,' I asked.

Bill sighed then looked at me. 'Not yet, Ma'am.'

Had I sensed a hint of condescension in his voice? I maintained eye contact, determined that I wouldn't be the first one to look away. He clicked his tongue and let his gaze drop once more to the paperwork in front of him. I didn't let it go. 'Keep me posted.' I waited until he raised his head again and nodded to acknowledge the request.

Turning towards Gary, I took in the young man with dark shoulder-length hair. He was wearing a pinstripe grey suit and a blue shirt open at the neck. He wouldn't have looked out of place in a car saleroom. I could see why he had a bit of a reputation for chatting up colleagues, given his good looks and easy smile. 'Carmel had better watch out,' I thought. Gary looked up as if surprised to see me, even though I could tell he'd been watching the exchange between myself and Bill. He jumped up from his seat and thrust out a hand to offer me a handshake. 'Gary Sutton, Ma'am. Pleased to meet you.'

I found myself smiling, liking the spark of confidence in meeting his new boss. 'And you, Gary. Any updates on what you've found so far?'

He grinned, enthusiasm oozing from him. 'I'm going through the statements. See if there's anything worth noting.'

I nodded and, without giving Gary a chance to say anything further, I headed for my office, aware of Bill's eyes on me as I made my way across the room. Knowing that he was reliable, able to take some responsibility and that he was meticulous in his approach to investigations, I remained hopeful that I would win his loyalty. And yet I couldn't shake the feeling that he doubted I could take charge of the team. I had to admit it irked me.

I helped myself to a drink from the vending machine and as I sipped the bitter coffee, I paused to gather my thoughts. I was keen to know if any connections between Mr Murdoch and his student could be found in the statements taken that morning. I decided that I would start sifting through some of that paperwork. It was the best way forward until we got some feedback from forensics, CCTV and any information that might be forthcoming from the house-to-house enquiries, which all seemed to take an age.

Retracing my steps, I lifted some folders from Bill's desk, the statements taken from students who had been in Mr Murdoch's class on his last day. Bill, Gary, and Carmel had been logging the statements and I wanted to read these ones first, considering the potential of them being witnesses or even suspects. It was painstaking work and I decided I'd share that with Pete. I pulled up a chair next to him and Carmel.

Pete looked up as I sat down and grinned. 'Decided to join the ranks?'

I smiled back, enjoying a glimpse of our old camaraderie. 'Keeping tabs on you all, Sergeant Fletcher.'

We had copies of Mr Murdoch's attendance sheets and class lists for the last two days. I glanced at the timetable and confirmed that he had been free the last period of the day he was murdered and so it made sense that he would have been taking books to the cupboard. The paperwork on his desk suggested he wasn't that keen to tackle marking and tidying up probably seemed a good show of doing something while waiting for the bell. I sat back, arms folded. That triggered something in my mind: surely, he must have been killed during that last period as he wasn't the type to be around for long after the school day. I made a note to double check the likely time of death with Duncan Cain.

Passing half the class lists to Pete, I suggested that he look at yesterday's morning classes while I took the ones from the afternoon. As I lined the lists up in front of me and began checking, I realised how tedious this would be. First, I would check whether a student had been present or not before perusing each statement. I was looking for anything they might have seen or heard, even if to them it seemed to have no significance. To us, any snippet of information could help.

Once we had gone through the statements and followed up any leads, we would question anyone in his classes who might have been absent that day. You never knew what might turn up and it was important to cover all angles. A crime like this, where there was no obvious motive, was usually a reaction to something. I felt in my bones that something had happened yesterday to trigger the murder. But what?

My ruminations were interrupted by an exclamation from Pete. 'Well. Who would've thought!'

My head snapped up. 'What is it?' I asked.

Pete handed me a sheet of paper. 'Shannon Birch was in Mr Murdoch's class first thing yesterday. Now there's a coincidence.'

I looked up and reached across to take the list from Pete. 'I don't believe in coincidences.'

Mr Murdoch had been killed and one of his students had been the victim of a stabbing on the same day, not a million miles away from each other and within hours. There had to be a connection. This was becoming more than a hunch. A glance at the attendance record revealed that Shannon had been late for school that day. We would need to interview her about both crimes but I decided to wait until we had more evidence. It was possible that others in the class would have something of interest in their statement.

Pete went to check with Gary and Bill to see how they were getting on. Mr Murdoch's students had been interviewed first so they could let them go and statements or details had been painstakingly taken from all the staff.

Now that I knew about Shannon, I was keen to find out if they had picked up anything relating to her.

So far, we had four persons of interest: Mr Murdoch, the murder victim, two suspects, the history teachers, Mrs Caldwell and Ellen Shaw and the stabbing victim, Shannon Birch. What was the connection between Shannon Birch and Mr Murdoch?

Until we could gather all the pieces that were needed to get the full picture, the best thing we could do was continue with the statements and notes so far. I took the statements from the students in Shannon Birch's class on the day of the murder, and retreated to my office. I needed a bit of space to think, away from the noise of Bill and Gary exchanging commentary and eating crisps.

The students had all been asked one question: had anything unusual happened during the lesson? It quickly became clear that Shannon and Mr Murdoch regularly exchanged banter; references to the fact that most days he would have to take her phone from her. However, everything pointed to it being good natured rather than acrimonious. There was no obvious indication that something could have gone wrong. It would be interesting to see what Shannon had to say about that.

A wave of tiredness hit me. I needed a break. It was almost seven o'clock so I put the statements to one side and stretched. Through the glass I could see Pete, Bill and Gary going through different stacks of papers. Carmel was still inputting data on her computer. Time for a quick drink and some food. I needed to relax and I couldn't do that with Bill, Gary, and Carmel around as well. It was time for a review of where we were and then I'd send everyone home apart from Pete. I hoped we could go over things in the pub. We could start afresh in the morning, no matter that it was the weekend. I called a meeting.

I began, 'We know that Mr Murdoch was murdered by a blow to the head but we'll have to wait for the post-mortem to get more information. Mrs Caldwell's alibi must be authenticated as well as the CCTV footage of Ellen Shaw's movements after school. Any progress on that?'

Bill stepped forward. 'There was a meeting on that day. I'm waiting for the records of who attended so that I can interview a few people, check if they remember Mrs Caldwell being there. I probably won't be able to follow that up until Monday though.'

'I've requested CCTV from the bus station. They have a lot of cameras and a photograph of Ellen Shaw has gone to the company. If I've not heard anything by tomorrow afternoon, I'll chase it up. They have twenty-four-hour surveillance and work weekends so if she was there, I'll find out,' Gary added, looking quietly confident.

I nodded. 'Right. I'll leave you two to follow up the alibi and CCTV. So far, the two teachers look like unlikely candidates for committing murder but we can't rule them out. Shannon Birch was stabbed by the river close to the pedestrian bridge to Holmston Road. It looks like the two events are linked: Shannon was a student of Mr Murdoch and the murder and attempted murder probably took place within hours of each other. Anything further on the stabbing, Carmel?'

Carmel shook her head. 'No, Ma'am.'

'Well, let me know if anything turns up.' I didn't sound hopeful. 'Any thoughts, Pete?'

Pete was rubbing his chin, deep in thought. 'I'd agree the two crimes are linked. But timings might be crucial. The post-mortem report should give a better indication of the time of Mr Murdoch's death and then we can see if someone would have been able to commit them both.'

I sighed. 'And we need to find out who was Mr Murdoch's night time visitor, starting with his fellow history teachers.' I paused before adding, 'I don't think we'll get much further today. Bill, Gary, you know what to do – follow up those alibis as much as you can first thing. Carmel, follow up the stabbing. Pete, we'll see how our colleagues in Cumnock are getting on. Get yourselves home and be here early in the morning.'

Bill and Gary didn't need telling twice. To them this was a bonus; they might not get another decent finish time before the case was solved. Carmel hesitated, looking from Pete to me. I asked her if something was on her mind. She looked at me as if deciding whether to say something or not.

After a few seconds, her mind seemingly made up; she spoke with confidence. 'You know I've been transferred from DI Burns' team. Well, he was working on some tip-offs of drugs activity in Ayr and the surrounding area; I was collating any information that came in to see if we could identify suspects, locations, that sort of thing. There were rumours of school students being involved. I wondered if there might be anything there.'

I knew DI Cliff Burns from the Specialist Crime Unit based in Glasgow. Cliff was a bit younger than me, and, although I was ambitious, he was more so. He was renowned for being very focused on getting promoted and was proud to be one of the youngest DIs in the Force.

This information from Carmel was interesting, possibly a link between the murder and the stabbing. But I couldn't see how Mr Murdoch could be linked to drugs. However, it could not be ruled out. He might have been a good teacher, but that didn't mean he couldn't have been a user or even a dealer. Ayrshire was second only to Greater Glasgow and Clyde in terms of drug related deaths. I had to take all of that into consideration and put my personal feelings aside. I looked at Carmel, who was patiently waiting for an answer. 'That's helpful to know. In the morning speak to DI Burns about that too. Ask if you can access the files. We can cross check anything that comes our way.'

Carmel smiled and nodded before picking up her coat and heading for the door.

CHAPTER 8

Pete and I walked to The Brig which was less than five minutes' away on Main Street. The pub was beginning to get busy but we managed to find a table. Pete checked that I wanted my 'usual' order. I nodded, thinking it was like old times. In Glasgow, Pete and I had often escaped the office to mull over a case. He went to get the drinks, soda and lime for me, alcohol free lager for him.

Looking around, I realised it had been a while since I'd visited a cosy, old-fashioned pub. Patrick and I had tended to head for the wine bars in the West End of Glasgow. Pete put my drink in front of me, carefully placing it on the beer mat, despite evidence of water stains on the wooden table. We didn't bother to look at the menu, instead ordering fish and chips because it wouldn't take too long. We looked at each other across the table.

'Quite the first day,' he said, 'glad to be here?'

''Nothing like diving into the deep end,' I responded. I smiled at him. 'Anyway, how've you been? Yvonne? The boys?'

Pete returned my smile. 'I get as much time as I can with the family when not on a case like this. Yvonne's great. Always has been. You know that. I couldn't do this job without her support. And the boys? Well, they're teenagers. Can't feed them enough. Loads of energy...' He caught my eye. 'What about you? The move here. How's Patrick?'

I looked away. 'Patrick didn't come with me. He's still in Glasgow.' I tried to keep my voice light, not showing too much emotion. Pete raised his eyebrows and I wondered how to avoid talking about it.

Luckily, our food arrived and I was able to deflect the conversation, although I could see Pete wasn't fooled. We reflected on the day, turned over what we had found out so far and shared our thoughts. The murder, the stabbing, and a possible link between the two.

The years fell away and I shed any remaining concern that Pete might be harbouring some resentment at my being his boss. I'd been right to get away from the station, to take a break and silence the inner critic. It was strange that I felt like this; during the whole time in Glasgow, I'd never questioned myself or my ability to do the job. Maybe it was being back here, dragging up memories, opening old wounds.

We polished off our food in silence and, draining our glasses, got up to leave. It was already half past eight and the pub was a hubbub of noise. Time to get back to work. I wanted to read through those statements one more time. I told Pete to go home but he insisted on coming with me. As I pushed back my chair to get up from the table something caught my eye. A party of three had come in and sat at the table next to us. They were looking at the menu and sharing something on their phones that they were obviously finding hilarious, evident from their laughter and the clinking of glasses. A server approached, ready to take the group's order and something clicked in my mind, something I needed to double check.

Back in the office, I asked Pete to hold on while I reread the statements. This time it was quicker because I knew what I was looking for; a particular reference. Once I found it, I cross checked and highlighted some of the others before heading out to the main room where I sat down opposite Pete and handed him the bundle. 'Take a look through these, Pete. I've highlighted some paragraphs.' I waited, the old-fashioned analogue clock ticking away the seconds. I could be patient when I wanted to be and it was important to see if Pete spotted what I had.

It took him five minutes to find it. He singled out one statement and handed the piece of paper back to me. 'A notebook, not a phone. You think it's important?'

I leaned back in my chair. 'Unusual, at least. It was at the pub it struck me, when the server flipped open his notebook to take the order at the next table. It is odd that all the statements bar one mentioned Shannon Birch having her phone taken from her.'

Pete was clearly impressed. 'Welcome to Ayr, Kim. Or, I should say, Ma'am.'

I smiled. I couldn't imagine ever getting used to Pete using that deferential title. 'Only in public, Pete. Only in public.' In that moment any remaining doubts that we would work well together again fell away. However, I'd still have to build my relationship with the rest of the team as well as impress my boss, DCI Lewis. Glancing at my watch, I decided we should call it a day. 'I think a visit to this student can wait until tomorrow.'

Pete smiled. 'I reckon Yvonne would appreciate me getting home, especially as I won't be taking the boys to football practice in the morning.' He paused, a look of concern crossing his face. 'You alright?'

His way of showing that he knew I would be going home to an empty flat, having told him that Patrick had stayed in Glasgow. I smiled at him. 'I'm fine, Pete. Honestly.' He looked at me, a doubtful expression on his face, as I kept smiling. It was fixed, and he knew it.

Eventually he nodded. 'If you say so.'

I picked up the paperwork so that I could check all the statements one more time and we made our way to the car park. As I got in my car, I looked across the fence to Lidl and wondered what I had in the fridge. Not that I needed food tonight. But it reminded me there would be no Patrick at home to do most of the cooking while I worked on a big case. Even if he was going out, he would usually have left something for me to put in the microwave.

I sighed as I reversed out of my space and pulled onto the main road. I drove north through Prestwick, circumventing the airport before choosing the A79, the quicker route home. I usually preferred the coast road to take in the views across to Arran. Even when it was dark, like tonight, I loved knowing that the sea and the mountains were there.

I'd decided to move to Troon rather than Ayr. Putting some distance between the police station and home was something I needed. It had worried me that Troon might be too quiet but I had been surprised to find I didn't miss Glasgow at all. My flat lay between the town centre and the harbour with the sea at the end of the road. There would always be easy access to the shore whenever I needed a walk to unwind.

I parked on the road outside and breathed in the salty smell before making my way up the path. Opening the front door, I was met with a silence that I hadn't yet got used to; the silence of living alone. Unexpectedly, tears sprung to my eyes. Whatever time I got in, I would tell Patrick about whatever case I was working on, well, as much as I was allowed, and he had a knack of knowing what to say. That was something I was going to miss. I took a deep breath, wiped away the tears, double locked the door, and kicked off my shoes. I'd find a different routine.

Throwing my jacket over the back of a chair in the living room and setting down my tote bag, I went through to the kitchen and opened the fridge. Finding yesterday's open bottle of wine, I poured myself a glass. Reminding myself that I probably shouldn't indulge tonight, I shrugged and went back into the living room. One glass wouldn't hurt. 'Was that what Mr Murdoch told himself as he poured his glass of whisky?' I asked myself. Sinking into my armchair, I turned on the news channel; the murder at the school and the stabbing by the river had made the local news. The journalists were making much of the fact that the girl had gone to the school where the teacher had been killed; that he was one of her teachers. That meant I'd have to deal with the communications team and possibly the media in my face as well as having my boss looking over my shoulder. None of which appealed. I'd much rather be left to get on with it. Taking the papers from my briefcase, I set to re-reading the statements.

The TV was still on when I woke up, cold and limbs aching, just after midnight. Journalists were still speculating about the teacher and the teenager; what the connection was, what their relationship might have been. The same news items on repeat. A sense of irritation crept over me, people putting two and two together and making ten. It made my job all the harder. I switched off the TV and putting the dirty wine glass in the sink, went to bed.

Saturday 15th October 2022

THE NOTEBOOK

CHAPTER 9

When I woke up the next morning, I wasn't in a good mood. I had drifted in and out of sleep, thoughts about the case going round in my head, colliding with memories of my time at Riverwood. Thankfully, the nightmare beginning to eat into my subconscious was interrupted by the alarm. That the case seemed to have triggered things I'd thought long forgotten was unexpected and unsettled me. I was usually good at not letting things affect me and getting on with it.

Dragging myself out of bed, I quickly showered and pulled on the first clean work clothes I came across in the wardrobe. Deciding what to wear was easy; I kept to my own uniform of black trousers and shirts of various colours so that I didn't have to think about what to wear. I bought a new pair of black brogues whenever they wore out: comfortable and practical given I never knew what terrain I might have to negotiate in this job.

I found some bread in the cupboard and not much else. Waiting for the coffee machine and the toaster, I resolved to take better care of myself including going to the supermarket and filling the cupboards with healthy food. Half an hour later, I retrieved my jacket from where I'd thrown it over the back of the chair when I got home, locked up and got into my Renault Clio. I love this car even though I've been teased about its colour - Valencia Orange – apparently not what people had in mind for an officer in CID. So what? It reminded me of glorious sunrises and sunsets. And holidays in Spain.

Pete was waiting in the car park when I arrived at King Street. Sensing my mood, he knew better than to say anything so we drove in silence to interview Shannon Birch's classmate. It took less than five minutes. The boy lived in a flat in Princes Court, on the ground floor of a four-storey, purpose-built block made of concrete. Like most of their neighbours, the family rented the flat from the Council. The starkness of the concrete was broken up by trees and, despite the potholes, the area looked well-maintained. Getting a whiff of rotting food as we passed the bins, we made our way into the building where a stressed-out looking woman probably in her late thirties opened the door, a toddler clinging to her leg.

I realised our timing wasn't good; the child was only wearing a nappy and likely we'd interrupted breakfast. The woman brushed hair back from her forehead with one hand as I checked whether I had the right house. Pete and I showed her our identity cards as I introduced us, explaining that we were there to speak to her son, Frankie. Following the death of Mr Murdoch at the school, we were following up statements from students in some of his classes. The woman nodded and indicated that we should go in, taking us into a small living room. I took in the surroundings, noting the cheapness of the furniture and the array of toys on the floor. It was, however, perfectly clean and nothing about this place indicated neglect.

She disappeared and returned after a few minutes with a teenager in tow, pushing the boy into the armchair opposite me. 'This is Frankie. I hope this won't take too long, I need him to get this little one her breakfast and go to the shops for me.'

I nodded. 'It'll take a few minutes.'

Frankie's mum lifted the toddler on to her hip and stood in the doorway, watching, as I turned my attention to the boy. He was tall for his age with mousy hair that reached his shoulders. He looked painfully thin with a torso that matched his long face. I hoped that this was a growth spurt and he would fill out as he got older, rather than due to lack of food.

Turning to the interview, Pete took notes as I asked the questions. Frankie looked nervous as I confirmed that he'd been in Mr Murdoch's first class of the day on Thursday and had given a statement to police following the discovery of the body on Friday morning. He wouldn't look at me and his hands gripped the cushions. I reassured him that he wasn't in any trouble but we needed to clarify a few things.

First things first, I asked whether he knew Shannon Birch. Frankie responded without hesitation, raising his head to meet my eyes. He said that everyone knew Shannon. She was popular, not just with fellow students but with some of the teachers too. She always seemed to be able to get herself out of any trouble. I pursed my lips, thinking about what he had said. In my view there were different types of popular; some people because they were genuinely liked, others because their peers were afraid of them, and those that had money they splashed around. I asked Frankie which category he thought Shannon Birch fell into.

He paused and shrugged his shoulders. 'Dunno. I wouldn't say she was a bully. As far as I know, no-one's scared of Shannon. She sticks to her own crowd and they respect her because she's got expensive stuff, the latest phone and that. She likes to think she's more grown-up than rest of us. Dunno where she gets the cash though.'

I wanted to establish Frankie's relationship with Shannon. That way I could see how much he might know about her life outside school. 'So, you and Shannon are friends?'

'Hell no!' Frankie twisted strands of hair round his fingers. 'No way. I'm not someone she'd be seen with.'

So, Frankie and Shannon were certainly not friends. I wanted to get to the crux of the matter. 'Did you know Shannon's in hospital? I asked. 'She was stabbed sometime Thursday afternoon or evening.'

Frankie looked at me. 'Yeah. I read about it online. We were all talking about it yesterday. Then Mr Murdoch...'

'Can you think of anyone at all who might want to harm Shannon?' I asked.

Frankie looked aghast at such a suggestion, 'Fu...! No, like I told you, she's popular. I can't believe that anyone would do anything to hurt her!'

I took a deep breath; I needed to get to the content of Frankie's statement, confirm what had happened in class yesterday, find the connection between Mr Murdoch and Shannon. I told him Shannon might have been stabbed around the same time as Mr Murdoch was killed. 'Any thoughts on that?' Frankie screwed up his face and shook his head. 'In your statement, you mentioned that Shannon and Mr Murdoch had a disagreement during the lesson.'

He visibly relaxed, obviously happier to talk about his statement. Apparently, it hadn't been a disagreement as such, more of a game. Every lesson Shannon would try to use her phone, waiting to see if Mr Murdoch would catch her and confiscate it. He paused, sat back in his chair, and watched Pete write up the conversation. After a few minutes, he said,

'Though, on Thursday... it wasn't her phone. She had a little notebook. Kept getting it out of her pocket. That was what Mr Murdoch took.'

I looked him in the eye. 'This is important, Frankie. Are you certain it was a notebook and not a phone?'

Frankie stared back at me, holding up his hands as if to emphasise his point. 'Totally. It was a black notebook about the size of a phone.' He illustrated the point by making a rectangle with his fingers.

I was watching Frankie's face intently. 'Why are you so certain it wasn't a phone?'

'I sit next to her. Not because she wanted to. Mr Murdoch put us there. She had the notebook under the desk but I could see it. That's what he took. Definitely.' He sat back in his chair, a confident smile on his face.

A black notebook about the size of a mobile phone; it would be easy for others to assume it was a phone. Especially if that was what you were expecting to see. 'Do you have any idea what was in the notebook?'

Frankie's response was quick and assured. 'No. And no way I'd ask. Shannon keeps a lot of things to herself. I pretended I hadn't noticed. But she was a bit agitated when Mr Murdoch took it. I think she asked him if he'd keep it safe. If his drawer was locked.'

I was satisfied that Frankie knew what he was talking about; there was no hesitation or changes to his statement. Pete and I glanced at each other, nodding in mutual agreement. It was time to go. We needed to find this notebook, the most likely connection between Mr Murdoch and Shannon Birch. Thanking Frankie for his help, we got up to leave. His mum moved into the room to let us pass and Frankie took his sister from her arms while we saw ourselves out. Catching a whiff of soiled nappy, I reckoned that would be Frankie's immediate task.

Pete and I looked at each other as we got back into the car. It went without saying that we needed to go back to Mr Murdoch's classroom and have a look in the desk drawers. Now that we knew what we were looking for, I wanted to find that notebook.

CHAPTER 10

It took about five minutes to get to the school via Craigie Road. As Pete pulled in to the car park, it struck me how it seemed to take no time at all to get anywhere here, unlike Glasgow where crossing the city could take ages.

I pressed the buzzer to gain entry and found Andy McGregor waiting for us on the other side of the door as we entered the lobby. He should have been at home, it being the weekend, the first day of his holidays, yet here he was on duty, having found himself dealing with lots of queries from parents and the media. Andy gave no hint of being put out by it all, looking relaxed in jeans and a hoodie. However, I couldn't warm to him. He gave the impression he was beginning to enjoy the attention, rather than appreciating the gravity of what had happened.

He started asking questions, trying to get an update on the investigation. That was not going to happen. There was too much media speculation already and I wouldn't risk snippets of information getting into the public domain. Quickly thanking him for his time, Pete and I headed towards the stairs, our footsteps echoing on the tiled floors.

As soon as we reached the History Department, we encountered Mrs Caldwell who had heard the swing doors to the corridor bang shut and come to check who it was. She appeared disconcerted, eager to explain why she and Ellen were there: tidying up, having not had the chance to do that the day before. I glanced towards the cupboard, still taped off.

Following my gaze, she said, 'We haven't gone near...' I put a hand up, indicating there was no need to confirm that. She continued, 'I heard what happened to Shannon. It's shocking that the media is trying to link her to Raymond...' Her voice tailed away.

I nodded. 'Was there any connection between Mr Murdoch and Shannon?'

She looked confused. 'Other than Raymond teaching Shannon, no. Not at all. They had their spats, usually over her phone, but never serious enough to involve me.'

That didn't surprise me. I changed the subject, keen to move on to why Pete and I were there. Thinking that the killer probably used Mr Murdoch's own keys to lock him in the cupboard, I asked her about them. She met my gaze, confirming there had been no sign of them and she had no idea where they might have gone.

I sighed. 'It's important that we find those keys. If we do, how will we know they are Mr Murdoch's?'

According to Mrs Caldwell, his keys are distinctive. A keyring of a metal saxophone with New Orleans etched on it. When he first got it, it was a bright gold colour, fake gold plating that had become tarnished. A souvenir from a rare trip abroad he had made many years ago to a festival. Apparently, Mr Murdoch was a big fan of jazz music. Inwardly, that made me want to smile. I could imagine him in his big armchair, feet up with a whisky, listening to jazz.

We were getting nowhere with the keys so I paused, considering how best to put my next question. It was a delicate matter and asking one of my old teachers about sexual relationships was somewhat embarrassing, even if she didn't know who I was. The hair in the shower trap at Mr Murdoch's house did not match Mrs Caldwell's colour but I couldn't assume that the stain on the sheet belonged to the same person, however likely that might be. Mr Murdoch might have had several visitors to his house on that day or on different days. If he was having an affair with Mrs Caldwell, though, why keep it so secret? He was single, she was a widow. Unless they didn't want to be the subject of school gossip? Regardless of what I thought, the question had to be asked.

I looked at Mrs Caldwell tentatively, aiming to be as tactful as I could, 'I need to ask you a personal question.' I paused. She looked at me quizzically. I swallowed. 'Were you in a relationship with Mr Murdoch?'

She stared back at me, obviously stunned. It took her a few moments to answer. 'A relationship? With Raymond? Inspector Berry, absolutely not. We were work colleagues, maybe even friends, but only at work. We never saw each other outside of school. Not even during the holidays. I have never been involved with anyone since my husband died. And before you ask, during my marriage too.' Her voice was high pitched, strained.

I believed her but we would still check the DNA and I asked her to give a sample. Whether she was upset or not couldn't be helped. I hoped that she was sensible enough to realise that we had to check every possibility. She became more relaxed when I asked whether she was aware of anyone with whom Mr Murdoch might have had an involvement. As expected, she didn't have a clue because he'd never mentioned anyone and kept his private life to himself, as did she. He used to talk about his parents when they were alive but since then no-one else. The impression was that he preferred his own company apart from Fridays in the pub with his friends.

A look of realisation crossed her face. 'On reflection,' she said, 'his car shouldn't have been in the car park yesterday because he'd usually get the bus so he could have a drink after school. She bit her lip and looked at the floor as if she was trying to hold back tears. I decided to leave her to her thoughts, thanked her and asked her to let us know if she came across the keys or had any further thoughts on where they might be. The exchange left me feeling odd, as if my teenage self was colliding with the woman I have become. The present confronted with the past.

Turning away from Mrs Caldwell, I headed into Mr Murdoch's classroom where Pete was waiting. Again, as I crossed the threshold, I got that feeling of being transported back in time. I couldn't help glance at the end desk, back row, next to the wall, seeing my teenage self, sitting there, gazing out the window or doing homework. If anyone had walked past in the corridor, I couldn't be seen. No-one needed to know I was there and that's how I wanted it.

Shaking my head to clear the memory, I turned towards Mr Murdoch's desk, the pile of marking still there, untouched. Pete and I had tried both drawers the day before and he had just tried again but they remained resolutely locked. He looked at me and smiled before producing a small screwdriver from his pocket. 'Thought I'd have a go at breaking in? These old desks are simple cam locks. I should be able to open them with this.' As always, he was prepared for most eventualities and a locked drawer wouldn't stand in his way.

I watched as he fiddled with the first drawer until it gave way and repeated the manoeuvre with the second one. Each of us took out a drawer, laying them out on the front desks. The insides of the drawers were a mess; old pens and pencils, paperclips, CDs, postcards, remnants of a teacher's life. A faint smell of extra strong mints. Nothing there that would suggest they even needed to be locked. However, there was no sign of a notebook.

Pete and I looked up simultaneously as a shadow fell across the room. Ellen Shaw was standing in the doorway. I beckoned her to come in. She looked even younger in sports clothes and her hair hanging loose. I was glad that she had saved me the job of looking for her to answer the two questions I'd posed to Mrs Caldwell. She couldn't remember the last time she'd seen Mr Murdoch with his keys. However, she could remember the last time she'd seen them. This was something, at least. On Thursday afternoon, the day of the murder, Mr Murdoch was in the cupboard and she'd caught a student, one of the boys in his senior class, rummaging in one of the drawers in the desk and challenged him. He claimed he was getting a marker pen for Mr Murdoch who was labelling items in the cupboard. The keys were lying on the desk.

I was intrigued, 'Did you believe him?'

Ellen shrugged. 'I couldn't see any reason why he would lie. Although, it did strike me as odd because it's not, it wasn't, like Raymond to be so organised. But as his keys were there...' She pointed to the desk. 'I assumed Raymond had given them to him.'

I asked, 'Do you know his name?' I couldn't expect her to know all the students in a school this size.

She nodded. 'Ben Chadwick. One of Raymond's star students. He should have been in his next class. I wanted to know why he was in the Department.'

I paused to gather my thoughts. This was a potential lead. Keeping the interest from my voice, I asked her what she had done next. In the end she'd taken the boy at his word and left him to it, going back to her own classroom. She assumed Ben would have returned the keys to Mr Murdoch. Pete and I glanced at each other. He waved his notebook; he had already made a note of the student's name.

Turning back to Ellen, I asked if she knew Shannon Birch and got the standard answer, that everyone knew her, she was confident and popular, stayed out of trouble. She also had seen what had happened to Shannon on the news and been shocked. Pushing for more information, I mentioned that she was also a student of Mr Murdoch's. However, she had no idea if there was a connection between Mr Murdoch, Shannon, and Ben.

It looked unlikely that she had anything more to offer. We would soon interview this Ben Chadwick and find out what he was up to. I moved on to the subject of how well she knew Mr Murdoch. Like Mrs Caldwell, I didn't think she was the visitor who had used the shower because the hair colour didn't match. But it still had to be checked out. In her case, I had no qualms asking her if she was in a relationship with Mr Murdoch and, as expected, she denied it. She wouldn't even say they were friends, just colleagues who got on well. They had never met up outside of school. I nodded and she turned away from me, leaving the scent of her perfume in the air as she left the room. It smelled expensive.

Given that we hadn't found anything; no sign of the keys and no notebook, it was time to go. We had a possible lead in Ben Chadwick and I asked Pete to contact Bill to get the file. I wanted to do some homework before we saw him.

As Pete disappeared into the corridor, I couldn't help making my way to the back of the room. I wondered if it was still the same desk; it certainly looked similar. Without thinking, I sat down on the hard plastic chair and placed my hands flat on the small, square table. The air was filled with that musty classroom smell of teenage body odour, sealed in by closed windows. Sitting at 'my' desk, I could picture Mr Murdoch smiling at me as he collected his lunch bag from his old briefcase. In my head I made a promise: 'I will get who did this, Sir.'

'What are you doing sitting there?' Pete's voice startled me. I jumped. I hadn't heard him re-enter the classroom.

I tried to laugh it off. 'Nothing, Pete. I was thinking about Mr Murdoch. Maybe trying a bit of divine intervention.' I could see Pete wasn't fooled, knowing how much this case meant to me, professionally. He didn't know it meant as much personally. At least not yet; I wasn't ready to own up to that. I got up from the desk and followed Pete into the corridor, quietly closing the door behind me.

CHAPTER 11

Fifteen minutes later, Pete and I entered the incident room to find that Bill and Gary were still going through statements. I called a team meeting. 'Anyone anything to report?' Silence. 'Assume nothing yet on the alibis?' Bill and Gary shook their heads.

'Sorry, Ma'am. Not heard back yet,' Gary said.

'Have you put together what we know about Ben Chadwick, Bill?' I asked. He nodded and handed me a file. He was polite enough but this relationship was going to require some work.

I turned to Gary. 'Check all the social media stuff. See what you can dig up about Ben and his interests.'

Gary smiled. 'I'll get on it right away.' This one was looking much more positive.

I asked Carmel to contact Cumnock police and see how they were getting on with identifying Mr Murdoch's mystery visitor. It might be the weekend but all the information was needed and I was willing to use my influence to get things moving if needs be. After checking that everyone knew what to do, Bill, Gary and Carmel got on with their allotted tasks. I looked at Pete. 'I think it's time we spoke to Shannon Birch.' I wanted to see if we could link the two crimes.

He nodded. 'Me too. Shannon had a notebook taken from her which Mr Murdoch locked in a drawer. Ben is found in Mr Murdoch's classroom with his keys. I think there might be a connection.'

'My thinking too, Pete.' I picked up my jacket and headed for the door, Pete following close behind.

When we drove into the hospital car park, I felt a pang of melancholia. The last time I was here was when my dad died from a heart attack. I had been accepted to join the police in Glasgow and was wondering whether to take it or not. I had been hoping to stay in Ayr because I was worried about whether he'd manage on his own. Dad had always wanted me to take any opportunities offered, but knew I wasn't sure about leaving him. We had been a team ever since Mum died from pneumonia, also in this hospital, a couple of years after we moved here.

As Pete and I passed the open door into the chapel on the way to the lift, I stopped for a minute, picturing my fourteen-year-old self sitting in there. I'd wanted peace and quiet to think; we'd come to Ayrshire for Mum and she was gone. I'd never been particularly religious but it had been comforting to be in the chapel at the time. I'd felt the same when Dad was here. After he died, I accepted the post in Glasgow and sold the house in the village.

'Excuse me.' A loud, but polite, voice close by. I was standing in the way of a porter pushing a patient on a trolley, the hustle and bustle of a busy hospital thoroughfare around me. I quickly apologised and caught up with Pete as he pressed the button and the lift door opened.

We showed our ID badges to the uniformed officer on the door of Shannon's room and went inside. The girl lying on the bed had long blonde hair spread out over the pillow and was deathly pale. By all accounts she was lucky to be alive. With a deep stab wound she had managed to pull herself out of the river and was found half out the water by a jogger early on Thursday evening. We had yet to establish how long she might have been lying there. Next to the bed sat a woman who was very thin with shoulder length, light brown hair that looked like it needed a wash. There was a faint smell of cigarette smoke in the air and her hands were shaking. My first thought was she may have a drink problem, but I'd find out for sure in due course. In this job, you get to recognise the telltale signs.

I introduced Pete and myself before confirming that she was Shannon's mother and gaining permission to speak to her daughter. The woman nodded and, as if on cue, Shannon stirred and I watched as she gradually opened her eyes, blinking rapidly at the overhead lights in the room.

Moving to the side of the bed, opposite the girl's mother, I waited for Shannon to focus on me before I spoke. I kept my tone as gentle as possible, aware that the girl had suffered a major trauma, physically and emotionally. 'Shannon, I am Detective Inspector Berry and this is Detective Sergeant Fletcher. We're here to ask you a few questions if you feel up to it.' She nodded slowly so I continued, 'Can you tell me what happened?'

She looked away, adjusted her position on the bed then let out a long breath. 'Dunno. Went for a walk along the river. The next thing I was in the water and after that all I remember is waking up here.'

It surprised me that she remembered nothing at all. There had been no reports of amnesia. 'You have no idea who stabbed you?' I asked.

Shannon lowered her eyes, her hands grasping the edge of the sheet. 'It happened so fast. One minute I was on the path, and as I said, the next, I was under the water.'

I found this hard to believe. I was sure the girl had to remember something. 'You have no idea at all of what they might look like? What they were wearing?' I didn't want to push too hard yet I felt she knew more than she was letting on.

'No.' Shannon sounded adamant.

I was certain she was lying. From the position of the wound, she had clearly been attacked from the front and, therefore, should have some idea of what her attacker looked like or at least the colour of their clothes. Turning to face her mother, I explained that we would take a copy of the medical records from when Shannon was admitted to see if there was any information that might help. We already had her clothes and belongings, currently with forensics.

Shannon's mother readily agreed. 'Whatever you need. I want whoever stabbed my daughter caught and off the streets. They might attack someone else.'

Shannon turned on her mother. 'Don't be so dramatic. It was random. I was in the wrong place at the wrong time.' The venom in her response bounced off the walls, leaving her mother aghast. Myself and Pete too.

This reaction was interesting. I wondered how she could sound so sure given that she claimed to remember nothing. What was more puzzling, however, was that she appeared more concerned by her mother's support for our investigation than the prospect of the perpetrator still being out there. She looked decidedly unhappy when her mother remained resolute; insisting that they'd do whatever they could to help. And that she would keep us informed if Shannon remembered anything.

Shannon might not want to say anything about being stabbed but I wanted to find out what she might know about Mr Murdoch. I asked if she knew that Mr Murdoch had been found dead at the school the previous morning, that he had been murdered. She nodded. 'It seems more than a coincidence to me that he's dead and one of his students has an attempt on her life. Don't you think?' Both mother and daughter stared at me, neither able to hide their shock. I looked at Shannon, allowing my words to sink in. 'If you remember anything at all, it's important to let us know.'

She seemed uneasy, almost imperceptibly shifting the position of her body, before finally speaking. 'It's sad. I liked him. He's - was - a good teacher. Not that I did much.'

It appeared she was willing to talk about Mr Murdoch. I asked, 'How did he seem to you in class on Thursday morning? I know you were there. You were late.'

Her face softened and I got the impression she had liked him, something I could understand. According to Shannon, Mr Murdoch had been his usual self that morning. It was a running joke that she was always late and he had never told her off about it. She would open the door and he would tell her to wait in the corridor, to make a point.

She glanced over at her mum who in turn was watching me intently. As far as Shannon was concerned nothing unusual had happened. Of course, I would have to jog her memory. 'What do you know about a notebook?'

Her face turned pale; the mention of the notebook had obviously caught her off guard. Watching her carefully, it looked to me that she was trying to come up with something to say. She shifted on the bed, her hands grasping the sheets. Her eventual response sounded like she was buying time. 'Mr Murdoch took my phone. It was a bit of a game; I'd always try to use it without getting caught. He knew it and would try to get it. He usually did.' She smiled weakly.

I asked her if he'd taken her phone on Thursday. She was sure that he had. I didn't believe her. Even though it was essentially Frankie's word against Shannon's that it was a notebook, I tended to believe Frankie's version of events. I could see no reason why he would lie and, given my hunch that the two crimes were connected, felt Shannon might have something to hide.

I decided to share with Shannon that we had a witness saying that Mr Murdoch didn't take her phone that morning. 'Our witness says that Mr Murdoch took a notebook from you to be returned at the end of the school day.' I didn't take my eyes off her. I could tell that she was thinking through her options. Was she going to lie and insist it wasn't a notebook, that Mr Murdoch had taken her phone? Shannon didn't know that we only had one witness and ultimately it would be her word against theirs. Or would she come clean? The seconds ticked away as I got up from my chair and wandered over to the window.

Her mum's voice eventually broke the awkward silence. 'Was it that girl who said it was a notebook?'

Spinning round to face them both, I caught how Shannon glared at her mother, struggling to contain the anger in her face, before blurting out, 'Shut up, Mum! She's got nothing to do with anything. She wasn't even there on Thursday.'

Pete and I exchanged glances, noting how mention of the girl had obviously riled Shannon. 'What girl?' I asked, not taking my eyes off Shannon's face even though she refused to look at me. The flash of anger turned to confusion. Again, I felt she was weighing up what to say.

Eventually she said, 'A friend came to see me.' She sounded deflated, like she had been caught out. Based on her reaction, this could be another lead.

'What's your friend's name?' I asked.

Shannon sighed. I could see in her face that she didn't want to tell me. Was she trying to cover up for someone? Or protect herself? At last, she provided a name. 'Katie Spencer. She's new to school.'

Spencer. I caught my breath. It couldn't be? Could it? My stomach turned over. This was a surname I recognised, one I knew had returned to Ayr recently. The stuff of nightmares. My nightmares. The reason for my doubts in taking this job. 'It must be a coincidence,' I thought, followed quickly by, 'you don't believe in coincidences.' I became aware that everyone was looking at me. I had to get a grip on myself. Think about the investigation.

I glanced at Pete standing in the doorway. A brief nod of agreement that this was another student of Mr Murdoch worth following up. Time to push on the notebook. 'What about the notebook, Shannon?' Her heart monitor beeped in the stillness of the room.

Mr Murdoch had indeed taken her notebook and not her phone. He had locked it in his drawer but when she went back for it at the end of the day he wasn't there and the drawer was locked. So, she left with the intention of getting it back the following morning. Instead, she'd ended up in hospital. The deflation in her voice was obvious. Shannon raised her head and we locked eyes. I decided to test her reaction to the news that the notebook had disappeared. 'Any idea where it might be?' I asked.

The look that crossed over her face wasn't bewilderment, or even shock. It was pure fear. Fleeting, but there, and at that point I realised I was on to something. Keep prodding and secrets are always revealed. Looked like there was a secret to uncover here. I wondered if there might be a connection between Shannon and Ben Chadwick. I asked if she knew him, but she looked genuinely baffled. Apart from knowing he was in the year above; she was more interested in why I would ask her about him. I didn't enlighten her.

Deciding that we likely had got as much information as we could for the time being, I told Shannon and her mother to get in touch if they thought of anything else. I also left them in no doubt that we would be back.

CHAPTER 12

As soon as we got back to King Street, I called another meeting; it was time to take stock of what we had so far and come up with a plan to take things forward. So much of an investigation was a waiting game. CCTV footage, mobile phone records, forensics, post-mortems, and so it goes on. We included Ben Chadwick and Katie Spencer on the list of suspects, together with Shannon Birch, Mrs Caldwell, and Ellen Shaw. I tried not to think about the surname Spencer, focusing instead on what we had so far, convincing myself I was wrong.

Turning my full attention to the meeting, I outlined my thoughts. 'By all accounts, Mr Murdoch was an ordinary bloke looking forward to retirement. The working assumption is that he was likely in the wrong place at the wrong time. That said, we can't rule out that he was involved in something that might have led someone to harm him.' Privately, I felt that wasn't the case, but it had to be considered, especially as I didn't want to leave myself open to accusations of not being thorough later. Or, of allowing my knowledge of the victim to get in the way. 'Anyone anything to report?'

Bill had been checking alibis. 'Mrs Caldwell's alibi is sound.' Instead of waiting until Monday, Bill had managed to track down someone who could check attendance at the meeting at the county buildings. 'I've spoken to some of the others who were there and they've vouched for her.' He paused and checked his notes. 'We've got Ellen Shaw on camera at the bus station, like she said, and the garage has confirmed her picking up the car.' I noted that Bill had picked up on how I addressed the suspects. Subconsciously, perhaps.

Although we couldn't rule out Ellen going back to the school after getting her car, I felt it was unlikely that Mr Murdoch would have been there that late if he were still alive. With both alibis checking out, we would need to look elsewhere for our killer.

Gary had been looking into Ben Chadwick's social media. 'He's not used his privacy settings. But there's nothing out of the ordinary to see. Usual stuff, photos, and banter with friends.' He frowned.

Carmel pitched in. 'I contacted Cumnock police but they've so far drawn a blank on Mr Murdoch's mystery visitor. They've agreed to investigate CCTV in the surrounding area to see if anyone could be seen hanging around, though.'

I sighed, unhappy at the lack of progress. It had only been a day or so but I wanted to show that we were getting somewhere.

As the team headed to their desks, I fetched a coffee from the machine, searched through the documents from the school and retreated to my office. We needed to check out Shannon's story, as well as interview Ben Chadwick and Katie Spencer. I wanted to find out more about this student before speaking to her. If Shannon's mother didn't know her, could she be a friend? And, if she wasn't a friend, what was the connection between Katie and Shannon? It only took a few minutes to check that Katie had been absent on Thursday as Shannon had claimed, and also on Friday. What had she been up to? I'd find that out but first, I would do some digging. I wanted to know if I was being paranoid or not.

I sipped my coffee as I fired up my PC. Logging into social media platforms, I typed in Katie Spencer. The girl hadn't made her profile completely private and I scrolled through her list of friends and photos. It didn't take too long. My blood froze as I stared at the face in the photo. More than twenty years may have passed but I was sure it was him. I felt the nausea rise in my throat and took a deep breath; this would have to be handled carefully. Whatever Katie's involvement in these crimes, if any, I'd have to make sure the evidence was watertight. I couldn't leave myself open to accusations of personal intent, possibly revenge. Shutting down the laptop and closing the folder, I drained my coffee, told the team to finish up for the day, and drove home as fast as I could.

After parking the car, I took the steps two at a time before thrusting my key in the lock. Slamming the door shut behind me, I rushed into the bedroom without stopping to take off my jacket and headed to the far side of the room. The box was in the bottom of my wardrobe, a collection of stuff I had kept when clearing out the house in Coylton. I'd often wondered why Mum kept so much, but found I couldn't part with some items either.

I took the box out and laid it on the bed before taking each item out one at a time until I found what I was looking for. It was my second-year group photo from Riverwood and I'd recently turned thirteen. I looked at my smiling face, remembering that time when I'd still been relatively happy, even thought that, maybe, given time, I might make some friends. Moving my gaze to the row behind, my eyes settled on a tall, broad boy with a mass of dark hair. The reason I had thought carefully about coming back here. A face from my nightmares. Richard Spencer. Katie Spencer's father. Ricky. One of the boys who had assaulted me at school.

Sunday 16th October 2022

A KNIFE

CHAPTER 13

I was running through the woods, my chest on fire, breaths coming in painful gasps. Behind me, the shadows were laughing, their shapes merging into the trees. Somewhere, a dog was barking. Then a buzzing from somewhere inside my head. The scene faded and I realised I was in bed, covered in sweat. I prised my eyes open, the grogginess from last night's wine keeping my head rooted to the pillow. Once again, I told myself I should be teetotal, especially during a case like this. Turning my head from side to side to gain some clarity, I realised the noise hadn't stopped. The alarm on my phone flashed at me; 8.30 am. I had arranged to meet Pete at 10am to interview Ben Chadwick.

Forcing myself to get out of bed, I headed for the shower, allowing the hot water to cleanse my skin for at least ten minutes. Pushing the images of my nightmare to the back of my mind, I turned the water to cold, shocking my system properly awake. In the kitchen, I downed a pint of cold water while waiting for the espresso machine to work its magic. Half an hour later, I was on my way to work, I hoped looking a lot better than I was feeling. Pete was already there, waiting for me in the car park. I got in his car and we set off in silence.

Ben Chadwick lived with his mother in Mossblown, a village about five miles from Ayr. Pete took the road towards Mauchline, green fields stretching out either side of the road. The clouds had cleared to reveal a sunny autumn day. I was reminded how much countryside was on the doorstep and how beautiful it was. It took less than ten minutes to reach the mid terrace, ex-Council house occupied by Ben and his mother, now owned by a private landlord who rented it to Mrs Chadwick.

Pulling up outside, I noted that the house was well kept, freshly painted with a neat front garden. At least the landlord appeared to be looking after the place on the outside. I knocked on the door which was answered by a woman wearing a smart cleaner's uniform. Having shown our ID badges, she confirmed that she was Ben's mother. She had just finished her cleaning shift at one of the local pubs. The uniform belonged to a private company. Pete and I stood on the doorstep until at last we were invited in.

The front door led into a tiny hallway that had barely enough space for the three of us. There were two options; either to go straight upstairs or turn right which took us into a compact living room. From where I stood, I noted that it was spotless, not a bit of clutter to be seen. An archway led through to a small dining room with a doorway off to the left which I presumed led to the kitchen. We sat down, Pete on the sofa, me on a chair opposite. That would give us different perspectives from which to gauge Ben's reactions to questions. Mrs Chadwick went to fetch her son who was apparently ensconced in his bedroom listening to music. The boy must have been wearing headphones, otherwise I reckoned we would have been able to hear it.

Mrs Chadwick eventually reappeared followed by Ben, a tall lad with fair hair. It looked like he usually wore it in a quiff but it needed a touch-up with gel. His piercing blue eyes met mine as I asked him to sit in the chair opposite me. A slight shake in his hands gave away that he was nervous but trying to not let us see it. His mother asked if we wanted a cup of tea and disappeared into the kitchen to make it. I realised I hadn't eaten anything and felt queasy.

I wanted Mrs Chadwick to be present while we talked to Ben, so focused on helping him relax. It would also take my mind off how I felt. Keeping it simple, I asked Ben to confirm that he was indeed a student of Mr Murdoch and that he knew his teacher had been murdered. Ben nodded; he'd seen it on the news. The room fell into silence, in the background the rattling of crockery and the rustling of wrappers. It was a relief when the tea and biscuits were served. Mrs Chadwick perched herself on the arm of Ben's chair, resting her hand on her son's shoulder. It made me think of a mother hen protecting her chick.

Pete took a mouthful of tea and ate a biscuit. I waited until he picked up his pencil, ready to go, before checking that Ben was in Mr Murdoch's class second to last lesson on the day his teacher died. He nodded. That was the warm-up. Bill had been through the statements from Ben's class as requested and had given us a few pointers from his notes. Therefore, I asked Ben if anything unusual had happened during the lesson.

His answer was short. 'No.'

From what I knew, that wasn't true, and I pointed out others had noticed Mr Murdoch confiscating his phone. It might seem a minor detail but sometimes that's where the clues lie. I asked, 'Why not mention it in your statement?'

He looked at me blankly. 'Didn't think anything of it. Teachers take phones all the time.'

I wasn't convinced. When challenged that taking his phone was unusual, he got agitated. He looked from me to Pete, and back again, as we waited for an answer. I glanced at Mrs Chadwick whose gaze rested on her son's head, also waiting for his response. The silence in the room was deafening, until Ben eventually broke it. The only thing he could come up with was that he didn't want his mum to find out. That she would get upset. He leaned forwards in his chair as if to pick up his mug but appeared to change his mind, letting his hand drop in his lap. An awkward silence filled the room again.

I might not know anything about parenting teenagers but the idea that he was worried about his mum finding out about the confiscated phone didn't sound right to me. I decided to change tack and come back to that if needs be. 'Why did you go back to Mr Murdoch's classroom the next lesson when you should have been in chemistry?'

Ben shot me a look of surprise. This was interesting. It looked like he had not expected us to know that. 'How...?' he rubbed his eyes and shrugged, trying to regain his composure. 'I went to get my phone back.' As soon as he said it, he turned away, looking flustered. He obviously knew he'd made a mistake.

I didn't take my eyes off him and asked to see Pete's notebook. Flipping back a couple of pages, I glanced through the notes, making a show of checking what Ben had said. I looked over again at Ben. 'Are you certain? Other statements from your classmates tell a different story.'

He gave a nervous laugh. 'Oh yeah, I remember. I already got my phone back.'

A bit of honesty at last. 'So, let's try again. Why did you go back to Mr Murdoch's classroom?' I wanted to find out if his version of events would agree with that of Ellen Shaw.

Ben took a deep breath, glanced at me but was unable to meet my eyes. He had been in chemistry period six and needed to go to the toilet. On his way he saw Mr Murdoch in the history cupboard putting books away. When he spotted Ben, he asked him to fetch a marker pen from his drawer and Ben went to his classroom to get one. He was waving his arms, getting into his stride, building a story. Pete and I glanced at each other, both of us sensing that he was becoming a tad agitated. I asked him how he had got into the drawer, hoping that he might provide information about the keys. Aware he might claim it was unlocked.

He became still and fixed his eyes on the floor, still avoiding my gaze. 'Mr Murdoch gave me his keys. I left them on his desk when I got the pen.'

If Ben had left the keys on the desk as he described, where were they? And who had taken them? I was certain that the killer must have used them to lock the cupboard door after committing the crime. 'And the keys were still there after you gave Mr Murdoch the pen?'

Ben raised his head, looked at me and shrugged. 'Assume so.'

He had gone back to his chemistry class, something he said his teacher could verify. After school he went with his friends to get something to eat up town. He was sounding increasingly sure of himself, confident in his story.

I was still not convinced. 'We'll be checking your movements, including any CCTV. We'll need a list of the friends you were with. And, of course, we may well need to talk to you again.'

At this, Ben went pale, looking increasingly uneasy. He responded in a thin voice. 'But I've told you everything I know.'

I could tell this boy was holding back, for some reason I couldn't fathom. But we would need more evidence of his story before we could press him further. Therefore, answering with a curt, 'I'll be the judge of that, Ben,' I got to my feet. As Pete followed suit, I could see the relief on Ben's face. Lifting a few biscuits from the pile on the plate, he quickly jumped ahead of us into the hallway and made a move for the stairs.

Mrs Chadwick was letting us out the front door when I paused and turned back towards Ben, who was almost at the top of the stairs. 'By the way, Ben...' He stopped at the sound of my voice and turned to look at me. 'When you got the pen out of the drawer, did you see a notebook, about the size of a mobile phone, with a black cover?'

I watched the blood drain from his face as he answered, 'No.'

We locked eyes. 'Are you sure? Think carefully.'

He was first to look away. 'Certain.'

I nodded. 'Right, thanks for your help. We'll be in touch.'

CHAPTER 14

Sitting in the car outside Ben's house, I remained certain that the boy had lied. I'd noticed the look of panic that flitted across his face when I'd mentioned the notebook and I was sure that he'd lied about a few other things too. I said as much to Pete who agreed that we needed to check out a few things about Ben and his story.

He suggested checking the route from chemistry to the boys' toilets. 'I'd like to see if he could happen to be passing.'

Before I could stop myself, I started to answer. 'He wouldn't have gone past the History Department to the toilets...' I stopped. My voice tailed off, realising I had probably given myself away. 'That is, I don't think he would....'

Pete gave me a quizzical look. 'You sounded pretty sure. How would you know that?'

I silently cursed myself because I hadn't intended to say anything yet. But this was Pete and I reckoned I could rely on him to keep quiet. And so, I came clean. 'It's my old school. Unless they've changed where everything is – and I doubt it – he should have gone straight down the stairs and bypassed history.'

Pete stared at me, clearly surprised. 'I know you lived round here before moving to Glasgow, but ... you went to Riverwood? Why didn't you say something?'

I didn't want to tell Pete that most of my memories of being at the school were not good ones. That it was a time in my life I preferred to forget. But I could tell him about not wanting to be taken off the case. I took a deep breath and told Pete how much I wanted to solve the case because I had recognised Mr Murdoch. He had always been a popular teacher, one of the good ones. 'It crossed my mind that, if Lewis thought I was too close to the case, he might think it would affect my ability to remain impartial. And pass the case to someone else.' I hoped Pete wasn't too offended as I waited for him to respond.

Pete shifted in his seat then turned to look at me. 'I wondered that something might be up when I saw your reaction to the body. And catching you sitting at that desk in his classroom.' Pete, as I'd suspected, perceptive as always. I relied on that for him to work things out on a case so why would I think he wouldn't have noticed my reactions to things right in front of him?

I bowed my head and took a breath before meeting Pete's gaze. 'Mr Murdoch, deceased. Not just a body as far as I'm concerned. It's important to me that we find out who did this. Well, I know every case is important. But this one is personal for me too.'

Pete nodded. 'I won't say a word. Unless I think it's affecting your judgement. There might come a time when it's best to let folks know though.'

I turned to look out the window. 'Maybe. Probably. But not yet. Not until I have more evidence, when it's too late for someone else to take it on.' Pete could tell I remained resolute in my decision. He set his eyes on the road, started the engine and we headed back to Ayr. I didn't feel great, perhaps because of my conversation with Pete reminding me of my nightmare or maybe because I still hadn't eaten. My stomach was growling. I glanced at Pete, his eyes peeled on the road ahead. 'Let's stop to pick up coffees on the way. I could do with some caffeine. And food.'

When we arrived back at King Street, we were accosted by the desk sergeant. A young man had come in having said he had found a knife in a bin close to the river. He had put him in an interview room. I thanked him and we headed upstairs. I needed time to drink my coffee and gather my thoughts.

Half an hour later Pete and I entered the interview room. At the table sat a young man in clothes that looked like they hadn't seen a washing machine anytime recently, emphasised by a sour smell that mingled with the stale air in the room. The young man looked up as we walked in, clearly worried that he was in trouble. I introduced myself and Pete. Keeping a friendly tone, I asked him what he'd been doing down by the river.

He took off his bobble hat and let his straggly hair fall around his face and shoulders. Lifting his head to look directly at me revealed brown eyes that showed more suffering than they should at his age. I couldn't help but feel sorry for him and gave him a reassuring smile.

Eventually he spoke. 'I was looking for food, searching in the bins. Not so many folks go looking for food in the bins down there, usually they stick to the town centre or by the big supermarkets, but sometimes I'll find something. Folks heading along the river walk, school kids go down there at lunchtime, students from the university maybe.'

This sounded reasonable enough. 'Where exactly did you find the knife?' I asked him.

The young man wrung his hands and pushed his hair out of his eyes. 'Friday morning. In the bin at the path going up to the footbridge across to Holmston Road. Wrapped up in a cloth. I was lucky I didn't cut my hand. I was going to leave it there but maybe someone would get hurt if I did.'

I leaned back in my chair and watched him. 'Friday, you said? Why wait two days to hand it in?'

His hands were shaking, his breath shallow. 'I didn't know what to do. I realised because I'd picked it up you might think it was mine. I was worried you might catch me with it. Better to hand it in. Maybe not get the blame. In case I'd been caught on CCTV.'

I searched the young man's face for clues as to whether he was telling the truth or not. Instinct told me he was; why bring the knife in and not leave it where it was if he had committed a crime with it? Or planned to. Also, it didn't seem like he had a violent nature, more someone down on his luck. Getting up from my seat, aware that he was watching me, I called the desk sergeant to bring him some food. After that we would take a statement and fingerprints. He would be allowed to go with the proviso of my knowing where to find him.

Leaving Pete to finish up, I went to the evidence store to check out the knife and rag. It was obvious the knife had been wiped clean, but whoever used it had made a mistake; they had wrapped it in the same rag used to clean it. That was clear from the dried blood on the fabric. I concluded this wasn't the work of a seasoned killer. I was certain that it would be Shannon Birch's blood and that I was looking at the knife used to stab her. I signed the paperwork to get the evidence sent over to forensics pronto.

By the time I got back to the incident room, Pete was already there. We agreed that the knife was almost certainly the one used on Shannon Birch. It was too much of a coincidence to find a weapon in the bin that close to the spot where she was found stabbed. We were also on the same wavelength about the profile of the attacker. That it probably was not a professional killer, more likely someone the victim knew and not that well planned. We noted that we were looking at a sloppy attempted murder. What we needed to find out was whether this was connected to Mr Murdoch's murder and, if so, how?

Nothing new had come in and, given it was Sunday, I sent Bill, Gary and Carmel home. Pete and I went through what we knew about Katie Spencer before deciding it was time to call it a day. Pete's wife, Yvonne, might be understanding of his job, having chosen to stay at home with the boys, but she would appreciate him being home for an early family dinner.

Pete shrugged into his jacket. 'Why don't you join us for dinner? Yvonne always makes loads. I'm sure she'd love to see you.'

When Pete became my mentor in Glasgow, Yvonne had taken me under her wing, even after the boys were born. I should have made a better effort to keep in touch after they moved back to Ayrshire. However, today I wasn't feeling very sociable. I looked up. 'No thanks, Pete. I'm going to look through this stuff again tonight. Another time.'

He gave me a long look. 'Don't turn into a hermit, Kim.' He didn't have to add 'now you're on your own.'

'I'm keeping my focus on this. When we're done, I'll come for dinner. Promise.'

Pete snorted and raised his eyebrows before waving and heading for the door.

I'd intended to work late to prepare for the visit to Katie Spencer but found I couldn't settle so, like the others, headed home. I felt the need to get out of the office, get a change of environment to think things through. Tomorrow, Monday, a new week, more people working and so hopefully get some answers. Or, at least, have something to report to my boss.

Instead of going straight home, though, I decided to drive to Coylton. I felt the need to reconnect with my old home, to remind myself of the house that had provided security for my teenage self. Fifteen minutes later, reaching the village, I took a left turn and parked at the top of the hill. That was where I used to live with Mum and Dad.

It was a beautiful autumn afternoon, cold but sunny and I wanted to get some air. Getting out of the car, I began walking down the farm track, to join the drive that led to Sundrum Castle. Mum and I used to pick brambles along here and she'd make jam. Closing my eyes, I could smell the boiling fruit that used to permeate the house. Almost twenty-five years since she'd gone. Dad died four years after her. I stopped, looking at the view, immersed in memories. I thought about how he had been so proud of me joining the police, even though he'd worried about my choice of career. 'You're such a slip of a thing, to be tackling criminals,' he would say. I smiled at the memory. A sheep in the field baaed, its bleat echoing across the still air, making me jump and forcing me back to the present. I made my way back to the car.

At home, I let the murder investigation crowd my mind again. It was rattling me, taking place in my old school, a teacher I had known and respected, who had cared about me. And the effort in suppressing bad memories. I'd known deep down that coming back might resurrect uncomfortable feelings but was sure I could handle it. I could not have anticipated my first case dredging up what had happened so many years ago. Events that I thought I had dealt with.

I wondered if Ricky Spencer would be there when I interviewed his daughter. Likely that he would be. Would he recognise me? I hoped not. Why had I come back here? Was the promotion worth it? Was it fate that I should be the person to find out who did this? I shook my head, telling myself to get a grip, to forget the melancholy and get on with the job.

Opening the fridge, I ignored the bottle of wine and contemplated what I could make to eat from its meagre contents. I hadn't found much time for grocery shopping these last few days. I opened the freezer instead, found a ready meal and put it in the microwave. While waiting for it to heat up, I went through to the bedroom to get changed.

My eyes were drawn to the small notebook I kept on my bedside table in case I came up with any ideas during the night. It wasn't unusual for me to have difficulty sleeping while churning over a case, nor to wake up in the night with a restless mind. It depended on how much the case I was working on got to me and I anticipated not getting much sleep until this one was solved. I suppose I should work on that, try to relax more, find other things to do.

Picking up my notebook, I thought about what Frankie had said, that Mr Murdoch had taken a notebook from Shannon Birch. I had a hunch that notebook was the key to everything.

Monday 17th October 2022

THE MURDER WEAPON

CHAPTER 15

Carmel was already there when I arrived at 7.30am the following morning. As if on cue, Pete, Bill, and Gary appeared carrying cups of coffee. I gratefully accepted my latte, took a sip, and retreated to my office to prepare for the day. When my phone rang, as expected, it was the DCI asking for an update. I noted that Lewis was in early too, obviously concerned about the media and what they would say about progress. I'd been surprised to not find a posse of reporters outside the building when I arrived. The Comms Team were evidently doing their job and keeping the press informed. As requested, I made my way upstairs to Lewis's office.

DCI Jack Lewis was standing looking out the window when I entered the room. A tall man with a commanding presence, he had the knack of making me feel even smaller than my five-foot-two frame. He'd made it clear that he had been willing to give me the chance in this job based on my reputation for getting results, even though there had been other, more experienced, candidates. I didn't want to let him down. Lewis turned to face me before taking a seat and asking how the investigation was going.

Sitting upright in his chair, his hands on his desk, fingers interlinked, I could feel his eyes boring into me. He didn't ask me to sit. 'The reporters are making a lot out of the link between the girl and the teacher. Anything in that?' He made it clear he was worried about media attention, that he wanted the case solved quickly.

Despite the scrutiny, I managed to remain calm. 'Absolutely not, Sir. There's no evidence of wrongdoing on the part of Mr Murdoch. Certainly, no rumours or suspicion of any relationship between him and the student, Shannon Birch. Apart from him being her history teacher.' What I'd said was true as far as we knew at this point, and I hoped that my instinct was correct, that nothing would come to light.

Lewis pursed his lips, never taking his eyes off me. 'Well, I hope you're right. Keep me posted. I want to know what's going on and not hear about it first in the news.'

I nodded. That was my cue to leave so I headed back to the incident room.

Going into my office, I closed the door and relished the silence. The glass wall did a decent job of keeping out most of the sound. I might want to see the comings and goings beyond it, but I didn't need to hear all the shenanigans as well. Office gossip and teasing were things that didn't interest me. Sinking into the large swivel chair, I kicked off my shoes before lifting the phone. The number I wanted was on speed dial and was soon picked up. 'Any progress with the post-mortem, Duncan?'

'Good morning to you, too, Inspector.' Again, Duncan met my rudeness with good humour and I could picture him smiling.

I had to get better at this; not allowing my need to get the answers quickly make me rude. 'Sorry, Duncan. Good Morning.' Thankfully, he'd worked with me enough times to remember I spent little time on pleasantries. Always keen to get to the details, my mind was fixed on that. If Duncan had nothing conclusive to report, he would at least give me his preliminary thoughts.

He didn't let me down, having come in on Saturday, anticipating a call from me sooner rather than later. I waited while he got his notes and organised his thoughts. 'The cause of death was as I'd thought, a contrecoup injury to the brain.' He paused before adding, 'There was considerable damage at the point of impact which resulted in bleeding. However, the opposite side of the brain has also been damaged. That means the impact was violent enough for the brain to slam against the opposite side of the skull.'

I shuddered, involuntarily picturing the violence of Mr Murdoch's last moments. 'What do you make of it?'

He took a deep breath. 'In my opinion, whoever did this wanted to make sure Mr Murdoch was dead. Even if he had survived the blow, and there was only one blow, to pull through that would have needed immediate medical attention and he'd been left there all night.'

I felt myself go cold, stunned, trying to take in what Duncan had said. 'Are you saying the blow might not have killed him? That he may have lain there in pain?'

His voice was quiet, knowing the implications of what he was saying. 'It's possible, but more likely that he would've been unconscious from the start and not known a thing.'

I was glad Duncan couldn't see me and turned to face the window to hide from the incident room. Tears pricked my eyes as the full horror hit me. In my mind I saw the young teacher, about the same age as me now, at the peak of his career, full of enthusiasm and fun who became the amiable, reliable, sometimes gruff, teacher who kept everything going, as his colleagues had described. The thought of him lying in that cupboard alive and in pain did not bear thinking about. He didn't deserve that. Keeping myself together, I listened carefully as Duncan gave his opinion on the likely murder weapon; something heavy would be needed to cause such damage to the head, probably flat and blunt, like a mallet. Trying to picture it, I asked, 'Something that an auctioneer would use?'

Duncan clarified. 'No. You're thinking about a gavel. Similar shape. Mallets are bigger, usually made of solid wood and are used for carpentry work. For woodwork...' His voice tailed off as he waited for his words to sink in.

I felt something click in my mind. 'A tool that might be found in a school's Technologies Department?'

I realised I'd said it out loud when Duncan responded. 'Absolutely, yes.'

He confirmed that the results of the DNA from Mr Murdoch's bedding should be through later that day. The results from the hair in the shower trap were in but had proved inconclusive in terms of identifying who it was. There were no roots so only mitochondrial DNA could be extracted, although it did confirm that it was a natural colour as there were no traces of chemicals. They could, however, compare the DNA extracted from the stain on the sheet to the hair to establish the possibility of it being the same person.

'In terms of the visitor to Mr Murdoch's house the night before his murder, can I assume from this evidence that we're looking for someone with auburn hair? And, also assume that it's one person?'

Duncan agreed. 'Yes, to both, Kim.'

I thanked him and ended the call. I took a moment to compose myself. My upset that Mr Murdoch may have lain there alive for some time morphed into increased determination that I would find out who did this. Heading out into the incident room, I updated Pete on what Duncan had said and asked him to go to the school and have a look round the Technologies Department, taking Gary with him. Follow the lead on the murder weapon. I wanted him to take charge of that.

The interview with Katie Spencer could wait. Although I could have taken Bill, given that Pete already knew I'd gone to Riverwood, I decided it was preferable to have him there in case Ricky Spencer recognised me.

CHAPTER 16

At Riverwood Pete and Gary showed their badges to the janitor who led them to the Technologies Department on the ground floor. Pete noted that it was two floors directly below the History Department. The door to Technologies led into a narrow corridor with two classrooms on each side. The corridor opened into a large workshop. Pete thanked the janitor who left them to it.

Gary chose this moment to suss out Pete. "How're you finding working for the DI? Was she not your DC a few years back? In Glasgow?"

Pete knew that Gary admired Kim because she had a reputation for being good at her job but had hoped Pete himself might have got the promotion instead. Gary had told him often enough that he thought Pete was a hard worker, a good cop, that he had proved his worth. Pete also knew that Gary would have wanted to step into his DS shoes. Gary also didn't seem to understand why Pete wasn't bothered about his former subordinate being his boss, having to call her Ma'am and follow her instructions. Pete didn't answer, preferring to let the comment go rather than explain himself again. In his view, less responsibility at work was better for family life. Gary would understand it one day, maybe when he had kids. Or maybe not. The young man was more ambitious than Pete had ever been. "Let's look around, Gary. See what we can find."

The two men turned in unison as the door opened behind them. A woman casually dressed in jeans and a black polo neck sweater stood with her hands on her hips. "Can I help you?"

Pete offered his badge and the woman visibly relaxed. 'And you are...?'

"Amanda Cairns,' she replied, 'I'm the technical assistant in this Department. I look after the equipment - make sure everything's clean and ready for lessons. Sometimes I help students if they need it."

Pete could not believe their luck. "Just the person we need to talk to. Why are you here, though? It's the holidays." Could she be here to dispose of a murder weapon? He made a mental note to check her statement back at King Street.

Amanda explained that she always came in the first week of the holidays to tidy up and make sure everything was in order; that all tools were accounted for and in the correct place. She kept an inventory of everything signed out for each lesson. Although things can get untidy, she made sure to check that they had been handed back in. There was always the risk that students would take them away. Pete asked to see the inventories for the previous week. If Amanda suspected it was to do with Mr Murdoch's murder, and she probably did, so be it. He didn't plan to enlighten her. She regarded him closely and said it wouldn't be a problem for him to see the paperwork.

Pete looked at Gary who nodded and headed off towards the classrooms to look around. He turned his attention back to Amanda. "How well did you know Mr Murdoch?"

Amanda looked directly at Pete. "Raymond? Not that well. Everyone knew who Raymond was, of course, and liked him. I only spoke to him a couple of times or so. Usually if I happened to sit next to him at something going on in the staff room. He never went to the end of term meals or Christmas parties. He was part of the group of older teachers who went to the pub instead. I've already said all that in my statement."

Pete followed Amanda to the back of the workshop where she opened a door to what turned out to be a large cupboard. He noted that it wasn't locked. Amanda confirmed that the room was never locked because they only had a couple of keys and it was inconvenient for staff if they had to find someone with a key every time they needed tools for lessons. She continued that there was usually someone around and they hadn't had a problem with things going missing.

'So far,' Pete thought.

Just inside the door of the cupboard was a filing cabinet. The rest of the room was floor to ceiling shelving round the walls and down the middle. The shelves were full of tools carefully stacked and labelled in boxes. It was obvious that Amanda was fastidious about her job. She flicked through folders in the cabinet, eventually pulling one out. "Here they are."

While Pete had been taking in the layout and contents of the room, she had pulled out the inventories, one for each day, from the top drawer of the cabinet. They were carefully typed with tools listed in alphabetical order. Against each there was a record of how many tools the department had, how many had been signed out, the dates and the lessons.

Pete perused the list until he reached the one for mallets. According to the list there should be twenty. Asking Amanda to show him where these would be stored, he followed her past rows of boxes before arriving at the correct one. He took a pair of gloves from his pocket, donning them before lifting the box from the shelf and putting it on the floor. He counted them laying each out as he did so. Nineteen mallets.

Amanda was taken aback. "That can't be right, Sergeant. The inventory says there were twenty mallets. And I remember, I counted them in myself."

Pete looked up at her. "Are you sure no-one borrowed one?"

"No. They would have to sign one out with me." She was adamant.

"You've never had an instance of someone borrowing tools for a DIY job with a promise to bring them back?" Pete knew there had to be some reason a mallet was missing but he was not going to share his suspicions.

"Well, yes, I have - but I always keep a note in the desk diary. Occasionally someone might borrow a tool and leave a post-it or something." Amanda was beginning to sound less sure of herself. Her system was obviously not as full proof as she had claimed.

Pete asked, "When were the mallets last used?"

Amanda checked the inventory. "The lesson before lunch last Thursday, the day before the last day of term."

"And they were all returned? No chance that one was borrowed?"

Amanda was insistent. "I counted them in myself. Lesson 4, ten mallets issued, ten returned. Twenty in box. Those are my initials."

"So, at some point since then, a mallet has gone missing." Pete waited for the penny to drop.

"Yes. You don't think ..." Amanda gasped as she looked at Pete, her eyes widening with shock.

Pete was still not going to enlighten her. Let her put two and two together. It didn't hurt to sometimes rattle people. "I'll need you to come down to the station to add to your statement so that we have all this on record." He replaced the mallets in the box and put it back on the shelf. He called King Street to arrange for Amanda Cairns to go to the police station and to organise forensics to take fingerprints and send uniform to secure the scene.

Gary appeared in the doorway. “I noticed something that might be helpful.”

Pete followed Gary into one of the classrooms. Gary pointed to an A4 sheet inside a polybag tacked to the wall to the right of the door. On closer inspection, Pete noted the sheet contained a table of pupil names against which were dates and times in and out of class. All the classrooms in Technologies had them. It looked like records of students leaving the classrooms so the teachers would know who had been wandering about if anything happened.

Pete was impressed. “As soon as uniform arrives, I think we head up to chemistry. Check if and when Ben Chadwick was signed out. Brilliant work, Gary.”

While Gary escorted Amanda to her car, Pete called Kim. She picked up on the second ring. “Assume you’ve something to report, Pete?”

“Oh, yes. The Technologies technician is on her way to update the statement she made on Friday. There’s a mallet missing from the store room. I’ve arranged for the area to be secured and forensics to come. And a search of the surrounding area.’ He paused. ‘But, even more interesting... Could be something, could be nothing.” Pete took a breath. “Amanda Cairns has auburn hair.”

CHAPTER 17

After Pete's revelation, I called Bill into my office. I wanted him to interview Amanda Cairns when she arrived to update her statement and carefully do some probing into her personal life. Was it a coincidence that the woman had auburn hair like that found in Mr Murdoch's shower? I didn't think so.

I was lost in thought, contemplating priorities, when Pete arrived back from the school and headed towards my office. I looked up, hearing the swing doors whoosh open and closed. Pete stopped to talk to Bill, referring to his notebook, no doubt giving him more detail for the Amanda Cairns interview. I watched as Carmel approached him, handing him a piece of paper, pointing out some information. Pete nodded and continued on his way. He saw me watching him and didn't bother to knock.

I waited until he sat down and got himself organised. 'What did you make of Amanda Cairns?' I asked.

He raised his eyebrows. 'Cool as a cucumber. At least, at first. She didn't like it when I discovered the flaw in her system.'

'Any chance she could be involved?' I was keen to hear what he had to say.

'Well, the auburn hair could be a coincidence?' I could tell he wasn't convinced though.

I sucked my teeth. 'Doubt it, Pete. I don't believe in coincidences. Let's see what more Duncan comes up with. In the meantime, ask Cumnock for any CCTV footage in the vicinity of Mr Murdoch's bungalow. See if her car appears.'

Pete nodded. 'Changing the subject... Mr Murdoch's bank records have come through. Carmel's had a quick look at statements for the last twelve months.' She's noticed a regular payment that doesn't look right.' He handed me a piece of paper. The one Carmel had given him.

My eyes were drawn to the areas Carmel had highlighted. Monthly payments of £131.25 to YouNeedCash.com. 'Why would someone on his salary with few outgoings need a loan? His house didn't strike me as a place he spent money on. There's nothing here to indicate expensive hobbies or holidays either. Any ideas?' I looked quizzically at Pete, leaning back in his chair.

He shrugged. 'Could be anything. Gambling addiction? Porn?'

I perused the information again. 'Can't see anything that looks dodgy here.'

'If he was involved in something illegal, it could be a way to transfer funds without raising questions. Or he took out a loan to hide his activities?' Pete suggested.

I opened and closed my mouth. I was working on the assumption that Mr Murdoch was an innocent victim. What if I was wrong? I didn't think I was but this we couldn't ignore. I scrutinised the page, not only the highlighted areas. And noticed that this last month there had been no payment. I showed it to Pete. 'Looks like he stopped the payments. I wonder why. Ask Carmel to keep digging into the bank account. And Bill to check out the loan company.'

Pete went to find out what kind of car Amanda Cairns drove and contact Cumnock to check if it had been caught on any CCTV footage in the vicinity of Mr Murdoch's house last Wednesday night. On the way he asked Bill to find out more about YouNeedCash.

I was trying to get my head around the possibility that Mr Murdoch might have been involved in criminal behaviour that got him killed when my phone rang, making me jump. The call was from the security company in Kilmarnock that monitored the CCTV cameras in the vicinity of the river. They kept everything for thirty days and, although the cameras didn't cover the exact spot Shannon went into the river, there were several nearby and at most access points to the path. The videos were ready for us to look at.

There could be hours of footage and I didn't want to take up my time on that. I called Gary for an update at the school. Given that uniformed officers were in place to wait for the forensics team, I asked him to go to Kilmarnock. I told him to start from when the school would have been out until the time Shannon was found.

I stood up and looked out of the window. There was a smirr of rain, making the view hazy. I knew what I needed to do and felt the uneasiness in my stomach.

This morning I'd planned to visit Katie Spencer, find out why she'd visited Shannon Birch and work out why Shannon had got so worked up when her mum mentioned the name. But what if her father was there? The thought of Ricky made my skin crawl. 'Stop thinking of him as Ricky. That's the boy who... Think of him as Richard, the father of a possible witness, even suspect,' I told myself.

I turned away from the window and rolled my shoulders, releasing some tension. I couldn't put this off any longer. It was time to find out what Katie Spencer had to say. And if he was there, I'd have to deal with it.

I waited until Pete put the phone down, picked up my coat and, passing through the office, asked him to meet me at his car in ten minutes. On my way to the lift, I stopped at the ladies' bathroom where I checked my appearance in the mirror. I had changed a lot since school, letting my hair go back to its natural colour and having a much shorter cut. I rarely wore make-up these days, certainly not the heavy goth stuff I had favoured as a teenager. Hopefully if Ricky – no, Richard – Spencer was there, he wouldn't recognise me or, at least, if he did find me familiar, be unable to place me. Mrs Caldwell hadn't, so why should he?

CHAPTER 18

The Spencer family lived in a detached house on Southpark Road, a tree-lined street of sandstone properties behind stone walls and security gates. My research revealed that Richard Spencer had joined the army and risen to the rank of officer. Having been invalided out with a substantial pension, he was now the owner of a security consultancy firm. It looked like he'd decided to move back home to Ayrshire, probably because of family, friends and house prices. For a lad from an upstairs Council flat in Annbank, a small village about five miles out of town, he'd done well.

Mrs Spencer answered the door, a short woman, smartly dressed, her hair tied back in a neat bun. Pete and I were shown into a large hall with high ceilings and a staircase that curved its way to the upper floor. The cloying smell of pot pourri in a cut glass bowl hung in the air. I almost wanted to choke, whether because of the perfume or trepidation at coming face to face with Richard Spencer, I couldn't say. We were left standing there until she returned with her husband and daughter.

I took a deep breath and did my best to keep my face expressionless as he appeared from a room at the back of the house. Inside, I felt like I was shaking. Richard Spencer looked every inch a soldier, close cropped hair and an upright posture that made him look like he was used to getting his own way. His appearance might have changed from the boy at school but I would have known him anywhere. He stared at me and I made the effort to meet his gaze. It took everything I had to remain professional when what I wanted to do was slap him. Or run. At last, he looked away and gestured towards a door to our left. First battle won. Inwardly, I breathed a sigh of relief that he didn't appear to have recognised me.

We were led into an opulent living room. No expense had been spared in the décor, although it wasn't to my taste. It was hard to tell whether it was decorated to impress others or because they liked it. The room looked barely used; perfectly arranged, it could easily be mistaken for a show house. The type of room that would always feel cold whether it was heated or not. Not what I would call a warm family home.

I reminded myself that we were here to interview Katie Spencer. Carefully avoiding Richard Spencer's gaze, I turned my attention to his daughter. Katie took after her father in height and features. Tall for her age with large eyes and a square chin. Her dark hair worn in a pixie cut, perfectly tousled, looking like it took minutes but more likely hours to get right. Dressed entirely in black and her natural face hidden behind layers of make-up, in some ways her style reminded me of myself at that age. The most important thing that I noticed, though, was that Katie looked nervous, maybe even a tad scared.

'You alright, lass?' Richard Spencer had evidently noticed too. His voice was softer than I expected.

Katie assured him she was fine. Pete and I exchanged glances, neither of us convinced. We were invited to take a seat and, as usual, positioned ourselves to get a good view of the set-up. Pete sat down at one end of a large four-seater sofa and I sat at the other end. Katie sat on the two-seater sofa opposite us, her mother next to her. Richard took the armchair in the corner where he could get a good view of everyone. To me it looked like he had put himself on high alert, back in army mode, surveying the territory, working out tactics. He spoke before I got the chance to, like it was important to get in first, asking us what we needed to know.

Already I felt rankled, the tone in his voice when he addressed me as 'Inspector' was downright condescending. I would have to tread carefully, not rise to the bait, nor let old ghosts get in the way. If Katie was involved, I would have to not allow myself any thoughts of revenge for what he did to me, or, more accurately, not open myself up to such accusations should he realise who I am.

I turned to look at him, trying to stop my stomach from rising into my throat. His experience in the army, having been injured in Afghanistan and by all accounts, a bit of a hero respected by his men, I reckoned he thought nothing would get past him. And, of course, I expected that he would do everything he could to protect his daughter. I wondered if he ever thought about what he'd done to me at school? When I was younger than his daughter is now? I turned away, ignored his question, and looked at Katie. 'We believe you're a friend of Shannon Birch?'

Before she could respond, Richard butted in, declaring, ‘We’ve not been living here that long. Katie hasn’t made friends yet.’

I continued to ignore him and, again, addressed her directly. ‘Katie, could you please answer the question? I’m suggesting that Shannon is a friend of yours because you visited her in hospital.’ I watched her take a deep breath, while avoiding my gaze. And the look of surprise on her parents’ faces didn’t escape my notice.

Eventually she spoke in a measured voice. ‘Not friends exactly. We know each other.’

I tried to place her accent but, apart from it not being Scottish, couldn’t pick up a regional tone. Presumably, given that the family had moved around a lot and had spent time abroad, she hadn’t lived anywhere long enough to pick up the dialect. At school, she was probably accused of being posh, a bit of an outsider. This fit with being there since August, it was now October and she still had no friends. I could empathise with that.

That said, it looked like I had another evasive teenager on my hands. I pointed out that she was the only friend who had been to see Shannon in hospital and there must be a reason for that. At this point, Richard intervened, clearly becoming exasperated, demanding to know what this was all about. I refused to look at him, determined that I wouldn’t let this man get to me. Feeling my resolve tighten, I at last turned towards him and looked him in the eye. ‘Have you seen the news, Mr Spencer? Shannon Birch is the girl who was stabbed by the river last week. The same day that Katie’s history teacher, Mr Murdoch, was murdered at the school. And according to Shannon’s mum, Katie is the only friend who has been to see Shannon in hospital.’

The room fell silent as my words sank in. Richard opened his mouth as if to speak, closed it again, dropping his gaze. After a few seconds that seemed like hours, I turned back to Katie. ‘I’ll ask you again to clarify your relationship with Shannon Birch and explain why you went to the hospital to visit her.’

Katie shrugged and glanced over at her dad. ‘I’ve spent time with Shannon. Wouldn’t call her a friend though. She’s in my history class. One day last week she came up to me in the canteen. No idea why she decided we could be friends but she invited me round to her house.’

At this point Richard loudly interjected, making the rest of us jump. 'That's right. Katie did go out last Wednesday evening. She went to study at a friend's house. It was nice to see her getting out. Normally we don't allow it on a school night but we let it go because we want her to make friends. She was home by eleven.' He grinned, pleased to have corroborated his daughter's story. That grin made me want to punch him. He clearly felt he had gained the upper hand.

I noted, though, how Katie sat biting her lip, to me a sign that she was hiding something. She hadn't been honest with her parents, of that I was certain. Ignoring Richard's comments, I asked again why she had visited Shannon in hospital when none of her close group of friends had.

Katie sat staring at her hands. 'I was shocked at what happened and thought I'd see how she was. Thank her for having me round. Didn't realise that she wasn't supposed to have visitors. Her mum went for a coffee and said I could keep Shannon company.'

When she insisted that they had only talked about how Shannon was feeling, not about what had happened, the stabbing, I wasn't convinced. And I wasn't happy. Here was a third teenager withholding information and I couldn't understand why. They all professed to like Mr Murdoch, so why not want to help find his killer? And why be so evasive about the stabbing? The only explanation I could think of was that one, two or all of them were somehow linked to these crimes.

Pete caught my eye and leaned over to show me something in his notepad. I nodded and he chipped in. 'According to our notes you were absent the day Mr Murdoch was killed?'

Katie flinched. 'Well, yes. What has that to do with anything?'

From her reaction, there was no harm in Pete doing a bit of fishing. 'It's unusual for you to be absent?' he asked.

This time it was Mrs Spencer who intervened, explaining that Katie enjoyed school and worked hard to keep on top of her studies, especially with changing schools so much. She wanted to do well and go to university. Even when she was ill, she would struggle on but last Thursday she couldn't get Katie out of bed. Her daughter was shivering and looked like she might be running a temperature so she told her to take the day off. It looked like flu, or at least, a bad cold.

The whole time her mother was talking, I didn't take my eyes off Katie. I wondered how someone who had been so ill on Thursday and Friday could be sitting here looking the picture of perfect health. I put it to her that she had recovered quickly, particularly given that she was well enough to visit the hospital. Katie caught my eye and looked away, decidedly uneasy. I carried on. 'So, let's get this clear. You were fine when you went to Shannon's house on Wednesday evening, then you had a couple of days feeling ill. One of them the day Mr Murdoch was likely murdered and Shannon was stabbed. On Saturday you felt better and went to see Shannon.'

Richard erupted. 'What is all this? Are you suggesting that my daughter has some involvement in these crimes?'

I turned to look directly at him. 'I'm not suggesting anything, Mr Spencer. However, you must understand we've two serious investigations here and we need to speak to everyone who might be able to help us put together what happened.' My voice was cold, but professional. I was proud of myself, that I had kept my composure. He sank back into his chair.

I changed tack, asking what time her parents had returned home the day Mr Murdoch was killed. Katie lifted her head and looked warily at me, then at her parents. Mrs Spencer confirmed that she'd arrived home about 6.30pm and her husband about 7pm. Katie was watching TV in the living room next door. It occurred to me that Katie had been on her own all day and could have left the house. I asked her if she had done so.

We all watched her, waiting for the answer. There was a pause before she responded, a feeble, 'I don't think so.'

'You don't think so?' I was unable to hide my disbelief. 'Surely you would know if you left the house at any time last Thursday. Or Friday and Saturday, for that matter.'

Richard had clearly had enough. He sat forward in his chair and stared first at me, then at Pete. He insisted that if Katie said she hadn't gone out, that was what had happened. And he could prove it. They had security cameras on the front and back doors which recorded everything and he could provide us with copies. I smiled inwardly. There was no need to rile him further when we would have the tapes.

While he was talking, I kept an eye on Katie. I noticed how the girl's face had changed when the cameras were mentioned. She must have forgotten about those and sat, her mouth opening and closing like a fish as if deciding whether to speak or not. In the end, she admitted that she had gone out because she'd felt a bit better and wanted to clear her head. She'd got up about lunchtime and gone for a walk on the beach in the afternoon. She hadn't met anyone while she was out so there was no-one to vouch for her whereabouts. When I told her we would be checking CCTV along the route she had taken, she sighed and looked at the floor. First, though, we would look at the tapes from the house. I handed Richard Spencer my card and asked him to email them as soon as possible.

CHAPTER 19

Pete and I got up to leave and Mrs Spencer rose to see us out. Reaching the door to the front room, I turned back towards Katie. She might not have been at the school long, but that didn't mean she didn't know what was going on. And I was a bit suspicious of her so-called illness and rapid recovery. Sounded like a hangover, or a comedown, to me. I waited until she looked up to meet my gaze. 'Do you know anything about drugs?' The look of shock on her face was at odds with her emphatic shake of the head. I continued. 'We've reason to believe that students in some schools are involved in a drugs racket. You would tell me if you knew anything, Katie, wouldn't you?' Katie stared and nodded as I continued, 'Oh, and you won't mind Sergeant Fletcher having your mobile number?' It wasn't a question and I watched as Pete made a note of the details. 'We'll be in touch.'

We were halfway across the hall when Richard called after me. I turned to face him, trying to remain impassive while my heart was pounding.

He was watching me intently. 'Why do I feel I've seen you before? Have we met?'

I met his eyes, and, without saying a word, turned for the door, resisting the desire to run. No way was I going to get involved in a conversation with him, one that might give me away. Reaching the car, I glanced back at the house. Mrs Spencer was still standing in the doorway, looking stunned, while Katie stood at the window watching us, misery written all over her face. Richard was standing behind her, a hand protectively on his daughter's shoulder, watching me.

Getting in the car, I took some deep breaths to keep calm, telling myself to focus on the case. I was convinced that Shannon Birch and Ben Chadwick were connected in some way and that was in turn connected to what had happened to Mr Murdoch. I still couldn't see the mild-mannered teacher involved in anything that had ended up getting him killed. I was sure that Katie Spencer was hiding something too. All students of Mr Murdoch. Could I be so wrong? I turned to Pete. 'You've got teenagers. Could any of these kids we've interviewed be killers? I've seen a lot in my time and know it's possible. But these kids all seem to have caring parents.'

Pete sighed. 'Anything's possible. We do our best as parents, but sometimes even Yvonne and I wonder if we get it right. If there's such a thing as getting it right. The boys are more interested in what their pals are thinking. Even the most stable homes have kids that go off the rails. You know that. We've seen it before.'

I knew he was right.

He started the engine and pulled away from the pavement. But then he parked further up the street, out of sight of the Spencer house. I could tell he had something to say. The wind whistled through the trees in the empty street, a solitary leaf falling onto the bonnet of the car. I waited.

Pete sucked in his breath, glancing at my hands which were inadvertently grasping the seat. He turned to look at me. 'What was going on in there? Something that's upset you.'

I tried to deflect the question. 'What do you mean?'

He was having none of it. 'I think you do. Richard Spencer. Do you know him? He seemed to recognise you.'

I sighed, looking out the window and bringing my hands to rest in my lap. I could never fault Pete's powers of observation. 'We were in the same year at school.'

He nodded. 'Riverwood. So, he did recognise you.' His voice was flat.

I rubbed my eyes. 'Probably. Yes. I don't think he's made the connection yet, though. But leave it, Pete. I don't want to talk about Richard Spencer. Let's say he wasn't someone I was a fan of at school. Some things are better left alone. It's his daughter and her involvement in these two cases I'm concerned about.'

Pete turned away, staring through the windscreen, deep in thought. At last, he switched on the ignition. 'Whatever you say. For now, anyway. But, if it's relevant, or clouds your judgement...'

I sighed. 'Yes, Pete, you'll be the first to know.' I sank into the seat. My heart was beating fast. 'Why did I come back here?' I thought again, suppressing the idea that flashed through my mind. Revenge? No, I could never have known that such an opportunity might present itself. I never expected things to resurface like they have. Pushing such thoughts to the back of my mind, I forced my attention back to the case. I needed to get a grip on myself.

We had interviewed those three teenagers, all of whom I was sure had an involvement in the murder case. I had seen enough during my career to know that sixteen- and seventeen-year-olds could kill, or at least, inflict serious injury which might lead to death. These three, however, didn't fit the usual profile. The unusual setting of the school and a teacher they all clearly liked threw in another conundrum. Where was the motive? When was the opportunity? If Katie had spent the evening at Shannon's house, why did Shannon's mum not recognise her when she appeared at the hospital? And on the day of the murder where did she go and how long for? Why were both Shannon and Ben so cagey about a notebook? Why is it so important? What is the connection between the murder and the stabbing? Who stabbed Shannon? And what about the mystery visitor and the payments from Mr Murdoch's account?

So many questions. The teenagers might help me piece the jigsaw together, but my gut told me I had to look deeper to find the killer. That would not stop me putting pressure on them, though, because they were all hiding something.

CHAPTER 20

When Pete and I got back to King Street, I called a meeting with Bill and Carmel. We had a lot to do. I started to speak but was interrupted by a flurry of activity as Gary burst through the doors of the incident room, obviously keen to share some news.

I waited for him to join the group. 'What have you got for us, Gary? You look like the cat that got the cream.'

He took centre stage, clearly pleased with himself. He had been at the CCTV company for a couple of hours and they had gone through reams of tape. They had started from the time the school would have been out, as I'd suggested. The cameras didn't cover all areas along the river so they had to focus on the likely direction the attacker had taken to get there. They could have come from either direction of the river walk, across the footbridge from Holmston Road or the path coming from the direction of the road that went to the school, university, and guest house.

The stabbing had taken place under the footbridge, out of sight of any cameras which were sporadically placed along the river. Gary had looked at the position of the cameras and realised that the attacker could have come across the footbridge and swung underneath the Craigie side without being caught on the one by the bin where the young man had found the knife. Therefore, he focused first on the last camera from the road to the school in case someone had parked there and walked to the river. There was nothing to note from that.

Next, he watched footage from the nearest camera on the route that someone would follow along the river walk from the town. Something had caught his eye and he'd asked the lad operating the equipment to zoom in for a closer look. We all waited with baited breath as, clearly, he was about to share a revelation. Looking proud of himself, he pulled a printout and copy of a tape from the folder he was carrying and held it up. 'Think we all know who this is.'

We certainly did and I felt a surge of anger which I couldn't disguise. 'I knew that boy was lying.' Pete and I exchanged glances, both of us astonished at how Ben could have lied, given the nature of these crimes. This was enough to, not only speak to Ben Chadwick again, but to search his house. Pete went to organise a search warrant. 'Bill, Gary, go through everything we have on Ben again. Talk to his friends. Whatever you need to do. Find out everything there is to know about him; anything that might be hidden.' I turned to Carmel. 'See if there could be a link to the suspected drugs activity at the school. Run the boy's name and photo past DI Burns's team to see if he's shown up at all.'

They all nodded, keen to get on with the job. This could be the breakthrough we needed. We could prove Ben Chadwick had lied. And now we had him in the area Shannon was stabbed and possibly around the time it took place. Tomorrow morning, we would interview him again and at least search his room, warrant or not. To get one could take days or longer, giving Ben the opportunity to destroy any evidence he might have that would link him to Mr Murdoch, Shannon, or drugs. If we had to bring him in I would do it. I asked Bill to chase up the warrant in the morning while Pete and I agreed to meet in Mossblown at 9am, late for us, early for a teenager on school holidays. I spent the next few hours going through what we knew, particularly examining Ben's movements, before deciding to call it a day.

The sun was about to set as I parked my car outside the flat. I walked to the end of the street and crossed the road to look over the wall at the beach and the sea. The clouds had been blown away by the wind, allowing the sun to sink spectacularly behind the mountains on Arran. As the last of the daylight faded, I felt an autumn chill and pulled my jacket closer around me. When the last of the orange had turned black, I retraced my steps and headed indoors. Keeping myself busy, preparing food, reading documents, catching up with the news, I stayed up late to avoid the time I dreaded. Today I had confronted one of the boys in my nightmares and during sleep I would be unable to control my subconscious mind.

Tuesday 18th October 2022

THE CODE

CHAPTER 21

Pete was already there when I pulled up outside Ben's house the following morning. He lived five minutes away in a bungalow in Tarbolton. Born and brought up in the village, he was proud of its heritage and association with the famous Scots poet, Robert Burns. When we worked together in Glasgow, I used to tease him about it and he'd laugh, saying that I should be more patriotic. He and Yvonne were childhood sweethearts and when the opportunity had arisen for them to move back to Ayrshire, they'd jumped at the chance. They wanted to bring their boys up in a more rural environment familiar to them and close to family and friends. And, even though Pete could have commuted, he liked to get home quickly at the end of a shift.

I parked behind Pete and turned my face away as I got out of the car, hopefully avoiding any comments he might make, even in jest. I didn't need reminding of how tired I looked. As expected, my sleep had been restless, punctuated by images that forced me wide awake to escape them. Checking my face in the mirror before I left, I could see that even concealer didn't hide the dark rims under my eyes. I hoped the team wouldn't think it was down to not being up to the job. Pete at least knew that there was a personal element to this case.

At last, I looked at Pete, ignoring the look of concern he gave me, and gave him a weak smile. 'Good morning,' I said.

'Good morning,' he replied. He paused and looked like he might say something else. Instead, he indicated that he would follow me along the path to the Chadwick's house. Our footsteps were heavy, neither of us happy to be interviewing a witness for the second time in as many days.

I knocked on the door and heard a bolt being drawn back and a chain unhooked; Mrs Chadwick being concerned about security. Pete remarked that we hadn't noticed that before. Had our previous visit made her nervous? She didn't look at all surprised to see us, almost as if our return visit was expected. We waited in the tiny hallway while she went to fetch Ben, the sound of heavy metal getting louder when she opened a door upstairs. Ben must not be wearing headphones this time.

After a few moments, the music abruptly stopped and she appeared at the top of the stairs. Behind her on the landing stood Ben, gazing down at us. I stood with one foot on the bottom step, looking up at him, and signalled him to come downstairs. He seemed rooted to the spot and it took him a few seconds to start moving. I watched as he slowly took one step at a time until he was standing in front of me. He was a tall lad and I had to tilt my head to see his face. It was expressionless.

His mother broke the silence. 'The police want to speak to you again, Ben. And have a look around your room.'

Although her voice was trembling, the look that passed between mother and son didn't escape my notice. It was like they knew something that we didn't, or some sort of code. Was she trying to tell Ben to be honest? Or to be careful? I couldn't decide, but I'd find out what was going on. Perhaps not today, but whatever they might have to hide would be uncovered. I was good at that, reading people, finding out their secrets.

'I thought you needed a warrant.' Ben looked nervous; his voice cracked.

'Not if I think you're hiding something which could help us solve two serious crimes.' I paused, holding his gaze until he was forced to look away. 'I'm going to have a quick look round your room, Ben. In due course, there will be a full search of the house.' Beside me I heard Mrs Chadwick gasp. It would seem she hadn't understood the full extent of the trouble her son might be in. She reached a hand out to him, which Ben ignored as he slunk past me into the living room.

She was left standing opposite me in the hall, Pete behind her, a wretched look on her face, wringing her hands. I nodded at Pete. He would take her into the living room and start questioning Ben while I had a snoop around.

I went upstairs. There were two bedrooms, one at the front of the house, the other, smaller one, at the back, next to which was the bathroom.

A typical two bedroomed terrace. I headed into the smaller bedroom at the back which was obviously Ben's. It smelled of stale pizza and sweat.

The room was a rectangular box. The bed was against the wall opposite the door with a window on the adjacent wall. To my left there was a wardrobe with a matching chest of drawers next to it. The furniture was coming apart in places. The floor was strewn with clothes, clean or dirty, it was difficult to tell. The top of the chest of drawers was covered with dirty plates and cups. Empty pizza boxes and fast-food cartons overflowed from the bin next to it. I wondered if any cooking went on in this house, although I was hardly one to judge given the contents of my own kitchen.

There was a small cabinet next to the bed, an expensive pair of headphones casually sitting on top of a pile of textbooks. I wondered how he could afford the headphones. For some reason that made me think of Ben's feet, the expensive trainers he was wearing, and I took a closer look at the clothes on the floor. Some were what I'd expect from the mother's income, cheaper high street attire. Yet some of the clothes were brands I'd have said were out of his reach: maybe even designer. Putting on my gloves, I bent down for a closer look. Something wasn't right here.

I looked inside the chest of drawers. The usual underwear and clothes, again a mix of cheap and expensive items. The wardrobe told a similar story. The bedside table had one small drawer full of pens, scraps of paper and an unopened packet of condoms. At least the boy was being sensible in that regard. Or maybe more like hopeful. We hadn't come across evidence of a relationship in his social media accounts.

So far, the only thing that bothered me was how he could afford any of the expensive stuff. Again, the rumours of drug dealing at the school crossed my mind. That could prove very lucrative. Taking in the posters on the walls, clearly Ben was a fan of Formula One as well as heavy metal. I turned to go downstairs. I'd leave the detailed search to Bill and see what else he managed to turn up.

When I entered the living room, Pete was asking Ben about why he was down by the river. His mother was watching, her brow furrowed, her body tense. I waited for Ben's answer but he remained silent.

From the doorway, I interrupted the conversation. 'You've got some expensive clothes, Ben. How can you afford them?'

His mother was quick to answer, jumping in before him, not giving him the chance to say anything. 'I work all the hours I can to make ends meet so I can't afford extras. Ben has a job working for a courier company and he buys his own clothes. They're all fake. Bought on the internet.'

Of course, this was likely to be the story Ben told her and she would believe it. There was a hopefulness in her tone and I wasn't sure who she was trying to convince, us or herself. Ben sat there, impassive, letting his mum speak.

I didn't respond to Mrs Chadwick. Instead, I addressed Ben. 'Come on, tell the truth. You know as well as I do that the designer clothes upstairs aren't fake.' Still, he wouldn't respond. 'Did you steal them? I asked. He shook his head, before insisting repeatedly that everything was fake, bought online. I was becoming more concerned about the boy lying than where he'd bought the clothes. Why had he not admitted to having a local delivery job unless it was illegal? Why not at least try to come up with a more credible story about the clothes that were clearly designer?

We were getting nowhere. Ben had refused to answer questions about being by the river and was clearly lying about the clothes. He was stacking up trouble for himself, yet appeared to not realise that. I thought I'd try another line of questioning. 'Do you know Shannon Birch?'

A flash of surprise passed across his face. Was he wondering why I would ask or did he know the girl? He looked me in the eye. 'I know who she is. The year below me at school.'

I walked across the room and sat down opposite him, in the same spot as the day before. 'Did you know that someone tried to kill her the day Mr Murdoch was murdered?'

Ben continued to look at me. 'I saw something about her being stabbed on the news.' He looked away.

My eyes never left his face. 'Sergeant Fletcher was asking why you were down by the river that day. Tell us, why were you down there?'

Ben looked at Pete, then at me. 'What d'you mean? I didn't go near the river!' He began to raise his voice, fists clenched, clearly agitated.

I watched his reactions carefully as I explained about the CCTV footage that put him in the vicinity of the river where Shannon was stabbed, possibly around the time of the attack. He kept looking from Pete to me and back again, the panic in his eyes plain to see. He glanced at his mother, who was sitting with a confused look on her face, and said he wouldn't answer any more questions.

I didn't know what to make of this. Why would he refuse to cooperate? Maybe he didn't know what to say, what story to tell. Or perhaps he was too scared to talk. If he was involved in drugs, it was likely he was frightened. Did his mother know? Whatever the truth, if Ben kept refusing to answer our questions, he would have to come with us to the police station and that would escalate things to a more serious level.

Despite warnings, he continued to refuse to say a word, staring into space. I asked Pete to read him his rights, hoping that would encourage him to talk. It had no effect.

'Ben,' I said, 'we have no choice but to take you into custody. Your mum or another adult can come with you...'

He interrupted me, shouting, 'I don't want anyone. Especially not Mum.'

That worried me, not because they appeared to be close and I'd have expected him to want her support, more because I got the impression that the mother knew more than she was letting on. The look between them I'd noted earlier crossed my mind. Maybe she knew too much and he was protecting her. Or maybe he was trying to protect himself in case she gave something away in the interview. I kept that thought to myself; it could be followed up later.

Pete took Ben gently by the arm and we made our way to the front door. Ben's mother put herself between me and her son, insisting that surely it wasn't necessary to take him away. I explained again there was no alternative. The evidence placed him at the scene of a crime and he was refusing to speak to us at home. Taking him into custody wasn't what I'd intended but we had no other option. Pete guided Ben out of the house and put him in a waiting patrol car, leaving his mother shouting at us to leave him alone. All I could do was reassure her that if he'd done nothing wrong, there was nothing to worry about. In the end I walked away, leaving her staring after us from the doorstep.

CHAPTER 22

By the time Pete and I arrived back at the station, Ben had already been shown into an interview room. Through the window we could see him sitting with his forearms on the table, head bent over. If he hadn't been so uncooperative, I might have felt sorry for him. But my annoyance at his silence outweighed that. The duty solicitor arrived and we entered the room. Pete and the solicitor took seats opposite each other. I remained standing. The atmosphere was tense. Outside it had started to rain, a steady pattering against the window.

I asked Ben to stand up and empty his pockets. The resulting look of panic etched on his face made me wonder what, or who, made him so scared. He tried to claim he didn't have anything on him but I could see the outline of a mobile phone in his right-hand back pocket. I looked at him for what seemed a long time, hoping that I would not have to seek permission to search him. At last, he capitulated, slowly removing the phone, and placing it carefully on the table in front of him.

'Given we've evidence linking you to two serious crimes, we'll be taking that,' I said. His face fell but he said nothing. I continued to look at him, certain from the way he held his hands to cover his front pockets, that he had something more to hide. 'Don't make me organise a search of your person, Ben. It's much better for you to cooperate.'

He looked at the solicitor, who nodded, indicating that she agreed with me. Keeping his eyes fixed on the table, he pulled an opened packet of chewing gum from his front left pocket. He paused, clearly uncomfortable, raised his head and looked at me, as if pleading to not have to do this. I nodded for him to continue, letting him know there was no way out.

He sniffed and let out a deep breath, reaching into his front right pocket. Finally, he pulled out an item which he carefully placed on the table. This seemed to be the most precious thing he had, his hand hiding it until the last moment. When he took his hand away, Pete and I looked at the object then glanced knowingly at each other. It was a notebook with a black cover the size of a mobile phone. This was the breakthrough. I felt it in my bones.

I picked up the notebook. Inside it was gobbledygook; a series of letters that made no sense. I handed the notebook to Pete. 'I think we've found what we've been looking for.' I looked back at Ben. 'What can you tell me about this?' He looked at me, saying nothing, and slumped back into his chair, staring at the objects on the table. I rested my gaze on his downcast head. 'We'll be taking this notebook as well.'

I decided to let Ben gather his thoughts before beginning the interview. I hoped that he might realise the seriousness of his situation and be more willing to talk. After organising tea and biscuits to be brought to him, Pete and I made our way upstairs to the incident room.

We agreed that the notebook was likely to be the one taken from Shannon Birch by Mr Murdoch. It was too much of a coincidence otherwise. We had to find out how Ben Chadwick had got hold of it. He had taken the detour, maybe to get it from the drawer. But how had he known it was there? And how could we prove anything unless Ben was willing to talk? There was nothing to identify who it belonged to and we couldn't make head nor tail of the letters inside it. Obviously, it was some sort of code. I urgently needed someone to decipher it.

I handed Gary Ben's phone to go through the contacts and cross reference those to his social media accounts. At least Ben had been compliant in providing us with the pin number. I wanted as much detail about him as Gary could find. Between that and the notebook we would hopefully get information to give us leverage and get Ben talking.

I sipped my lukewarm coffee, lost in thought. I'd have to find someone who could work out the code. Someone with a mathematical brain, or logical enough to sit with it, see if they could see a pattern. Then it clicked. Carmel had a degree in computing and she had a logical approach to solving problems. I knew she would take responsibility for a task that could be crucial to the case. I called her in, handed her the notebook and asked her to set about cracking the code.

Pete and I sat in my office, mulling over what we knew about Ben Chadwick. He had a notebook that fit the description of the one taken from Shannon which, in my view, wasn't a coincidence. It had to be the same one that had been in Mr Murdoch's drawer. I picked up my cup of coffee as a piece of the jigsaw fell into place. I took a couple of gulps. 'I think when Ben said he went to the toilet, he went to look for the notebook.'

A puzzled look crossed Pete's face. 'Why would he go looking for it in Mr Murdoch's drawer?'

'I reckon he saw the notebook when he had his phone confiscated the lesson before and, for some reason, decided to retrieve it,' I said. 'What I'm not so sure about is whether he would have known that the notebook was Shannon's. Or maybe he did and wanted to get it before she did.'

We agreed that the notebook was the connection between these two teenagers and we needed to find out what that link was. It was time to talk to Ben yet again.

We entered the interview room to find him with his head in his hands, a disposable cup on the floor and drips of tea creeping down the wall. He must have lost control and thrown his cup of tea across the room. We decided to ignore it. Pete took a seat opposite the boy as I paused, standing, looking at him. He was clearly distressed but I refused to feel sorry for him, sure that he had something to hide, had lied to us, and the best thing he could do to help himself was talk. I nodded at the solicitor, reached over, and turned on the tape before taking a seat next to Pete.

Pete led the questioning this time, starting off with a reassuring tone to try to put Ben at ease. 'Tell us about the notebook, Ben. Where did you get it?'

'I thought you wanted to know about my stuff?' He sounded petulant, avoiding the question.

Pete persisted, his voice becoming a tad firmer. 'We'll get to that. First, tell us about the notebook.'

'It's mine.' Ben looked from Pete to me before settling on a spot on the table.

Pete continued. 'OK. There seems to be some sort of code. Could you decipher it for us?'

Ben was quick to respond. 'No. I meant I found it. I don't know what any of it means.'

Pete looked thoughtful as he came back at Ben. 'Where did you find it?'

'I can't remember.' His voice was beginning to rise.

Pete was unperturbed. 'Can't remember? Or don't want to remember?'

'I can't remember.' Ben's eyes remained fixed on the spot on the table, beads of sweat forming along his hairline.

I decided to butt in, my voice colder than Pete's. 'Did you know that Shannon Birch had a notebook like that?'

Ben's head snapped up in shock. He stared straight at me. 'No way Shannon would have that notebook.'

I kept looking straight at him until he turned away, obviously realising he had made a mistake. His reaction had shown me that he knew more than he was letting on about the notebook. A gamut of emotions passed over his face, from annoyance to confusion to fear. I could only wonder at what he was thinking. Annoyed at being careless? Confused about Shannon and the notebook? Fear about being questioned and what to say? Time would tell. 'Did you know that Mr Murdoch took a notebook exactly like the one you had from Shannon Birch the morning he was murdered?' I asked.

Ben's mouth dropped open. For a moment I felt a tad of sympathy towards him, but my determination to get answers took over. All I wanted was a bit of honesty so I took him through what we knew of his movements. 'You left your chemistry class and went to the History Department. You were caught in Mr Murdoch's classroom and told Miss Shaw that you were getting a marker pen for Mr Murdoch. Why did you really go to history? We know it wasn't to get your phone.' Sometimes, the small details yield results, but he sat there, saying nothing. The noise of the rain against the window reverberated around the room. He lowered his head to stare at his hands, tightly clenched in his lap.

I decided to go for it. 'I'll tell you what I think, Ben. I think you saw the notebook in Mr Murdoch's drawer and went to retrieve it. The only thing I can't work out is why. Why would you go to get a notebook that had been taken from Shannon Birch earlier in the day? It must be important. To you? To someone else? Are you protecting someone?'

He remained silent, refusing to meet my gaze. Very quietly, I asked, 'Did you kill Mr Murdoch?'

Raising his head to look directly at me, he yelled, 'No! No way...!'

I said, 'In that case, help me find who did kill him.'

He put his head in his hands. 'I've no idea.'

I leaned back in my chair. It didn't feel good, given that Ben was distressed but he'd left me no choice. As far as I was concerned, his refusal to talk and the circumstantial evidence we had, made him a suspect in both the stabbing and the murder. I decided to detain him for the twenty-four hours we were allowed for further questioning. After that I would have to see if I had enough to press charges. I arranged for him to be taken to the detention centre, making it clear he could change his mind and speak to me at any time. If I'd hoped that would get a response, I was disappointed. He refused to look at me.

I waited but he didn't lift his head so I gave him my parting shot. 'By the way, with regards to your purchases and how you can afford them, none of the local delivery companies have heard of you. Why is that?' Without waiting for an answer, I got up and left the room.

CHAPTER 23

I hadn't been sure what to expect with Ben Chadwick, but a continuing refusal to say nothing wasn't on my list. I paused in the corridor and took a moment to remind myself that this was a teenage boy, seventeen years old. One of Pete's sons was seventeen too. Maybe Ben had got himself involved in something way over his head. On the other hand, I'd been in this game long enough to know what some seventeen-year-olds are capable of and the crimes they commit. Although my gut told me Ben was in the former category, it was obvious he was still lying. I couldn't understand why. But I would find out.

Leaving Pete to sort out the paperwork and contact Mrs Chadwick, I headed back upstairs. As soon as I walked through the door of the incident room, I spotted Carmel sitting at the desk opposite Pete's, oblivious to my presence as she scrutinised the notebook.

Heading to my office, I glanced at the view of the town before sinking into my chair to review the evidence so far and think about what we needed to do next. Unable to settle, I got up again and stood by the window looking towards the river. The area where Shannon Birch had been stabbed was further along, away from the town centre and not that far from Riverwood. I'd read through the reports compiled by Pete and the team, but visiting it might give me some inspiration. Part of me knew I should have done this sooner but it was an area I preferred to avoid. Rather than taking the car, I decided to go along the river walk. The rain had stopped and it would be good to get some air.

After letting Pete know where I was going and to keep me informed of developments, I made my way out of the station. Crossing the main road, I headed for the aptly named River Street where I accessed the river walk. The air felt fresh, like the rain had cleansed it.

Since moving back, I hadn't walked along the river and I'd forgotten how wide it was. It took my breath away as I gazed along the river towards the sea, before turning onto the path to walk in the opposite direction. I followed the route past flats and high rises interspersed with green spaces. Beyond the road and railway bridges, as I carried on past the college, sports stadium and university, the landscape became less urban, the river flowing through parkland. The school couldn't be seen from the river, yet the closer I got to its location I felt myself becoming tense. An image of Richard Spencer popped into my mind and my stomach lurched. I fought back my feelings, reminding myself I was here to inspect the scene of the stabbing.

I finally reached the pedestrian bridge that led across to the woods on the other side of the river and the path to Holmston Road. Shannon had been stabbed near the bushes and trees that would have hidden her and her assailant from the sight of passers-by. I walked to the middle of the bridge and looked upstream then downstream, taking in the sound of the running water and the scent of the foliage. Not a building in sight, I felt like I was in the countryside.

I noted there were a few security cameras in the area. Gary had picked up Ben on the main path, but I felt we should get a screenshot of everyone who had been in the vicinity at the time. No-one had come forward despite appeals for information so we would go to them. I turned to head back the way I'd come, passing the bin where the homeless young man had found the knife.

Leaving the crime scene behind me, I went back the way I'd come as far as the railway bridge where I exited to the road. Taking the route back along John Street, I was soon back in the office and asked Gary to contact the security company to get the screenshots. I went to my office and started to look again through everything we had so far, to put together a likely timeline of events.

I was completely absorbed and had no idea of how much time had passed when the door opening startled me. I looked up to see Carmel standing in the doorway, a look of contained excitement on her face. Without waiting for me to speak, she blurted out that she had tried to knock but I hadn't heard her. I nodded, sensing that she wouldn't have barged in like that if it wasn't important. 'What can I do for you, Carmel?'

She smiled at me. 'I think I've cracked it.'

I met her gaze, unable to hide my scepticism that she could have cracked the code so quickly. Yet she stood there, oozing confidence. 'It was easy once I'd worked out the logic of it. It couldn't have been created by an expert because the code's so simple.' She passed me a document with the printout of a table, a jumble of letters and numbers and a note of what it all meant.

Letters of the alphabet had been converted into numbers. Take every second letter of the alphabet: B, D, F, H, J, L, N, P, R, T, V, X, Z. Add 9 down to 0 steps to get a new letter so B plus nine steps down the alphabet becomes K, D plus eight steps down the alphabet becomes L, F plus seven steps down the alphabet becomes M and so on. Next take the new letter and add 0 to 9 steps to get another new letter. Therefore, K remains the same, L becomes M, M becomes P, N becomes Q etc. That leaves K, M, P, Q, S, U, W, Y, A, C. Give these letters numbers 0 to 9 and it looks like mobile phone numbers. KYCSA is 07948, KYACS is 07894, KYCUP is 07952, KYYSA is 07748 and KYYCC is 07799. Once she'd worked out 07 the rest had been easy.

I was impressed. 'This is great, Carmel.' She beamed at me. 'It gives us loads of leads to follow. Speak to Pete, work with him to run all the numbers through the system, and let me know if anyone of significance turns up.' She nodded, looking pleased with herself, and went back to her desk, closing the door behind her.

I got up and gazed out the window. I could feel myself becoming impatient even though we were making good progress. Finding the numbers in the notebook, waiting for this and that evidence, teenagers lying; it was all frustrating. I desperately wanted to solve this case quickly. Like Shannon, Ben and Katie, I'd sat in Mr Murdoch's class, and he'd listened to me when I'd needed it, got me some help. I was convinced that at least one of those teenagers had put him at risk. Maybe even killed him. Why would they do that? What was it I couldn't yet see? I sighed, sat back down at my desk, and started to review what we had yet again.

Having spent another couple of hours reading through the statements and reports, I was glad when my thoughts were interrupted by a knock at the door. Lifting my head, I saw Carmel looking in, waving the notebook and a sheet of paper at me. When I beckoned her to come in, she almost threw the door open before quickly reaching my desk. It seemed she had more exciting news for me and I wasn't wrong.

She placed the notebook and a sheet of paper in front of me. There appeared to be some two hundred names and so Pete had organised for himself, Carmel, and Gary to divide the numbers up and find out who they were. He reckoned that if anyone had a record; arrest, interviews or whatever, their number should appear in the database. After that, they would start on phone company records.

They had checked the numbers of the teenagers, all of whom were there, Katie Spencer being the final entry. Given that we had already connected Ben Chadwick and Shannon Birch to the notebook, it didn't surprise me that their names were in it. It seemed Katie was linked to whatever was going on as well. Carmel paused, making me wonder what was coming next. I waited. You could have heard a pin drop.

She tapped her finger next to a number and name on the sheet. 'I think this one is interesting.'

I was studying the sheet intently. 'Go on.'

She didn't move her finger. 'Stevie Nicolson. He's a serving traffic police constable. Number came up on the staff database.'

I looked at Carmel, caught the look of confidence on her face. 'I've cross-checked it and looked him up on social media too. Nothing untoward there.'

I nodded. 'Great work again, Carmel. You've used your initiative and you're thorough. Qualities we need here.' She smiled at me. As she turned and left my office, I'd swear that she walked a little taller. And no wonder, she had nailed potential breakthroughs in the case.

Looking at my watch, it was time to call a meeting and set out a plan for the next morning. Gary and Carmel would continue working together on the notebook to get a name and profile for every entry. Bill would follow up forensics and any updates on CCTV. And Pete would track down the traffic officer and arrange for him to come in for a chat.

Half an hour later, as I neared Troon, instead of going straight home, on a whim I drove to the car park at Barassie Beach. Although it was already dark, I got out and leaned against the bonnet, ignoring the autumn chill on my exposed skin. Walking across the narrow patch of shrubland onto the beach, I could sense the expanse of sand and taste the salt in the air. I churned things over in my mind. The notebook had proven to be significant and today we'd made real progress. A whole list of potential suspects and witnesses. A jigsaw to solve. And a serving police officer one of the pieces. I took several deep breaths of the sea air before turning back towards the car. Another ready meal awaited, another late night hoping that sleep without nightmares would follow.

Wednesday 19th October 2022

THE PARTY

CHAPTER 24

I gathered the team round Pete's desk in the incident room. We needed to update each other on any progress that had been made, before going through the list of what to do next.

I began. 'Right, given that Shannon Birch, Ben Chadwick, and Katie Spencer are in the notebook, they are likely all connected in some way to the murder. And Shannon Birch may well have been stabbed because of that connection.' Everyone nodded in agreement. I continued, 'Whether the notebook or the connection between them was a catalyst for murder remains to be seen. My guess is with Katie being the last entry, that makes her involvement in whatever it is more recent. She might be the one most likely to crack.' I asked Gary for an update on the footage from Richard Spencer's CCTV.

He reached into his pocket and pulled out his electronic notebook which was part of the Police Scotland digital roll-out scheme. 'The door cameras produced some interesting results,' he said, checking his notes. 'Last Wednesday, the day before the murder, Katie left the house about 7.30pm and returned about 11.00pm. I know she said she went to Shannon's but, to me, she wasn't dressed for studying at a friend's house. I'd say she was going to a party.'

This was interesting. We already had Shannon's mum contradicting Katie's account and the CCTV seemed to back that up. 'Anything else significant?' I asked.

Gary nodded. 'Well, coming home she looked worse for wear. She practically stumbled into the house. Ties in with me thinking she went to a party.'

‘So her ‘illness’ was more likely a hangover or comedown. I’m surprised her parents hadn’t noticed that,’ I said. ‘Especially given her father’s protectiveness.’ I suppressed a shudder at the thought of Richard Spencer. ‘OK. I think we can all agree that Katie didn’t go to Shannon’s house that night.’ Everyone nodded. ‘So, the question is, where did she go last Wednesday? Check CCTV around the Spencer house, particularly bus stops, Gary. What about Thursday?’

Referring to his notes again, he said, ‘Thursday, the day of the murder, she left the house about 2.45pm and didn’t return until 6.20pm.’

Again, interesting. She’d made it home not long before her mother arrived to find her watching TV. Yet she’d told us that she’d gone for a short walk, later changing her mind to say it might have been longer. But no indication it was that length of time, some three and a half hours. What was she playing at? We would need to find out where she’d gone because that was within the time frame that Mr Murdoch was killed. Possibly the stabbing too.

Gary added, ‘She didn’t go out on Friday. But what’s interesting is that on the Saturday, she left the house not long after her mother went to work, yet didn’t arrive at the hospital to visit Shannon until the afternoon.’

‘Pete and I must have just missed her. We need to find out where she went that morning,’ I said, ‘and, as far as the visit to the hospital is concerned, I don’t buy the ‘to see how Shannon was’ story.’

We concluded that we still had a lot of questions for Katie Spencer. And we needed answers.

Pete talked through the visit to the school and meeting the tech assistant, Amanda Cairns. It looked like one of the mallets from the Technologies Department went missing shortly before the murder and wasn’t returned. The mallet was there at lunchtime and no-one had signed it out. ‘Amanda thought she had a perfect system to record everything and got a bit flustered when she realised she hadn’t a clue who’d taken the mallet. Unless it was herself, of course.’ He glanced at each of us. ‘I think it’s too much of a coincidence that it matches the description of the likely murder weapon.’

We all agreed. I was willing to bet the missing mallet was used to kill Mr Murdoch and we needed to find it. Having checked the class sign-out sheets, it transpired that Ben Chadwick was out of class for twenty minutes that day. That was more than enough time to take a detour to Mr Murdoch's classroom, even via the Technologies Department.

Bill had interviewed Amanda Cairns to update her statement, including all the details about the inventory. He'd also asked her about Mr Murdoch. 'She reiterated that he was a colleague. And insisted she's happily married. To be honest, I'm not sure I believe her. But when I said we'd need a DNA sample, she didn't flinch.' He looked at me and I nodded, indicating my agreement. If Bill thought Amanda was being less than honest, I tended to think he was right. Of course, he hadn't told her about the stain on the sheet or the hair in the shower.

Carmel had requested CCTV footage from the vicinity of Mr Murdoch's house to see if Amanda Cairn's car had been in the area the night before he was murdered. So far there had been no sightings. 'We'll have to wait for those DNA results. Bill, I'll leave that to you. Carmel, keep following up the CCTV. We need more evidence before deciding whether she's in the frame or not.' I paused. 'And Carmel. Any progress on the bank accounts for the loan company?'

She picked up her phone and did a quick search. 'Sorry, Ma'am. Nothing yet. I requested their accounts for the last twelve months.'

I sighed. 'OK.' I turned to Bill. 'Found anything on them?' He shook his head. 'Looks like you need to go round there. Pay them a visit.'

He nodded. 'Righto.'

For the first time, I felt a thaw in Bill's attitude towards me.

My priority was to get the three young people talking. There was enough circumstantial evidence to put Ben Chadwick at the scenes of both Mr Murdoch's murder and Shannon Birch's stabbing. He would have to be interviewed again at some point to decide whether to charge him or not. It was clear he had lied and knew more than what we had found out. We'd have to keep digging and I felt the more pieces we had, the more likely he was to talk. Also, we had a possible motive: drug dealing. 'I'm certain Ben's so-called delivery job is couriering drugs. But where did he get them from? Who is the supplier? If this is organised around schools, the other two might be involved as well. Carmel, keep in touch with your ex-colleagues. Let me know as soon as anything comes in.' She nodded.

Katie had lied about her whereabouts and was not at home when the murder took place, maybe the stabbing too. She would have to be brought in for further questioning to explain what she was up to during those long periods out of the house. 'If we can show she could have been in both places, set out the consequences for her if she was involved or for withholding information, that should get her talking.' Turning to Gary, I continued, 'Anything you can find on CCTV will be helpful.' He gave a small salute.

'Shannon could have been involved in killing Mr Murdoch; she was around school that day. We'll put that to her and see if it jogs her memory. I want to see her reaction to all of this. Pete, we'll visit her again in due course.' He caught my eye and nodded.

There were a lot of comings and goings with potential suspects. We needed to put together a detailed timeline to establish the order in which the incidents happened. Work out exactly, or as much as we could, who was where and when. 'Bill, work on the order of events, knowing what we know now, double check who could have been at the scenes of both crimes.' The detail, Pete said that was one of his strengths. Bill's nod of assent was almost imperceptible. But it was there.

The working assumption was that the missing mallet from the Technologies Department was the murder weapon, given the provisional post-mortem findings. All three teenagers, as well as Amanda, were likely to have had access to that. It had to be found. Now that we knew what we were looking for, the search of the school grounds and surrounding area could focus on that. And a weapon that size was unlikely to have been carried too far from the scene of the crime.

I paused to gather my thoughts. Mrs Caldwell was at a meeting, borne out by other attendees, Ellen Shaw had got the bus, as she had said, so that ruled them out. I couldn't see Ben Chadwick, Katie Spencer, and Shannon Birch as cold-blooded murderers but, on the other hand, as I've said before, I had seen stranger things happen. The assumed motive was drugs and I still felt the key to it all lay in the notebook. 'Carmel, once you've chased up our colleagues, keep working on the notebook. Get names for as many numbers as you can.'

Was Mr Murdoch's mystery visitor auburn-haired Amanda Cairns? Could Mr Murdoch be the victim of a crime of passion? But where did that leave the stabbing? I remained convinced they were connected. And what about the loan? Could Mr Murdoch have been involved in something criminal? Enough to get him killed?

Gary had finished going through Ben's contacts, cross checking names with social media and school lists. There was one contact that was only on his phone, someone called Jake. My gut told me that was significant. I asked Gary to try calling Jake's number and put a trace on it. I wanted to find out who this Jake was.

After checking that everyone was clear about what to do, I ended the meeting, got a coffee from the machine, and returned to my office. It struck me that we were forming a pretty good team. Everyone was putting a lot of effort into investigating these crimes.

Turning my attention back to the investigation, I pondered the amount of information we had to digest and follow up. I took a sip of coffee and opened the folder in front of me, a copy of Stevie Nicolson's staff file. The traffic police officer whose name was in the notebook was coming in for a chat.

CHAPTER 25

Half an hour later Stevie Nicolson entered the incident room. I recognised him from his staff photograph: tall, early twenties, short brown hair and with a build that indicated he went to the gym a lot. I watched him stride past the desks, eyes looking right and left, a clear sign that he felt out of place. He would be nervous because I hadn't given any indication as to why I wanted to talk to him. And he was right to be concerned. Although he didn't yet know it, he was a potential link to two serious crimes. I expected, for once in this investigation, that someone would tell the truth. His future in the police force depended on what he had to say. His willingness to cooperate would be a factor too.

Pete stepped out from behind his desk and intercepted him, forcing the young officer to stop and meet his gaze. They stood facing each other, almost the same height. They shook hands as Pete introduced himself before heading towards my office, Stevie falling into step behind him. As they came in, I signalled to Stevie to take a seat directly opposite me. Pete sat down too, moving his chair so that he was to the side of Stevie but able to see his face. I wanted Stevie to feel a bit cornered, under observation, friendly, yet not quite.

I waited until he met my gaze. 'No doubt you're wondering why we've called you in for a chat, PC Nicolson? Or shall I call you Stevie?'

He nodded. 'Yes, Ma'am, Stevie. It came as a bit of a shock, to be honest. I've no idea why you'd want to talk to me.' He was clearly uncomfortable.

I raised an eyebrow. 'Really? Why so shocked?'

He looked from me to Pete. 'Well, we've not had any incidents these last few days that we thought should be reported to CID.'

Never taking my eyes off him, I watched carefully for his reaction to what I had to say next. 'This has nothing to do with your police duties, Stevie. This is to do with you personally.'

His face dropped. 'I'm not sure what you mean.'

I glanced at Pete, notebook on the table, pencil in hand, then looked back to Stevie. 'Why did you join the police?'

He leaned forward. 'I wanted a career where I could do some good and didn't need a degree.'

'Do you think you made the right decision?' I asked.

'Oh yes, Ma'am. Definitely.' His enthusiasm seemed genuine. But he was blinking rapidly. The nerves remained. I could tell he had no idea where this was headed.

'Good. I take it you'll fully cooperate with us.' I continued to watch him.

He frowned. Silence filled the room, the atmosphere tense. Outside a car backfired. Stevie jumped. I remained still and waited. At last, his voice filled with anxiety, he asked, 'If I've done something wrong in the past could that end my career?' He looked at me.

I met his gaze. 'Depends what it is.' I was intrigued by his question. Even a criminal record doesn't prevent someone joining the police force, depending on what they've done, and as long as they declare it. What did he have to hide? I got the impression that he had something he wanted to get off his chest. He continued to meet my gaze, his face a picture of uncertainty.

Pete and I exchanged glances, indicating that we were on the same page. I nodded to him to make a start. The plan was to show Stevie photographs of the three teenagers and gauge his reaction. Pete retrieved a file that he had brought with him into the room. He reached into it and slowly pulled out a photograph of Shannon which he placed on the desk in front of Stevie. I watched him as Pete showed him the photograph and asked if he recognised the girl. He let out a long sigh, like he'd been holding his breath. Looked like he might, indeed, be willing to offload whatever was on his mind.

Looking carefully at the photograph, he told us he recognised Shannon but, until seeing her face in the newspapers after the stabbing, he hadn't known her name. He faltered, admitting he'd wondered whether to come forward, but wasn't sure if it would help. I told him he should have done so and I would have to think about what to do about that. There was no harm in indicating the seriousness of his situation. I wanted to find out everything he knew.

Pete pulled out another photograph. Stevie studied the photo intently before insisting that he had never seen Ben before. However, when the final photo, Katie, was placed in front of him, his face went pale. I was surprised to see how visibly shaken he was by it and wondered why, when he hadn't appeared so bothered by the photo of Shannon. He took a sharp intake of breath before admitting that he'd seen Katie before, although, again, he didn't know her name. He'd seen Shannon a few times but Katie only once and that was last week. He dropped his gaze to avoid looking at either me or Pete. Behind him, on the other side of the glass wall, Bill, Gary and Carmel were chatting and laughing together. A sharp contrast to this meeting.

I turned my attention back to Stevie. 'How do you know these girls?' I kept my voice quiet, probing. The tension in the room increased as he stared at his hands, resting in his lap, continuing to avoid my gaze. I waited for him to say something. He looked pensive, perhaps weighing up his options.

Eventually, he looked again at the three photographs, turned to look at Pete's notebook, raised his eyes to meet mine. 'I've seen them at parties.' His voice was barely a whisper.

I gave him an encouraging nod. 'Tell us about the parties, Stevie.'

The flood gates opened. He sat up in his chair and began to talk.

He was seventeen when he and his friends had been approached by a young man offering to get them alcohol and later, drugs. He used to supply them whatever they wanted, usually beer and soft drugs, for camping trips or gatherings on the beach. The first couple of times they'd been given them for free but after that they'd started paying.

When his friends left for university, he didn't see the supplier for a while. A couple of years ago he'd bumped into him in the supermarket where he was working. It had looked like the guy was doing well. He'd said that he had a new events business organising parties and had invited Stevie to the next one. By the time he'd got there the alcohol was flowing and he was already drunk when someone had offered him drugs. That was when he'd realised there were a lot of drugs on offer, including some hard stuff, mainly cocaine. He admitted he'd indulged and had a good time.

The next day he'd got a shock when the supplier contacted him and told him that he'd filmed him at the party. Selling drugs was a sideline, a way of finding clients for the parties which would draw them in to his main business. The idea being to film them taking drugs and blackmail them to get a regular income, threatening to post the videos online. There were a lot of people who wouldn't want their drugs habit or history known and were willing to pay to have it kept quiet. Including him.

This was a massive breakthrough. I had in front of me a reliable witness who had provided a link between two of the teenagers connected to both crimes. On top of that, the link was, as suspected, drugs, which could prove the suspicion of organised activities in schools.

Stevie looked relieved, a man who had unburdened himself. He had no idea how vital the information he'd provided was to our investigation. I smiled at him. 'Tell me, Stevie, do you have a name for this supplier?'

He looked scared. 'You won't let him know it came from me?'

'I can't make any promises. But you do need to tell us his name.' I watched as he struggled with his predicament. Giving up a name meant the supplier would likely come after him. Unless we got him first. 'Come on, Stevie, you don't have a choice here.'

He stared past me, through the window. The sun was trying to break through the clouds. Time stood still. After what seemed a long time, he turned his head to look at me. 'Jake. Jake Devaney.'

Jake. The name that appeared in Ben's contacts. I was right to think that was significant. It couldn't be coincidental.

Pete produced a thin, black notebook from the file and placed it on the table. 'Do you recognise this?'

He looked carefully at the notebook. 'That looks like Jake's. I assume that's how you found me? My name's in it?'

I looked at him. 'Yes.'

He sank back into his chair. He'd seen Jake with the notebook and believed it was a list of his clients, those being blackmailed as well as users, and people who worked for him. He'd stopped doing drugs after deciding to join the police but he'd had to keep paying. I asked him about the teenagers he'd recognised from the photos. He thought that Shannon helped to organise the parties as well as doing deliveries and collecting money. He'd seen Katie at a party last Wednesday.

That was the night she said she was studying at Shannon's house. A piece of the jigsaw fell into place. Stevie reckoned that was Katie's first time because he'd seen Jake film her. He'd wanted to get her out of there. He gulped and stopped speaking, swallowing hard.

Pete cut in, unable to keep the coldness from his voice. 'Why didn't you?'

Stevie turned to look at Pete. 'It was already too late. And, to be honest, I didn't want to get involved.' He paused. 'I'm not proud of myself…'

He'd gone to the party to talk to Jake. He wanted a career in the police without the blackmail hanging over him, the constant threat of exposure. I wondered how successful he'd been, but bided my time, letting him get on with his story. By the time he'd arrived, Katie was already out of her head and he'd thought stepping in wouldn't have made a difference. He returned his gaze to the photographs still lying on the desk. The girl had been dancing on her own in the middle of the room smoking weed and Jake was filming it all on his phone.

I couldn't help picture the scene in my head and felt a pang of sympathy for Katie. I wondered what I would have done in Stevie's position. Would I have jumped in to save her? I couldn't honestly answer that. I surmised that Shannon must have invited Katie to the party and set her up. I was confident that when we confronted Katie with what we knew she would talk. I nodded at Stevie to continue.

He'd watched from the doorway until Jake noticed him and they'd met up in the kitchen where they could be alone. He'd made it clear to Jake that he wanted out but Jake had smirked, insisting that he would have to keep paying. They'd argued. He'd even tried threatening Jake, telling him he'd shop him to the police. But Jake had taunted him, playing the video taken at that first party, of him swigging back vodka and coke followed by a line of cocaine on a dirty coffee table which he sucked up his nose with a straw.

Stevie had realised how naïve he'd been. Of course, there was no way Jake would let him off the hook. He'd been left with two choices: keep paying or come clean and risk his career. He hadn't yet decided which it would be. And then we'd called.

There was a lot to take in here but before I'd time to gather my thoughts, he leaned forward and looked me directly in the eye. 'What happens now?' Concern about the impact on his future in the police was written all over his face.

I didn't have a choice. I'd have to report him. I returned his gaze. 'It's out of my hands. I'll have to inform Professional Standards. It'll be up to them to decide what action to take. Whether to suspend you or not. But I'll let them know that the information you've provided today is very helpful to us. You're a witness in a murder investigation.'

Stevie was completely shocked, his eyes wide. 'I thought this was about that girl being stabbed.'

Knowing it had never been mentioned, I said, 'We're also investigating the murder of a teacher at the high school. I'd like to speak to this Jake Devaney about both crimes.'

He pushed his chair far enough away from the desk to put his head in his hands. Pete collected the photographs and the notebook to put them back in the folder. I asked him to find out where Jake Devaney lived.

Stevie raised his head to look at me. 'Inspector Berry.' I met his gaze. 'I might be able to save you some time.'

I glanced at Pete who had paused, waiting for what Stevie had to say, then back to Stevie. 'Go on…'

He smiled. 'You see, when I threatened to grass on Jake… I'd followed him. I know where he lives…'

July 2012

TEN YEARS BEFORE

CHAPTER 26

Jake Devaney decided that he was going to be rich. He'd watched the kids whose parents had money have a life that he yearned for; nice houses, the best gear, holidays and, most of all, respect. The thing that nagged at him was how to do it. School didn't interest him much as he knew he wouldn't be able to afford to go to college or university. And he didn't see how any job he could get would pay him enough to get what he wanted. Resentment and jealousy burned in him, making him determined to find a way.

After school and during the holidays, he'd follow the rich kids and their friends, trying to work out what made them tick, find a way into the groups, initially wanting to be part of it. And it dawned on him that he could make money exploiting them instead. They liked to gather in parks or go camping in the woods around the reservoirs, getting drunk on cheap vodka and smoking weed.

It was the cannabis that gave him the idea. If they wanted it, he could work out how to supply it, and maybe something stronger too. He could make it easy for them; a one-stop shop. The morals of it didn't bother him. As far as he was concerned, everyone has a choice. Don't they? He wouldn't be forcing the drugs down peoples' throats; just making them available at a price and a tidy profit for him. He paid special attention to those whose wealthy parents tended to work lots of hours, some hardly seeing their kids. A lot of them were given generous allowances without their parents looking too closely at how they spent it. It had turned out to be easy. Of course, he never took drugs himself.

Getting in was easier than he thought. At first, he would suss out potential customers and offer them beer; he knew which places would sell to underage drinkers or give commission to folks who got it for him. He approached dealers who didn't look too heavy handed and buy the drugs. He'd bide his time, raise the topic of maybe liking something a bit stronger than beer and would they like to try? And he happened to have that something on him. After they were hooked, some more than others, and wanted a regular supply, he'd be the dealer. He was sixteen when he started and worked on the advantage of being about the same age and, therefore, less suspicious. He grew up with his customers and blended in, especially as his bank account grew and so did the quality of his attire. He made deals with his dealers, giving them a cut of his sales, keeping them happy. However, Jake couldn't see a long-term future or the means to get rich. Nor could he get away with hanging around parks and alleyways forever. He had to come up with a different plan.

By July 2012 he'd been supplying drugs for two years. He stood by the water's edge at the reservoir, bored by the noise of the twelve or so revellers behind him. Someone slapped him on the shoulder, asking if he was alright. Jake turned, smiled. A tall lad with a mop of blonde hair, eyes dilated to pinpricks reflected in the moonlight. 'Great party, mate,' he said. He looked at Jake and smirked, pushing his face closer so that Jake could smell the weed on his breath. 'Just want to say thanks for everything in case I don't get another chance. After the summer I'm off to uni. No offence but...' He put his hand on Jake's shoulder. 'I won't be keeping in touch. You're not one of us... Don't want any of this to get out... If we ever come across each other again after this summer, I've never met you...' Slapping Jake on the back, he walked away.

Jake stood there, fuming. That lad had made him feel like shit and his anger fuelled his determination to get the upper hand and keep it. His mind raced, turning over and over in his head how to do it. And then it struck him. The lad had said it was a great party. Why not make it a bigger party? He smiled to himself as the idea took shape. The lad had mentioned not wanting anyone to know about his antics. He must have a big career planned. Plans which might suffer if they knew about his drugs activities. Smoking weed round a campfire could be put down to one night of teenage antics but, if Jake organised it properly, he could make it look much worse. And he could film it, see how much these kids would be willing to pay for him to keep their secrets. Blackmail. There must be money in that. His smile got wider. He had a plan.

Wednesday 19th October 2022

THE PHOTOGRAPH

CHAPTER 27

Jake Devaney lived in a penthouse overlooking Barassie Beach. It struck me how close he lived to me, that many times I had walked along the beach past that block of flats or parked in the car park across the road to take in the view. Only last night on my way home I had stood in that very place opposite his penthouse and watched the last of the sunset. The thought that he might have looked out of his window and watched me gazing out to sea, even though he wouldn't know who I was, sent shivers up and down my spine. I might have past him in the street, in the supermarket, never giving the stranger a second glance.

He would also have the beautiful views over to Arran, a picture postcard every time he opened his curtains. I couldn't help but think he didn't deserve that. Someone like him, who made a living through ruining the lives of others, sharing such a view, made me angry. I wanted to put Jake Devaney behind bars where he wouldn't see such beauty for a long time. Even if he hadn't killed Mr Murdoch, he was still a drug dealer making a living from the misery of others.

On the way there Pete hadn't said a word, sensing my mood. We arrived at the beach car park. Getting out of the car, I crossed the road and studied the block of flats in front of me. I could see the appeal. The flats were modern and designed to take full advantage of the views, the frontage mainly windows and balconies. Bill and Gary had already checked the car park at the back. Jake's car, an Audi Sportback, wasn't there. I'd thought he might have gone for something more glamorous, but maybe he didn't want to draw too much attention to himself.

I would have preferred to get hold of Jake first and question him before searching the flat. But, according to the neighbours, he hadn't been seen for a few days and I had enough evidence to force entry, given he was a suspect in a serious crime. I had already put Jake and the car on the wanted list so forces across the UK should be on alert as well as the authorities at ports and airports. I had to be thorough; not leave myself open to scrutiny later.

Waving our badges at the police officer on duty at the front door to the block, Pete and I got in the lift, donned overshoes and gloves, before alighting on the top floor. We crossed the landing and entered the hallway of the penthouse. The door opposite led to a large living room with an open-plan dining area and kitchen where we joined Bill and Gary. The four of us paused and took in the view of the sea through the windows and double doors that led onto a large balcony. It had taken a few hours to get sorted and the early evening sun was going down, glowing orange and red across the Firth of Clyde to the mountains of Arran. The changing colours of October would never disappoint and we had to tear ourselves away. We had a job to do.

I reflected on what Jake had achieved, living in this place. How exactly he had done it was another question. Could the drug dealing and parties fund this lifestyle? I'd have to find the answer to that. I left the room to have a quick look round the rest of the apartment.

The whole place exuded luxury. All the rooms led off the T-shaped hallway including the one I had just vacated. A master bedroom, a study, a bathroom and second bedroom were located at the back to allow the living areas full access to the views to the front.

Unexpectedly, I felt a pang of envy. If something like this had been on the market it was the kind of place Patrick and I might have liked. I shook my head; this wasn't a train of thought I wanted to dwell on. The murmurs of Pete, Bill, and Gary in the background reminded me we needed to make a start on the search. We needed to look for anything that could link Jake to the school, the three teenagers and/or drugs. I felt there had to be something because, after all, Stevie had confirmed the notebook belonged to Jake.

I asked Pete and Bill to search the living/dining room and kitchen while Gary went to the second bedroom and bathroom. I'd take the master bedroom and study. There was silence as we started in our respective rooms, punctuated only by rustling and sometimes clanging sounds as we deftly worked our way through cupboards and drawers.

The master bedroom could be described as minimalist. Another place not to my taste, it was too functional. The walls and carpet were white while the black furniture provided a sharp contrast. A king-size bed, which was neatly made, dominated the space. Glossy side tables with a single drawer either side of the bed matched the built-in wardrobes that ran the length of one wall opposite.

A door to the left of the bed led into an ensuite shower room while another to the right led on to a small balcony with views to Troon harbour. I imagined Jake sitting at the small bistro table watching the boats coming and going. I pursed my lips and turned my attention back to the room. It was clean and exceptionally tidy. Either Jake was fastidious in his housekeeping or he paid someone to do it for him. 'Probably the latter,' I thought. In the ensuite, I poked around the shelves and in cupboards, noting an array of expensive grooming products. Jake apparently took care of his appearance. Picking up a bottle of aftershave, I couldn't resist pushing the nozzle and the room filled with the scents of lavender and mint.

Moving back into the bedroom, I slid back the wardrobe doors to reveal the contents. There were drawers down one side, double hanging space in the middle with a shoe rack underneath and shelves at the other end. It struck me immediately that there was something odd about the assortment of clothes. On closer inspection I saw that the top rail had expensive looking suits, shirts, and leisure wear while the bottom rail had cheaper high street stuff. I wouldn't call myself an expert on designer brands but, like at Ben Chadwick's, I could tell the difference in the quality even before checking the labels. Why would Jake have two sets of clothes?

I ran my fingers along some shirts and pulled out a Ralph Lauren which still had its £129 price tag. I slid the shirts along the rail to put that one back in its place and something caught my eye. Pulling them further apart revealed a safe built into the wall, the front protruding into the wardrobe. Of course, I would have expected a dealer like Jake to have a safe. Wanting to find out what was inside, I made a call to colleagues who could sort that out.

Moving over to the nearest bedside table, I opened the slim drawer and rummaged through the contents. Inside were a couple of pens, some loose change, and condoms. I was about to close it again when I noticed an envelope tucked away underneath the other items. Intrigued, I pulled it out and scrutinised it. It had been handled a lot but there was no writing to indicate the contents. The flap was tucked in and I carefully opened it out. Inside was a polaroid photograph, a bit faded and dog-eared.

The photograph showed a couple, probably in their early fifties, and two children, a boy, and a girl. They were all smiling at the camera, wearing shorts and t-shirts, the sea visible in the background. It looked like it had been taken on a family seaside holiday. I supposed the boy must be Jake Devaney. Why else would he have it? I looked closely at the photograph. There was something about the girl that disturbed me. I felt like I had seen her before.

'Ma'am! Through here!' I put the photograph back in the envelope and followed Pete's voice to the kitchen. He was kneeling on the floor in his shirtsleeves, flanked by Bill and Gary, two drawers full of pots and pans piled one on top of the other behind him. Pete pointed out that the back of the unit that housed the drawers had been taken off and put back. It looked like a bit of a botched job because there was a gap where it hadn't been properly fitted. He'd spotted it when he opened the drawers. If it had happened because the drawers were overfull or stuff had fallen down the back and they were being forced shut, the panels would be bent but that wasn't the case. Pete reckoned someone had removed the panel and put it back.

He asked Bill to pass him his jacket and, reaching into the inside pocket, he pulled out the mini screwdriver he'd used to open the drawers in Mr Murdoch's desk. Bill, Gary, and I watched as, lying on his back to get inside the space under the worktop, Pete loosened a couple of the screws. The panel creaked as he pulled it back enough to fit his arm behind it.

It was like time stood still as we waited for him to confirm whether he'd found anything. After what felt like ages, he said he could feel something but couldn't reach it. He undid the remaining screws and pulled the panel loose, passing it to Bill. The three of us watched as he managed to grab the object, hidden behind the adjoining unit, pulled it towards him and slowly edged himself out from under the counter. He held the object in his hands and, at first, we all stared at it, then looked at each other. It was a mallet like one a carpenter might use, or one that might be used in a school woodwork classroom. And there were specks of what looked like dried blood on it.

This was hard to believe. From what Stevie had said, I'd expected to find evidence of drug dealing, at least something that would link Jake to the three teenagers. That I was probably looking at the weapon used to murder Mr Murdoch was an incredible find. I took the mallet from Pete, examined it, and put it in an evidence bag before handing it to Gary to take to the laboratory to confirm if it was, indeed, Mr Murdoch's blood. I instructed Bill to keep searching. We were particularly looking for a set of keys with a New Orleans keyring which would provide evidence if Jake had been the one to lock Mr Murdoch in the cupboard, dead or still alive. He would also work with the forensics team and the safe-breakers when they arrived. I contacted the team at the school grounds to call off the search for the murder weapon.

As Gary headed out, I turned to Pete and Bill. 'I found this photograph in a drawer in the bedroom. I'd like to find out more about it; who these people are and why Jake has it. I'm guessing the boy is him.' I passed it to Pete and to Bill before taking it back to study it myself again. There was something at the back of my mind. Whatever it was, it would come to me. I'd ask Carmel to scan the photo and send it to Stevie to see what he thought because he knew what Jake looked like.

I put the envelope in my pocket. 'Right. Let's go, Pete. We need to think about how that mallet got into this flat. Jake Devaney has become our lead suspect. We need to find him and he's several days ahead of us.'

'Righto, Ma'am.' Pete smiled as he saluted me.

I laughed. 'Enough of the cheek, Sergeant Fletcher. I'll let you away with it this time, given how clever you were in finding that mallet.'

We took the quick route back to Ayr.

CHAPTER 28

Later, standing at the window in my office, looking out at the darkness, knowing the river was there but not being able to see it, I couldn't stop thinking there was something I was missing. Gary was back from the lab; those results would be through tomorrow. Bill had secured Jake's flat. The safe had contained several thousand pounds in cash but no drugs. Yet the volume of money in small denominations pointed to drug dealing. That fit with Stevie's story. There had to be a hiding place for the drugs somewhere. There was a lot to do but I didn't think we'd get any further tonight. We had a brief meeting, after which I told everyone to go home, and that we would regroup early in the morning.

It was late and I should have headed home myself but I wanted to go through again what we had so far. I liked the solitude of the office when it was empty because it gave me a quiet space to think. Sometimes I'd even talk out loud to myself, testing my theories. Cross-checking could take me a few hours but, the quicker the case was solved, the better for me and the team. The buck stopped with me. I needed to make sure that nothing had been missed.

I sat down at my desk, holding my cup of hot coffee, letting it warm my hands and relax me a bit. I took a sip. It tasted bitter but I hoped the caffeine would help me stay alert. The photograph from Jake's flat lay in front of me. I picked it up. There was something familiar, something I couldn't quite see. My gut told me it was important but I couldn't work out what or why. Something that I was missing was staring me in the face. But I was confident I'd find it. I laid the photo back down, just out of sight, and turned my attention to the evidence we had so far.

The next time I raised my head it was well after ten and, after locking the files away, I made my way out to the car. The car park was deserted and poorly lit. The silence was eerie, the only sound the crunching of my feet on the gravel. As I put my key in the lock, I paused, certain I had heard something. 'Who's there?' I called. No answer. I couldn't pinpoint the sound but felt the hairs on the back of my neck bristling. I shuddered. Things like this don't usually bother me and I tried to ignore it. But I heard it again. And the feeling that someone was watching me. Jake? But surely he wouldn't know that we were after him? At least not yet. Richard Spencer? But he hadn't recognised me. Or maybe he had? Had our enquiries about the loan unleashed something? Fumbling with my keys, I got in the car, breathing hard. As I slammed the door shut, a cat jumped off the wall and onto the bonnet, for a second its bright eyes staring into mine. I screamed. Then breathed a sigh of relief. 'Get a grip on yourself, Kim,' I said out loud to myself, 'I know this is getting to you but really? A cat?' I turned on the engine and pulled away, the tyres spinning on the gravel as I crunched the gears. I still felt rattled.

It was after eleven o'clock by the time I got home. Walking into the empty flat I was overcome by a sense of aloneness, the quietness of the place. Still feeling out of sorts, I switched on the overhead lights and the television, needing light and noise. The news on the TV reminded me that I'd need to update Lewis and the Comms team to brief the press on progress. The investigation never far from my mind.

The microwave pinged. I barely remembered putting something in there. I poured myself a glass of water, resisting the temptation to open some wine, and decanted the chicken curry onto a plate, yet another ready meal. Sitting down at the kitchen table, I robotically ate one forkful after another, not tasting the food, telling myself I should get some shopping done, start to look after myself. I took the dishes to the sink, contemplated washing up but left them to soak. I went to bed, plunging the flat into silence and darkness once more.

Thursday 20th October 2022

THE HOUSE

CHAPTER 29

The next morning, I woke up before six o'clock, feeling unrefreshed, the late meal sitting heavy in my stomach. I'd tossed and turned most of the night. Faces of hatred screaming at me, bony fingers pulling at my clothes. The shadows, the dog barking. One of those faces was not that of teenage Ricky, but that of Richard Spencer, grown-up, retired soldier, Katie's father. I'd thought I was over what had happened, that I'd put it behind me. But seeing Richard Spencer must have exacerbated the trauma more than I thought. As much as I tried to suppress my feelings, my subconscious mind would not let them go. Like I had opened Pandora's Box.

Sipping a peppermint tea to settle my stomach, I inhaled its freshness as I looked out at the early morning darkness of the garden, watching as lights came on in the flats and houses opposite. Another day dawning. Time to get myself together. I was here and I had a job to do. I reminded myself that this was where I was meant to be and I had to keep focused on the investigation. Suppressing any further maudlin thoughts, I headed for the shower.

Pete was already at King Street when I arrived just after seven. He smiled at me. 'Late night?'

I wasn't in the mood for humour. 'I look that bad, do I, Pete?'

He had the grace to look embarrassed. 'That's not what I meant. It was already late when we left last night and you were still here.'

I was sorry for snapping at him and sighed. 'Yeah, I know. Something about this case is bugging me.' I tried to smile. 'Anyway, we've a lot to do.'

Pete was arranging to bring Katie in for questioning, making sure her parents were aware of the CCTV so they'd understand why she was being interviewed at the station. Shannon Birch would also need to be interviewed again now that we knew about the parties. We were building up portfolios of the names for the phone numbers in the notebook. Progress was needed on Amanda's car and its whereabouts as well as whether the number Ben had in his phone for Jake had been traced. Once everyone had arrived and were set on what they needed to do, I headed for Riverwood. I wanted to go back to the school to have another look around, revisit the scene of the crime, and think things through from the start, knowing what I did now.

.oOo.

When I arrived in Mr Murdoch's classroom, I was surprised to see Mrs Caldwell and Ellen Shaw there again. Mrs Caldwell was standing by the desk, looking upset, her hands resting on Mr Murdoch's sweater flung over the back of the chair. The room was freezing. The heating had been switched off for the holidays and the windows were fully open, causing a draught that rustled the papers in front of her. Obviously unaware of my presence, she picked up a stack and started to sort them into piles.

Ellen Shaw was at the back of the room, emptying the old metal book cupboard. She was the first to notice me and when she called my name, Mrs Caldwell looked up to see me standing in the doorway.

A guilty look crossed her face. 'Inspector Berry. I'm sorry... I thought it was alright to sort out Raymond's things...'

I raised a hand, signalling her to stop, reassuring her that what she was doing was fine. I asked both whether they had come across Mr Murdoch's keys, receiving the expected negative response. Glancing at the two women, one then the other, I decided to gauge what they had to say about the idea of students being involved in drug dealing. However, I thought I'd approach it from a more dramatic perspective. 'I think you should both be careful.' Maybe I thought it would provoke a reaction, provide some answers, inform my gut feelings.

Mrs Caldwell's eyes widened and I could see the shock on Ellen's face as she met my gaze. She made her way to the front of the classroom, coming to stand next to Mrs Caldwell, before asking, 'What do you mean?'

I thought I would shake things up a bit, see what response I got. 'I'm convinced the murder of Mr Murdoch and the stabbing of Shannon Birch are connected. We are, of course, looking at motives but couldn't rule out a grudge against the school or even the Department. Any ideas?'

As anticipated, both women remained silent and shook their heads. It was time to see their reaction to the more likely motive. Making sure I had their full attention, I continued. 'Have either of you heard anything about students here being involved in dealing drugs? Could someone at the school be involved in that? Could Mr Murdoch have known about that?' Ellen stared at me and shook her head.

'There were rumours,' said Mrs Caldwell. 'I did mention to Raymond that we were to report anything suspicious.' She turned to Ellen. 'I was going to say something at the next meeting...'

'But you hadn't seen anything suspicious?' I asked.

Ellen shook her head again. 'No. Nothing at all. This is the first I've heard of it.'

Mrs Caldwell put her hand on Ellen's arm. 'I'm sure they were rumours. I haven't come across anything to make me think otherwise.'

'Well, if either of you do think of anything, please let me know.' I turned and left the room.

I walked along the corridor to the cupboard, the door propped open. The crime scene remained the same, untouched. The stench of dried blood mixed with the musty dampness of a space that was never heated, the dust of a place that was never properly cleaned. I surveyed the packed shelves and piles of books and stationery, like I was willing them to talk to me, provide me with answers.

In my mind I saw Mr Murdoch as he was more than twenty years ago stacking books on to a shelf while I hid round the corner trying to stifle sobs. I'd come out of the girl's toilet by the stairwell and there he was in the history cupboard, the door wide open. I'd desperately hoped he wouldn't see me but I hadn't been quiet enough. He'd led me to his classroom and arranged that I no longer had to spend breaks and lunchtimes outside where I no longer felt safe. Instead, I retreated to his classroom while he went to the staffroom.

I'd refused to tell anyone the full story of what had happened and they'd decided it was bullying, like kids do. I'd also not given names. Ricky and his pals had told me they'd say I'd asked for it and it would be their word against mine. But Mr Murdoch had sensed I wasn't telling the full truth. His classroom became my lifeline at that time and I was damn well going to find out who killed him and why. I was still certain he'd been inadvertently caught up in something; I just didn't know what that was yet.

I took one last look around and slipped away via the side stairs.

CHAPTER 30

As soon as I got back to the incident room, Pete told me Katie was downstairs with her father waiting to be interviewed. For the moment, a solicitor had not been requested. Deciding the Spencer's could wait another ten minutes, I got a coffee and retreated to my office to gather my thoughts. After my start to the day and that nightmare, I wanted to make sure I could keep my cool in front of Richard Spencer. I knew I was on edge, wondering if he would recognise me. Knowing that was only a matter of time.

Half an hour later, when Pete and I entered the interview room and sat down opposite Katie and her father, it was the two of them that looked agitated. I began by wishing them a good morning and thanking them for coming in.

Despite Pete explaining about the CCTV, Richard was obviously annoyed, clearly looking for an argument. He leaned forward in his chair, elbows on the table, 'You didn't give us any choice!'

I smiled, retaining my poise. 'We've had a look at your CCTV, Mr Spencer.' It wouldn't do any harm, repeating what he already knew.

'So, I gather.' Anger clouded his eyes.

I ignored his attitude and continued. 'And I'd like to clarify a few things with Katie.'

'What kinds of things? If you overstep the mark, I've told Katie to say nothing and we'll contact my lawyer.' A note of superiority had entered his voice. I could feel his eyes boring into me. 'I've done my homework.' A pause. 'I know who you are.'

He leaned forward, attempting to get closer to me. Was this a threat? Who the hell did he think he was? I wasn't the one with something to hide. I'd done nothing wrong. I stared at him until he dropped his gaze. Glancing at Katie, I noted the quizzical look on her face. Determined that he would not get the better of me and, reminding myself that I was the one in charge here, driving this investigation, I decided to confront him. I looked at Pete then at Richard. 'Mr Spencer.' I waited for him to look at me. 'I'd like a quiet word. Outside. Now.' I kept my voice low but cold. Rising from my chair, I held the door open, beckoning him to step outside. Katie was looking from me to her dad, confused. Pete looked at me with concern but I gave him a nod and he did the same. I waited. Eventually, Richard got up and followed me into the corridor. I closed the door and made sure that we could both see through the window as Pete sat opposite Katie, noting for the tape that we had left the room.

Richard was about a foot taller than me and I had to crane my neck to look at him. 'Would you like to elaborate on that last comment?' My voice was ice cold. 'Or would you prefer me to do that?' I paused, getting into my stride. 'You know what you did. You and your friends. You think you can sit there, with your arrogance, and talk to me like that?' I met his eyes, before looking back into the room at his daughter. 'I might have let you get away with it at the time. But not today. Do you want Katie to know what you did? Even if she doesn't believe me, there will always be that niggle of doubt.'

I didn't believe for a minute that he'd admit to what he'd done. But I was equally sure he would not want me to make accusations in front of his daughter.

He looked through the window at Katie, who, at that moment, raised her eyes to meet his, before turning to glare at me. 'Have it your way,' he said through gritted teeth. I held my ground until he looked away. A win for me.

I opened the door and told him to go first into the room, watching him sit down, his demeanour less imperious. I took a deep breath before following him and taking my seat opposite him, feeling more confident that I could deal with this. I had jumped a hurdle, confronting him like that. We glared at each other across the table until he dropped his gaze.

'Right, let's start again. I'll ask the questions. And I'd like Katie to answer them.' I looked directly at her. 'If you are honest with us, have nothing to hide, you will be fine. On the other hand...' I left the sentence hanging, giving Richard Spencer something to think about. He frowned and looked at his daughter.

I gave Katie my full attention. 'The night before you were ill, you said you went to Shannon's house. CCTV shows you leaving the house about 7.30pm and returning around 11.00pm.' Katie looked at me and shrugged.

I sensed the 'so what' and fought back irritation at this response. 'The only thing is Shannon's mum didn't recognise you when you turned up at the hospital. Why was that?'

Katie made a face. 'I don't know. Maybe because we were in Shannon's room the whole time.' Her tone was clipped, precise.

I was becoming increasingly impatient at the constant lying. 'I'm pretty sure if you'd been in that house Mrs Birch would have seen you.' Katie didn't respond. I pressed on. 'From the clothes you're wearing in the CCTV images, you don't look like someone going to study at a friend's house. I'd say you were going to a party.' Katie opened her mouth to speak but, having decided to let that one rest, I carried on. 'The next day, the day that Mr Murdoch was killed and Shannon was attacked, you woke up late and, when prompted, remembered going for a walk.'

Katie looked at me. 'That's right.' She might have sounded confident but lowered her gaze. She evidently wasn't as sure as she was trying to make out.

I was getting fed up with her attitude. She was clearly lying and I found it unbelievable that she could remain so calm and almost rude. I'd felt sorry for her when I'd found out she'd been filmed at the party but was finding it difficult to have even an iota of sympathy now. Somehow, I had to get her to talk. The only way was to keep pushing the evidence. 'It must have been a long walk. You left the house at 2.45pm and returned at 6.20pm. You got home not long before your mum got in from work. Where were you?'

She glanced at me, briefly meeting my eyes before fixing her gaze on the tea stains caused by Ben throwing his cup at the wall. She claimed she had been walking and lost track of the time. I'd had enough. 'For about three and a half hours? We need details, Katie. You do realise that you were out and about at the times these crimes took place.'

Richard suddenly interjected. 'You're not seriously suggesting that Katie had anything to do with the murder and stabbing!' He looked like he was about to explode.

I met his gaze, fury in his eyes. He didn't have a clue what his daughter had been up to and I wondered what was going through his mind. Did he think I was using Katie to get back at him? Revenge may have flitted through my mind, but this would never be a way to get it. In time he would see that. 'I'm not suggesting anything at this stage. We're gathering information.

And Katie's whereabouts are important to the investigation. Which will become clear.'

I turned back to face Katie. I wanted to know exactly where she'd gone on her walk, pointing out that it would be better if she told me, rather than us having to piece it together from CCTV. Katie looked back at me, blinking rapidly, fidgeting with the buttons on her shirt. I got the feeling that she didn't know what to do or how to respond, her confidence dissipating. 'Don't push it,' I thought, 'this has turned into a waiting game.' The room fell into an uncomfortable silence. Along the corridor, a door opened and closed.

Richard was the first to speak. I watched as he reached over and took her hand. He must have picked up on her discomfort. 'Tell the truth, Katie. We've always said that's what to do. Whatever it is we can support you. If you tell us the truth.' The bravado was gone. His voice tender. This was a different man to the one who had challenged me. A man protective of his daughter.

Katie looked at her dad. I watched as their eyes met and he nodded at her, not letting go of her hand. She turned to me, this time holding my gaze. 'I've been so stupid.' Tears pricked her eyes.

At last, we were getting somewhere. Inwardly, I felt relieved and hoped that this time we would at least get something resembling the truth. I kept my tone light. 'Do you want to talk about it?'

She lowered her eyes, found a spot on the table, and stared at it. 'I saw Shannon straight after school last Thursday. She was fine.' She looked at me. 'I didn't stab her.'

'Why did you go to see Shannon?' I asked. The tension in the room rose as Katie hesitated to give a response. I decided to help her along. 'We know about the parties.' I paused. 'And the videos.'

A look of horror swept over her face. 'How...?' Her voice trailed away.

'We have a witness who saw you at a party the night you said you went to Shannon's house to study. The same witness saw you being taped.' I let that sink in. 'So, why did you go to meet her the next day?'

Katie let go of her dad's hand, sat upright in her chair, and placed her hands on the table, fingers interlinked. She took a deep breath and met my eyes. 'I wanted to see Jake again.'

I didn't let on that I knew about Jake because I wanted to find out what she could tell me. And, of course, see how much that corroborated the information we already had. Therefore, I asked, 'Who's Jake?'

Following a sideways glance at her dad, she said, 'He's a drugs dealer. He organises parties.'

Pete and I glanced at each other. Without saying a word, we knew what the other was thinking, that here we had a witness who could substantiate the evidence we already had. We could use this to build the case against Jake and, hopefully, get Ben and Shannon to talk as well. Richard was sitting there, clearly stunned. Silent. He obviously had no idea what his daughter had been up to those few days. 'Go on,' I said to Katie.

She had only been to a party that once, last Wednesday. Before that she had never tried anything apart from alcohol, not even cigarettes. Shannon had approached her at school and invited her to the party. It was Shannon's idea to say that she was going to her house to study. The day after the party she decided she wanted to see Jake again and the only way to do that was through Shannon. He was attractive and had been nice to her. But Shannon had confronted her, saying she owed money for drugs she'd taken at the party and offered her more. She'd told her Jake had a video that he'd taken that night. He'd post it on social media if she didn't pay what she owed or buy more drugs. Katie raised her head and looked at her dad. 'If I'd known, or even suspected, there would be drugs, I wouldn't have gone.' She turned to me, obviously relieved to get it all out in the open.

Richard didn't say a word, his face unreadable. The tears ran down her face as Katie hugged herself. Richard put an arm round his daughter's shoulders. What was I to make of this Ricky Spencer? In my mind, and nightmares, he was always a monster. Pete and I sat in silence, giving her time to compose herself. Shannon had obviously targeted Katie and Jake had exploited her. What could have led Shannon to this? Eventually, I asked Katie, 'Do you still have the drugs?'

Katie looked at her dad. 'I'm sorry.' She looked back at me. 'Yes. But I don't want them. It's not worth it. All this.' She waved her arms around the room. The party was one thing. I sensed the repercussions were quite the other. The tape machine whirred gently in the background. The interview was not over yet. We took a break.

CHAPTER 31

When Pete and I returned to the interview room half an hour later as promised, Katie's eyes were swollen and red from crying but she appeared calm. Richard sat with his arm around his daughter's shoulders. He smiled weakly at me as we entered the room. I didn't smile back.

I waited until Pete had settled in his chair and switched on the tape before sitting down myself and picking up the thread of questioning. 'Are you okay to continue, Katie?' She looked at me and nodded. 'OK. Let's start with you telling me why you went to see Shannon in the hospital?'

She sighed. There was no sign of her previous bravado. 'When I heard that she'd been stabbed, I wondered if she still had her phone. Maybe it was damaged and she wouldn't have a copy of the video. I thought maybe she could get in touch with Jake, or give me his number. I could get him to delete the video. But she had no idea how to get in touch with him.'

I nodded. This seemed reason enough to have visited Shannon.

There was still a chunk of the day missing. 'Where did you go before the hospital?' I noted a worried look pass over Katie's face when I asked the question. There was clearly something else on her mind.

'What do you mean?' her voice was a whisper.

I jogged her memory. 'You left the house after your mum went to work. But visiting at the hospital is not until the afternoon. Where were you all morning?'

Her eyes swept the room. Eventually she said she'd gone to the hospital café. I couldn't believe that she had sat there the entire morning. Watching her closely, I explained that we would check the hospital CCTV to confirm it. I hoped, since we had got this far, that she wouldn't start lying again. She was biting her lip, clasping, and unclasping her hands on the table. 'Do I have to tell you?' she asked.

I was intrigued. What could still be bothering her so much at this point in her confession? 'Like I said before, better that you tell me... Better for you, that is.'

I could see she was becoming increasingly agitated. 'I don't want to get anyone into trouble.'

'Who?' I asked.

'Someone who's done nothing wrong, I'm sure.' She paused and took a deep breath. 'I'm worried she could lose her baby.'

This I had not expected. Another angle, the potential for another witness or suspect. I tried to reassure her. 'That should only happen if she's broken the law or if the baby's been neglected. Think about it, Katie, what life is it for a child brought up amongst drug dealing?' I hoped this was enough to convince her that she was doing the right thing.

Katie gave me a pleading look. 'She cares about her baby.'

'How do you know that?' I asked.

She looked at me. 'Because I saw her on Thursday and again on Saturday. Before the hospital.'

I held her gaze. 'That's where you were after seeing Shannon on Thursday?'

'Yes.' She bowed her head.

I leaned across the table. 'If that's the case, maybe we can help her. You've done well, Katie. Tell us about the baby and its mother.'

Katie looked from me to Pete and then her dad before sitting back in her chair, her hands flat on the table in front of her. She stared into space. 'When Shannon told me about the video and handed me the drugs, I was frantic. Didn't know what to do. I got the idea to go back to the house in Kincaidston. Maybe Jake would be there and make it all go away.'

'Kincaidston? That's where the party was?' She nodded. 'But Jake wasn't there,' I suggested.

'No,' she said. 'It was a girl not much older than me. And her baby. She claimed she knew nothing about parties. And that didn't know Jake.' Katie looked at me. 'I was sure I had the right house but the girl kept insisting I was wrong. Telling me there was no way I could have been at a party there. But I knew I was right.' She paused, running her fingers through her hair, and I allowed her a moment to settle before asking her to go on.

'I told her if she let me have a quick look for my peace of mind, that would be the end of it. So, she let me in.' Her face clouded over. 'It looked different inside but it was definitely the same place.' She stopped speaking, took a sip of water, and put her head in her hands.

I realised that we may have another young person caught in Jake's web. The girl at the house may or may not be an accomplice. Whatever the truth, we would need to find out what had brought her into Jake's orbit.

It was important to get the rest of Katie's story, so I pushed her to continue. 'Why did you go back on Saturday?' I sat back in my chair and took a sip of coffee.

She shook her head. 'I couldn't relax. I had to do something. Try to sort it out.' She paused. 'I saw on the news about Mr Murdoch. And Shannon...'

I interrupted her. 'You have no idea how Shannon ended up in the river?' I asked. 'You were with her...' I let the inference hang in the air. Her father sat there, looking shocked.

Katie stared at me. 'Honestly, I've no idea. I was flabbergasted when I saw it. But maybe... Shannon's a drug dealer. Maybe she upset someone.'

It sounded like these kids had got themselves involved in stuff they couldn't handle. And thought they could lie their way out of it. 'Let's be clear. You decided to visit Shannon in hospital but go and see the other girl first?' It seemed Katie had been busy.

'I couldn't sit around all morning. The only two people I knew with connections to Jake and maybe help me find him were Shannon and the girl at the house in Kincaidston. So, I decided to go back.' She smiled weakly at the memory. 'And this time I would stand my ground.'

When she got to the house, the girl didn't want to let her in but she'd kept banging on the door until the girl answered. 'I told her I'd go away if I was allowed in to talk.'

I could imagine Katie turning up again like that would have been a shock and I couldn't blame the girl for not wanting to let her in.

'Can you give us a name?' I asked.

She nodded. 'Said her name was Jaz. Didn't tell me a surname. Or her baby's name.' She paused.

I gave it a couple of minutes before asking Katie to go on.

She'd explained to the girl that she was there to find Jake but the girl reiterated she didn't know anyone called Jake, only she and the baby lived there. 'I could tell she was lying. She couldn't look me in the eye.'

We exchanged looks. The irony of that statement wasn't lost on me, given the runaround I'd had the last few days.

Katie continued. 'I told her everything. Even about Shannon being stabbed. I think that gave her a shock. In the end she said she'd make a call. She didn't say Jake but I'm pretty sure it would've been him.'

I listened carefully to the way she spoke about Jaz and her visits to the house. I believed her when she said she hoped that I might be able to help Jaz and her baby. However, I made it clear we would be checking her story, looking at CCTV, speaking to people who might be able to corroborate her movements. 'What about Mr Murdoch?'

She looked surprised. 'Mr Murdoch?'

'You were out and about at the time he may have been killed,' I said.

Her mouth opened and closed but it took a few seconds for any sound to come out. 'It's sad. I didn't like the class but he was a good teacher. Surely, you can't think...'

I was matter of fact. 'I hope you're not lying to us, Katie. The thing I don't get is, given how much trouble you were in, you didn't come to us? Tell us what happened and let us investigate. When we came to the house, you should have been honest. Until we verify where you say you were last Thursday afternoon, we need to consider the possibility that you were in the vicinity of both the murder and the stabbing.'

She looked stunned. 'I promise I'm telling the truth. There's no way I could hurt anyone. I didn't say anything because... It seems so silly now...' She glanced at her dad. 'I didn't want Mum and Dad to find out how stupid I'd been. They'd be disappointed in me. And I honestly thought I could sort it, persuade Jake to destroy the video, let me off the hook. But it was too late.'

Too late for what? I was intrigued. 'What do you mean?'

She looked at me. 'By the time you came to our house, Jake had been in touch.'

A call came through from a number she hadn't recognised and she had debated picking it up, thinking it might be a scam. However, not knowing Jake's number and hoping Jaz would come through on her promise to contact him, she had answered it. 'It was Jake but he sounded so different from the man I met at the party. When he'd been so nice, so friendly...'

Her voice faded to a croak. On the phone, he was so cold that it frightened her. She had asked him if he would destroy the video, that it had been that one mistake. But he'd shown no warmth, insisting that he hadn't forced her to take the drugs and that she'd had a good time. When she told him she couldn't afford to give him money, that she only had a small allowance, he said she should have thought of that before. That was when the penny dropped. 'When I realised I was a source of income to him, I felt a complete idiot.'

'That's putting it mildly,' I thought.

She sighed and looked at the ceiling, tears pricking her eyes. When she'd threatened to get the police involved, he'd laughed, reminding her that her video was easy to upload and it would go viral. Katie stole another glance at her dad. He'd told her she should get her parents to help with the payments. She'd become distraught, pleading that her parents couldn't know. It had taken him ages to answer and she thought he was going to put the phone down. In the end, he said he might take a one-off payment. The condition was that she wouldn't go back to the house. He rang off and when she'd called back, the number was withheld. She'd been waiting for him to call again and, in the meantime, was too scared to do anything.

Pete and me turning up at their house had given her a real shock. She was worried about the drugs hidden in her bedroom, what we might know, what Shannon might have said, especially when she realised that Shannon had given us her name. She had decided to say as little as possible, knowing that it was all being written down and she wanted to be able to remember everything to be able to give the same answers. She looked from me to Pete, who gave her an encouraging smile. 'It was hard because I didn't want to lie. But I was too scared to tell the truth.' And her dad had mentioned his CCTV which she had forgotten about. Katie let out a sigh before sitting back in her chair, chewing her lip. 'I'm glad you know everything. It's a relief.'

Richard Spencer was watching his daughter intently. I nodded to Pete to switch off the tape and we got up to leave the room. Some time alone would not do father and daughter any harm. They would have a lot to talk about. Pete could come back in a bit and arrange for them to go home. There wasn't enough to charge Katie with anything yet. At least we had her side of the story and it was a big piece of the jigsaw. Things were starting to come together. However, I still couldn't fathom how Mr Murdoch could have been involved in, or linked to, any of this.

CHAPTER 32

Pete and I sat on either side of the desk in my office going over the evidence and making plans. We would have to interview both Shannon and Ben yet again. Now that Katie had given her side of the story, which tied in with what Stevie had said, it would be interesting to see what Shannon had to say about Jake, the drugs, and the parties. Katie might be denying involvement in either crime but, given that she didn't have a verified alibi for the stabbing or the murder, she still couldn't be ruled out.

We knew there was a number for someone called Jake in Ben's phone, so we could confront him about that. We would also pay a visit to the house in Kincaidston, see if the girl there confirmed Katie's version of events. Forensics had found traces of Mr Murdoch's blood on the mallet discovered in Jake Devaney's flat. The weapon had been wiped clean of fingerprints. That meant Jake could argue that it had been planted in his flat by someone else. However unlikely that was, we would have to prove he knew it was there. That he was the one who put it there.

Pete and I looked up as Gary knocked on the door and didn't wait for a reply before he opened it and came in. I noted the look of excitement on his face. I'd asked him to do a search on Jake Devaney, to see if anything at all came up that might prove to be useful. I'd also put in a call to Cliff Burns to see if Jake was known to the drugs team.

Gary was eager to tell us what he had uncovered. He'd been unable to find any records of a Jake Devaney going back more than a couple of years which is when he bought the flat in Troon and the car, both in cash. Therefore, he assumed that Jake may have gone by a different name in the past and contacted the deed poll service. However, that could take a while and was unlikely to give us any results unless he'd changed his name legally.

It had occurred to Gary that if someone changes their name, they are likely to have a reason. It might be they didn't like their name but there was always the chance they wanted to become someone else, for example. This was an interesting line of thought. We had all agreed that the boy in the photograph was likely to be Jake but, given that there was no evidence of a Jake Devaney at that age, Gary had searched the newspaper archives. Maybe the change of name was linked to something that might have been reported at some point. And so, he followed this hypothesis.

Gary had our full attention. Keen to hear where this was going, I indicated to him to take a seat beside Pete. He clearly could hardly wait to share what he had discovered. He had come across an article about an accident that had happened on the M74 twenty years ago. The family involved were from Edinburgh and they had been on holiday in North Wales. He placed the printout he'd been holding on the desk in front of me. I picked it up and quickly skimmed it, the headline read: 'Couple Die in Horror Smash.' There had been a horrific car crash involving a lorry and a car. The driver and front passenger had been killed instantly. Two children travelling in the back had miraculously escaped without a scratch.

Gary had found out more details about the accident. The couple killed were called Devaney and the children were called John and Danielle Crichton, a brother and sister. He had cross checked police archives and the report stated the children were fostered. After being examined at the hospital, they were handed over to social services. They would have ended up back in care.

I didn't doubt Gary's enthusiasm but was beginning to wonder where this was going. 'What makes you think any of this is relevant?'

Gary smiled. 'There's something that's too much of a coincidence. A photo with the article. Not the children. The couple, Gerard, and Karen Devaney. I think it's the same people in the photo you found in the flat. If I'm right Jake Devaney used to be John Crichton.'

Gary placed a photo on top of the printout. I looked at it and it seemed like time stood still. I looked across the desk at him, visibly impressed. 'I don't believe in coincidences. This is good work, Gary. Get in touch with social services. See what we need to do to get access to the records relating to the Crichton children. Keep me updated.'

Gary smiled, pleased with himself.

I called a team meeting to set out the latest plan. Bill would do some digging on Amanda Cairns and keep in touch with forensics. Gary would follow up the lead on the Crichton children and Carmel would liaise with Cumnock police. Pete and I would speak to Ben Chadwick and Shannon

Birch yet again, given what we knew about Jake Devaney. But those interviews could wait until tomorrow.

Everyone prepared to go. 'Bill,' I said. He turned back to face me. 'Any news on the loan company?'

'Oh, yes,' he responded. 'They have a small shop on the high street. I was there yesterday when you called to go to Troon. Sorry, forgot to say with all the excitement of the weapon...and that photo.' His gaze went to where Gary was sitting typing away on his keyboard.

I smiled at him. 'No problem. There's a lot going on. What did they say?'

'A new set up. The main office is in Paisley. They do same day, pay day... all the usual loans.' He paused. 'They weren't pleased to see me.'

'I don't imagine they would be,' I replied with a shrug. 'Whether it's legal or not, it doesn't look good, us turning up. What about Mr Murdoch's account? Get anywhere there?'

'Nah. Spoke to a young lass... Said she didn't have the authority... And the manager wasn't there...' He gave me a 'why does that not surprise me look' and raised his eyebrows.

I had to agree. 'Go back and see if you can speak to this manager. If not, I'll give Cliff Burns a call. See if he's heard of them. Thanks, Bill.'

He nodded and left.

Before seeing Ben or Shannon again we were going to visit the house in Kincaidston to interview the girl, Jaz, and see how much she corroborated Katie's story. We should also be able to find out more about Jake. The drug dealer and his possible link to a tragedy years before was a conundrum; what could that have to do with our investigations? I couldn't shake the feeling that something was just out of reach, pieces of the puzzle missing and, if Jake proved to be John Crichton, that could be one of them.

CHAPTER 33

The house in Kincaidston was a small terrace that, from the outside, looked like it needed some maintenance; the paint peeling on the front door and evidence of rotting wood in the window frames. I noted this contrasted with the properties surrounding it.

The young woman that answered the door almost jumped out of her skin when I showed her my ID. She didn't look much older than Katie, certainly still in her teens. 'Jaz?' I asked.

She stared at Pete and me, clearly confused. A look of fear settled on her face. 'Please, don't take my baby.' Her accent wasn't what I expected. She didn't have an Ayrshire twang. If I were a betting woman, I'd say she'd gone to a private school around Glasgow.

I looked at her, taking in the cropped blonde hair and thin frame, knowing I could not give reassurances. 'Why don't we come in for a chat?'

She stood back to let us into the long, narrow hallway before showing us to a living room that was neat, clean, and sparsely furnished. It smelled of polish and air freshener. The interior so far was in sharp contrast to the outside. The room fitted the description given by Katie when she had visited in the days after the party. Jaz invited us to sit down.

The baby was asleep in a bedroom upstairs so I decided to get straight to the point. 'What do you know about Jake Devaney?'

She looked at the floor. 'Jake ...?'

I wasn't prepared to have someone else try to convince me that they didn't know Jake. 'We have witnesses who say someone called Jake organises parties in this house.' I paused, allowing that to sink in. 'Listen, Jaz. It's important you tell the truth. Tell us what you know, if you're in any trouble... That's the best way of keeping your baby.' I didn't like making veiled threats but I'd had enough of being led around by young people who seemed hell bent on protecting a drug dealer. That fear might be stopping them talking, but this man needed to be off the streets. For all I knew, Jaz could be involved in running some sort of drugs racket with Jake. I watched her carefully, knowing that, like the others, she was weighing up her options, trying to decide what to say. I thought I'd give her a push. 'The polish. The air freshener. Are you hiding something?' I paused. 'Drugs?'

Her eyes widened in shock. Finally, she spoke. 'Jake owns this house.'

She was aware he used it for something but claimed that she didn't know what. Katie had turned up saying she'd been at a party there but Jaz hadn't known whether to believe her. Jake would tell her to go away for a couple of days, which he paid for, and when she came back the house would look the same. Whatever he was up to, it was always meticulously clean. She was allowed to keep the two bedrooms locked, for herself and her baby. The dining room next door, at the front of the house, was used by Jake. She thought he stored stuff in there but had no idea what. Without a key she couldn't look even if she wanted to.

I leaned towards her and waited until she met my eyes. 'Are you trying to tell me that you have no idea what Jake was up to while you were away?' We continued to look at each other. 'Be careful, Jaz. It won't look good if you lie to us.'

She turned away, looked at Pete, standing in the doorway. 'I...' Turning back to me, she averted my gaze. 'I suspected but... I thought maybe it was best to not know. And Jake... Well, he keeps a lot to himself. I don't ask questions...'

I remembered noticing as we approached the house that the blinds to the front were closed. Pete caught my eye, I nodded to him and he left the room. I called Bill to organise a search warrant and a forensics team before telling Jaz that she and her baby would have to move out. Her distress was obvious as she told me she had nowhere to go. She sunk into the nearest chair.

The silence in the room was broken when Pete put his head round the door. There was something I needed to see. I was aware of Jaz's eyes on me as I followed him into the hall. The door to the dining room next door was open; he'd obviously worked his magic on the lock. However, this was no dining room. Here were the things that Katie had described at the party. An old couch with broken springs, a rolled-up carpet which, on closer inspection, was a threadbare pattern of swirls, and a scratched table which I suspected would show signs of cocaine when examined in the lab.

The room also contained a lot of boxes. Pete opened one to find that it contained padded envelopes and blank address labels that could be used for concealing deliveries of drugs, made to look like normal parcels. In another he found a stash of cocaine, double vacuum sealed to minimise the risk of odour leakage. There was an unpleasant whiff of burnt plastic, chemicals, rotten eggs, and herbs; the sofa and carpet betraying the effects of marijuana and crack cocaine which even the air freshener in here could not fully mask.

Behind me, I heard Jaz gasp, not realising she'd followed me from the living room. I shook my head, wondering for the umpteenth time how these young people get caught up with criminals like Jake. I asked Jaz to put the kettle on and make some tea, relax her a bit, and hopefully then she could tell us everything.

She nodded and I followed her to the kitchen. We didn't speak as she busied herself with the drinks, her hands shaking as she poured the boiling water into mugs. Settled back in the living room, I made it clear I wanted to know about her relationship with Jake and what she knew about his activities. 'You suspected something was going on, but claim to not know exactly what? No amount of air freshener would mask those smells. Maybe for a few days, but after that? Are you saying you didn't know he was dealing drugs from here?'

She took a deep breath. 'As I said... I did suspect but...' She bit her lip. 'I didn't want to lose this house. I told you I've nowhere else to go... Jake said there was nothing to worry about... I had to believe that...'

I did feel sorry for the girl. She seemed genuinely distraught. 'I need the truth, Jaz.' If she gave me that and it transpired she wasn't involved, I hoped that we could help her keep her baby. First things first, though. 'Tell me how you met Jake.'

She gripped her cup of tea. 'Inspector Berry...' Her voice trailed off as she waited for me to meet her eyes. 'Before I answer more of your questions... I'd prefer you call me my proper name. Jasmine. I only told Jake my name was Jaz because... well, I guess I didn't want him to know who I really am...'

Jasmine was brought up in Newton Mearns and wanted for nothing. So, I was right about the accent. When she got pregnant, a complete accident, she couldn't bring herself to have an abortion. Her father said she had brought shame on the family and, after a heated argument, told her to leave. She had gone to see the father of her baby but he'd wanted her to get rid of it. Too ashamed to call on other family or friends, she got the bus to Ayr, thinking it would be far enough away and she'd feel safer in a small town. She had ended up on the streets but, no matter how desperate she'd felt, never tried to contact her parents, remaining convinced they wouldn't want her. She had changed her appearance in case someone came looking for her.

Jasmine ran her hands through her hair as she described how much she used to love it when it was long and dark. She'd left behind a wardrobe full of designer clothes and now bought from charity shops. She gave me a small smile. 'But I have my baby.'

I couldn't help but warm to this girl. Maybe it was the way she looked when she mentioned her baby. I smiled back at her. 'And Jake?'

She had met Jake when living on the streets. Every day she had gone for a meal at the homeless centre. One day Jake had been there as she was leaving, like he'd been waiting for her. She had thought it a bit creepy. He'd approached her, looked at her bump, and told her he could help. She had said she didn't need his help, trying to sound confident. But every day after that he'd be there waiting, and her belly was getting bigger and bigger. The closer it got to when she was due, the more insistent he'd become, repeatedly asking what would happen to her when it was born. If she was going to bring it up on the streets or maybe leave it in a doorway when she found she couldn't cope.

Tears began to slide down her cheeks. She hadn't wanted to think about what would happen when the baby was born. If she went to social services, they might contact her parents and that was the last thing she wanted. She had decided she could never forgive them. But the thought of giving up her baby had been tearing her apart. Jake had said he'd help if she wanted to keep it.

They had come to an arrangement. Jake would pay for them to live in this house, making sure they had enough to live on. She raised her head and looked directly into my eyes. 'Don't you think...' She took a deep breath. 'Don't you think, the main thing was I would be able to look after my baby?'

It felt like a rhetorical question so I didn't answer. She had suspected Jake was up to no good, probably involving drugs, but didn't know what else to do. She didn't ask him any questions because she wouldn't have to lie if she was confronted about what he did. As time went on and everything was working out, she had settled into a routine. Jake would come to the house when she and the baby were out and they went away overnight about once a month. When they got back everything looked the same, even cleaner than how she had left it. And there would be money in an envelope on the table for essentials and a few treats. Cash for no questions. She reckoned she was better off than a lot of the other mums living on benefits. She thought she had made it work for them, despite her doubts.

There were several options here. She could be actively involved in Jake's business, fully aware of his stash. However, she had looked me in the eye when she had said he kept the room locked and she didn't have access. Plus, she had appeared totally shocked when we'd entered what turned out to be a store for his drug dealing business. My gut was she had kept out of illegal activity and so far, there was no evidence to suggest otherwise. Perhaps she was completely naïve, unaware of what Jake did when she went away. However, I thought that unlikely. She had been savvy enough to enter into an arrangement which she might not like, but it suited her. More likely that she'd turned a blind eye to what might be going on in order to look after herself and the baby without the involvement of the authorities. I had to admit I could see her dilemma when Katie had appeared on her doorstep.

Jasmine gave a brittle laugh. 'Thing is... When I agreed to his proposal, part of me wondered if the price might someday turn out to be too high.'

Strangely, if she was referring to possibly not being allowed to keep her baby, I hoped she would be proved wrong.

CHAPTER 34

That day arrived when Katie turned up at the house, not once, but twice. It was the first time someone had come looking for Jake and it had forced her to think about things, about what was going on, something she didn't want to do. It had been better to not know, keep things in the background, keep going as they were. But Katie had talked about parties, drugs, and blackmail, beyond anything she could imagine.

Jasmine sat with her hands in her lap, gazing out the window. 'That first time, I watched her run out of the house, thinking I might have easily ended up taking drugs to cope with everything... I hadn't allowed myself to think about what Jake might be up to. But she came back. I couldn't get what she'd said out of my head. What Jake had done. Especially when I looked at my daughter. So, I said I'd phone him.'

Surprisingly, I felt my heart clench. The job didn't usually affect me like that. I didn't know who I was most angry with - the parents who had abandoned their pregnant daughter or the drug dealer who had taken advantage of the desperate girl. I wanted to do my best for Jasmine and offered to put her in touch with a shelter as a temporary measure. What would happen to the house in the longer term, I had no idea.

Before making the call, I wanted to follow up one other possibility, 'Are you sure you can't get in touch with your parents? Once they see you and your baby, they might change their minds?'

Jasmine looked at me. 'I don't know.'

'Worth a try?' I asked. At least she would know for sure.

She shook her head. 'I don't think so. They probably think I'm dead. I've had no contact with them since they threw me out. Since I left.'

I was determined that this was worth a shot. 'A lot could have happened, Jasmine. Maybe they were in shock and may well have been looking for you all this time. How long since you left?'

'Two years.' She slouched in her chair and ran her fingers through her hair.

I looked across at Pete, hoping he'd be thinking the same as me. He nodded and went into the hall, phone already in hand. I turned back to Jasmine, suggesting that we could contact them for her, check things out. She looked at me, uncertainty written all over her face. As we fell into silence, the cries of the baby started up and Jasmine left the room to fetch her.

I contemplated the offer I'd made; it was out of my remit but somehow, I felt the need to reunite this girl with her parents. To let them meet their grandchild. Was it too much to ask for one happy ending? I didn't think Jasmine was actively involved in whatever Jake was up to although she did benefit financially from it. With her parents' support and somewhere to go, she could be given a caution to stay out of further trouble.

Pete came back into the room. Two years ago, a missing person's report was filed for Jasmine Anand in Glasgow. He showed me the photo; apart from the long, dark hair, it was the girl here with us. It's easy for people to disappear, even if they don't go far.

We looked towards the door as Jasmine came back into the room, carrying the baby. I could tell straight away that the little girl was well looked after, clean, and beautifully dressed. She sat down with the baby propped on her knee, bottle in hand. I let her settle the baby before telling her that her parents had filed a missing person's report two years ago, at the time she had left home. It was still live. 'That says to me they want you back. We can't tell you what to do. And we can't let your parents know that we've found you unless you say so. It's up to you.'

A whole gamut of emotions passed over Jasmine's face. What was she feeling? Relief that she could maybe go home? Fear that her parents would no longer want her? Worry about where else to go? Concern for her baby? I watched as Jasmine looked at her daughter and hugged her even closer.

At last, she smiled and turned to look at me. 'Inspector Berry, will you take me home?'

I opened my mouth to tell her that I couldn't, it wasn't part of my job, especially in the middle of a murder investigation. Somehow, though, the words wouldn't come out and, instead, I thought, what the hell, maybe I could do the right thing. It would be a better outcome than transferring mother and baby to a shelter. I had to hope it would work out. I asked Pete to wait at the house until Bill arrived with the forensics team. He could call a patrol car to take him back to the station. I'd take Jasmine and the baby home.

Less than an hour later we pulled up in front of a smart detached property in Newton Mearns. We parked on the road outside instead of the drive to not attract close attention. Jasmine wanted me to sound things out before she was spotted. I felt uncharacteristically nervous getting out of the car. The blood and guts of serious crime didn't bother me but dealing with relationships and families did.

The woman who answered the door was dressed in loose trousers and matching blouse, effortlessly smart. She looked suspiciously at me until I showed her my ID, at which point her manner abruptly changed. She stood back politely, allowing me to step into the house. I checked that her husband was at home before asking to speak to them both.

Having led me through a large hallway and into a sitting room, she went to find her husband. I took in my surroundings; an elaborately decorated room, high ceilinged with a large window that overlooked the garden. I moved over to the window and remained standing to take a closer look. I was still gazing out over the lawn when Jasmine's mother re-entered, a man I presumed to be Jasmine's father close behind.

They sat close together on the sofa while I took an armchair opposite. Both looked at me expectantly. 'I'm here about your daughter, Jasmine.' I watched closely for their reactions. The mother's eyes opened wide. Was it shock or surprise? A good sign? Or not? I decided the best thing to do was come right out with it. 'Your daughter has been found.'

Jasmine's father's eyes met mine, his wife clinging onto him. He admitted that the last time they had seen Jasmine they had rowed and said a lot of things they had always regretted. The air in the room was thick with apprehension.

'How is our daughter, Inspector?' Jasmine's father asked.

I looked at him. 'She has a lovely baby. And she needs support.'

'Where is she?' Jasmine's mother couldn't keep the nervous excitement from her voice.

This was a positive sign. 'Jasmine is in my car parked on the road outside. With her baby.'

'Can she come home?' A note of hope had crept into the mother's voice.

I appraised them of the facts before suggesting they ask Jasmine to fill them in with the details.

Jasmine's mother rose from the sofa, looked at me then her husband. 'We've been given another chance, Caleb. This time I'm doing right by my daughter.'

I followed her as she retraced her steps through the hall towards the front door and caught up as she reached the car. Mother and daughter's eyes met as Jasmine got out, the baby in her arms.

Jasmine's apprehension was written all over her face. 'Hi, Mum,' she said tentatively, 'this is Olivia.'

Mrs Anand gasped. 'She's beautiful.'

Jasmine put her baby into her mum's arms. 'Say hello to Grandma.'

It was time for me to go, I still had a job to do. I reminded Jasmine that I would arrange for her to pop down to the station in Ayr over the next few days to give her statement.

As I got in the car, she shouted, 'DI Berry.' I turned to look at her. 'Thank you.' We smiled warmly at each other.

'Sometimes it's good to step out of the box,' I thought.

Taking in the views as I sped over the Fenwick Moor on the way back to Ayr, I made two calls. Hands free, of course. First, to Cliff Burns to hand over the discovery of drugs at the Kincaidston house. He could take that over and keep me up to date on anything I needed to know. Second, to Pete to let him know that it was time to call it a day; he and the team should be in early in the morning. Reaching the junction that would take me home, I turned off. It had been a long day and there was a lot to digest. With Katie's confession and what we had learned from Jasmine and the contents of the house, a lot of progress had been made.

On impulse, I drove to Barassie Beach and parked up opposite Jake's penthouse. There was a uniformed officer outside in case Jake came back but I doubted that he would. Where are you, I wondered? My resolve tightened. I would catch him and bring him to justice. Whatever it took.

Friday 21st October 2022

THE JIGSAW

CHAPTER 35

The next morning everyone was in early. Now that we had Katie's statement and Jasmine's story, it was imperative to speak to Ben and Shannon again. I couldn't see how either of them could still deny knowledge of Jake and his activities.

I'd released Ben into his mother's care pending further enquiries but arranged for him to be brought back in for further questioning. When he arrived, he was put in an interview room and Pete and I headed downstairs to talk to him. He still didn't want anyone with him, but I'd organised a solicitor anyway. It was important to cover ourselves as much as anything else. And maybe it would help Ben see the gravity of his situation. When we entered the room, he looked even more downcast than usual. Pete sat opposite the solicitor and I took a seat opposite Ben. As my chair scraped the floor, Ben looked up.

'How are you, Ben? I asked. He shook his head and looked away, saying nothing. I was going to give him one more chance to tell me the truth now that he'd had time to think and came straight to the point. 'Who's Jake?'

A look of fear passed over Ben's face. Fleeting, but it was there. 'I don't know anyone called Jake.'

I persevered. 'I'll ask you one more time. Who is Jake?'

'I told you I don't know.' Ben sounded even less convincing, unable to look at me.

I felt a sense of disappointment, I thought he might have owned up to knowing Jake. What kind of a hold did Jake have over him? I reminded him that we had his phone and had obviously checked his call records and contacts. Ben put his head in his hands and I thought I'd help him out by telling him what we knew.

He had a notebook in his possession and Shannon had a notebook taken from her by Mr Murdoch. He was signed out of chemistry for twenty minutes to go to the toilet, yet was seen in Mr Murdoch's classroom. CCTV places him near the river and text messages show him arranging to meet someone called Jake there. And his number was in the deciphered notebook.

There was silence as I let all of that sink in. I pressed home the point. 'We can place you at the scene of two crimes on that day, Ben. Mr Murdoch's murder and Shannon's stabbing.'

He stared directly at me. 'I didn't kill anyone. I didn't stab anyone.'

Holding the boy's gaze, I persisted, 'The evidence suggests otherwise, Ben. So, tell me. Who is Jake?' I paused and told him Jake had disappeared. 'Is he expecting you to take the rap for him? Are you protecting him? Do you know who killed Mr Murdoch? Was it Jake?' The tension in the room increased and Ben looked worn out. I spoke quietly. 'Ben, if you didn't kill Mr Murdoch, I ask you again to help me find out who did. If you tell us what you know, maybe I can help you not ruin your life.' Ben and I stared at each other, both waiting for the other to flinch. I almost admired his tenacity. But no way would he win this stand-off.

It seemed like hours but at last Ben started to talk. His voice wavered. He was obviously finding it difficult to remain in control. He kept his eyes on me. 'D'you know what it's like to not be able to afford anything? To see everyone else with stuff I couldn't have? I want to go to university. How am I supposed to do that?' He glanced out the window and ran his hands through his hair. 'We don't have enough money and I can't take on the debts.'

'Why don't you tell me about it, Ben.' The frustration I had felt receded. What I saw in front of me was a kid caught up in something he couldn't handle, all the false bravado knocked out of him. He went limp and leaned back in his chair. Laying his hands flat on his knees, his fingers twitching, he, at last, began to talk. 'I saw a notebook in Mr Murdoch's drawer when I got my phone. I wasn't a hundred percent sure. But it was black and tatty. Like Jake's. I've no idea why he kept the notebook but it never left his sight.' He paused. 'So, I asked out of Chemistry to see.' He let out a deep breath, like a weight being released from his chest. 'I took the keys from the cupboard door. Mr Murdoch didn't even see me. I saw the notebook and ... instinct, I suppose, I took it. Miss Shaw caught me...'

'Did you ever think Mr Murdoch was involved in whatever Jake was up to? That was why he had the notebook?' I asked.

Ben looked aghast. 'Mr Murdoch! No way. He was always on about rights and wrongs. If he knew what I was up to... I know he thought highly of me, expected me to get an A...' He sighed.

I nodded. 'Go on.'

He took a deep breath. 'I texted Jake and he told me to meet him by the river.'

'Where you were picked up on CCTV,' I said.

Ben nodded. 'Yes.'

'Do you know anything about the contents of the notebook? What it means?' I asked.

He laughed. 'Jake asked me the same thing.' When Jake had asked him if he had looked in the notebook, he had seen no point in lying. He had told Jake he'd looked to check that it was his. 'I told him the same as I'm saying to you. I didn't have a clue what all the letters meant.' Jake had seemed happy with that and wanted Ben to keep hold of the notebook for another day. He said he had been let down by someone he trusted, so he was going to trust Ben. The notebook was important, Ben had to keep it safe. Ben looked at me and almost laughed. 'At that point, I felt happy I'd done the right thing. Almost proud. Stupid, looking at it now...' After seeing Jake, he'd gone to meet his friends up town.

I got the impression that working for Jake was more than a job to Ben. That Jake's validation was important to him. 'How did you end up working for Jake?' I asked.

Ben rubbed his eyes before resting his hands on his knees. 'It was at the bus stop. A few months ago. I'd been in town with my mates and I'd decided to head home. I was on my own and this guy started chatting to me. I'd never seen him before but he seemed nice enough, not that old, maybe twenty-something.' He turned and looked at the solicitor. 'I know the rules but...' Looking back at me, he continued. 'I thought ... I'm not a kid. It wasn't like he was trying to kidnap me.'

I nodded. 'No-one's blaming you for talking to Jake at a bus stop, Ben. What I want to know is how he drew you in from that first approach.' I was pretty sure he'd been targeted by Jake and wanted to find out what the hook might have been. Apparently, Jake had overheard him talking with his friends about not being able to afford decent trainers and thought he might be up for earning some extra cash. They'd gone for a coffee and that was it; Jake had offered him a job and he'd started delivering parcels the next day.

This confused me. 'It didn't occur to you that he must have been in the Arcade? And followed you to the bus stop?'

Ben shrugged. 'Not really. At the time I didn't think about it. He seemed cool, wanted to help me out. Listened when I told him about my dad.'

Jake seemed to have picked out Ben because he was vulnerable. First, that he needed money and, second, that his dad had left, leaving Ben hurt and bitter. For Ben, Jake's apparent concern for him, as well as the cash, would have been a powerful draw.

At first, he had been fooled, believing the business was above board. He let out a long breath and met my eyes. 'Call me naïve. Or a sucker.' He looked away.

However, it hadn't taken long, a few weeks, for it to dawn on him that he was probably carrying drugs. Everything might have looked above board, normal brown packages, but delivering similar sized parcels to the same addresses on a regular basis had set alarm bells ringing. By then, though, he was in too deep. He had begun to rely on Jake's friendship and the pay was so good, it was great to be able to afford what he wanted. As far as his mum and friends were concerned, he worked for a courier company and made enough to buy fake designer stuff online. He had also been saving for university. 'I didn't like what I was doing. But, well, although Mum works hard, we don't have much...' His eyes scanned the room before resting on the tea stains on the wall.

In my view, the generous level of pay on its own would have been reason enough to keep Ben's mouth shut. But he obviously also looked up to Jake. Or, at least, had done. I sighed. 'Look, Ben. From what you say, I can understand the temptation to get involved with Jake. What I don't get, is your continued stubbornness in not telling us the truth. After all, Jake left you high and dry.'

He looked at the cracked tiles on the floor. 'Dunno. Panic, I suppose.' He smiled to himself. 'I wasn't able to fool my mum, though.'

‘I assume that’s why you didn’t want your mum to come here with you. She might say too much,’ I said.

He nodded. ‘You came back… I was arrested…’ In the interview room, everything was going round and round in his head and I told him to empty his pockets. ‘You had my phone. You had the notebook. Jake would be mad because I’d promised to look after it. But I was furious too. Jake had left me in it. If he’d taken back the notebook, I wouldn’t be in this mess.’

I didn’t say anything but, in my head, I agreed with him. The more questions I had asked, the more confused he’d become, trying to remember what he’d previously told us and his mum.

I nodded. ‘Are there others in the school working for Jake?’ I asked.

He looked me in the eye. ‘Dunno. Didn’t know about Shannon. If there’s anyone else?’ He shrugged. ‘No idea. When I realised Jake must’ve given Shannon the notebook… It’s obvious how stupid I’ve been. If I’d left it where it was, Shannon would’ve gone back for it and I’d be in the clear.’

He stopped talking. We all knew that, instead, he was in the frame for killing Mr Murdoch and stabbing Shannon because that notebook was in his possession. He covered his face with his hands before linking his fingers and resting his elbows on his knees, staring at the floor. In the corridor, someone started shouting, angry at being detained next door, their screeches echoing off the walls. We were all waiting for Ben to speak.

At last, he raised his head to look at me, clearly struggling to say what was on his mind. ‘When I realised Shannon might have gone back for the notebook… Knowing that you had asked me about it… Maybe it had something to do with what happened to Mr Murdoch…’ His eyes were wide, realisation dawning. ‘If I’d left it there…’ A gulp. ‘Would he still be alive…?’

Pete and I exchanged glances before I said gently. ‘I assume that’s why we have those tea stains down the walls of the interview room.’

He nodded; eyes downcast. ‘When you left me there, I’d never felt so alone in my entire life. I felt so frustrated. And scared. And angry. I couldn’t help myself, like everything exploded inside me.’

I couldn’t help but feel sympathy for him, as well as glad that he’d decided to tell us the truth. We would check it all out but I was fairly certain that, although Ben’s actions might have been a catalyst, he wasn’t Shannon’s attacker nor Mr Murdoch’s killer. Coming to terms with his role in what had happened, I felt he would need help to work through that. I couldn't reassure him that if he'd left the notebook in the drawer, Mr Murdoch might still be alive because I didn't have the answer to that. He would remain a person of interest but I felt that he could go home for the time being. I handed over to Pete to make the necessary arrangements. As I left the room, Pete explained to Ben that he would arrange for him to update his statement and contact his mum.

Climbing the stairs, I was thinking what to do about Ben. He was a crucial witness, not just for us but also for the drugs investigation. I might be able to arrange for leniency based on him helping bring a drug dealer, who was possibly a murderer, to justice. I felt no sense of triumph at having been proved correct.

But first, we would have to find Jake.

CHAPTER 36

Sitting in my office, preparing to visit Shannon again, Pete and I agreed on two things. First, that, for some reason, Shannon was protecting Jake. Second, that she didn't have a good relationship with her mother.

I'd asked Bill to visit Shannon to try to get her to talk, if necessary, by outlining the trouble she was in given we knew about her drug dealing activities. She had insisted that she still didn't remember anything and couldn't give a description of her attacker. Bill, like Pete and I, was convinced she was lying.

When asked about Jake, she had been adamant she didn't know him, even when Bill told her we had a witness saying she helped Jake to host parties where drugs were available and that she was a courier. Shannon had blamed Katie for pointing the finger at her and accused us of bluffing. She had shown no fear when he explained that Katie wasn't the witness nor when he'd mentioned the notebook and all the names in it, still insisting it wasn't the one that would have been in Mr Murdoch's drawer. She had no idea why her name was in it. Even when Bill explained there was a connection between Mr Murdoch's murder and the notebook, she had been shocked but refused to say anything.

He had been left with no choice but go with my last resort; caution the girl on suspicion of soliciting drugs and extortion.

Following Bill's report and the further evidence we had, it was time to put even more pressure on Shannon. I'd start by having a quiet chat with Shannon's mum, who seemingly had no inkling of what her daughter had been up to.

When Pete and I arrived at Shannon's room, she was sleeping so I signalled to her mum to follow me and we went to the café. Pete took a seat by her bedside in case Shannon woke up.

After fetching the coffees, I sat down opposite her weary looking mother. 'You had no suspicions at all about what Shannon was up to?'

She nodded, staring into her coffee cup. Working back shift meant she was out most evenings and Shannon came and went as she pleased. She was in last Wednesday because she was ill. She looked up at me. 'I would have known if Katie was there. I might've had a couple of drinks but I remember... Shannon made me a sandwich and a bit later I heard her go out.'

I wasn't in the mood for a soft approach. 'And you don't know where she went? Parties? Drugs?' She kept shaking her head. It seemed she had no idea about any of it.

Wiping her eyes to stem the flow of tears, she admitted that, since her husband, Shannon's dad, had died, she hadn't paid much attention to her daughter. His death had been a shock and she hadn't known how to handle it. It wasn't Shannon who had gone off the rails, at least not in those first few months. 'I started to drink as a way of coping, to take the edge off my grief.' Before long, she couldn't get through the evenings without a drink, although she assured me, she hadn't touched a drop since Shannon had been in hospital. As I'd suspected the first time we met, the tremors and restlessness were down to alcohol withdrawal.

She was weeping, insisting that she had failed her daughter. She wasn't wanted at the hospital but was too scared to go home in case she started drinking again. She relied on friends to bring in what they needed.

I looked at the woman opposite me. Who was I to judge? Who knows what anyone's tipping point is? My mum died when I was fourteen and I was lucky because Dad and I had got through it together. The first few weeks he'd reach for the whisky bottle in the evenings but stopped when I'd discovered him asleep in an armchair in the middle of the night, a half empty bottle in his hand. I can still see the shame on his face when I woke him up and he never touched another drop after that. I was always able to count on him and Shannon had not had that. This mother and daughter couldn't change the past, but the main thing was to look forward.

I leaned across the table. 'Shannon could be in a lot of trouble. We need to find out what she knows. She may well be in danger. Mr Murdoch's murder may be connected to her being stabbed. And, if she's honest with us, I can maybe take that into account, given the charges she's facing.' I waited. At last, she raised her head. 'Will you help me persuade Shannon to talk?' I asked.

She sighed. Around us the café was filled with noise. Chatter, crockery, cutlery, somewhere someone dropped a tray. She met my gaze. 'Inspector Berry, I'll do my best. But I doubt my daughter will listen to me.'

When we entered the room Shannon launched into a tirade of anger, shouting at me to leave her alone. I watched as her mum approached the bed and laid a hand on her daughter's shoulder. For the first time using a firm voice, she told Shannon that she should speak to us. Shannon looked up into her face and shifted away, letting her mum's hand fall to the pillow. The girl's voice was icy. 'You haven't been there for me for years. You've no right telling me what to do.'

I stepped in to try and convince Shannon that things can change; they would get support for what she had been through and for her mum's drinking. She stared at me, maintaining that they didn't need any help from us. I had to admit, I'd rarely seen such a level of determination in a youngster to stick to their story, even in some of the toughest cases in Glasgow. I told her the hospital would allow her to continue her recovery at home but I had requested that she stay for her own safety. Her look of defiance changed to one of puzzlement as that information sank in.

I met her gaze. 'We can link Jake Devaney to the murder of Mr Murdoch. And we can link Jake to you. He's disappeared and we don't know what he might be capable of...'

The words burst out of Shannon, reverberating around the room. 'Jake would never...!'

I had caught her out. 'Jake would never what, Shannon? I thought you didn't know anyone called Jake? And if he's the one who stabbed you – and I think he is – there's every reason to assume he killed Mr Murdoch. And every reason to assume he'll come for you. He must know that you survived the attack. Why would you protect him?'

Shannon's mum reached out and took her daughter's hand. 'Tell the truth, love. Please. We can get through this.'

I watched the myriads of emotions pass over Shannon's face as the girl looked at her mother, clearly confused. I spoke quietly, hopefully to encourage her to talk. 'Come on, I think it's time for the truth. Better for you if you talk.' The equipment hummed. She closed her eyes. I tried again. 'How did you meet Jake, Shannon?'

She opened her eyes and looked at Pete, who had remained in the chair at her bedside. She glanced at his notebook. She took a deep breath in, letting it out slowly, and looked at me. I pulled up a chair next to Pete. When she started to speak, her voice almost a whisper, the stubbornness was gone. She sounded exhausted.

Maybe a year or so ago, she had spotted him across the road from the school gates and wondered who it was. He'd stood out; older, tall, dark hair, a fringe that fell over his eyes, she'd thought he was gorgeous. Still did. They had locked eyes as she walked past with her friends. A couple of days later he was there again and a few times after that. She had decided to find out who it was so hung back, letting her friends go on ahead and started talking to him. Shannon smiled to herself. He'd asked her to meet for a coffee and she'd felt flattered, thinking he was interested in her. They had met a few times and she'd found she could talk to him about anything, including her dad. She stole a glance at her mum.

Shannon stared at the opposite wall, biting her lip. When her mum had started drinking, she had got used to dealing with things on her own. She had met Jake and he'd listened to her. Much the same as Ben, Jake had used her vulnerability to draw her in and get her to the point where she had broken the law and repeatedly lied for him. 'I can see that it would have been good to talk to someone. How did you end up working for him?'

Shannon regained her composure. 'He told me he was setting up an events business, asked if I wanted a job. Of course, I said yes. I liked the idea of having money to buy what I wanted. Not having to ask Mum all the time.'

I nodded. 'That's how you got involved in helping at the parties. What about the drugs? The dealing?'

Shannon sighed. She hadn't realised until she'd helped at the first party that drugs were involved. She didn't take any herself and, in her opinion, what others did was up to them. As Jake always said, everyone makes their own choices and he was giving people what they wanted.

It was an effort for me to suppress my anger. 'And you believed him?' Shannon nodded and looked me in the eye before stating that she loved him. To me that explained a lot; she was heavily under his influence. I needed her to consider the reality of the situation. 'Why did he stab you, Shannon?'

She took a deep breath, a look of resignation on her face. At least this time, she didn't deny knowing her attacker. 'Because I didn't look after his notebook. He didn't trust me anymore.'

'Progress,' I thought, 'she has at last confessed to having the notebook. And that Jake stabbed her.' I leaned towards her. 'You're doing well. Take your time and tell us as much as you can remember.'

After meeting Katie, she headed home and was surprised when Jake had contacted her again, asking to meet by the river, at the bridge over to Holmston Road. The location had puzzled her because they'd never met there before. As soon as she saw him, he challenged her about the notebook, saying that the fewer people that knew about it the better. She tried to tell him it was safe and she could get it the next morning. But Jake had told her he knew she didn't have it and the teacher might have seen inside. It could only be a matter of time before he might work it out. He was so angry and said she could have ruined everything he had worked for.

'And that's why he stabbed you?' I asked.

'Not only that,' she replied, 'he said he could accept a mistake, having the notebook taken from me but I'd lied and that's why he could no longer trust me. The last thing I saw was Jake turning away as I rolled backwards into the river.'

I took a few moments, weighing it all up. 'Why wouldn't you tell us this before?'

She sank further into the pillow. 'I didn't know what to think, didn't know what to say. I couldn't believe that Jake had meant to kill me so decided to keep my mouth shut. Think about myself. I am – was - part of his business, finding customers, helping at parties, delivering drugs. With one word he could ruin my life, the respect I have at school, the money. If I said nothing, maybe I could talk to Jake, things could go back to how they were...'

But Katie had turned up, asking about her phone, demanding to get in touch with Jake, wanting to destroy the evidence that Jake had to blackmail her. However, Shannon had no idea where Jake was nor how to get in touch with him. Everything was arranged by text and she no longer had her phone. She thought she would wait and see if he got in touch and brazen it out in the meantime. She got used to keeping quiet, scared that she would be blamed for everything, by Jake, by us. Maybe Jake would turn up, tell her what to do, make things right.

Now she realised that things couldn't be put right, couldn't go back to how they were. We knew about the notebook; her number was in there and she had been charged with serious crimes. It had all become too much and getting it out in the open, being honest about what had happened, had been a relief. She looked at me then Pete, and managed a faint smile.

We had Ben and Shannon's stories. More pieces of the jigsaw to decipher.

Saturday 22nd October 2022

A PHONE CALL

CHAPTER 37

I hadn't slept well again. This case was bringing back too many bad memories. For what seemed like the umpteenth time, I found myself wondering if I should have held out for a promotion in Glasgow, or anywhere else for that matter. Had I been dreaming, was my memory playing up or was it that in-between state between sleep and being awake? Running through the woods, a dog barking, Richard Spencer's face haunting me... Somehow, I would have to settle those demons. It was only 5am, but I got out of bed anyway.

I squeezed the memories of the assault from my mind as I stirred my coffee and buttered my toast. Having spent so many years trying to forget what happened at school, I wouldn't let it get to me. I piled the dishes in the sink and got ready for work. I took the bypass and made it in less than twenty minutes.

Sipping coffee at my desk, I thought about Ben, Shannon, and Katie and how they had become involved with Jake Devaney. They were teenagers. Sixteen. Seventeen. How do parents not know what their kids are up to? Pete and Bill always said it was impossible to keep them on a leash and maybe I was being over judgemental because, not having kids, I didn't know what it was like. The balancing act between giving them freedom and keeping them close. Anyhow, these three weren't out of the woods; it was still possible that one or more of them was involved.

The door to my office swung open. I looked up and smiled. 'Couldn't sleep either, Pete?'

Pete had also woken early. 'For some reason, Shannon's statement was going round in my head. I can't help feeling sorry for her, losing her dad. And I'm amazed how she was able to save herself.'

'D'you think any of them is capable of murder?' I asked.

He sat down opposite me. 'To be honest, I can't see any of them killing Mr Murdoch. But, they're all tied in with Jake, so I think they're involved somehow. With the drugs, anyway. Katie, maybe less so.'

I opened my mouth to agree, but was interrupted by the arrival of Bill, Gary, and Carmel. It seemed everyone was being kept awake by this investigation. As soon as they got their coats off, I asked them to join Pete and me to gather thoughts and update progress.

Bill reported that CCTV footage of Mrs Caldwell and Ellen Shaw had confirmed their statements on the day of the murder. Forensic results established that the blood on the mallet was Mr Murdoch's and toxicology gave no indication that he was a heavy drinker. Time of death was estimated to be give or take a couple of hours around 3.30pm. 'That means any of those teenagers could be involved. I think we need to pin down their movements more accurately,' he said. I asked him to go through their statements to get as accurate a timeline as he could and double check if there was CCTV available.

Bill continued. 'I also went back to that loan place. Spoke to the guy in charge.'

'Any progress?' I asked.

He shrugged. 'Nah. He said they organise cash loans for local customers or help them set up payments. All the paperwork goes through the Paisley office. They have all the records.'

'What was your impression of the place? The people there?' I trusted Bill's instincts on this.

'I'd say there's something off although he – Geoff Barrett, the guy in charge, that is – gave me the impression he didn't know much. Might be small scale. Could be the start of something bigger.'

I nodded. 'OK. I'll call Cliff Burns later.' I couldn't help but feel a bit uncomfortable that this might lead somewhere I had hoped it wouldn't; that Mr Murdoch was involved in something illegal. But I had to do my job and if that's what I found, I'd deal with it.

I turned to Carmel. She hadn't yet heard from Cumnock Police and was still going through the notebook, deciphering names, and constructing profiles.

She didn't sound happy. 'Sorry, I don't seem to be making much progress.'

I reassured her that it might be painstaking work but it was important to get the details of as many names as possible. They were the means to work out how Jake made his living and were witnesses to his blackmailing racket and drug dealing.

I turned to Gary who was looking pleased with himself, clearly, he had something to say. 'Ma'am? I had a thought...' Gary looked around as everyone laughed before joining in himself. 'I know, I know. Could hear my brain creaking... Look, I was wondering about the number for Jake in Ben Chadwick's phone so I tried calling it. It was switched off and went to voicemail. But I contacted the service provider and the last time it was switched on was last Saturday, a week ago, in North Wales. Llandudno specifically.'

I was impressed. 'This is good work, Gary. Using initiative.' I paused and a thought popped into my head. 'This gives us somewhere to start looking for Jake.' The photograph from the flat, what Gary had found out about the car accident and the identity of the children had been bothering me. 'I don't think it's a coincidence Jake might've headed for North Wales because, if he's the boy in the photograph, that's where they'd been on holiday.'

I paused before continuing, having made my decision. 'Gary, get in touch with the police in North Wales. Work with them to identify places Jake might be staying.' I reckoned he might have headed for the same guest house or hotel, if it still existed. Given that the Devaney couple were fostering the boy and the girl in the photograph, if it was Jake, his name in those days would have been John Crichton. 'Ask them to check for a guest called either Jake Devaney or John Crichton, possibly a hybrid of both.'

We were so immersed in planning, it took a few seconds to realise a phone on Gary's desk was ringing. Gary rushed to pick it up but didn't get there in time. 'Damn.' He looked over at us. 'That's Ben Chadwick's phone.' He brought the phone and handed it to me. 'Caller ID withheld.'

I turned the phone over in my hand. 'My guess is this is Jake.' The others nodded in agreement. 'But why would Jake be calling Ben now?' We all looked at each other. 'He can't know that we have Ben's phone...' I was cut off as the buzzing started again. I pressed the green button. 'Hello?' My voice was cool, abrupt.

There was a pause at the other end before the line went dead. 'If that was Jake, he now knows that Ben doesn't have his phone. And may well work out we know about him. If he is in Llandudno, he's been there a week maybe. But I suspect not for much longer. That's upped the stakes for us.' I handed the phone back to Gary and asked him to find out what he could about that phone call.

The room fell silent. I looked around. We were all thinking the same thing; time wasn't on our side as Jake was a few days ahead. The clock was ticking.

Friday 14th October 2022

REWIND 11 DAYS

CHAPTER 38

Jake lay in bed contemplating the events of the day before and trying to work out how things could have gone wrong. He had done what he set out to do. He was rich with the lifestyle to match.

Ten years ago, he had made his plan, amended as he went along, and it had worked. After that night at the reservoir, he searched venues and hired a barn in a farmer's field near Edinburgh. It had been hard work but he'd organised a party, putting the word around his groups of clients, telling them to bring their friends. The next day he'd presented a select view with evidence of what a good time they'd had, including the snotty bastard that had made him feel like shit. They'd been paying him to keep his mouth shut ever since.

That party had taken a lot of effort and he'd wanted an easier way to find clients, whether to feed their habit and/or to blackmail. At the time he was claiming benefits and looking for a job, not because he wanted to but because he had to keep getting the money. One day he got chatting to a teenage mum in the queue at the Jobcentre. She had offloaded her troubles to him; that she was struggling on her benefits and her parents refused to help. It occurred to Jake that she found him easy to talk to and maybe he could gain her trust. So, he had asked if he could use her flat for a night, in return for a generous sum and as well as a B&B. Her part of the deal was to ask no questions and say nothing; that way she wouldn't be able to answer any questions about his business. They agreed it was win/win.

That had been his first house party and the two of them had kept the arrangement going for a few months. But one of her neighbours reported her to the landlord. The nosy cow had been watching. The landlord threatened to throw her out and the arrangement stopped. By then though Jake had several regular payments coming in and could see the potential in the business. Indeed, several of the first customers had turned out to have high profile careers and provided him with a good monthly income.

The only problem as far as he could see was using rental properties but he couldn't afford to buy in Edinburgh. So, he'd looked around, done his research and settled on moving to Ayrshire. He'd set up several properties, all single teenage mums desperate for extra cash and he chose girls that had no contact with parents and few friends. That way they were dependent on him. And a couple of nights staying somewhere nice was a fair exchange for moving out. Ten years on from his first party, he had achieved the lifestyle he wanted. And still only twenty-eight. He wasn't planning on losing it any time soon.

He rolled out of bed, pushed the button to open the blinds and stood at the floor to ceiling windows gazing out over the bay. Turning back towards the bed he told Melanie to get up and make him a pot of coffee. He watched her throw on a robe and leave the room, one of several girls willing to get their fix for services rendered.

His thoughts turned to the day. He would have to go and see Jaz; calm her down. She'd called him yesterday, crying on the phone about some girl who said she'd been at a party at the flat. Apparently, the girl had turned up looking for him. Jaz said she'd tried her best to convince the girl that she was in the wrong place but she wasn't sure it had worked. Eventually she had got her to leave. Jaz was angry that she might get caught up in whatever he was up to, though she didn't know the details, and worried about losing her baby. Jake had promised to sort it out, feeling annoyed at having to smooth things over. The description fit the girl Shannon had brought two nights ago. Damn it! She brings someone and it leads to trouble. On top of losing the notebook.

Melanie put a steaming mug of fresh coffee in his hand. Their eyes met and he told her to leave; he had a busy day ahead. She nodded, dressed, and left. He'd call her later, maybe.

The coffee tasted good and helped to calm his hangover. He had drunk a bit more than usual last night. He never touched anything else though; that was for other people, his way to make a living. Defeats the purpose if you use it yourself, reduces the profits and fogs the mind. Jake took his coffee through to the bathroom, showered then decided on his outfit for the day. To see Jaz, it wouldn't be an expensive one. He couldn't let on to her how rich he was; she might ask for more money. And he didn't want to stand out in her neighbourhood. Too many nosey parkers. It would have to be a high street jeans and shirt ensemble.

As he selected his shirt, something caught his eye on the TV screen. Melanie must have turned it on before she left. Breaking news. Local teacher found dead. Jake picked up his phone. He texted Ben to tell him to hold onto the notebook. Best not take any chances for a couple of days or so. Maybe he should wait before going to see Jaz too.

In the end, he threw on some old joggers and a t-shirt, switched off the TV and fired up his laptop to catch up with some emails. He couldn't concentrate though; he was on edge and kept revisiting the decision to go see Jaz and sort things out. Maybe organising the next party at a different location would take his mind off things.

He picked up his phone and dialled the number before remembering that Shannon would no longer be there to answer at the other end. What's more he didn't have his notebook as he'd told Ben to keep hold of it. He would have to keep away from that school for a while which was a shame because it had been easy to set things up there.

Glancing at the time, he realised it was mid-afternoon already. Opening the fridge, he grabbed some food, subconsciously noting that he needed to stock up. He decided against having a beer; last night's consumption still hung heavy in his head. He filled a glass with cold water from the fridge tap and took a long slug. In the living room, he sank into the sofa and turned on the TV again. The run of afternoon quiz shows droned on as he finished his food and set the plate to the side. Briefly he closed his eyes to try and get rid of the thickness in his head.

Jake woke up to find the news on the TV. He must have been asleep for two hours or more. He was about to switch off when something the presenter said caught his attention. Sinking back into the sofa he realised with horror that he was staring at a picture of Shannon. Rewinding, he listened carefully as the newsreader explained that a young local girl had been found left for dead on the banks of the river. So far, she had no memory of what happened but told police she thought it was a random stabbing. Police were appealing for witnesses. The telephone number appeared on the screen.

Jake's blood ran cold. He decided that the best thing he could do was disappear for a few days and hope things would die down. When he got back, he'd visit Shannon in hospital, they'd have a chat and sort things out. She worshipped him, after all.

Switching off the TV, he headed to the bedroom to pack. On the way, he dug out his rucksack from the back of the cupboard in the hall. That would do.

Opening the wardrobe, he ignored the designer gear hanging from the rails, instead pulling cheap stuff from the shelves below, packing enough to last him a few days. In the ensuite he picked up the necessities and put them in a toilet bag before heading back into the bedroom. Returning to the wardrobe, he pushed back the row of shirts and keyed in the code. The safe door swung open and he reached in to take out a couple of the envelopes. Opening it up, he flicked through the notes inside even though he knew how much was there, a thousand in each. Enough to last a few days at least. Relocking the safe, he pulled the shirts back into place, his fingers lingering on Ralph Lauren cotton, and closed the wardrobe doors.

He took some cash and put it in his wallet before placing the envelopes on top of his clothes followed by the toilet bag and his phone charger. Looking into the bag, he wondered what else he might need. On impulse he opened the drawer of his bedside table and took out a blue and tan checked scarf which he carefully placed on top of the other items. Finally zipping up the rucksack, he was ready to go.

He paused in the doorway, taking in the room, before finally closing the door and exiting the flat.

Saturday 22nd October 2022

A NEEDLE IN A HAYSTACK

CHAPTER 39

Gary went to call our colleagues in North Wales while the rest of us returned to our desks, each deep in thought. I picked up the phone and made the call to Cliff who agreed to have a look at the activities of YouNeedCash before immersing myself in what we had so far. It didn't surprise me that Cliff was also working on a Saturday.

The silence was broken by Carmel's telephone ringing. We waited while she took the call. It was Cumnock police who had been doggedly revisiting properties where no-one had been at home during the initial house-to-house enquiries. A car the same make, model, and colour as none other than Amanda Cairns, the auburn-haired technician at the school, had been parked outside a house on Holmhead Road, around the corner from Mr Murdoch, last Wednesday night. The occupant remembered seeing a car he didn't recognise parked close to his driveway when he put his bin out about ten o'clock and it wasn't there the following morning.

'Is he sure about it? The time, the make, the model?' I asked.

'Oh yes, Ma'am,' Carmel replied. 'There's no doubt. He has footage from his security cameras.'

Pete and I looked at each other, knowing we were thinking the same thing. Amanda Cairns had said she didn't know Mr Murdoch that well. Yet it was auburn hair found in his shower and likely that her car had been parked near his house. I perched on the end of the desk and crossed my arms. 'So, she might have been in a relationship with Mr Murdoch. She had easy access to the murder weapon. Could a love triangle or scorned woman be the key to this murder?'

'I wasn't sure I believed her when she said she didn't know him that well,' said Bill.

I replied, 'I remember that. The idea of – let's say lover's revenge – hadn't occurred to me. It doesn't fit what we already know.' What I didn't say was that Mr Murdoch didn't seem the type to have an affair. But what did I know about a teacher I hadn't seen for more than twenty years? I continued. 'If Amanda did kill Mr Murdoch, it might rule out links between the murder and the stabbing. Yet so many other things show they are connected. Whatever, Amanda Cairns has lied, even by omission, and missed two chances to come clean.'

I asked Bill to collect Amanda and bring her in for questioning, confront her about her affair with Mr Murdoch and see what she had to say for herself. Gary would liaise with colleagues in North Wales to try and track down Jake while Carmel kept going with the notebook and chase up any information on the Crichton children. Pete and I would review everything and come up with the timeline, try to find the holes.

It was over a week ago that Mr Murdoch was murdered yet, although we were making progress, I felt no closer to finding the killer, especially as the main suspect had disappeared. 'Right, let's get to it. Pete. Could you grab us some coffees? Not the vending machine, though.' He nodded and headed for the kitchen.

As soon as I sat down at my desk and opened the first file, the phone rang: DCI Lewis was looking for an update. I made my way upstairs. Lewis would be concerned that the press would find out about Jake and that it looked like he was on the run. That wouldn't look good for his reputation.

He was sitting at his desk, drinking a cup of tea, when I went in. He didn't offer me a seat. I could tell he wasn't in a good mood; probably because he'd decided to come in on a Saturday. 'Any progress, Kim? It's been over a week, time's getting on.' He looked at me. 'I need something to tell the press.'

Taking a deep breath, I said my piece. 'We're going through the names in the notebook, all possible suspects, including those three teenagers. I've not ruled them out yet. We're making progress but it's going slower than I'd like.' He indicated for me to take a seat and I sat down opposite him, the other side of his huge desk.

After telling him about the North Wales connection and the decision to look for Jake there, I took a deep breath. 'It's a hunch but the phone means it's the best we have to go on.' I could only hope Lewis would back me. The whole time I was talking I kept my eyes on him, trying to read his thoughts.

He sucked in his teeth. 'I'll tell the press we have a suspect but enquiries are ongoing. Hopefully, that will keep them at bay. He picked up his tea and turned his attention to the stack of papers on his desk which I took as my cue to leave.

I closed the door to his office and breathed a sigh of relief.

The incident room was relatively quiet when I got back. Bill was on his way with Amanda and Pete had gone downstairs, ready to join him in the interview. Gary had received a list of hotels and guest houses in Llandudno and had started ringing round the ones allocated to him, North Wales police dealing with the others for the time being. Carmel was checking names in the notebook and waiting for calls about the Crichton children.

I went into my office to carry on reviewing the evidence we already had and look at the timing of events. I stood looking out of the window over the town. Lewis asking about progress reminded me that the media wasn't letting up about the connection between the murder and the stabbing, speculation about the teacher and his student. That's how it would be until we solved it. It piled on the pressure and I felt my stomach muscles contract involuntarily as the thought floated in and out of my mind: 'Are we, am I, going to solve this?' I rubbed my temples, taking steady breaths. 'Of course, you are,' I said out loud to the voice in my head.

I turned away from the window, sat down and picked up the file I had started to read before going upstairs. 'Get a grip,' I told myself, 'Being back here has unsettled you, that's all.'

I was absorbed in the paperwork when Pete and Bill appeared having finished their interview with Amanda. Glancing at my watch I saw it was almost lunchtime already. I waved at them to come in and take a seat. Amanda had apparently burst into tears when asked if it was her car parked on Holmhead Road the night before Mr Murdoch was killed. The implication had evidently not been lost on her.

Bill scoffed. 'She tried to defend herself. Said she didn't think it was relevant. But, when we pointed it out, of course, she could see how suspicious it looked.' She'd been having an affair with Mr Murdoch for about two years, not long after she started at the school, even though he was a lot older than her. 'She says it wasn't serious, just company and sex because her husband is away a lot. She didn't say anything because she doesn't want him to find out.'

I felt no sympathy for her in that regard; the investigation came first and any fallout from her behaviour wasn't my concern. 'Any reason to think she could've done it?'

Both Bill and Pete shook their heads. She had insisted there had been no recent change in her relationship with Mr Murdoch and nothing had happened that would have made her angry with him. She described him as a lovely, gentle man, and, of course, was adamant that she hadn't killed him. According to her, the entire Technologies Department had left early last Thursday and gone for drinks to celebrate that it was nearly the holidays.

'I've already checked the others' statements and they were in the pub. I need to contact them to verify that she was there with them the whole time,' said Bill. If her colleagues could vouch for her, she had an alibi for the murder.

'What do you think, Pete?' I asked.

Pete inclined his head towards Bill, acknowledging agreement. 'It looks like her alibi is sound. This might be a red herring.'

I thought for a moment. 'OK. Finding Jake Devaney remains our priority.'

There was no point holding on to Amanda. We knew where she lived and she would be unlikely to run if she was trying to keep her husband out of it. I told Bill to let Amanda go then help Gary out with contacting the hotels and guest houses. Given the number of them, it was an onerous task.

I asked Pete to check how Carmel was getting on. Both men nodded and left me alone. I picked up the last thing I had been looking at; the photo of the Devaney couple with the children. Something was bothering me about the girl, John Crichton's sister. I felt certain I had seen her somewhere before. Something about her eyes. I picked up the phone and asked Carmel to come into my office. Within seconds, she appeared in the doorway. 'Take a seat. I want you to run a background check on someone for me.'

She nodded and sat down. 'Actually, when you rang, I was coming to ask for a word with you.'

I was intrigued. 'Have you found something?'

Carmel leaned forward. 'The records for the Crichton children came through from social services. This one proves the boy is who we know as

Jake Devaney. And it confirms that the Devaney couple planned to adopt the children. Look here…'

She handed me an A4 document: 'Application for an adoption order Section 46 Adoption and Children Act 2002.' I scanned the document. Gerard and Karen Devaney had applied to adopt a child. Flicking further through the document there it was: John Crichton. She continued. 'And the other one, here. This shows they were going to adopt the girl as well. They planned to keep the siblings together.' She sat back in her chair, put a hand to her heart. 'What a tragedy that accident was for those kids.'

I agreed. 'Yes, unimaginable.' For a moment there was silence, each of us lost in thought. I broke the spell. 'The sister, Danielle Crichton. Do we know what happened to her?'

Carmel looked at me. 'I'm still checking that. I've found the name of the home they were in after the accident. The records should be archived with the local authority so I've requested them.'

'Great. Keep going with that. And make sure you also do that background check.' I smiled. 'Let me know as soon as you have something. Oh, and ask Pete to come in with what you've got so far from the names in the notebook. I'd like to see where that's going.'

Carmel smiled back at me. 'Of course.' She closed the door quietly as she left the room.

CHAPTER 40

A few minutes later Pete came in and plonked himself down opposite me, a pile of papers in his hand. He'd looked through some of the profiles from the notebook and thought there was enough to get a picture of Jake's activities.

I was keen to find out how someone in their late twenties could afford the penthouse, the car, designer clothes and the latest gadgets. I reached over to take a couple of sheets from Pete. Each one was headed up with a name and a short biography: age, location, job and so on. The top sheet was an index. Carmel had been thorough, going through the notebook in order, trying to get the story behind a name, look for patterns.

'I recognise a few names on there,' Pete said.

I perused the list. 'I see what you mean. A few of the rich and famous among his clients. We'll make a few calls, get some ammunition for when we catch him.' I refused to consider the idea of if we caught him.

Pete leaned back in his chair and smiled at me. 'You're sounding positive.'

I shrugged. 'Have to be, Pete, have to be. Come on, let's see who we should call first.'

The hours ticked by fuelled by strong coffee and takeaway food. The names in the book went back at least ten years, each one seemed to have been added chronologically. By eight o'clock Pete and I felt we had built up a reasonable picture of how Jake had made his money but there was still no feedback from Llandudno.

From what we could piece together, Jake's story started in Edinburgh when he had become the supplier of alcohol and drugs to teenagers for parties and camping trips. From there he'd organised parties to set up a blackmailing racket. We think he must have invested quite a bit of money from what he made dealing to hire the venue etc. Those we spoke to who had been at his first party remembered having a great time. This corroborated what Stevie had said; it sounded like Jake had used similar tactics when he moved to Ayr.

The problem for the partygoers was what happened the next day. They had trusted Jake but everything changed when a few people received a photo from him showing them taking drugs together with a demand to pay up. He had threatened to make those photos public. Jake had chosen wisely and worded it well. Although each of them had suspected that others had received the same threat, none of them had spoken about it just in case.

The blackmail victims from those first years all came from wealthy families and had ambitions to do well at school, go to university and fund the same lifestyles that they were used to, or maybe move into politics. No-one wanted to risk it ending before it had begun. Some of them had gone on to be successful: a famous actor, a politician, and the director of a company producing ethical clothing among them. As time went on it had become imperative that their past not be brought into the limelight, so they continued to pay. The more successful they got, the more money he wanted; there were a few paying around two thousand pounds a month, the average around five hundred to a thousand. With the expansion of social media platforms, the stakes got higher.

Jake had set up a sole trader business, Crichton Financial Consulting, and every month they received an invoice, apparently for financial advice. The money was paid by direct debit into an offshore bank account, a blackmailing racket that had already given Jake a regular substantial income over the last ten years. Supplying drugs to regular clients appeared to be a sideline. Pete and I discussed how easy it would have been for him to set it all up, agreeing that we didn't have a clue. If it hadn't been illegal and hurt so many people, we might be admiring his ingenuity and business acumen.

I was keen to find out more about how the financial side worked. Of course, I knew a good accountant who could give the information I needed. But, did I want to speak to him? Running my fingers through my hair, I turned to look out the window. I watched the gathering clouds and listened to the seagulls screeching between the sea and the river. Could I put my personal feelings aside? My gut told me I could because solving this case was so important to me. I swung round, leaned back in my chair, and looked at Pete. 'You know who could tell us how this works?'

Pete returned my gaze, concern reflected in his eyes. 'Are you sure you want to do that? There must be someone else?'

I hadn't discussed my situation with Pete but he knew I'd moved to Troon on my own. I shook my head. 'Not someone that can get us what we need to know quickly. And I want to understand all this. Have as much information as we can when we get him.'

Pete nodded. 'It's your call. Excuse the pun.' He was trying to lighten the mood.

I gave a weak smile, took a deep breath, and lifted the phone to call the person who would be able to tell me what I needed to know. He answered on the third ring. 'Hello, Patrick.'

'Kim. How are you?' He couldn't keep the surprise from his voice.

'I'm fine. Busy.' I didn't ask how he was. If I were honest, I didn't want to know. Why would I need details of how well he was doing with the new woman? I got straight to the point. 'I'm hoping you could shed some light on offshore back accounts.' He didn't need to ask why I was enquiring about that because he would know it would be linked to the current investigation, that I trusted him to keep his mouth shut. At least, I hoped I could. Surely, he owed me that? 'I'm putting the phone on speaker so that Sergeant Fletcher can listen in.' I wanted to keep this formal.

Patrick told us that opening an offshore account is easy. The documents required depend on where the bank is based and the country the person lives in. But it can be done online with ID such as a passport and proof of address like a bill or bank statement. Everything can be done via an app. The accounts are legal, unless they are used to hide assets to avoid, for example, paying tax, and can make someone's money untouchable by the authorities. This is exactly what Jake would want. It was likely he already had a lot stashed away. If we didn't catch him, he'd be able to set up a new life.

I thanked Patrick for his help and made to put the phone down. He butted in before I got that far. 'Are we still on speaker, Kim?'

I turned it off. 'No.' I waited. Pete pretended to sort through the papers, shuffling them about on the desk. The murmur of phone conversations, Bill and Gary's calls to LLandudno, were just audible through the walls.

'How are you?' Patrick asked. It sounded like he cared. Really?

I didn't have time for this. 'As I said, I'm fine.' My tone was cold, clipped.

'We should meet. Discuss things. We've a lot to sort out.' An almost businesslike tone crept into his voice.

I felt my hackles rise but kept my voice cool. 'I have to go. I'm at work. Thanks again for your help. Goodbye, Patrick.' I quickly ended the call to avoid further conversation.

'Are you alright?' Pete looked worried.

'Honestly. I'll be fine. Let's get back to the case. Catch this bastard.' I picked up the folder in front of me.

'OK,' said Pete. He understood there was no point pursuing the topic of Patrick.

We had already established that John Crichton had a passport, but what address had he used? Pete called one of the names on the list and asked her to send a copy of one of Jake's invoices. Within minutes his phone pinged and we had it up on the screen, checked an online map and found the address was a small flat in Moredun, one of the less well-off areas of Edinburgh. If he'd left care at the age of sixteen, it was possible that was where Jake - or John - had moved to; the question was did he still pay rent on it or own it?

I was curious. 'Why would Jake move from Edinburgh? There's a massive drugs scene there.'

Pete had a simple theory. 'Living in Ayrshire's much cheaper than Edinburgh. The penthouse in Troon would cost a small fortune there. Out of his reach. Same to buying or renting properties for his parties. If he'd done his homework, which he probably had, he'd know there was a market in Ayrshire for his services.'

That all made sense to me. 'Big fish in a small – or, at least, smaller pond.'

'Yep,' he said.

I wanted to check progress on tracking Jake down. If he was heading abroad, he could easily disappear. If that happened, it would become an international search and he would be much harder to find. I pushed to the back of my mind the thought that he may well have already left the country. I clung on to the belief that he had headed to North Wales to lie low. Hopefully, he suspected we wouldn't know to look for him there. And we would get him. Standing up and stretching, I headed for the door. 'We've got to catch him, Pete.'

Bill and Gary were still making phone calls to hotels and guest houses. North Wales police had put on extra patrols in the town overnight and were monitoring transport routes in and out, watching for anything suspicious. I decided we would give it until midnight before starting again first thing in the morning. Right now, it felt like looking for a needle in a haystack.

Saturday 22nd October 2022

MAKING A MOVE

CHAPTER 41

Jake had made the decision to come to Llandudno on impulse. No-one would look for him here so he could relax and work out what to do. Driving towards the seafront, he parked up outside the guest house. He hadn't given much thought to where he would stay and yet, now he was here, it was obvious. Looking around the basic but comfortable room, he thought it would do; clean enough with its own bathroom.

Putting down his things, he wandered over to the bay window. Although it was dark, he felt the sea match his mood, brooding and unsettled. The streetlights emitted a glow and he could make out white waves crashing on the shore. He left the curtains open and pulled the armchair over to the window, uncapping a bottle of beer. Taking a long drink, he allowed himself to see his eight-year-old self on the beach. A police siren made him start, bringing him back to the present. Checking the street below, he realised it was some distance away. Shrugging off the feeling of nostalgia, he downed the last of his beer and closed the curtains.

He stretched out on the bed, the springs creaking as he shuffled to get comfortable, and checked his phone. There were several texts and missed calls from Ben. He didn't respond. Over the next few days, he'd have to decide what to do about Ben, Shannon, Jaz and the other houses. In the meantime, it was late, he'd get some rest and some time to think. He took a long, slow breath and felt himself relax.

The buzzing was somewhere close to his head. Slowly opening his eyes, it took a few seconds for Jake to remember where he was. Daylight filtered through the thin curtains. He took in the room and it came back to him. The journey here, and the reason. His phone was buzzing on the bed next to him but he let it go to voicemail. It occurred to him he should have been more careful and switched it off, not left a possible trail. But this call was from Jaz. The last party had been at her house and she had no reason to call him this soon. So, something must have happened and that didn't bode well.

Jake looked at his watch; it was already past noon; he must have slept a straight ten or eleven hours. He got up, noting that he'd fallen asleep on top of the bed, fully clothed. He was also hungry, time to get moving.

Half an hour later, showered and changed, he emerged from the guest house, glanced across the road to the promenade but, instead, headed for the high street. Much as it would be nice, he didn't have time yet for a stroll by the beach. The first thing to do was buy a cheap pay-as-you-go phone and call Jaz to find out what was going on.

On the high street he found a repair shop for all sorts of techie stuff. He picked up a second-hand Alcatel for a fiver and put some money on it. All paid in cash. He got Jaz's number up on his usual phone and put it into the one he'd bought. Hopefully she would answer a number she didn't recognise. The phone rang out so he tried again. If he persevered, she might pick up to get rid of the nuisance caller. It worked fourth time.

'Who the hell is this? If you call again, I'll report you to the police!'

'Jaz, it's Jake.'

'Jake! What the hell! What are you trying to pull? Not using your usual number.'

'I'm on holiday, Jaz. Having a break. I'm only calling you back because you sounded so worried. What's up?'

'What's up? You always told me there would be no hassle. Leave it all to me, you said. I've had a sixteen-year-old girl at my door twice, Jake, and she's not for fooling. Told me about drugs, parties and being blackmailed. What the hell is this all about? What am I supposed to say?'

'Did you admit to knowing me?'

'Is that all you're worried about? Of course, I didn't – though she was having none of it. Insisted I must know you and if she doesn't hear from me in a couple of days she's going to come back. What am I supposed to say? What do I do?'

'Did she leave a number?'

Jake noted the number on the receipt for the Alcatel, told Jaz he'd take care of it, hung up and put the number into the new phone. Things had become complicated; Mr Murdoch, Shannon, this girl Katie. It was like all his careful plans had begun to unravel. He thought that a walk on the beach would clear his head and made his way back to the promenade, stopping at a café to buy some breakfast. He would have to call this girl Katie, somehow calm her down. That should make her and Jaz go away. What to do about Ben, Shannon and Mr Murdoch's murder was a lot more complicated. That would take time. And, in the meantime, he'd have a few days or so break, confident that no-one would be able to find him.

He spent the days in his room or walking on the beach. Some of the time he almost forgot why he was there. With his phone switched off, he had no contact with anyone. But he couldn't stay here indefinitely. He needed to work out a plan. How to save his business. Jake stepped onto the beach and despite the chilly autumn sunshine, took off his shoes and socks to stand barefoot on the sand, letting the grains squirm between his toes. It was in that moment, looking out to sea, that an idea came to him.

He remembered sitting on the beach with his dad describing a comedy TV series about a man who had faked his own death to get away from his current life. What was it called? Jake turned it over in his mind until it came to him: 'The Fall and Rise of Reginald Perrin'. He sat down and mulled it over. Was it possible? Why not? He had plenty of money in foreign accounts, as well as the contacts to wind up his business and get more funds. How difficult could it be? People went missing all the time. Feeling reenergised now that he had a plan, he stood up, dusted the sand from his feet and, donning his socks and shoes, headed back to the guest house. He had to work out how to make it happen. At least he'd had the sense to pick up his passport and no-one would be looking for him. They would be looking for Jake Devaney who didn't officially exist.

Picking up supplies on the way, he prepared to hole himself up in his room until he was ready to go. He made a list of what he needed to do. He would contact Katie and tell her he was deleting the evidence and she wouldn't see him again. Jaz and the others could stay in the houses until he was settled when he'd decide what to do about them. Shannon hopefully wouldn't talk but even if she did, he would have gone. He shouldn't have trusted her with the notebook; a momentary lapse of judgement after Stevie threatened to tip off the cops.

Every morning Jake woke up and switched on the TV to hear the news. He was always relieved that there was no mention of events in Ayr on the national news nor the local Welsh news. No-one was looking for him. This morning, he switched on and it was the usual Saturday morning cookery programme. That made him realise he had already been here a week. Over the last few days, he had put most of his plan into action. There was one last thing to do, get rid of the evidence. He had to call Ben and tell him to destroy the notebook. The first time there was no answer. But he had a plan and wanted it sorted sooner rather than later. He would feel a lot happier once he knew the notebook had gone. And it was possible Ben was asleep. So, a few minutes later, he tried again.

There was a pause. A woman's voice said: 'Hello?'

Jake ended the call and stood there, staring at the phone.

He knew he was in trouble. He had to assume the phone had been answered by the police. If they had Ben's phone, they would have spoken to him. And likely the lad had talked. The only hope he had was that Ben didn't know where he lived and no idea where he had gone. But it wasn't worth taking any chances. He had to make his move.

Sunday 23rd October 2022

THE CHASE

CHAPTER 42

I was in a reflective mood driving to work the following morning. Daylight was trying to break through, the sun obscured by clouds. I couldn't help but hope that this was not a metaphor for the day ahead. That, instead, more light would be shed on this investigation. That Jake Devaney would be caught.

When I entered the incident room, Gary was already there, hoping for a call from North Wales. He looked up as I came in. 'Sorry, Ma'am. Nothing yet.'

I nodded, got myself a coffee and headed to my office. I had no idea where to start if we discovered that Jake hadn't gone to Llandudno after all. Yet I couldn't help feeling that he had. I sat at my desk, taking in the silence before everyone else arrived and the place filled with activity. Opening the file in front of me, I tried to concentrate on something else. The minutes ticked by.

I was alerted by Gary shouting 'Yes!' and went to see what the fuss was about. He got up from his desk and met me halfway, unable to contain his excitement. 'Ma'am. North Wales has been on the phone. A John Crichton checked in to a small hotel about a week ago. Late Friday night. Someone's on their way round to investigate.'

My heart skipped a beat. I pictured the sun breaking through those clouds. 'Don't get ahead of yourself, Kim,' I thought. I said, 'Great, Gary. Keep on it. Any calls, put straight through to me.'

'Should we send someone down there?' asked Pete.

'Let's wait and see what turns up. It's a four- or five-hour drive if the traffic's alright. And what if he's no longer there?' I responded. North Wales would detain Jake if they found him and involve the local CID if there was evidence he'd been there but gone. If he wasn't there, he could be anywhere and I'd have wasted time and money focussing resources into looking for him in Llandudno. Pete and I exchanged glances; he could tell how I felt. 'Keep me posted.' Retreating to my office, I waited for news.

At quarter past ten DS Barry Williams of the North Wales Police called in his report. He had only phoned about ten places before landing on the Bellevue. Having looked carefully at the photograph we had sent of the family on holiday, he had worked out roughly the area in which it had been taken and focused on the nearest hotels and guest houses. He was Llandudno born and bred and there was a lot to be said for detailed local knowledge. It was a shame yesterday had been his day off.

At first, the landlady had been a bit reluctant to confirm the name of one of her guests, but soon cooperated when she was told she was helping with a murder enquiry. Barry had gone to check it out and, although the owner had played the client confidentiality card again, when he'd reiterated that she would be helping with a murder enquiry, she confirmed that a John Crichton who matched the man in the driving licence photograph had checked into the guest house. He had been there about a week but kept himself to himself. He didn't eat breakfast in the dining room. The guest register confirmed John Crichton had checked in last Saturday.

At that stage, Barry didn't know if John Crichton was still there and put a call through to his own boss to see if they should get a search warrant. However, he'd thought it worth seeing if the owner would let him check the room. With any luck Crichton might get a surprise.

'Well done, Barry, a man with instincts,' I thought. If he'd asked me, that's what I'd have told him to do.

The owner wasn't sure what to do because she hadn't seen John Crichton that morning. Barry reminded her that they would have a warrant soon enough. After a few minutes, she had placed a key on the counter, given him a quick nod and walked away. The room was on the first floor, to the front overlooking the sea. As soon as he entered Barry could tell that Crichton had gone. It looked like he'd left in the early hours, given that the bed looked slept in but he hadn't checked out. There was no sign of personal items. The room smelled of stale pizza. There was a wad of cash on the bedside table, evidently payment for the room.

I thanked Barry for his help, put down the phone and went into the incident room. I updated everyone, asked for ideas. 'Where would you go, if you didn't want to be found?' We agreed most likely London, however obvious it might seem. A city big enough to easily get lost in before finding a way to leave the country. Given we hadn't found a passport in the penthouse, it was likely Jake had it with him. We had to hope he had not already used it.

As well as upping the alert on the ports and airlines, we would have to check the bus routes and rail services from Llandudno to London as well as motorway cameras in case he had taken his car or hired one. If he had hired one, we'd have to check companies and that would cost us more time. The only consolation I had was that, even though he had left Troon over a week ago, it looked like he had only left Llandudno this morning. There was still a chance we could intercept him. All we could do was follow the leads and wait.

A knock on the door and I looked up to find Gary standing in the doorway, letting me know that forensics had arrived at the guest house. Also, a car matching Jake's had been found parked about a ten-minute walk away and they were looking at that too. North Wales police had checked out the railway station and the staff were certain a man that matched John Crichton's description had bought a ticket to London Euston as soon as they had opened that morning at 8.30. 'The thing is, Ma'am, he wasn't happy when he found out that the first train out on a Sunday was 10.18 and there were three changes to get to London.' He looked at me and smiled. 'That means he couldn't get away early.'

This was another chink of light. Gary had already established that the 10.18 train went via Llandudno Junction, Chester and Crewe. Fewer changes would mean waiting until 11.07. I looked at my watch. It was quarter to eleven. If Jake had waited for the 11.07, he could still turn up. I asked Gary to speak to North Wales again, have someone keep an eye on the station there.

If, as I suspected, Jake got the first train available, he would already be through Llandudno Junction and on his way to Chester. I turned to Pete and asked him to speak to the forces in Cheshire and Staffordshire to ask if they could look out for him if he changed trains between 11.33 and 11.42 in Chester and 12.04 and 12.23 in Crewe. I was conscious there wasn't a lot of time to set that up. Our best chance to get everything in place was when the train was due to arrive in London at 14.04. I called the Metropolitan Police. If none of this worked, I would have to accept we were back to the drawing board.

The clock ticked slowly. Gary confirmed that Jake hadn't appeared for the 11.07 so we had to assume he had got the earlier train. At noon Pete took a call from Cheshire to say they hadn't had time to get an officer there so it was likely he had got the train to Crewe. At half past twelve, the call came in from Staffordshire to say he hadn't been sighted at Crewe. We were relying on catching him at Euston. If he was on the train at all. In that moment, I refused to consider that buying the train ticket might have been a ruse to deflect our attention. I would have to wait and see what happened in the next couple of hours. I picked up a file and put it down again. I got up and looked out of the window, sat down again. I stared at my cup of cold coffee. I opened another file.

Sunday 23rd October 2022

THE RACE

CHAPTER 43

At six am Jake crept out of the B&B. Leaving some cash on the bedside table, he packed his rucksack and walked out, taking care to check that no-one saw him. He drove his car and abandoned it with the keys in the ignition next to the Lifeboat Station. He walked back along the beach and dumped his rucksack with a pile of clothes on top. Next, he crushed both phones and threw them in the public waste bin at the play area by the beach. He took one last sweeping view of the sea before pulling his hood up close around his face and down over his brow, walking swiftly towards the railway station.

It took under half an hour to get there and he couldn't believe it when he saw that it was closed until 8.30am. It wasn't yet 7am and he'd have to kill time. It was infuriating to not have his phone to look things up. Maybe he should have bought a better second phone but didn't want to waste the money. He found a café that was open, bought some food, and headed back to the beach to wait, consoling himself that tomorrow he would be sitting on a different beach, looking at a different sea.

The minutes ticked by until the station opened, only to find that the first train out didn't leave until 10.08. Jake had to contain his anger. He wouldn't get to London until after two o'clock. 'Calm down,' he kept telling himself. He was certain that the police would be looking for Jake Devaney, not John Crichton. He should be fine. The minutes ticked away until at last the train arrived. He found his seat, dumped his bag under the table and slumped into the chair, glad he'd opted to pay for first class. It was a shame the train didn't go straight through. Although he was confident the police wouldn't know where to find him, or even where to start looking, that woman answering Ben's phone had given him a shock.

Just before half past twelve, the London train pulled out of Crewe. Jake leaned back into his seat and smiled. An hour and a half and he'd be at Euston. From there he'd head to Heathrow and fly to Spain, disappear there before deciding on a final destination. By the time the train pulled into the station, Jake was feeling good. In a few minutes, he'd be on his way to starting a new life.

Sunday 23rd October 2022

SECRETS

CHAPTER 44

At last, the phone rang. 'DI Berry? This is DS Crawford, Metropolitan Police.'

'Yes. This is DI Berry.' I held my breath.

'We got him, Ma'am,' said DS Crawford.

I let out a long, slow breath and felt my shoulders loosen.

Jake had been caught going through the exit barrier at Euston. They had closed all barriers except for one and he'd tried to hide behind a group of teenagers. He was on his way to Scotland Yard where they would arrange his transfer from London back to Ayr. With luck he could be back late today and ready to interview in the morning.

Thanking the sergeant and replacing the handset, I spun round in my chair and looked up at the sky. Was that sunshine breaking through? I didn't realise how tense I'd been feeling until I felt myself relax.

Smiling with relief, I got up to share the news. All eyes turned towards me as I entered the incident room. 'They got him.'

A cheer went up. Everyone was as relieved as me. This was our big breakthrough. I asked Gary to call Barry, let him know our suspect had been apprehended and ask for an update on forensics in Llandudno. Bill would organise the transfer of Jake back here while Pete and I would prepare to interview him, making sure our paperwork was watertight.

While Pete went to get us some coffee, I called Lewis to bring him up to speed, let him know we would be interviewing Jake tomorrow. As expected, he was delighted that the case might be solved, although decided he would wait until Jake was here before putting out a press release. I was glad about that. The boss's congratulations still ringing in my ears, I looked up as Pete put a fresh cup of coffee in front of me. 'Thanks, Pete. Lewis is very pleased. Job done, in his eyes. But I'm not inclined to agree. At least not yet. We need to be well prepared for this interview, look for any flaws.'

Pete gave me a quizzical look. 'You're not entirely sure it's him, are you?'

I met his gaze. I couldn't rid myself of the feeling that I was missing something and had gone back to the beginning. I had reread the key statements: Mrs Caldwell, Ellen Shaw, Amanda Cairns, Ben Chadwick, Katie Spencer, and Shannon Birch. I had revisited the timeline, looking for gaps, putting things together. Shannon asking Katie to the party, Mr Murdoch taking the notebook and Ben finding it, the stabbing, and the murder. Or maybe the murder then the stabbing.

'Thing is, Pete,' I replied, 'the question that nags me is: did Jake have time to get from killing Mr Murdoch at the school to stabbing Shannon by the river? Or vice versa?'

I was sure he'd stabbed Shannon Birch but had he killed Mr Murdoch? I wasn't yet convinced. Should I pass on my concerns that Jake might not be the killer? All I had to go on was a hunch because it looked like there was enough evidence to convict him. Yet, there was something in my mind and I couldn't put a finger on it. However, this was Pete, so in the end I said, 'No, I'm not.'

Pete's face was serious. 'Enough to stake your reputation on it?'

The room fell into a tense silence. I took a minute to think before responding, 'Enough to make sure I get who did this to Mr Murdoch. And if it does turn out to be Jake, so be it. But there's more to it, of that I'm certain. However, I'm not going to share my doubts with Lewis yet. Until... unless I can back them up.'

We were immersed in putting together the case against Jake when Carmel appeared at the door. I waved her in and she stood behind Pete, for once looking indecisive. She had found some information and wasn't sure if it was relevant to the case. She was going through the social services report on the Crichton children. After the accident they had been taken to a care home in Liberton, Edinburgh. John and Danielle had been fostered by the Devaney's at the ages of six and two respectively. They were the children in the photograph which had been taken the day before the car accident two years after they went to live with the couple. This confirmed what we knew already.

However, Carmel had something to add. 'The report says there were three children. A half-sister with the same father as John and Danielle but a different mother. She was sixteen when they were orphaned so was put in a hostel.' I wondered where this was going and could see why she questioned its relevance to the case. However, anything connected to Jake Devaney could be relevant. Carmel continued, 'I was intrigued so followed it up. It's amazing what you can find online if you know where and how to look. I've managed to trace the older sibling. Her name was Amanda Crichton.'

The atmosphere in the room was like a collective holding of breath as Pete and I waited for what we suspected was to come, anticipating what she was about to say. 'Her married name is Cairns. Amanda Cairns. Same as the tech assistant at the school. Maybe it's a coincidence?'

We all looked at each other and I could tell Pete and Carmel were thinking the same thing as me. 'Like I always say, I don't believe in coincidences. Thanks, Carmel. Another great job.' She headed out of the office, followed by Pete who overtook her, striding towards his desk to collect his jacket before turning to wait for me. Without me saying a word, he knew I would want to speak to her this time.

CHAPTER 45

Minutes later we were on our way to pay Amanda a visit. I was interested to meet this woman who had been giving us the runaround. And determined to get the whole truth. If we upset her husband in the process, so be it. Her marriage, or her extramarital activities, were no concern of mine, unless they were relevant to, or interfered with, my investigation. And she had been less than honest with us.

The Cairns lived at West Court, a small development of houses on the drive leading to the 12th century Sundrum Castle. A tall man with dark hair and matching close-cropped beard answered the door. Pete and I glanced at each other, knowing the havoc we were about to wreak. 'Not my problem,' I thought. Amanda Cairns would have to pay the consequences for her deceit and lies.

'Mr Cairns? Detective Inspector Berry and Detective Sergeant Fletcher. We would like a word with your wife.' He looked warily at us, clearly not happy that we were on his doorstep, and insisted that his wife had said all she had to say in her statement. I sighed, not trying to hide my annoyance. 'New information has come to light and we need to speak to your wife. Again. We can either do that here or she can come with us to the station.' I was being abrupt but time was of the essence and I wasn't about to have her waste any more of it.

He reluctantly stepped back to allow us into the hall, a spacious square-shaped space with white walls and a chessboard tiled floor. To one side an open tread staircase with wrought iron spindles rose to the first floor and there were several doors of varnished oak. A woman, whom I assumed to be Amanda Cairns, appeared from the back of the house, unable to hide her surprise when she recognised Pete.

Pete introduced me and informed her we had more questions. She remained calm and turned to me. 'I don't see how much more I can do to help.'

I regarded the woman in front of me and wondered if she'd told her husband about being at the station yesterday. 'Mrs Cairns, despite the statements you've already given, both at the school and the station…' I paused to note the reaction of Mr Cairns and didn't miss the look of confusion on his face at the mention of statements, plural, and the station, nor the glance at his wife who remained stony faced. 'Information has come to light that could be crucial to solving Mr Murdoch's murder.'

At the mention of Mr Murdoch's name, Amanda winced. 'I told the police officers the other day everything I know.'

I doubted that and remained unrepentant. 'If you would prefer to speak privately, Mrs Cairns, that can be arranged.'

The four of us stood in the hallway in silence. The body language between husband and wife was illuminating. He was leaning towards her as if to provide reassurance, she leant away from him, trying to put distance between them. He clearly didn't have a clue about the affair as well as her leading us a merry dance.

I broke the silence, suggesting that we sit down somewhere. Amanda turned and led us through into a large sitting room. Patio doors faced to the garden, beyond which were the woods and farm fields beyond. Two sofas were placed adjacent to each other; Pete and I sat on one, Amanda and her husband on the other. She asked her husband to leave the room. He looked at her, clearly puzzled. We watched with interest as the couple exchanged words; he didn't want to go but she insisted.

As her husband closed the door on the way out, she turned to us, 'There are things Alistair doesn't need to know. I told Constable Purves that. And you, Sergeant Fletcher.' She looked at Pete.

I scoffed. 'I know what you said. However, as I said, new information has come to our attention. It's unlikely that we, or you, will be able to keep your secrets.' She stared at me, her mouth opening and closing. I got straight to the point. 'Do you know a John Crichton, also known as Jake Devaney?'

The shock on her face was clear to see. 'I…'

I cut across her. 'Don't try and lie about it. We know he's your brother.'

'John is my brother,' she admitted, 'but I haven't heard of Jake Devaney. In fact, John is my half-brother. My dad married his mum when I was nine and they had John and Danielle.' A look of confusion crossed her face. 'Isn't… Isn't Devaney the name…'

I interrupted her. 'Yes. The couple who was going to adopt them.' I told her we knew about the accident and that Danielle was subsequently adopted without John and asked her to fill in the gaps.

A hand floated up to her throat, her brow creased, remembering. 'Dad had died of a heart attack. I was fourteen. John was four and Danielle a baby. Things were never the same after that. I didn't feel Janet wanted me even though I helped a lot with the kids. When she died from breast cancer two years later I was sixteen. I was put in a hostel and they went into care. I heard they'd been fostered. And later, I heard about the accident, of course.'

'Did you keep in touch?' I asked.

She sighed. 'I was allowed to write letters. After the accident, I asked if I could look after them but they said I was only eighteen, I was too young and didn't have a suitable home or income.' She laughed wryly. 'Yet younger kids than that were having babies, families...' She shrugged wearily.

I thought about Jasmine and her baby and couldn't disagree with Amanda about that. 'So, you didn't keep in touch?'

She looked at me. 'After Danielle was adopted, I kept tabs on John but, when he turned sixteen, he left care and disappeared. I got on with my life and after school, got a job working for Standard Life in Edinburgh. That's where I met Alistair. We moved here about two years ago. Alistair got a consultancy job with a firm in Glasgow. It was his idea to come here. His family are close by.'

'You didn't move here to be close to your half-brother?' I asked.

She let out a deep breath and leaned forward. 'Honestly? I didn't want to leave Edinburgh. That's where my friends are. But Alistair's the bread winner.' She sank back in her chair. 'I had no idea John was here until about a year ago.'

Out of the blue, she came out of school and saw someone who looked like him near the university campus. 'I wasn't sure but there was only one way to find out. If it was him, I didn't want to lose him again.' She had shouted his name. 'He didn't respond so I assumed I'd got it wrong.' She'd got in the car and made to drive off. 'But he tapped on the window. Gave me the fright of my life. We've been in touch ever since.'

I found it hard to believe it was a coincidence that they had ended up living so close to each other. Trying to work out if I believed her or not, my thoughts were interrupted by the phone ringing. It was Carmel. Knowing she would only call when we were out if it was important, I excused myself and went into the hall.

CHAPTER 46

Carmel apologised for interrupting the interview before launching into what she had discovered. 'The girl in the photo, Jake's sister, who was adopted. And the background check you asked me to do. I think you'll be very interested to know what I've found out.' She paused, making sure she had my full attention.

'Go on,' I said.

She continued, 'Like you thought. They are one and the same person.'

'Are you sure?' I felt myself relax. My instinct proven correct.

Carmel was emphatic. 'There's no doubt.'

I ended the call, delighted that she had confirmed the nagging suspicion that I'd found the girl in the photo familiar. I sent Pete a quick text which he was reading as I re-entered the sitting room. Amanda sat staring into space. I turned my attention back to her and Mr Murdoch. In terms of the Crichton siblings, I had a lot to think about before pushing that further so changed the direction of my questions. 'How did your relationship with Mr Murdoch start?'

She looked at me indignantly. 'I've already told you all this.'

My response was curt. 'I want you to tell me.'

Her voice was cool. 'One time I happened to sit next to Raymond in the staff room. We chatted and became friends. It went from there. He never wanted more and I get lonely stuck here on my own. I know he is – he was – about twenty years older than me but such a lovely, understanding man. Alistair is away a lot and I haven't made many friends since we moved here.'

I didn't need to hear the excuses. 'Tell me about last Wednesday.'

They had arranged to meet at Mr Murdoch's as usual. She always parked her car round the corner to try and avoid being seen by the nosey neighbour next door. She would normally stay the night and sneak out early in the morning, but Alistair had called from the hotel in Dundee to say he was coming home. His meeting had finished earlier than expected so he'd decided to drive home rather than wait until the following morning. She'd showered at Mr Murdoch's and told Alistair she'd been to the gym.

That she went to those lengths to dupe her husband wasn't exactly endearing. 'And as far as you were aware, your ... friendship ... with Mr Murdoch hadn't changed in any way?' I didn't care if she caught a note of disapproval in my voice.

She looked horrified. 'What are you implying? That I'd harm Raymond?'

I was unperturbed. 'It wouldn't be the first time that the woman, or person, scorned has turned to murder.'

She was almost in tears and stuck to what she had said in her previous statement, that everything was fine between them when she last saw him. I sat back in my seat, taking time to think, before leaning forward again to look her in the eye. 'Do you know anything about a notebook?'

'A notebook?' She sounded perplexed.

From her reaction, it seemed she might be telling the truth about that.

'Yes,' I said. 'A notebook belonging to a drug dealer called Jake Devaney, birth name John Crichton.' A look of shock passed over her face. 'You had no idea your brother was dealing drugs? You didn't wonder why he was hanging around the school the first time you spotted him?' She caught my eye and shook her head. I had one last question. 'When was the last time you saw Danielle?'

'Danielle? I told you. Danielle was two when they were fostered and I didn't see her again after that. She was adopted and I lost all contact. I've no idea where she is.' Amanda appeared genuinely confused.

I glanced at Pete and nodded; it was time to go. 'We'll leave it there. But don't go anywhere. Your relationship to John Crichton, also known as Jake Devaney, and your affair with Mr Murdoch connect you to his murder. And, for good measure,' I paused to make sure she looked at me, 'it appears the murder weapon is the missing mallet from your store cupboard.'

She looked horrified as she digested what I had said. Pete and I got up. 'We'll see ourselves out.' Alistair Cairns was waiting in the hall. I'd no idea how much he'd overheard but, as I said before, their marriage wasn't our problem.

Pete and I looked at each other as we got back in the car.

'Pub?' asked Pete.

This time I went to get the drinks while Pete got a table. Once settled in our seats, we discussed our visit to Amanda Cairns. It was possible she had committed the murder. She had access to the murder weapon and we were yet to verify the time she had arrived at the pub to join her colleagues.

The problem was motive; she appeared genuinely fond of Mr Murdoch. Would she commit murder to protect a half-brother she hadn't seen for years? Assuming the latter part was true. And she claimed to know nothing about the notebook so where was the need for protection? Or was she lying – she had form on that – and was angry if Mr Murdoch had wanted to end the relationship?

We turned to the information Carmel had uncovered. 'Finding Jake's siblings has changed the scope of the investigation. Especially the younger sister,' I said. Pete nodded in agreement as I continued. 'I think there's likely to be more loyalty between the two in the photograph.'

He jumped in. 'Yeah. If Amanda's telling the truth, she's been in touch with Jake only recently. Doesn't know Danielle at all. Depends if the other two have kept in touch.'

I said, 'We'll need to speak to Danielle before drawing any conclusions. If Jake has kept in touch with her, if he knows who she is... Things could be coming together, Pete. Could she be involved in Jake's activities? Could all three of the Crichton siblings be involved?'

We looked at each other across the table, lost in thought. Finishing our drinks, we headed back to King Street. I wanted an update on where we were with transferring Jake from London. Pete would arrange a search warrant for the younger sister's house.

Tonight, I would go through everything we had on the Crichton family. I wanted to be well prepared to interview Jake tomorrow and for my planned visit to Danielle. The pieces of the jigsaw were falling into place. But, I didn't yet have the full picture.

Monday 24th October 2022

LOYALTY

CHAPTER 47

The next morning, I woke up from another fitful sleep. For once, it wasn't my recurring nightmare. Instead, I tossed and turned, the evidence and doubts playing with my mind. Everyone would most likely have been celebrating last night, believing that we had our killer. Not me. I would never uncork the champagne until I was sure we had enough for a conviction. And that nagging doubt remained, especially as we were now dealing with three Crichton siblings.

As far as the case was concerned, I reckoned there was still a lot to do. Throwing back the duvet, I jumped out of bed, determined to focus on what needed to be done. I was convinced that my instincts were right. My first task was telling Lewis that I wanted more time on the case; that I wasn't convinced Jake was the murderer. I wasn't sure he would agree given the evidence so far. But I had to go with my gut.

Pete was already at his desk when I got in. I handed him a coffee. 'Thought it was time I brought you one for a change. Americano with milk?'

He nodded and took the coffee with a smile. 'Jake arrived in the early hours. Ready for questioning whenever we're ready.'

An hour later Jake looked dishevelled but calm when we entered the interview room. He appeared younger than his twenty-eight years and I found myself thinking about what he had managed to achieve by such a young age. I didn't approve of how he'd done it, but to have come up with the ideas showed a considerable amount of intelligence. It was a shame he hadn't directed that in pursuing a career on the right side of the law.

I took a seat opposite Jake while Pete sat opposite the duty solicitor. That surprised me; I thought Jake might have called upon one of his clients in the notebook but, on the other hand, that might be considered an admission of guilt. And why would any solicitor admit to knowing Jake? Pete had already checked the credentials of the duty solicitor that morning and he wasn't in the notebook. For the record, Pete turned on the tape machine and gave our names, why we were there and checked that Jake Devaney understood his rights.

The whole time I watched Jake carefully. His dark blue eyes moved around the room, taking in the bare white walls and the bars over the window before settling back on my face. He was waiting for me to speak but I would be taking my time. He was a drug dealer who had dragged teenagers into his schemes and made a lot of money exploiting people. Maybe even a murderer. If not, I was convinced he had at least stabbed Shannon.

Eventually, I slid the notebook across the table. 'I believe this is yours.'

Jake didn't flinch. 'Never seen it before.'

'Really?' The disbelief was evident in my voice.

Jake countered. 'I just said so. It's not mine.'

'We've at least three witnesses who say this notebook is yours. We know about the drugs, the parties, the blackmail.' I paused. 'A murder weapon found in your flat.' I didn't take my eyes off him. He looked at me, his face blank, refusing to say a word. 'That makes you a murder suspect.'

He smirked. 'And you have to prove it.'

'If you didn't kill Mr Murdoch or stab Shannon Birch, why did you run?' I asked.

He laughed. 'Who said anything about running? I went on holiday.' He didn't budge and continued to stare at me.

I could feel myself losing patience, fed up with lies and refusals to talk. I said coldly, 'Whatever you're hiding, we'll find it. Whoever murdered Mr Murdoch will have the book thrown at them. That I can guarantee.'

He raised his eyebrows as he met my gaze. 'Sounds personal.' I hoped my expression didn't reveal how close he was to the truth.

This was going nowhere. I needed some time to think. I motioned to Pete to switch off the machine and we left Jake with the solicitor.

As soon as we got back upstairs, I made myself a strong coffee in the kitchen and retreated to my office. I'd barely sat down when the phone rang. It was Cliff. I imagined him relaxed as usual, reclining in his chair, feet up on the desk, tie loosened.

I put the phone on speaker and hugged the warm mug. 'Got something for mc, Cliff?'

'Always straight to the point, Kim.' I could hear the smile in his voice. It reminded me of Duncan Cain.

'Just focused on the job, Cliff, focused on the job,' I replied.

He laughed. 'Of course.' The sound of papers being shuffled his end. 'Right... We've looked into your loan firm. Fairly new as you know. Been operating in Paisley a few months, Ayr a few weeks. They haven't come under our radar until you asked about them. They've been helpful which is a good way of keeping us off their backs.'

I took a sip of coffee and straightened up, keen to hear what Cliff had to say. From the tone of his voice, I guessed I would find it informative. 'So, sounds like you have something for me...?

'You know what it's like, Kim. We told them it involved a murder investigation, we could always get a search warrant etc. Anyway, turns out your Mr Murdoch was paying off a loan for someone else.'

I was intrigued. 'Why would he do that?' I thought. To Cliff, I asked, 'Assume you have a name?'

'Danny McCall. Ring any bells?' Cliff sounded curious.

Indeed, it did. I enlightened Cliff before hanging up the phone and heading into the incident room to update the others.

No sooner had I done that than Carmel informed me that Lewis had been trying to get hold of me. I went into my office and called him, having to report that our suspect was admitting nothing.

Lewis was convinced Jake needed more time to think through his options and I had to keep up the pressure. 'We've enough evidence to charge him without a confession. I think it's time to release the news we've got the killer and the attacker. That we've solved both crimes.'

I wasn't so sure. 'Probably, but ...' I hesitated, still uncertain as to whether to share my doubts.

'But what, Kim?' Lewis had obviously picked up the tone in my voice.

'Never mind, Sir. Let me have another go at Jake before going public, just in case? We don't want to have to backtrack later.' I needed more evidence that I was right before speaking to my boss. 'Also, I've spoken to Cliff Burns. Mr Murdoch was paying off a loan for someone else.'

'Who?' demanded Lewis.

'Danny McCall,' I said, 'his sister's grandson. He died a couple of months back which would tie in with the payments stopping.'

He went silent. Eventually he sighed. 'Might be something, might be nothing. Follow it up. Speak to Devaney one more time. After that, regardless of whether he confesses or not, charge him. We have enough evidence.'

I took a deep breath. 'I'll let you know how we get on.'

Leaning back in my chair sipping my lukewarm coffee, I called Bill and told him to find out more about Danny McCall. In the meantime, I needed to find Jake's weak spot. What would get him talking? Suddenly, it occurred to me. Of course! It was time to speak to his sister. The one in the photo.

CHAPTER 48

The neat terraced house was in a cul-de-sac about a quarter of an hour's drive away. We made our way to the front door and, not having called ahead because we wanted the element of surprise, hoped she would be in. We rang the bell and waited. After a few minutes we heard footsteps and the door being unlocked. The occupant was shocked to find us on her doorstep.

'DI Berry. DS Fletcher. I wasn't expecting you.' Ellen Shaw was clearly just out of the shower; her hair was damp and ruffled like she'd towelled it dry. She was wearing a long dressing gown that might have been cashmere. 'Apologies for the state of me but I've been for a run. Perhaps you could come back another time?' Not exactly a warm greeting and very cool in comparison to the young teacher we met the day Mr Murdoch's body was discovered.

I was having none of it. 'No, Miss Shaw, we'd like to ask you a few questions. We wouldn't be here if it wasn't important. Can we come in?'

Ellen stared at me, sighed, opened the door wide and led us through to a small living room which was neat and clean. It had a citrusy smell. She remained aloof as she invited us to take a seat before disappearing upstairs to get dressed.

I positioned myself in an armchair in a corner by a door leading to the kitchen. Pete sat on the two-seater sofa opposite. While waiting for Ellen to come back, I took in the room. It made me feel like I was in a show house. The walls were painted magnolia and there were no personal items such as photographs on display.

'Bit impersonal in here,' said Pete.

I nodded. 'Funny that. I was thinking the same thing.' I was curious as to why there were no photographs, no indication of family, adopted or otherwise, no sign of friends. A couple of diffusers, though, hence the smell.

My observations were interrupted when Ellen re-entered the room. She offered to make tea or coffee which we refused. 'Why don't you sit down?'

I indicated a chair directly opposite me; I wanted Ellen to be where I could watch her face and body language.

As soon as she settled into her chair, she asked, 'What can I do for you, Inspector?'

Did I detect a hint of sarcasm in her voice? I felt my hackles rise but kept my cool. 'Like I said, we've some questions for you.' Our eyes met. I had felt compassion for this young woman but, now I knew she hadn't been entirely truthful and given her attitude, my feelings were rapidly changing.

She didn't flinch. 'I've told you everything I know. It's in my statement.'

I didn't flinch either. 'Are you sure?'

Ellen cast her eyes downwards as I continued to stare at her, before nodding and answering in the affirmative. I cut to the chase. 'Have you heard of Jake Devaney?'

Ellen abruptly looked up at me then across to Pete. 'I....'

I continued without giving her time to reply, outlining what we had discovered about the car accident twenty years ago, that two children, John, and Danielle Crichton, were to be adopted but had ended up back in care. John had remained in care while Danielle had been adopted six months after the accident and given her new family's surname. I kept my eyes on her. 'Their surname was Shaw. And they changed the girl's first name to Ellen. That's you. You are Danielle Crichton. You never said.'

She looked at me and shrugged. 'Why would I? What has me being adopted to do with anything? That accident... traumatic. I've spent my life trying to get over it. And being adopted, separated from my brother. I didn't want to leave John behind.'

I took my time to answer. The accident would have been a trauma. I needed to be careful. But what I wanted to know was if she had remained in contact with her brother. 'Did you keep in touch with John after the adoption?'

She nodded. 'Yes, we were allowed letters and visits. I still see him.'

Time to go digging. 'Right, you'll know that John later decided to use the surname of your foster parents – Devaney – and the first name Jake?'

Ellen sat there with her hands in her lap. Eventually, looking me in the eye, she insisted she didn't know a Jake Devaney, that her brother John was a local businessman, mainly dealing in loans and financial consulting and was very successful. 'He's helped me out a lot financially.'

'Including buying you this house?' I asked. She nodded.

Not for a minute did I believe that she didn't know her brother used the name Jake Devaney but I needed to get her to admit it. 'Come on, Ellen. He's a drug dealer using students at your school to set up new clients and courier drugs. Don't tell me you knew nothing about it.'

She denied it. 'Jake Devaney is not my brother. I've no idea who he is. And, if I thought someone was dealing drugs at the school, I would have told you.' Her face was indecipherable. She was persistent. I'd give her that.

I remained unconvinced. We would have to interview her under caution, hoping that would get her to talk. Just how deep she was in all this would come out. We would have to revisit the timeline and her alibi. I would make sure of that. In the meantime, I wanted to get her thinking. 'We have evidence that John Crichton and Jake Devaney are the same person. And that person is your brother.'

Ellen stared at me. 'What evidence? What makes you think this Jake Devaney is my brother?'

I held her gaze. 'I found a photograph in Jake Devaney's flat of a family group on holiday at the seaside. The boy in the photo is John Crichton who is also Jake. The girl in the photo, his younger sister, bothered me. She reminded me of someone and it took me a while to figure it out. When I came in to the school the other day, I realised she reminded me of you. It's your eyes; they haven't changed.'

CHAPTER 49

At the police station Pete took Ellen to be processed while I arranged for Jake to be brought to an interview room. I called Gary to go through Ellen's statement line by line with her while Pete and I would talk to Jake again. With Bill finding out more about Danny McCall, I arranged for a uniformed officer to sit in too.

I wondered how Jake would feel if he knew we were holding his sister along the corridor? The sister who worked at the school where Mr Murdoch was killed? I had an idea, made a couple of calls and we were ready to go. The trick was to make sure that Jake saw his sister but she didn't see him.

At the end of the corridor to the interview rooms, I met the duty sergeant bringing Jake back from his toilet break. Right on cue Pete emerged from Room One and nodded at me before standing outside the room diagonally opposite. As we passed the door to Room One, I glanced through the window to see Ellen sitting behind the table, her face unreadable, Gary and the uniformed officer opposite her. I sensed Jake start to move towards the door; he'd obviously followed my line of sight and spotted Ellen in the room. Before he could speak, Pete was ready and grabbed his arm, bundling him out of view and into Room Three. 'That worked a treat,' I thought.

Jake stood, fists clenched, his face contorted with hatred. 'What the hell are you playing at, Berry?'

I pretended to look confused. 'What do you mean, Jake? Is there a problem?'

He glanced towards his solicitor. 'You well know that's ...'

I persevered, not giving up. 'That's what? Or who?'

He sank into the plastic seat, furious but knowing he was outwitted. It was evident I'd done my homework. 'My sister.'

A flicker of the boy in the photograph, the big brother wanting to protect his sister after their dream of family life had been cruelly snatched away. The boy who had turned into the criminal in front of me. He would be punished for what he had done. 'So, Jake. I assume I can call you Jake? Or do you prefer John?' I paused but got no response. 'Let's start again.'

He glared across the table at me. 'This has nothing to do with my sister. Keep her out of this. Let her go.'

I gave a wry smile. 'Which sister, Jake?'

His surprise was obvious. 'What d'you mean?'

Pete made a show of rifling through his notebook. 'Well,' he said, 'there's Amanda who works in the Technologies Department at Riverwood. We know the murder weapon was taken from there. Did you know she was having an affair with Mr Murdoch?' Jake stared at Pete; his face emotionless. Flicking forward a few pages, Pete continued. 'There's Danielle, known to us as Ellen Shaw, another colleague of the deceased. Sitting in a room across the corridor.'

All the while I carefully observed Jake's reactions. His face was set. 'This has nothing to do with either of them.' He claimed he hadn't seen Amanda for years before she suddenly popped up at the school, wanting to play the big sister. They had met up a few times but he owed her nothing, she had gone her own way, not been there. Danielle had been in the care home until she was adopted. As soon as he could, he had left the care system. 'Once out, I never looked for help from anybody.' There was self-assurance in his tone.

I noted he appeared to be much less concerned about Amanda. Would I have to start believing in coincidences? So far, his story corroborated what Amanda had said. It didn't sound like she knew what he was up to.

Ellen Shaw was a different matter though. She was involved somehow, I felt it in my bones. I reminded him that, as well as drug dealing and blackmail, he'd been arrested on suspicion of the murder of Mr Raymond Murdoch and the attempted murder of Shannon Birch. I looked him in the eye. 'We're speaking to Danielle, or should I say Ellen, about all of this as well.' I paused, watching as he lowered his eyebrows and tilted his head to the side. Something was making him think. 'Are you ready to talk?' I asked.

CHAPTER 50

The room filled with silence. Still, he said nothing. I spoke again. 'Jake? Should we speak to Ellen – Danielle - again first? See what she has to say when we tell her you're here?' He looked down at the table. His eyes were obscured by the dark fringe that fell over his forehead. I had to suppress the urge to lean over and push the hair back off his face so that I could read his eyes. I waited.

He placed his forearms on the table and leaned towards me, his eyes boring into mine. 'I did it.' His voice was low.

I wanted to be sure about what he had said. 'Did what, Jake?'

His eyes didn't leave mine. 'Killed the teacher. Stabbed Shannon.'

Seconds passed as we looked at each other. A door slammed along the corridor. He looked away first, staring down at his hands. 'What happened?' I asked.

'I heard that the teacher had my notebook and wanted to check it out. Things got out of hand. Shannon lost the notebook in the first place and I got annoyed...And she lied to me about it...'

'Because she's scared of you,' I thought.

He was still talking. 'I wanted to frighten her but I always carry a knife.' He smirked. 'For protection, you know... It wasn't planned, but the knife was in my hand...' The callousness of his tone, so matter-of-fact, turned my stomach. 'It was a shame... She'd done a great job up to then. But needs must.' He gave me a mocking look. 'She's devoted to me, you know. Well, she was. It was obvious she wanted to be my girlfriend. As if...'

I had to contain the anger I felt bubbling inside me, feeling nothing but contempt for this man and his lack of remorse. The solicitor coughed, holding a handkerchief over his mouth.

After stabbing Shannon, he claimed he had gone home and phoned one of his girlfriends to keep him company for the night. 'We had a few drinks. I can give you her number.' He shook his head, gave a small laugh and looked at me. 'Believe it or not, I've never hurt anyone before...'

'Not hurt anyone? Dealing drugs, blackmail. That's not hurting people?' I could hear the anger in my own voice.

'You know what I mean, Berry. Violence isn't my thing.' The use of my name sounded scornful. There was mutual contempt in the room. 'Anyway, I couldn't change it. I needed to focus on the business, how to keep it going. I wasn't about to lose everything...'

It wasn't a surprise that, ultimately, his priority was to think about how to save himself. Swallowing my revulsion, I continued. 'Why did you give Shannon the notebook, if it was so important?'

Jake shrugged. 'Someone said they'd grass. If you found the notebook on me or in my flat, that would be that. So, I gave it to Shannon until things settled down. Seemed like a good idea at the time...'

'And now someone is dead. Who told you they would come to us?' I wasn't going to let on that I already knew the answer.

'A traffic cop who came to the parties. Stevie Nicolson.' Jake smiled to himself. 'Stevie thought he had something on me. Let's see how he feels to have his precious career ended.'

I didn't say a word. I couldn't, even if I wanted to. Time would tell what would happen to Stevie. I hoped he wouldn't be sacked, but I wasn't going to share that with Jake.

I wanted to pin down the timings. He claimed he had delivered the drugs to Shannon at the end of the school day, then killed Mr Murdoch. By the time he met Shannon again it was late afternoon, possibly early evening, and that's when he'd stabbed her. He couldn't remember the exact times nor if he'd gone somewhere else in between the killing and the stabbing.

His lack of memory was unconvincing and, when he leaned back in his chair, his demeanour was annoying. I could barely hide my contempt. 'Why hide the mallet in your flat?' I asked.

He almost laughed. 'I didn't expect you to find out I existed. At least so soon. I reckoned I'd have time to work out what to do with it.' He sighed. 'Then I heard on the news that Shannon was alive so I decided to buy some time to work things out.'

I kept my eyes fixed on Jake's face as I returned to the subject of Mr Murdoch. 'Exactly how did Mr Murdoch die, Jake?'

He gave me a half smile. 'You know. I hit him on the head with the mallet.'

'Where precisely did you hit him?' I was anxious to know if his answer would fit with what Duncan had said about the fatal blow.

His reply was astonishing. 'I can't remember.' He tossed his head back to look at the ceiling.

'You seem to have a bit of memory loss.' I studied him in silence for a few seconds before getting to my feet. I needed to take some time to go through what he had said; get the timeline clear in my mind, decide if his version of events was possible and consider his lack of detail about the blow from the mallet. Pete switched off the tape and we rose to leave.

I had my hand on the door handle.

'Does this mean you'll let Danielle go?' he asked.

I turned back and looked him in the eye. 'No, Jake. At least not yet.' Was his sister his main concern? Why? I wasn't convinced by his confession but wasn't going to tell him that. 'We're taking a break. Mull over what you've told us. We'll be back in due course.'

I opened the door, let Pete go ahead of me before closing it firmly behind me, all the time feeling Jake's eyes boring into my back.

Thursday 13th October 2022

THE DAY OF THE MURDER

CHAPTER 51

The bell went and Ben shuffled up to the teacher's desk. Mr Murdoch looked at him disapprovingly, before opening the drawer and retrieving his phone. Ben remained by the desk, having spotted something in the drawer. Mr Murdoch followed his gaze towards the notebook. 'Who does that belong to, Sir?'

Mr Murdoch was emphatic. 'None of your business, Ben. Away you go to your next class. You're already late.'

Ben had got a real shock when he spotted the notebook. Although he wasn't a hundred percent certain, it had to be the same one. Black. A bit tatty. And nobody used notebooks like that anymore. He had no idea why Jake kept it but Ben knew it never left his sight. What was it doing in Mr Murdoch's drawer?

Next, he had chemistry, the last lesson of the day. He asked to go to the toilet but, instead, went back to the history department. Pleased to find Mr Murdoch's classroom empty, he tried the drawer. It was locked. Back in the corridor he spotted Mr Murdoch in the history cupboard, mending a shelf. His keys swung from the lock. He sneaked up to the cupboard and carefully released the keys from the lock. Mr Murdoch didn't even turn around.

Ben held his breath as he tiptoed back the way he had come and turned into the classroom. Unlocking the drawer, he pulled it out a bit and there it was. He picked up the notebook and opened the first page. It was Jake's. How had it come to be there? On impulse, he took it and put it in his pocket. As he closed the drawer, he spotted someone the other side of the desk. Miss Shaw. He had no idea how long she had been standing there.

'What are you doing?'

Thinking on his feet, Ben said, 'I'm getting a marker pen for Mr Murdoch. He's labelling stuff in the cupboard.'

She stared at him before, after a moment, letting him go. It was only when he got back to chemistry with the notebook safely in his pocket that he realised he must have left Mr Murdoch's keys on the desk.

The clock had never moved so slowly, waiting for the final bell. His friends pressed ahead out the door, planning to go up town and get a burger or pizza. Ben decided not to join them and said he would get the bus home. He wanted to meet Jake to hand over the notebook and sent him a message.

Jake told Ben to meet him down by the river at the pedestrian bridge to Holmston Road. Ben felt deflated because he'd hoped Jake would be pleased with him. Instead, all Jake was concerned about was that he hadn't mentioned the notebook to anyone. Jake told him he would have a lot to lose if it got into the wrong hands; it felt like a threat. For the first time since getting involved with Jake, he'd felt a stirring of anxiety in his stomach.

.oOo.

Shannon texted Jake to tell him about Katie, anticipating how pleased he was going to be. She had done a good job; the fish was hooked and just had to be reeled in. After school, she hurried to the usual meeting point by the university halls of residence. Jake pulled up within ten minutes and she got in the car.

'You got my notebook, Shannon?' he asked.

She bit her lip, forgetting he would ask her about that. 'I've got it hidden at home. Didn't want to take it to school.'

She didn't like lying to him, convinced he'd see right through her, but he seemed to believe her. He passed her a small packet; she got out the car and watched him drive off. She tucked the packet in her bra and set off for home, the meeting point with Katie about half way.

.oOo.

Walking towards the river to meet Jake, Ben wondered who else in school might have been given the notebook. He wasn't naïve enough to think he was the only one Jake used to organise things and do deals, but was a bit surprised that it might be someone else at Riverwood. Jake was already there and asked him if he had looked in the notebook. Ben nodded, deciding there was no point in lying, telling Jake that he didn't have a clue what all the letters meant. Jake told Ben to hold on to the notebook for another day. He was going to trust Ben to keep it safe.

Ben's anxiety dissipated, replaced by a sense of pride at being given this level of trust. Promising to keep the notebook with him, he walked away along the river towards the high street. Glancing back to where he had left Jake, he could see him talking to someone on his phone.

.oOo.

Jake headed towards the school, trying to work out the best way of getting in without being seen. It shouldn't be too difficult. He made for the fire exit by the old gym. The alarms would not be on yet and the door was easy to prise open from the outside. He kept close to the walls, under the radar, as he approached the door and got inside. Heading for the stairs, he made his way quickly and soundlessly to the history corridor. The place was silent as a morgue.

.oOo.

Shannon was almost home when her phone buzzed. She was surprised to hear from Jake again so quickly. He said he needed to see her urgently and told her to meet him by the pedestrian bridge over the river to Holmston.

Reaching the meeting point, Shannon couldn't see him at first. As she got nearer, however, he appeared from the dimness of the bushes, smoking a cigarette. He offered her a drag. She shook her head.

'How did it go with the new girl? Katie, is it?' Jake asked.

The meeting with Katie had unnerved her. She hesitated and she could see Jake didn't like the uncertainty in her not answering straight away. 'It was fine. I gave her the stuff. You can have cash now if you like. The only thing is she wants to go to another party already.'

Jake shrugged. 'I'm sure you can deal with it.'

Shannon felt a surge of relief. It was short-lived, though, because he asked her again about the notebook. She apologised again, compounding the lie, saying that she had not had time to pick it up after seeing Katie but it was at home for safe-keeping. She promised to get it to him the next day. Inside her stomach was churning. Not only that she had failed Jake but also that he was the last person she wanted to have to lie to. However, she could not risk him knowing that she had let him down. Tomorrow morning, she would get to school early for once and get the notebook back from Mr Murdoch. And everything would be fine.

But Jake wouldn't let it go. 'Are you sure it's safe? Do you know how important it is?' His eyes bored into her.

Shannon felt her insides contract. She started to stutter, dropping her gaze. Suddenly, he grabbed her arms, linking them behind her back and forcing her to look at him. They stared at each other for what seemed like ages, fear in Shannon's eyes, Jake's indecipherable. He suddenly let her go and Shannon could not take it anymore. She began to shake. 'I'm sorry, Jake. I don't have it. Sorry I messed up. Sorry I lied. Mr Murdoch took it off me, thinking it was my phone. I begged him not to take it but he wouldn't listen. I went back at the end of the day but he'd already gone home. I know it's safe though, locked in his desk drawer.'

Jake did not take his eyes off Shannon. 'Thing is, Shannon, it's not there.'

Shannon could not hide her shock. He kept talking, telling her that this teacher might have seen inside and it might only be a matter of time before he worked it out. The anger in Jake's voice cut through her as he said everything that he had worked for could be ruined. 'Do you realise how careless you've been?'

She kept saying sorry, trying to reassure him that Mr Murdoch wasn't the type to interfere. She knew she'd made a mess of things and could hear the tears in her voice as she spoke. Her stomach would not stop churning; the anxiety, the fear of losing everything, losing Jake. She pleaded with him for forgiveness, that she could make it right. That she would do anything for him.

Shannon watched as Jake's face softened and she began to cry, tears of relief flowing down her cheeks. He took her in his arms, pulled her close and held her tight with his left hand across the small of her back. She tilted her head and met his eyes. He spoke, softly, into her ear. 'The only thing is, I trusted you. You made a mistake, fair enough. But you lied and the question is, what else have you lied about? I've given you chances to come clean and you didn't take them. Even when I met you earlier to give you the stuff for that new kid, I knew you didn't have it. So how can I trust you? You might lie to me again. You might give me up. And I can't have that. I must be able to trust the people that work for me.'

She was still gazing adoringly at him and didn't feel a thing as the knife pierced her skin below her ribcage. Falling to her knees, she felt the hot blood on her hands. The last thing she saw was Jake turning away as she rolled backwards into the river.

.oOo.

Jake wiped the knife clean with an old rag and wrapped it in a plastic bag before putting it in the bin. It was a shame to have to get rid of Shannon. But she'd messed up with the notebook and now he couldn't trust her. There was too much at stake. Taking off his gloves, he turned up the collar of his jacket and put on his baseball cap. Without a backward glance, he made his way back past the school to where he had parked his car away from CCTV. He decided that when he got home, he would ring Melanie and invite her round for a few drinks.

Monday 24th October 2022

MOTIVES

CHAPTER 52

Pete and I sat in my office, mulling over what Jake had said. There were inconsistencies in his confession which needed to be addressed. But I also wanted to find out more about what made him tick. What made the boy who had suffered such a trauma turn into a drug dealer and possible murderer?

When we re-entered the interview room, he looked relaxed, with a smile on his face. He thanked me for providing lunch and I suppressed the urge to punch him. He wasn't worth me losing my job. Determined to remain unmoved, I sat down next to Pete and placed my folder on the table. Pete indicated to the solicitor that we were about to start and switched on the tape.

I looked at Jake. 'What made you decide to deal drugs?'

He met my gaze. 'D'you know what it's like to be brought up in care?'

Suffering a tragedy as a child and being brought up in care. How much had that affected him? 'Stop it, Kim,' I thought, 'you've come across a lot of kids in your time who've been through the care system and not ended up with Jake's history. This man has made choices.'

As I shook my head, he continued, a sneer coming into his voice. 'Of course, you wouldn't. Unless you've had to come through the system, you wouldn't have a clue what it's like.'

'Why don't you tell me about it?' I asked.

'Being in care taught me the only person I can rely on is myself,' he said. 'After Danielle was adopted, I was on my own. I decided I would find a way to get rich. And I did.' He paused, making sure I was watching him. 'You know, Berry, everyone has a choice and I never forced drugs down peoples' throats; just made them available at a price.' He shrugged.

I thought about all the vulnerable people I had seen succumb to the likes of Jake over the years and what he said turned my stomach but I kept quiet. I needed to get as much information as I could and he was talking freely.

He had never taken drugs himself but found out that he could make plenty of money from them. 'There are loads of kids with cash looking for a fix. I watched and waited. Got to know them and went from there.'

He looked pleased with himself. I felt nauseated. Pete took notes with a cold expression on his face. The solicitor cleared his throat and stared at the wall.

'Go on,' I said.

He leaned back in his chair, stretching his legs, getting into his stride. 'But I wasn't going to be hanging around parks and alleyways forever,' he said.

'So, you came up with the idea of parties?' I asked.

'Yep,' he replied. 'People relax at parties and, after a few drinks or whatever, lose their inhibitions.' He laughed. 'Easy to film. Some people pay a lot for me to keep their secrets.'

We knew from our investigations that some had proved exceedingly lucrative. Several of those first customers provided him with a good monthly income. Given that we had already worked out how he earned his money, it was incredible how easy it had been for him to set it all up.

Thinking that parties on a smaller scale would be a more manageable way forward, he'd had to find a way to do it. House parties, single mums. 'I pay them a fee plus the cost of a guest house. Win/win arrangements.'

'Like Jasmine,' I thought, and wondered how many others he'd exploited over the last ten years. I glanced at Pete, the furious scratching of his pencil revealing his revulsion.

'You moved to Ayr,' I said to Jake.

He smiled. 'Yeah. I did my homework and decided to come here. Shouldn't need to spell out why to you. Plus it's more affordable than Edinburgh.'

Pete and I glanced at each other. We'd been right about the reasons for the move here. Apart from the much lower property prices, Ayr had a growing problem with drugs. 'So, you thought you'd come here and take advantage…' I couldn't finish, bile rising in my throat.

He looked wolfish. 'Go where the market is. First rule of business.'

'Your exploitation is well thought out.' Pete's voice was icy, clearly disgusted, not only by Jake's activities, but by his attitude, his pride, in describing them.

'Where's the money then?' I asked.

We knew he'd set up his own company to send invoices for financial services, using the address of his rented flat in Edinburgh. Payments went direct to overseas bank accounts. Mail forwarded to a PO Box. He folded his arms across his chest. 'You won't be able to find my money.'

Something else we had been right about; he was clever. He appeared to have thought of everything. Apart from one thing. I smiled. 'But you won't reap the benefits. You're going to prison for a long time.' Our eyes met. 'Tell me about Llandudno.'

He looked away. 'Thought I'd disappear for a few days, hoping things would die down.' His callousness almost took my breath away.

'And Llandudno?' I asked.

He looked back at me, his expression unreadable. 'I thought no-one would find me there.'

'Did you think you could have a holiday at the seaside and it would all go away?' I said, glancing at Pete and I could tell he had been thinking the same.

Jake laughed. 'Here was me thinking, if the kids didn't talk, no-one would be looking for me.'

'You never once thought about what you were doing to them and anyone else caught up in your so-called business?' I asked.

He sat up, leaned forward, put his elbows on the table. 'I didn't expect everything to get so complicated. What mattered was finding a way out. So, I guess the answer to your question is, no.'

'You decided to disappear for good?' I stared at him until he was forced to look away.

'Yeah. Why not? A new start. I've plenty of money overseas. How difficult could it be? No-one would trace Jake Devaney; he doesn't officially exist. I hardly know Amanda. Danielle, though...' He raised his eyes, looked towards the window where he would only have a view of the grey sky.

'You thought you had it all worked out.' I smiled. 'But... you reckoned without me and my team.'

He looked at me. 'Got to hand it to you. Very clever.' He leaned back in his chair. 'Right. You know I did it. All of it is down to me. Let Danielle go.'

I met his gaze. 'I can't do that, Jake.'

July 2002

TWENTY YEARS AGO

CHAPTER 53

The two children played happily on the beach. It was July but the sea breeze still made it a bit chilly. They hadn't a care in the world as they knelt on the sand, buckets in one hand and spades in the other, oblivious to the screaming of the seagulls overhead. The moat they'd dug was far from the water's edge but Gerard had told them the tide would be in later and fill it without demolishing it. He was considerate like that; thinking of everything and trying to make sure things worked out.

Gerard wasn't their real dad and they didn't know how much longer they would be with him. That was the thing with foster care. You never knew when you might have to leave and couldn't get too attached, just in case. But they liked this place and didn't want to mess it up. They loved that Gerard wanted them to call him Dad.

Having filled their buckets with wet sand and made towers, piling one on top of the other, they went searching for shells to decorate the castle, Gerard following in their wake and Karen shouting at them to not go too far. Karen, their foster mum, was nice too. She could be a bit of a nag at times, but she made them feel warm with a smile that lit up her eyes.

They clambered through rock pools and felt the cold water fresh on their feet. The sun was getting higher in the sky and the breeze turned warmer. They made their way back to their sandcastle and took off their t-shirts, ready to run into the sea. This was their second summer with Karen and Gerard and they knew he would chase them when they started running, pretending to be a sea monster. They'd wait for the big waves and splash each other until they were sore laughing. Last year had been the first time they'd laughed like that, until it hurt. It was a good feeling.

In the late afternoon Karen packed up their stuff and they made their way to the guest house they'd rented for the week. Karen and Gerard saved all year to afford it and the children knew the allowance they got for fostering helped with the cost. They sometimes wondered whether they would still have a home with them without the money. Yet, their foster parents were so nice, surely that couldn't be the case. Gerard and Karen were older than the other parents at the school gates and they didn't have any children of their own. It gave them hope that they would be allowed to stay.

The family made their way up the beach towards the promenade, Gerard striding ahead with the bags while Karen ushered them from behind. Gerard had promised ice cream on the way back and they could feel the excitement to the tips of their toes. Before they got to the ice cream van they were accosted by a photographer, stopping people to take instant photos with an old-fashioned polaroid camera. They all smiled in the picture and the children waited for the photo to appear; a memory fixed in time.

Arriving back at the guest house with sticky hands from the overflowing cones, Karen put them in the bath one at a time and laid out clean clothes. This was the last day of their holiday and, instead of the usual meal in the dining room, they'd been promised fish and chips which they could eat sitting on a bench overlooking the sea. They sat side by side, their bottoms turning a bit numb with the discomfort of the wood and the chill that permeated it. They occasionally glanced at each other as they ate their food, sharing the incredulity of the luck of where they had found themselves. They watched the waves lap the shore and hoped it would never end.

It was late when they got back and they were put to bed in their twin room. Once the door was closed, they shared stories of their day, until they fell asleep, safe, and contented, comforted by the quiet voices of Gerard and Karen chatting as they sipped cups of tea in the lounge downstairs.

The next morning, they had their final cooked breakfast of the holiday. Gerard watched as Karen cut their pieces of toast into soldiers and they dipped them into the soft egg yolks.

They paused and glanced at each other as Gerard opened his mouth to speak, his eyes looking from one to the other. He told them he had something to say and they caught their breaths, time standing still amid the chatter of the other diners. Instinctively both felt shivers of fear running through their bodies. This was it, the final holiday before they were to be moved on.

It took a few seconds for what he was saying to sink in; Karen and Gerard loved them, they wanted them to stay together, brother and sister. They wanted to adopt them. Would that be OK? Karen and Gerard had loved having them these last two years and wanted to be their proper mum and dad. The other guests stared as the children squealed with delight and jumped up and down in their seats.

After breakfast they went upstairs to their rooms, packed their things, and got in the car to go home, a permanent family-to-be.

.oOo.

Like all accidents, it was sudden. The lorry hit the car with such vengeance that Gerard and Karen would not have felt a thing. That's what the police had said and the children wanted to believe it. They woke up to find their foster parents dead, the front wheels of the lorry almost on their laps. It took two hours to cut the children from the wreckage, almost unscathed apart from a few cuts and bruises. No-one mentioned the mental scars.

The social worker was waiting for them when they emerged from Accident and Emergency. There was no other foster home for them, there would be no adoption. They were unlikely to be lucky twice and resigned themselves to years in care. In the car on the way to the home, they held hands tightly, trepidation in every muscle.

The police had given them their suitcases and they unpacked them in their dormitories. Clothes that smelled of the sea and shoes with sand still sticking to them. The other children hung around them, poking about and picking up their stuff.

The boy hugged the scarf more tightly, feeling the soft cashmere against his cheek and Gerard's smell in his nostrils. It would always remind him of the seaside, of happier times, of what might have been. Before the others spotted it, he snatched the photo from the bottom of the case and put it in his pocket. The only real things left from the time they had with Karen and Gerard. From now on they only had each other and he promised himself that he would always look out for his little sister. Their parents would have wanted that.

.oOo.

Six months after the crash, the girl clung to her brother's arm, her belongings in a suitcase already taken out to the car. She didn't want to go and leave him behind. The boy stood still, emotionless, telling her she would have to go. Living in the home was hard with its rules and lack of privacy. They had never stopped grieving for Gerard and Karen and the future that had been so cruelly snatched away. The other children seemed to resent them, maybe because they'd had those two years on the outside, a taste of proper family life. The others stood, silent, watching, waiting for his reaction, ready to tease him should he get upset.

The girl had been offered another chance; a family willing to adopt a four-year-old girl but with no room for her eight-year-old brother. This was her second chance at family life and they were old enough to keep in touch. When she got in the car, he remained impassive, hands in his pockets. Tears poured down her face, watching him through the window as the car pulled away, pummelling the glass as she screamed his name. He remained aloof, feeling the pain as he dug his nails deep into his palms, unwilling for the other kids to see his emotions. Now that he only had himself to worry about, he resolved to make his own way in life and promised to find a way to provide whatever he, and his sister, needed and wanted.

Monday 24th October 2022

REVELATIONS

CHAPTER 54

I went to see how Gary was getting on interviewing Ellen about her statement. Watching through the window, I waited until I caught his eye and signalled for him to come out, leaving the uniformed officer with Ellen and her solicitor for a few moments.

'Any progress?' I asked.

Gary shook his head. 'She's not moving an inch from her statement. Maintains Jake Devaney can't be John Crichton. Insists her brother, who she admits is John Crichton, is not connected to the school and certainly not the murder. So, questions why she would have mentioned him to us.'

'What do you think, Gary?'

'I think she's either duped or lying. About something.' He glanced through the window to where she was sitting looking at her hands.

'OK. Give it a break. Jake's confessed but I don't want her to know that yet. Surely, once she does, she'll have to admit that they're one and the same person.'

Gary looked excited. 'That's great. A confession.'

I put my hand up. 'Not yet. There's a few things that don't hang together. Wind up this interview and we'll regroup upstairs.'

He gave me a quizzical look but nodded and re-entered the interview room.

In my office, I took off my shoes and jacket, sank into my chair. We might have a confession but I didn't feel triumphant. Something wasn't right, that niggle that I hadn't yet got all the pieces. I was convinced Ellen fitted in somehow and that Jake's account wasn't entirely true. Although a lot of the statements, or bits of them, could be corroborated, there were things that didn't add up. I needed more time to investigate the loopholes and I would need to work out how to approach that with the boss.

I also wanted to see what Bill had to say about Danny McCall, the grandson of Mr Murdoch's sister. We knew his death certificate cited heart failure. Maybe there was more to it than we thought. As if on cue, Bill called from the car. 'Danny was well known to our colleagues in Cumnock. In and out of the cells since school. Word is he owed some nasty people money. His heart failure was a result of drug abuse.'

Drugs, again. 'Had Mr Murdoch got himself killed over something his nephew had done? Money the nephew owed?' I wondered to myself. 'Does his grandmother – Mr Murdoch's sister - have any idea as to whether that might have to something to do with her brother's murder, Bill?' I asked.

The background music cut out as Bill switched off the radio. 'She knew about the loan. Apparently, about five years ago, the grandson owed a lot of money to his dealer. Her brother stepped in and took on the loan to help them out. The deal was the lad was to get clean, go to college, get a job, and pay him back.'

That sounded to me like the kind of thing Mr Murdoch would do. It also made sense with the bank statements. He must have kept paying until the debt was settled. Or maybe because the boy had died. Avoiding trouble, rather than becoming embroiled in it. 'Double check everything, Bill, but it sounds like a dead end in terms of suspects. Seems the boy didn't stick to his part of the bargain, though.'

'We've got who did it anyway, Ma'am,' Bill said, 'sitting in an interview room.'

'I know, Bill, I know that's what you think.' I ended the call.

No sooner had I put the phone down than it rang again. I had a summons to see Lewis. Sighing, I picked up the jacket I'd taken off and put it back on, same for the shoes I'd kicked off. I ran my fingers through my hair, debating what to say to Lewis, whether to go for it, or not. 'Sod it,' I thought, 'I know I'm right.' I would do what was necessary to prove it.

Lewis was sitting behind his desk, reclining in his chair. He put the phone down as I entered and gestured to me to take a seat, smiling, clearly pleased with progress. He offered his congratulations again at catching Jake Devaney, recognising the good thinking on my part to check the guest houses and the trains. I sat and took all this in, telling him it was a team effort, that I would pass it on to everyone. All the while I was unable to rid myself of the nagging doubt about Jake's guilt on the murder charge. In the end, I had to say something. 'Thank you, Sir, however ...' I paused and looked at him.

Our eyes met. Sensing my hesitation, he asked, 'What is it, Kim?'

I took a deep breath, aware that he was watching me intently. 'I'm convinced Jake stabbed Shannon. We have his confession, plus she's changed her story to identify him. However, I can't say the same about him being Mr Murdoch's killer.' I paused, waiting for his response.

He was clearly taken aback. 'Give me your reasons. As far as I'm concerned, we have a case to convict him of murder. The confession, the murder weapon at his flat and plenty of witnesses to his activities. Not forgetting the motive. The teacher had the notebook in his possession.'

It was strange but, now that I had voiced my doubts, I felt even more certain there was something amiss. 'I'm concerned about the timings. I'm convinced Mr Murdoch was murdered before the end of the school day. I can't see how Jake could've been in the school before 3.30 without someone seeing him. No-one mentions a stranger wandering about. He admits he went there after school was out. No evidence to suggest he was there before.'

Lewis remained unconvinced. 'Come on, Kim, we all know that determining time of death is not an exact science.' I bristled at that, something I didn't need to be told.

But the more I thought about it, the more I became convinced that Jake might not be our killer. I could feel a flutter of nerves in my stomach and pressed ahead. I was new to the job and defying my boss, but in my gut, I knew I was right. So, I stood my ground. 'Furthermore, I don't think Mr Murdoch would have been there at that time, Sir. By all accounts, he was always away on the bell. And if he had been locked in alive, someone would have heard him. If he had been gagged there would have been signs on the body. I don't buy that Jake met Shannon to hand over drugs before killing Mr Murdoch. I think that by the time he met Shannon the murder had already taken place. That he did go to the school, but later.'

Lewis looked pensive. 'Anything else?' he asked.

I nodded. 'The motive. Jake knew Ben had the notebook. Even if he was concerned that Mr Murdoch had read it, even tried to decipher it, why take the risk of going to the school to talk to him? Why not wait it out? If anything happened, he would have it back from Ben and could destroy it. Evidence gone.'

We sat in silence for a couple of minutes before Lewis asked, 'What are you thinking?'

I shared my theory that Jake disposed of the murder weapon, which was why he went to the school and later hid it in his penthouse. Maybe he was supposed to dispose of the body too. But that I suspected he wasn't the killer, that his confession was a cover for someone else. I didn't want to say anymore until I had more evidence. All I wanted was his permission to keep the case open a bit longer to give me more time to put things together. I wanted to prove who I thought was the real killer.

He leaned back in his chair and took a moment. 'We have enough evidence to throw the book at Devaney. The media would love it; not only do we solve a murder and a stabbing; we take a drug dealer off the streets at the same time.' He paused, watching me carefully. Then, letting out a long, slow breath, he eventually said. 'OK, if you think someone else is the killer, I'll run with it. You can have more time, as requested, to prove it.' As he continued to stare at me, I could feel the skin on my face start to redden. At last, he said, 'I sense there's more to this than you're letting on.'

It was time to admit my personal connection to the case. Better that he heard it from me, especially if I turned out to be wrong and Jake was the killer after all. 'Riverwood is my old school; Mr Murdoch was one of my teachers and he was kind to me when things took a nasty turn. So, yes, there's a personal element to the investigation. But it hasn't clouded my judgement. I want to make sure we get the right person for the crime. I'd want that for anyone.'

He got up, walked round his desk, came to a halt beside my chair and looked down at me. I was forced to look up at him. 'You can have a couple of days at most before we go public. However, if you're wrong, it's on you.' He retraced his footsteps, sat down, leaned back in his chair, and turned to pick up his phone, a signal that the meeting was over.

I quickly got up and left the room. I was out in the hall before it struck me that I might have put my career on the line. Pausing briefly to ensure my emotions were in check, I headed for the stairs. I had to go and tell the team that the investigation wasn't over yet. I wasn't sure how that would be received.

They were all waiting for me in the incident room. Bill, especially, looked like a man ready to wind everything up and start preparing the case for the prosecution. I didn't blame them for thinking that the case was closed and it was time to celebrate before the slog of preparing the evidence for the Procurator Fiscal began. I hated to break up the party but I was certain that we had more to do.

After gathering them together in my office, I broke the news. 'Lewis has given me more time on the investigation.'

Everyone looked at me. Bill spoke first. 'But we've got him, Ma'am. For both crimes. You can't get better than a confession.'

We exchanged glances. 'I disagree, Bill. We need to make sure the evidence to support that confession is watertight. And something doesn't feel right to me. We need to look at everything again. Lewis has given us a couple of days. Anything from the search of Ellen's house?'

'Nothing at all. I'm telling you. We've got him.' He continued to look intently at me.

I sighed, thinking through this information. Had I expected to find anything at Ellen's house? I didn't know, maybe because I wasn't sure what I was looking for. 'Well, keep putting together the evidence against Jake, Bill. If I'm wrong, we need to make sure we have everything we need to build the case; that it will stand up in court.'

I turned to Gary. 'Anything from Ellen's phone?'

Gary had found nothing useful. 'Contacts have John Crichton but not Jake Devaney.' Being the same person, it would make sense that she would have her brother's real name in her phone. 'Usual messages about meeting up, been too long since they'd seen each other and so on. Nothing to indicate she's aware of what he was up to or was involved in any way. No contact details for Amanda Cairns so it looks like she didn't know about her.'

It was disappointing that there was nothing there but I asked Gary to keep checking anyway.

Carmel was doing a timeline of Danielle Crichton/Ellen Shaw's life since being adopted. I wanted to find out everything we could, from school to university, but particularly anything that indicated the siblings were keeping in touch all these years. 'Anything to report?'

Carmel shrugged. 'Sorry, Ma'am. Not a lot. She was in Aberdeen and by the time she went to university in Edinburgh, John – or Jake – was here. Looks like they got back in regular touch when she got the job at Riverwood. After that it's what Gary says from her phone.'

I was beginning to feel out on a limb with my hunch that Ellen was somehow involved. I turned to Pete. 'What are you thinking?'

So far Pete had sat back. He would have been watching and listening to everything that was said, weighing up the evidence and going through his notes. He would tell the truth if he thought I was wrong or if he had doubts and felt things needed to be checked out. I also knew he would have my back if he agreed with me and that's what I hoped for because I could do with him on my side. The silence was deafening, everyone looking at Pete.

At last, he spoke. 'I'm with you, Ma'am. I think Jake's confession is too neat. And, as you've said, for one thing, the timings don't add up.'

I hadn't realised I'd been holding my breath. I relaxed, letting my shoulders drop. 'Right. Bill, work through the evidence against Jake. Gary and Carmel, keep seeing what you can dig up about Ellen. Pete, you and I are going back to Riverwood. This time we're searching Ellen Shaw's classroom.'

CHAPTER 55

Ten minutes later we were outside the school. The place was deserted, the eerie silence of an empty building. The staff should have been in for the new term but, thankfully, I hadn't given permission for them to enter the building yet. I got out of the car and couldn't help myself turn towards the woods. I caught my breath and put a hand to my throat. Why this time? I had reacted on my previous visits but not as strongly as this. An eerie feeling crept into my bones and I shuddered.

Pete put a hand on my shoulder. 'What happened here, Kim?' he asked.

I took a few steps forward and turned to face him. His hand dropped to his side. Should I tell Pete? I'd told no-one; not my parents who would have wanted me to take it further, not even Patrick. When I went to Glasgow I wanted a new start, to put it behind me. And now? Maybe, it would be good for someone to know. I felt we were close to solving Mr Murdoch's murder. Was I supposed to get closure for me too? I looked at Pete and sighed. 'They assaulted me. Richard Spencer – Ricky, as he was back then – and a couple of his pals. Tried to get my clothes off. Said they 'just wanted a look'. They ran when they heard someone calling their dog.'

'You didn't report it?' He sounded surprised.

'No. Thing is, they made me feel like I was to blame. If I told anyone, it was my word against theirs. And they'd say I wanted it. You see, they were supposed to be my friends. Or... At least I thought they were. We had hung out together.' I paused, unable to look him in the eye. 'I get it, Pete. Why so many women and girls don't report attacks. It's the guilt. The shame.'

'But they got away with it. What if they did it again?' he asked.

'They've not appeared in the system. I check now and then. I have to hope...' I couldn't finish. I'd had to live with the thought they might have done it to someone else who hadn't reported it either.

Pete looked at me. 'Where does Mr Murdoch fit in?'

'He found me in a state. I'd sneaked into the toilet near his classroom. It was lunchtime and I thought no-one would be around. I got cleaned up but was still upset. He heard me crying in the corridor.' I shook my head as memories came crowding back. The wind whipped up leaves, swirling around my feet, reminding me of being held down under the trees. 'I told him I was scared because I was being bullied and stuck to that story. He allowed me to be in his classroom instead of going outside. I think he suspected I wasn't telling the whole truth.'

'Why come back?' he asked gently. 'Surely the promotion isn't worth it?'

I let out a deep breath, the soft sound carrying on the breeze. 'I've asked myself the same question since moving to Troon, especially turning up here that first day. Finding out that Mr Murdoch was dead.' I looked up and around me, taking it all in. 'Maybe this opportunity came up because it's time to face my demons. And, maybe, I'm the one who's meant to find my teacher's killer.'

Pete sighed. 'I hope you're right, Kim.'

We turned as another car pulled up, the engine rumbling as the ignition was switched off, catapulting us back to the investigation. The headteacher got out, waved at us, and made his way to the front door, quickly joined by Pete and me. I smiled politely at Andy Macgregor, thanking him for coming to let us in. 'We'll make our own way upstairs.'

He nodded, letting us know he would be in his office if we needed anything.

Pete and I headed to the History Department, our footsteps echoing on the tiled floor. I paused outside Mr Murdoch's classroom, the cupboard straight ahead, still roped off, and tried not to think of the image of him lying there face down, dead. I wanted to remember him as he had been in my school days. A glance into his classroom showed that Mrs Caldwell had finished tidying up. Had Ellen helped? If I was right, the irony of that wasn't lost on me. Pete touched my arm, jolting me out of my reverie, and we turned into Ellen's classroom opposite Mr Murdoch's.

'We'll start with the desk, Pete,' I said, 'take it you brought a screwdriver if we need it?'

Pete pulled the screwdriver from one of his pockets and waved it at me. We made our way to the desk and I tried the first drawer. Locked. I tried the second drawer. Also locked. Pete took seconds to pick both locks and we pulled out the drawers, laying them on the desk side by side.

In contrast to Mr Murdoch's, these drawers were well organised. Everything was sorted into boxes and tins. We laid them out on the desk. Mostly they contained stationery sorted into similar items: paper clips, erasers, sharpeners, colouring pens etc.

A pink tin with a picture of a teddy bear on it which looked like it had once contained sweets had been tucked at the back of one drawer. I opened it and couldn't believe what I was seeing. 'Bingo, Pete. Look at this.' I showed him the open tin. Here was evidence almost hidden in plain sight. Or maybe more accurate to say, hidden under our noses. 'I should have had the neighbouring classrooms searched before.' I sucked my teeth in annoyance. 'But Ellen Shaw's alibi had checked out...and we had no reason to suspect she might be involved...' I sighed. 'At least, though, we've got there.'

Pete looked at me and smiled. 'No, Kim. You got there. Lewis would have had the rest of us go with the confession.'

I shrugged. 'I'm not popping the champagne yet, Pete. Come on, let's get back and see what Ellen has to say. We won't let her know what we've found here – at least not yet. Give us time to do a bit more digging.'

The evidence bagged, we headed back to the office.

'You OK?' he asked as we got in the car.

'I'm fine, Pete.' I smiled and corrected myself. 'I'll be fine.' He nodded.

On the short trip to King Street, we discussed strategy. Pete would start the interview and I would watch through the window from the room next door. I wanted to scrutinise the young woman's reactions to every question and intervene when the time was right.

CHAPTER 56

Pete entered the interview room and sat down opposite Ellen. She stared at him, twisting her hands in her lap. 'I have nothing to add to my statement. I want to go home. You can't force me to stay here.' She glanced at her solicitor, who said nothing.

Pete was unperturbed. 'We want to go over a few things again. For one, your relationship to Jake Devaney. I'll remind you, it's much better for you to help us voluntarily. But there's no way we can let you go home yet. We've too many questions for you.'

She looked down at the table and up again at Pete. 'I told you I've nothing more to say.'

He persisted. 'Jake Devaney is your brother. A drug dealer who blackmails people.'

Her voice was calm. It was hard to believe this was the young teacher upset by her colleague's death that we met only a week and a half ago. 'You asked me about the murder of my colleague. I told you I don't know a Jake Devaney. John Crichton is my brother. I don't know exactly what he does for a living. Some sort of financial consulting, I think. He helps me out financially, that's all. He had nothing to do with Raymond's murder.'

Pete was firm. 'Are you certain of that?'

Ellen lifted her gaze to meet Pete's. 'Absolutely.'

Ellen Shaw was clearly lying. The way she sat so still, repeating the same things, the way she kept her eyes fixed on Pete. I couldn't watch anymore of this. I entered the room, nodded at the solicitor. Pete pulled out a chair for me to sit beside him and we exchanged glances as I did so. I could see we were on the same page. His patience was wearing thin too. It was time for me to play our cards.

I took in her appearance. Dressed in a cashmere sweater and tailored trousers, her hair tied neatly in a ponytail and her make-up subtle, she looked like she was being interviewed for a job rather than as a suspect in a crime. There was an air of preparedness about her.

My voice was cold. 'There's no doubt that Jake Devaney and your brother John Crichton are one and the same person. I find it hard to believe that you didn't know your brother was using the Devaney surname, the surname of your foster parents.' Next a key question. I stopped talking and waited for her to look at me. 'If Jake, or John, had nothing to do with the murder of Mr Murdoch, why was the murder weapon found in his flat?'

Ellen couldn't hide the shock on her face and, for the first time, lost some of her composure. 'You're lying.'

I was unfazed. 'Why would we lie? Shall we bring your brother in here to tell you himself?'

'What do you mean? You don't know where John is. I don't know where he is.' But a hint of doubt had crept into her voice.

I kept my voice crisp. 'Oh, didn't I say? We found him. He went on holiday to the seaside. I think you might know where. Once we knew he was involved somehow, that he's a drug dealer with links to the school, we put two and two together. And we were right.'

She closed her eyes. Maybe it was cruel to bring up painful childhood memories; she had suffered a trauma. But then again, an innocent man had been killed. So, I was unrepentant.

'Your brother – let's call him Jake - is running a drugs racket involving students at Riverwood. He attempted to murder one of those students,' I said. 'He's confessed to that ...' Pausing for effect, I added, 'And to the murder of Mr Murdoch...'

I was cut off by a sharp intake of breath from Ellen who opened her eyes and raised her head to stare at me. 'No. No way ...' This was intriguing, an acknowledgement of her brother?

I ignored her and plodded on, in full flow. 'What we don't know yet is your involvement in all of this. We know you've profited from his dealings. Yet you continue to deny any knowledge of him and his activities. We're talking about children, young people in your care being exploited and an innocent man killed. Are you trying to tell us you know nothing about it?'

Ellen pushed her hands against the table as if starting to rise from her chair, thought better of it and slumped back down. I decided to leave it there for now, give myself time to think things through and we needed an update on the items we had found in the school. 'We're keeping you overnight and will interview you again in the morning.' I looked from her to her solicitor. 'If you object to that, I'll charge you with perverting the course of justice. And that's just the start.' Without waiting for a response, I rose from my chair, headed for the door, nodding at Pete to follow me, then turned back to speak to her. 'Have some time to think. A night in the cells alone might improve your memory.' Her solicitor and I exchanged glances; he didn't raise any objections.

Ellen shook her head and looked at me. 'I want to see my brother. I want to be sure it's him.'

I met her eyes. 'That's not possible.' I opened the door and beckoned Pete through before closing it softly behind me.

.oOo.

'What do you make of Ellen Shaw, Pete?' We were sitting in my office discussing the interview.

'I don't know, to be honest. It's a bit odd. The persistent lying. Her coldness. How different she seems to when we spoke to her that first day,' he replied.

'I agree.' I picked up her file and leafed through the adoption records, settled on a contact number and address, deciding it was worth a shot. I asked Pete to check progress on the evidence we needed for tomorrow and he left the room. I picked up the phone and dialled the number in the file.

'Hello?' A tentative voice, probably expecting a scam call.

'Mrs Shaw?' I asked.

'Who is this?' Her voice full of suspicion.

'Detective Inspector Kim Berry, based at Ayr Police Station. I'd like a word with you. But if you're worried whether this call is genuine, please call the station at the number listed online and ask to be put through to me.' The line went dead. I sipped my coffee and waited, hoping she would call back.

The phone rang. 'Mrs Shaw?' I asked for the second time.

'No. This is Gordon Shaw. What do you want with my wife?' He sounded self-assured, yet with an underlying note of concern.

'Mr Shaw, I can speak to either yourself or your wife. It's more a case of whether you are willing to speak to me.'

Silence. A sigh. 'What's this about, Inspector?' he asked.

'Your daughter, Ellen,' I replied.

'Oh. I thought as much. I called back because you said you're in Ayr.' A sharp intake of breath followed by a brief conversation of which I could make out bits and pieces. Mr Shaw informing his wife of the reason for my call. Next a question that took me by surprise. 'What's Ellen done?'

I didn't exactly respond to this. 'I thought I'd let you know that Ellen is helping us with our enquiries...' I didn't get the chance to finish.

'I assume to do with the teacher at her school? And the pupil? We saw it on the news,' he interrupted.

'Yes,' I responded. 'Mr Shaw...' I paused until he indicated that he was listening. 'When I mentioned this call was about Ellen, why did you ask me what she had done?'

'Look, Inspector,' he replied. 'We've not heard much from Ellen since she moved to Ayr. If you want to know about her, ask her brother. Her biological brother.'

'You mean John Crichton?' It was worth checking.

'Yes. After we adopted her, he kept in touch. He would even come for visits. She worshipped him.' He stopped and took a breath. 'She didn't get on with our kids. And didn't make many friends here.'

'That must have been tough,' I said.

He snorted. 'That's putting it mildly. All we wanted was to give her a home and make her happy. But it didn't work out as we hoped.'

'If you don't mind, could you tell me what happened?' I asked.

'There was no one thing, Inspector. It was constant. She would lie to us and steal, not only money from my wife's purse, my wallet, the kids' piggy banks, but also things from the house that she could sell. We tried talking to her but she wouldn't accept that she'd done anything wrong. There was no guilt, no remorse. In fact, sometimes she would have this smirk on her face, like she enjoyed upsetting us.' His voice became increasingly strained.

'Was she ever violent? Aggressive in any way?' I was trying to form a picture of Ellen Shaw as a child.

'She wouldn't do what she was told and sometimes lashed out, punching and kicking. We found her temper tantrums almost impossible to control at times... It was exasperating.' His voice faded, as if remembering those incidents.

'Yet Ellen went on to do well. University. Teaching. How did she achieve that if she was so disruptive?' I asked.

'We got help. We were lucky because social services were already involved in the adoption. No-one wants to see that fail. By the time she got to high school she had regular therapy and medication if needed. Things got better although we were always on tenterhooks, never knowing if it would all keep working. They said a lot of kids grow out of it.' He sounded like he knew what he was talking about.

I was intrigued. 'And do you think Ellen did?'

'Well,' he replied. 'I know she kept up the therapy through university and teacher training. We used to visit her then. In Edinburgh. She rarely came home, maybe Christmas. But, as I said, once she moved to Ayr, she met up with her brother. We've not seen her since. And, to be honest, Inspector...I know this will sound horrible...but it's a bit of a relief.'

I felt a surge of sympathy for this couple I had never met. They had taken on a child who had suffered a terrible trauma with a view to giving her a loving home. And all it appeared she had done was cause them anxiety and trouble. 'I understand. You said you've not seen her. But have you been in touch at all since she moved here?'

'A handful of phone calls,' he replied.

'And how did she sound?' I asked.

He gave a short laugh. 'She always sounded fine. She said she was happy. But look, Inspector, Ellen could charm the birds off the trees sometimes. But with us...'

'Yes?' I prompted.

'She never stopped lying. She never stopped being angry. And when she got angry, she always said it was our fault,' he responded.

'Your fault?' I was curious.

'Yes,' he said. 'You see, I don't think she ever stopped being angry at us for taking her away from her brother. I guess she had to lash out at someone and that was usually us. We tried our best but...I don't know what else I can tell you.'

'Thank you, Mr Shaw. I appreciate your time. You've been very helpful.'

We said our goodbyes and I ended the call. Cupping my hands on my chin, elbows on the desk, I reflected on what Ellen's adoptive father had said. There was a lot to think about and I wanted to be prepared to take her on the next day. After updating the team on my telephone conversation, I told everyone to call it a day, picked up the files and headed home.

Putting my key in the lock, for the first time, I didn't mind that the flat would be dark and empty. Instead, relishing the silence, I poured myself a small glass of wine, ran a bath and sank into the scented bubbles, allowing myself to relax. Before I interviewed Ellen again in the morning, I'd need to present my version of what happened to Lewis. He would have to give permission to lean on Ellen and somehow get brother and sister to tell the truth. I also hoped that, with the three teenagers providing witness statements, I could persuade him to let them go with a caution and give them a chance to not mess up the rest of their lives. I was certain I had cracked the case and needed to persuade my boss that I was right.

Tuesday 25th October 2022

THE TRUTH

CHAPTER 57

I woke up feeling refreshed for the first time since the investigation began, even though it had been a late night. I'd sat up until after midnight going through all the evidence again, adding in what we'd found in Ellen Shaw's drawer. For the first time since this investigation began, the bad dreams and images didn't go round and round in my head. Instead, I'd fallen into a deep sleep, brought round by the alarm on my phone. I wondered if that was because I had opened up to Pete about the assault? Or because I was convinced of my theory about the murder? Probably a bit of both. Getting justice for Mr Murdoch helping to lay to rest old ghosts.

Stretching, I got out of bed and prepared myself for the day ahead. I was confident that Lewis would agree with my line of enquiry given the evidence we had found in Ellen's classroom. The notebook may have been the motive for the murder but the photograph had been the key to finding out who did it. The items in the sweetie box solved the case. Knowing that I was close to getting a result for Mr Murdoch kept me focused and positive about the outcome.

I arrived early and was in my office reflecting on all the information as the others arrived one by one. I'd already met with DCI Lewis and got his official approval to carry on. I called a briefing with Pete, Bill, Gary and Carmel.

'Ma'am,' said Bill, 'It seems your instincts proved correct.' He caught my eye and gave me a quick nod.

I smiled at him, knowing for Bill that was a compliment, an admission I'd been right to pursue the case, take the risk of being wrong. 'Thanks, Bill.' I meant it.

Turning to Pete, I asked him to arrange for Ellen to be brought to an interview room ready for questioning. Then, I took some time to myself and sat in my office, taking my time to gather my thoughts before heading downstairs. A week and a half ago, Pete and I had spoken to Ellen Shaw for the first time. We had thought she was a young teacher upset at the murder of her colleague with a cast iron alibi. I remembered Mrs Caldwell's concern for her, thinking about the support Ellen would need to continue her job. I wondered how Mrs Caldwell would feel when she found out that Ellen's behaviour that morning might have been a charade.

When I entered the interview room, I was reminded of how young Ellen was. She was wearing the same clothes and devoid of make-up, looked different to the composed young woman of the day before. When I suggested she looked like she hadn't slept much, her expressionless eyes met my gaze and turned away. I took that as agreement. 'Would you like to talk about what kept you awake?' I asked. She stared at the table and refused to say a word. This was going to be painstakingly slow.

I checked that she was watching what I was doing. Her eyes followed my hands as I reached into the evidence bag in front of me. I pulled out a set of keys which I carefully placed on the table, directly in her line of vision. The key ring was a metal saxophone etched with New Orleans. I never once took my eyes off her face and the look of surprise that passed over it when she saw the keys was plain to see. 'Can you identify this set of keys?' Ellen looked away, remaining silent. I tried again. 'Ellen? Have you seen these keys before?'

She wouldn't look at me, kept me waiting but eventually said, 'They're Raymond's.' At least an admission that she recognised them.

'Why were they in the drawer of your desk?' I asked.

'I don't know,' she responded.

This was unbelievable! I scoffed. 'Come on. Do you expect me to believe that? A crucial piece of evidence that you know we've been looking for, which you consistently denied seeing, or knowing where they were? And we find them hidden in your desk?'

She looked at me. The coldness in her eyes was striking as she described Ben Chadwick leaving them on the table. 'I put them in my drawer for safe-keeping.'

No way that was true. 'Why not give them back to Mr Murdoch? And why didn't you tell us this before? We asked several times.'

She stared at me, clearly not knowing what to say, then turned her gaze to the small window close to the ceiling. I decided to leave the topic of the keys, yet to reveal my full hand.

So, I bided my time, in no rush to play my trump card, all the time watching her. The silence in the room was palpable, broken only by the sound of the rain pattering against the window. The overhead light flickered. Slowly, I removed another object from the evidence bag and placed it on the table. 'Can you tell us what this is?'

She shrugged. 'It's a mobile phone, of course.'

'Whose mobile phone?' I asked.

'How should I know?' She had the nerve to look confused.

I was astonished that she could sit there and pretend not to recognise it. This woman was a tough cookie and I had to admit she'd had me fooled. 'We found it in one of your locked desk drawers. Why do you have a second phone? And one that's pay-as-you-go, more difficult to trace?'

She hesitated. Her eyes scanned the room, refusing to look at me. 'I ...' She fell silent.

Aiming to get a response, I reminded her that her brother, Jake, had confessed to killing Mr Murdoch and would go to prison for a long time.

She met my gaze. 'You've got it wrong. I told you I don't know Jake.' There it was again, the lie.

It looked to me she was trying to keep herself under control, I could sense suppressed anger. Her hands gripped the edge of the table and she was biting her lip. So, I kept pushing. 'If you don't know him, why did you call Jake from this phone, just after quarter past three last Thursday?' Gary had already checked that out. 'And why are there calls to him from this phone going back about a year? The phone we took yesterday, your smartphone, has calls to John Crichton. So, why a second phone for calls to Jake?'

Ellen found a spot on the wall and fixed her gaze on it. 'I didn't make the calls. I remember, I took that phone from one of my students and they didn't collect it.'

I was incredulous. 'You're denying this is your phone? Even though we found it hidden, tucked away in a box, in your drawer?' I was reaching boiling point. I'd had enough of lies and deceit.

Her eyes swept around the room again, like she was hoping the walls would come up with answers. The silence hung heavy but this time neither Pete nor I would be the one to break it. She looked from one of us to the other then glanced at her solicitor before releasing her grip on the table. She sighed. 'OK, have it your way. It's mine.'

I slid the photograph of the family on holiday across the table. She stared at it for what seemed a long time. 'That's John and me.'

'At last,' I thought, before asking her, 'And you admit you know he uses the name Jake Devaney?'

She nodded. 'He told me when I found out I would be coming to Ayrshire and gave me the phone when I started at Riverwood. I was to use it to contact him in an emergency. I had no idea what he'd meant at the time.'

Finally, we were getting somewhere. 'What was the emergency last Thursday?' I asked.

She looked me in the eye. 'I found Raymond in the cupboard. He was dead.'

I had to stop my questions coming out in a rush. Remain in control. 'Why didn't you call an ambulance or get some help? Why call your brother instead?' At this point I paused, feeling the need to keep a check on my emotions. 'And,' I took a deep breath, 'how did you know he was dead?'

Her eyes widened in shock. 'What do you mean?'

I continued. 'It's a simple enough question. When you found Mr Murdoch that afternoon, how did you know he was dead?'

Her eyes bore into me. 'You mean he wasn't dead?'

My voice was ice cold. 'We don't know. He might have been but, it's not conclusive. He might not have been. The pathologist can't say for certain that the blow to the head killed him straight away.' I hoped he had been killed outright, and Duncan had assured me he was unlikely to have survived, nor suffered for long. But I wasn't going to tell her that.

She continued to stare at me. 'I thought he was dead.'

'And your brother killed him?' I asked.

She was defiant. 'You can't prove that.'

I returned her glare. 'We have the murder weapon found at his flat.'

'Even so.' She turned away.

I could no longer feel anything but anger at her. She hadn't stopped to check that Mr Murdoch was dead. She showed no remorse that he might have lain there alive for hours, that she might have left him to suffer. It was time to put an end to this. I might be taking a risk, but her demeanour throughout these interviews and the mood changes we had seen convinced me that my gut was right. Therefore, I went for it. 'And if you had thought he wasn't dead, what would you have done? Smacked him a second time with the mallet?'

She looked at me like I had slapped her. But I had had enough. It was time to get to the truth.

CHAPTER 58

Ellen Shaw and I stared at each other across the table. Her face was unreadable, like she had put on a mask. Or maybe I should say a different mask. I was trying to contain my anger but knew that I couldn't hide the hostility in my eyes. To have been taken in by this young teacher to the extent I had not considered searching her classroom until yesterday irked me, even though it made no difference to the outcome. We had still got there. I could sense it. All I needed was a confession.

I considered taking a break but decided that might give her time to think, to come up with another story. I put a finger on the photograph and she lowered her eyes to look at it. 'Tell me about this photograph,' I said. 'Get her talking, admit who her brother is and see where it leads,' I thought.

She looked at me. 'A holiday in Llandudno. The Devaneys. And John and me. They were going to adopt us. Keep us together. Be our forever parents and then... the accident. I was only four. John was eight. Sometimes it feels like yesterday. It never goes away. Not really.'

I was weighing her up. Was her sadness genuine? I couldn't tell. 'It must have been hard, going back into care?'

She caught my eye, and glanced quickly away, resting her gaze once again on the window high up the wall. 'They said I was lucky, given a second chance. But I didn't want to leave John. It wasn't fair, me being adopted and him left behind.' They were allowed to keep in touch, but the Shaw family lived in Aberdeen so initially it was only letters. 'I was happy enough and was well treated but missed my brother.' Her being 'happy enough' was not exactly the impression I had got from Gordon Shaw.

When John had left the care home and got his independence, he'd visit about once a month. He'd always said he'd look after her and had kept that promise. Not only financially, helping with university fees and buying the house, but with advice and support. 'He was always there when I needed him.' She smiled to herself. 'And I'm all he has.'

She obviously didn't know he was in touch with Amanda and I didn't enlighten her. Time enough for her to find out the half-sister she hadn't seen since the age of two worked two floors below her in the school. But I did wonder why Jake hadn't told her about Amanda. I came back to my accusation. 'Did you kill Mr Murdoch to protect your brother? Is your brother confessing to protect you?' Again, I had to remain patient as the room fell into silence, expectation hanging in the air.

At last, she looked at me and said, 'Yes.'

I persisted. 'Yes, to what exactly?'

She continued looking at me. 'I killed Raymond. But I didn't plan it...'

'Why don't you tell me what happened?' I asked.

She had spotted Ben Chadwick with the notebook in Mr Murdoch's classroom and recognised John's handwriting. She couldn't understand why it was in her colleague's drawer because John always kept it with him. That had bothered her.

If seeing the notebook had worried her, I reckoned that was enough to confirm she must have known about Jake's activities. However, she still claimed to not know what he was up to. When she had got the job at the school, he wasn't pleased and she'd had to convince him it wasn't her choice. After training, she had been placed there. I asked her if she was aware that students at Riverwood were involved in dealing drugs for Jake.

She smiled. 'No.'

'If you knew nothing about it, why have the hidden phone?' I asked.

John had told her that not all his business dealings were strictly legal and, for some things, he was using the name Jake Devaney. He had also told her not to worry but not to ask questions because it was better not to know. He had given her the phone with the name and number in it and she was to call if she was concerned about anything.

It had never been specified what she might be concerned about but when she saw Ben with the notebook, she knew her brother was precious about it and that it was crucial it be kept in safe hands. She used to tease him and he'd get annoyed, saying that if anyone found it, he'd be done for. It didn't make sense that Mr Murdoch would have the notebook and she needed to find out why. She had no reason to think he was involved in whatever her brother was up to, but him having the notebook worried her that someone knew about it and might come after John. When she later saw him fixing a shelf in the cupboard, she decided to ask him about it.

I leaned towards her. 'What happened?'

She put her elbows on the table, the tips of her fingers holding her head and took a deep breath, perfectly calm. 'I asked Raymond what Ben Chadwick was doing in his classroom, that the boy had taken a notebook from his drawer. That's when he told me he'd taken one from Shannon Birch.' She'd become even more concerned, realising that three people knew about the notebook.

Mr Murdoch must have wondered what all the fuss was over a tatty notebook. 'Was Mr Murdoch curious about why you were asking about it? About why you were so interested in Ben Chadwick's movements?'

She shook her head. 'Not at first. He asked me why it mattered. I wasn't sure what to tell him but he noticed that his keys were missing and that Ben Chadwick must have taken them.' She fell silent.

I wanted to find out more about the conversation that led to the murder. She shifted in her chair. 'Raymond decided that if Ben took his keys to get into his drawer to steal the notebook, it must have some significance.'

She leaned back in her chair, resting her hands in her lap. Given that Ben had stolen his keys to acquire the notebook he decided he should investigate further. She paused to take a deep breath. 'I tried to deflect him but he insisted on going to find Ben straight away.'

She abruptly stopped talking. I asked for some fresh water to be brought in. It was difficult to keep my own emotions in check, finding out the last moments of Mr Murdoch's life. The water arrived and I poured her a glass but she ignored it. I prompted, 'What did you do?'

She took another deep breath, releasing the air slowly through her mouth and shrugged. 'It was instinct. I had no idea why these kids would have John's notebook. It's important. I didn't know what would happen to him if someone like you…' I could see the contempt in her eyes when she looked at me. '…If someone like you got hold of it. And… what about me, my career… We would lose everything.'

'Here was the motive,' I thought. 'So, you thought you were protecting your brother, yourself, both?' She nodded. 'What did you do?' I asked, finding myself almost unable to speak, clutching my fists under the table.

She looked at me, a veiled expression on her face. 'It wasn't my fault... I couldn't let him start asking questions... It was an impulse. I spotted the mallet on a pile of books. Raymond turned his back on me. So, I hit him.'

The confession reverberated noiselessly around the room. It took a few minutes for me to speak. 'You killed him.' My face was grim and my voice icy. I wanted the details of what happened next.

Her eyes were far away. She'd looked at his body, knowing it couldn't be undone. 'I didn't know what to do, I needed to breathe, to think. I dropped the mallet, checked that no-one was around, left the cupboard and locked the door.'

The corridor had been silent with Mrs Caldwell out of school and the classrooms empty of students. She had gone to her classroom, got the phone from the box in the drawer and called John. She had used the pay-as-you-go because he would know it was an emergency, that she was in trouble and maybe he would be too. 'He'd help me, know what to do, be able to think straight.'

I was aghast that she thought her brother could somehow fix it, that he could make it go away. It was one thing for her to kill someone in the heat of the moment. Another to shut the door and try to save herself. I couldn't help but think about what Duncan had said, that Mr Murdoch might have still been alive at that point. But I had to keep going. 'Where was your brother when you phoned?'

She rubbed her temples. He had been parked a short distance from the school and picked up the phone immediately. He had asked her what had happened and she had told him she thought Raymond Murdoch, the history teacher was dead. 'I told John I'd killed him. That Mr Murdoch might have found out about him. He'd looked in his notebook. Was going to investigate further. I'd panicked and hit Raymond and was sure he was dead.'

She looked at me. 'You're saying he might not have been...if he suffered... that's too bad... But if he'd let me deal with it...' Still no sign of remorse.

'You killed him. You contacted your brother.' My tone remained cold, abrupt. 'Then what happened?'

John had given her instructions on what to do. She was to go home as normal at the end of the day and he would sort it out. If she let him handle it, they could walk away, no-one need know she was involved. She was genuinely shocked when Mrs Caldwell found Mr Murdoch's body because she had expected John to have moved it.

Unbelievably, she smirked. 'I thought John was so clever, leaving Mr Murdoch where he fell and disposing of the weapon. No-one knew about him. Who would suspect me? But you...' Her voice faded to nothing. She sat back in her chair and sighed.

I stood up, my chair scraping along the tiled floor, causing her to look up at me. 'Yes, Ellen. You, and your brother, reckoned without me.'

I quietly paced the room, needing to think. Something was bothering me. I was still struggling to grasp why the stealing of a notebook could lead to such a violent crime. What had triggered her to do such a thing? Surely more than protecting her brother and his business?

The stain on the wall caused by Ben throwing his tea caught my eye and I stared at it. Teenagers accused of involvement in crimes committed by one of their teachers and her brother. It beggared belief.

I sat down again and met her gaze across the table. 'The thing I don't understand is why you didn't let it be. I mean, let Mr Murdoch talk to Ben. Take the risk that he'd get the notebook and speak to Shannon. Then, if he'd thought it suspicious enough to hand in, it would only be Jake here. He's the drug dealer, the one breaking the law. He'd always promised to look after you, after all. No reason to mention you.'

Our eyes met and the look she gave me chilled me to the bone. 'Oh, Inspector Berry. Maybe I could have done that. Should have done that. It makes sense when you say it. But...in that moment...' She paused and pursed her lips. 'You see... did you think that Jake randomly selected the Riverwood students that worked for him?' She paused again, allowing that to sink in. 'Don't you see? I couldn't let Raymond take everything away from me.' She sat back in her chair. 'Raymond, though. I genuinely did like him.'

I glared at her. She was the first to look away. Beside me, Pete switched off the tape. I couldn't stay in the same room as her a second longer. I rose from my chair, turned, and walked out. Pete could take it from here.

Thursday 11th October 2022

MR MURDOCH'S FINAL DAY

CHAPTER 59

Raymond Murdoch woke to the sound of jazz. He lay in bed soaking up the mellowness of the tunes and smiling at the memories of last night. Amanda Cairns was so much younger than him and he couldn't believe his luck. It had all been her idea; she had pursued him after they got chatting in the staff room. She was lonely and wanted to have some fun whenever her husband was away. And Mr Cairns was away a lot.

Last night had been cut short, however, because her husband had called to say that he would be home late that evening instead of staying over at the hotel in Dundee. Amanda had arrived after nine o'clock and didn't even have a drink. It was straight to bed and they had a quick shower before she headed home about eleven o'clock. Raymond wasn't complaining; he preferred to sleep alone.

Chuckling to himself, enjoying the secret they had managed to keep from the gossips at school, he could delay getting up no longer. With a grunt, he swung his legs out of bed, put on his slippers and dressing gown, made his way along the hall to the bathroom and peed. He avoided looking in the mirror; his once dark, curly hair confined to old photos, replaced by a thinning cover of grey.

Once in the kitchen, he switched on the TV to get the news, turning it off again as soon as he got the headlines. He didn't like the commentary and chat as well as everything being repeated over and over. Pouring a bowl of cornflakes, he considered his timetable for the day; deciding whether it was likely to be a good or not so good one.

He recalled that the first lesson was his bottom set. They had caused a bit of hassle at first but once they had agreed a truce that he would make it as easy as possible for them if they behaved themselves, it had worked a treat. Sometimes he would chat to them for a bit. Other times they would do the simple tasks and he could plan his next class. It was an easy start to the day.

He had reached the point of being able to do his job without too much preparation but that didn't mean he didn't care. It was years of experience that made it easier. He wasn't interested in promotion, having given up on that idea a while ago. He had spent a lot of years caring for his parents and, in the meantime, there had been too many changes, too many new ideas, too much jargon and he hadn't kept up with it all. He didn't regret the choices he had made in putting his parents first and would do it all again in a heartbeat. His sister had a family and he didn't, so it had made sense for him to move in with them. Instead of management responsibility, he enjoyed doling out advice and having a laugh. He was under no illusions about his reputation. But he was content with his life and how many people could say that?

Smiling to himself, he found his uniform of chinos, shirt, and sweater, got dressed, picked up his jacket and made his way out of the house, checking the lock three times to make sure that it was secure. He pulled into the car park at quarter to seven as usual. He liked to get in early, check his pigeon hole and make himself a cup of strong coffee before the others arrived.

By the time Marina and Ellen came in he was usually on his second cup. He had a lot of time for Marina, with whom he had worked for many years, mainly because she wasn't some bright young thing who thought she knew everything. Marina had been promoted above him and as his boss for more than ten years, they trundled along nicely because she knew her stuff, respected his experience and they made a good team. Ellen Shaw, on the other hand, was quiet and studious. This was her first permanent job, having done her probationary period with them last year. She was keen on perfection, always asking questions which he was happy to answer.

Before he knew it, the bell had gone and it was time to start the day. Registration over, he prepared to welcome the bottom set. Shannon Birch was late as usual. The class had already started when she pitched up and threw open his classroom door. It was no surprise; he had never known her to be on time for the first lesson of the day. She paused in the open doorway to make sure everyone was looking at her; short skirt, tight jumper, and trainers; her take on school uniform. They went through the usual rigmarole. He always liked to make her apologise for being late and promise she wouldn't do it again before he let her in.

'Wait outside the door, Shannon.'

'Why, Sir? What have I done?'

'You know very well, young lady.'

He knew she didn't mind waiting because it was an opportunity to check her make-up for the umpteenth time. Who knew mobile phones could double as mirrors? The rest of the class also didn't mind and neither did he. It all made the lesson that little bit shorter.

He gave the class their first task, which they wouldn't even look at, before heading to the door and speaking to Shannon in the corridor. A few minutes later he re-entered and beckoned her to follow him into the room. Running her fingers through her long blonde hair, her eyes swept over everyone as she moved towards her desk at the back next to Frankie. Raymond knew he would likely have her phone before the end of the hour too, part of the routine.

It didn't take long. There she was fiddling with her phone under the desk. Except, when he went to confiscate it, it turned out to be a notebook. He took it anyway and locked it away in his desk drawer, a bit surprised at how concerned she was that the drawer would be locked. He assured her that it would be.

At half past twelve he made his way to the staffroom where he joined his pals in their usual spot. They always met there for lunch and, every Friday, they went to a local pub for a quick drink after work. Sometimes they would spend the whole afternoon; it could turn into a bit of a session. The topic of conversation usually turned to the prospect of retirement, counting down how many years they each had to go and whether they could afford to go early. Raymond had a couple of years or so left and nothing would keep him any longer; luckily, he was able to retire at sixty. He always said he wouldn't mind working in a shop or some such job to top up his pension if he had to.

Straight after lunch he had his brightest and best class. This was one of those classes where he had known a lot of the kids since they had started at high school and he knew they thought he was a legend. They were all expected to get good grades and hung on his every word. That was why he was so surprised to spot Ben Chadwick using his mobile phone when he was supposed to be writing an essay. 'Mr Chadwick. Hand it over, please.'

Ben reluctantly handed over his phone. Raymond thought the boy should have known he wouldn't get away with it in his class. 'Come and see me at the end of the day. No, wait a minute. I'm heading off early today so you can have it back at the end of the lesson. Lucky for you I don't want to end up with your phone overnight.' He never liked having to take responsibility for students' phones.

Taking the phone away, he locked it in the drawer next to Shannon's notebook. That was when he remembered he had forgotten he wouldn't be around to give it back to her that day so it would have to wait until the next morning. He wasn't going to search the school to find her for the sake of a notebook. As soon as the bell rang at 3.30pm he planned to be out the door fast.

The bell went for the start of the last period of the day and he was glad to be free. He sent the class off to their next lesson and surveyed the carnage of his desk. The pile of marking that should be done before the holidays beckoned but he wasn't in the mood. Instead, he decided he would put away textbooks he wouldn't be using next term. At least he could surprise Marina by trying to tidy up his classroom and create a bit of space which no doubt would soon be filled by even more clutter after the holidays.

He gathered up a pile of books and made his way to the cupboard at the end of the corridor. He put them on the floor so that he could unlock the door. Leaving his keys in the lock, he propped open the door with the pile of books. He soon realised there wasn't much space in the cupboard because it was full of outdated textbooks they no longer used but hadn't thrown away. There never seemed to be time to sort them out.

Looking around he noticed the only available space was an empty shelf that looked precarious. A couple of dowels had come loose so it wouldn't take much weight. He decided he would try to fix it and headed down to the Technologies Department to see if they had any spare dowels and borrow a mallet. Might as well delay the actual tidying up.

Downstairs the Technologies Department was empty. Of course, Amanda had told him last night everyone was leaving early and going to the pub. He thought he might join them later. It was always fun to spend time with Amanda while concealing their relationship from the rest of the group. In the meantime, he knew where the storeroom was so could help himself to what he needed. It didn't take him long and ten minutes later he was back in the cupboard working out the logistics of repairing the shelf.

He was disturbed by someone calling his name and turned around to find Ellen in the doorway. His first thought was that she would have more questions for him; probably already thinking ahead to next term. She didn't always like to ask Marina in case the boss thought she wasn't up to the job. Raymond hadn't been too sure of Ellen at first but had become quite fond of her and her keenness to do a good job. Sometimes, though, he felt she needed to calm down and take a break.

But Ellen wasn't asking about work. She stood in the doorway smiling at him. He smiled back and put the mallet he was about to use on top of a pile of books.

CHAPTER 60

'What can I do for you, Ellen?' he asked.

She smiled. 'I've just seen Ben Chadwick in your classroom.' Her voice was light, casual.

He was puzzled, not only because he couldn't think why Ben would be there, but also by the fact she was mentioning it. He shrugged. 'I took his phone from him last lesson but gave it back at the end.'

She continued to look at him. 'I caught him with a notebook and it looked like he'd taken it from your drawer.' She seemed unduly interested in what Ben had been up to.

'If it was a notebook, it couldn't be Ben's. I took a notebook from Shannon Birch this morning, though. Made a change it wasn't her phone.' He chuckled, trying to lighten the atmosphere which, for some reason, had become tense.

She stood stock still, her tone serious. 'It was definitely a notebook.' She stuck out her chin and it reminded him of all the defiant teenagers he had taught over the years.

He met her gaze. 'It can't be the same notebook. I locked it away.'

'It was,' she said.

He paused, putting a hand to his chin. 'How do you know it's the same one? How did Ben get into the drawer if that's the case? I'm sure I locked it.' He instinctively put his hand in his pocket to check for his keys, before remembering they should be in the lock. Glancing towards the cupboard door, he saw they were missing.

Ellen followed his gaze. 'They're on your desk,' she said. 'Ben must've taken them.'

He was curious. 'Why does it matter so much to you?'

She ignored the question. 'Have you read it?' There was a hint of anxiety in her voice.

This conversation was strange. 'I've flicked through it, in case there was something that caused concern. That might need reporting... Child protection – you should know that.' He paused, unable to fathom why she was so interested. 'I haven't worked it out, though. It's some sort of code. I was going to speak to Shannon about it in the morning.'

Her hands clenching and unclenching by her sides, she said, 'Ben's got it. He took it.'

His brow creased, wondering what all this was about, becoming a bit exasperated. 'I'll go find him and get it. I need to do that anyway. It's not his. And if he took my keys to get it...' He rubbed his temples. 'Why are you so concerned? Is it important? Do you know something I don't?' He tried to keep his tone light, quizzical. But her concern about this notebook and the fact Ben had stolen it from his desk meant it must be important in some way. Her attitude was disconcerting. He'd have to do something about it.

'You've read it,' she repeated.

This was becoming ever stranger. 'I've glanced through it and it's gobbledygook.' He looked at her, trying to work out the expression on her face. 'You're obviously worried about something. And you've made me think. A notebook with a code. One of my students had it, another stole it.' He blew out his cheeks and looked at her. 'There are rumours about kids being involved in drugs here. Marina mentioned something, she was going to talk to us both, something about anything suspicious being reported to the police. Maybe this is a coincidence but... I'll head off, speak to Ben, take it from there.'

He was taken by surprise when she moved quickly, blocking the doorway. 'No, Raymond. It's fine. I'll handle it.'

He shook his head. 'I didn't see Ben. I didn't hear him take the keys. He's stolen something. I need to find out what's going on.'

She didn't move. Her face had become unreadable. 'Look, Raymond. I'll be honest with you. I only wanted to know if you'd read it. If you'd worked anything out. You know how good you are at problem solving.' A coldness in her tone, at odds with the attempted compliment.

He was completely baffled. 'You're not making any sense.' He tried to smile at her. 'I don't understand what's going on here.' He didn't like the expression on her face. It was like her mind was somewhere else. She was making him feel uncomfortable. This wasn't the young teacher he had come to know. He felt the need to diffuse the situation. 'Let me pass and

I'll get the notebook back from Ben. We can have a look, see if we can work it out. Pass it to the powers-that-be if we think it's dodgy.'

She sighed and put her hands on her hips. 'I don't think you get it Raymond. You've seen it. Even suggested there might be a link to students and drugs. Have you shown it to anyone else? Told anyone?'

This was getting out of hand. She was becoming agitated, raising her voice, and rocking from one foot to the other. Confused and becoming increasingly anxious, he asked, 'Ellen, what's going on?' He took a step forward, hoping she would move and let him pass. She didn't. He stopped, tried another tack, keeping his voice friendly, despite the knot of worry growing in his stomach. Concern that she might be in some sort of trouble. 'Tell you what. Let's go get a cup of tea, sit down and talk about this.'

'Raymond,' she shouted, 'there's nothing to talk about. I can't have you working things out. Going to the police.'

He had never seen her like this before. Where was the colleague he would share a joke with? They stood in silence, face to face. Surrounded by the smell of old books and dust. 'Come on. Ellen. What's up with you? This isn't like you. Let's get it sorted out. Whatever's bothering you. We'll lock up here and get a cup of tea.'

He turned his back on her to move the pile of books he had used to prop open the door. As he pushed them forward, he moved further into the room and the door began to close behind him.

He didn't have a clue what hit him.

Six Months Later

EPILOGUE

I stood at the back, taking in the crowd of people who filled the room. The walls of the assembly hall were adorned with pictures of Mr Murdoch throughout his career as well as photographs and messages. There were notes, letters, and cards from current and former students, from staff and from parents. Lots of people with fond memories like mine. He was a good man who had found himself in the wrong place at the wrong time, as I had thought.

I had done what I had said I would do and found his killer. Who would have thought it would turn out to be the young teacher he had worked with and helped?

On the stage sat the three young people who had organised the memorial event. Katie Spencer had learned her lesson. She had made a mistake and been lucky. No-one knew of her involvement in the case. There was no concrete proof; the evidence had disappeared when Jake destroyed his phone although there was still the possibility that it was stored somewhere in the cloud. I had given her a warning with regards to withholding information and a lecture on cooperating with the police. The girl up there today looked relaxed. Her acceptance in the school was assured now that she was friends with Shannon Birch. It had taken some persuading Katie's dad, Richard Spencer, to allow his daughter that association but he had given in eventually. Keeping risks close was how he had looked at it in the end.

If it were possible, Shannon's popularity had gone up a notch. The full details of her involvement in Jake's activities hadn't been made public, so she enjoyed the status of stab victim and bringing down a local drug dealer. Better to make a deal with me than have your life ruined. Shannon was also rebuilding her relationship with her mum who was attending AA meetings every week. She had the incentive to keep Shannon on the straight and narrow and not allow any more 'Jakes' in her daughter's life. She sat in the front row, watching proudly as her daughter delivered a speech.

The person I worried about most was Ben. Repeatedly he had asked me if he hadn't stolen the notebook would Mr Murdoch still be alive. That was a question I couldn't answer. He might not have wielded the weapon, but Ellen had caught him with the notebook and that triggered the murder. What if? What if? But I could tell him that no-one told Ellen Shaw to kill; she had made that decision when she lifted the mallet and struck her colleague. Regardless, it would take a lot of counselling for Ben to come to terms with what had happened. I had arranged that, in return for being a witness for the prosecution, Ben wouldn't face charges himself. I hoped that he would one day achieve his dream of university.

Across the other side of the hall, I caught sight of Amanda Cairns, someone else having to live with their actions. Her husband had left her and at the end of the school year she was moving back to Edinburgh. She also felt guilty, however unfounded, that she hadn't fought harder to take in her half siblings after the accident. To find them years later and learn that one made money from drugs and blackmail while she had worked alongside the other who turned out to be a killer was something with which she would have to come to terms. With regards to Amanda, I had to admit that sometimes coincidences do happen. There was no evidence to suggest that she knew anything about her half-brother's activities and she had been shocked to find that she had worked in the same place as Danielle for more than a year.

After the memorial, I couldn't resist making my way to the History Department one last time. I needed to quietly spend some time there to pay my respects and say goodbye. I waited as people filed their way out of the main entrance before crossing the foyer towards the stairs.

Reaching the first step, I heard a voice say my name. 'DI Berry!' I didn't turn round but then a second time, a more insistent tone, 'DI Berry! Kimberley... Kim...'

I felt like I was moving in slow motion, unwilling yet compelled, as I spun through one hundred and eighty degrees to face the man calling for my attention. Richard Spencer. Ricky. I felt every muscle stiffen. 'What do you want?'

A muscle twitched in his cheek as he looked directly at me. Tension hung between us. He moved closer and I had to stop myself from recoiling from him. 'I wanted to... I wanted to say thank you. For what you did for Katie. Keeping her out of it. Giving her another chance.'

I scoffed. 'What did you expect? That I would use your daughter for revenge?' I looked past him, my gaze seeing beyond the door, to the car park, to the woods.

He looked at his feet, took a deep breath, raised his head to look at me. 'No, never that. No... But... I'm sorry. For what happened. For what we did. It was never meant to go that far. We were stupid kids. Got carried away. We wouldn't have touched you... Wouldn't have hurt you... We just wanted to ...'

I glared at him, eyes blazing, my voice low and cold. 'But you did hurt me. Not cuts and bruises, maybe. But you wanted to strip me. Are you trying to say that leaves no hurt, no scars? And how do I know, how will I ever know? How will you ever know... what would have happened if you hadn't heard that dog walker come into the woods? When she called her dog and it made you run? You say you'd never have touched me? Neither of us will ever know if that's true.'

Our eyes locked. He had no answer. He opened his mouth to speak but no sound came out. I turned away, climbed the stairs. I felt his eyes on me until I turned the corner and was out of sight. I didn't look back. If he was looking for forgiveness, he wasn't going to get it from me. Certainly not today. I had got a result for Mr Murdoch but absolution for Ricky Spencer, I wasn't ready for that. Maybe I never would be.

At the top of the stairs, I took a deep breath and gave myself a hug before opening the doors into the History Department. Pausing once again on the threshold, I could see that Mr Murdoch's classroom looked completely different; walls painted cream with blue poster boards. Desks were arranged in groups and there was no paperwork strewn over the desk. A new teacher was obviously making their mark.

'Quite a change, don't you think?' I turned to find Mrs Caldwell in the corridor behind me.

I smiled. 'Yes. Huge changes for you, having two new members of staff.'

She returned my smile. 'We keep going. Children need to be taught. They've exams to sit. Raymond would want them to have the best chance in life. He sometimes appeared gruff, especially in recent years. He might not always have shown it but he always cared about the students.' Mrs Caldwell paused and looked at me. 'Like he did for you.'

I stared at her. Did she know? How did she know?

She continued. 'Inspector Berry, Kimberley, I did some digging of my own. I thought you were familiar but couldn't put my finger on it. Then, when I was clearing Raymond's desk, I found a newspaper, a copy of the Ayr Advertiser from a couple of months before... before he died. Raymond was always interested to know what happened to former students. We often talked about it. The newspaper was open and folded at a page with an article about you. The first woman to get the rank of DI in Ayr, a local girl coming home. I wondered if you might have come to this school so I looked up the records and there you were. Kimberley Atkins.' She paused and smiled. 'You do look different.'

I met her eyes. 'Yes, well, I did like my Goth look for a while and the colourful hair...' I stopped, caught my breath. 'Mr Murdoch saved me, you know. Gave me somewhere to go. I was assaulted. I didn't want to go to court; it was their word against mine and there were three of them. I said I had been bullied. But I was always scared to go outside and he arranged for me to come in here.' I paused and looked around the classroom. 'Mr Murdoch said the best revenge for whatever happened to me would be to work hard, make something of myself. He encouraged me to do that. I think it's because of him, I'm here. Life is strange, isn't it? He helped me and I end up with the job of finding his killer.'

She smiled. 'Sometimes it's best not to try and make sense of things. You decided to give those students another chance. That won't make sense to some people.'

I nodded. 'I reckon Mr Murdoch would've wanted me to.'

She continued. 'You know, what happened to Raymond brought to light what was going on with them. Maybe in some strange way, he saved them, from a life of crime, from drugs. Who knows?'

I was reflective. 'That's one way of looking at it, I suppose. But it shouldn't have happened. One tragedy leading to another. Siblings making promises that end up in murder.'

We looked at each other, a gamut of emotions passing between us. Eventually I broke the silence. 'Good luck, Mrs Caldwell. If you ever need me, you know where I am.'

I took one last look around the classroom before heading back into the corridor. I paused by the recess between the history cupboard and the stairs, by the toilets, waiting for the memories to engulf me. It didn't happen. Instead, I felt a lightness, like something being lifted from my shoulders. Perhaps solving this crime, confronting Ricky, telling Pete and Mrs Caldwell would end my nightmares once and for all. I continued downstairs and into the playground towards the car park.

.oOo.

When I got back to King Street, I went straight to my office to pick up any messages and gather my thoughts. Sipping my coffee, I turned my attention to the folder that had been left on my desk, an official prison stamp emblazoned on the front. It contained a copy of a letter, the contents of which took me back to Ellen Shaw's trial and sentencing. Despite her confession, the young woman had changed her plea to not guilty to murder. Her lawyer had requested psychiatric reports based on the trauma she had suffered as a child and the influence of her brother, arguing that diminished responsibility should reduce the charge to culpable homicide.

Two months ago, I attended the High Court in Edinburgh for her trial. Each day the court room had been packed. Etched in my memory is her brother's attendance, there to give evidence in her defence. Currently serving ten years in prison, I had watched him brought into the courtroom. He had looked straight ahead as the prison officers accompanied him to take his place in the witness box. It was only after he had been seated and taken the oath that I saw him look around, watched him look towards the public gallery and catch my eye before quickly turning his gaze on Amanda, the supportive sibling, sitting six feet away from me. Lastly, he had looked to where Ellen was sitting in the dock. I noted how their eyes met and the faintest of smiles had passed between them. Here was the sister John Crichton had promised to protect, charged with killing Mr Murdoch.

In the end, the plea of diminished mental capacity had been accepted and Ellen had, indeed, been convicted of culpable homicide. At sentencing, the judge recommended that she spend a minimum of eight years in prison after which she might be released on license if she underwent appropriate counselling and was deemed no further risk in the community. I could see Amanda was pleased. I felt Ellen had got off lightly. To add insult to injury, if her brother was on his best behaviour, he might serve half of his term and be out in five years. I sighed and turned my attention to the letter.

Dear Danielle,

I feel I've not done a good job of keeping my promise to look after you but one day I'll fix it. It's great that you got off so lightly. I'm behaving myself, might even be called a model prisoner. I should be out in five years. Seems ages away but it'll pass and I'll still be young enough to start somewhere else. I've plenty of money they can't get hold of so I'll head abroad, buy a bar or something. I'm worried about how you're holding up. I know how you can let things get to you. Take each day as it comes and you'll get there. Amanda says she's been to see you too so that'll help. Keep focused on when you get out. By then I'll be set up and I'll find a way for you to join me. I know you won't be allowed but I'll find a way. Whatever it takes. That's a promise.

Love John x

I put the letter back in the folder, smiling to myself. 'We'll see about that,' I thought.

Leaning back in my chair, I observed the team through the glass wall of my office into the incident room and felt lucky to have them. Pete caught my eye and smiled. The last six months had been good, working with him again. Bill seemed to have accepted me, hopefully we had mutual respect to build on. Gary and Carmel were two young people with talent and ambition, two things I could identify with and nurture. Looking from Pete to Bill, Gary, and Carmel, I allowed myself to think that maybe they all felt as lucky to have me.

I stood up, taking a moment of silence to appreciate what I had. From the window I looked out over the town, taking in this view while I still could. We were packing up to move to our new offices at Newton House. I stretched and yawned before picking up my jacket, and heading to the car, now certain that I had made the right decision coming home.

ACKNOWLEDGEMENTS

This novel has been several years in the making. I wrote a draft of the first chapter in 2017 but didn't pick it up again until 2021. In February 2022, my eldest sister, Margaret McBlain, to whom the book is dedicated, was given a terminal diagnosis: a brain tumour. Having been a keen supporter of my wish to write, I wanted her to read a completed story. My thanks to her and her husband, Brian, for reading the first draft manuscript in the spring of 2022 and encouraging me to continue. Margaret died in November 2022. She will always be in the hearts of her family and friends.

Over the last couple of years or so, several people have provided me with editing skills or feedback, and I couldn't have completed this book without their contributions.

Best-selling author of *The Bigamist* and *The Psychopath* Mary Turner Thomson for her early editing, formatting and cover design. Author of *The House Beside the Cherry Tree* and *Blossom on the Wind,* Lea Taylor, for her detailed read-through and, in particular, for suggesting that Kim Berry's voice be heard in the first person, which transformed the narrative. Dilys Leonard, Sandra Davidson, Karen Fairbairn, Sonia Masson and Graham Reid for their comments on an earlier version. Eileen Reid, Claire McBlain, and Kath Paterson for reading it twice and providing even more constructive feedback. Joyce Nisbet for detailed editing and Alan Donald for his overview and comments on the final manuscript. Thanks also to Alan for sharing the manuscript with members of his book group, providing me with further suggestions and encouraging feedback. I am immensely grateful to you all.

Last and not least, thanks to my family and friends who have supported and encouraged me on this writing quest, including my husband, Doug, and daughter, Heather.

ABOUT THE AUTHOR

Mamie Philp was a civil servant, then a teacher but her dream from the age of eight was to write stories. Having written two non-fiction books and three memoirs for clients, *Mr Murdoch is Dead* is her first novel.

Printed in Dunstable, United Kingdom

66621222R00160

AJ PEARCE

BESTE MEVR. BIRD

'Geestig, ontroerend en hartverwarmend.'
– **John Boyne**, auteur van *De jongen in de gestreepte pyjama*

Uitgeverij Mozaïek, Utrecht

ISBN 978 90 239 5901 4
ISBN 978 90 239 5902 1 (e-book)
NUR 302

Vertaling: Roeleke Meijer-Muilwijk
Ontwerp omslag: bij Barbara
Lay-out en dtp binnenwerk: Gewoon Geertje
Auteursfoto: Alexander James

Oorspronkelijk uitgegeven door Picador, eem imprint van
Pan Macmillan, Londen, Verenigd Koninkrijk,
onder de titel *Dear Mrs Bird*.

www.uitgeverijmozaiek.nl

Uitgeverij Mozaïek vindt het belangrijk om op milieuvriendelijke en verantwoorde wijze met natuurlijke bronnen om te gaan. Bij de productie van het papieren boek van deze titel is daarom gebruikgemaakt van papier waarvan het zeker is dat de productie niet tot bosvernietiging heeft geleid.

Londen, december 1940

I

Een advertentie in de krant

Toen ik de advertentie in de krant las, dacht ik echt dat ik zou ontploffen van geluk. Ik had toch al een behoorlijk vrolijke dag, ondanks dat de Luftwaffe weer eens roet in het eten gooide zodat we allemaal te laat op het werk waren gekomen, en ik had zowaar een ui te pakken gekregen, wat goed nieuws was voor m'n stoofpotje. Maar toen ik die aankondiging zag, was ik helemaal hoteldebotel.

Het was kwart over drie op zo'n akelige dag in december, als het al donker lijkt te worden voordat het echt helemaal licht is, en je zelfs met twee vesten en een lange jas aan onmogelijk warm kunt worden. Boven in de dubbeldekker, lijn 24, kon ik wolkjes condens zien als ik uitademde.

Ik was onderweg naar huis na mijn werk als secretaresse bij Strawman Advocaten en verheugde me erop nog even te kunnen zitten voor mijn nachtdienst in de telefooncentrale van de brandweerkazerne begon. Ik had alle nieuwspagina's van *The Evening Chronicle* woord voor woord gelezen en keek nu naar de horoscopen, waar ik niet in geloofde, maar je wist maar nooit... Voor mijn beste vriendin Bunty stond er: 'Binnenkort heb je veel geld tot je beschikking. Geluksdier: bunzing.' Bepaald veelbelovend! Voor mij: 'Het komt vast allemaal goed, uiteindelijk. Geluksvis: makreel.' Nogal een sof, vergeleken met dat van haar.

En toen zag ik het staan, onder *Vacante Betrekkingen*, ingeklemd tussen een vacature voor jamkokers (geen ervaring vereist) en een voor een volwassen opzichter in een overallfabriek (bij voorkeur met referenties).

ASSISTENT GEZOCHT
Parttime Assistent gevraagd bij Launceston Press Ltd.,
uitgevers van *The London Evening Chronicle.*
Eisen: capabel, enthousiast en hardwerkend,
60 w. p. min. typen/110 w. p. min. steno.
Brieven z.s.m. richten aan: Mevr. H. Bird,
Launceston Press Ltd., Launceston House, EC4 Londen.

Het was de beste baan waarvoor ik in mijn hele leven ooit een advertentie gezien had.

Als ik íéts het allerliefste wilde – behalve natuurlijk dat de oorlog afgelopen zou zijn en dat Hitler liefst op zeer onverkwikkelijke wijze aan zijn eind zou komen – was het journaliste worden. Of, om precies te zijn, het soort journaliste dat door mensen-die-het-weten-konden 'oorlogscorrespondente' genoemd werd. Al tien jaar – sinds ik als twaalfjarig meisje een uitstapje naar de lokale krant gewonnen had als prijs voor het schrijven van een nogal beroerd gedicht – droomde ik van een carrière in de journalistiek.

Nu sloeg mijn hart op hol, bonkte dwars door de vesten en de jas heen en dreigde uit mijn borstkas te springen, boven op de dame naast me. Ik was dolblij met mijn baan bij Strawman, maar ik snakte ernaar te leren hoe ik verslaggeefster kon worden. Zo iemand die altijd een notitieboekje paraat heeft en te allen tijde klaarstaat om Politieke Intriges op te sporen, moeilijke vragen te stellen aan volksvertegenwoordigers, of – het allerbeste van alles – op het laatste vliegtuig naar een ver land te springen om belangrijke verslagen over oorlog en verzet naar huis te sturen.

Op school hadden mijn leraressen gezegd dat ik bij zinnen moest komen en niet zo hoog van de toren moest blazen, ook al was Engels mijn beste vak. Bovendien weerhielden ze me ervan de minister-president te schrijven om hem namens de schoolkrant vragen te stellen over zijn buitenlandbeleid. Dat was een ontmoedigend begin geweest.

Sinds die tijd had ik volgehouden, maar een baan vinden terwijl ik bijna geen ervaring had, bleek nogal hoog gegrepen, vooral omdat ik per se voor een krant in de Londense Fleet Street wilde werken. Doorgaans ben ik een optimist, maar zelfs ik geloofde er niet in dat het enkele feit dat ik ooit drie keer tijdens de zomervakantie artikeltjes voor de *Little Whitfield Gazette* geschreven had voldoende was om in Berlijn terecht te komen.

Maar nu zag ik mijn kans schoon.

Ik bestudeerde de advertentie nogmaals en vroeg me af of ik aan de vereisten kon voldoen.

Capabel

- Dat was ik beslist, al was het nog even afwachten welke capaciteiten ze van me verwachtten.

Enthousiast

- Zeg dat wel! Ik gilde bijna de bus bij elkaar van enthousiasme.

Hardwerkend

- Tot diep in de nacht zou ik doorwerken, desnoods op kantoor blijven slapen, onder mijn bureau.

Ik kon niet wachten om me aan te melden.

Ik drukte op het knopje om bij de volgende halte uit te stappen en al tijdens het vrolijke belletje minderde de bus vaart. Ik graaide mijn handtas, gasmasker en ui bij elkaar, schoof de krant onder mijn arm, verloor een handschoen – merkte ik later – en roffelde het trapje af.

‘Dank u wel,’ riep ik tegen de conductrice; ik drukte haar nog net niet plat terwijl ik achter uit de bus sprong.

We waren nog niet helemaal bij de halte naast Apotheek Boots, die nog altijd geopend was, ondanks het feit dat alle ramen twee weken geleden gesprongen waren, maar ik sprong op de restanten van de stoep en begon naar huis te lopen.

Boots was niet de enige winkel die tijdens de luchtaanvallen een oplawaai gekregen had. De hele straat was er beroerd aan toe. Van de kruidenierszaak was niet veel meer over dan een halve muur en wat puin, vier van de appartementen ernaast waren helemaal weggebombardeerd en op de plek waar de wolwinkel van meneer Parsons gestaan had, was een gapende leegte. De wijk Pimlico hield nog altijd stand, maar er was veel verlies geleden.

Over kraters heen springend alsof het horden waren, rende ik de straat over; ik vertraagde mijn pas en riep een groet naar meneer Bone, de tijdschriftenverkoper – ‘Met mijn naam zou je toch denken dat ik slager was!’ – die een stapel kranten voor zijn winkel neerlegde. Hij had zijn opzichtersuniform al aan en blies op zijn vingers om ze warm te houden.

‘Middag, Emmy,’ zei hij tussen twee puffen door. ‘Heb je daar de vroege editie? Prachtige foto van Hunne Majesteiten op de voorpagina.’ Hij glimlachte stralend. Ondanks alles wat de oorlog hem had aangedaan was meneer Bone de vrolijkste man die ik kende. Het maakte niet uit hoe vreselijk het nieuws was, hij wees zijn klanten altijd op iets leuks. ‘Nee, sta maar niet stil; ik kan zien dat je haast hebt.’

Meestal bleef ik even staan om over het nieuws van de dag te kletsen. Soms gaf meneer Bone me een overgebleven exemplaar van een krant of van de *Picture Post* als iemand er een gereserveerd had maar vergeten was die op te halen – eigenlijk moest hij ze terugsturen naar de uitgeverij – maar vandaag moest ik meteen naar huis.

'Pagina twee, meneer Bone,' riep ik dankbaar. '*The Chronicle* heeft een assistent nodig. Dit zou hem weleens kunnen zijn!'

Meneer Bone steunde me door dik en dun in mijn droom om oorlogscorrespondente te worden, ook al maakte hij zich ongerust omdat ik achter de vijandelijke linies wilde gaan. Nu glimlachte hij nog breder en zwaaide triomfantelijk met een exemplaar van de avondkrant.

'Zo mag ik het horen, Emmy!' riep hij. 'Veel geluk. Ik zal de *Times* van vandaag voor je bewaren.'

Ik schreeuwde een bedankje en zwaaide verwoed met mijn vrije hand terwijl ik doorholde naar het eind van de straat. Nog een paar minuten en daarna een scherpe bocht naar rechts. Ik ontweek twee bejaarde dames die veel belangstelling toonden voor Walter, de man die gepofte aardappelen verkocht, waarschijnlijk vanwege de warmte die om hem heen hing. Nu nog langs de tearooms, dan was ik thuis.

Bunty en ik deelden een appartement op de bovenste verdieping van het huis van haar oma in Braybon Street. Bij elke luchtaanval moesten we als een haas naar de tuin van de buurvrouw zien te komen en de schuilplaats van gebogen golfplaten in duiken, maar daar waren we inmiddels aan gewend, dus we maakten ons niet onnodig ongerust. Het was een reuzebof dat we daar gratis mochten wonen.

Ik gooide de voordeur open en vloog de betegelde gang door, en de trappen op.

'Bunty!' riep ik, in de hoop dat ze me drie verdiepingen hoger zou horen. 'Je raadt het nooit. Ik heb het beste nieuws aller tijden.'

Tegen de tijd dat ik boven was, kwam Bunty in haar duster uit haar slaapkamer tevoorschijn, de slaap uit haar ogen wrijvend. Ze werkte 's nachts als secretaresse voor het ministerie van Oorlog, maar ze moest natuurlijk altijd haar mond stijf dichthouden over wat haar werk precies inhield.

'Hebben we de oorlog gewonnen?' vroeg ze. 'Daar zeiden ze niks over op het werk.'

'Alleen maar een kwestie van tijd,' zei ik. 'Nee, maar kijk: het op een na beste.'

Ik duwde de krant in haar hand.

'Jamkoker?'

'Nee, gekkie. Daaronder.'

Bunty grijnsde en bekeek de krantenpagina nogmaals. Toen ze de advertentie zag sperde ze haar ogen wijd open. 'Grote griebels!' Bij elk woord werd haar stem luider. 'Emmy, dit is jouw BAAN!!!'

Ik knikte heftig. 'Vind je? Echt? Ja toch?' vroeg ik, totaal onlogisch.

'Natuurlijk! Precies iets voor jou!'

Bunty was dan ook de loyaalste vriendin ter wereld. Ze was ook ontzettend praktisch ingesteld, en ze kwam onmiddellijk in actie.

'Je moet vandaag nog schrijven. Zorg dat je de eerste bent. Meneer Strawman zal je wel een referentie geven, toch? En kapitein Davies van de brandweer. O, lieve help... Kun je daar je diensten dan nog wel draaien?'

Naast mijn werk bij het advocatenkantoor was ik al voor het begin van de Blitzkrieg bij de vrijwillige brandweer gaan werken. Mijn broer Jack had zich een slag in de rondte gevlogen en gevochten en het was hoog tijd geweest dat ik ook mijn steentje bijdroeg. Bunty's vriendje William – Bill voor zijn vrienden – was fulltime brandweerman en toen hij me voorstelde om als vrijwillige telefoniste bij de brandweerkazerne op Carlton Street te gaan werken, leek me dat ideaal. Een sollicitatiegesprek bij kapitein Davies van de kazerne, een medisch onderzoek om zeker te weten dat ik niet op het punt stond de pijp uit te gaan, en klaar was Kees. Drie nachten per week werken, dat kon ik prima in mijn leven inpassen naast mijn baan als secretaresse. Ik kreeg een keurig marineblauw uniform met glanzende knopen en stevige zwarte schoenen en ik was zo trots als een pauw op mijn pet met de badge van de Vrijwillige Brandweer.

Bunty en ik kenden William al sinds we kinderen waren, en toen ik bij de brandweer ging, was onze dorpskrant naar Londen gekomen om een foto van ons drieën te maken. Die drukten ze af met de kop 'Little Whitfield schiet te hulp' eronder. Het bijgaande artikel klonk alsof William, Bunty en ik met ons drietjes verantwoordelijk waren voor de veiligheid van heel Londen en voor de voortgang van het ministerie van Oorlog. Ze hadden ook mijn verloofde Edmund genoemd omdat ook hij uit Little Whitfield kwam – heel lief, al deden ze het een beetje voorkomen alsof hij de halve koninklijke artillerie aanvoerde, wat volgens Edmund nogal bezijden de waarheid was. Ik had hem het krantenknipsel opgestuurd en hij had er veel plezier om gehad. Het was leuk dat de krant ons alle vier had genoemd. Dat voelde als in de goede oude tijd, voordat de oorlog ons leven overhoop gooide en Edmund naar de andere kant van de wereld gestuurd werd.

Binnen twee weken nadat ik bij de brandweer was gekomen, begonnen de Duitsers met hun aanvallen op Londen, en ik was blij dat ik me enigszins nuttig kon maken. Mijn vriendin Thelma, ook bij de brandweer, zei dat ik tenminste mijn steentje bijdroeg, al was het dan niet als oorlogscorrespondente.

'O mooi, het is parttime,' zei Bunty. Ze had de advertentie nog eens doorgelezen en beantwoordde haar eigen vraag. Ze was inmiddels opgehouden met schreeuwen en nu was ze volkomen serieus. 'Echt waar, Emmy,' zei ze, 'dit kon weleens jouw grote kans zijn.'

We keken elkaar even aan en lieten tot ons doordringen hoe kolossaal dit was.

'Ik durf te wedden dat jij helemaal op de hoogte bent van het laatste nieuws,' zei Bunty. 'Ze zullen echt zó onder de indruk zijn.'

'Ik weet het niet, Bunts,' zei ik, plotseling nerveus. 'Ze zullen wel akelig hoge eisen stellen, zelfs voor een assistent. Wil jij me eens testen?'

We liepen de woonkamer in. Op de salontafel balanceerden twee stapels tijdschriften en drie plakboeken met krantenknipsels. Ik zette mijn hoed af en haalde het notitieboekje uit mijn tas – ik had het altijd bij me voor het geval dat... – en bladerde door naar achterin, waar ik met grote rode letters 'appendix' geschreven had en daaronder, op de volgende regel, 'leden van het oorlogskabinet'.

Ik overhandigde het Bunty, die op de sofa neergeploft was.

'Ik zal doen alsof je bij mij komt solliciteren,' zei ze, wijzend op de minst comfortabele stoel in de kamer. 'En ik zal heel streng zijn. Om te beginnen: wie is de minister van Financiën?'

'Sir Kingsley Wood,' zei ik terwijl ik de knopen van mijn jas losmaakte en ging zitten. 'Makkie.'

'Goed zo,' zei Bunty. 'Goed, wie is de voorzitter van de kroonraad? Weet je, ik kan niet wachten tot je daar begint. Je ouders zullen zo blij zijn.'

'Sir John Anderson,' zei ik als antwoord op haar vraag. 'Rustig aan, ik heb die baan nog niet. Ik hoop maar dat moeder en vader er gelukkig mee zullen zijn. Ze gaan zich waarschijnlijk zorgen zitten maken of ik gevaarlijke dingen moet doen.'

'Maar ze zullen doen alsof ze er absoluut geen probleem mee hebben,' zei Bunty.

We grijnsden allebei. Bunty kende mijn ouders bijna even goed als ik. Onze vaders waren vrienden geweest tijdens de Eerste Wereldoorlog en Bunty hoorde helemaal bij de familie.

'Nu een echt moeilijke vraag,' zei ik.

'Doen we,' zei Bunty en zweeg toen weer even. 'O, wacht eens. Wat zal Edmund zeggen, denk je? Hij is vast woest,' voegde ze eraan toe voordat ik antwoord kon geven.

Ik wilde hem graag verdedigen, maar Bunty had wel een punt. Edmund en ik hadden al eeuwen verkering en sinds anderhalf jaar waren we verloofd. Hij was geweldig – slim en attent en zorgzaam – maar hij moedigde mijn hoop op een carrière bij de krant niet bepaald aan. Soms was hij een beetje een conservatieveling.

'Dat valt heus wel mee,' zei ik uit loyaliteit. 'Hij is vast blij voor me.'

'En jij neemt die baan gewoon aan, zelfs als hij niet blij is,' vulde Bunty vol vertrouwen aan.

'Reken maar,' zei ik. 'Als ik hem aangeboden krijg.' Ik was dol op Edmund, maar ik vertikte het om over me heen te laten lopen.

'Ik hoop zo dat ze jou die baan geven,' zei Bunty, terwijl ze begon te duimen. 'Dat moet gewoon.'

'Stel je voor: assistent bij *The Evening Chronicle*...' Ik staarde in de verte en zag mezelf in gedachte Londen rondscheuren in een taxi, op het punt een primeur te bemachtigen. 'Het begin van een journalistieke carrière.'

'Goed van je!' zei Bunty ernstig. 'Ga je je specialiseren als oorlogscorrespondente, denk je?'

'O ja, dat hoop ik wel. Ik ga broeken dragen en als we de oorlog gewonnen hebben, ga ik sparen voor mijn eigen auto en dan kunnen Edmund en ik een appartement in Westminster huren, en ik ga natuurlijk roken, en waarschijnlijk ga ik elke avond naar het theater, of naar Café de Paris om daar allerlei amusante opmerkingen te gaan zitten maken.'

Bunty keek enthousiast. 'Ik kan gewoon niet wachten,' zei ze, alsof we plannen aan het maken waren voor over twee weken. 'Als Bill me niet ten huwelijk vraagt, ga ik misschien wel de politiek in.'

Voordat de oorlog uitbrak, studeerde Bunty's vriendje architectuur. Hij was van plan geweest eerst af te studeren en vast wat geld te verdienen voordat ze zich zouden verloven.

'O, Bunts, wat een mieters idee,' zei ik, onder de indruk. 'Ik wist niet dat jij daarin geïnteresseerd was.'

'Nou ja, niet zo heel erg; in elk geval nu nog niet. Maar als we eenmaal gewonnen hebben, willen de parlementsleden natuurlijk massaal stoppen, en stel je voor, dan kom ik op de radio – het idéé!'

'Slim bedacht. En iedereen zal je respecteren omdat je bij het ministerie van Oorlog gewerkt hebt.'

'Maar daar zal ik nooit over praten.'

'Uiteraard.'

Het begon inderdaad goed te komen. Ik zou journaliste worden en Bunty ging voor de BBC werken.

'Goed,' zei ik en stond op. 'Ik ga mijn sollicitatiebrief schrijven en daarna ga ik bij de kazerne proberen kapitein Davies te spreken te krijgen. Wat een getuigschrift van een vrijwillige telefoniste gaat helpen voor een baan bij *The Evening Chronicle* weet ik niet, maar het kan vast geen kwaad.'

'Larie,' zei Bunty. 'Het is perfect. Als jij telefoontjes kunt beantwoorden terwijl Hitler probeert ons allemaal de lucht in te blazen, zul je als oorlogscorrespondente onder vuur absoluut de allerbeste zijn. William zegt dat je het dapperste meisje in de nachtdienst bent en dat je zelfs geen spier vertrok toen Derek Hobson zwaargewond terugkwam van een klus.'

'Nou ja, ik ben eerste-hulpmentor,' zei ik. Ik dacht er niet graag aan terug. Je maakt geen nodeloze drukte over zoiets, maar het was een afschuwelijke nacht geweest en Derek was nog steeds op ziekteverlof.

Bunty pakte de krant weer op. 'Jij bent hartstikke dapper,' zei ze. 'En je bent gewoon geknipt voor die baan. Nou, schiet maar een beetje op,' zei ze terwijl ze mij de krant overhandigde. 'Er staat "brieven zo snel mogelijk..."'

'Eerlijk gezegd,' zei ik, en met een glazige blik pakte ik de krant aan, 'kan ik nog niet geloven dat dit echt zou kunnen gebeuren.'

Bunty grijnsde. 'Wacht maar af.'

Ik pakte mijn tas, haalde mijn beste vulpen eruit en begon te schrijven.

2

Dhr. Collins, Hoofdartikelen & Algemene Redactie

Een week na de krantenadvertentie deed ik verschrikkelijk mijn best om rustig te blijven. Sinds mijn brief aan mevrouw H. Bird had ik mijn op-de-hoogte-blijven-van-het-nieuws opgevoerd tot een ongekende graad van geestdrift, en nu was ik zowaar echt op weg naar een sollicitatiegesprek bij *The London Evening Chronicle.*

Bunty was me blijven testen tot het op een politieverhoor begon te lijken, en toen ik mijn familie en de meisjes bij de brandweer erover vertelde, was iedereen vervuld van enthousiasme en een nogal zorgwekkend vertrouwen over mijn vooruitzicht op de baan. Ik had Edmund geschreven om hem over mijn sollicitatiegesprek te vertellen. Zijn reactie was nog lang niet te verwachten, maar ik werd door anderen van alle kanten gesteund. De vorige dag hadden de meisjes na mijn nachtdienst op de brandweerkazerne 'Succes!' geroepen, William en de jongens schreeuwden: 'Stop de persen!' en: 'Moedig voorwaarts!' in een enthousiaste poging te klinken als de krantenmensen uit de films. Heel lief van ze: ik had het gevoel dat half Londen – en heel Little Whitfield – achter me stond.

Vandaag ging Londen gebukt onder een lage en sombere grijze lucht, alsof een reusachtige jongen zijn schooltrui had uitgetrokken en die per ongeluk over de hele wijk West End gegooid had. Ik trotseerde de kou in mijn keurige blauw kamgaren mantelpakje met enkele rij knopen, met mijn allerbeste schoenen aan en een klein zwart hoedje dat ik van Bunty geleend had op. Ik hoopte dat ik er zowel zakelijk als alert uitzag. Als iemand die een primeur kon ruiken en onmiddellijk op waarde kon schatten. Als iemand die niet het gevoel had dat haar hart elk moment kon ontploffen.

Ik had die dag vrij van mijn werk en hoewel ik het binnen een uur had kunnen lopen, nam ik twee bussen om niet helemaal verwaaid aan te komen, want dat stond zo sjofel. Zodoende was ik afschuwelijk veel te vroeg aangekomen, dus ik bleef buiten staan, voor Launceston House, en keek nerveus omhoog naar het kolossale gebouw in art-decostijl.

Dat ik misschien híér zou gaan werken… Het was een duizelingwekkende gedachte.

Met mijn hoofd in mijn nek, terwijl ik met mijn ene hand Bunty's hoedje tegenhield en met mijn andere mijn handtas omklemde, was ik al lichtelijk uit balans toen een bijzonder boze stem bulderde: 'Aan de kant! Je houdt het verkeer op!'

Een stevige dame was uit het gebouw gekomen en stevende mijn kant op. Haar hoed leek op een gleufhoed voor mannen, met een kort fazantenveertje op de rand, waardoor hij op het platteland thuis leek te horen. Een ander deel van die dode vogel had de krachten gebundeld met een stuk konijnenbont om een fraaie broche te vormen die op de revers van haar jas prijkte. Ze deed me aan mijn tante Tiny denken, die als driejarige voor het eerst meegegaan was op korhoenjacht en sindsdien allerlei beesten uit de heg schoot.

'Het spijt me echt,' zei ik. 'Ik stond alleen…'

De dame grimaste en stoof langs in een wolk van carbolzeep.

'... te kijken.'

Ik keek haar na terwijl ze kordaat de weg overstak en ineens had ik het eigenaardige gevoel dat ik weer op school zat. De bel voor gymnastiek kon elk moment gaan.

Ik schudde het gevoel van me af. Ik was hier voor een baan waarbij ik aan 'serieus nieuws over zaken van vitaal belang' zou werken; ik moest dus voortmaken. Ik haalde diep adem, keek voor de honderdste keer op mijn polshorloge, liep de brede marmeren trap op en ging de draaideur door.

De entreehal was bijzonder chic, en het was hier binnen bijna even koud als buiten op straat. De muren hingen vol met portretten van grimmig kijkende mannen; in olieverf vereeuwigde uitgevers van tweehonderd jaar geleden keken vol minachting neer op een jonge vrouw met een geleend hoedje, die ervan droomde correspondente te worden. Elk moment kon er één afkeurend gaan mompelen.

Vurig hopend dat ik niet zou uitglijden op de glad gepoetste vloer liep ik op de hoge, notenhouten receptiebalie af.

'Goedemorgen. Mijn naam is Emmeline Lake en ik kom voor mevrouw Bird. Het is voor een sollicitatiegesprek.'

De jonge vrouw achter de balie schonk me een meelevende glimlach.

'Vierde verdieping, juffrouw Lake. Met de lift naar de tweede verdieping, linksaf de gang door, twee trappen op en als u daar bent, is het achter de dubbele deur. U kunt meteen doorlopen. Er is niemand om u binnen te laten.'

'Dank u wel,' zei ik en glimlachte terug. Ik hoopte dat iedereen hier zo aardig was.

'Vierde verdieping,' zei ze weer. 'Heel veel succes.'

Haar behulpzaamheid was zo bemoedigend dat ik de verontrustende dame buiten al bijna vergeten was. Opgewekt sloot ik me aan bij twee heren van middelbare leeftijd met lange jassen aan, die op de lift stonden te wachten, al discussiërend over de radiotoespraak die de minister-president de vorige avond gehouden had. Een van hen maakte zich druk over de activiteiten van de geallieerden in Afrika en stond met zijn handen te wapperen tot de as van zijn sigaret bijna op zijn vriend terechtkwam. De andere man leek niet echt naar hem te luisteren, maar riep toch telkens luid: 'Poeh!'

Ik luisterde mee met het gesprek, want de koperen pijl boven de liftdeur bleef maar op de derde verdieping staan en de mannen bleven maar bekvechten.

'Het is een belachelijke zet. Ze maken geen schijn van kans. En Selassie heeft geen idee wat hij doet.'

'Flauwekul. Je raaskalt.'

'Poeh! Ik durf er vijf shilling om te verwedden dat je het mis hebt.'

'Ik zou me schamen om die van je aan te nemen.'

Ik realiseerde me pas dat ik hen stond aan te gapen toen de man met de sigaret een blik in mijn richting wierp.

'En wat denk jij, snoes? Is Eritrea al verloren? Moeten we daar wel moeite voor doen, nu we daar toch zijn?'

Lieve help! Nu werd mijn mening over een politiek onderwerp al gevraagd nog voordat ik aan mijn sollicitatie begonnen was.

'Nou,' zei ik met het gevoel dat ik goed voorbereid was, 'ik weet het niet helemaal zeker, maar als meneer Churchill het een goed idee vindt, zou ik zeggen dat we ze het beste vanaf Soedan kunnen aanpakken.'

De man slikte zijn sigaret haast in.

Zijn vriend aarzelde even en begon toen bulderend te lachen. 'Dat zal je leren, Henry! Ze zijn niet allemaal zo suf als ze eruitzien.'

De andere man sneerde: 'Iedereen kan een zin die ze op de radio gehoord heeft herhalen.'

'Eigenlijk heb ik er in *The Times* over gelezen,' zei ik naar waarheid.

Geen van beiden reageerde; ze waren weer begonnen met bekvechten. Intussen was de lift eindelijk gearriveerd.

Ik volgde de mannen de lift in en vroeg de liftbediende beleefd of hij me naar de tweede verdieping wilde brengen. Daarna hief ik mijn hoofd en wierp de mannen van onder de rand van mijn hoed een strijdlustige blik toe. Het zou nog niet meevallen om oorlogscorrespondente te zijn, maar dat verbaasde mij niets. Veel mannen denken dat iedereen met een boezem een idioot is, zei mijn moeder altijd. Het is het slimste om ze maar in die waan te laten tot je ze allemaal het tegendeel kunt bewijzen.

Ik was dol op mijn moeder, niet in de laatste plaats omdat vader, elke keer als ze een woord als 'boezem' in het openbaar gebruikte, met zijn ogen rolde en met een theatraal gebaar naar zijn hart greep.

De gedachte aan mijn ouders kikkerde me op. Ik stapte op de tweede verdieping uit, liep de gang uit en ging de trappen op. Boven stond ik even stil om mijn neus te poederen en een verdwaalde pluk haar achter mijn oor te duwen, en ik probeerde niet al te onzeker te worden bij de aanblik van een grote, ingelijste afbeelding van een nogal strenge heer met wit haar en krachtige wenkbrauwen. Ik herkende hem onmiddellijk. Het was Lord Overton, miljonair, filantroop en eigenaar van Launceston Press. Hij en zijn vrouw waren altijd in het nieuws vanwege hun liefdadigheidswerk en ik bewonderde hen reusachtig.

Even verloor ik bijna de moed. Ik aarzelde bij de dubbele zwaaideur die naar mevrouw Bird en naar mijn sollicitatie leidde.

Diep ademhalen, schouders naar achteren.

Ik duwde de deuren open en liep een smalle, donkere gang in. Het leek totaal niet op de indrukwekkende entreehal beneden. Zoals ik al gehoord had, was hier geen receptioniste. Voor me was een rij deuren, op twee na allemaal dicht, en op het gedempte geluid van een typemachine na was het hier stil. Hier geen drukke nieuwskamer vol mannen zoals die twee in de lift. Maar misschien was iedereen buiten aan het verslaggeven.

Ik omklemde mijn handtas en zag dat er een eindje verderop, links, een deur half open stond; ik vroeg me af of een bescheiden 'Hallo daar' te brutaal zou zijn om mee te beginnen.

Dat idee verwierp ik. Ik besloot op een van de deuren te kloppen. Als ik deze baan zou krijgen, zou ik misschien wel naar Amerika moeten bellen om te vragen of ze me wilden doorverbinden met het Witte Huis. Dit was geen plaats voor angsthazen.

Op de deur van het kantoor aan mijn rechterhand was een kaartje geplakt met daarop in een keurig handschrift 'juffrouw Knighton'. Op de muur ernaast hing een ingelijste modeprent van een vrouw die een poedel uitliet en daar zo te zien grenzeloos opgewekt van werd. Ik snapte niet wat dat met belangrijke wereldgebeurtenissen te maken had. Maar goed, over smaak valt niet te twisten. Op de tegenovergelegen muur hing een soortgelijke prent; alleen stond daar een vrouw met een zomerjurk aan hartelijk te lachen om een jong katje.

Ik fronste mijn wenkbrauwen. Ik was dol op dieren, maar wat moest een belangrijke krant in deze zware tijden met zulke plaatjes? Een portret van de koning of van iemand uit het oorlogskabinet zou toch veel gepaster zijn?

Misschien betekende het dat de mensen hier vrolijke types waren. Maar vrolijk of niet, het was nog steeds akelig stil.

'JUFFROUW KNIGHTON!' bulderde een man achter de andere, half geopende deur. 'JUFFROUW KNIGHTON! O, in vredesnaam...

JUFFROUW KNIGHTON! Waar hangt ze nu weer uit? Ik praat blijkbaar tegen dovemansoren. GEEN PROBLEEM; IK DOE HET ZELF WEL!'

Er klonk wat gerommel en daarna een klap.

Toen een krachtterm, gevolgd door: 'Idioot!'

'Hallo?' riep ik en zette koers in de richting van het lawaai. 'Gaat het? Kan ik u misschien helpen?'

'Natuurlijk gaat het. Kathleen, ben jij dat? Wacht even.'

Er klonk geschuifel en daarna struikelde een magere heer van ergens in de veertig de gang in. Hij was keurig gekleed, met een tweed pantalon en bijpassend mouwloos vest over zijn overhemd, maar zijn aanblik was bepaald slonzig. Zijn hemdsmouwen waren opgerold, zijn bruine haar moest nodig geknipt worden en zijn handen zaten onder de zwarte inkt.

Dit was beslist een journalist. Wat spannend! Hij keek nogal moordlustig, maar dat hoorde er waarschijnlijk bij.

De journalist, die zichzelf niet voorstelde maar me woedend aankeek omdat ik juffrouw Knighton niet was, veegde zijn haar uit zijn ogen en smeerde tegelijkertijd zijn hele voorhoofd vol inkt. Fatsoenshalve deed ik alsof dat me niet opviel.

'HOE MAAKT U HET?' vroeg ik luidkeels – als ik zenuwachtig ben, heb ik de neiging te schreeuwen. 'Ik ben Emmeline Lake. Ik heb een sollicitatiegesprek met mevrouw Bird.'

'Nee toch.' Hij keek me enigszins gealarmeerd aan. 'Nu al?'

Ik probeerde enthousiast, maar intelligent te glimlachen. Hij leek in elk geval te weten dat ik zou komen.

'Om twee uur,' zei ik in een poging behulpzaam te zijn.

'Juist, ja. Nou, ik ben bang dat ze er niet is. Ze is er natuurlijk nooit, dat is een voordeel. Tel je zegeningen, en zo. Waarschijnlijk is ze bij het een of andere goede doel dingen aan het organiseren tot ze erbij neervallen, maar ja, zo gaat dat.'

Hij hield op met praten. Mijn mond was opengevallen van verbazing.

'Juist,' zei ik in een poging positief te blijven.

'Dus u bent hier voor het sollicitatiegesprek, juffrouw…'

'Lake. Ja. Maar ik kan wel wachten, als dat helpt.' Ik keek om me heen op zoek naar een plek om te gaan zitten, maar de gang was leeg.

'O, dat is geen probleem,' zei hij, niet onvriendelijk. 'Ik ben bang dat u het met mij zult moeten doen. Maar mijn handen zitten onder de inkt…' Hij zei een lelijk woord.

Ik besloot niet te melden dat de inkt ook op zijn gezicht zat, voor het geval hem dat sterkere termen zou ontlokken, grabbelde in mijn tas en bood hem mijn zakdoek aan. Mijn moeder had er een bloem en mijn initialen op geborduurd; het was een kerstcadeautje.

'Dank u wel. Ramp afgewend!' Hij begon vol overgave mijn moeders handwerk te bederven. 'Mooi. Nou, kom dan maar binnen.'

Ik volgde hem zijn kantoor in en zag in het voorbijgaan het versleten naambordje op de deur.

Dhr. Collins
Hoofdartikelen & Algemene Redactie

'Kijk uit, het zit overal,' zei meneer Collins, en ik baande me een weg door de rommeligste kamer die ik ooit gezien had.

Hij perste zichzelf achter een bureau waarop zich hoge stapels boeken en kranten bevonden, samen met een overvolle asbak en de zo ongelukkig omgevallen inktpot. Het hele tafereel kreeg een dramatisch tintje door het felle licht van de enige lamp in de kamer, een verstelbare bureaulamp die eruitzag alsof hij opgevorderd was bij een verbeurdverklaarde fabriek van medische hulpmiddelen.

Ik zag een lichtblauw inktvloeiblok op de grond liggen,

bukte om het op te rapen, en overhandigde het hem alsof het mijn getuigschrift was.

'Aha, mooi. Ja.' Met een ontmoedigd gezicht begon hij de gemorste inkt op te deppen.

Na een paar seconden – ik had intussen om me heen gekeken en vroeg me af of journalisten altijd halflege flessen sterkedrank als boekensteun gebruikten – zuchtte hij diep, gaf de moed op en keek me doordringend aan.

'Juist,' zei hij. 'Laten we dit afhandelen. Goed. Juffrouw Emmeline Lake. Hier prompt om twee uur aanwezig om bij mevrouw Bird te solliciteren. Eigenares van een kleine, maar op dit moment hogelijk gewaardeerde zakdoek...'

Ondanks al zijn gestuntel was de redacteur hoofdartikelen blijkbaar niets ontgaan.

'Vertel eens,' zei hij, 'wat bezielde u in vredesnaam om hier te willen werken?'

Zo had ik me het begin van het sollicitatiegesprek niet voorgesteld.

'Nou,' zei ik en herinnerde me hoe Bunty en ik dit gesprek thuis geoefend hadden. 'Ik ben zeer hardwerkend en ik kan vijfenzestig woorden per minuut typen en honderdvijfentwintig woorden per minuut stenograferen...'

Meneer Collins gaapte, wat me even van mijn stuk bracht, maar ik zette door.

'Volgens mijn referenties ben ik bijzonder capabel en...'

Hij deed zijn ogen even dicht.

Ik probeerde wat meer gewicht in de schaal te leggen. 'De afgelopen tweeënhalf jaar heb ik op een advocatenbureau gewerkt, dus...'

'Laat maar zitten,' zei hij. 'Ter zake nu.'

Ik zette me schrap voor een mondelinge overhoring over de meest effectieve leden van de regering.

'Bent u snel bang?'

Dat was gelukkig meteen ter zake. Ik zag mezelf al tijdens

een luchtaanval door Londen stormen om mensen te interviewen en probeerde niet al te enthousiast te kijken.

'Volgens mij niet,' zei ik, mijn eigen – naar ik hoopte – onmetelijke moed onder moeilijke omstandigheden bagatelliserend.

'Hm. We zullen zien. Goed in dictaat opnemen?'

Oftewel: als een schaduw achter een topcorrespondent aan lopen en elk woord noteren, speurend naar zaken van nationaal belang.

'Absoluut. Honderd...'

'... vijfentwintig woorden per minuut, ja, dat zei u al.'

Meneer Collins raakte niet bepaald in vervoering. Zelf zou ik het ongetwijfeld ook saai vinden om assistenten te ondervragen als ik zelf redacteur hoofdartikelen was en me in het zweet zat te werken in een race tegen de klok om de dodelijke deadlines te halen. Geen wonder dat zijn kantoor een troep was. Het viel vast niet mee om de boel in het gareel te houden met die onbetrouwbare juffrouw Knighton. Hij moest uitgeput zijn.

Mijn gedachten dwaalden af. Misschien zou dit mijn baan worden... Meneer Collins helpen zijn Deadlines te halen. Opschrijven wat mensen-die-het-weten-konden zeiden, terwijl hij hen aan een genadeloze ondervraging onderwierp om het allerbeste nieuws te pakken te krijgen. Hem eraan herinneren dat hij om drie uur een geheime vergadering met een parlementair secretaris had.

'Dat betekent in essentie: kunt u overweg met ruziezoekende oude vrouwen – akelige oude tangen, om precies te zijn?'

Ik besefte dat ik niet had opgelet.

Wat was het verband tussen oude tangen en *The Chronicle*? Ik dacht aan mijn grootmoeder, die volgens mijn vader sinds het begin van de vorige oorlog niet meer geglimlacht had.

'O ja,' zei ik vol zelfvertrouwen. 'Ik kan heel goed overweg met akelige oude... eh... met dat soort mensen.'

Meneer Collins trok een van zijn wenkbrauwen op en glimlachte bijna, maar blijkbaar bedacht hij zich. Hij voelde in zijn vestzakje en viste daar een sigarettenetui uit.

'Juist,' zei hij en leunde op zijn elleboog terwijl hij een sigaret opstak. Hij nam een flinke trek en trok een grimas. 'Nou, juffrouw Lake, u lijkt me aardig genoeg.'

Ik probeerde niet te laten merken dat ik me gevleid voelde.

'Weet u zeker dat u dit wilt? De vorige assistent is maar een week gebleven. En die daarvoor haalde de middag niet eens. Let wel, dat was deels mijn fout.' Hij zweeg even. 'Mij is verteld dat ik bij gelegenheid schreeuw,' voegde hij er ter verduidelijking aan toe.

'Daar klopt vast niets van,' loog ik, denkend aan de misthoornachtige geluiden waarmee hij juffrouw Knighton geroepen had. 'Trouwens, het doet geen zeer.'

'Hm?'

'Schelden doet geen zeer,' waagde ik. 'Slaan zoveel te meer.'

Meneer Collins keek me weer aan, en ik had het gevoel dat hij iets dacht wat hij me niet wilde vertellen. Uiteindelijk kneep hij zijn lippen op elkaar en knikte.

'Ik denk dat u het misschien wel aan zou kunnen,' zei hij na een korte stilte. 'Ja, ik denk dat u het echt wel aan zou kunnen. Wanneer kunt u beginnen?'

Als ik hem niet verkeerd verstaan had, was dit de mooiste dag van mijn leven. Hij had me dan wel niet bevraagd op de onderwerpen waarop ik al dagen had zitten studeren, maar alle inzichtelijke vragen die ik had willen stellen, waren als sneeuw voor de zon verdwenen toen hij het woord 'beginnen' gebruikte.

'Sjonge,' zei ik, waarmee ik niet bepaald een ontwikkelde, wereldwijze indruk maakte. Ik probeerde het nog een keer. 'Dank u wel, meneer. Heel hartelijk bedankt. Ik kan meteen mijn ontslag aanbieden, als dat de bedoeling is. Is dat goed?'

Nu zag ik een zweem van een glimlach. 'Dat zou ik wel zeggen,' zei hij. 'Al zult u me misschien niet meer bedanken als u hier eenmaal bent, weet u.'

Ik durf te wedden van wel, dacht ik, maar dat zei ik niet, want het enige wat telde, was dat ik nu echt bijna tot het personeel van een beroemde krant behoorde. Meneer Collins leek me een ironisch type en zijn waarschuwingen hoorden vast en zeker gewoon bij zijn manier van doen.

'Dank u wel, meneer Collins,' zei ik terwijl we elkaar de hand schudden. 'Ik beloof dat ik u niet zal teleurstellen.'

3

Hoogachtend, Mevr. H. Bird

Achteraf bekeken was het toch een beetje een vergissing dat ik meneer Collins geen enkele vraag gesteld had over de baan. Maar vanwege het 'Juffrouw Knighton'-gebulder, de vragen naar het overweg-kunnen-met-oude-tangen en de ontzaglijke sensatie dat ik me nu echt in een uitgeverij bevond, was het me helemaal ontschoten. Toen ik drie weken later, enigszins nerveus, in mijn nieuwe bruin geruite mantelpakje, waarvoor ik een van mijn moeders oude mantelpakjes had laten vermaken, en gewapend met mijn favoriete vulpen, drie nieuwe potloden en een reservezakdoek in mijn tas arriveerde om te beginnen, ontstond er dan ook enige verwarring.

Ik had mijn baan bij Strawman verlaten – met veel goede wensen van mijn werkgevers en instructies om hen niet te vergeten – en was naar Little Whitfield vertrokken om kerstfeest bij mijn ouders te vieren. Met mijn nieuwe baan in het vooruitzicht en de winkels die ondanks alles mooie etalages wisten te maken, was het een vrolijk kerstfeest geworden, ondanks het feit dat mijn broer Jack geen verlof had kunnen krijgen. Omdat het Kerst was, deden we allemaal alsof we daar niet verdrietig over waren en ons geen zorgen over hem maakten, en Tweede Kerstdag kwamen Bunty en haar oma op bezoek. Daar knapte iedereen van op. Ik had nog steeds niets van Edmund gehoord, maar gaf de moed niet op, want soms hoorde je wekenlang niets en daarna konden er ineens vier brieven tegelijk komen. Ik zou vast gauw bericht van hem krijgen, waarschijnlijk met een tekening van een kerstboom of een sneeuwtafereel, omdat Edmund zo graag tekende. Natuurlijk had ik hem over mijn nieuwe baan geschreven, en hoewel hij in het verleden de draak had gestoken met mijn droom om oorlogscorrespondente te worden, zou hij vast blij voor me zijn. Ik probeerde niet te piekeren over de vraag of hij zou willen dat ik ophield met werken als we eenmaal getrouwd waren. Aangezien we nog steeds geen datum voor de bruiloft hadden afgesproken, zette ik die gedachte maar snel van me af.

In Londen was het nieuwe jaar bitter koud begonnen. Daar hadden we niet bepaald behoefte aan, maar de meisjes van de brandweerkazerne rekenden erop dat de Luftwaffe, die de stad meteen na Kerst zwaar gebombardeerd had, nu door het weer afgeschrikt werd. Thelma wist zeker dat dit een heel goed teken was en Joan was ervan overtuigd dat de oorlog niet lang meer zou duren als de Duitsers door een beetje kou al ontmoedigd raakten.

Wat er ook gebeurde, niets kon mijn opperbeste humeur bederven toen ik bij Launceston Press arriveerde met in mijn hand beslist de wonderbaarlijkste brief ter wereld.

Launceston Press Ltd.,
Launceston House,
Londen EC4

Maandag 16 december 1940

Beste juffrouw Lake
Onder referte aan uw sollicitatiegesprek met

dhr. Collins bevestig ik uw aanstelling als parttime assistent met ingang van maandag 6 januari 1941.
U zult elke dag van negen uur tot één uur werken. Hierbij inbegrepen is een theepauze van tien minuten, maar geen lunchpauze.
Uw salaris zal negentien shilling per week bedragen en u zult ieder jaar zeven dagen betaald verlof krijgen als vakantie.
U dient zich bij mij, mevr. Bird, te melden om negen uur precies op de dag waarop uw tewerkstelling aanvangt.
Hoogachtend,

Mevr. H. Bird,
waarnemend redactrice

Waarnemend redactrice! Ik had er geen idee van gehad dat mevrouw Bird waarnemend redactrice was en dat mijn baan betekende dat ik voor zo'n belangrijk persoon zou werken. En dan ook nog een dame! Ik was enorm onder de indruk. Hoewel de meeste jongemannen opgeroepen waren door het leger, was het toch nog heel vooruitstrevend van *The Chronicle* om een vrouw de leiding te geven.

Ditmaal was ik meer enthousiast dan nerveus toen ik bij Launceston House aankwam. Het liefst zou ik alle trappen op gestormd zijn, met twee treden tegelijk, maar dat stonden mijn nette schoenen – en het decorum – natuurlijk niet toe. Daarom nam ik heel verstandig de lift naar de tweede verdieping en liep de overige trappen zo rustig mogelijk op om niet buiten adem aan te komen. Ik wist dat ik als assistent helemaal onderaan begon, maar dat vond ik helemaal niet erg. Ik zag voor me dat ik goede maatjes zou worden met energieke types, met wie ik het nieuws van de dag zou bespreken. Tegelijkertijd zou ik bewonderenswaardig hard werken, typend dat de stukken ervanaf vlogen of onmogelijk snelle dictaten opnemend. Misschien zou ik – als de tijd rijp was – een idee voor een nieuwsartikel opperen, of kon ik, mocht iemand zo ongelukkig zijn ziek te worden, voor diegene invallen op een gruwelijke plaats delict of tijdens een luchtaanval midden in de nacht.

Ik arriveerde op de vierde verdieping, geestdriftig, maar klaar om meteen teruggestuurd te worden naar de grotere, lichtere verdiepingen van het gebouw, waar het kantoor van mevr. Bird moest zijn. Mij maakte het niets uit, al moest ik in een bezemkast zitten, maar de waarnemend redactrice had vast en zeker een heel belangrijk kantoor, met misschien zelfs een aantal vertrekken.

Nadat ik de dubbele deur opengeduwd had, werd ik begroet door een lege gang. Ik had verwacht dat het in de kantoren een drukte van belang zou zijn op maandagochtend; tenslotte was er genoeg nieuws om verslag van te doen. Het hoorde waarschijnlijk bij mijn werk om behoorlijk akelige kopij te moeten uittypen, maar die gedachte duwde ik weg. Dat was wel het minste wat ik kon doen.

Tot mijn vreugde concludeerde ik dat juffrouw Knighton aanwezig was, want de deur van haar kantoor stond op een kiertje en ik hoorde haar typemachine – ze typte vreselijk snel.

Ik nam het risico iets van 'vitaal belang' te onderbreken en klopte op haar deur.

'Hallo,' zei ik en tuurde de piepkleine ruimte in. 'Het spijt me dat ik u lastigval, maar ik ben de nieuwe assistent. Zou u me alstublieft kunnen vertellen op welke verdieping ik moet zijn voor mevrouw Bird?'

Juffrouw Knighton, een sproetig meisje van mijn leeftijd, met mooie groene ogen en betreurenswaardig haar, keek me uitdrukkingloos aan.

'Verdieping?'

'Ja, op welke verdieping is haar kantoor?'

'Eh...' Ze zweeg even, alsof het een strikvraag was. 'Deze.'

Juffrouw Knighton leek me eigenlijk te jong om een excentriekeling te zijn, maar ik zei: 'Puik', want ik was nieuw en je maakt geen vrienden door afstandelijk te doen.

'Aan de overkant van de gang,' vervolgde ze. 'De deur zonder naambordje. Dat is er vorige week af gevallen en niemand is eraan toegekomen om het weer op te hangen.' Dat laatste vertelde ze fluisterend, alsof dit de vreselijkste misdaad was.

Plotseling hoorden we het geluid van een deur die krachtig opengegooid werd; juffrouw Knighton sprong bijna van haar stoel van schrik en begon daarna nog sneller te typen dan tevoren. Dat leek me een hint, dus ik vloog het kamertje uit en botste meteen tegen degene die de deur geopend had op.

'Goeie genade,' zei ik terwijl ik een stap achteruit deed en opkeek naar de dreigende gestalte. 'Het spijt me verschrikkelijk.'

'En terecht,' zei de vrouw. 'Dat was mijn voet.'

Ik keek naar beneden, naar een volmaakt gepoetste, stevige schoen met mijn voetafdruk erop, en probeerde niet ineen te krimpen. Ik had haar onmiddellijk herkend. Dit was de opmerkelijke dame die me op de dag van mijn sollicitatiegesprek op de stoep van het gebouw bijna onder de voet gelopen had. Uitgedost met dezelfde hoed-met-veer en met ongeveer dezelfde gezichtsuitdrukking als meneer Churchill vertoonde in het bioscoopjournaal als Hitler hem had lopen vervelen.

Ze leek mij ook te herkennen, wat mij nog minder reden tot optimisme gaf. Ik keek weer naar haar schoen en overwoog een aanval van hysterie voor te wenden.

'Het spijt me echt heel erg,' zei ik. 'Mijn naam is Emmeline Lake. Ik kom voor mevrouw Bird.'

Nu liet ik mijn voorzichtigheid varen en glimlachte bemoedigend. Waarschijnlijk kwam ik over als een onnozele ziel.

‘Ik ben mevrouw Bird,’ kondigde de vrouw aan.

‘Hoe maakt u het?’ vroeg ik met een klein stemmetje en probeerde tegelijkertijd verbazing, enthousiasme en enorm respect uit te drukken.

Mevrouw Bird bekeek me alsof ik zojuist van de maan gekomen was. Ze was een opvallende vrouw van achter in de zestig, met een rechthoekig hoofd, een angstaanjagend vierkante kin en donkergrijs, golvend haar. Ze leek een beetje op koningin Victoria op haar oude dag, maar dan nog nijdiger. Het was moeilijk om niet bang te worden.

‘Juffrouw Lake, stelt u zich altijd voor door mensen te verwonden? Wacht hier,’ voegde ze eraan toe voordat ik een antwoord kon bedenken. ‘Deze jas is te warm.’

Indrukwekkend mobiel voor een vrouw van haar formaat en haar leeftijd draaide ze zich op haar hakken om, marcheerde het tegenoverliggende kantoor in en trok de deur stevig achter zich dicht.

Met bonzend hart bleef ik in de ijskoude gang staan.

‘U mag binnenkomen!’ bulderde ze even later door de deur heen, zoals mensen doen die geen megafoon willen gebruiken omdat ze dat een teken van zwakte vinden.

Ik haalde diep adem en stelde me een kamer voor met een kolossaal mahoniehouten bureau en een manhaftig buffet vol zilveren presenteerbladen en kristallen karaffen om met de journalisten te proosten als iemand een ‘geweldige primeur’ binnenhaalde. Maar dat had ik helemaal mis. De kamer was even groot als het kantoor van meneer Collins, maar dan met een raam en zonder de anarchistisch aandoende rommel. Mevrouw Bird troonde niet op een kolossale leren stoel achter een schitterend bureau, maar zat gewoon achter een ordinair houten geval.

Het raam, dat de helft van de achtermuur besloeg, stond wijd open, ondanks het feit dat het januari was, en ijskoude buitenlucht kwam met vlagen binnen. Dit leek mevrouw

Bird niet in het minst te deren. Ze had zich al ontdaan van haar jas en hoed; die namen nu een staande kapstok in de hoek van de kamer in beslag.

Op een grote stalen archiefkast en twee stoelen voor stenotypistes na was de kamer uitgesproken sober; bijna niets getuigde ervan dat een vrouw hier de scepter zwaaide over de drukte van een dagblad. Het bureau was bijna helemaal kaal; erop prijkten slechts een onaangeraakt inktvloeiblok met een omlijsting van groen leer, een telefoon en een grote ingelijste foto van mevrouw Bird voor een decoratief meer. Ze was informeel gekleed in een dik wollen kostuum, ze droeg leren handschoenen en werd omringd door een grote groep jachthonden, die stuk voor stuk vol stomme devotie naar haar opkeken.

'Aha,' zei mevrouw Bird. 'U hebt de kerels ontdekt. Simpele zielen.'

Aan mevrouw Birds gezicht was duidelijk te zien dat ze iedereen die er ook maar aan dacht die beesten aan te raken met haar blote handen zou vermoorden. 'Totale sukkels,' voegde ze eraan toe. Haar borstkas zwol van trots.

'Zijn ze allemaal van u, mevrouw Bird?' vroeg ik, erop gespitst iets van mijn verloren terrein te herwinnen.

'Inderdaad,' zei ze. 'Eén goede raad, juffrouw Lake.' Ze leunde naar voren, wat nogal alarmerend was. 'Honden zijn net kinderen. Lawaaiig, opvoedbaar, maar dom, en geneigd om onaangenaam te ruiken zodra er gasten komen.' Ze fronste haar wenkbrauwen. 'Ik heb er acht.'

Ik keek weer naar de foto.

'Hónden,' snauwde mevrouw Bird ter verduidelijking. 'Wat kinderen betreft, is vier ruimschoots voldoende. Met meer komt men in de arbeidersklasse of in het katholicisme terecht.'

Ik knikte, hoewel ik niet helemaal zeker wist wat het meest gepaste antwoord zou zijn. Maar mevrouw Bird was al op een ander onderwerp overgegaan.

'Als we in Duitsland waren, zouden de kerels natuurlijk allemaal afgemaakt zijn. Vijftig centimeter schofthoogte. Groter dan dat, tenzij het Duitse herders zijn: vermoord.' Ze sloeg met haar vuist op het bureau.

'Wat vreselijk,' zei ik en ik dacht aan Brian, de Deense dog van mijn tante Tiny, waar we allemaal dol op waren. Ik vroeg me af of hij het erg zou vinden om te leren kruipen.

'Zo zijn de nazi's,' zei mevrouw Bird dreigend.

Ik knikte weer. De Führer had geen idee tegen wie hij het hier zou moeten opnemen.

'Goed.' Mevrouw Bird schraapte haar keel. 'Genoeg gebabbeld. Juffrouw Lake. Ik begrijp dat u ervaring hebt bij tijdschriften?'

Het zou een beetje ongeloofwaardig zijn om de *Little Whitfield Gazette* als 'tijdschriften' te bestempelen.

'Niet echt,' zei ik. 'Maar ik wil al eeuwen voor een krant werken. Ik hoop op een dag oorlogscorrespondent te worden.'

Nu speelde ik open kaart. Ik voelde me behoorlijk dapper.

'Oorlog?' bulderde mevrouw Bird alsof dit als een donderslag bij heldere hemel kwam, terwijl heel Londen zich dag in, dag uit schrap zette bij het geluid van vijandelijk vuur. 'Daar willen we niet over doorzeuren. U weet toch dat u alleen brieven gaat typen, of niet?'

Ik keek verbijsterd.

'Meneer Collins heeft u toch verteld wat uw rol is?' Mevrouw Bird fronste haar wenkbrauwen en tikte geïrriteerd met haar rechterwijsvinger op het bureau.

Ik aarzelde. Nu ik erover nadacht: nee, dat had hij niet verteld.

'Brieven typen,' zei ik, meer omdat ik hardop nadacht dan als antwoord op de vraag.

'Precies. En natuurlijk alle andere typewerkzaamheden waarvoor ik u nodig zou kunnen hebben.'

'Typen,' zei ik weer.

Mevrouw Bird keek naar me alsof ik een idioot was, en ik had het akelige gevoel dat ze daar weleens gelijk in kon hebben.

'Alleen typen. Niet, eh... de verslaggevers helpen?'

Door het raam kwam weer een ijskoude windvlaag binnen.

'Verslaggevers? Bespottelijk,' snauwde mevrouw Bird. 'U bent assistent-typiste, juffrouw Lake. Ik begrijp niet wat daar verwarrend aan is.'

Ik dacht razendsnel na. Hier klopte iets niet. Niet dat ik iets tegen typen had; in feite had ik al verwacht dat ik dat veel zou doen.

Ik haalde diep adem. Ik wilde meneer Collins niet de eerste dag al teleurstellen. Ik had het tenslotte aan hem te danken dat ik hier was. Dus vermande ik me. Als het werk een beetje minder spannend was dan ik gehoopt had, was dat geen probleem. Ik was nog steeds bij *The London Evening Chronicle.* Ik maakte nog steeds mijn entree in de wereld van de journalistiek. Misschien zou het een beetje langer duren dan ik verwacht had, maar dan moest ik maar gewoon nog harder werken.

'Ja, mevrouw Bird,' zei ik en ik probeerde energiek te klinken. 'Nee. Ja. Absoluut.'

Ik voelde me verre van energiek.

Mevrouw Bird bleef met haar vinger tikken. 'Hm,' zei ze. 'We zullen zien hoe u het doet. Juffrouw Knighton zal u wegwijs maken. U moet de vertrouwelijkheidsovereenkomst vandaag ondertekenen, en geen getreuzel bij het lezen van de brieven. Geen woord erover buiten dit kantoor en bij het eerste teken van onaangenaamheden gaat het de prullenbak in. Is dat duidelijk?'

'Doen we,' zei ik krachtig, al had ik geen flauw idee wat ze bedoelde. Van de woorden 'vertrouwelijkheidsovereenkomst' en 'onaangenaamheden' kikkerde ik toch ook weer op. Dat klonk opwindend. Ze mocht er dan niet van houden om over de oorlog door te zeuren, maar het was duidelijk dat ze met behoorlijk sterk nieuws te maken kreeg.

'Mooi zo. Als u niet voor mij aan het werk bent, zult u meneer Collins helpen. Juffrouw Knighton zal wel aangeven wanneer u gemist kunt worden.' Mevrouw Bird zette een strenge blik op. 'U zult merken dat ik het bijzonder druk heb. Dit is niet mijn enige taak.'

'Natuurlijk,' zei ik vol eerbied. 'Dank u wel.'

Ze wierp een blik op haar polshorloge. 'Ik moet opschieten. Goedemorgen, juffrouw Lake.'

Bijna had ik een knicksje voor haar gemaakt, maar ik herinnerde me net op tijd dat mevrouw Bird niet mijn schooldirectrice was; ik trok me terug in de gang.

Het was bepaald anders dan verwacht allemaal. Maar dan nog...

Vertrouwelijkheidsovereenkomst. Geen woord erover buiten dit kantoor. We zullen zien hoe u het doet.

Het was nog steeds de spannendste dag die ik ooit beleefd had.

'Ik heet Kathleen,' zei juffrouw Knighton verlegen toen ik weer in haar kantoortje stond. 'Ik hoop dat we vriendinnen worden.'

Kathleen was opgewekt en intelligent, al fluisterde ze bijna de hele tijd en was het moeilijk voor te stellen hoe ze die bulderende mevrouw Bird het hoofd kon bieden. Haar krullende rode haar leek te stuiteren terwijl ze sprak; het stak aan alle kanten wijd uit, zodat je de indruk kreeg dat ze met haar vingers in een stopcontact klem gezeten had.

'Dank je wel,' zei ik. 'Dat hoop ik ook. Noem me alsjeblieft Emmy. Wat een prachtig vest heb je aan.'

'Dat heb ik dit weekend gebreid,' zei ze stralend en daarna keek ze zenuwachtig in de richting van de deur. 'Is mevrouw Bird weggegaan? Want ze houdt niet van geklets.' Ze trok een bezorgd gezicht. 'Ik val altijd in als iemand niet blijft, dus ik kan je wegwijs maken. Dat is jouw bureau.'

Kathleens gehavende eikenhouten bureau stond recht tegenover de deur en het mijne stond daar vlak achter. Naast elk bureau, zo dichtbij dat je je er maar net tussendoor kon wringen om op je stoel te komen, stond een hoge houten kast met archiefladen. Kathleen had een pot met een plant op haar kast gezet, die enigszins belemmerend werkte op mijn uitzicht: een prikbord met een maandkalender waarop elke donderdag omkringeld was, verschillende tijdschriftfoto's van wollen kledingstukken en een lijst namen met telefoonnummers. Op beide bureaus stonden drie gestapelde houten brievenbakjes en een typemachine. De mijne was enorm groot, oud en groen; het merk *Corona* stond in gouden letters op de voorkant. Ze had maar drie rijen toetsen en zag eruit alsof er een stormram voor nodig was om ermee te typen. Ik wist vrij zeker dat dit apparaat nu al voor de tweede keer een oorlog meemaakte, dus ik nam maar aan dat het een heel degelijk ding was.

Ik ging zitten en haalde mijn potloden tevoorschijn.

'Kathleen, wat voor soort artikelen schrijft mevrouw Bird?' vroeg ik.

Kathleen keek verward. 'Wat voor soort artikelen?' herhaalde ze. 'Het is "mevróúw Bírd,"' voegde ze eraan toe, op een toon alsof ik een beetje achterlijk was.

'Nou ja,' zei ik, 'ze zei iets over geen woord buiten het kantoor.' Ik ging zachter praten. 'Is haar werk strikt geheim?'

Je kon wel zien dat Kathleen gewend was aan mensen die vragen stelden over gevoelige informatie. Haar gezicht bleef volkomen uitdrukkingloos. 'Wat?'

Dit meisje was echt professioneel. De vertrouwelijkheid bleef volkomen intact.

'Natuurlijk begrijp ik dat we het waarschijnlijk niet mogen zeggen,' zei ik terwijl ik steeds meer voor mijn nieuwe baan ging voelen. 'De muren hebben oren, zelfs hier.'

Kathleen fronste haar wenkbrauwen en trok rimpels in haar neus. Ze zag eruit als iemand die een buitengewoon moeilijke som uit haar hoofd moest uitrekenen. Ik was helemaal voor geheimhouding, maar ik hoopte dat we dit niet te allen tijde hoefden vol te houden, want het was nogal ingewikkeld om zo ook maar iets verder te komen met het gesprek.

'Sjonge,' zei ze uiteindelijk. 'Ik snap wel waarom jij de baan gekregen hebt. Jij bent echt heel goed met vertrouwelijke informatie.'

Ik voelde mijn gezicht een beetje warm worden bij dit compliment.

'Nou,' zei ik heldhaftig, 'ik doe mijn best.'

'Je moet de overeenkomst natuurlijk nog wel tekenen.' Ze wroette wat rond in een la. 'Alsjeblieft.'

Bliksemsnel pakte ik mijn nieuwe vulpen uit mijn tas en zette mijn naam op het document. Daarna begon ik te lezen wat er allemaal stond.

> **Ik, ... (naam invullen), verklaar hierbij dat ik als werknemer van Launceston Press Ltd. alle correspondentie van lezeressen van *Vrouw & Vriendin* met uiterste vertrouwelijkheid zal behandelen. Ik verklaar dat ik de inhoud van brieven niet zal doorvertellen aan iemand anders dan aan permanente stafleden van *Vrouw & Vriendin*...**

Helaas, Kathleen had me de verkeerde overeenkomst gegeven.

'Gommie,' zei ik. 'Het spijt me echt, maar dit lijkt over *Vrouw & Vriendin* te gaan, wat dat ook is.'

'Ja.' Ze schonk me een brede, bemoedigende glimlach. 'Maak je geen zorgen; het gaat er echt alleen maar om dat je niet overal moet rondvertellen waar de lezers over schrijven. Mevrouw Bird is daar heel streng in.' Ze zweeg even. 'Sommige dingen zijn vreselijk persoonlijk, dat kun je je wel voorstellen.'

Ik beantwoordde haar glimlach, maar ik kon me helemaal niets voorstellen.

Kathleen vatte mijn zwijgzaamheid op als bezorgdheid. 'Maak je geen zorgen, Emmy,' zei ze. 'Mevrouw Bird zal nooit iets pikants beantwoorden, dus je zult niet in een ongemakkelijke situatie terechtkomen.'

Ik keek naar een boekenplank rechts van Kathleen. Die lag vol met stapels tijdschriften. Het begon tot me door te dringen dat een van ons het weleens bij het verkeerde eind zou kunnen hebben.

'Kathleen,' zei ik, 'wat doet mevrouw Bird precies?'

Ze lachte en pakte een kleurig tijdschrift van een van de stapels.

'Je hebt toch weleens gehoord van "Henriëtta Bird weet raad"? Ze was al een beroemdheid bij *Vrouw & Vriendin* voordat jij en ik geboren werden.' Ze leunde voorover en overhandigde mij het blad. 'De een na laatste pagina.'

'Het spijt me,' zei ik, nog steeds vol onbegrip. 'Wat heeft "Henriëtta Bird weet raad" te maken met *The Evening Chronicle*?'

Kathleen lachte weer, maar hield toen opeens op en hapte naar adem. 'O, nee! Je dacht toch niet dat dit een baantje bij *The Chronicle* was? Goeie grutten, dat dacht je wel!'

'Maar dit ís *The Evening Chronicle*,' zei ik met meer hoop dan overtuiging.

'Nee. Zij zitten beneden. In het chique gedeelte. Wij zijn

allebei eigendom van Launceston Press, maar zij praten nooit met ons. Wij zijn de ongelukkige, arme tak van de familie.' Ze bleef er opmerkelijk opgewekt onder. 'Goeie grutten. Ik heb die advertentie voor mevrouw Bird opgesteld. Daar stond het niet echt in, of wel?'

Ik keek naar de voorkant van het tijdschrift. Daar stond het, apetrots, met afschuwelijke, ouderwetse letters:

VROUW & VRIENDIN
Weekblad voor de moderne vrouw

Haak uw eigen toilettafelkleedje.
Snoezig patroon ingesloten!

Onder de kop stond een krullerige tekening van een kanten kleedje. De rest van de omslag werd in beslag genomen door een foto van een vrouw die een ontstellend grote zuigeling vasthield, en een cirkel met daarin de tekst: 'Zuster McClay zegt: "Doe dat raam open en geef kindlief wat lucht!"'

Dat was nogal een stevige benadering voor in januari, maar ik was natuurlijk geen expert op dat gebied.

'Mevrouw Bird is meer dan twintig jaar de meest geliefde adviezenschrijfster van *Vrouw & Vriendin* geweest,' legde Kathleen behulpzaam uit. 'Ze ging in 1932 met pensioen, maar Lord Overton heeft haar persoonlijk teruggevraagd toen onze redacteur vorig jaar opgeroepen werd.'

Lord Overton. Eigenaar van Launceston Press. Eigenaar van *The Evening Chronicle*. Heeft mevrouw Bird persoonlijk teruggevraagd.

Ik gaapte de reusachtige zuigeling aan.

'Emmy,' vervolgde Kathleen op de toon die je gebruikt voor mensen die niet helemaal honderd procent zijn, '*Vrouw & Vriendin* is een damesweekblad. Jouw baan is het uittypen van de brieven voor de adviesrubriek.'

Ik knikte, sprakeloos. Kathleen wachtte geduldig tot het tot me doorgedrongen was.

Eindelijk wist ik een hopelijk kranige 'helemaal tiptop'-glimlach op te brengen.

Maar het was allemaal verre van tiptop. Mijn moreel begon hopeloos te verpulveren.

Terwijl Kathleen aanbood me rond te leiden, probeerde ik goed na te denken. Niets leek minder op de eerste stap naar een journalistieke carrière dan dit. Van het achtervolgen van verslaggevers of het telefoneren met het Witte Huis was het lichtjaren verwijderd.

Ik had de verkeerde baan aangenomen.

4

Mevrouw Bird weet raad

Kathleen hield er flink de pas in tijdens haar wervelwindrondleiding langs de redactionele kantoren van *Vrouw & Vriendin*. Ik liep achter haar aan door de smalle, naargeestige gang en dacht verwoed na. Welke idioot gaf een prima baan bij een advocatenkantoor op om suffe brieven voor een damesblad uit te typen? En nog wel voor een damesblad dat, als ik mijn nieuwe collega goed begreep, op zijn laatste benen leek te lopen.

'Vroeger, toen *Vrouw & Vriendin* nog massa's exemplaren verkocht, hadden we veel meer journalisten en zat iedereen hier, maar nu niet meer, dus staat het leeg,' zei Kathleen terwijl we langs het kantoor van meneer Collins – dat volgens haar op slot was – liepen. Ze deed de volgende deur rechts open. 'De typistes hadden de kamer aan de andere kant van de gang. Maar nu zijn alleen jij en ik er nog.'

Ik keek de lange, smalle ruimte van de journalisten in, waar twee rijen verlaten bureaus stonden. Het dichtstbijzijnde bureau was volgestapeld met kartonnen dozen, wat beslist brandgevaarlijk was, maar alle andere bureaus waren helemaal leeg, zonder een spoor van typemachines, inktpotten of brievenbakjes. Aan de muren hingen rijen prikborden, sommige nog met uit weekbladen gescheurde artikelen erop geprikt, een aanwijzing dat dit ooit een rumoerig centrum van activiteit was. Sommige papiertjes begonnen langs de randen om te krullen en de kamer rook beschimmeld, naar een gekke combinatie van tabak en boterhammen met kaas en augurk.

'Hoelang is het geleden dat hier iemand werkte?' vroeg ik.

Kathleen sloeg haar armen over elkaar en staarde peinzend in het niets. 'Eeuwen.' Ze ging zachter praten. '*Vrouw & Vriendin* is niet erg bij de tijd gebleven. Het is een beetje ouderwets, denk ik. Al lees ik het wel altijd,' voegde ze eraan toe.

Ik knikte, nog somberder dan tevoren, en Kathleen babbelde verder.

'Bijna iedereen is bij het leger gegaan en niemand is ooit vervangen. Meneer Collins schrijft alle fictie en daar is hij ontzettend goed in. De rest laten ze door anderen opsturen, omdat dat goedkoper is. Hoe dan ook, laat me je iedereen voorstellen.'

Terwijl ze de gang weer in marcheerde, keek ik even op mijn horloge. Het was twintig over negen, maar meneer Collins was nergens te bekennen. Ik had het gevoel dat ik rondliep in een museum na sluitingstijd.

'Aan de andere kant van de gang is het advertentieteam. Dat is alleen meneer Newton.' Kathleen ging zachter praten terwijl ze doorliep naar de volgende deur. 'Hij is er vandaag niet. Hij heeft niet veel te doen, want zoveel adverteerders zijn er niet. En dit is de afdeling kunst. Hier worden de illustraties en de foto's van japonnen gemaakt.' Ze klopte op de volgende deur en liep binnen zonder op een reactie te wachten.

'Morgen, meneer Brand. Hoe gaat het met u? Dit is juffrouw Lake, onze nieuwe assistent.'

Ik liep achter haar aan het kantoor in, dat net als alle andere kantoren nogal somber was, maar er tenminste uitzag alsof er iets gebeurde. Een oudere man, met een dikke bril met schildpadmontuur op zijn neus en veel brillantine in het haar, was een prachtig tafereel aan het uittekenen van een man in marine-uniform, die een nogal zwak uitziende vrouw ondersteunde.

'Hoe maakt u het?' zei meneer Brand. 'We hebben gisteren nog gelachen.'

Dat was een ongebruikelijke groet, maar hij was overduidelijk een creatief type.

'Hoe maakt u het?' antwoordde ik. 'Neem me niet kwalijk… u hebt gisteren nog…?'

'Gelachen. Dat is het belangrijkste verhaal voor volgende week. Daar werk ik op dit moment aan.'

'Ik begrijp het,' zei ik en probeerde te kijken alsof ik het weten kon. 'Het is heel mooi.'

Meneer Brand straalde.

'En dit is mevrouw Mahoney,' zei Kathleen. Een mollige dame van middelbare leeftijd met een geruststellend gezicht zwaaide naar me van achter een stapel kolossale vellen papier.

'Hallo, juffrouw Lake,' zei ze. 'Ik ben de afdeling productie. Ik ben heel aardig, maar haal alstublieft uw deadlines.' Ze schonk me een bemoedigende glimlach toen ik 'Hallo' zei en daarna leidde Kathleen me weer de gang op.

Op de angstaanjagende mevrouw Bird na leek iedereen heel vriendelijk. Ik probeerde weer moed te vatten, maar de waarheid was afschuwelijk ontmoedigend. Terwijl de rest van het land Hitler het hoofd bood en alle mogelijke inspanning in de oorlog stak, zou ik de problemen van lezeressen en frivole verzonnen verhalen uittypen. Dat leek helemaal niet op het werken bij een krant. Had ik Edmund er maar niet over geschreven. Hij zou me zo'n sufferd vinden. En Bunty ook. En de meisjes van de brandweerkazerne – vooral vreselijke Vera in de A-wacht. Dit was een buitenkansje voor haar. Het was mijn verdiende loon; dan had ik maar niet moeten denken dat ik op weg was naar een dramatisch spannende carrière.

Terug in ons eigen kantoortje begon Kathleen het intercomsysteem uit te leggen en ik deed mijn uiterste best om te doen alsof ik leergierig was. Mijn kortstondige ervaring met het volume van mevrouw Bird leek erop te wijzen dat een intercom nauwelijks noodzakelijk was.

'Het eerste wat je moet doen,' zei Kathleen, 'is de post openmaken en de brieven op het bureau van mevrouw Bird leggen. Maar alleen de acceptabele brieven. Absoluut niets onfatsoenlijks.' Haar gezichtsuitdrukking werd bloedserieus.

Ik keek naar het tijdschrift dat ik opengeslagen op mijn bureau had laten liggen. Naast een rond 1915 genomen foto van een vastberaden mevrouw Bird, die op het punt leek te staan iemand een stomp te geven, stond een kort stukje kopij dat alles verklaarde.

> Mevrouw Henriëtta Bird weet raad
> Er bestaat geen probleem dat niet opgelost kan worden met gezond verstand en een sterke wil.
> Mevrouw Bird is altijd bereid om uw vragen te beantwoorden. Als u een vertrouwelijk antwoord via de post wilt ontvangen, sluit dan een aan uzelf geadresseerde en voldoende gefrankeerde envelop in, maar houd er rekening mee dat de postzak van mevrouw Bird vol is, dus er kan vertraging optreden.

Ik dacht aan Bunty die correspondentie uittypte op het ministerie van Oorlog. Daarmee vergeleken sneed dit niet bepaald hout.

'Ik zal het vast reuze druk krijgen,' zei ik opgewekt. 'Hoe groot is de postzak van mevrouw Bird precies?'

Kathleen haalde haar schouders op. 'Niet zo groot.'

'Maar er staat toch dat hij vol is?'

'O, dat hebben we erin gezet omdat alle andere tijdschriften dat ook doen. We krijgen niet zo veel brieven.'

'Juist,' zei ik en las in het tijdschrift een brief van iemand die zich 'Onzeker' noemde en die worstelde met dikke armen. Mevrouw Birds advies was kordaat.

Doe alsof uw armen de wieken van een vliegtuigpropeller zijn en zwaai ze met enige kracht rond boven uw hoofd.

Ik voelde me hopeloos terneergeslagen. Groot-Brittannië was nog geen vierendertig kilometer verwijderd van het zwaar gehavende Europa en *Vrouw & Vriendin* gaf zijn weinige resterende lezeressen advies over dikke armen. Ik had gedacht dat ik nu wel zo ongeveer bezig zou zijn met het uittypen van nieuws over Mussolini.

'Het belangrijkste,' zei Kathleen, nog steeds volkomen serieus, 'is dat mevrouw Bird geen brieven wil beantwoorden waar onaangenaamheden in voorkomen. Daar is ze volkomen duidelijk over.' Kathleen zweeg en keek even naar de deur. 'Mevrouw Bird zegt dat onze generatie alles ernstig heeft laten afglijden.' Even later voegde ze eraan toe: 'Mevrouw Bird wil daar niets mee te maken hebben. Zodra je iets ziet wat op de lijst van onacceptabele onderwerpen staat, moet je de brief weggooien.'

Ze trok een la van haar bureau open en rommelde daarin rond terwijl ik me verdiepte in een brief van een jonge lezeres die last had van ontstoken tandvlees. Mevrouw Bird had geantwoord dat dit haar eigen schuld was omdat ze snoepjes gegeten had en dat ze er maar mee moest leren leven. Dat was niet bepaald een meelevende reactie.

'Dus als iemand een onacceptabel probleem instuurt, wordt haar brief in stukken geknipt, en als ze een postzegel ingesloten heeft voor het antwoord, geven we die aan een van de "goede werken" van mevrouw Bird. Dat betekent:

haar liefdadigheidsinstellingen.' Kathleen wees op een grote kartonnen doos met 'Postzegels' erop geschreven en dook daarna weer de la in.

Ik las de volgende brief, afkomstig van een dame die drie evacués opgenomen had en hoewel het erg lieve kindjes waren, maakte ze zich zorgen omdat haar eigen kinderen nu begonnen te vloeken. Het verbaasde me niets dat mevrouw Bird niet dol was op vulgaire taal en haar antwoord was bijzonder raak.

Ik vroeg me af wat ze van mij zou vinden.

Beste mevr. Bird,
Ik heb per ongeluk een onzalige baan aangenomen, wat te wijten is aan het niet luisteren tijdens mijn sollicitatiegesprek.
Ik blijk nu op een zinkend schip te werken en brieven te moeten typen voor een dame die dwars door massieve muren heen kan schreeuwen.
Ben ik een vreselijke idioot geweest? Vertel me alstublieft wat ik moet doen.
Hoogachtend,
Meestal niet zo onnozel

Ik zag het antwoord helemaal voor me.

Beste Onnozel,
Dit is helemaal uw eigen schuld. Ik stel voor dat u ophoudt met jammeren en de schouders eronder zet.
Hoogachtend,
Henriëtta Bird

'Eureka,' zei Kathleen en overhandigde me een document met de titel 'VOOR MEVR. BIRD ONACCEPTABELE ONDERWERPEN'. Iemand had er met rode inkt de tekst 'HOOGST VERTROUWELIJK' op gestempeld.

Onderwerpen die niet gepubliceerd of beantwoord worden door mevr. Bird
(NB: lijst is niet exclusief en zal aangevuld worden indien nodig.)
Echtelijke omgang
Voorechtelijke omgang
Buitenechtelijke omgang
Lichamelijke omgang
Seksuele omgang in het algemeen (alle kwesties, vermeldingen, suggesties of resultaten van)
Illegale activiteiten
Politieke activiteiten en opinies
Religieuze activiteiten en opinies (m.u.v. vragen aangaande kerkelijke groeperingen en samenkomsten)
De oorlog (m.u.v. vragen aangaande rantsoenering, vrijwillige diensten, clubs en praktische zaken)
Koken

'Koken?'

Misschien had ik tijdens de lessen huishoudkunde op school iets bedreigends gemist, maar dit onderwerp leek nogal saai, naast buitenechtelijke relaties en illegale activiteiten.

'Doorsturen naar mevrouw Croft,' zei Kathleen. 'Zij schijft WAT DE POT SCHAFT. Dat gaat voornamelijk over de rantsoenering. Alsjeblieft.' Ze overhandigde me een klein stapeltje brieven. 'Voorzichtig maar. Sommige dingen vind je misschien choquerend.' Kathleen beet op haar lip. 'Meestal proberen ze een oudere, getrouwde vrouw te rekruteren om deze uit te typen. Jij ziet er nog jonger uit dan ik.'

'Ik ben bijna drieëntwintig,' zei ik, in de hoop dat het volwassen klonk.

Kathleen grijnsde en zei dat ik alles aan haar moest vragen als ik het niet helemaal zeker wist.

Met niet bepaald damesachtig enthousiasme richtte ik mijn aandacht weer op het document. Ik was niet het soort meisje dat graag in losbandig gezelschap is, maar een lijst met te vermijden 'pikante elementen' doorlezen klonk als dikke pret.

Woorden en zinnen die niet gepubliceerd of beantwoord worden door mevr. Bird
Voor verdere referenties zie *Van meisje tot vrouw: Praktisch advies door een arts* (1921)
A–C
Affaire
Amoureus
Bed
Bedjasje
Berlijn

De lijst besloeg nog een aantal pagina's.

Sodom en Gomorra zouden niet bepaald wakker liggen van wat mevrouw Bird als perversiteit beschouwde. Natuurlijk stond 'Te ver gaan voordat je getrouwd bent' niet op het menu. 'Meegesleept worden' beslist ook niet en als je 'In problemen' raakte, was dat gewoon je eigen schuld.

Eigenlijk kon je, zodra je ook maar op de onschuldigste wijze in de richting van een relatie neigde, beter meteen maar weer afkoelen, want het was hoogst onwaarschijnlijk dat mevrouw Bird – 'altijd bereid om uw vragen te beantwoorden' – terug zou schrijven.

Na het lezen van de lijst voelde ik me enigszins gekortwiekt, maar ik wilde mijn werk serieus nemen en begon de brieven open te maken.

Sommige waren zorgvuldig met inkt geschreven, met een echte naam eronder, terwijl andere brieven met potlood gekrabbeld en niet ondertekend waren, of met verzonnen namen zoals 'Bezorgde Verloofde' of 'Matrozenmeisje'. Andere briefschrijvers hadden een aan zichzelf geadresseerde en gefrankeerde envelop ingesloten, duidelijk in de hoop rechtstreeks antwoord te krijgen. Bijna alle brieven waren van vrouwen en meisjes, een paar van mannen die over hun vrouw geschreven hadden.

Ik las een brief van een dame die Florence heette en wiens calciumtabletten helemaal niet geholpen hadden tegen haar wintervoeten. 'Wandelen is nu zo'n beproeving,' vertelde ze. Ik had er alle vertrouwen in dat mevrouw Bird dit onderwerp niet zou verbieden en daar vrolijkte ik een beetje van op. Daarna was een optimistische dame, mevrouw Ditton geheten, zo vriendelijk geweest te schrijven: 'Mijn dochter heeft haar EHBO-diploma gehaald. Denkt u dat ze carrière zou kunnen maken als verpleegster bij het leger?'

Ik hoopte dat dit als dienst aan de oorlogsinspanning zou tellen en legde de brief op die van Florence in mijn acceptabel-brievenbakje.

Naarmate ik meer brieven opende, werd het moeilijker om er nog meer bij te leggen. Eén lezeres was verliefd geworden op een man die gescheiden was, wat volgens de lijst van mevrouw Bird absoluut verboden terrein was, en een andere lezeres vond een jongeman aardig maar had gehoord dat hij 'genegenheid op gênante wijze toonde'. Ik hoefde de lijst er niet eens bij te halen om te weten dat deze twee op de onaangenaamheden-stapel gelegd moesten worden. Ik vond een schaar in mijn bureaula, knipte de brieven vlijtig in stukjes en deed ze in de prullenbak.

In andere gevallen vond ik het niet zo gemakkelijk. Sommige vragen klonken, zelfs als ze op de lijst 'voor mevr. Bird onacceptabele onderwerpen' voorkwamen, eigenlijk helemaal niet onredelijk.

Beste mevr. Bird,
Ik ben vijftien en mijn vriendinnen zeggen dat ze zich door jongens een kus laten geven als ze welterusten zeggen. Heb ik gelijk dat ik dat weiger? En is er verschil tussen kussen voordat je getrouwd bent en erna?
Ik ben bang dat ik goedkoop lijk als ik me door jongens laat kussen.
Groeten
Verlegen Tiener

Voor een vijftienjarige leek me dat een heel fatsoenlijke vraag. Ik wendde me tot het gedeelte J tot L op de lijst van mevrouw Bird. Kus, Kusjes en Kussen waren allemaal beslist verboden onderwerpen. Met tegenzin voegde ik Verlegen Tiener toe aan de stapel brieven die ik moest weigeren, in stukken knippen en in de prullenbak gooien. Het was nauwelijks een schandalig onderwerp en ik voelde me beroerd omdat zij niet geholpen zou worden.

Aangezien meer brieven niet voldeden aan de maatstaven van de lijst van mevrouw Bird, begon ik ze aan Kathleen voor te lezen, in de hoop dat zij me kon helpen.

'Beste mevrouw Bird,' waagde ik, 'mijn echtgenoot zegt dat ik onsympathiek en kil ben.'

'Oe, nee,' zei Kathleen, nog voordat ik aan de vraag toe kon komen.

Ik scheurde de brief doormidden en probeerde er nog een. 'Beste mevrouw Bird, ik ga met mijn verloofde trouwen zodra hij met verlof thuiskomt uit het leger...'

Kathleen keek optimistisch. Dat was bemoedigend.

'"... maar ik heb het gevoel dat ik nogal onwetend ben wat het Huwelijksleven betreft." Huwelijksleven is met een hoofdletter,' zei ik terwijl Kathleen met een woeste blik – dat moest het gezicht zijn dat ze trok als ze diep nadacht – in het niets staarde.

‘Ik weet vrij zeker dat huwelijksleven niet mag,’ zei ze.

‘Dat geldt specifiek voor de intieme kant…’ las ik behulpzaam verder.

‘Och, lieve help! Nee!’ hijgde Kathleen en ze wierp een snelle blik op de deur, alsof mevrouw Bird weleens op het punt kon staan in vreselijke razernij naar binnen te stormen. ‘“Intiem” kan echt helemaal niet.’ Ze ging zachter praten. ‘Mevrouw Bird zegt dat ze dat soort akeligheden in 1911 niet hoefde te beantwoorden en dat ze niet van plan is om dat nu wel te doen.’

Kathleen haalde deze opgelegde regel zo ernstig aan dat ik het niet in mijn hoofd haalde om met haar in discussie te gaan.

Ik probeerde er nog een. ‘“Beste mevrouw Bird, hebt u misschien advies over de manier waarop men verbrand braadvet uit de koekenpan kan krijgen?” O, die is zeker voor mevrouw Croft.’ Ik beantwoordde mijn eigen vraag en ging door met het uitzoeken van de overgebleven post.

‘Wat de pot schaft,’ zei Kathleen zwakjes, met een opgelucht gezicht.

Ik vouwde een brief met het opschrift ‘Matte omgang’ open. Hij was in een elegant handschrift geschreven door een keurige dame die zichzelf ‘Teleurgesteld in het Noordoosten’ noemde.

Teleurgesteld was getrouwd met een beste man, maar hij toonde bijzonder weinig interesse in het ‘met elkaar vertrouwd raken’ als de lampen eenmaal uit waren. De brief was heel fijngevoelig geschreven, dus dacht ik dat we nu wel een kansje maakten.

‘Nee, natuurlijk niet,’ zei Kathleen en ze friemelde ondertussen aan een pluk haar die overboord sprong uit haar ontoereikende knotje. ‘Er staat “omgang”. Mevrouw Bird houdt niet van “omgang”.’

‘Maar ze zijn getrouwd!’ wierp ik tegen.

'Daar gaat het niet om.'

'En hij toont geen interesse.'

'Emmeline!'

'En dat is vast geen pretje.'

'Wacht eens even,' zei Kathleen. 'Je mag geen details lezen. Je had na de derde regel moeten ophouden met lezen.'

'Dat heb ik gedaan,' loog ik.

'Weet je dat zeker?'

'Nou, goed dan, misschien een beetje later. Maar het klinkt beroerd. Ze zijn al een jaar getrouwd en ze heeft hem nog nooit zonder pyjama aan gezien.'

'Emmeline!' Kathleen werd vuurrood en ik besloot niet over de volgende zin te praten, want die zou haar helemaal de stuipen op het lijf jagen. 'Echt, je mag niets lezen wat mevrouw Bird op de lijst gezet heeft. Daar ben je veel te jong voor.'

Ze stond op en keek bezorgd.

Dat vond ik een goeie, aangezien Kathleen niet ouder leek dan ik, maar ik wilde niet nog een flater slaan op mijn eerste dag. Dus bood ik mijn excuses aan en zei dat ik in het vervolg beter zou opletten.

Maar ik voelde me ongemakkelijk. Niet alleen voor de dame van deze brief, maar ook voor Verlegen Tiener en de andere lezeressen wier problemen als verboden beschouwd werden.

Ik zag dat mensen vreselijk openhartig waren in hun brieven, en dat vond ik echt behoorlijk dapper. Mevrouw Bird was maar een vreemde die voor een tijdschrift werkte, maar lezeressen vertelden haar toch hun geheimen. Sommige lezeressen leken echt in de knoei te zitten: ze waren eenzaam omdat hun man vertrokken was om te vechten, of iemand had hun het hoofd op hol gejaagd, of soms waren ze gewoon alleen maar jong en wilden ze een beetje goede raad. Iedereen had het op dit moment moeilijk en ik vond het echt verkeerd van mevrouw Bird dat ze niet terugschreef. Het tijdschrift heette tenslotte *Vrouw & Vriendin*. Nou, wat een vriendin was mevrouw Bird! Bijna alle brieven die ik gelezen had, zouden in stukken geknipt in de prullenbak belanden.

Ik maakte de laatste envelop op mijn bureau open. Deze lezeres had met een potlood dunne lijntjes getrokken langs een liniaal en hoewel het handschrift bijzonder netjes was, kon ik zien dat ze er eeuwen over gedaan had om de brief te schrijven.

Beste mevr. Bird,
Ik ben zeventien en verliefd op een jongeman bij de marine, die vriendelijk en royaal is en zegt dat hij ook van mij houdt. Hij neemt me mee uit dansen en nu heb ik hem daarvoor beloond op een manier waarvan ik weet dat het helemaal verkeerd is. Mijn vriendin Annie staat er hetzelfde voor met haar jongeman en we maken ons allebei zorgen en Annie is bang dat haar pa erachter komt. Kunt u ons helpen, alstublieft? We willen onze vriendjes niet kwijtraken.
Ik heb een gefrankeerde en aan mezelf geadresseerde envelop ingesloten en een postbestelling voor het patroon voor een overjas van vorige week, zodat mijn moeder denkt dat het daarvoor is.
Met de meeste hoogachting,
In de War

Kathleen zat een lastig, over twee pagina's gespreid radeerpatroon voor lentejaponnen te controleren, dus las ik in stilte de brief van In de War nog een keer door. Met de andere lezeressen leefde ik al mee, maar over haar en haar vriendin was ik echt bijzonder bezorgd. Als ze zo doorgingen, kwamen ze tot over hun oren in de problemen.

Bunty en ik hadden zelf ook over soortgelijke zaken gepraat terwijl we avond aan avond in de bomschuilplaats zaten te babbelden, zoals beste vriendinnen doen. Bunty was smoorverliefd op William, en hoewel Edmund misschien bekrompen reageerde op mijn carrièredromen, was hij altijd attent en vriendelijk. En ook heel aantrekkelijk met zijn uniform.

Ik klonk bijna net zo als die arme In de War. Maar het verschil was dat wij wisten waar de grens lag, en of we nu wilden of niet, die zouden we niet overschrijden. Het was waarschijnlijk vreselijk provinciaal om zo vastberaden te blijven, oorlog of geen oorlog. Maar Bunty en ik hadden gezien hoe afschuwelijk alles mis kon gaan op dit front, en dat was voor iedereen akelig.

Ik ging aan mijn bureau zitten en deed alsof ik de brief van In de War voor de derde keer las, maar eigenlijk was ik mijlenver weg.

Tijdens onze hele schooltijd hadden Bunty en ik ons eigen kleine clubje gehad: Bunty, Olive, Kitty en ik. We deden alles met ons vieren: we gingen naar dezelfde schoolclubs, hoorden bij dezelfde sportteams, zwijmelden over dezelfde filmsterren, stelden ons aan bij dezelfde jongens. Niets bijzonders, gewoon alle normale dingen die iedere tiener deed.

Maar toen we zestien waren en alle vier net ons diploma gehaald hadden, begon Kitty om te gaan met een jongen die ouder was dan wij. Hij heette Doug en hij was twintig. Kitty zei dat hij heel volwassen was en ons allemaal nogal kinderachtig vond, waar hij waarschijnlijk gelijk in had. Maar hoe dan ook, terwijl wij allemaal verliefd werden op Gary Cooper en Errol Flynn, werd Kitty verliefd op Doug. Ze zei dat hij ook van haar hield. Toen werd ze zwanger. En toen Doug daarachter kwam, verdween hij spoorloos.

Ik beet op mijn onderlip en staarde naar de brief van In de War. Kathleen had gelijk: ik was nog jong. Maar dat betekende nog niet dat ik mijn hele leven onder een steen had doorgebracht.

Kitty was naar Edinburgh uit logeren gestuurd, naar een tante die ze nog nooit ontmoet had. Wij mochten niet bij haar op bezoek, dus ze was helemaal alleen. Ze wilde haar kindje wanhopig graag houden, maar vier dagen nadat hij geboren was, haalde iemand hem weg. Ik was samen met Bunty naar Kitty's ouders gegaan om hun te smeken er nog eens over na te denken. Maar zij schaamden zich voor haar, waren woedend op haar en ze zeiden nee.

Kitty had haar zoontje Peter genoemd. Hij zou inmiddels bijna zes zijn.

Ik zette mijn ellebogen op het bureau en leunde met mijn kin op mijn handen, want ik was vergeten dat ik net een nieuw baantje had en moest proberen een goede indruk te maken.

'Gaat het een beetje, Emmeline?' Kathleens gezicht stond weer vriendelijk. 'Maak je geen zorgen. Je krijgt alles wel onder de knie.'

'Absoluut,' zei ik. 'Het is alleen allemaal nog een beetje nieuw.'

Kathleen keek meelevend. 'Is dat weer een "onacceptabele"?' vroeg ze toen ze de gefrankeerde en geadresseerde envelop van In de War zag. 'Zal ik de postzegel in de doos doen?'

'Nee, nee,' zei ik, bliksemsnel nadenkend. 'Deze is van "Bezorgd over een Kat". Ik denk dat mevrouw Bird deze wel leuk zal vinden.'

Kathleen aarzelde even en glimlachte toen. 'Goed zo. Huisdieren doen het altijd kolossaal.' Ze zweeg weer even. 'Emmy, ik weet dat het hardvochtig klinkt om sommige brieven te negeren, maar mevrouw Bird zegt dat als mensen zich in de problemen werken, het gewoon hun eigen schuld is.'

Ik vond niet dat In de War degene was die de schuld moest krijgen. Zij was ervan overtuigd dat iemand van haar hield, dat was alles. Het enige verschil tussen haar en mij was dat ik wist wat ik wilde en dat Edmund geen gladde jongen was zoals Doug. Als niemand In de War hielp, kon het met haar weleens net zo aflopen als met Kitty.

'Natuurlijk, Kathleen,' zei ik. 'Ik zal ze allemaal in stukken knippen.'

Kathleen glimlachte hartelijk en ging door met typen. Ik wachtte even en deed alsof ik de papieren die over mijn bureau verspreid lagen, opruimde.

Daarna stopte ik de brief van In de War in mijn la.

5

Beste In de War

In de daaropvolgende weken stortte ik me enthousiast op mijn werk en probeerde ik er het beste van te maken. Bunty had me geweldig gesteund toen ik haar vertelde dat *The Evening Chronicle* in feite *Vrouw & Vriendin* was. Het klonk evengoed kolossaal, vond ze. Thelma en Joan en Mary van de brandweerkazerne hadden ook steengoed gereageerd door te zeggen dat het tot grootse dingen kon leiden. Daar kikkerde ik echt van op. Ik had Edmund geschreven en er een komisch verhaal van gemaakt, in de hoop dat hij er de grappige kant van zou inzien, maar hij had niet geantwoord. Eigenlijk had ik, op een kort kerstbriefje dat midden januari gearriveerd was na, al eeuwen niets meer van hem gehoord en ik begon me zorgen te maken. Misschien zat hij wel ernstig in de problemen. Ik wilde geen zenuwpees lijken, dus ik had er maar één keer iets over gezegd toen William en Bunty me op pruimentaart trakteerden, maar ik merkte best dat zij er ook aan dachten. Bunty zei net iets te snel dat het leger je altijd meteen op de hoogte bracht als er iets vreselijks gebeurd was, dus 'geen nieuws is goed nieuws' en daarna nam Bill het stokje over met: 'Maak je geen zorgen, Emmy;

Edmund is voor geen kleintje vervaard.' Daarna, toen ze dachten dat ik het niet zag, keken ze elkaar even aan.

Toch wilde ik hen op hun woord geloven. Ik besloot me niet te laten kennen en zei dat ik me helemaal geen zorgen maakte. Dat was wel het minste wat ik kon doen, want die arme Bunty moest zich altijd maar flink houden als het over Williams werk als brandweerman ging, terwijl we allebei wisten dat dat ontzettend gevaarlijk was. Toen het leger hem niet wilde hebben omdat zijn oren niet pluis waren – vanbinnen, bedoel ik; aan de buitenkant zag je er niets van – was Bill bij de brandweer gegaan. Het was echt beroerd voor hem geweest toen Edmund en mijn broer Jack bij het leger gingen en vertrokken, maar hij had er het beste van gemaakt. En ik wilde niet over Edmund zaniken terwijl Bunty bijna elke nacht vanuit haar raam de bommen en branden en andere vreselijke dingen kon zien waar haar vriendje mee te maken kreeg.

Op de tijdschriftredactie was mevrouw Bird vrijwel altijd nogal nijdig op bijna alles en iedereen, in het bijzonder op de lezeressen. De meesten stelden haar diep teleur. Ik keek uit naar de post die een handjevol problemen binnenbracht en bleef vastberaden en optimistisch op zoek naar interessant en toch acceptabel materiaal, maar het liep niet bepaald storm. Tenslotte kon het tijdschrift niet elke week iedereen aanraden om zich bij een jeugdvereniging aan te sluiten om het moreel hoog te houden.

De brief van In de War lag nog steeds in mijn bureaula. Ik wilde haar dolgraag helpen, maar Kathleen had de regels heel duidelijk uitgelegd en ik wist dat mevrouw Bird er geen moment aan zou willen verspillen. Ik overwoog haar zelf een brief terug te schrijven, zoals een vriendin zou doen, maar daar kon geen sprake van zijn. Om te beginnen zou In de War zich afvragen wie ik in vredesnaam was. En trouwens, wat zou er gebeuren als mevrouw Bird daar ooit achter kwam? *Vrouw & Vriendin* mocht dan niet mijn droom-baan bij een krant zijn, maar ik werkte tenminste in hetzelfde gebouw als *The Evening Chronicle.* Op een dag kon er een mogelijkheid zijn om bij de krant te gaan werken, en een goede referentie van mevrouw Bird kon weleens de doorslag geven. Kathleen had gezegd dat Lord Overton en mevrouw Bird persoonlijk met elkaar bevriend waren, dus je wist het maar nooit.

Toch wenste ik in stilte nog steeds dat ik iets kon doen. In de War was niet de enige lezeres die het moeilijk had, maar mevrouw Birds lijst van onacceptabele onderwerpen maakte het bijna in alle gevallen onmogelijk hen te helpen.

Beste mevr. Bird,
Ik ben eenentwintig en heel erg verliefd op een jongen van mijn leeftijd. Ik weet dat hij ook van mij houdt en hij heeft me gevraagd of ik met hem wil trouwen voordat hij naar het buitenland gestuurd wordt, maar ik weet niet zeker of ik dat wel moet doen. Weet u, hij heeft me verteld dat hij heel dik met een ander meisje geweest is en al is dat een tijd geleden, voordat we elkaar ontmoet hebben, ik vraag me toch af of het wel juist is om hem te vergeven dat hij intiem met iemand anders geweest is.
Kunt u me alstublieft vertellen wat ik moet doen?
Heel hartelijk bedankt,
Juffrouw D. Watson

Juffrouw Watson leek me fatsoenlijk genoeg, en dat gold ook voor haar vriend. Het leek mij niet zo'n vreselijke misdaad; het was tenslotte verleden tijd en hij had haar de waarheid verteld, terwijl hij gemakkelijk zijn mond had kunnen houden. Ik had het erop gewaagd en de brief aan mevrouw Bird gegeven, maar ze wilde er niets van weten. De brief was in vier stukken geknipt teruggekomen met in grote letters 'Nee' erop geschreven en het woord 'intiem', nijdig omcirkeld met rode inkt.

Beste mevr. Bird,
Ik ben al vijf jaar getrouwd met een man van wie ik dacht dat hij van me hield. Nu vertelt hij me dat hij als een blok gevallen is voor een meisje dat hij ontmoet heeft terwijl hij voor het leger werkte. Hij zegt dat hij me niet wil verlaten, maar ik weet dat ze in de weekends samen weggaan en nu heb ik ontdekt dat ze zwanger is. Ik kan de gedachte met hem samen te wonen niet verdragen. Wat moet ik doen?
Zou u mijn brief alstublieft willen afdrukken? Ik durf u niet te vragen mij terug te schrijven, voor het geval hij uw brief in huis ziet liggen.
Hoogachtend,
Ongelukkige Echtgenote

Wat een ontzettend treurige brief! Ik had geen idee welk advies ze zou moeten krijgen, maar aangezien Ongelukkige Echtgenote absoluut niets verkeerd gedaan had, zou zelfs mevrouw Bird toch wel met haar meeleven? Ik stopte de brief tussen twee bijzonder saaie brieven en duimde ervoor, maar hij maakte geen kans. Nu stond er een grote rode streep door de hele brief en mevrouw Bird had het woord 'Nee!' er zo ferm op geschreven dat de inkt uitliep op het papier. Daaronder had ze het woord 'Affaires' geschreven en dat drie keer onderstreept.

Het was behoorlijk frustrerend. Voor zover ik in mijn korte periode bij *Vrouw & Vriendin* had gezien, stond Ongelukkige Echtgenote niet bepaald alleen. Ik was niet zo naïef om te denken dat dit soort problemen niet van alle tijden was, maar je hoefde geen bolleboos te zijn om te begrijpen dat de oorlog alles nog moeilijker maakte.

Op veel van de problemen had ik geen antwoord, maar ik wist wel dat een vriendelijke reactie beter was dan niets. Ik vond het vreselijk dat ik die brieven moest weggooien.

Kathleen begon me bergen werk voor meneer Collins te

geven. Zij gaf veruit de voorkeur aan het uittypen van de patronen en het schoonheidsadvies van mevrouw Bird, dat vanzelfsprekend heel kernachtig was en bijna volledig gebaseerd op het niet dragen van make-up en op het aanbrengen van iets alarmerends waar je een pasta van moest mengen. Meneer Collins schreef de artikelen en de fictie en ik moest toegeven dat dit, hoewel het niet bepaald leek op uittypen dat de RAF de vijandelijke bommenwerpers van katoen gaf, toch een stuk leuker was dan de juridische documenten van mijn vorige baantje.

Mevrouw Bird bracht meer tijd door buiten dan binnen het kantoor omdat ze de leiding had over een kolossaal aantal 'goede werken'. Telkens als ze naar een vergadering vertrok, hoorden we een machtig gebrul in de gang: ze kondigde zowel haar bestemming als de ingeschatte tijd van terugkeer aan. Dat was wel even wennen, want een joviaal geloeid 'Stapelbedden voor metrostations, kwart over drie' was echt wel iets om van te schrikken.

Op een ochtend, een paar weken nadat ik met mijn nieuwe baan begonnen was, klonk er een zachte klap in de gang, gevolgd door het geluid van rollende wielen.

'Dat zal Clarence zijn,' zei Kathleen toen een bijzonder hoge stem piepte: 'Tweede post,' en een zeer diepe stem daaraan toevoegde: 'Bestelling, juffrouw Knighton.'

'Kom binnen, Clarence,' riep Kathleen.

'Vooruit dan maar,' klonk het paniekerig en de stem schoot weer omhoog naar sopraan.

Clarence was de meest toegewijde en gemakkelijkst in verlegenheid te brengen postjongen van Launceston. Hij was vijftien jaar oud en nu al één meter tachtig lang, en had een onrustige huid – waaronder hij zichtbaar leed. Een aantal keer per dag deed hij zijn rondes. Hij werd heen en weer geslingerd tussen zijn intense interesse in de oorlog en de tragedie van de bijna volledige verlamming die zijn hopeloze verliefdheid op Kathleen teweegbracht.

Aangezien Clarence sprakeloos werd als ze ook maar in zijn richting keek, richtte hij alles wat hij tegen haar zou willen zeggen maar tot mij.

'Morgen, juffrouw Lake,' zei hij over drie octaven. 'Juffrouw Knighton,' voegde hij eraan toe. Dat laatste klonk bijna hoog genoeg om een gesprek met een vleermuis te beginnen.

'Goedemorgen, Clarence,' zei ik.

'Hallo, Clarence,' zei Kathleen.

Clarence keek alsof hij wenste dat hij dood was.

'Pakje voor u, juffrouw Lake,' zei hij en hij keerde Kathleen de rug toe zodat hij het aandurfde om eraan toe te voegen: 'We hebben ze op de vlucht gejaagd in Ethiopië.' Het klonk alsof die twee zaken alles met elkaar te maken hadden.

'Onze jongens zijn niet te verslaan,' zei ik, in de wetenschap dat Clarence me stralend zou aankijken.

'Ga maar gauw verder, Clarence,' zei Kath vriendelijk. 'Anders krijg je mevrouw Bird op je dak.'

Clarence wierp een blik in haar richting, maar werd met stomheid geslagen door het resultaat; hij wuifde onhandig en haastte zich weg.

Ik begon meteen aan de correspondentie van de dag en werd beloond door een brief waarin mevrouw Birds advies gevraagd werd over postzegels waarvan de opbrengst ten goede kwam aan de oorlog. Dat was een leuk en veilig onderwerp, dus ik begon goed. De tweede brief kwam van een dame die sinds kort geteisterd werd door een kropgezwel. Dat was geen ontspannend onderwerp om over te lezen, al was ik niet snel misselijk. Ik controleerde de brief tweemaal aan de hand van 'de lijst' en besloot dat hij, als we een paar medische elementen schrapten, wel door de beugel kon.

Natuurlijk ging de daaropvolgende brief over een dame

die echtscheiding wilde aanvragen; met tegenzin knipte ik die in stukken en gooide hem in de prullenbak. Nu lag er alleen nog een briefkaart, met grote letters geschreven, die meteen ter zake kwam.

> *Beste mevr. Bird,*
> *Weet u een oefening voor de enkels? Alles is op dit moment nog acceptabel omdat ik overdag bontlaarsjes draag en alleen in avondjapon naar evenementen ga, maar de zomer is een marteling die ik nauwelijks kan verdagen. Kunt u me alstublieft adviseren?*
> *Hoogachtend,*
> *Betreurenswaardige Benen*

Ik voelde met Betreurenswaardige Benen mee, aangezien het leven momenteel al moeilijk genoeg leek zonder de pret te moeten beperken tot uitgaan in een lange japon, maar ze had me wel uit de penarie geholpen. Er zouden genoeg brieven zijn voor de volgende adviesrubriek.

Ik deed ze allemaal in een stevige kartonnen ordner voor mevrouw Bird en wrong me langs Kathleens bureau de gang in, die zoals gewoonlijk verlaten was. In de gang hing altijd de flauwe geur van gekookte kool en zeep. Dat was een mistroostige mengeling die ik aan slechte afvoerpijpen toeschreef.

Mevrouw Bird was naar een bijeenkomst van Evacuatie van katten, dus legde ik de ordner op haar bureau en ging toen even langs bij de afdeling kunst om mevrouw Mahoney te vertellen dat ik tot zover op tijd was voor de deadline van deze week. Zij stond meneer Brand net te vertellen hoe hij een lekker pasteitje zonder vlees kon maken en ik ging er gezellig bij zitten. Ik mocht hen allebei graag en vond het jammer dat we niet allemaal samen in de oude journalistenkamer zaten, want dat zou stukken leuker geweest zijn dan opgesloten zitten in onze duffe kamertjes.

Mevrouw Mahoney vroeg me om meneer Collins even aan te sporen op tijd te komen met zijn filmrecensiekolom, dus verliet ik het gesprek – met tegenzin – en klopte op zijn deur. Ik was nog steeds op mijn hoede voor zijn onvoorspelbare gedrag, maar vandaag zat hij niet in zijn eentje somber te wezen; hij leek in een joviale bui.

'Juffrouw Lake, ben jij dat?' vroeg hij zonder op te kijken van zijn bureau. 'Kom binnen.'

Hij werkte in het halfdonker, omringd door chaos, wat – zoals ik al snel ontdekt had – zijn favoriete manier van werken was. Ik was al gewend aan zijn handgeschreven teksten, rommelig en verfrommeld, en af en toe doormidden gescheurd en vervolgens weer aan elkaar geplakt. Op één manuscript had hij een halve pagina doorgekrast en was opnieuw begonnen. Ondanks zijn cynische houding had ik het gevoel dat hij het echt belangrijk vond wat hij schreef en nooit zomaar iets inleverde.

'Zo,' zei hij. 'Hoe gaat het? Je hebt het al langer uitgehouden dan de twee voorgaande assistenten. Gedraagt Henriëtta zich een beetje?'

Meneer Collins was de enige die mevrouw Bird ooit bij haar voornaam noemde, zelfs achter haar rug.

'Iedereen is zo lief,' zei ik diplomatiek. 'En ik leer bendes over de problemen van de lezeressen.'

'Aha,' zei meneer Collins. 'Kathleen vertelde me dat het een hele uitdaging is om de pagina vol te krijgen.'

Ik knikte. Ik vroeg me af of hij wist hoeveel brieven genegeerd werden.

'Er zijn wel genoeg brieven,' zei ik. 'Maar mevrouw Bird wil de meeste niet beantwoorden. Sommige mensen zitten echt in de knoei, maar zij zegt dat het allemaal onaangenaamheden zijn.'

'Ja, zo is ze wel,' zei meneer Collins. 'Eerlijk gezegd: ik snap er geen jota van. Daarom houd ik me bij fictie. Dingen verzinnen is toch wel iets gemakkelijker dan het echte leven ontwarren.'

Ik keek naar de boekenkast. De cognacfles stond er nog steeds.

'Ik heb medelijden met hen,' zei ik treurig en dacht aan In de War. 'Het lijkt me zo spijtig voor hen dat ze niets horen.'

Meneer Collins ging rechtop zitten en wreef peinzend over zijn kin. Zo te zien had hij zich niet geschoren. Daarna leunde hij weer naar voren.

'Zit maar niet in de put, Emmeline. Henriëtta deed dit adviesgedoe al toen ik nog een klein jongetje was en ik ben bang dat jij haar niet kunt veranderen. Eerlijk is eerlijk, onze geliefde waarnemend redactrice laat mij met rust zodat ik aan de verhalen en artikelen kan werken, want ze weet dat dat mijn werk is, en ik probeer goed werk te leveren. Geloof het of niet, maar ik hoop echt dat de lezeressen ze mooi vinden.'

Dat laatste zei hij meer tegen zichzelf dan tegen mij. Ik knikte en begon te zeggen hoezeer ik van zijn werk genoot, maar dat wuifde hij weg.

'Het is niet bepaald literatuur,' zei hij. 'En lieve help, we worden verpletterend verslagen door de concurrentie. Het arme oude tijdschrift knijpt er langzaam maar zeker tussenuit. Maar wij, de weinige overgeblevenen, doen wat we kunnen. Kijk maar naar de illustraties van meneer Brand. Prachtig spul, echt. Emmeline, maak je maar geen zorgen over Henriëtta. Doe gewoon wat je kunt, en doe het zo goed als je kunt. Op een dag zal het de moeite waard zijn, dat beloof ik je.'

Hij krabde in zijn nek en rekte zich vervolgens uit alsof hij begon te gapen. 'Lieve help, ik loop gevaar ons allebei te vervelen. Preek voltooid. Zoek uit waar jíj goed in bent, juffrouw Lake, en word daar nog beter in. Dat is de sleutel.'

Hij keek weer naar de rommel op zijn bureau. Dat vatte ik op als een teken dat hij weer aan het werk wilde gaan, dus gaf ik hem de boodschap van mevrouw Mahoney door en zette koers naar mijn kantoor. Vreemd genoeg voelde ik me een heel klein beetje opgekikkerd… bemoedigd zelfs.

Zoek uit waar jíj goed in bent, juffrouw Lake, en word daar nog beter in.

Het was eigenaardig om geïnspireerd te worden door een cognac drinkende cynicus van onduidelijke, middelbare leeftijd, die soms nog ongelukkiger leek te zijn met *Vrouw & Vriendin* dan ik, maar dat was ik wel. Meneer Collins had gelijk over zijn verhalen: hij stelde de lezeressen van *Vrouw & Vriendin* nooit teleur. Hun helden waren dapper, hun heldinnen kranig, en het liep altijd goed af. Dat was meer dan je van mevrouw Birds reactie op hun problemen kon zeggen.

Kathleen had een briefje op mijn bureau gelegd met de mededeling dat ze even een boodschap buiten de deur moest doen, dus ging ik in mijn eentje zitten nadenken, kauwend op de achterkant van een potlood.

Ik had geen idee waar ik goed in was. Nog niet. Ik wist alleen dat ik oorlogscorrespondente had willen worden om belangrijk nieuws te vertellen en op de een of andere manier iets te veranderen. Nu was ik hier vastgelopen bij *Vrouw & Vriendin* en negeerde ik zelfs de weinige mensen wier leven door mevrouw Bird veranderd had kunnen worden.

Doe wat je kunt, en doe het zo goed als je kunt.

En toen nam ik een besluit. Met snel kloppend hart draaide ik, me afvragend hoe snel ik eigenlijk echt kon typen, een nieuw vel papier in mijn typemachine en haalde daarna de brief van In de War uit mijn la. Lezeressen als Ongelukkige Echtgenote hadden problemen waar ik nog helemaal niets van begreep, maar ik wist wel wat ik tegen In de War moest zeggen. Ik had mijn vriendin Kitty in dezelfde situatie gezien en toen het voor haar afschuwelijk misgegaan was, had ik lang niet genoeg gedaan om haar te helpen.

Ik las de brief van In de War nog eens door, beet op mijn lip en probeerde te denken als een ervaren persoon, zo iemand tot wie je je in een crisis zou wenden. Een vriendelijke versie van mevrouw Bird als het haar echt iets zou kunnen schelen. Er zou absoluut wat voor me zwaaien als dit ooit ontdekt werd, maar ik moest het op zijn minst proberen. Ik begon te typen in een schrijfstijl die op mevrouw Birds nuchtere manier van schrijven leek, maar dan niet zo meedogenloos. Het was gemakkelijker dan ik dacht: ik vertelde In de War dat ze haar jonge man absoluut op geen enkele manier hoefde te 'belonen' – uitstapjes naar de bioscoop en cadeautjes of niet. Ze moest voet bij stuk houden en als hij het daarom uitmaakte, moest hij het zelf maar weten. Dan was hij niet de moeite waard.

Ik had bijna het gevoel dat mevrouw Bird dit antwoord zou goedkeuren.

Maar aan het eind van de brief hield ik op met typen. Hoe moest ik dit in vredesnaam ondertekenen?

Ik hoorde de deur van de gang met een klap opengaan. Dat zou Kathleen zijn, die terugkwam van haar boodschap. Ik kon niet riskeren dat zij zag wat ik gedaan had. Ik rukte het papier uit de typemachine, graaide mijn vulpen naar me toe en schreef snel:

Heel veel succes,
Mevr. Henriëtta Bird

6

Niet iedereen is goed volk

Tegen de tijd dat Kathleen binnenkwam en vertelde dat ze bijna haar gasmasker in de metro had laten liggen, had ik de brief in mijn tas gestopt en zat ik nonchalant een artikel uit te typen alsof er niets ongewoons gebeurd was. Afgezien van het feit dat ik de brief aan In de War had ondertekend met 'Mevr. Henriëtta Bird' was het bijna alsof ik echt gewoon een brief aan een vriendin geschreven had.

Maar niet heus. Ik had mevrouw Birds handtekening vervalst. En het briefpapier met de kop *Vrouw & Vriendin* gebruikt. En de brief geschreven in de door *Vrouw & Vriendin* betaalde tijd. Dus eigenlijk was het helemaal niet alsof ik gewoon een brief aan een vriendin geschreven had.

Toen ik die middag om één uur vertrok, durfde ik Kathleen nauwelijks aan te kijken. Ik had het gevoel dat ik een toneelstuk opvoerde.

'Loopt de klok gelijk? Ik ben zo laat, ik moet naar huis, tot morgen, dag,' zei ik veel te luid, zonder tussendoor adem te halen.

Daarna stoof ik met mijn hoed en jas in de handen het kantoor uit voordat ze kon zien dat ik knalrood was geworden van schuldgevoel.

Het duurde oneindig lang voordat ik het gebouw kon verlaten. Ik stond in de lift en zweette overmatig, telkens als hij stilhield – op elke verdieping – en daarna zwalkte ik de grote hal door in een onzekere combinatie van half wandelen, half draven, terwijl ik elk moment een zware hand op mijn schouder en onmiddellijke arrestatie verwachtte.

Tegen de tijd dat ik buiten was, waar de straat kleddernat was van de natte sneeuw, kon ik nauwelijks wachten om me van het bewijs te ontdoen door het in de brievenbus te deponeren. Daarna sprong ik per ongeluk in een dubbeldekker die ik helemaal niet moest hebben: om thuis te komen moest ik precies de andere kant op.

Dit moest ik nooit meer doen. Het was verschrikkelijk verkeerd. Hoewel ik erop vertrouwde dat mevrouw Bird het nooit zou ontdekken, was het nog steeds krankzinnig dat ik het gedaan had.

Ik vroeg me af wat Bunty zou zeggen. Ik had het gevoel dat ze me zou vertellen dat ik geen greintje verstand had en dat ik ontslagen zou worden als iemand erachter kwam. Daar zou ze nog gelijk in hebben ook. Ik hoopte dat ik In de War misschien wel kon helpen, maar doen alsof het advies van mevrouw Bird kwam? Bunty zou beslist denken dat ik gek geworden was. En Edmund... Aan zijn reactie durfde ik helemaal niet te denken.

Ik besloot dat het beter was om het aan niemand te vertellen.

De rest van de week werkte ik me drie slagen in de rondte, in een poging een goede beurt te maken. De teleurstelling omdat ik er een warboel van gemaakt had en bij *Vrouw & Vriendin* terechtgekomen was, bleef steken, maar ik draaide nog steeds mijn diensten op de brandweerkazerne, dus ik probeerde wel mijn steentje bij te dragen. Ook bleef ik alle kranten lezen, erop gespitst evenwichtig en vol bedachtzaam politiek inzicht te zijn voor het geval zich ook maar de kleinste kans zou voordoen om naar *The Chronicle* over te stappen. Ik bleef elke dag aan Edmund schrijven en hield mijn brieven luchtig en licht.

Op kantoor typte ik de problemen voor de pagina van mevrouw Bird met dubbele snelheid uit, timmerde twee romantische verhalen door meneer Collins uit de stokoude typemachine en bood me vrijwillig aan voor elk karweitje waar Kathleen of een van de anderen niet zo veel zin in had. De tijd tikte door en toen mevrouw Mahoney, die ik heel graag mocht, me 'een parel' noemde, begon het leven bij *Vrouw & Vriendin* beter aan te voelen.

En toen, een week later, werd het weer riskant.

Ik deed oprecht mijn best om onaangenaamheden uit de brieven voor mevrouw Bird te houden, maar met de armzalige hoeveelheid correspondentie en het feit dat de lat voor immoraliteit zo vreselijk laag lag, viel het niet mee om aan het juiste aantal te komen. Elke brief begon ik vol hoop te lezen, bemoedigd door een milde openingszin, maar dan werd mijn hoop wreed stukgeslagen door een 'wil de liefde niet meer met me bedrijven' of 'en nu verwacht ik een kindje' die halverwege de tweede alinea de kop opstak. Mevrouw Bird was ervan overtuigd dat een gezonde kijk op het leven en een stevige wandeling alle problemen konden oplossen, maar de meeste lezeressen van *Vrouw & Vriendin* hadden beproevingen waar zelfs een hele buslading frisse lucht niets voor kon betekenen.

Ik kon het nog steeds niet opbrengen om sommige onacceptabele brieven in stukken te knippen. In het geheim hield ik ze in mijn bureaula, hoewel ik er niets mee kon.

Op maandag kreeg ik een flink standje van mevrouw Bird omdat ik haar een brief gegeven had van een dame wier echtgenoot een affaire gehad had. Ik had zo'n medelijden met haar. 'Mijn hart is gebroken,' schreef ze, 'aangezien ik onlangs ontdekt heb dat mijn echtgenoot, van wie ik na twintig jaar nog altijd houd, met een vriendin van mijn werk op stap geweest is…'

Maar dat kon mevrouw Bird niets schelen. 'Juffrouw Lake,' snauwde ze. 'Affaires. Bent u helemaal gek geworden?'

Twee dagen later raakte ik in de problemen met een jonge vrouw die zich zorgen maakte over haar huwelijksnacht. 'Mijn vriendin zegt dat haar huwelijksnacht niets bijzonders was, maar ik maak me zorgen over wat ik kan verwachten' riep weer een gedecideerde reactie op.

'Juffrouw Lake, mag ik u vragen: staat "Genot" op de lijst of niet?'

Af en toe boekte ik succes. Een uitzonderlijke vraag naar mevrouw Beeton – 'Heeft zij echt bestaan en is het waar dat ze jong gestoven is?' ('Natuurlijk heeft ze echt bestaan, juffrouw Lake. Negenentwintig.') – en een verre lezeres die het leven in Canada nogal eenzaam vond ('Met somberheid bereik je niets, juffrouw Lake, we moeten duidelijk maken dat ze het hoofd niet moet laten hangen.') kwamen tamelijk goed over, maar slechts zeer weinig brieven waren in acceptabele mate vrij van onaangenaamheden.

'Echt, Kathleen,' zei ik op een ochtend toen ik moeite had genoeg post te vinden die ik aan mevrouw Bird kon geven, 'als we niet op echte problemen reageren, is het geen wonder dat niemand meer schrijft.'

'Toch doen sommigen dat nog wel,' zei Kathleen. Ze droeg een ingewikkeld dubbel gebreid vest en zag er verfomfaaid uit.

'Niet veel,' zei ik. 'Andere weekbladen staan vol adviezen over beroerde echtgenoten en zwanger zijn of geen kinderen krijgen, en wat je moet doen als je vriendje al een jaar weg is om te vechten en je je afvraagt of je hem ooit nog terug zult zien.' Ik dacht aan Edmund; meestal wist ik niet eens waar hij was. 'Daar maken mensen zich zorgen over, niet of we in juni een mierenplaag zullen krijgen. Wie kan dat nu nog iets schelen?'

Kathleen keek zenuwachtig naar de deur.

'In vredesnaam, Kathleen, ze is weg,' zei ik.

Het was niet eerlijk om te snauwen, ook al was ik moe. De luchtaanval van de afgelopen nacht was zwaar geweest, en ik had een lange dienst op de brandweerkazerne gedraaid, maar waarschijnlijk had de helft van de Londenaars evenmin geslapen. We zaten allemaal in hetzelfde schuitje. De lezeressen negeren voelde echter nog steeds verkeerd.

'We zouden mensen zoals deze dame moeten helpen,' zei ik en begon een brief voor te lezen van iemand die ondertekend had met 'Verbijsterd'.

Beste mevrouw Bird,
Ik ben heel erg verliefd op mijn verloofde, maar hij is opeens heel kil tegen me. Hij zegt dat hij gek op me is, maar niet hartstochtelijk.

'Emmeline,' fluisterde Kathleen, die wit wegtrok. 'Niet doen!'

Ik ging door.

Moet ik met hem trouwen en hopen dat hij bijdraait?

Ik keek Kathleen woedend aan, wat volkomen onterecht was, aangezien zij niet degene was op wie ik kwaad was.

'Waarom kan mevrouw Bird niet helpen?' vroeg ik. 'Dit meisje gaat een ellendige tijd tegemoet als hij niet echt van haar houdt. We zouden alleen maar hoeven zeggen dat er nog veel meer mannen rondlopen. Of, of... Wat dacht je van deze?' Ik trok de bureaula open waarin ik een wanhopig trieste brief had gestopt die ik niet kon weggooien.

Beste mevrouw Bird,

Ik ben moeder van drie kinderen, weduwe sinds voor de oorlog. Ik heb niet veel vrienden en toen een bijzonder aardige soldaat bij ons ingekwartierd was, zijn we intiem geworden. Nu ontdek ik tot mijn afgrijzen dat ik zwanger ben van zijn kind. Ik heb hem geschreven, maar hij heeft me niet geantwoord. Ik ben wanhopig... Vertel me alstublieft wat ik moet doen.

'Emmeline, hou op,' zei Kathleen, die haar geduld begon te verliezen. 'Je weet dat mevrouw Bird niet over dit soort mensen wil nadenken.'

'Dit soort mensen?' vroeg ik en ik dacht aan Kitty en haar zoontje. 'In vredesnaam, Kathleen! Dat zou jou en mij ook kunnen overkomen. Het gaat niet alleen om een bepaald soort mensen. Luister maar eens naar deze brief:

Beste mevrouw Bird,

Toen ze de kinderen uit Londen begonnen te evacueren, kon ik het niet opbrengen om mijn zoontje te laten gaan. Twee maanden geleden werd ons huis gebombardeerd en nu is mijn zoon voor de rest van zijn leven gehandicapt.

Ik hield op met lezen. Ik was geen huilebalk, maar mijn stem stokte. Deze brief had ik aan mevrouw Bird laten zien. Zij had gezegd dat deze vrouw het niemand anders kwalijk kon nemen. Het was haar eigen schuld.

'Echt, Kathleen,' zei ik, 'wat heeft het voor zin dat *Vrouw & Vriendin* een adviesrubriek heeft als we helemaal niemand helpen?'

Ik wist dat ik tegen de verkeerde sprak. Eigenlijk zou ik moeten proberen mevrouw Bird te overtuigen.

Kathleen zuchtte. 'Emmy, hoor eens,' zei ze met haar rustige stem. 'Ik weet dat het akelig kan zijn. Soms word ik er ook afschuwelijk somber van. Maar er is niets aan te doen. Als mevrouw Bird zegt dat je iemand moet negeren die een... eh... je weet wel... een kindje verwacht, dan moeten we dat gewoon doen.' Ze schudde haar hoofd en haar haar deed meelevend mee. 'Zelfs als we dat niet leuk vinden.'

Ik bukte om een envelop die onder het bureau gevallen was op te rapen.

'Als ik een kindje verwachtte,' zei ik tegen de donkere houten vloer, 'zou ik graag het gevoel hebben dat iemand me wilde helpen.'

Ik hoorde Kathleens stoel over de vloer schrapen. Toen hoorde ik een andere, beslist ijzige stem vragen: 'En is dat een reële mogelijkheid, juffrouw Lake?'

De klok aan de muur achter Kathleens bureau begon te slaan om me eraan te herinneren dat mevrouw Bird om elf uur terug zou zijn op kantoor, nadat ze een alcoholist die op straat aangereden was op zijn falie gegeven had.

Ik hield mijn hoofd onder het bureau terwijl de klok doorging met slaan. Ik vroeg me af of het me zou lukken elf slagen lang ondergedoken te blijven.

'Juffrouw Lake?'

'Ja, mevrouw Bird?' zei ik, terwijl ik eindelijk tevoorschijn kwam.

Kathleen stond in de houding. Ze was net zo bleek als een dame die ik tijdens de tentoonstelling over dokter Crippen had zien wegvluchten bij Madame Tussaud.

'Juffrouw Lake,' zei mevrouw Bird, bewonderenswaardig kalm in aanwezigheid van potentiële verdorvenheid, 'ik mag hopen dat het hier om een hypothetische situatie gaat?'

'O ja, lieve help, natuurlijk!' zei ik in de zekerheid dat mijn dagen geteld waren. 'Kathleen en ik waren alleen een van de brieven van de lezeressen aan het bespreken.'

Ik zag Kathleen zowaar nog meer verbleken en herinnerde me – te laat – dat het bespreken van de brieven streng verboden was.

'Ik begrijp het,' zei mevrouw Bird met een gezicht alsof ze er helemaal niets van begreep.

'Nou, als ik zeg dat we die brief bespraken,' zei ik, snel terugschakelend naar de eerste persoon, 'bedoel ik eigenlijk dat ik er iets over zei. Kathleen kon geen kant uit, ze moest wel luisteren.'

Ik hoopte dat ik mijn vriendin in ieder geval uit de penarie kon houden.

'En wat zei u dan wel, juffrouw Lake?' vroeg mevrouw Bird, die het klaarspeelde om tegelijkertijd woedend en ijzig te kijken. Ze droeg een stokoude, kolossale bontmantel, waardoor ze uiterlijk iets weghad van een grote beer die zojuist een bijzonder sappige vis net niet gevangen had. 'Want ik wist niet dat u als parttime assistent-typiste aangenomen was om wát dan ook te zeggen.'

Ik zette me schrap. Ik werkte nog geen maand bij *Vrouw & Vriendin* en nu zou ik de zak krijgen.

Aan de andere kant: als ik mijn baan zou verliezen, kon ik niet anders dan bij het leger gaan, zelfs als mijn ouders daardoor waanzinnig ongerust zouden worden. Ik zag geen alternatief. Dan zou ik tenminste echte oorlogservaring opdoen en daardoor zou ik misschien op een dag toch oorlogscorrespondente kunnen worden.

Misschien kon ik me bij de Vrijwillige Luchtmacht voor Vrouwen aansluiten. Dat was een kolossaal idee. Ik zou getraind kunnen worden om de parachutes in te pakken en me dan bij het eskader van mijn broer Jack aansluiten en zorgen dat ik zijn parachute veilig inpakte. Of misschien kon ik wel vliegtuigen rond gaan brengen als vrouwelijke piloot, al was het natuurlijk wel tegen de regels als ik vijandelijke vliegtuigen neerschoot.

Terwijl mevrouw Bird op dreef kwam met haar uitbrander, dacht ik over andere mogelijkheden na. Misschien kon ik ook bij de brandweer blijven en de motorcursus volgen om als motorkoerierster berichten over te brengen. Ik had een paar meisjes ontmoet die dat deden en zij waren echt mieters: opgewekt en ijverig, en altijd snel op weg naar de plaats-waar-alles-gebeurde. Jack zou dubbel liggen als ik leerde motorrijden, maar dat zou ook betekenen dat ik in Londen kon blijven wonen en daar was ik echt op gebrand. Dan zouden Bunty en de meisjes van de kazerne er nog zijn, en ook William en zijn vrienden voor de bioscoop en dansavondjes en zo, dus dan zou er eigenlijk niets veranderen. We zouden Kathleen ook kunnen meevragen.

Misschien zou het juist goed zijn om bij *Vrouw & Vriendin* weg te gaan. Al zou het feit dat ik al na een paar weken ontslagen werd, natuurlijk geen goede indruk maken bij een eventuele volgende sollicitatie. Ik zou kunnen zeggen dat het allemaal een vergissing geweest was en dat ik er eigenlijk vooral ontzettend op gespitst was om meer bij te dragen aan de oorlogsinspanning. Ik zou het naar vinden dat ik de lezeressen die mevrouw Bird negeerde in de steek liet, maar ik kon toch niets doen om hen te helpen.

'En ik denk niet dat de lezeres van *Vrouw & Vriendin* haar middag door dit soort zaken wil laten bederven, denkt u wel?'

Mevrouw Bird was aan het eind van haar toespraak gekomen. Het was een flinke slagbeurt geweest.

'Nee,' zei ik flink. 'Nee, vast niet.'

Ik maakte me klaar voor vertrek, maar nu bleek dat mevrouw Bird slechts tijdelijk het spel gestaakt had en nu weer stevig aan slag was.

'Juffrouw Lake, u bent nog jong en onschuldig!' bulderde ze op een toon alsof dat een misdaad was. 'Maar u zult het nog wel ontdekken: niet iedereen is goed volk!'

Mevrouw Bird deed haar handen op haar rug, zodat ze eruitzag als een generaal die de troepen inspecteert. 'Dat geldt in het bijzonder voor dit soort,' zei ze met een hoofd-knik in de richting van de rommelige brieven op mijn bureau.

'Affaires... hun hoofd op hol... zwangerschappen... onaangenaamheden!' daverde ze en zweeg even om de gruwel goed tot me te laten doordringen. 'En zelfs, juffrouw Lake... zénuwen.'

De blik die ze me bij dit laatste woord toewierp, suggereerde dat we inmiddels op het niveau van landverraad beland waren.

'Deze vrouwen hebben de tijd van hun leven, terwijl onze mannen weg zijn om te strijden voor de toekomst van de vrije wereld. Dat vind ik niet iets waarmee zij onze hulp verdienen, u wel?'

Afgaande op wat ik gelezen had, dacht ik niet dat hier ook maar een woord van waar was, maar als mevrouw Bird uit volle borst tekeerging, had het niet veel zin om ertegenin te gaan. En eerlijk gezegd: waarom zou ik ook maar iets moeten geven om die suffe adviesrubriek?

Maar terwijl mevrouw Bird op stoom kwam voor het tweede deel van haar lezing over hoe vreselijk deze mensen waren, realiseerde ik me dat ik er wel degelijk om gaf. Echt, eerlijk waar! Ik gaf om de vrouwen die brieven schreven naar dit ouderwetse, op sterven na dode weekblad. Mevrouw Bird kreeg zo weinig post dat ze echt wel voldoende tijd kon vrijmaken om alle brieven te beantwoorden. Maar nee, ze liet de meeste brieven in stukken knippen door een onbelangrijke assistente als ik, terwijl zij Londen rondstruinde met haar liefdadigheidscomités. Als je huis gebombardeerd werd, was dat volgens mij al erg genoeg zonder dat mevrouw Bird ter plekke verscheen en per se een toespraak moest houden om je eraan te herinneren dat je ruggengraat moest tonen en je hoofd niet mocht laten hangen.

Zij mocht dan niet om die lezeressen geven, maar ik wel.

Bij *Vrouw & Vriendin* gaan werken was een vergissing

geweest; dit baantje zomaar opgeven zou echter nog erger zijn. Misschien kwam ik niet zo ver in mijn poging om mevrouw Bird het hoofd te bieden, maar als ik mijn baan verloor en de volgende assistent-typiste het niet eens probeerde, wat zou er dan gebeuren? Als niemand ooit opkwam voor de vrouwen die zo wanhopig waren dat ze haar schreven…

Ik had altijd gedacht dat de echte oorlog datgene was waarvan de kranten verslag deden: de veldslagen en vijandelijke slachtoffers en belangrijke aankondigingen van politici en leiders. Daar had ik deel van willen uitmaken. Nu begon ik te denken dat ik het bij het verkeerde eind gehad had. De regering zei altijd dat iedereen thuis van vitaal belang was voor de oorlogsinspanning, en dat we moesten doorgaan met het steunen van onze jongens en het normale leven voortzetten alsof er niets aan de hand was, zodat Adolf Hitler niet zou denken dat hij ons eronder kreeg. En we moesten vrolijk en stoïcijns zijn, echt geschikte lui, en lippenstift opdoen en er leuk uitzien voor als de mannen op verlof waren, en we mochten vooral niet huilen of somber zijn als ze weer weggingen om te vechten. En natuurlijk was ik het daarmee eens, natuurlijk! Maar hoe zat het dan als het moeilijk werd of misging? Vrouwen zoals de lezeressen die mevrouw Bird schreven, kwamen nooit in de krant. Vrouwen wier wereld op z'n kop gezet was door de oorlog, die hun echtgenoot misten of zich alleen voelden en verliefd werden op de verkeerde man. Of die gewoon jong en naïef waren en zich het hoofd op hol lieten brengen in een tijd van beproeving. Het waren problemen die mensen altijd al gehad hadden, alleen werd er nu, nu alles zo chaotisch was, verwacht dat deze vrouwen gewoon verder ploeterden.

Wie steunde hén?

Ik wilde nog steeds een echte correspondente worden. Een oorlogsjournaliste zoals de vrouwen over wie ik gelezen had, die op pad gingen om verslag uit te brengen van de Spaanse Burgeroorlog met niets bij zich behalve twee bontjassen en een kolossale vastberadenheid om de waarheid te ontdekken. Ik wilde deel uitmaken van de actie en opwinding.

Maar dat kon wachten! Mevrouw Bird was in een andere eeuw blijven steken. Haar opvattingen mochten dan dertig jaar geleden gemeengoed geweest zijn, nu waren ze verouderd. Dit was niet alleen háár oorlog, iedereen had eronder te lijden. Het was ónze oorlog.

Ik wilde hier een succes van maken. Ik wilde voor *Vrouw & Vriendin* blijven werken en proberen de lezeressen te helpen. Ik wist nog steeds niet precies hoe ik dat zou doen, maar ze hadden een helpende hand nodig.

Het werd tijd om een toontje lager te zingen, om zoete broodjes te bakken.

'Mevrouw Bird,' zei ik flink, 'ik bied u mijn nederige excuses aan. Ik ben bang dat ik nog steeds de slag niet helemaal te pakken had.' Een domme indruk maken leek me de beste benadering. 'Nu begrijp ik het allemaal veel beter. Het spijt me echt dat ik zo vreselijk traag van begrip was. U hoeft het me geen twee keer te vertellen. Mag ik u deze brief laten zien? Deze is van Teleurgesteld in Frankrijk.'

Ik hield mevrouw Bird een brief voor die ze aanpakte, nog altijd met een vervaarlijke blik. Na een hele tijd knikte ze even.

'Juffrouw Lake, uw morele maatstaven zijn buitengewoon laag. Ze horen in de goot thuis.'

Ze liet het klinken alsof ik opgevoed was door een groep uitzonderlijk losbandige prostituees of er een gewoonte van gemaakt had gehandicapten te stompen. Niettemin keek ik zo berouwvol mogelijk.

'Ik wil dat soort brieven niet meer zien,' zei ze, op mijn bureau wijzend, bij wijze van slotverklaring. 'Ik zal ze niet lezen, ik zal ze niet beantwoorden. Ze zijn niet afkomstig van goed volk.'

Met die woorden pakte ze een handvol van de brieven die ik Kathleen voorgelezen had en gooide die allemaal in de prullenbak. Daarna voer ze met opgestoken zeilen, als een galjoen dat onder moeilijke omstandigheden een vijandelijke vloot verslagen had, de kamer uit. Het was een vorstelijke aftocht, voor zover de geringe afmetingen van ons kantoor dat toelieten.

Kathleen en ik bleven zwijgend zitten tot we de deur van mevrouw Birds kantoor hoorden dichtslaan.

'Sjonge,' zei ik, duizelig van triomfantelijkheid.

'Nou ja,' fluisterde Kathleen met ogen als schoteltjes. 'Dat was moedig van je.'

'Zouden we het gelijkspel kunnen noemen, denk je?' vroeg ik, opeens giechelig.

'Ik dacht dat ons laatste uur geslagen had,' zei Kathleen. 'Heel erg bedankt dat je zei dat ik het niet gedaan had.'

'Nou, zo was het ook,' zei ik. 'Jij zei nog dat ik mijn mond moest houden. Het spijt me dat ik jou hierin meegesleept heb. Ik zal niets meer over die stomme brieven zeggen.'

'Het geeft niet,' zei Kathleen. 'Eerlijk gezegd heb ik er echt van genoten. Nu ga ik naar de postkamer.' Ze keek ontzettend opgelucht omdat de rel voorbij was en haastte zich naar de trap.

Zodra Kathleen weg was, leunde ik achterover op mijn stoel en zuchtte.

Ik wil dat soort brieven niet meer zien. Ik zal ze niet lezen, ik zal ze niet beantwoorden.

Het leek allemaal volkomen duidelijk. Ik zou meteen inbinden. Ik zou de instructies van mevrouw Bird tot in de puntjes volgen en haar nooit meer een brief laten zien die niet precies voldeed aan haar lijst.

En als mevrouw Bird ze niet wilde beantwoorden, zou ik de lezeressen zelf schrijven.

Dat was riskant natuurlijk. Ontzettend riskant. Maar ik had In de War teruggeschreven en mijn brief ondertekend met 'Mevr. Henriëtta Bird' en daarna was er niets vreselijks gebeurd. Niemand had er ook maar iets van geweten. Ik beet op mijn lip terwijl ik erover nadacht. Ja, ik kon dit. Als ik reusachtig voorzichtig was, kon ik dit doen, dat wist ik zeker.

Ik haalde een grote stapel van meneer Collins' werk uit mijn bak met ingekomen stukken en schikte die zo aan de voorkant van mijn bureau dat Kathleen, als ze binnenkwam, niet kon zien waarnaar ik keek. Daarna viste ik de brieven die mevrouw Bird in de prullenbak gegooid had er weer uit en las ze allemaal nog eens.

Sommige problemen gingen me vreselijk boven mijn pet. Ik had geen idee wat ik erop moest zeggen. Mijn persoonlijke ervaring schoot schromelijk tekort. Ik leunde tegen mijn rugleuning, beet op de nagel van mijn duim en dacht aan wat meneer Collins gezegd had: ik moest doen wat ik kon, zo goed als ik kon.

Ik zou er hard voor moeten werken. Research doen, uitzoeken wat een fatsoenlijke adviescolumnist zou zeggen, om niet te riskeren dat ik alles nog erger maakte voor de lezeressen in kwestie. Onmiddellijk voelde ik me gerustgesteld, want dat was echt iets voor journalisten: research doen voor een groot verhaal. Oorlogscorrespondenten wisten alles van undercover gaan. Ik zou het helpen van mijn lezeressen op precies dezelfde manier aanpakken.

Zelfs als ik geen antwoord op hun problemen had, waren er bendes veel populairdere tijdschriften die dat wel hadden. Ik zou die antwoorden niet kopiëren, maar ik kon er wel van leren. Ik voelde me het meest op mijn gemak als ik met meisjes van mijn eigen leeftijd praatte, dus al deed ik verder niets, ik kon beginnen met hen te helpen.

Tegen de tijd dat Kathleen verscheen met mevrouw Bussell, de theedame, die zenuwachtig was omdat ze te laat kwam, was ik helemaal enthousiast. Mijn prullenbak zat vol met een overtuigende hoeveelheid versnipperde enveloppen van lezeressen, terwijl drie brieven zich in het donker in mijn tas verschuilden om mee naar huis genomen te worden. Ik zou alle andere damesweekbladen kopen die ik te pakken kon krijgen, en Bunty en de meisjes van de brandweerkazerne vragen of ik hun bladen ook mocht lenen. Ik kon brieven schrijven en versturen vanaf de postbus die buiten voor de deur stond, en zelfs als iemand terugschreef om mevrouw Bird voor 'haar' advies te bedanken, kon ik ervoor zorgen dat mevrouw Bird dat niet te zien kreeg. Tenslotte maakte ík alle brieven open. Zij hoefde er nooit iets van te weten. Dit was spionage van de hoogste orde!

Waarschijnlijk zou ik misselijk geworden zijn van enthousiasme als mevrouw Bussell niet net op dat moment begonnen was aan haar gebruikelijke waarschuwing over de gevaren van thee met koekjes midden op de ochtend.

'Wacht maar tot je veertig bent,' verkondigde ze. 'Dan ben je halverwege de overgang en dan gaat alles op je heupen zitten.'

Ik uitte een gepaste reactie op dit angstaanjagende vooruitzicht en toonde een overmatige belangstelling in het uitzoeken van het juiste koekje. Aangezien de keuze beperkt was, zat ik een paar tellen later weer achter mijn typemachine met een kopje thee en een slechts lichtelijk kapot gemberkoekje.

Ik was helemaal in de wolken met mijn plan. Ook Kathleen was in een jubelstemming, omdat ze een kwijtgeraakt pakje voor mevrouw Bird had weten op te sporen. Ze begon erop los te babbelen.

'Ik ben blij dat ik het gevonden heb,' zei ze nadat mevrouw Bussell ons had verlaten om een andere afdeling dik te maken. 'Er zitten een heleboel nieuwe patronen en staaltjes in. Mevrouw Bird zou beslist stapelgek geworden zijn als we dat kwijtgeraakt waren. Na vanmorgen is het waarschijnlijk beter als jij en ik ons koest houden.'

Ik liet een schril lachje horen, wat helemaal niets voor mij is. 'Zeg dat wel!' brulde ik met volle mond.

Kathleen hield haar wijsvinger voor haar lippen en zei: 'Sst.'

Ik richtte me weer op het werk van meneer Collins.

Hoofd in de wolken. Het volgende hoofdstuk van onze nieuwe, onstuimig romantische serie.

Ik typte netjes volgens script:

> **Lichtzinnige jonge Clara. Zoveel om zich op te verheugen in haar welvarende, gelukkige leven. Ach, wilde ze haar ogen maar openen, dan zou ze zien hoeveel de jonge kapitein van haar zou kunnen houden.**

Het was een smartelijke, duizelingwekkend aangrijpende tekst. Ik typte verder terwijl het verhaal steeds dramatischer werd. Tenslotte was ik niet meer dan een parttime assistente die vlijtig haar werk deed.

7

Een dilemma over volgende stappen

Het enige wat me echt dwarszat aan mijn beslissing de lezeressen terug te schrijven, was dat ik het niet aan mijn beste vriendin kon vertellen.

Bunty en ik hadden geen geheimen voor elkaar. Je kunt niet je hele leven met iemand bevriend zijn en voor diegene verzwijgen wat je van plan bent. Ik was ervan overtuigd dat ze mijn plan zou afkeuren, maar ik snakte ernaar het haar te vertellen. Ik hoopte dat ze, als ik goed uitlegde dat ik er mensen mee hielp, het zou begrijpen.

Aan het eind van mijn ochtend bij *Vrouw & Vriendin* kwam ik thuis met een klein pakje brieven – diep in mijn tas verstopt – en met een stapel damesbladen van meneer Bone, de tijdschriftenverkoper, onder mijn arm. Het had weer flink gesneeuwd en ik stampte met mijn voeten op de mat bij de voordeur. Zodra ik boven was, zou ik mijn schoenen volproppen met krantenpapier om ze droog te krijgen. Terwijl ik de drie trappen naar ons appartement op stommelde, riep ik 'Hallo' naar Bunty, maar ze reageerde niet. Ze had weer nachtdiensten gedraaid, dus het was best mogelijk dat ze een dutje deed. Ik liep door naar boven en ging de woonkamer binnen.

Maar Bunty sliep niet; ze stond bij de open haard met

een bezorgde uitdrukking op haar gezicht en ze had haar op een na beste blauwe rok aan.

'Emmy, ik vind het zo erg,' zei ze en overhandigde me een envelop, nog voordat ik mijn hoed afgezet had. Het was een telegram, aan mij geadresseerd. We kregen nooit telegrammen. Ik kon maar aan één ding denken: Edmund.

Ik voelde het bloed uit mijn gezicht wegtrekken. Ik keek naar Bunty en toen weer naar de envelop. Daarna haalde ik diep adem.

Bunty bleef om me heen hangen terwijl ik de envelop openmaakte en de vijf zinnen van het telegram las.

Het was niet wat ik gevreesd had.

In feite was ik na het lezen van het telegram – de inhoud onthulde dat Edmund echt helemaal tiptop in orde was – nogal in tweestrijd. Ik was ontzettend blij dat hij niet door een Duitser neergeschoten was, maar over de rest van het bericht was ik niet bepaald in de wolken.

'Ik vind het echt heel erg voor je,' zei Bunty weer. 'Wil je misschien een zakdoek hebben?'

Ze bood me haar eigen zakdoek aan. Die was keurig schoon, met citroengele randen.

'Nee, dank je,' zei ik beleefd, al was dit overduidelijk een moeilijke situatie.

Bunty keek diepbedroefd. 'Wil je misschien gaan zitten?' vroeg ze. 'Misschien ga ík wel zitten. Is het Edmund? Arme, lieve Edmund.'

Bunty zette de radio, die een bemoedigend deuntje speelde, uit. Zoals iedereen wist ze dat telegrammen uit het buitenland altijd, zonder uitzondering, bijzonder slecht nieuws bevatten.

'Was hij verschrikkelijk dapper?' vroeg ze, blijkbaar hopend op verdere informatie over Edmunds waarschijnlijke dood. Bunty was altijd vreselijk goed in een crisis, maar ze stond niet bekend om haar geduld.

'Nee,' zei ik langzaam. 'Nee, dat zou ik niet willen zeggen. Eigenlijk is hij ervandoor met een verpleegster, Bunts.'

'Wat?' Bunty's wenkbrauwen deden gymnastiekoefeningen. 'Ik dacht dat hij dood zou zijn.'

Ik overhandigde haar het telegram en probeerde te bedenken wat ik nu hoorde te zeggen.

Ze las de inhoud en reageerde vrij levendig. 'Hoe haalt hij het in zijn hoofd jou telegrammen te sturen terwijl hij blijkbaar tiptop in orde is?'

Ik gaapte haar met open mond aan. Dat toonde niet veel ruggengraat van mijn kant, maar het was het enige wat ik kon opbrengen.

Bunty propte de citroengele zakdoek nijdig in haar mouw, alsof die haar op akelige wijze herinnerde aan haar voorbarige, verkeerd geïnformeerde rouw.

'EEN TELEGRAM!' Haar stem klonk snerpend. 'Hoe haalt hij het in zijn hoofd een telegram te sturen terwijl hij niet eens DOOD is?'

Ze begon het telegram voor te lezen; ik wist niet zeker of dat wijs was, aangezien ze er nu al uitzag alsof ze een beroerte zou krijgen.

'... gevallen voor Wendy. Trouwen zaterdag. Even goede vrienden. Tabee dan. Edmund. PS...' Bunty hield op met lezen en keek op. 'Emmy, hij heeft je de bons gegeven. Wat een VARKEN!'

Bunty zorgde altijd dat haar mening volkomen duidelijk was. Daar was ze goed in.

Ik pakte het telegram van haar af voordat ze het in woede zou verscheuren en legde het daarna op de schoorsteenmantel, wat geen goed idee was, want nu zag het eruit als een uitnodiging voor een spannend evenement – wat het voor Wendy waarschijnlijk ook zou zijn.

Ik probeerde rustig na te denken. Het was echt een kolossale opluchting dat Edmund niets mankeerde. Maar verder was het vooral alsof iemand me een dreun in mijn maag gegeven had. Ik had het gevoel dat ik misschien echt zou moeten overgeven.

'Nou,' wist ik eindelijk uit te brengen, 'we moeten blij zijn dat alles goed is met Edmund. En dat hij niet dood is. Dat is echt kolossaal goed nieuws.'

'Nou ja. Ja. Natuurlijk.' Bunty knikte. 'Ja,' zei ze nogmaals, in een poging goed mee te doen. Daarna gaf ze het op en voegde eraan toe: 'Maar het is nog steeds echt afschuwelijk van hem.'

Bunty had gelijk. Ik probeerde het tot me te laten doordringen. Edmund had me de afgelopen weken nauwelijks geschreven, maar ik had me voorgehouden dat hij druk bezig was met de vijand in de pan te hakken – zou meneer Bone zeggen. Dat was beter dan me zorgen maken of het wel goed met hem ging. Het was niet bij me opgekomen dat hij ook druk bezig kon zijn met verliefd worden op iemand anders.

'Hoe kón hij? Je hebt hem pas nog dat wollen hemd gestuurd,' zei Bunty, op een toon alsof ik het klaargespeeld had een tank voor hem te bouwen.

Ook hierin had ze weer gelijk. Met de naaimachine kon ik bijna alles maken wat je maar leuk zou kunnen vinden, maar ik was vreselijk slecht in breien en ik had een eeuw over dat wollen hemd gedaan.

'Misschien heeft hij dat niet ontvangen,' zei ik.

Treurig ging ik zitten, want mijn knieën besloten het te begeven.

'Ik zal een borrel voor je pakken,' zei Bunty. Onder gunstige omstandigheden dronken we geen van beiden veel, maar aangezien alles vandaag niet bepaald gunstig verliep, was dit misschien een goed moment om daarmee te beginnen.

Ze tilde het deksel van ons drankkastje, dat de vorm van een globe had, op. Het was een kolossaal, foeilelijk ding, maar Bunty's grootmoeder had gedacht dat wij het modern zouden vinden. Bunty en ik hadden besloten dat we het, als de Duitsers Londen binnenvielen en bij ons inbraken, van de trap zouden duwen, naar hen toe. Het hele Britse Gemenebest stond er in een nogal zelfverzekerde kleur oranje op en wij dachten dat ze daar echt kolossaal boos van zouden worden.

'Ik maak een whisky-soda voor je,' zei Bunty, die dol was op Amerikaanse films.

Het was twintig over drie in de middag en we dronken geen van beiden ooit whisky, laat staan overdag. Waarschijnlijk was dit iets wat filmster Bette Davis altijd deed, en het zou heel opwindend geweest zijn als het maar niet voortgekomen was uit het feit dat Edmund niet met mij wilde trouwen. Hoe bestond het dat ik dat niet doorgehad had? Ik legde mijn hoofd in mijn handen en probeerde niet te huilen. Ik voelde me zo stom. En gekwetst.

Bunty overhandigde me mijn borrel. Ik durfde te wedden dat Bette Davis zich niet gekwetst zou voelen. Eigenlijk durfde ik te wedden dat zij zich om te beginnen al helemaal niet met Edmund verloofd zou hebben. Hij was waarschijnlijk een beetje te verstandig voor haar en bovendien zou hij het feit dat ze een beroemde actrice was waarschijnlijk kolossale aandachttrekkerij gevonden hebben. Tenslotte had hij mij ook uitgelachen toen ik vertelde dat ik oorlogscorrespondente wilde worden.

Ik snoof eens aan de whisky. Bunty, die me angstvallig in de gaten hield, hief haar glas en ik volgde haar voorbeeld. Daarna namen we een flinke slok, als echte vrouwen-die-van-wanten-weten.

Binnen de kortste keren begonnen mijn longen te branden en we kregen allebei een flinke hoestbui. Na een tijdje veegde ik mijn ogen af en probeerde me te vermannen.

'Wat zou Bette Davis doen?' vroeg ik. 'Met Edmund?'

'Hem neerschieten met een pistool en daarna op de vlucht slaan,' hijgde Bunty terwijl ze naast me op de bank kwam zitten en haar rok gladstreek. 'Em, ik weet best dat dat hemd eruitzag alsof het door een waanzinnige gebreid was tijdens de verduistering, en misschien was hij daardoor wel een beetje minder dol op je, maar er met iemand anders vandoor gaan slaat echt alles.'

'Ja hè?' zei ik instemmend.

De waarheid was dat ik van Edmund gehouden had, of op zijn minst gedacht had dat ik van hem hield, en dat we al eeuwen met elkaar gingen, dus had het volkomen verstandig geleken om ons met elkaar te verloven. Ik vroeg me af wat er precies gebeurd was zodat hij van gedachten veranderd was wat met mij trouwen betreft. Had ik iets verkeerd gedaan, of was Wendy zo volmaakt mieters dat hij haar niet kon negeren? Ik wist niet wat ik ervan moest denken.

Ik voelde me als een van de lezeressen die brieven aan mevrouw Bird schreven.

In de schemerige woonkamer overwoog ik nog een slok van mijn borrel te riskeren. Nu het branden van mijn longen gekalmeerd was, smaakte de drank helemaal zo slecht nog niet, en ik had het gevoel dat het me hielp om een enigszins filosofische instelling aan te nemen.

Ik knikte naar het telegram op de schoorsteenmantel. 'Ik vraag me af wat Wendy voor iemand is,' zei ik.

'Ik durf te wedden dat ze vreselijk is,' antwoordde Bunty, loyaal tot op het bot, maar zonder een greintje bewijs.

We bleven allebei zwijgend zitten en overpeinsden de kolossale omvang van deze situatie.

'Ik zal het iedereen moeten laten weten,' zei ik.

Bunty trok een meelevend gezicht. 'Ze begrijpen het vast wel. Iedereen zal je alleen maar willen helpen en opvrolijken. Ik kan het wel vertellen, als je dat wilt. Ik zal het William in elk geval vertellen,' zei ze. 'Hij zal Edmund waarschijnlijk om zeep willen brengen. Tenzij je broer hem als eerste te pakken krijgt.'

Ik glimlachte halfhartig en begon op te sommen wie het allemaal moesten weten – mijn stem klonk niet zo dapper als ik gehoopt had. 'Moeder en vader en oma en dominee Wiffle.'

Dominee Wiffle was onze predikant. Hij had jicht en keek scheel, maar als je eenmaal wist welk oog je aankeek als je hem sprak, bleek hij reuze aardig. Hij zou een verbroken verloving bijzonder ongemakkelijk vinden.

Eigenlijk zou het beroerd zijn om het iedereen te vertellen. Vader zou zeggen: 'Emmy, die jongen is een sukkel van de eerste orde,' en moeder zou hem in de rede vallen met: 'Volgens mij helpt het niet om te schelden, Alfred, maar ik moet toegeven dat Edmund zich buitengewoon dwaas heeft gedragen.'

Al met al zou het niet meevallen.

'Bunts,' zei ik, 'ik word een oude vrijster.'

'Rustig aan,' weersprak Bunty. 'Je maakt best nog kans.'

'Nee, ik heb de boot gemist. Ik moet voortaan alleen door het leven.'

Ik probeerde uit alle macht Edmunds afwijzing sportief te incasseren. Zwelgen in je ellende deed je niet, en al voelde ik me nogal verpletterd, toch wilde ik vooruitkijken. Tenslotte was ik degene die de oorlog wilde in marcheren als verslaggever. Ik kon niet bij het minste of geringste in een hoekje gaan zitten huilen.

Ik stond op van de bank en begon met grote stappen door de woonkamer heen en weer te lopen terwijl ik verder sprak. 'Ik kan dit soort toestanden niet nog eens doormaken, Bunts. Van nu af aan is het huwelijk streng verboden toegang voor mij. Ik ga me volledig op mijn carrière concentreren.'

'Goed zo!' zei Bunty, opgewekt over mijn recente rampzalige beroepskeuze heen stappend. 'Wat kan die rot-Edmund je ook schelen?'

Ze nam nog een slok whisky en stond op.

'Sorry,' hijgde ze daarna. 'Volgens mij kan ik niet meer ademhalen.'

Ik sloeg haar op haar rug, wat niet hielp, en zette daarna de radio aan, wat misschien wel zou helpen.

Het was nog te vroeg om me klaar te maken voor mijn nachtdienst in de telefooncentrale van de brandweerkazerne, maar zodra ik mijn borrel ophad, ging ik naar mijn kamer om mijn uniform vast aan te trekken. Intussen probeerde ik alles op een rijtje te zetten. Hoewel ik het klaargespeeld had me dapper voor te doen – ik had zelfs geen traan gelaten – voelde ik me eigenlijk totaal verpletterd. Ik ging op mijn bed zitten, naast de stapel tijdschriften die ik meegenomen had, en wenste in stilte dat ik gewoon een maand zou kunnen slapen tot alles een beetje beter aanvoelde. Hoe had ik kunnen denken dat ik advies zou kunnen geven aan mensen die brieven schreven naar *Vrouw & Vriendin*? Dat was echt bespottelijk. Ik kon mijn eigen verloofde niet eens bij me houden. Nee, ik was volkomen ongekwalificeerd.

Aan de andere kant: nu kon ik nog beter sympathiseren met lezeressen die in hetzelfde schuitje zaten. Ik was zojuist botweg gedumpt, maar ik had vriendinnen en familieleden op wie ik kon rekenen, wat er ook gebeurde en hoelang ik hen ook nodig had. Terwijl ik me in mijn slaapkamer vreselijk zat te voelen, was Bunty in de keuken een boterham voor me aan het klaarmaken met het laatste restje vleespastei – wat mijn lievelingskostje was – in de hoop dat het me zou opvrolijken. En hoewel het moeilijk zou worden om mijn ouders over Edmund te vertellen, wist ik dat ze zouden luisteren en me zouden verzekeren dat alles uiteindelijk minder pijn zou gaan doen. En Thelma en de meisjes van de kazerne zouden me vertellen dat Edmund een volslagen idioot moest zijn en dat ze hem trouwens, afgaand op wat ik in het verleden over hem had verteld, toch al nooit gemogen hadden.

Het mocht dan vreselijk pijn doen, ik had bendes mensen die naar me zouden luisteren. Ik hoefde dit niet helemaal alleen te verwerken.

Wat moest het akelig zijn als je niemand had die naar je luisterde! Stel je voor dat ik om geruststelling en advies te vragen geen andere keuze had dan een brief schrijven aan een volkomen vreemde bij een tijdschrift… En dat ze me zou negeren en geen antwoord wilde geven… Dat zou alles nog erger maken.

Ik veegde mijn ogen af en snoof. Ik mocht niet zomaar neerslachtig in een hoekje blijven zitten. Edmund had me de bons gegeven en ik voelde me een mislukkeling, maar hij was niet dood. En hij klonk ontzettend gelukkig in dat telegram, dus moest ik hem maar gewoon het beste wensen en mijn eigen leven leiden. Ik was nog altijd beter af dan bendes andere mensen. En mijn oma had zich niet haar halve leven laten vastketenen voor de rechten van de vrouw om daarna weg te kwijnen en af te wachten tot de een of andere kerel voor haar kwam zorgen.

Zo was dat!

'Goed,' zei ik hardop. 'Kop op!'

Ik snoot mijn neus. Daarna haalde ik de brieven van de lezeressen, mijn pen en mijn notitieboek uit mijn tas. Ook pakte ik het bovenste tijdschrift van de stapel. Vervolgens sloeg ik de adviesrubriek – ook hier op de op een na laatste pagina – op, haalde de dop van mijn pen en begon aantekeningen te maken. De adviezen waren praktisch en in het algemeen sympathiek, en ze beantwoordden vragen over ontzettend veel onderwerpen waarmee mevrouw Bird niets te maken wilde hebben. Vrouwen die hun hoofd op hol hadden laten brengen door een man, die teleurgesteld waren door een man of zich zorgen maakten over een andere man. Anderen waren bang dat hun kinderen iets zou overkomen, of ontevreden over hun ouders. Sommige lezeressen waren dom geweest, maar geen enkele brief was schandalig. Een paar tijdschriften beloofden folders te sturen met uitleg over onderwerpen die ze niet in het tijdschrift konden behandelen.

Ik keek naar het stapeltje brieven dat ik mee naar huis genomen had. Het leek verschrikkelijk onbetekenend om te proberen die een of twee lezeressen te helpen die een postzegel en hun adres ingesloten hadden, terwijl deze grote, kleurige tijdschriften door duizenden en nog eens duizenden mensen gelezen werden.

Wat *Vrouw & Vriendin* eigenlijk zou moeten doen, was fatsoenlijke adviezen publiceren, zodat meer lezeressen ze zouden lezen. In stilte wenste ik dat mevrouw Bird de andere tijdschriften zou kunnen zien.

Ik herlas de brief van Verbijsterd, het meisje van wie de verloofde geen belangstelling meer voor haar had. *Hij zegt dat hij gek op me is, maar niet hartstochtelijk.* Had Edmund zo over mij gedacht? En als ik echt helemaal eerlijk was: had ik misschien ook zo over hem gedacht? Plotseling was ik bijna opgelucht omdat we niet met elkaar zouden trouwen. Stel je voor dat hij Wendy ontmoet had en uit plichtsbesef toch met mij getrouwd was. Dat zou afschuwelijk geweest zijn. Misschien kon ik dit alles echt van de zonnige kant bekijken.

Ik voelde me voldoende toegerust om Verbijsterd terug te schrijven en besloot een bemoedigende volgende zet te bedenken. Maar toen ik nog eens goed keek, zag ik geen adres of gefrankeerde envelop voor het antwoord. Mijn moment van triomf was meteen voorbij; ik voelde me ontmoedigd. Dit was juist een probleem dat ik echt kon begrijpen en waarschijnlijk zou ik haar ook kunnen helpen, maar nu kon ik haar niet terugschrijven.

Treurig smeet ik de brief weer op het bed.

De combinatie van een nare dag en een groot glas whisky bezorgde me een koppige, optimistische kijk op het leven.

Waarom zouden we niet proberen Verbijsterd te helpen? Of een ander meisje in haar positie dat *Vrouw & Vriendin* las? Het kon mevrouw Bird toch niets schelen. Haar zou het waarschijnlijk niet eens opvallen als er een extra brief in de adviesrubriek terechtkwam.

Dus waarom niet?

Nee, dat zou echt een kolossaal risico zijn. Idioot en roekeloos. Zoiets als tot achter de vijandelijke linies doordringen en verslagen sturen onder het oog van de vijand. Alleen de krankzinnigste of de allerdapperste oorlogscorrespondent zou zoiets doen.

Voor het eerst sinds Edmunds telegram glimlachte ik breeduit.

8

Een gerucht over stukjes ananas

Gedumpt worden door Edmund betekende dat mijn onbedoelde carrièreswitch naar damestijdschriften inmiddels nauwelijks nog enige nieuwswaarde had, wat mijn familie betrof. Toen ik vertelde dat ik niet meer verloofd was, hadden mijn ouders voorgesteld dat ik het weekend bij hen thuis zou doorbrengen, en het vooruitzicht op een zeldzame strooptaart en het laatste blik met stukjes ananas was te mooi om af te slaan. En wat nog beter was: mijn broer Jack had voor het eerst in eeuwen verlof, dus ik zou ook hem weer zien.

Ik was de afgelopen week op mijn werk een toonbeeld van deugd geweest voor zover het mevrouw Bird betrof, en had haar vlijtig een handjevol veilige brieven gegeven waar zelfs zij geen bezwaar tegen kon hebben. Veel belangrijker was dat ik in het geheim drie lezeressen teruggeschreven had; ik had diep nagedacht over de antwoorden die ik thuis in klad geschreven en vervolgens uitgetypt had en probeerde ze met vaste hand te ondertekenen met de tekst: *Hoogachtend, mevr. H. Bird.*

Ondertekenen met mevrouw Birds naam was het moeilijkste, en het was geen werkwijze die ik licht opnam. Als ik bij het terugschrijven aan In de War betrapt was, had ik misschien nog kunnen doen alsof ik onschuldig was, maar schrijven aan meerdere lezeressen was een stap verder op bijzonder gevaarlijk terrein. Het was natuurlijk heel iets anders dan Duitse tanks of vijandelijk vuur trotseren, of proberen Londen elke nacht te beschermen tegen afbranden in de Blitzkrieg. Als je het zo bekeek, nam ik eigenlijk helemaal geen ernstig risico. Dus ondertekende ik de brieven als mevrouw Bird en deed ze stuk voor stuk op de post.

De brief van Verbijsterd had ik nog steeds, en ik had een korte reactie geschreven die gemakkelijk op de wekelijkse 'Henriëtta Bird weet raad'-pagina zou passen, maar ik had nog niet het initiatief genomen om die echt aan mevrouw Mahoney te geven om te laten zetten. Ik vermoedde dat mevrouw Bird niet de moeite nam het eindproduct te lezen – de exemplaren die Kathleen in haar postbakje legde, leken altijd onaangeraakt – maar dat wist ik niet helemaal zeker. Verder onderzoek was dus vereist.

Ik vertelde Bunty niets van dit alles. Ik vond het vreselijk dit voor haar achter te houden, maar ze was zo bezorgd over me vanwege Edmund dat ze vast en zeker zou denken dat ik leed aan een of andere hersenstoring. En eerlijk gezegd, hoewel ik dacht haar er wel van te kunnen overtuigen dat het niet zo onbezonnen was om af en toe een behulpzaam antwoord op te sturen, wist zelfs ik dat het veel te ver ging om een brief het tijdschrift binnen te smokkelen zonder medeweten van mevrouw Bird.

Een week nadat ik een vrijgezelle carrièrevrouw werd, gingen Bunty en ik op weg naar Little Whitfield. Ik zag enigszins op tegen de partijdige beroerte van mijn ouders over Edmund, maar het was fijn om uit Londen weg te gaan. Het dorp was gelukkig nauwelijks geraakt tijdens de luchtaanvallen die hadden plaatsgevonden, al was er wel een weiland opgeblazen toen een bommenwerper uit koers geraakt was na het bestoken van een van de kleinere steden. Al met al lokte de gedachte aan twee nachten in een lekker warm bed, zonder naar beneden te moeten slaapwandelen om in de bomschuilplaats te komen of mijn helm te moeten opzetten in de brandweerkazerne, me meer aan dan een week in Monte Carlo.

Bunty en ik namen op zaterdagmorgen een trein vanaf Waterloo Station. Het station krioelde van alle troepen op weg naar of van hun kwartieren en mensen die het weekend naar hun familie gingen. De trein zat stampvol militairen op weg naar Weymouth en Bunty zag dit als een ideale gelegenheid om een vervanger voor Edmund te zoeken, of ik er nu een wilde hebben of niet. In een volle coupé genoten we van de rit door het platteland van Hampshire in gezelschap van een paar bijzonder aardige officieren die erop stonden ons hun zitplaats te geven en daarbij nog een reep chocola, twee sigaretten – hoewel we niet rookten – en verschillende adressen om hun te schrijven.

Terwijl de sneeuw gestaag viel – het was februari – maakten we knerpend de korte wandeling van het treinstation van Little Whitfield naar ons huis. Deze route hadden Bunty en ik al honderden keren samen afgelegd. Bunty, ik en Jack trokken al samen op sinds haar beide ouders gestorven waren, nog voordat zij op school zat, al was ze niet helemaal een wees omdat ze haar oma nog had.

Bunty kende mijn familie dus door en door; nu nam ze de rol van hoofd morele steun met verve op zich met het oog op de naderende lawine van medeleven en mogelijke toorn.

'Je ouders zullen enthousiast zijn over *Vrouw & Vriendin*,' zei ze. 'Ze zijn vast blij dat je nu veel minder kans loopt gewond te raken tijdens journalistieke plichten dan wanneer je bij *The Chronicle* had gezeten, dus zo erg is het allemaal niet.'

'Hmm,' zei ik, 'ik denk niet dat ze zich zorgen maken over mijn werk. Ze zijn allemaal zo woedend over Edmund dat we waarschijnlijk het hele weekend op hen moeten inpraten om te voorkomen dat ze hem over de kling jagen.'

Bunty lachte. 'Dat is anders geen slecht idee.' Ze schopte met haar overschoenen een klont sneeuw weg om haar woorden te benadrukken.

Vlak voor Vicarage Hill liepen we de brink op en daar zagen we tot onze blijdschap de Wildhay Oaks groot en stoïcijns onder hun zware sneeuwlaag staan. Jack, Bunty en ik hadden onze hele kindertijd tussen deze bomen gespeeld; we joegen achter elkaar aan en renden in volle vaart door tot iemand 'thuis!' kon roepen. Als je een boom aanraakte, was je veilig; dan mocht je niet gevangen worden. Voordat de oorlog begon, hadden Jack, Edmund en William een circuit rondom de bomen gemaakt en er dagelijks rondjes omheen gerend; alle drie de jongens waren erop gespitst in topconditie te zijn voor het leger.

Als de luchtaanvallen in Londen echt hevig waren, deed ik soms mijn ogen dicht en dan zag ik de Wildhay Oaks voor me, kalm en betrouwbaar als altijd. Zolang deze eiken nog standhielden, dacht ik dan, zou alles met ons ook wel goed aflopen.

Toen we de laatste hoek omsloegen en Glebe Lane op liepen, kwam Pennyfield House in zicht. Het was een lief, klein huis uit de tijd van koning George, omringd door treurwilgen en met zulke symmetrische ramen dat het eruitzag alsof een kind de architect precies verteld had hoe een huis ontworpen moest worden. Ik vond die eerste aanblik van mijn ouderlijk huis altijd geweldig. Vandaag werd mijn gemijmer echter onderbroken door een kolossale sneeuwbal die me precies op mijn hoofd raakte, zodat mijn baret op de grond viel en ik sputterde als vaders oude automobiel.

'Jack Lake!' bulderde ik, want er was geen grote intelligentie voor nodig om te begrijpen waar de sneeuwbal vandaan kwam. 'Jack Lake, als je soms denkt dat je –'

Mijn broer gooide nog een sneeuwbal precies raak, midden in mijn gezicht.

'Hij staat bij de zijpoort, Em,' gilde Bunty, die, niet in het minst van slag door de aanval, enthousiast munitie aan het verzamelen was. Haar koffer lag al op de grond. Zij was de helft van haar kindertijd het doelwit van mijn broer geweest en ze kende de strategie van onze tegenstander. 'Ik zal hem wel krijgen.'

'Heel onwaarschijnlijk, Bunts, ouwe oma!' schreeuwde mijn broer terwijl een volgend projectiel rakelings langs Bunty's hoofd zoefde.

'Mis!' brulde ik terwijl ik sneeuw opschepte. 'Noem jij jezelf een gevechtspiloot? Jij gooit als een klein meisje!'

Jacks reactie bestond uit een waar spervuur van sneeuwballen, stuk voor stuk midden in de roos.

'Dames,' treiterde hij met een heel vrolijk stemmetje, 'ik probeer jullie nog een kans te geven.'

De sneeuw op mijn jas begon te smelten – hij was niet waterdicht – en mijn wollen handschoenen waren doorweekt.

'Zwijn!' schreeuwde ik. 'Misbaksel!'

'Hoe komen we binnen?' fluisterde Bunty, die minstens één voltreffer in haar gezicht te pakken gekregen had en nu op een knipperbol bij een zebrapad leek. 'Hij zal de achterpoort wel gebarricadeerd hebben.'

Ik bedwong een enthousiast gesnuif. Natuurlijk had hij dat gedaan. Het was volmaakt! Terwijl Europa geteisterd werd door een krankzinnige en Engeland zijn best deed de hoop op een vrije wereld levend te houden, waren wij drieën als kinderen in de sneeuw aan het spelen. Even was het alsof er niets veranderd was sinds de tijd dat alles nog eenvoudig was en je ouders er waren om alle gruwelen gewoon te laten verdwijnen.

'Er zit maar één ding op, Bunts,' fluisterde ik terug. 'Stormram. Sjaals omhoog.'

We wikkelden allebei onze druipende sjaal om ons gezicht. Bunty drukte haar hoed plat op haar hoofd en ik wenste in stilte dat mijn baret niet midden op de weg lag.

Het was je reinste zelfmoordmissie, maar we zetten door en tien meter verderop deden we ons best om zo veel mogelijk sneeuw in het gezicht van mijn broer te keilen. Omdat hij werd beschermd door zijn lange uniformjas en zijn leren handschoenen hadden onze pogingen Jack tot op dat moment nog helemaal niet weten te treffen, maar nu lachte hij zo uitbundig dat hij een grote klont sneeuw inslikte. Hij vocht dapper terug en presteerde het ons allebei op een armlengte afstand vast te houden, zodat we enkel met onze armen in het rond konden fladderen, als twee jonge vogeltjes die zijn gevangen door een grote hond.

We gilden en lachten en schreeuwden alle drie even hard.

'Kinderen toch! Jullie worden doodziek zo.'

Mijn moeder stond bij de deur van het huis en ze verhief haar stem nauwelijks, maar we stopten allemaal meteen met knokken.

Keurig als altijd, een toonbeeld van kalmte in haar lichtblauwe geribbelde vest en plooirok, schudde moeder haar hoofd, maar ze glimlachte erbij.

'Jullie gedragen je stuitend, alle drie. Ik heb jammerlijk gefaald. Jack, ga de baret van je zus oprapen, Emmeline, hou op met je broer te plagen, en Bunty, kom meteen hierheen zodat ik kan zien hoe het met je gaat. Kom… voorwaarts, mars.'

Gehoorzaam lieten we elkaar los en begonnen hoeden, koffers en tassen die we tijdens het handgemeen hadden laten vallen op te rapen. Bunty werd hartelijk op beide wangen gekust door mijn moeder, die verklaarde dat ze even aantrekkelijk was als altijd. Intussen zette Jack mijn baret zwierig scheef op mijn hoofd en omhelsde me stevig.

'Fijn je te zien, zus,' zei hij. 'Beroerd om je nieuws te horen. Die man is een sukkel. Gaat het een beetje?'

'Het gaat prima, dank je,' zei ik, getroffen door zijn medeleven.

'Was het dat hemd? Volgens moeder was het niet duidelijk of hij het aan moest trekken of als een soort matrozenpetje moest gebruiken. Nou ja, je bent nu tenminste wel op weg naar *The Times*.' Hij grijnsde naar me; zijn blauwe ogen glansden en zijn oren waren felrood van de kou. Hij leek niet ouder dan een jaar of tien. 'Als je wilt, zal ik Edmund opsporen en buiten westen slaan, weet je. Echt.'

Ik schudde mijn hoofd. 'Het gaat wel, bedankt. Eigenlijk is het ook maar beter zo.'

'Wat? Om een oude vrijster te zijn?' Hij leek niet echt overtuigd. 'Nou ja, hoe dan ook, maak je geen zorgen: ik kan altijd nog een goed woordje voor je doen bij de jongens. Jocko Carlisle is misschien de moeite waard. Nee, wacht. Jocko niet, die is net verloofd. Of Chaser, dat is ook een fijne vent.' Hij dacht even na. 'Eigenlijk toch niet... De naam zegt het al: een rokkenjager.' Hij fronste zijn wenkbrauwen, maar daarna vrolijkte hij weer op. 'Laat het maar aan mij over, Em. Ik zal er eens goed over nadenken.'

Ik knikte dapper. Dat was gemakkelijker dan hem ervan te overtuigen dat ik geen man nodig had.

'Kom, we gaan naar binnen,' stelde ik voor. 'Het gerucht gaat dat er stukjes ananas zijn.'

Dat was genoeg om Jack af te leiden; hij hield op me uit te huwelijken aan zijn halve eskader en samen liepen we de gang in.

Moeder hielp Bunty uit haar jas en zei, op een toon die ze normaal gesproken nooit gebruikte: 'Is het niet geweldig dat het echt helemaal goed gaat met Emmy?'

Bunty wist natuurlijk dat dit codetaal was voor: 'Zeg eens eerlijk, het hart van mijn dochter is gebroken, of niet soms?'

Ik kuchte. Moeder draaide zich snel om, gooide Bunty's jas over haar arm en pakte vervolgens mijn gezicht tussen haar handen om me stralend aan te kijken. 'Lieveling, wat zie je er goed uit!' riep ze. Ik wist natuurlijk dat ze eigenlijk bedoelde: 'Als ik Edmund Jones ooit nog eens ontmoet, sta ik niet voor mezelf in.'

'Bedankt, mam; het gaat goed met me.'

'Ja, het gaat goed met je!'

'Inderdaad.'

'En dat is fijn!'

'Nou en of!'

Moeder leek niet bepaald van plan het gesprek op een ander onderwerp te brengen. Als we in dit tempo doorgingen, stonden we hier met Pasen nog.

Maar toen trok ze me naar zich toe en hield mijn armen zo stevig vast alsof ze me nooit meer los wilde laten.

'Mannen zijn zulke imbecielen, lieve schat,' fluisterde ze. Het klonk fel, maar daarna veranderde ze van toon. 'Behalve je vader, natuurlijk. Maar de rest: imbecielen.'

Ik kon nauwelijks ademhalen. Als mijn hele familie dit bleef doen, had ik grote kans een paar ribben te breken.

'En Jack,' hijgde ik in moeders haar, 'Jack is best prima. En Gregory mogen we ook graag, toch? Dus niet alle mannen...'

Moeder drukte me nogmaals tegen zich aan. 'Grote meid,' zei ze. 'Zo is dat. Niet allemaal. Goed zo.'

'Houdt je moeder de imbecielentoespraak?'

Mijn vader was de gang in komen lopen.

'Hallo, Bunty. Hoe gaat het met jou?' vroeg hij en kuste haar op de wang. 'Houd je het ministerie van Oorlog goed op gang? Ik hoop dat je Churchills grammatica controleert. Duitsers doen nogal laatdunkend over dat soort dingen.'

Bunty verzekerde hem dat de grammatica van meneer Churchill tiptop was, verzwijgend dat ze absoluut niets met hem te maken had en hem zelfs nog nooit in het gebouw van het ministerie gezien had. 'De muren hebben oren, dokter Lake,' voegde ze eraan toe om de ernst van haar werk te benadrukken.

Dat maakte kolossaal veel indruk op mijn vader. 'Je vader zou trots op je zijn,' zei hij en Bunty keek blij, zoals altijd wanneer hij iets over haar ouders zei, al kon ze zich geen van beiden echt herinneren.

Toen was ik aan de beurt.

'Hallo, pap,' zei ik terwijl hij me een kus gaf, zijn wenkbrauwen fronste en me over zijn brillenglazen heen aankeek.

'Ik heb hem nooit gemogen,' zei hij, wat een pertinente leugen was. 'Een absolute kluns. Je moeder maakt zich natuurlijk zorgen, maar ik heb gezegd dat ze het van de zonnige kant moet bekijken, want nu zullen we in ieder geval geen achterlijke kleinkinderen krijgen.' Hij gaf me een knipoog. 'Volgens mij vrolijkte ze daar van op.'

'Bedankt, pap,' zei ik. Dit was de langste toespraak die ik ooit van mijn vader gekregen had. Daarna kneep hij me nog eens hartelijk in mijn arm en zei: 'Goed gedaan, kindje,' hoewel ik niets gedaan had.

Ik trok mijn jas en sjaal uit, hing ze op de hoge victoriaanse kapstok die vroeger van mijn grootouders was en liep achter mijn vader aan de woonkamer in.

Ik hoorde hem in zichzelf mopperen. 'Afschuwelijke toestand,' zei hij. 'Ik jaag hem nog eens over de kling.'

Tijdens een eersteklas lunch, bestaande uit aardappelpuree zonder veel gehakt eronder, gevolgd door naar keuze een plak strooptaart of stukjes ananas met een lepel zorgvuldig opgespaarde custardpudding, werd ik door mijn ouders ondervraagd over – en door Jack geplaagd met – *Vrouw & Vriendin*. Tegen de tijd dat ik enthousiast verteld had hoe aardig iedereen was en hoe stevig het kantoor in elkaar zat, was iedereen het erover eens dat ik een lucratieve baan bemachtigd had bij een pioniersbedrijf voor vrouwen op de werkvloer en, wat mijn moeder nog veel belangrijker vond, bij het minst interessante doelwit voor de Luftwaffe in heel Londen.

'*Vrouw & Vriendin* helpt mensen, en dat is geweldig,' zei mijn moeder, alsof ik geld uitdeelde aan daklozen. 'En aangezien we nu eenmaal in deze dwaze toestand zitten, kunnen jullie, meisjes, er evengoed een carrière aan overhouden.'

Mijn moeder noemde de oorlog standvastig 'deze dwaze toestand', waardoor het klonk alsof het een milde ruzie over een sinaasappelcake was. Maar dit terzijde. Ik bofte dat mijn ouders zo'n moderne kijk op het leven hadden. Mijn vader stemde met haar in.

'Emmy,' zei hij, 'je bent de volgende in een lange rij formidabele vrouwen.'

'Hoe gaat het met oma, moeder?' vroeg Jack.

Mijn ouders wisselden veelbetekenende blikken.

'Stapelgek,' beantwoordde Jack zijn eigen vraag.

'Knetter,' zei ik tegelijkertijd.

'Wat vind jij ervan, Bunty?' vroeg mijn vader. 'Zeg het maar gerust.'

'Eh... Is ze nog steeds zo gek als een deur, dokter Lake?' vroeg Bunty, die mijn grootmoeder goed kende.

Vader brulde van het lachen. 'Ik denk dat dat wel een goede samenvatting is,' zei hij. 'Arme bevolking van Exeter. Ze zijn vast buitengewoon opgelucht als het vrede is en zij weer naar huis gaat.'

Moeder keek ons allemaal een voor een aan. 'Jack en

Bunty, jullie ruimen de tafel af, en Emmy gaat met me mee het dorp in, want ik moet een boek terugbrengen naar de bibliotheek.' Ze keek op haar polshorloge. 'Ze zijn maar tot twee uur open.'

Bunty begon met grote aandacht dessertschaaltjes te verzamelen, vooral omdat ze mij niet wilde aankijken, wist ik. Zij had om drie penny met me gewed dat moeder een gesprek met me zou willen voeren over Edmund.

Moeder werkte me de eetkamer uit en trok me mijn overjas aan op ongeveer dezelfde manier als ze gedaan had toen ik drie was. Even later liepen we arm in arm door de sneeuw naar de bibliotheek, zonder een boek om terug te brengen, merkte ik.

Ze babbelde vrolijk en bracht me op de hoogte van het plaatselijke nieuws; ze deed duidelijk haar best om me op mijn gemak te stellen en me ten onrechte het gevoel te geven dat ik veilig was.

'Hè bah,' zei ze toen we de weg naast de eendenvijver overstaken. Ze stond stil en zette haar handen in haar zij, wat een beetje overdreven geacteerd was, vond ik. 'Ik ben dat bibliotheekboek vergeten, vrees ik. Ach, nou ja, zullen we dan maar gewoon een eindje gaan wandelen?'

De sneeuw wervelde om ons heen terwijl we langs de High Street liepen, en moeder trok me dichter naar zich toe.

'Eigenlijk wilde ik je nog even onder vier ogen spreken.'

Bunty had de weddenschap gewonnen. Ik vroeg me af of we dit een beetje konden versnellen. Het was afgrijselijk koud.

'Moeder, het gaat prima met me. Echt. Ik vind het helemaal niet erg, van Edmund.'

Mijn moeder keek alsof ze zich geen zorgen maakte. 'Ja, lieveling, dat merk ik wel. En daar ben ik heel blij mee. Zo'n domme jongen. Vertel eens, hoe gaat het met die lieve Bunty? Mevrouw Tavistock heeft me uitgenodigd om op bezoek te komen en ik zou haar graag verslag uitbrengen.'

Toen de oorlog uitbrak, was Bunty's grootmoeder verhuisd naar haar kleine landgoed. Mevrouw Tavistock wilde Bunty niet verbieden om in Londen te blijven wonen, maar ze maakte zich voortdurend zorgen over haar kleindochter.

'Het gaat heel goed met Bunty,' zei ik, want dat was ook zo.

'Dat is mooi. En hoe gaat het met haar werk?'

'Druk,' zei ik. 'Diep geheim.'

'Natuurlijk,' zei mijn moeder. 'En William, hoe gaat het met hem? Denk jij dat ze met elkaar zullen trouwen?'

'Dat mag ik hopen,' zei ik en ik stapte voorzichtig om een bevroren stuk van de stoep heen.

'Ze hebben allebei geweldig geboft dat hij niet ergens naar het buitenland gestuurd is,' zei moeder uit de grond van haar hart. De zoons van haar vriendinnen waren over het algemeen allemaal in het buitenland.

'Ik denk niet dat William het met je eens is,' antwoordde ik. 'Hij lijdt er nog steeds onder dat het leger hem niet wil hebben vanwege zijn oren.'

Mijn moeder trok haar sjaal nog iets dichter om haar hals terwijl we verder liepen naar de Fox and Thicket, aan de oostkant van de brink.

'Brandweerman zijn is zulk gevaarlijk werk,' zei ze, alsof dat niet overduidelijk was. Daar hoefde ze mij niet aan te herinneren. Ik wist op welk soort oproepen hij moest reageren. Ik had zo het gevoel dat het gesprek in de richting ging van een toespraak over 'Jullie passen toch wel goed op jezelf?' Ik probeerde de boel een beetje te bagatelliseren. 'Moeder, alles is gevaarlijk.'

Ze stond stil, draaide zich naar me om en pakte mijn handen.

'Lieveling, we zijn allemaal ontzettend trots omdat jullie alles in Londen draaiende houden, maar willen jullie extra voorzichtig zijn? Mevrouw Tavistock maakt zich vreselijk ongerust over Bunty.'

'Moeder, Bunty en ik kunnen best voor onszelf zorgen,' zei ik.

Ze glimlachte, want ze wist dat ik gehapt had. 'Dat weet ik. Ik weet alleen niet wat mevrouw Tavistock zou doen als er iets gebeurde. Of wij. Niemand wil iemand kwijtraken. We houden allemaal zielsveel van jullie.'

Ze marcheerde verder en onder de rand van haar hoed deden haar blauwe ogen, die precies op die van Jack leken, hun best onbezorgd te kijken.

'Wij redden ons wel,' zei ik ferm.

Dat overtuigde haar helemaal niet. Moeder kneep haar lippen op elkaar.

'Ik meen het, Emmy,' zei ze na een korte stilte, terwijl ik met mijn ogen rolde als een tiener. 'Jullie moeten goed op elkaar passen. Mevrouw Tavistock kan geen ellende gebruiken. En ik ben niet zo jong als ik eruitzie.'

Ze keek me van opzij aan, waarna we allebei in de lach schoten.

'Laten we het over iets anders hebben,' zei moeder, die wist dat ik haar begreep. 'Je weet toch wel dat je op een dag een geweldige man zult ontmoeten?'

Ik begon aan mijn goed voorbereide toespraak over alleen blijven en carrière maken, maar ik kwam niet ver.

'Doe niet zo absurd,' zei moeder. 'Je kunt het allebei krijgen. Zodra deze dwaze toestand helemaal opgelost is, kunnen Bunty en jij en al jullie vriendinnen doorgaan en alles bereiken wat je maar wilt. Anders is het tijdverspilling dat we tegen die waanzinnige vechten.' Ze stak haar kin in de lucht op een manier die politiemannen tot stilstand gebracht moest hebben in haar onconventionele jeugd. 'Emmy, laat je door Edmund niet ontmoedigen. Echt, dat is helemaal niet de juiste mentaliteit.'

Ik grijnsde, want ik wist wanneer ik verslagen was.

'Op een gegeven moment komt er wel een of andere

fatsoenlijke jongen langs, en wat er ook gebeurt, maak er gewoon wat moois van bij dat tijdschrift van je. Je mag dan misschien niet overal rondstruinen om over de strijd te schrijven, maar het is een begin. En het is echt een leuk tijdschrift. Ik heb me erop geabonneerd.'

'Echt waar?' vroeg ik verbaasd. Mijn moeder zou eerder met een roman van Virginia Woolf aangetroffen worden dan met *Vrouw & Vriendin*.

'Natuurlijk, lieveling,' zei moeder met een tamelijk verontwaardigd gezicht. 'Dit is jouw carrière. En er staat veel leuks in. De WAT DE POT SCHAFT-pagina staat vol met geweldige ideeën.'

Ze ploeterde voort en deed haar uiterste best om positief te zijn. 'Die verpleegster is echt informatief, de verhalen zijn behoorlijk meeslepend, en HENRIËTTA WEET RAAD lijkt heel...' Ze raakte uitgeput.

'Hardvochtig?' suggereerde ik.

Mijn moeder lachte. 'Ik wilde "flink" zeggen. Maar het is vast ontzettend behulpzaam voor de mensen die brieven insturen.'

Ik zei: 'Hmm.' Het was eigenaardig om mevrouw Bird geprezen te horen worden.

'Eigenlijk lijkt mevrouw Bird te denken dat mensen – vooral jonge mensen – meestal kwaad in de zin hebben.' Ik trapte een homp sneeuw plat.

'Dan moet jij haar maar laten zien dat ze het mis heeft, hè?' antwoordde mijn moeder. 'Laat haar zien wat een fatsoenlijk jong mens kan doen.' Ze pakte mijn arm. 'Een beetje van die oude vastberadenheid van de familie Lake is daar wel nodig, denk ik. Denk je ook niet?'

Ik glimlachte in mijn sjaal. Mijn moeder gaf de moed nooit op. Een van vaders vrienden had eens gezegd dat als moeder het voor het zeggen gehad had, de Eerste Wereldoorlog al in 1916 afgelopen zou zijn. Waarop mijn vader had geantwoord dat die stomme oorlog, als mijn moeder het voor het zeggen gehad had, überhaupt helemaal nooit begonnen was. Moeder zei altijd dat je niet alleen moest doorgaan, maar dat je bovendien moest blijven staan voor waar je in geloofde.

Ik knikte. Ze had gelijk. Hier was een beetje van die oude vastberadenheid van de familie Lake nodig.

Terwijl de sneeuw weer begon te vallen en wij terugliepen naar Pennyfield House, popelde ik om weer achter mijn bureau te zitten, hoe fijn het ook was om thuis te zijn.

9

Wij kennen geen Harold

Bij het antwoorden van lezeressen was voorzichtigheid geboden en niet alleen omdat ik me zorgen maakte dat ik tegen de lamp zou lopen. Nog erger zou het zijn als ik waardeloze adviezen gaf en mijn lezeressen van de wal in de sloot hielp. Ik hield mijn reacties daarom algemeen, moedigde iedereen aan om de tijd te nemen om over de zaak na te denken, niet overhaast te handelen, en zeker nooit te zwichten. De andere tijdschriften waren heel bruikbaar: ik kwam te weten wat anderen zeiden en hoe ze het formuleerden en ik probeerde het ook zo te doen, zonder te kopiëren.

Beste mevr. Bird,
Ik ben tweeëntwintig en dol op mijn moeder, maar zij wil altijd mee als ik met mijn vriend naar de bioscoop of naar een dansfeestje ga. Ze geeft hem altijd complimenten en maakt ook altijd zijn lievelingseten voor hem klaar. Ik wil haar gevoelens niet kwetsen, maar ik vraag me af of ze af en toe niet een beetje al te vriendelijk is.
Wat moet ik doen?
Hoogachtend,
Juffrouw Joyce Dickinson, Preston

‘Weerzinwekkend,’ zei mevrouw Bird. ‘Nee.’

> *Beste juffrouw Dickinson,* schreef ik terug.
> *Uw moeder bedoelt het vast heel goed, en jullie zijn vast erg op elkaar gesteld. Toch stel ik voor dat u eerlijk met haar in gesprek gaat en haar uitlegt dat u uw eigen vrienden nodig hebt…*

Ik nam de brieven mee naar huis en aangezien Bunty nu in de dagdienst werkte bij het ministerie van Oorlog, zat ik ’s middags achter mijn typemachine in de woonkamer en schreef mijn reacties zorgvuldig op. Zodra ik tevreden was met mijn werk, typte ik het uit, ondertekende de brief met mevrouw Birds naam, wat nog steeds het ergste was, en de volgende dag deed ik ze in de brievenbus die bij het gebouw van Launceston Press stond.

Tot zover was het allemaal vlot verlopen en heel soms kon ik bijna vergeten dat dit niet echt bij mijn baan hoorde en dat het eigenlijk niet kon, wat ik deed. Mevrouw Bird had het drukker dan ooit; ze marcheerde van het ene naar het andere liefdadigheidswerk of haastte zich naar het treinstation om ‘hachelijke noodsituaties aan het thuisfront’ op te lossen – ‘Drachtige koe klem in een greppel. Die uilskuikens kunnen haar er niet uit krijgen.’ Behalve gebrulde instructies voor iedereen tijdens de wekelijkse redactievergaderingen liet ze ons eigenlijk allemaal onze eigen gang gaan.

Dat was maar goed ook, want op een ochtend, vlak voordat *Vrouw & Vriendin* ter perse ging, bleek een van de adverteerders vergeten de deodorantadvertentie op tijd in te sturen. Het was een doodzonde om de laatste deadline niet te halen en meneer Newton van de afdeling advertenties schrok zich bijna dood.

‘Grote griebels, grote griebels,’ bleef hij maar zeggen terwijl iedereen zich op de afdeling kunst verzamelde, nogal van streek. ‘Als er geen Odo-Ro-No is, valt er een gat van twee kolommen op pagina twaalf. Dan staat daar niets. Helemaal niets. Wat zal mevrouw Bird zeggen? Wat zal ze daarvan zeggen?'

'Mevrouw Bird maakt niet uit,' zei mevrouw Mahoney, die zich nu toch echt van haar strenge kant dreigde te laten zien. 'Het is mijn deadline die ze verknoeid hebben.'

'Wacht even, allemaal,' zei meneer Collins, de enige die kalm bleef. 'Mevrouw Mahoney, mag ik voorstellen dat we de advertentie voor Bile Beans van vorige week nogmaals plaatsen? Volgens mij heeft die ongeveer hetzelfde formaat.'

Mevrouw Mahoney werd milder en meneer Newton begon een beetje kleur terug te krijgen en was in staat namens ons allemaal te spreken.

'Maar wie vertelt het aan mevrouw Bird, meneer Collins? Wie vertelt het aan mevrouw Bird?'

Meneer Collins leek onbezorgd. 'Niemand,' zei hij terwijl we hem allemaal ontzet aankeken. 'We zullen Odo-Ro-No er volgende week in zetten. Met een beetje geluk komt ze het nooit te weten. O, schei uit, jullie!' voegde hij eraan toe, aangezien er paniek leek uit te breken. 'Heeft iemand onze redactrice ooit echt naar een voltooid exemplaar van het tijdschrift zien kijken? Steek dan je hand op.'

Niemand stak zijn of haar hand op. Ik wist het niet zeker, dus keek ik Kathleen aan. Zij schudde haar hoofd.

'Zie je wel,' zei meneer Collins. 'Bile Beans – afgesproken. Als iemand zich zorgen maakt, kom dan maar met mij praten. Of nee, doe maar niet,' voegde hij er rustig aan toe. 'Het komt allemaal goed.'

Daarna marcheerde hij de kamer uit en ging terug naar zijn eigen kantoor.

'Sjonge,' zei Kathleen.

'Die krijgt alles erdoor als hij wil,' zei mevrouw Mahoney.

'Ik word vast ontslagen,' kreunde meneer Newton.

Maar meneer Collins bleek gelijk te hebben. Mevrouw Bird merkte er niets van.

○

Dat was het bewijs dat ik nodig had. Ik had allang het idee dat onze redactrice geen gedrukte exemplaren las, maar dat was nauwelijks meer dan een vermoeden. De wens was de vader van de gedachte, eerlijk gezegd, en dat was beslist niet genoeg om er ook naar te handelen. Het absolute zelfvertrouwen van meneer Collins, gecombineerd met het feit dat mevrouw Bird niet opmerkte dat er een grote advertentie voor maagtabletten in plaats van een voor okselfrisheid was opgenomen, overtuigde me. Niets kon me nu nog tegenhouden.

Met een droge mond en klamme handen stopte ik de brief van Verbijsterd tussen de andere brieven die volgende week in Henriëtta weet raad afgedrukt zouden worden. Ik had de woorden een beetje veranderd zodat Kathleen de brief niet zou herkennen en het woord 'hartstochtelijk' door iets anders vervangen omdat ik wist dat alles daardoor zou uitkomen. Maar het ging nog steeds duidelijk over een verloofde die niet meer verliefd was. Als Verbijsterd mijn antwoord las, zou ze gerustgesteld zijn. Dat hoopte ik in elk geval van harte.

Het was simpel om de brief en mijn antwoord in de map met kopij te stoppen die naar mevrouw Mahoney zou gaan om gezet te worden, maar het was ontzaglijk moeilijk om die map ook echt uit handen te geven. Ik wist dat mevrouw Bird nooit naar drukproeven keek voordat het tijdschrift verscheen, dus vanaf dit punt kon ik niet meer terug.

Mijn plan voor onvoorziene gebeurtenissen was niet bepaald indrukwekkend. Als ik betrapt werd, zou ik beweren dat mevrouw Bird vergeten was dat ze dit advies geschreven had. Ontzettend zwak, maar het was het enige plan dat ik had. Als meneer Collins er alle vertrouwen in had dat mevrouw Bird een advertentie van een halve pagina niet zag, zou één briefje toch wel veilig zijn?

Ik besloot het risico te nemen.

Het werd hoog tijd dat ik Bunty over mijn geheime activiteiten vertelde. Ik had het lang genoeg uitgesteld. Bunty was beslist geen Brave Hendrik, verre van dat, maar ze was vreselijk gespitst op eerlijkheid en zou misschien niet meteen onder de indruk zijn van het idee. Ze zou het vast puik vinden als ik haar alles vertelde, dus besloot ik de volgende zaterdag de gok te wagen.

De zon deed goed zijn best aan de bijna wolkeloze winterse lucht, dus gingen Bunty en ik een wandeling door Hyde Park maken. Zij had voorgesteld eerst een stevige mars rondom de Serpentine te maken, voor theetijd naar Kensington te lopen om de laatste bomschade te bekijken en daarna naar de bioscoop te gaan. Na een grote luchtaanval was de aanblik van platgeschoten gebouwen en uitgebrande kerken die honderden jaren staande gebleven waren treurig, maar de monumenten en standbeelden, zelfs de parken en de grote warenhuizen die er nog waren en gewoon doorgingen, hadden echt iets triomfantelijks. De Luftwaffe mocht dan proberen ons in stukken te schieten, maar iedereen bleef gewoon weer overeind komen. En als je zag dat ze zelfs geen deukje in de Big Ben hadden kunnen schieten en dat we hadden voorkomen dat Saint Paul's Cathedral afbrandde, werd je echt weer vrolijk.

Bunty wilde niets liever dan erop uitgaan, dus vertrokken we zonder geluncht te hebben en kauwden we onderweg op een stuk oud brood dat voor de eendjes bestemd was.

'Denk je dat mevrouw Bird je aardig begint te vinden?' vroeg Bunty terwijl ze een korst naar een eend gooide. De keiharde korst stuitte tegen de kop van de eend af en viel in de vijver. Het dikke beestje peddelde dapper weg om de korst te redden.

'Dat denk ik niet,' zei ik en ik blies op mijn handschoenen. 'Misschien slikt ze mijn aanwezigheid. Ze is eigenlijk op niemand bijzonder gesteld. De meeste lezeressen inbegrepen.'

Het park was vol mensen die van deze heldere dag in februari genoten. Ik stapte opzij voor een oudere heer die een klein meisje op een driewieler begeleidde en keek naar een jonge vrouw met een dunne jas aan, die een kolossale kinderwagen voortduwde. Ze probeerde de wagen aan de overkant van het grasveld te krijgen terwijl ze ook nog twee onbesuisde zoontjes binnen handbereik moest houden. Ze was niet veel ouder dan Bunty en ik, maar ze zag er uitgeput uit. Een van de jongens duwde zijn broertje in de sneeuw en binnen een paar tellen waren ze aan het vechten en brullen.

'Vorige week was er een brief van iemand die een kindje verwacht van de verkeerde man,' zei ik, nogal plompverloren. 'Maar dat mag je aan niemand vertellen, hoor,' voegde ik eraan toe; ik klonk precies als Kathleen.

'Mondje dicht,' zei Bunty en trok een gek gezicht.

Ik grinnikte even, maar ploeterde door. 'Mevrouw Bird wilde haar niet helpen. Ze is nogal bekrompen.'

'Mm-mm,' zei Bunty, die op zoek leek naar iets of iemand in de verte.

'En dat is nogal oneerlijk,' hield ik vol. 'Sommige mensen hebben het zo beroerd.'

'Het is oorlog,' zei Bunty, volkomen terecht.

'Dus ze hebben hulp nodig,' zei ik verlangend. 'Vind je ook niet? Ook daaraan moeten we ons steentje bijdragen, toch?'

'Nou, ja,' zei Bunts, nog altijd in de verte turend. Ze leek nogal verstrooid. 'Maar als mevrouw Bird dat niet wil, kun jij daar niet veel aan doen, of wel?'

'Eigenlijk wel,' zei ik. 'Soort van.'

Bunty draaide zich naar me om. Ik keek naar de kinderen die nog steeds tegen elkaar liepen te gillen.

'Emmy,' zei Bunty, 'wat voer jij in je schild?'

Ze kende me langer dan vandaag.

'Ach,' zei ik. 'Het is helemaal onder controle.'

Bunty deed haar ogen dicht en zuchtte. 'Dat vroeg ik niet.'

Ik keek naar haar gezicht en besloot dat het goed zou zijn om alles te bagatelliseren.

'Eén meisje klonk net als Kitty,' zei ik. 'Of eigenlijk alsof het weleens op Kits situatie uit kon lopen...'

Bunty deed haar ogen open, langzaam, alsof ze bang was voor wat ze te zien zou krijgen.

'Dus heb ik haar geschreven,' flapte ik eruit.

Bunty gaapte me aan.

'Alsof ik mevrouw Bird was,' voegde ik eraan toe.

Bunty's mond viel zo mogelijk nog verder open. Een eenzame eend kwaakte alsof hij 'grote griebels' wilde zeggen.

'Em,' zei Bunty. 'Nee toch. Je... Lieve help.'

Ik besloot niet te vertellen dat ik de brief van Verbijsterd in het blad van volgende week gezet had.

'Het komt allemaal goed,' zei ik opgewekt. 'Ik probeer gewoon een beetje te helpen.'

'Dat lijkt me geen goed idee.' Bunty keek me aan alsof ik waanzinnig was; ze had haar grijze ogen wijd opengesperd, als een stripfiguur. 'Emmy, dit is je grote kans. Een stap dichter bij wat je echt wilt gaan doen. Hoezo komt het helemaal goed?' Haar stem schoot omhoog. 'Je maakt er weer eens een zootje van. O, Em...' Ze leek nogal sceptisch.

Ik begon aan mijn ingestudeerde argumentatie. 'Mevrouw Bird leest die brieven niet eens. Zij zal nooit weten dat ik ze beantwoord.'

'Maar als ze erachter komt?'

'Dat gebeurt niet. O, Bunts, je zou die brieven moeten zien,' zei ik. Begreep ze het nou maar! 'Zo treurig. Mensen maken zich vreselijk zorgen over alles... Je zei net zelf nog dat het oorlog is. Iedereen zet z'n beste beentje voor, maar sommigen zitten echt in de penarie. En mevrouw Bird gooit hun problemen zomaar in de prullenbak. Zo oneerlijk.'

'Emmy,' zei Bunty, 'ik weet dat het moeilijk is. Maar je moet ermee ophouden. Serieus.'

Ze keek weer over me heen en ik draaide me om.

'Nee maar,' zei ik. 'Is dat William?'

Ik was nog nooit zo blij geweest Bunty's vriendje te zien.

Bunty zelf leek absoluut niet verrast te zijn, vreemd genoeg. Ze keek al eeuwen die kant uit.

'Begin nou niet ineens over iets anders,' zei ze. 'Emmy, je moet het me beloven.'

'Hij ís het,' zei ik, verrukt over deze kans om haar te negeren. 'Of niet soms? En wie heeft hij bij zich?'

'Niemand,' zei Bunty nijdig. 'Niks.'

'Niks?'

'Ik weet van niks,' zei Bunty.

'Wat is er?' vroeg ik en keek haar strak aan. Ik rook lont.

Ze bloosde diep. 'Niks,' zei ze. 'Nou ja, misschien wel iets. Hoe dan ook, Emmy, bemoei je niet met de problemen van de lezeressen. Dat kan echt niet.'

Bunty keek me nog één keer streng aan, trok mijn sjaal recht alsof ze mijn moeder was en pufte geërgerd. 'Nu lief kijken en glimlachen,' beval ze.

William marcheerde met flinke tred op ons af. Naast hem liep, in legeruniform gestoken, de langste man die ik ooit gezien had.

Eigenlijk vond ik thuis al dat Bunty de voorbereidingen voor het eendjes-voeren nogal overdreef. Mijn verstelde wollen rok en warme trui waren echt wel goed genoeg, maar van haar moest ik zo nodig een andere rok en een veel te dunne mohair trui aan, alsof het al lente was.

'O zeg, dat moet Harold zijn,' zei ze nu uitbundig.

'We kennen helemaal geen Harold,' zei ik. 'Bunty, heb jij dit bekokstoofd?'

William wuifde vrolijk, en de grote kerel ook.

'Niet echt,' zei Bunty met een schuldig gezicht. 'Nou ja, eigenlijk wel. Maar William zegt dat-ie heel aardig is. Harold.'

'Heb jij hem al eens eerder gezien?' vroeg ik.

'Nee. Maar hij is lekker lang, zie je wel?'

Dat kon je wel zeggen. De dapper doorzettende winterzon riskeerde een onmiddellijke verduistering.

'Ze zijn al vlakbij,' zei Bunty, woest wuivend en opgewekt kijkend. 'Glimlachen.' Zelf had ze een idiote grijns opgezet en praatte ze als een buikspreker tussen haar opeengeklemde tanden door.

Braaf deed ik wat me opgedragen werd.

'Schaterlachen om zijn grappen,' adviseerde Bunty, blijkbaar in de veronderstelling dat Harold die zou maken. 'En laat je wimpers fladderen.' Toen ik niet reageerde, keek ze me streng aan. 'Knipperen. Zo veel mogelijk.'

'Hoor 'ns, Bunts,' zei ik, nog altijd idioot glimlachend, volgens instructie, 'ik vind het vreselijk aardig van je, maar ik heb geen belangstelling, dat zei ik toch. Ik concentreer me op mijn carrière.'

'Da's een goeie,' zei Bunty. 'Volgens mij probeer je die juist te ruïneren. Trouwens,' voegde ze eraan toe, 'ik durf te wedden dat hij verrukkelijk is.'

Bunty had het woord 'verrukkelijk' haar hele leven nog niet gebruikt. Bovendien sloeg ze een eigenaardige toon aan: heel hoog en echt veel te hard.

De jongens hadden een flinke afstand afgelegd en stonden nu voor onze neus. Voordat ik nog een woord kon zeggen, bulderde een zware stem: 'VERRUKKELIJK? HEBBEN JULLIE HET OVER ONS? MIETERS!'

Werd Harold geleverd met misthoorn?

Het was te laat om te ontsnappen. Ik was er vierkant ingeluisd, zou meneer Bone, de tijdschriftenverkoper, zeggen.

'Hallo Bunty, hallo Emmy,' zei William.

Ik gaf het op.

'HÉ DAAR!' schreeuwde Harold.

'Hallo,' zei ik flauwtjes. Hopelijk kwam dat niet over alsof ik zwijmelde van louter enthousiasme.

'Dit is Harold,' zei William.

'JA!' bulderde Harold zonder enige noodzaak.

'En dit is Emmeline,' zei William.

'Hoe maak je het?' zei ik. 'Dit is Bunty.'

Tot zover onze namen, met een boel geschreeuw over en weer. Natuurlijk wilde ik niet onbeleefd zijn tegen Harold, maar ik had echt geen idee wat ik moest zeggen.

Harold was beslist een opvallende verschijning. Hij was minstens twee meter lang; hij had in het nationale rugbyteam kunnen zitten. Hij droeg waarschijnlijk het grootste uniform dat het Britse leger ooit verstrekt had. Nu grijnsde hij van oor tot oor. Vervolgens stak hij me een ham met het formaat van een tennisracket toe die bij nader inzien zijn rechterhand bleek te zijn.

'KOLOSSAAL!' schreeuwde hij, nog luider dan tevoren. Hij schudde me energiek de hand en ik probeerde goed weerwerk te geven, al dreigde hij mijn schouder te ontwrichten. Ik concludeerde dat Harold een enthousiast type was.

'Harold en ik hebben samen gestudeerd,' zei William. 'Nu zit hij bij de koninklijke genie. Explosievenopruimingsdienst.'

Hij zei het met bewonderenswaardige trots. Voor William was het nooit gemakkelijk om eraan herinnerd te worden dat al zijn vrienden bij het leger gegaan waren. Hij was niet door de selectie gekomen. Bunty tobde er voortdurend over dat hij zichzelf een mislukkeling vond. Ik ontkende dat altijd, maar we wisten allebei dat zij gelijk had. En nu deed hij zijn best om met zijn kolossale makker te pronken voor het geval ik hem leuk zou vinden, omdat Bunty blij zou zijn als het zo was. Dat was echt verschrikkelijk aardig en ik kon niet boos op hem zijn. Of op Bunts. Harold was bepaald geen kneus, integendeel.

'Echt leuk om je te ontmoeten, Harold,' zei ik, waardoor Bunty bijna flauwviel van blijdschap. 'Zullen we een eindje gaan wandelen?'

Iedereen verklaarde dat dit een ontzaglijk goed idee was. Harold vertelde het laatste nieuwtje: de boekwinkel was eergisteravond getroffen, maar niemand was gewond geraakt, en we waren het erover eens dat dat een kolossale opluchting was. William droeg zijn steentje bij en vertelde dat de mensen die in de metrotunnel van Kensington sliepen door een ukelelespeler vermaakt werden. Dat zal hun een hart onder de riem gestoken hebben, zeiden we allemaal. Ook al waren de nieuwsberichten van de luchtaanvallen behoorlijk ontnuchterend geweest, we deden alle vier dapper ons best alles van de vrolijke kant te bekijken. En tegen de tijd dat we High Street in wandelden, vormden we echt een opgewekt gezelschap.

Harold leek een toffe kerel, al deed zijn bulderende lach pijn aan je oren. Hij presteerde het zelfs op een geloofwaardige manier interesse voor *Vrouw & Vriendin* te tonen. En hij kon ertegen als er een stilte viel wanneer ik even niets wist te zeggen. Maar ik kreeg geen last van knikkende knieën en bespeurde ook geen aandrang om met mijn wimpers te knipperen.

Waarschijnlijk vond hij mij ook niet vreselijk interessant, vermoedde ik. Tenslotte had ik alleen maar een heleboel gegrijnsd, volgens de instructie van Bunts, en over de mensen op mijn werk gepraat. Toch hoopte ik dat hij me niet helemaal een sukkel vond, want William had de moeite gedaan ons aan elkaar voor te stellen. Het zou jammer zijn als hij hierdoor een flater sloeg bij zijn vriend.

'Wat een toeval dat we jullie tegen het lijf liepen,' zei ik tegen William terwijl we naast elkaar langs Barker's warenhuis liepen – en ik plotseling bedacht dat mijn blauwe katoen op was. 'We gaan zo theedrinken. Gaan jullie mee?' vroeg ik. Aangezien alles toch al gepland was, zou ik hun spelletje maar meespelen.

'Alleen als jij dat wilt,' zei William en hij keek me daarbij ernstig aan. Daarna keek hij naar Bunty, die Harold een grappig verhaal vertelde. 'Bunty wilde zien of jullie het een beetje met elkaar zouden kunnen vinden. Ik heb alleen maar tegen Harold gezegd dat we een ommetje zouden maken. Geef hem een kans, Emmy. Hij is een fijne vent. Heeft massa's van zijn eigen mannen gered. Vreselijk dapper.'

Ik zuchtte. Dapperheid was voor William het belangrijkste in de wereld.

'Bill, lieveling, ik wil je een jas laten zien,' zei Bunty en sleepte hem bij me weg. Harold en ik keken elkaar aan.

'ZULLEN WE DOORLOPEN?' stelde hij luid voor. 'HET IS TE KOUD OM STIL TE STAAN!'

'Doen we,' zei ik hulpeloos. Ik had geen idee wat ik nog meer moest zeggen.

'We zijn belazerd, hè?' vroeg Harold bijna op normaal volume.

Weer keken we elkaar aan. Hij trok een quasi-zielig gezicht en ik schoot in de lach.

'Sorry hoor,' zei hij. 'Eergisteren kwam ik Bill in de pub tegen. Hij vertelde een heleboel over Bunty en stelde voor dat we jullie tegen het lijf zouden lopen. Vind je dit erg vervelend?'

'O nee, helemaal niet,' zei ik. 'En jij?'

'ONTZETTEND!' zei hij, weer op zijn gebruikelijke volume, en daarna lachte hij net zo luidruchtig. 'NEE, NATUURLIJK NIET. TREK HET JE NIET AAN,' voegde hij eraan toe toen ik ineenkromp. 'IK BEN WAARDELOOS IN DIT SOORT GEDOE. GEEF MIJ MAAR EEN NIET-ONTPLOFTE BOM, DAAR RED IK ME WEL MEE. SCHREEUW IK TROUWENS?'

'Een beetje wel,' zei ik.

'SORRY. GALMEND GELUID IN MIJN KOP. NIET BLIJVEND. IK HEB TWEE WEKEN VRIJ GEKREGEN, EN DAN MOET HET OVER ZIJN.'

'Gommie, wat erg voor je,' zei ik. Nu schaamde ik me een ongeluk dat ik hem een schreeuwlelijk gevonden had.

'Geeft niks,' zei hij weer wat zachter. 'Zo gaan die dingen. Het is allemaal een beetje luidruchtig en zo. Zal ik een tijdje fluisteren, of klinkt dat helemaal getikt?'

Ik lachte weer. Harold was aardig. Ik voelde nog steeds geen romance opbloeien, maar hij evenmin, dat wist ik bijna zeker. Dus dat zat wel goed.

'Min of meer,' zei ik.

'Hoor 'ns,' zei hij. 'Vind je me erg onbeleefd als ik voorstel dat we gewoon vrienden worden?'

Ik kon hem wel zoenen. Wat een kolossale opluchting.

'HAROLD!' schreeuwde ik; drie voetgangers draaiden zich om. 'IK ZOU HET ERG FIJN VINDEN OM VRIENDEN TE WORDEN. DANK JE WEL!'

'MIETERS!' schreeuwde hij terug, zo te zien even verrukt als opgelucht.

We marcheerden terug naar Bunty en William en ik vertelden tactvol het nieuws dat onze hofmakerij al gestrand was. Bunty nam het sportief op en Bill vroeg Harold of hij zin had om naar de pub te gaan. Eerst brachten ze ons naar The Tea House. Ik zette me schrap, want ik wist dat fase twee van Bunty's verhoor over *Vrouw & Vriendin* me boven het hoofd hing. Zodra de mannen weg waren, zou ik aan haar overgeleverd zijn.

‘Kom op, Bunts,’ zei ik terwijl we hen uitwuifden. ‘Ik trakteer. Zoveel broodjes als je op kunt.’

‘Vooruit dan maar,’ zei Bunty met een onheilspellend gezicht. ‘Maar omkoperij zal je niet helpen. Ik ben diep terneergeslagen over Harold.’

Ik knikte en dacht even dat ik uit de problemen was.

‘En denk erom,’ zei Bunty, ‘ik wil precies weten wat je op je werk uitspookt. Het hele verhaal, graag.’

IO

Zeg maar Charles

Bij The Tea keken we – letterlijk – reikhalzend naar de vitrine om te zien of er misschien nog taartjes te koop waren. Dat viel nog niet mee, want we stonden in de rij voor zitplaatsen. De rij was lang en bewoog tergend langzaam; heel ontmoedigend allemaal, vooral omdat we inmiddels allebei uitgehongerd waren. Bunty en ik mopperden tegen elkaar en wierpen de mensen die al zaten knorrige blikken toe.

'Moet je die twee zien,' zei Bunty. 'Aan een tafel voor vier personen. En ze zitten niet eens te eten.'

Ik keek in de richting van haar priemende wijsvinger en schrok me een hoedje. 'Goeie genade, dat is meneer Collins,' zei ik, want hij was het.

Hij zat met zijn gezicht naar ons toe en had zijn eeuwige tweedkostuum aan, maar zijn haar zat ietsje netter dan gewoonlijk. De twee mannen – de andere man, in uniform, zat met zijn rug naar ons toe – waren in gesprek. Meneer Collins zat meelevend te knikken, wat me volledig in verwarring bracht.

Bunty nam hen kritisch op. 'Jóúw meneer Collins?' vroeg ze, en ik werd zonder enige noodzaak knalrood.

'Nee,' zei ik natuurlijk. Voordat ik nog iets kon zeggen, keek hij op en zag ons. Even leek hij me helemaal niet te kunnen plaatsen. Toen hij besefte wie ik was, wuifde hij, kort maar vriendelijk. Daarna richtte hij zijn aandacht weer op zijn vriend, zei iets tegen hem, en tot mijn stomme verbazing wenkte hij ons.

Verlegen wuifde ik terug. Bunty was zo bijdehand om giechelend te zeggen: 'Zo te zien ben jij wél zijn juffrouw Lake!' Die ongepaste opmerking negeerde ik uiteraard.

'Toe nou,' zei Bunty. 'Misschien kunnen we bij ze gaan zitten, dan hoeven we niet meer in de rij te staan. Zeg, wie is die andere knul?'

De man in uniform had zich half omgedraaid om te kijken naar wie meneer Collins zo lichtvaardig gebaarde. Hij had hetzelfde donkere haar en dezelfde tengere lichaamsbouw als meneer Collins, maar was stukken jonger, eind twintig misschien.

Bunty en ik baanden ons een weg naar hun tafel.

'Juffrouw Lake,' groette meneer Collins beleefd. Beide mannen waren opgestaan. 'Wat aardig om u te zien.'

'Hallo, meneer Collins,' zei ik. 'Dit is juffrouw Marigold Tavistock, mijn beste vriendin.'

'Hoe maakt u het?' vroeg Bunty verrassend netjes. 'Zeg maar Bunty, dat doet iedereen.'

'Aangenaam kennis te maken, Bunty,' zei meneer Collins. Hij schudde haar de hand en gedroeg zich zo galant dat ik me begon af te vragen of ik wel de juiste persoon voor me had. 'Mag ik u mijn halfbroer voorstellen? Kapitein Charles Mayhew. Charles, dit is juffrouw Lake, een collega. Ik heb haar wellicht al genoemd: de jongedame die Henriëtta tegenwoordig waar voor haar geld geeft.'

Ik werd nogal verlegen van de gedachte dat ik genoemd was. We schudden elkaar de hand. Kapitein Mayhew zei: 'Zeg maar Charles,' en meneer Collins zei: 'Dat doet iedereen,' en we lachten allemaal. Het was een eigenaardig idee dat meneer Collins een broer had, dat hij buiten het kantoor ook nog een leven had. Je had altijd het gevoel dat hij louter en alleen bestond om verwoed schrijvend achter zijn bureau te zitten, in de vreselijke rommel.

Aangezien we met ons vieren om de tafel heen stonden, konden de serveersters er niet meer door. Er kon elk moment een scène ontstaan.

Meneer Collins redde de situatie door als een dolle te gaan praten, net zoals hij op kantoor soms deed. 'Dames, dit gaat tegen elke vorm van etiquette in, omdat we elkaar nog maar net ontmoet hebben en juffrouw Lake en ik collega's zijn, maar mag ik u uitnodigen om bij ons te komen zitten? Ik loop gevaar mijn broer zodanig te vervelen dat hij zichzelf uit het raam werpt als hij niet snel door een jonger iemand toegesproken wordt. We hebben taart besteld,' zei hij tot slot, met een zwierig gebaar.

'Dat is heel aardig. Dank u wel,' zei Bunty keurig. Elke kans om te weigeren was meteen verkeken.

Ik voelde me ongelooflijk opgelaten. Hoe zou ik dit spontane theekransje met een hooggeplaatst lid van het personeel en zijn broer, op zaterdag nog wel, ooit kunnen verklaren? Kathleen zou in shock raken als ze dit wist, en mevrouw Bird zou waarschijnlijk uit haar voegen barsten. Maar ik viel bijna flauw van de honger.

'Dank u wel, meneer Collins,' zei ik, dankbaar omdat hij nog niet helemaal gek geworden was en 'Zeg maar Guy' gezegd had – dat was zijn voornaam, wist ik – want dan zou ik me echt de ogen uit mijn hoofd geschaamd hebben. 'Dat lijkt me leuk.'

'Gelukkig,' zei meneer Collins. 'Dan kunnen we gaan zitten. Al dat getwijfel…'

Bliksemsnel zwiepte Bunty haar hoed af, vloog om de tafel heen en ging naast meneer Collins zitten, zodat ik naast kapitein Mayhew – die ik nog geen Charles kon noemen, vond ik – moest zitten.

'Ik wil graag even zeggen,' zei de kapitein, 'dat ik me niet in het minst verveeld heb. Al is het natuurlijk erg leuk dat jullie bij ons komen zitten,' voegde hij er snel aan toe. Zijn stem klonk rustig, maar vriendelijk. 'Hebben jullie gewandeld, dames?'

Meneer Collins was in stilzwijgen verzonken. Om pijnlijke stiltes in het gesprek te vermijden, begon ik maar te praten. Ik voelde me verplicht te proberen een interessante indruk te maken, want ik wilde hem niet teleurstellen.

'Ja, inderdaad,' bevestigde ik. 'We zijn even gaan kijken bij de boekwinkel die er nu niet meer is, en daarvoor hebben we brood naar de eenden gegooid. Bunty heeft er een geraakt,' voegde ik eraan toe. Dat klonk alsof dat onze bedoeling geweest was.

'Twee, eigenlijk. En ik deed niet eens echt mijn best,' zei Bunty in een vergeefse poging de boel te redden.

'Juist,' zei kapitein Mayhew met de moed der wanhoop. 'Dat is, eh…'

'Een milde versie van de eendenjacht,' zei meneer Collins.

Bunty denderde voort.

'Echt niet,' zei ze. 'Alleen de korsten zouden pijnlijk geweest zijn, en die hadden we onderweg al grotendeels opgegeten.'

'We hadden de lunch overgeslagen,' zei ik.

'Lieve help,' zei meneer Collins en wenkte de dichtstbijzijnde serveerster. 'Zou u onze bestelling willen verdubbelen? Het is nogal dringend. Dank u wel. Ik trakteer.'

Hij wierp Bunty een blik toe waaruit de gedachte leek te spreken dat ze in staat was elk moment een vuilnisbak in te duiken op zoek naar voedsel.

'O, wat vreselijk vriendelijk van u,' zei ze met majesteitelijke waardigheid, en ze schonk hem haar lieflijkste glimlach. 'Het waren maar heel kleine broodkorsten.'

Ik keek naar kapitein Mayhew met het gevoel dat ik hem

mijn verontschuldigingen moest aanbieden. Maar voordat ik iets kon zeggen, realiseerde ik me dat hij vreselijk zijn best deed om niet in de lach te schieten.

Dat mislukte jammerlijk. 'Het spijt me,' zei hij schaterend. 'Maar het is net of we met Laurel en Hardy aan tafel zitten. Niet dat u er zo uitziet, natuurlijk. Grote griebels, dat komt er helemaal verkeerd uit.' Hij hield abrupt zijn mond en keek ontzet. 'Vergeef me alstublieft,' zei hij blozend. 'Ik bedoelde alleen maar dat jullie me echt opgevrolijkt hebben. Mijn regiment heeft nogal een beroerde tijd achter de rug en die arme Guy zit al de hele dag met een stuk verdriet opgezadeld.'

'Het geeft niets, kapitein Mayhew,' zei ik en bedacht dat hij echt heel geschikt leek. 'U zult wel denken dat we nooit uitgaan.'

'Dat heb ik geen moment gedacht,' zei hij. 'Maar noem me alstublieft Charles.'

'Goed dan, Charles,' zei ik roekeloos. 'En noem mij alsjeblieft Emmy. Zullen we maar helemaal opnieuw beginnen?'

'Graag,' zeiden Charles en Bunty tegelijkertijd.

'Moet dat echt?' vroeg meneer Collins. 'Ik weet niet zeker of ik dat verhaal over die eend nog een keer aankan. Gelukkig, daar is de serveerster.'

Hij wuifde verstrooid naar het meisje dat een dienblad vol eten op tafel gezet had. Daarna schonk hij ons allemaal een van zijn meest theatrale boze blikken. 'Kom op allemaal, hou nu eens op met die idiote beleefdheid. Laten we aanvallen.'

Hij hief een theepot alsof het een wijnglas was. 'Hulde, dames. Dit is de eerste keer dat ik mijn broer heb zien lachen sinds hij thuisgekomen is. En, wie wil als eerste aanspraak maken op de mosterd en de tuinkers?'

Nu het ijs gebroken was en met voedsel in het vooruitzicht kwamen Bunty en ik weer bij ons verstand en gedroegen we ons niet langer als babbelzieke onnozele halzen. Al bleef het eigenaardig om met meneer Collins te babbelen – ik vóélde gewoon dat hij elk moment 'VLOEIBLOK, JUFFROUW LAKE!' kon bulderen – morgen waren we misschien allemaal dood, dus we konden net zo goed genieten van dit moment, zei ik tegen mezelf. Kapitein Mayhew was rustiger dan zijn halfbroer en leek een beetje verlegen. Toch nam hij deel aan het gesprek dat, zoals alle gesprekken met mensen die je niet echt kent, verschrikkelijk opgewekt en monter was. We bagatelliseerden alles wat met de Blitz te maken had – 'Het huis van Gwyneth, een vriendin van mijn tante, werd platgebombardeerd, maar de kat vonden ze terug… wat een geluk!' – en beperkten ons tot veilige onderwerpen.

'Blijf je nog lang in Londen, Charles?' vroeg Bunty.

'Nog een paar dagen,' zei hij. 'Als mijn broer het zo lang met me uithoudt.'

'Is dat niet verschrikkelijk saai voor je?' vroeg meneer Collins met een oprecht bezorgd gezicht.

'Guy,' zei Charles hartelijk, 'je bent zesenveertig. Niet bepaald een museumstuk uit de Griekse Oudheid. Dames, let niet op hem, alstublieft.' Hij nam een slokje thee, trok zijn ene wenkbrauw omhoog en keek me over de rand van zijn kopje aan. Ik glimlachte.

'Hou je van films?' flapte Bunty eruit, als een donderslag bij heldere hemel.

Ik keek haar gealarmeerd aan.

'We waren namelijk van plan om na de thee naar de bioscoop te gaan om *The Mark of Zorro* te zien, en ik vroeg me af of je het misschien leuk zou vinden om mee te gaan. U bent natuurlijk allebei welkom,' voegde ze eraan toe terwijl ze meneer Collins aankeek. Daar meende ze niets van.

Charles lachte. 'Dank je wel, Bunty, dat is vreselijk aardig van je. Ik wil me alleen niet opdringen, en evenmin mijn broer in de steek laten.'

Bunty zei heel opgewekt: 'Natuurlijk niet,' en meneer Collins zei: 'Helemaal niet' en keek tevreden.

'Dat is dan geregeld,' vervolgde meneer Collins. Hij fronste zijn wenkbrauwen. 'Jullie weten toch wel dat er vanavond zwaar gebombardeerd kan worden?'

'Dat geeft niet,' zei ik terwijl ik mijn spullen verzamelde. 'We kennen alle schuilplaatsen op weg naar huis.'

'Ik bewonder jullie lef, moet ik zeggen,' zei Charles. 'Ik vind het hier alarmerender dan wanneer ik aan het front ben.'

'Dat zegt mijn broer ook,' zei ik. 'Maar ik vind dat je net zo goed een bewegend doelwit kunt zijn, dan maak je het ze niet te makkelijk.'

'Juffrouw Lake,' zei meneer Collins, 'al vinden jullie het nog zo leuk om een bewegend doelwit te zijn, ik voel me een stuk beter als Charles met jullie meegaat. Ik zou het bijzonder irritant vinden als u opgeblazen werd. Ik reken hier wel af. Wees voorzichtig,' zei hij tegen ons alle drie.

We bedankten hem om het hardst uitbundig voor de thee en het eten, maar met een Europees aandoend gebaar wuifde hij ons weg.

Het was al verduisteringstijd en buiten was het pikkedonker, maar we hadden zaklantaarns en Bunty en ik hadden onze witte hoofddoeken omgebonden zodat we niet door een bus verpletterd zouden worden. Niettemin wilde Charles per se aan de buitenkant van het trottoir lopen.

'Hoffelijkheid is natuurlijk mooi en aardig,' zei ik door mijn hoofddoek heen terwijl we voorzichtig verder liepen. 'Maar als jij overreden wordt, is dat niet best voor de oorlogsinspanning.'

'Ik word niet overreden,' zei Charles vriendelijk. 'Trouwens, jullie zijn allebei ook belangrijk door het werk dat jullie doen, dus het zou even erg zijn als het een van jullie was.'

'Ik typ alleen teksten uit,' zei ik.

Charles antwoordde: 'Daar komt vast meer bij kijken,' en

Bunty wierp me een strenge blik toe alsof ze wilde zeggen: 'Ik ben ons gesprek niet vergeten, als je dat maar weet.'

We liepen een tijdje vriendschappelijk zwijgend door en ik wenste in stilte – en niet voor het eerst – dat ik mijn praktische trui nog aanhad. Het was akelig koud. De afgelopen weken was het voortdurend bewolkt geweest, maar vanavond was de lucht zo helder als wat. Meneer Collins had gelijk: de Duitsers zouden het later nog druk krijgen.

Aangezien oudere mensen en ouders met kinderen al voor zonsondergang naar huis gegaan waren, was de bus vol jonge mensen zoals wij, die met elkaar kletsten en zich verheugden op hun zaterdagavond. Winkelmeisjes die met lippenstift op en pumps met naaldhakken aan van hun werk gekomen waren, praatten over jongens en dansen, en jongens in uniform voerden gesprekken over meisjes en de oorlog. Terwijl de bus langzaam en voorzichtig om Hyde Park heen reed, hoorde Bunty Charles uit over de oorlog. Ik keek uit het raam de diepe duisternis in.

Zodra we in de Odeon-bioscoop waren en zitplaatsen gevonden hadden, kondigde Bunty hardop aan dat ze naar het toilet moest. Ze bleef eeuwen weg. Charles en ik keken naar het bioscoopjournaal, dat halsstarrig optimistisch bleef over alles. Er was een korte film over de meisjes die chauffeerden voor de transportdienst van het leger, die hen liet zien terwijl ze de motorkap van een vrachtwagen openmaakten en vol vertrouwen in de motor porden. Een groep mensen in de voorste stallesplaatsen begon te juichen toen deze film begon en iemand riep: 'Dat ben jij, Mavis!' en een vrouwenstem zei: 'Nee, Vincent, ik ben veel slanker,' en iedereen in de zaal lachte. Maar ik voelde me opgelaten, vooral omdat ik naast Charles-in-uniform zat. Tijdens het theedrinken had ik hem over de brandweerkazerne verteld en nu fluisterde ik hem toe dat ik erover dacht op een dag motorkoerier voor de brandweer te worden als ik tot die cursus toegelaten werd.

'Goed van je,' fluisterde Charles terug. 'Heel spannend.'

'Ja toch?' zei ik. 'Ik moet alleen leren motorrijden, dan begin ik, al denk ik wel dat ik lang moet wachten.'

Daarna zei Charles op luchtige toon: 'Ik zou het je wel kunnen leren als je het leuk vindt. Als je het niet erg vindt om op een nogal oude motor les te krijgen.'

'Gommie,' zei ik, diep onder de indruk. 'Dat is vreselijk aardig van je.'

Op dat moment kwam Bunty eindelijk weer op haar stoel zitten.

'Gaat het een beetje?' vroeg ik zo onopvallend mogelijk.

'Ja, natuurlijk. Puik,' zei Bunty alsof het volkomen normaal was om twintig minuten op het toilet door te brengen.

'Charles gaat me leren motorrijden.'

'Sjonge,' zei Bunty zo vol ontzag alsof hij een uitstapje naar de maan voor me georganiseerd had.

Ik draaide me half om en keek naar haar. Zij tuurde aandachtig naar het filmscherm, waar Max Miller een veldkantine vol nonnen opvrolijkte. Hij moest wel een eersteklas komiek zijn, want Bunty's grijns was bijna nog breder dan haar gezicht.

'Echt kolossaal,' zei ze bijna binnensmonds. 'Wie had dat gedacht?'

Halverwege de hoofdfilm kwam de bioscoopdirecteur op het podium en kondigde aan dat er een luchtaanval was. Een jaar geleden zou iedereen zijn gasmasker gepakt hebben en naar de dichtstbijzijnde schuilplaats gevlucht zijn, maar nu verroerde niemand een vin en verschillende mensen op het balkon riepen: 'Gewoon doorgaan' en: 'Breng Tyrone Power terug.' Zo ging het tegenwoordig overal. De bioscoopdirecteur werd door twee mensen uitgefloten en kreeg een mager applaus. Bunty en ik bleven met alle plezier zitten, want we zaten midden in een bijzonder aangrijpend stuk van het verhaal. Aan het eind van de film was het signaal 'alles veilig' nog niet gegeven.

Bunty kondigde aan dat ze weer naar het toilet ging.

'Tot ziens, Charles,' zei ze en schudde hem de hand. 'Ik hoop echt dat we je nog eens zullen zien. Emmy, zeg Charles gedag, en als hij weg is, wacht dan hier op me,' eindigde ze nogal bazig. Dat was niks voor haar. Daarna verdween ze achter een dikke vrouw met een bontjas.

Hoewel de films altijd op hoger volume dan normaal gedraaid werden, had zelfs *The Mark of Zorro* het dof dreunende geluid van de bommenwerpers boven de stad niet helemaal kunnen overstemmen. Nu we de zaal uit waren en vlak bij de voorkant van het gebouw stonden, was het geluid nog veel harder. Charles en ik moesten tegen elkaar schreeuwen om boven het kabaal uit te komen.

'Jullie gaan toch niet echt met de bus naar huis?' riep Charles.

'O, dat doen we altijd, niks aan de hand,' schreeuwde ik terug. Net op dat moment klonk er een afschuwelijk fluitend geluid. Iedereen in de foyer stond even stil tot een kolossale dreun het hele gebouw deed schudden. 'Dat was een joekel,' zei ik ten overvloede.

'Ach ja,' zei Charles boven het lawaai uit. 'Ik wil niet overdreven doen over veiligheid, en het maakt me niks uit of jullie gewoonlijk ligstoelen buiten zetten om te kijken hoe de stad in vlammen opgaat, maar vanavond gaan we met de taxi, als ik er een kan krijgen.'

Hij glimlachte nog steeds en was nog altijd even beleefd. Ik deed mijn mond open om tegen hem in te gaan, maar bedacht me en klapte mijn mond weer dicht, als een goudvis. Ondanks zijn vriendelijke ogen en rustige charme leek Charles me een man die wist wat hij wilde.

Er klonk weer een gefluit, ditmaal lager van toon, dus verder weg, maar ook dit werd gevolgd door een sidderend geknars. Een nabijgelegen gebouw was getroffen. Hoewel de glazen pui van de bioscoop volledig met planken afgetimmerd was en we hier best veilig waren, was Charles tussen mij en een eventuele luchtstroom in gaan staan.

'Goed,' zei hij, alle lawaai negerend. 'Zou jij even kunnen controleren of alles goed is met Bunty, denk je?'

Ze was alweer eeuwen weg.

'Puik idee,' zei ik terwijl Charles me bij de arm pakte en we ons een weg baanden tussen de rij voor de kassa door. 'Die gaat nog liever dood dan dat ze op het toilet opgeblazen wordt.'

Charles keek me van opzij aan. We schoten allebei in de lach.

'Goeie genade,' zei ik. 'Meestal ben ik niet zo stom.'

'Jij bent minder stom dan iedereen die ik ken,' antwoordde Charles. 'Kijk, daar staat ze.'

Bunty stond te treuzelen achter het kraampje met verfrissingen, alsof het volkomen normaal was om je te verstoppen als het tijd werd om naar huis te gaan.

'We nemen een taxi,' zei ik terwijl we rechtsomkeert maakten. 'Anders krijgt Charles een beroerte, zegt hij.'

'Inderdaad,' zei Charles. 'Wachten jullie hier, dan ga ik een taxi zoeken.'

Charles haalde een kleine legerzaklantaarn uit zijn kolossale jaszak en marcheerde vol zelfvertrouwen over de marmeren vloer naar buiten, tussen de verduisteringsgordijnen bij de uitgang door.

'Goeie genade,' zei Bunty. 'Hij is echt aardig, vind je niet?'

Buiten klonk alweer een onheilspellend gerommel.

'Bunty,' vroeg ik nu we eindelijk alleen waren, 'heb je last van je buik?'

Bunty keek me verbijsterd aan.

'Je blijft maar naar het toilet gaan,' fluisterde ik. 'En dan blijf je daar eeuwen.'

'O, dat,' zei ze grinnikend. 'Goed excuus, vind je niet?'

Nu keek ik haar niet-begrijpend aan.

'Ik laat jullie met elkaar alleen, idioot,' kreunde ze. 'Hij vindt je aardig.'

'O, hou op,' zei ik. 'Dat is absolute flauwekul.'

'Nee. En trouwens, jij vindt hem leuk. Dat zie ik. Ik probeer hem zover te krijgen dat hij je mee uit vraagt voordat hij vertrekt.'

'Bunty...'

'Goed.' Ze schonk me een samenzweerderige blik. 'Als we bij oma's huis aankomen, hol ik als een haas naar de voordeur omdat ik me vreselijk ziek voel. Jij moet achter me aan snellen, maar eerst zeg je hoe vreselijk het je spijt om hem zo achter te laten.'

Ik rolde met mijn ogen.

'Dan zegt hij dat hij je absoluut nog eens moet zien en dan kun je hem lieflijk aankijken en zeggen dat je meteen moet gaan omdat ik weleens ernstig ziek kon zijn – dat maakt een zorgzame indruk – maar dat je hem je telefoonnummer kunt geven als hij wil.'

'O, Bunts,' zei ik. 'Niemand zegt in het echt: "Ik moet je beslist nog eens zien." Jij hebt veel te veel films gekeken.'

'Nou en of,' stemde Bunty in. 'Daar heb ik bendes goede ideeën opgedaan. Wat is dit spannend. Ik ben die arme Harold al bijna helemaal vergeten, en jij?'

'Ik ben al bijna helemaal vergeten dat je mijn vriendin bent,' zei ik streng.

'Charles!' riep Bunty, alsof ze te midden van een ruwe zee op een rots gestrand was.

Ze haakte haar arm door de mijne en sleurde me mee naar de hoofdingang. Daar was Charles opgedoken, met rode oren van de kou.

Schaamteloos greep Bunty zijn arm. 'Dank je wel, Charles. Je hebt mijn leven gered!' kweelde ze. 'Ik voel me namelijk niet zo lekker, zie je.'

11

Een zware nacht in de kazerne

De volgende avond liep ik met grote stappen door Rowland Street in mijn heerlijk warme lange overjas van de vrijwillige brandweer; het boodschappennetje met mijn boterhammen voor de komende nacht slingerde heen en weer aan mijn hand. Het was al de tweede heldere nacht achter elkaar en de maan gedroeg zich nogal verraderlijk door de meest geschikte doelwitten in Londen te verlichten. Ik had andere zaken aan mijn hoofd. In gepeins verzonken marcheerde ik naar de brandweerkazerne.

Ik zat midden in een aanval van gemengde gevoelens, zoals artistieke mensen dat noemen. Zaterdag was de leukste dag van mijn leven geweest. Ik had geaccepteerd dat Bunty bij het appartement als een ongeleid projectiel de taxi uit schoot – omdat ze zich zogenaamd beroerd voelde. Charles zei: 'Lieve help' en dat het zo leuk geweest was en vroeg of we het nog eens over konden doen, op Bunty's ziek-zijn na. Ik zei dat Bunty dol op de bioscoop was. Charles zei dat hij Bunty erg graag mocht en hoopte dat ze snel helemaal beter zou zijn, maar misschien – als Bunty en ik het niet erg vonden – konden hij en ik samen een keer uitgaan.

Ik gaf Charles dus mijn telefoonnummer en daarna schudden we elkaar langer de hand dan strikt noodzakelijk was, en zo namen we afscheid. Het was echt een groot succes.

Daar was Bunty natuurlijk dolenthousiast over. Dat was slechts uitstel van executie; de volgende dag gaf ze me alsnog een stevig standje over mijn brievenschrijverij op het werk. Zij vond het volslagen krankzinnig dat ik dat deed. Zelfs al probeerde ik alleen maar te helpen, dan nog zou het mogelijke verlies van mijn baan me op andere gedachten moeten brengen.

Het was dus niet zo gek dat het me een beetje duizelde over Charles, maar dat ik tegelijkertijd nogal zenuwachtig was. Morgen zou het nieuwe nummer van *Vrouw & Vriendin* op het kantoor afgeleverd worden, compleet met de brief die ik Henriëtta weet raad binnengesmokkeld had.

Al had ik brieven geschreven aan alle lezeressen die ik dacht te kunnen helpen, ik was me er pijnlijk van bewust dat een brief in het blad plaatsen een totaal andere zet was. Ik zei tegen mezelf dat ik er niet aan moest denken. Als er vannacht een luchtaanval kwam, zou ik veel meer reden tot ongerustheid hebben.

De brandweerkazerne in Carlton Street was maar drie straten bij het huis van Bunty's oma vandaan en ik wist de weg zelfs met mijn ogen dicht. Dat was maar goed ook. Als het me onderweg te heet onder de voeten werd, als de straten verlicht werden door de oranje gloed van de branden die de Duitse bommen in Londen ontstaken, kon ik het hele eind naar huis hollen. Ik was niet paniekerig aangelegd, maar volgens mij zou zelfs meneer Churchill het in zo'n situatie verstandig vinden om op te schieten. Als ik eenmaal in de kazerne was en de kanonnen van de luchtafweer in topvorm waren, zou ik binnen blijven tot het signaal 'alles veilig' afging. Het had geen zin om naar buiten te gaan als het granaatscherven regende, en het afweergeschut maakte bovendien een oorverdovend kabaal.

Ik liep om een grote krater in het plaveisel heen, stak de straat over en riep een groet naar meneer Bone, die de deur van zijn met planken dichtgetimmerde nieuwsagentschap afsloot. Hij had zijn opzichtersuniform aan. Terwijl hij zich naar me omdraaide, blies hij op zijn vingers om ze warm te houden.

'Avond, meneer Bone,' zei ik. 'Geen handschoenen? Zo bevriest u nog.'

'Avond, Emmy. Die stomme krantenjongen heeft ze meegenomen. Hoe gaat het met die broer van je? Nog steeds de vijand in de pan aan het hakken?'

'Hij doet z'n best, meneer Bone,' zei ik bagatelliserend.

'Goeie knul,' zei meneer Bone vriendelijk en ik vroeg naar zijn vrouw. Herbert, hun enige zoon, was boordschutter bij de Koninklijke Luchtmacht geweest. Hij was boven Het Kanaal neergeschoten en nooit teruggevonden. Ik probeerde niet terug te denken aan de dag waarop zijn ouders dat hoorden. Meneer Bone bleef maar kranten opstapelen, zodat je zijn gezicht niet kon zien, en mevrouw Bone stond bij de kassa – zoals altijd – maar de tranen liepen over haar wangen en de blik in haar ogen zei dat echt alles verloren was. Bert was hun enige kind.

'Je gaat toch niet naar huis vóór het alles-veiligsignaal, hè?' vroeg meneer Bone met een bezorgde blik.

Dat beloofde ik hem. Daarna zei hij dat hij best wist dat ik achter mijn rug mijn vingers gekruist hield – omdat ik niet aan mijn belofte gebonden wilde zijn – wat ook zo was.

Ik wuifde ten afscheid, ging de hoek om en liep naar Bellamy Street, vlak langs een kolossaal gat waar de fietsenwinkel geweest was. Nu kon je de straat erachter zien, maar daar keek ik niet naar. Zoals altijd begroette ik in stilte het handgeschreven bordje 'OP VAKANTIE – KOMEN SNEL TERUG!'

dat tegen het puin aan gezet was. Vroeger woonde meneer Dennis, de eigenaar, met zijn gezin boven de winkel, maar tijdens het bombardement waren ze gelukkig uit logeren geweest bij zijn zus in Southsea. Meneer Dennis was teruggekomen om te zien of er nog iets te redden viel, wat niet het geval was, maar hij had het geweldig flink opgenomen.

'Ik heb altijd gezegd dat we er vaker tussenuit moesten,' had hij gezegd, en de mensen die naar buiten gekomen waren om hem te begroeten, hadden hem toegejuicht. Daarna had hij iedereen de hand geschud. Een paar van zijn vrienden hadden hem meegenomen naar de pub voordat hij weer op de trein naar Southsea stapte. 'We komen snel terug,' had meneer Dennis gezegd. 'Als Hitler naar me vraagt, zeg dan maar dat ik op vakantie ben.'

De volgende dag had een plaatselijke grappenmaker het bordje neergezet. Het riep een glimlach op, maar was vooral een manier om aan de familie Dennis te blijven denken. We wisten zeker dat ze terug zouden komen.

William zou vannacht in de kazerne dienstdoen, zoals bijna altijd. Hij was gepromoveerd tot onderofficier van de B-dienst. Dat verdiende hij echt en we waren allemaal hartstikke blij voor hem. Hij werkte het hardst van iedereen en was ook kolossaal dapper, al moet ik toegeven dat ik daar soms bang van werd. Ik had niets tegen dapperheid, dat hoorde nou eenmaal bij zijn baan. Maar ik had er ook niets op tegen dat Bunty uiteindelijk nog lang en gelukkig zou leven met de knul die haar grote liefde was.

Ik haastte me verder. Thelma en Joan waren vast al in de kazerne – zij waren de vaste krachten in de B-dienst – en dan kwamen Mary en ik, de vrijwilligsters. We zaten altijd in een rij achter onze bureaus te kletsen en te doen alsof alles helemaal normaal was, tot de sirene afging en de telefoons begonnen te rinkelen. Mensen belden om ons te vertellen dat hun huis gebombardeerd was of dat de helft van de straat in lichterlaaie stond door een brandbom. Dan werd het druk. Mary en ik werkten drie nachten per week, al draaide dat vaak uit op vier of vijf. Maar dat was nog niets vergeleken bij William en de jongens. Als het in het westen van Londen rustig was, kon je er je laatste penny om verwedden dat de havens om hulptroepen zouden bellen. Aan het begin van mijn dienst zag ik William altijd wel, maar het kwam zelden voor dat hij aan het eind, om zes uur 's morgens, al terug was. En dan was hij vaak doorweekt, uitgeput, en met zijn gedachten nog in een andere wereld. Als ik thuiskwam, maakte ik altijd expres een beetje kabaal, zodat Bunty wist dat ik terug was; dan schoot ze haar kamer uit en bood aan om thee te zetten. Dat betekende dat ik haar kon geruststellen zonder dat een van ons er overdreven veel aandacht aan besteedde. Wat er 's nachts ook gebeurd was, ik vertelde haar altijd dat William zo te zien gezond en wel was.

Nu deed ik – mooi op tijd – de zijdeur van de kazerne open en liep langs twee jongens van de B-dienst. Ze waren bezig met het repareren van een brandweerwagenpomp waar vorige week een muur boven op gevallen was.

'Morgen, jongens!' riep ik, al was het avond.

'Avond, engel!' riep een van de jongens van onder de pomp. 'Bedankt dat je even aanwaait. We komen hier om van de dorst.'

'We gaan meteen theezetten, Fred,' zei ik tegen zijn voeten, terwijl ik mijn witte sjaal uit de knoop haalde. 'Jij ook, Roy?'

'Dat zal helpen. Goed zo, meid.' Roy klonk nogal buiten adem. 'Met de klok mee, Fred! Als je 'm die kant op draait, word ik nog verpletterd.'

Ik wrong me langs de krakkemikkige machine en beklom de steile trap naar de telefoonkamer; daar zaten de andere meisjes al met elkaar te kletsen. Thelma trok de ceintuur van haar uniformrok strak en liet zien hoeveel ruimte ze overhield.

'Kijk, dat komt ervan als je geen kaas eet. Zodra ze snoepjes gaan rantsoeneren, geef ik dit werk op en word ik fotomodel.' Ze grijnsde breed.

'Hallo, meisjes. Je ziet er geweldig uit, Thel,' zei ik. Ik wist dat Thelma bijna geen kruimel at omdat ze haar kinderen zo veel mogelijk van haar rantsoen gaf. 'Gebeurt er al iets spannends?' Ik deed mijn jas uit en mijn pet af.

'Adolf heeft op je gewacht,' zei Joan. 'Volgens mij kan het nu elk moment beginnen.'

'Dan kunnen we maar beter een beetje theedrinken en kletsen nu het nog kan,' zei Thelma. 'Hoe was jullie wandeling gisteren, Emmy? Ben je nog iemand tegengekomen buiten?'

Sinds Edmund het met me uitgemaakt had, waren de meisjes onophoudelijk campagne aan het voeren om een vervanger voor hem te vinden. Ik vond het wel best; zo hadden we iets frivools om over te praten. Als er geen luchtaanvallen waren, mochten we in de vrijwilligersruimte slapen. Dan zaten we op onze stapelbedden, dronken chocolademelk en kraamden onzin uit. Een echtgenoot voor mij zoeken was daar een perfect onderwerp voor.

'Eigenlijk wel,' zei ik. 'Een hele lange man die Harold heet.'

Alle drie keken me onschuldig aan en zeiden tegelijkertijd: 'Nou ja, zeg,' en 'Mieters!' Ze waren vast en zeker allemaal bij het plan betrokken.

'Maar hij is niet de ware jakob,' zei ik, waarmee ik hun hoop in duigen sloeg. Ik had besloten niet over Charles te praten. We hadden elkaar nog maar net ontmoet en ik wilde niet dat de halve B-wacht zich er uit louter enthousiasme tegenaan bemoeide.

'Was hij afschuwelijk?' vroeg Joan, die mannen meestal niet de moeite waard vond. Vooral haar eigen echtgenoot niet, als het erop aankwam. Ze gaf me een bemoedigend schouderklopje. 'Het geeft niet.'

'En je bent nog best jong,' zei Mary, die negentien was en mij stokoud vond.

'Er is echt wel iemand die jou wil hebben,' verzekerde Thelma me.

'Hé, waar blijft onze thee?' riep een mannenstem van beneden.

Joan zette een zachte, gevoelige stem op. 'Geef de hoop niet op, Emmy,' zei ze met een ernstig gezicht.

Ik was een oude vrijster, geen invalide... Maar zoals altijd ging dat aan iedereen voorbij.

Joan en Mary haastten zich weg om thee te zetten en Thelma en ik begonnen onze gebruikelijke bezigheden, zodat we op tijd klaar zouden staan voor onze dienst. William stak zijn hoofd om de hoek van de deur en begroette me; aan zijn vastberaden blik was te zien dat hij liever bij zijn mannen was. Hij verdween meteen weer.

Thelma was dol op tijdschriften en de laatste tijd kocht ze *Vrouw & Vriendin*. Als ik zei dat mijn baantje echt verre van aantrekkelijk was, dacht ze dat ik overdreven bescheiden deed.

'WAT DE POT SCHAFT van vorige week...' zei Thelma peinzend. 'Die stoofpot van lamshersenen... Die stank krijg ik niet meer weg.' We lachten allebei. 'Toch hadden de kinders eindelijk weer 'ns genoeg te eten,' voegde ze eraan toe. 'Hoe gaat het met de problemen? Zit er iets smakelijks bij?'

Grinnikend wachtte ze op mijn opmerking dat ik het niet mocht vertellen. Daar was ze inmiddels mee vertrouwd geraakt. Mijn maag kwam in opstand en niet vanwege de stoofpot. Natuurlijk had ik Thelma niet verteld dat ik zelf brieven schreef, al zou het echt handig zijn als ik haar om raad kon vragen. Thelma was bijna dertig en had drie kinderen. Zij was massa's beter gekwalificeerd om mensen te helpen dan ik.

'Eigenlijk mag ik dat niet zeggen,' zei ik. 'Maar...'

Thelma zette grote ogen op. Ze trok een stoel bij en ging naast me zitten.

'O, het is niets vreselijks,' zei ik op luchthartige toon. Ik dacht aan een lezeressenbrief die ik niet had weggegooid omdat ik het niet over mijn hart kon krijgen.

Beste mevr. Bird,
Ik ben achttien en mijn ouders zijn vreselijk streng. We wonen vlak bij een militair kamp en de mannen zijn altijd heel aardig. Ik ben bevriend geraakt met een soldaat die even oud is als ik. We zijn gewoon vrienden, maar mijn ouders zeggen dat ik niets met soldaten te maken mag hebben en dat ze me anders zullen verbieden alleen de deur uit te gaan. Ik ben met deze jongen naar de film geweest, maar dat weten ze niet. Al mijn vriendinnen gaan met jongens uit, en ik wil hem niet kwijtraken. Wilt u me alstublieft vertellen wat ik moet doen?
Ontevreden, Hull

Mevrouw Bird zou vast onmiddellijk korte metten maken met Ontevreden, maar ik had met haar te doen. Toch wist ik niet precies wat ik moest adviseren. Achttien was in mijn ogen beslist oud genoeg om met iemand uit te gaan, maar ik wilde haar zeker niet aanmoedigen om tegen de wensen van haar ouders in te gaan. Wat moest ik voorstellen? Daar liep ik op vast.

In de vrijwilligersruimte hoorde ik Joan en Mary kletsen en lachen tijdens het theezetten. De jongens waren nog steeds beneden en kapitein Davies had zich opgesloten in zijn kantoor. Ik leunde naar voren en ging zachter praten.

'Thel, wat zou jij zeggen als iemand van achttien met een soldaat wilde uitgaan? Als het jouw Margaret was?' Thelma's dochter was nog maar negen, maar dat deed er niet toe; ik gaf haar alle informatie zonder het over Ontevreden te hebben.

Thelma kneep haar ogen tot spleetjes.

'Ik zou haar het liefst in haar kamer opsluiten tot het vrede is,' zei ze glimlachend. 'De schat. Toen ik Arthur voor het eerst ontmoette, droeg hij zijn marine-uniform. Joeg meteen mijn hoofd op hol. Als haar ouders haar opsluiten, klimt ze gewoon het raam uit.' Ze dacht er eens grondig over na, zichtbaar genietend van de uitdaging. 'Ze zou haar moeder zover moeten krijgen een of twee van die jongens op de thee uit te nodigen... helemaal onder toezicht en zo. Ook zo draag je je steentje bij.' Thelma zweeg even. 'En dan kan haar moeder hem meteen de stuipen op het lijf jagen.'

We lachten allebei, maar in gedachten maakte ik aantekeningen. Thelma's advies klonk praktisch, maar niet overmatig streng.

'En,' vroeg Thelma, 'ben ik goed genoeg voor HENRIËTTA WEET RAAD?'

Ze moest eens weten... Ze zou het massa's beter doen dan mevrouw Bird. Als Thelma de baas was over *Vrouw & Vriendin*, zou ik er niet over denken daar een brief binnen te smokkelen.

Opnieuw kwam mijn maag in opstand.

'Goed,' zei Thelma. 'Waar blijven ze met die thee? Wacht even...'

We luisterden allebei. De sirenes jammerden.

Joan en Mary kwamen haastig terug, Mary met het dienblad met thee. Bijna onmiddellijk hoorden we het geluid van vliegtuigen en van het afweergeschut, en daarna de eerste bommen van deze nacht.

Mary bracht de thee rond, Thelma stak een sigaret op en zette haar helm op. Ook ik zette mijn helm op en trok het riempje strak onder mijn kin.

'Klinkt vlakbij,' zei Joan. Ze kneep haar lippen op elkaar en voegde er na een poosje aan toe: 'Het wordt druk vannacht.'

Ze had gelijk.

Binnen de kortste keren rinkelde mijn telefoon, als eerste. Ik nam snel op. 'Brandweer. Waar belt u vandaan?' vroeg ik. Precies op dat moment klonk er een reusachtige klap buiten, en de hele brandweerkazerne schudde. Mijn theekopje liet zich vreselijk kennen door zenuwachtig van zijn schoteltje te springen en zijn gloeiende inhoud te lozen.

'Neem me niet kwalijk, wilt u dat nog eens zeggen?' vroeg ik. De andere telefoons in de ruimte rinkelden nu ook. De dame aan de andere kant van de lijn schreeuwde de informatie door. Twee huizen verderop bij haar in de straat was een bom ingeslagen.

'Weet u hoeveel mensen daar wonen?' vroeg ik en krabbelde het adres van een straat die ik kende, ongeveer achthonderd meter verderop, neer. 'En hoeveel kinderen?'

'Zes,' vertelde ze. 'We kunnen niets zien vanwege de rook.'

'Maak u geen zorgen,' zei ik. Mijn stem klonk rustig, maar ik was blij dat de beller niet zag dat ik ineenkromp. 'Blijf waar u bent. Ze zullen zo snel mogelijk bij u zijn.'

Vervolgens bedankte ik haar en rondde het telefoongesprek af alsof ik de reservering van een tafeltje in mijn restaurant noteerde in plaats van de akelige details over een straat waarin alle gebouwen met de grond gelijkgemaakt waren. Toen ik net begon als vrijwilligster, leek dat me hardvochtig, maar we moesten absoluut rustig blijven, hoe vreselijk de oproepen ook waren. Dat hoorde bij ons werk. Je kon het je niet permitteren overal over na te denken als je een drukke nacht had. Daarmee was niemand geholpen, zei kapitein Davies altijd. Natuurlijk deden we dat wel achteraf, vooral als je te weten kwam dat het misgegaan was.

Ik scheurde het blaadje uit mijn notitieblok en duwde het stevig op de pin waar alle oproepen terechtkwamen. Thelma en Mary duwden hun blaadjes er ook bij en kapitein Davies kwam uit zijn kantoor.

‘Twee pompen en een zware eenheid, Mary,’ zei hij. Hij keek op het krijtbord en begon schijven te verplaatsen om te laten zien welke groepen waarheen moesten. Mary stond al en liep naar de deur om buiten de brandweerklok te luiden. Een van de mannen holde naar binnen om orders in ontvangst te nemen. Hij had een gezichtsuitdrukking die ik hier al maanden zag: een gekke mengeling van ernstig kijken en niet kunnen wachten om tot actie over te gaan. Daar zou ik nooit aan wennen, al duurde de oorlog nog twintig jaar.

‘Helmen op, meisjes,’ zei kapitein Davies met een boze blik naar Mary.

Mijn telefoon rinkelde weer en die van Thelma ook. Joan probeerde iemand die zij aan de telefoon had te verstaan. Door de bominslagen aan de andere kant van de lijn en het onophoudelijke geratel van het afweergeschut boven ons hoofd was het een wonder dat iemand nog iets hoorde.

‘Brandweer. Waar belt u vandaan?’

We bleven dezelfde zinnen herhalen. Thelma’s sigaret brandde op en stierf stilletjes in de asbak. Mary bleef de klok luiden tot er geen mannen meer waren om weggestuurd te worden en kapitein Davies gaf Thelma opdracht naar Lambeth te bellen om versterking. Iedereen kreeg gelijk: dit was een van de drukste avonden sinds Nieuwjaar.

In de loop van de avond kwam het geluid van de bommenwerpers dichterbij en klonk het steeds luider. We bevonden ons in het heetst van de strijd. Het gejammer van de vliegtuigen boven ons hield niet op en werd alleen onderbroken door het kabaal van het afweergeschut en van nog meer bommen.

‘Ze moeten ons echt hebben vanavond,’ zei Thelma op zakelijke toon toen het even rustig was tussen de telefoontjes door. ‘Ik hoop dat mijn moeder de kinderen naar de kolenkelder gebracht heeft.’

‘Ik hoop dat Bunty veilig is,’ zei ik. Ze zat waarschijnlijk in de bomschuilplaats van de buren. Dat was de afspraak: als een van ons alleen thuis was, rende diegene door onze tuin naar die van mevrouw Harewood. Mevrouw Harewood was een alleenwonende weduwe, maar omdat haar man lid van het Corps Diplomatique geweest was, stelde ze haar kamers beschikbaar aan hoogwaardigheidsbekleders die tijdelijk in Londen waren. Volgens Bunty wist je nooit naast wie je kwam te zitten. Het kon Maureen zijn, de huishoudster van mevrouw Harewood, of iemand met een pijp, die in het diepste geheim opereerde. Op een avond als deze maakte het natuurlijk niet uit naast wie je zat, al was het de koningin van Sheba. Het was heel waarschijnlijk dat er iemand geraakt zou worden.

Het ergste was nog als er een bommelding kwam uit de nabije omgeving van je familie of een van je vrienden. Dan kon je niet veel doen, hooguit een schietgebedje plegen en doorgaan tot je dienst voorbij was. We wilden de jongens niet in de steek laten – tenslotte waren zij buiten branden aan het blussen terwijl de granaatscherven hun om de oren vlogen en het bombardement doorging.

Tegen middernacht waren we allemaal toe aan een opkikkertje en ik probeerde tussen de telefoontjes door mijn boterhammen op te eten, want die begonnen al om te krullen aan de randen. Eigenlijk mocht je niet aan je bureau eten, maar kapitein Davies was nu zelf buiten met zes pompwagens voor een brand waar alle hens aan dek nodig was, dus ik dacht dat ik het me wel kon veroorloven.

Thelma stond bij het krijtbord en keek naar de aantekening van kapitein Davies: ‘Church Street, 20.15 uur’. Zwijgend wierp ze een blik op de grote klok bij zijn kantoor. We wisten allemaal wat ze dacht.

Je zorgen maken over de brandweerploegen was het ergste van dit werk. Dus begon ik maar over *The Mark of Zorro* te praten om ons allemaal af te leiden van de vraag hoelang de jongens al weg waren. Het lawaai van de vliegtuigen dreunde maar door. Joan en Mary hielden hun vrije oor dicht terwijl ze belden en leunden dicht naar hun telefoons toe om nog iets te verstaan. Tevergeefs. De bommenwerpers waren pal boven ons en het kabaal was oorverdovend.

Net toen ik *Zorro* opgegeven had, kwam de ontzagwekkendste klap: alsof je midden in een onweerswolk zat. We doken onder de tafel terwijl het hele gebouw schudde op zijn grondvesten. De grote klok viel van de muur, met een brok pleisterwerk eraan, en theekopjes, schoteltjes en borden kletterden neer; mijn kopje en schoteltje vielen van het bureau en vielen vlak naast mijn hoofd in diggelen. Mary slaakte een gil en keek beschaamd, maar we konden het haar niet kwalijk nemen. Het lawaai kwam overal tegelijk vandaan, alsof we verslonden werden door het geluid. Nog een ontzettende explosie en weer schudde het gebouw.

Als deze bom niet ons einde betekende, dan was iemand heel vlakbij de klos. Zelfs Joan keek ongerust.

Thelma, die naast me op de vloer lag, stootte een heel lelijk woord uit. 'Die was dichtbij. Gaat het een beetje?'

Ik knikte. 'Helemaal.' Met een geforceerde grijns keek ik naar de andere meisjes. 'Vingers en tenen nog compleet?'

De anderen knikten en Thelma en ik knikten terug.

'Die smerige mestbuil van een Hitler,' brulde Joan boven het afweergeschut uit.

'Volgens mij ben ik op mijn potlood gaan zitten,' schreeuwde Mary gemaakt joviaal en draaide zich zo dat ze naar haar achterwerk kon kijken.

'Pech,' riep ik. Daarna stak ik mijn duim omhoog en vroeg geluidloos: 'Gaat-ie?'

Ze stak haar duim omhoog en knikte verwoed.

Nog een kolossale klap en weer schudde alles. Ditmaal was het iets minder dichtbij en het was ze blijkbaar niet gelukt om de telefoonlijnen te raken, want we hoorden weer gerinkel vlak boven ons.

'Waarschijnlijk de mijne,' schreeuwde Joan. Ze begon onder de tafel vandaan te kruipen om de telefoon op te nemen. Wij keken toe. 'Oef, mijn knieën.' Ze hees zichzelf op, terwijl het luchtgevecht doorging. Joan was voor niets en niemand bang.

'Donder op, Hitler,' schreeuwde ze terwijl ze onze tijdelijke schuilplaats verliet.

De telefoons gingen als razende tekeer. Wat dacht Joan te kunnen beginnen? We konden elkaar nauwelijks horen terwijl we uit volle borst schreeuwden. Maar zij was de taaiste van ons allemaal, onze aanvoerder.

Mary, Thelma en ik keken elkaar aan. We konden de hele nacht onder de tafel blijven liggen, of doen wat we moesten doen.

'Klaar?' riep ik. De anderen knikten.

'Donder op, Hitler!' brulden we en we krabbelden overeind om onze telefoons op te nemen.

12

De helft is gewoon naar de gallemiezen

Hitler was niet onder de indruk van onze forse taal en bleef tot diep in de nacht het westen van Londen de stuipen op het lijf bombarderen.

Urenlang namen we aan een stuk door telefoontjes aan. Een man gaf me zijn adres, Latham Road, maar zei dat het in feite niet uitmaakte hoe de straat heette. We mochten nog van geluk spreken als we íéts konden terugvinden.

'De helft is gewoon naar de gallemiezen, schat, het is allemaal naar de gallemiezen,' zei hij door de telefoon.

Overal om ons heen werden branden gerapporteerd. Alle koeriers die hun neus in de kazerne lieten zien, werden erop uitgestuurd om de brandweerploegen op te sporen. Die moesten niet naar de kazerne terugkomen, maar rechtstreeks naar de branden gaan die het meest uit de hand liepen. Tegen kwart over drie – nadat ze zo te horen alles verwoest hadden wat ze maar konden – was de vijand naar huis teruggekeerd. Kort daarna klonk het signaal 'alles veilig' en iemand belde de dienst van vrouwelijke vrijwilligers om te zorgen dat die mobiele veldkeukens op pad stuurde om onze jongens op gang te houden.

Om zes uur 's morgens begon de dagdienst binnen te

komen. Eindelijk kon ik mijn stoel verlaten; ik draaide mijn schouders naar achteren, want ik had een stijve nek gekregen van het over de telefoon gebukt zitten. Ik snakte ernaar om naar huis te gaan en me ervan te verzekeren dat Bunty, mevrouw Harewood en Maureen in veiligheid waren. Het was een lange nacht geweest.

'Hoe laat moet je op je werk zijn?' vroeg Thelma, toen ze me in mijn ogen zag wrijven.

'Negen uur,' zei ik. 'Ik kan nog een paar uur pitten.' Ik sprak Joan aan. 'Is er nog nieuws over de jongens? Ik wil Bunty graag verslag uitbrengen.'

Joan had vannacht het bord met oproepen beheerd; ik was al uren niet meer op de hoogte.

'Ze zijn nog buiten, in Church Street,' zei ze en keek op haar polshorloge. 'Daar zijn ze al een tijd.' Ze zag mijn gezicht en zei op luchtiger toon: 'Het gaat vast goed met ze.'

'Niet als Bill zo tekeergaat als vorige week. Ik heb verhalen gehoord...' Vreselijke Vera, een van de vaste telefonistes in de A-dienst, was zojuist binnengewandeld. 'Tommy Lewis zei dat Bill zo fanatiek bezig was met een oproep dat hij bijna zijn been kwijtgeraakt was. Dat scheelde niks,' voltooide Vera haar verhaal met een zwierig handgebaar.

Ze zette haar pet af en schudde nonchalant haar haar naar achteren. Vera en ik konden niet zo best met elkaar opschieten. Iedereen wist dat ze een zwak voor William had en achter Bunty's rug om valse dingen over haar zei.

'Hou je mond, Vera,' zei Thelma.

Vera trok een onschuldig gezicht – wat voor haar een hele toer moest zijn.

'Nou ja, dat wil Emmeline vast graag aan die Bunty vertellen. Dat zou ik tenminste wel doen als het mijn beste vriendin was.'

Volgens mij moest ik zelf beslissen wat ik aan 'die Bunty' vertelde, maar Vera denderde door.

'O, wist je dat niet? William is maar nét aan de dood ontsnapt bij die pakhuizen aan Shepherd's Bush Road. Tommy zei dat er een kolossale dwarsbalk naar beneden kwam zetten, zo dichtbij dat ze geluk hadden dat ze niet allemaal dood waren. Zo terug.' Met een flauwe glimlach liep ze de controlekamer uit.

Ik hield me koest en begon mijn verslagboeken op te ruimen.

'Ze loopt gewoon te stoken, Emmy,' zei Thelma. 'Je weet toch hoe ze is. Zo erg was het allemaal niet.'

Ik beet op mijn lip en vroeg me af waarom iedereen behalve ik hiervan op de hoogte was. Geen wonder dat Bill zich gisteravond gedeisd gehouden had en niet even was blijven kletsen.

'Gewoon negeren,' beval Joan en ging op haar tenen staan om de klok weer aan zijn haakje aan de muur te hangen. 'Vera deugt voor geen cent, dat weet je.'

'Een deugniet met een krullenpruik op,' zei Thelma en we grinnikten alle drie. 'Wegwezen jij, voordat ze terugkomt. Schiet op. Zorg maar dat je vannacht wat rust krijgt. Morgenavond zien we je wel weer verschijnen.'

Ze joeg me de controlekamer uit.

Afkeurend met mijn tong klakkend graaide ik mijn overjas en pet van de haak in de hoek en kloste de trap af en de kazerne uit. Ik was moe, en nu ook nijdig omdat ik me door Vera op stang had laten jagen. Die maakte van een mug een olifant, dat wist iedereen. Ik durfde te wedden dat alles dik in orde was.

Aan de andere kant: Church Street lag bijna op de route naar huis; ik kon er best even langslopen. De zon was nog niet op, maar binnen de kortste keren waren mijn ogen gewend aan het donker en kon ik het resultaat van de nachtelijke activiteiten zien.

Zo'n puinhoop had ik nog nooit gezien! Geen wonder dat de kazerne vannacht trilde als een espenblad.

Hatch Road was er eigenlijk niet meer. De gebouwen bestonden alleen nog uit verkoolde geraamtes, met nog smeulende bergen rommel en overal brandlucht. Sommige huizen waren half ingestort en in het schemerige begin van het ochtendlicht zag je dat sommige kamers nog deels intact waren. Een slaapkamer klampte zich vast aan de zijmuur van een huis, met een ladekast die gek genoeg onbeschadigd leek, maar de rest van de kamer ontbrak – alsof die met een bot mes weggehakt was. Twee brandweermannen stonden boven op een berg rokend afval en spoten die nat met een brandslang. Ze waren door en door nat en zeiden geen woord, volkomen geconcentreerd op het afmaken van dit karwei. Ik herkende hen niet, dus ze moesten afkomstig zijn uit een van de andere kazernes. Gelukkig waren ze ons te hulp gekomen.

Onopgemerkt door de reddingswerkers liep ik door. Een ambulancechauffeur hielp een oude man in zijn wagen instappen en zei dat hij zich geen zorgen moest maken, dat alles goed zou komen. De man zei dat hij wel oud was, maar niet gek, en wat zou er gebeurd zijn met de mensen die vermist werden? De ambulancebroeder negeerde zijn vraag en beloofde hem een kop thee.

Ik ving de blik op van een vrouw van middelbare leeftijd. Ze zat in een donzen deken gewikkeld op een keukenstoel, midden op wat eens het trottoir was. Ze was helemaal alleen.

Ik ging naar haar toe. 'Hallo, ik ben van de brandweer,' zei ik, alsof mijn uniform niet voor zichzelf sprak. 'Kan ik u helpen?' De vrouw was van top tot teen bedekt met roet en as en ze had een grote snee in haar kin.

Ze schudde haar hoofd en schonk me een vermoeide glimlach. 'Maak je geen zorgen, lieverd, ik kom gewoon even op adem,' zei ze. 'Dit is de derde keer dat ik mijn huis uit gebombardeerd word. Het komt wel goed.'

'Weet u dat zeker?' vroeg ik. Ik voelde me nutteloos.

'Ja, hoor. Loop jij maar door. Zo te zien had je haast om ergens heen te gaan.'

Daar had ze gelijk in, moest ik toegeven. Ik wilde naar huis. Ik wilde me ervan verzekeren dat mijn vrienden in veiligheid waren. Daarna wilde ik mijn nette werkkleren aantrekken, naar een kantoor gaan dat niet midden in een luchtaanval stond, en als een gewone burger over patronen en romantische verhalen praten, en over de manier waarop je een ons pens het beste kon klaarmaken.

Nu schaamde ik me. Als oorlogscorrespondente zou ik geen best figuur slaan.

Ik had al massa's uitgebrande gebouwen, bomkraters en zelfs brandende huizen gezien, en huizen die uit elkaar getrokken werden om instorting te voorkomen. Maar nog nooit had ik de verwoesting met eigen ogen gezien terwijl ik er zelf doorheen liep. Niet als er nog mensen op brancards lagen en Burgerwacht-opzichters ernaast hurkten om hun naam op identificatiestrookjes te schrijven.

Ik haalde diep adem en zette me schrap. Daarna vroeg ik de vrouw op de keukenstoel nogmaals of ik haar nergens mee kon helpen, en toen ze me verzekerde dat ze het wel zou redden, zette ik koers naar Church Street om William en de jongens te zoeken.

'Kom op, Lake,' fluisterde ik tegen mezelf. 'Doe maar alsof je aan het werk bent.'

Ik ging rechtop lopen en stak mijn kin een beetje naar voren.

'Daar wilt u niet heen, juf,' zei een opzichter van de Burgerwacht toen ik bij de hoek van de straat kwam. 'Als ik u was, zou ik de andere kant op gaan.'

'Dank u wel, maar ik ben door de kazerne hierheen gestuurd,' loog ik en ik klopte op het brandweerinsigne op mijn jas. 'We hebben geen koeriers meer.'

Hij keek aarzelend, maar zei: 'Goed zo, meisje' en: 'Vooruit dan maar,' dus liep ik door.

Hatch Road was al macaber geweest, maar dat was nog niets vergeleken bij het tafereel dat ik aantrof toen ik de hoek omsloeg. Het was nooit een heel grote straat geweest, en nu was het middelste gedeelte helemaal verdwenen. Waar eens een rij met kleine, maar vol trots onderhouden huizen uit de tijd van koning George stond, lagen nu alleen bergen bakstenen en glas, waar de rook uit kwam omdat het daaronder nog altijd brandde. Overal was water, en niet alleen omdat de brandweer aan het blussen was. Aan het opspuitende water in het midden van de straat te zien was de voornaamste buis van de waterleiding gesprongen.

Ik liep door en zag dat er nog steeds vier pompwagens en twee zware eenheden stonden, en brandweermannen waren nog druk bezig. Ik had nog steeds geen spoor van William en de jongens gevonden. Er stond een veldkeuken geparkeerd en vrijwilligsters deelden boterhammen uit aan een paar politieagenten, maar onze jongens hielden niet op. Een van de ploegen spoot met volle kracht water op een brand in een ingestort gebouw. De vlammen verlichtten de hele straat en toen ik dichterbij kwam, voelde ik de enorme hitte. Ik probeerde er kordaat en efficiënt uit te zien voor het geval iemand zou vragen wat ik daar deed, maar niemand had tijd om notitie van me te nemen.

Iemand smeet het portier van een ambulance dicht en gaf een klap op de achterkant; de ambulance reed netjes tussen een krater en de overblijfselen van een huis door. Toen de ambulance weg was, kwam er een busje met een ploeg van Zware Reddingsacties aanrijden. Grote kerels met spades sprongen eruit, met opgerolde mouwen en een vastberaden blik in hun ogen.

Ik bleef toekijken.

Een brandweerkapitein begroette de ploeg en schudde de leidinggevende man de hand.

'Wees echt voorzichtig, jongens,' zei de kapitein. 'Het is zo instabiel als wat. We denken dat er nog steeds mensen onder zitten; een van de jongens probeert bij ze te komen.'

Een van de grote mannen mompelde een krachtterm. 'Willen ze dood of zo?'

'Kijk naar die muur,' zei zijn buurman. 'Kapitein, dat ding komt over zo'n drie minuten naar beneden. Uw jongens moeten daar als de bliksem uit komen.'

Ze tuurden naar de overblijfselen van een woonhuis: de helft van een huis met twee verdiepingen, dat eruitzag alsof het elk moment kon omvallen. Een muur die er voorheen aan vastzat, helde nu akelig over naar rechts, slechts ondersteund door een enorme berg rokend puin en versplinterd hout. Twee brandweermannen lagen boven op de berg met een touw om hun middel geknoopt in een gat te turen. Twee collega's stonden boven hen om het andere eind van het touw vast te houden. Mijn maag kneep samen toen ik zag dat Roy van onze kazerne een van die twee was. Hij was een toonbeeld van opperste concentratie. Volslagen anders dan de Roy die ik kende, die altijd om meer thee vroeg en grappige verhalen over zijn fretten vertelde.

Ik aarzelde even, maar sloop toch dichterbij, me verstoppend achter de ploeg reddingswerkers omdat ik heel goed wist dat ik als vrouwelijk personeelslid van de kazerne hier niet zou mogen zijn, laat staan buiten diensttijd. Als Roy me zag, zou hij woedend worden en me naar huis sturen.

'Wacht!' riep de andere man die bovenop stond, en ik realiseerde me dat het Fred was. Hij gebaarde dat de reddingsploeg moest ophouden en wees daarna naar beneden, in het gat. 'Ik kan hem niet horen. Kunnen ze die pompen even uitzetten?'

Een paar tellen later hield het gesis van de waterstralen op en de mannen met de brandslangen deden een stap achteruit.

'Hou je waffel, allemaal,' riep Fred, want de mannen van de reddingsploeg stonden nog steeds tegen elkaar te mompelen. Zijn stem klonk zo dringend dat iedereen zijn mond hield en stokstijf stilstond. Je kon het vuur dat nog niet geblust was, horen knetteren en toen de dame in de veldkeuken een roestvrijstalen theepot neerzette, hoorde je dat ook.

De reddingsploeg keek grimmig toe terwijl de oudste man voorzichtig om het puin heen liep en de overhangende muur bekeek. Volgens de etiquette mochten de jongens van de reddingsploeg geen bevelen uitdelen aan de brandweer. Maar iedereen nam hun advies serieus, wist ik, en de brandweerkapitein wachtte op zijn inbreng.

Hij was snel klaar.

'Die muur begeeft het,' schreeuwde hij. 'Haal ze eruit. Nu!'

De kapitein knikte.

'Fred,' riep hij naar boven. 'Hij heeft lang genoeg de tijd gehad. Haal hem naar boven. Zo snel als je kunt.'

Fred stak zijn duim omhoog en boog zich voorzichtig voorover in het gat. Eigenlijk wilde ik niet blijven kijken. Wat ik vooral niet wilde, was blijven luisteren. Ik wist wat ik te horen zou krijgen.

'Bill,' schreeuwde Fred. 'Bill, makker, ben je daar?'

Niemand verroerde een vin terwijl Fred zweeg om te luisteren. Daarna draaide hij zich om en riep naar beneden: 'Er zitten twee kinderen beneden. Levend. Hij gaat ze naar boven sturen. Gooi nog 'ns wat touw.'

Even klonk dit als goed nieuws. Maar mijn optimisme was van korte duur.

De leidinggevende man van het reddingsteam zei een lelijk woord. 'Dat houdt het nooit. Niet als het er drie zijn.'

Hij keek omhoog naar de overhangende muur. 'Als er ook maar íéts beweegt, komt de hele donderse boel naar beneden.'

Daar stond ik, alleen. Ik wilde wel helpen, maar ik was me er maar al te zeer van bewust dat ik een reserveonderdeel was.

'Iedereen behalve de brandweer en de redding achteruit,' beval de kapitein en ze stuurden de opzichters, de politie, de vrijwilligers en mij weg. Alle brandweerjongens bleven staan; zelfs de jongens uit andere kazernes dan de onze weigerden een voet te verzetten. Samen met de kerels van de reddingsploeg probeerden ze van hout een stellage te maken die het puin overeind zou kunnen houden.

Roy liet het eerste touw in het gat zakken. 'Goed, kinderen,' riep hij. 'Wees lief en hou je stil voor de brandweerman. Voorzichtig, Fred.'

Ze begonnen het touw omhoog te trekken en ik duimde voor ze.

'Goed zo, kleintje, rustig maar.' Roy riep het kind bijna zingend toe. 'Nee, liefje, niet schoppen. Mooi zo, als een engeltje. Daar zijn we dan.'

Toen zagen we haar. Een doodsbang klein meisje klemde zich in haar nachtponnetje aan het touw vast. Het kindje was van top tot teen bedekt met grijs stof, zodat ze eruitzag als een kleine geestverschijning.

'Blijf stil hangen, prinses,' zei Roy.

Het kind deed wat haar gezegd werd. Ze knipperde met haar ogen in het grauwe ochtendlicht en deed haar ogen wijd open toen ze de groep mannen boven op het puin zag. Haar gezicht begon te vertrekken.

Fred tilde haar uit Roys handen. 'Het is al goed, oom Fred heeft je vast.'

Het kind klauwde met haar handjes naar zijn uniformjas.

'Mabel,' begon ze te jammeren. 'Mabel.'

‘Het komt goed, we halen haar op,’ beloofde Fred terwijl hij het kind wist door te spelen aan de anderen.

Ik sprong naar voren, maar een dame van de ambulance legde haar hand op mijn arm. ‘Ik heb haar,’ zei ze en liep voor me langs; een van de mannen gaf haar het kleine meisje dat nog steeds om Mabel riep.

Roy en Fred hadden het touw alweer naar beneden laten zakken, naar Bill. Oneindig lijkende seconden gingen voorbij. Toen zagen we ze een jongen uit het gat trekken, groter dan het meisje, maar met hetzelfde onnatuurlijke uiterlijk door al het stof. Zijn rechterarm hing slap langs zijn lichaam en hij kon zich niet goed aan de mannen vasthouden terwijl ze hem eruit tilden. Zijn rechterbeen zag er ook akelig uit.

Voorzichtig haalden de mannen de jongen van de berg af en een verweerd uitziende brandweerman droeg hem weg. Ik bleef toekijken met bonzend hart, misselijk van angst over de jongen en over William die nog steeds nergens te zien was.

Van het naburige huis begonnen bakstenen naar beneden te vallen, en de grote muur begon te wankelen.

‘Bill,’ schreeuwde Roy het gat in. ‘We halen je naar boven. Het is hier gevaarlijk. Pak dat touw.’

Ik hield mijn adem in. Kinderen van hooguit twintig kilo ophijsen was één ding, een volwassen man zou een heel ander geval zijn.

‘Wat is het probleem?’ riep de kapitein. ‘Gaat het wel goed met hem?’

‘Als ik hem te pakken krijg wel,’ zei Fred tegen zijn superieur. ‘Al heb ik zin om hem meteen daarna een optater te verkopen.’

De grote muur helde over. Alle toeschouwers hapten naar adem.

Roy leunde in het gat.

‘Daar komt hij,’ riep hij. ‘Rustig aan, Fred, voorzichtig.’

Nu trokken ze allebei aan het touw. Het regende bakstenen: de berg puin onder hen begon te bewegen.

'Wegwezen, jongens!' riep de aanvoerder van de reddingsploeg. 'Iedereen wegwezen!'

De mannen die de muur met hout en balken probeerden te ondersteunen, begonnen achteruit te lopen. Ze waren ontzaglijk dapper geweest door te doen wat ze gedaan hadden, maar nu riep hun baas hen weg. De stenen begonnen te vallen, en ze hadden geen andere keus dan zichzelf in veiligheid brengen.

Boven op de berg puin zagen we dat Roy en Fred Bill eindelijk naar buiten sleepten. Hij was nauwelijks te herkennen.

'Ik ben eruit, jongens. WEGWEZEN!!!'

Zo hard had ik van mijn leven nog niemand horen roepen.

Alle drie de mannen klauterden half struikelend, half vallend de berg af en daarbij vielen bakstenen, glas en stukken hout naar beneden. Het leek wel een vulkaan, maar dan andersom: het puin leek naar binnen gezogen te worden. De hele berg begon in te storten, met de grote muur er meteen achteraan; het was een kabaal van jewelste.

Roy en Fred kwamen eerst overeind en renden weg, zo snel ze konden. Blijkbaar bewoog ik in hun richting, want een opzichter van de Burgerwacht pakte me bij mijn overjas en trok me met zich mee achteruit.

William kwam een tel later. Terwijl het laatste stuk van het gebouw op de grond stortte en een kolossale wolk van stof en rook opsteeg, verscheen hij, vreselijk hoestend, met bloed op zijn uniform en met een kleine bundel in zijn armen geklemd.

Ik schudde de opzichter af en rende tussen de anderen door naar hem toe.

'Het gaat goed met hem, liefje,' zei Roy terwijl ik hem opzij duwde. 'Het komt helemaal goed.'

‘Wat haal jij je in vredesnaam in je hoofd?’ gilde ik. ‘Je had dood kunnen zijn.’

William hield het bundeltje omhoog. Het was een pop, in een deken gewikkeld.

Toen zag ik écht bloed.

‘Moet ik Bunty echt vertellen dat je bijna doodging bij het redden van een pop?!’ schreeuwde ik.

‘Waar is die kleine, Roy?’ vroeg William, mij volledig negerend. Hij kwam langzaam op adem. ‘Die wil haar Mabel hebben.’

Ik keek hem woedend aan. Kinderen redden was één ding, dat was kolossaal. Maar bijna de helft van zijn ploeg het risico laten lopen verpletterd te worden om een stuk speelgoed uit het puin te krijgen was heel wat anders.

Fred zat op zijn knieën op de restanten van het plaveisel. Hij hield zijn arm vast en mompelde een reeks buitengewoon onfatsoenlijke woorden.

Ik probeerde eraan te denken dat ik nog in uniform was en dat ik geen scène mocht schoppen.

‘Je hebt hun leven gered, je hoefde niet terug te gaan voor hun speelgoed.’ Ik veegde in mijn ogen – overal zat stof van het ingestorte gebouw. ‘Je had wel dood kunnen gaan.’

‘Kalmeer, Emmy,’ zei William. ‘Ze zijn alles kwijtgeraakt. Je begrijpt niet hoe dat is.’

‘Nee,’ zei ik en ik probeerde kalm te klinken. ‘Waarschijnlijk niet. Maar je hoeft niet te doen alsof dit iets eenmaligs was, want ik weet wel beter. Heb je me niks te vertellen over zaterdagavond, toen je nog maar net op het nippertje kon ontsnappen uit dat pakhuis?’

Terwijl ik Vera’s woorden herhaalde, wist ik dat ik fout zat. William was een held en ik bedierf het voor hem. Maar ik had doodsangsten uitgestaan, ik had niets kunnen doen en de hele situatie was veel te moeilijk voor me.

‘Emmy,’ zei hij, ‘je gaat dit niet tegen Bunty zeggen, toch?’

Ik kon hem wel slaan. Hij had volkomen onnodig risico gelopen, en nu wilde hij ook nog eens dat ik deed alsof het niet gebeurd was!

'Denk jij ooit aan iemand anders dan aan jezelf?' vroeg ik en keek hem vernietigend aan. 'Volgens mij niet.'

William wierp me een woedende blik toe.

'O, maak je geen zorgen,' zei ik. 'Ik zal niks zeggen. Maar alleen omdat ik niet wil dat mijn beste vriendin weet dat je vandaag je leven geriskeerd hebt voor een pop. Maar jij moet eens goed naar jezelf kijken, Bill. Je denkt niet aan háár en dat is niet eerlijk.'

Toen keerde ik hem de rug toe, veegde het stof uit mijn ogen en liep met grote stappen naar huis.

13

Een hele troost om te weten

Tegen de tijd dat ik thuiskwam, was Bunty al naar haar werk. Dat maakte het gemakkelijker om me te houden aan mijn belofte om de reddingsoperatie en Williams aandeel daarin te verzwijgen. Ook hoefde ik niet uit te leggen waarom ik van top tot teen bedekt was met stof en roet. Ik stroopte mijn kleren af en permitteerde me de weelde van een bad. Het bodempje water dat ik uit de kraan wist te persen was weliswaar bijna koud, maar toch was het beter dan niets. En het koude water hield me wakker en hielp me om mijn gedachten op een rijtje te krijgen.

Ik was fout geweest, dat besefte ik maar al te goed. Ik had niet midden op straat tegen Bill moeten schreeuwen. Zijn gedrag was onbezonnen en roekeloos geweest, dat vond ik nog steeds, maar zodra het een beetje rustig was in de kazerne, wilde ik hem mijn excuses aanbieden. Ik wilde geen ruzie met hem. Dat ik zo nijdig op hem geworden was, kwam ook doordat ik me zo nutteloos gevoeld had. Ook dat besefte ik nu. De dame die thee uitdeelde, had meer gedaan dan ik.

Terwijl ik het stof uit mijn haar waste, sprak ik mezelf streng toe. Ik had het vreselijk gevonden toeschouwer te zijn tijdens een noodsituatie. Nu schaamde ik me wezenloos omdat ik zo overdreven emotioneel gereageerd had. Ik had verschillende autobiografieën van onbevreesde vrouwelijke journalisten die tijdens de Spaanse Burgeroorlog ter plaatse waren geweest verslonden. Nu verwonderde ik me over de vraag hoe zij het klaargespeeld hadden objectief te blijven, hun werk te doen en hun verslagen op te sturen zonder zich ermee te willen bemoeien.

Zou ik dat kunnen? Dat wist ik niet zeker. Ik bleef de gezichten van de kinderen terwijl Roy en Fred ze uit het puin trokken voor me zien. Hoe kon je afstand houden van zoiets? William was vannacht te ver gegaan, maar zelfs als je die stomme pop vergat: Roy, Fred en hij – en álle mannen – hadden zichzelf in gevaar gebracht om de kinderen te redden. En vannacht zouden ze dat weer doen. Ik was natuurlijk trots op mijn werk in de kazerne, waar ik samen met de andere meisjes de telefoon opnam, maar eigenlijk wilde ik meer doen.

Het werd tijd om mezelf te vermannen.

Op kantoor deed ik extra veel moeite om energiek en monter over te komen. Ik wilde Kathleen niet te veel vertellen over de afgelopen nacht, dus zwakte ik mijn avonturen tijdens de luchtaanval af tot een paar klappen en dreunen bij de kazerne. Om een ander onderwerp aan te snijden, zei ik terloops dat ik zaterdagmiddag meneer Collins en Charles tegengekomen was, alsof we alleen maar 'hoe maakt u het?' tegen elkaar gezegd hadden. Dat bleek bij nader inzien niet zo'n goede zet te zijn.

'Nee zeg.' Kathleen hapte naar adem en keek me met uitpuilende ogen aan bij het idee dat meneer Collins een familielid had, alsof het al eigenaardig was dat hij buiten het werk echt bestond. 'Ik zou het gewoon bestorven hebben. Was hij een schreeuwlelijk zoals je-weet-wel-wie af en toe is?' voegde ze er fluisterend aan toe.

'De broer van meneer Collins was heel beleefd,' zei ik, in de hoop dat dit genoeg informatie was. Maar nee.

'En hoe zag hij eruit? Ouder of jonger?' Kathleen streek op de rand van haar bureau neer, een ronduit roekeloze zet als – je wist maar nooit – mevrouw Bird plotseling binnen zou stormen.

'Gommie, dat weet ik niet meer, hoor,' zei ik zo vaag dat het op geheugenverlies zou kunnen duiden. 'Nogal lang. Nogal jong. Eigenlijk net als iedereen.'

'Stel je voor!' zei Kathleen. 'En wat zei hij?'

'O,' zei ik. 'Je weet wel. "Hallo."'

Kath schudde haar hoofd over mijn onthulling. 'Niet te geloven! Meneer Collins met een broer.'

'Halfbroer,' zei ik nogal stijfjes. 'Dat is volslagen normaal.'

Kathleen kneep haar ogen tot spleetjes en glimlachte. Ik had mezelf in verlegenheid gebracht.

'Je kijkt net als Clarence,' zei ze.

Ik snoof minachtend om aan te tonen hoe bespottelijk dit was en begroef me in mijn werk.

Zoals altijd waren er niet veel acceptabele brieven. Er waren er maar een paar geweest die ik aan mevrouw Bird kon geven en zelfs toen had ze er nog verscheidene geweigerd als volkomen onacceptabel. De enige problemen die ze meteen wenste te beantwoorden waren een vraag van een verlegen veertienjarig meisje – 'Je gedraagt je nogal dwaas; ik stel voor dat je je aansluit bij de padvinderij' – en een nuttige wenk voor een vrouw wier fietszadel glimmende plekken op haar opzichtersuniform achterliet – 'We zijn in oorlog. Het maakt nauwelijks uit of uw uniform glimt of niet. Als u dat niettemin per se wilt voorkomen, bedek uw zadel dan met een oude baret.'

Er was nog een brief geweest die de moeite waard was om haar voor te leggen en tot mijn aangename verrassing had die haar fiat gekregen. De brief kwam van een meisje wier vriendje steeds naar andere meisjes keek.

Beste mevr. Bird,
Vertel me alstublieft wat ik moet doen. Mijn vriend kijkt altijd naar andere meisjes als we op straat lopen. Hij zegt van niet, maar ik heb het zelf gezien. Moet ik hier aandacht aan besteden of het negeren? Als hij nu eens iemand ziet die hij aardiger vindt dan mij, wat dan?
Hoogachtend,
In de Kou

Ik had geriskeerd dat mevrouw Bird de fiolen van haar toorn over dit wulpse gedrag op míj uitstortte, maar 'mannen die naar andere vrouwen kijken' bleek een van haar lievelingsonderwerpen te zijn. Haar antwoord – 'De jongeman in kwestie is een door en door onverkwikkelijk sujet. Als hij dit blijft doen, stel ik voor dat u ofwel hem vergeet, ofwel de politie belt' – was krachtig, zij het aan de dreigende kant.

Om halftien, net toen ik dit had uitgetypt, hoorden we de gangdeur met een klap opengaan en meneer Collins binnenkomen. Hij neuriede iets van Mozart; ik kon niet precies thuisbrengen wat het was, maar het was een teken dat hij in een goede bui was. Als hij niet floot of neuriede, ging hij altijd rechtstreeks naar zijn kantoor, stommelde daar een beetje rond en gaf dan een van zijn schreeuwen ten beste. Vandaag daarentegen stak hij zijn hoofd om de hoek van de deur van ons knusse hokje en leek warempel bijna te glimlachen.

'Goedemorgen, dames. Hoe gaat het met jullie? Het doet me deugd te zien dat jullie de festiviteiten van de afgelopen nacht overleefd hebben.' Zo noemde hij de luchtaanvallen altijd.

'Ja, meneer Collins, dank u wel,' zei Kathleen beleefd, terwijl ik een aanval van afgrijselijke verlegenheid kreeg. Tenslotte hadden we afgelopen zaterdag cake met elkaar gedeeld.

‘Hebt u het veilig doorstaan, meneer Collins?’ informeerde Kathleen. ‘Ik hoop van wel.’

Gewoonlijk was Kathleen muisstil zodra meneer Collins in de buurt was, aangezien ze hem behoorlijk geschift vond. Ze snakte er vast naar om hem naar Charles te vragen.

‘Veilig in mijn warme bed, Kathleen. Dank je wel.’

Ze keek hem stralend aan. ‘En hebt u een leuk weekend gehad, meneer?’

Eerlijk, ze deed me steeds meer denken aan een serveerster die op een vette fooi aast.

‘Ronduit kapitaal, Kathleen, dank je wel,’ zei meneer Collins, die gedurende de weken dat ik hem kende nog nooit toegegeven had iets kapitaal te vinden. ‘En jij?’

Kathleen deed er nog een schepje bovenop. ‘O, heel fijn, dank u wel. We hebben helemaal geen last gehad van de bommen, moeder en ik. Mijn jongere broer was thuis, ziet u, en we voelen ons altijd heel veilig met hem in de buurt, al is hij een stuk jonger dan ik.’

Even overwoog ik me uit het dichtstbijzijnde raam te storten.

‘O, is dat zo?’ vroeg meneer Collins. ‘Stel je voor.’ Hij keek naar mij, maar ik zat met open mond naar de potplant te kijken.

‘Goed weekend gehad, Emmeline?’ vroeg hij.

‘Eh... ja, dank u,’ wist ik uit te brengen. Wat zou er gebeuren als hij over Charles begon? Of erger nog: over het uitstapje naar de bioscoop? Kathleen zou beslist een appelflauwte krijgen.

‘HOE GAAT HET MET UW BROER,’ gilde ik plotseling zo hard dat iedereen schrok, ‘DIE WE OP STRAAT TEGENKWAMEN?’

Het klonk alsof ik in East End rondgehangen had, daar een hondengevecht georganiseerd of op paarden gewed had en patat verpakt in krantenpapier had lopen eten.

Meneer Collins leek van zijn stuk gebracht, wat goed

bekeken een begrijpelijke reactie was, maar vermande zich meteen. Hij stak zijn hand in zijn zak om zijn sigaretten te pakken en richtte zich weer tot Kathleen.

'O ja. Heeft Emmeline al verteld dat ze zaterdagmiddag mij en mijn jongere broer toevallig tegen het lijf liep?' vroeg hij.

'OP STRAAT!' schreeuwde ik, voor het geval dat dit nog niet duidelijk was.

'Ja. Zoals Emmy geografisch correct opmerkte, vond deze gebeurtenis op straat plaats.' Meneer Collins glimlachte.

'ZO IS DAT!' brulde ik. In stilte vroeg ik me af of het werkelijk mogelijk was om te sterven van verlegenheid.

'Op straat,' herhaalde Kathleen fluisterend, blijkbaar in de hoop dat ze hiermee het hele kwellende gesprek tot een goed einde kon brengen voordat iemand bloedende oren kreeg van het kabaal.

Meneer Collins grinnikte, stak een sigaret op en creëerde – nadat hij blijkbaar besloten had dat we allemaal genoeg doorstaan hadden – een welkome afleiding door mij te vragen waaraan ik op dat moment werkte.

'Dit is de adviesrubriek van volgende week, meneer… eh… Collins,' zei ik en probeerde het te laten klinken alsof ik alles onder controle had. Het zou me bijzonder slecht uitkomen als meneer Collins zich ineens voor de brieven ging interesseren. Ik gaf mezelf de opdracht kalm te blijven.

'Aha,' zei hij terwijl hij de aantekeningen pakte. 'Grote griebels,' vervolgde hij toen hij mevrouw Birds antwoord op In de Kou zag. 'Dat kunnen we niet afdrukken. Dan wordt de helft van alle jonge mannen in Groot-Brittannië gearresteerd. Emmy, haal deze eruit. Henriëtta zal het niet merken. En als ze zich toch boos maakt, vertel je maar dat ik gezegd heb dat je het moest doen.'

Blijkbaar keek ik nogal onzeker. Meneer Collins blies een rookwolk uit en trok een ongeduldig gezicht. 'De zetters kunnen er altijd wel voor zorgen dat alles past. Ik ga naar mijn kantoor.' Daarop snoof hij geïrriteerd en liep met grote stappen de kamer uit.

'Doen we,' zei ik. 'Ik hoop maar dat hij gelijk heeft,' vervolgde ik tegen Kathleen, die potloodslijpsel uit haar puntenslijper probeerde te peuteren.

'Volgens mij wel,' zei ze peinzend. 'Mevrouw Bird heeft niets gezegd over die Odo-Ro-No-advertentie die verviel. En toen ik een keer vergeten was of ik haar een exemplaar gegeven had en het haar vroeg, zei ze dat ze geen tijd had voor kletspraatjes over lezen en dat ze trouwens alles al gezien had behalve de romantische verhalen en meneer Collins' wissewasjes-die-geen-aandacht-behoefden.'

Kathleen zweeg, zichtbaar getraumatiseerd door de herinnering.

'Zware tijden,' zei ik meelevend. 'Toch fijn om te weten dat het, als er per ongeluk iets fout gaat, heel onwaarschijnlijk is dat mevrouw Bird erachter komt, vind je niet?'

'Ja.' Kathleen keek me stralend aan. 'Dat is een hele troost om te weten.'

'Toch?' zei ik, al even stralend.

In de Kou had de perfecte hoeveelheid ruimte ingenomen op de HENRIËTTA WEET RAAD-pagina. Terwijl mijn vriendin het uittypen van 'Hoe maakt u het? Een bekoorlijk kleedje voor uw dienblad' hervatte, haalde ik de map met 'onaangename brieven' uit mijn la en vond de brief van de achttienjarige Ontevreden, waarmee Thelma me vannacht geholpen had. Ik probeerde me precies te herinneren wat Thelma gezegd had en begon een antwoord te typen.

Beste Ontevreden,
Wat moet het teleurstellend zijn dat uw ouders voor uw gevoel te streng zijn. Ze hebben vast en zeker het beste met u voor, dus misschien kunnen jullie elkaar enigszins tegemoetkomen...

Je zou toch denken dat het feit dat ik niet in de problemen was geraakt na het plaatsen van één brief in *Vrouw & Vriendin* het gemakkelijker zou maken om dat een tweede keer te doen, maar dat was helemaal niet het geval. Al had ik er alle vertrouwen in dat mevrouw Bird het niet zou zien, het was ronduit verkeerd dat ik Bunty's advies negeerde. Ik had niet echt beloofd dat ik geen lezeressen meer zou schrijven, maar ik had heel vaak geknikt en 'Je hebt natuurlijk gelijk, Bunty' gezegd, wat in feite hetzelfde was. En dat ging alleen nog maar over het sturen van brieven aan de lezeressen. Ze wist niets over het laten afdrukken van antwoorden in het tijdschrift.

Wat was erger, vroeg ik me af, iets voor je beste vriendin verzwijgen of mensen die naar hulp smachten negeren? Volgens mij zou Bunty, als ze die brieven elke dag las, zoals ik, vast en zeker toegeven dat ik probeerde het juiste te doen.

Ik had een pauze nodig, dus mompelde ik iets tegen Kathleen en haastte me naar het trappenhuis, waar ik even rustig kon nadenken. Omdat ik mijn hoofd er niet bij had, knalde ik boven aan de trap tegen meneer Collins op.

'Aha. Blij dat ik je gevonden heb, Emmeline,' zei hij toen ik mijn excuses aanbood. 'Hm.' Hij zweeg even, staarde naar de muur en haalde zijn hand door zijn haar, waardoor het rechtop ging staan. 'Zo. Ja. Dit is hoogst onprofessioneel, om van akelig ongemakkelijk nog maar te zwijgen, maar ja, zo zie je maar weer. Charles zou woedend zijn als hij dit wist. Hm...'

Hij hield op en keek schaapachtig.

'Hm...' zei hij weer. 'Zo. Ja.'

'Wat wilde u zeggen, meneer Collins?' vroeg ik toen zijn stem weer wegstierf. Toen drong het tot me door. 'O. Gommie. Gaat het over kapitein Mayhew?' vroeg ik snel, voordat ik met stomheid geslagen werd door de maatschappelijke gruwel van dit alles.

'Aha,' zei meneer Collins. 'Ha. Ja.'

We keken allebei naar de vloer, hopeloos van ellende. Eindelijk deed meneer Collins wat een heer betaamt en vermande zich. Hij keek even achterom voor het geval er iemand aan kwam, wat niet zo was.

'Zo,' wist hij met enige inspanning uit te brengen. 'Niet eerder over begonnen. Realiseerde me dat het wel moest. Om maar te zeggen, Emmy, eh... Emmeline, of beter gezegd, juffrouw Lake, dat mijn jongere broer Charles gelukkiger was dan ik hem in lange tijd gezien heb, na afloop van jullie uitstapje naar de bioscoop, bedoel ik.' Hij schraapte zijn keel. 'En. Zo. Juist. Ik wilde alleen zeggen dat als u, om welke reden dan ook, vindt dat werken voor, of náást, moet ik zeggen, in veel opzichten, eh... mij, hier...'

Hij kneep zijn lippen op elkaar en keek me recht aan. Toen slaakte hij een diepe zucht en dook in het diepe. 'Emmeline, Charles heeft er heel erg van genoten om jou te ontmoeten. Hij zou vast en zeker opgetogen zijn als dat nogmaals zou gebeuren en ik wil niet dat je denkt dat je dat niet moet doen, alleen omdat wij op hetzelfde kantoor werken. Ik vind niet dat de mensen hier er iets van hoeven te weten en ik zal het er zeker nooit meer over hebben. Dus als je wilde...' Hij zweeg even. 'Of misschien niet...'

Dit was ondraaglijk.

'Het zit wel goed, meneer Collins,' zei ik snel. 'Volgens mij zou ik het best leuk vinden,' wist ik ook nog uit te brengen.

Daarna hervatte ik het vernederd wegkijken. Dit was erger dan die keer dat Bunty en ik door vader betrapt werden op het giechelen om de tekeningen in een van zijn medische boeken – we waren twaalf.

'O juist. Mooi. Ja. Mooi zo,' zei meneer Collins met een ontzaglijk opgeluchte blik. 'Dat is dan weer geregeld. Het spijt me echt dat ik je dit moest aandoen. Afgrijselijk. Geen idee hoe ouders dat klaarspelen. Echt niets voor mij. Hm.' Maar hij glimlachte erbij en keek me trots aan. 'Hij is een fijne kerel, die Charles,' zei hij. 'Fijne kerel. Dat spreekt natuurlijk vanzelf.'

En daarna marcheerde meneer Collins kordaat de trap af, precies zoals hij bovenaan verschenen was.

Het was een hele opluchting om weer achter mijn bureau te gaan zitten en te beginnen aan het uittypen van een nieuw romantisch vervolgverhaal. Net toen ik bezig was met een episode waarin een jongen op een marinebasis geplaatst wordt en ogenblikkelijk op twee officieren tegelijk verliefd wordt, arriveerde Clarence. Hij pronkte met een nieuw kapsel waarin een enthousiaste hoeveelheid Brylcreem de hoofdrol speelde en sidderde zichtbaar van de hoop dat dit misschien indruk op Kathleen zou maken.

'Goedemorgen,' riep hij op barse toon – wat een goed begin was – om vervolgens het woord 'dames' uit te gillen, als een onverwacht hoge finale. 'Exemplaren voor het huis,' voegde hij er plechtig aan toe. 'En post.'

Als de bliksem stond ik op en ik duwde mijn stoel achteruit zodat die luid over de houten vloer schraapte.

'Het nieuwe nummer. Dank je wel, Clarence!' brulde ik, terwijl ik de stapel uit zijn handen trok. 'Post. Denderend!'

Dit was het nummer met de brief van Verbijsterd. Zojuist had ik nog zorgeloos een antwoord aan Ontevreden geschreven en gedacht dat het een makkie was om van alles binnen te smokkelen in Henriëtta weet raad. Nu het bewijs van mijn muiterij zwart-op-wit gedrukt stond, was ik zo schichtig als een veulen.

'Gommie, Em, wat een ijver,' zei Kath. 'Hallo, Clarence, wat zie jij er leuk uit.'

Clarence zag eruit alsof hij tot in het diepst van zijn hart getroffen was.

'Dank je wel, Clarence,' zei Kath vriendelijk, omdat ze met hem te doen had. 'Gaat het een beetje, Emmy?'

'Puik, dank je,' zei ik. 'Massa's te doen.'

Ik voelde het zweet over mijn rug lopen terwijl ik de stapel tijdschriften op de vloer naast mijn bureau legde en begon met het doornemen van de post. Als mevrouw Bird nu eens besloot de *Vrouw & Vriendin* van deze week te lezen, als iets eenmaligs, wat dan? Of misschien las ze het tijdschrift in feite altijd, maar liet ze het heel netjes op haar bureau liggen zodat het er alleen maar uitzag alsof ze het niet gelezen had. Wat moest ik dan beginnen? Streng zei ik tegen mezelf dat ik een beetje ruggengraat moest tonen. Iedereen was ervan overtuigd dat mevrouw Bird niet naar het eindproduct keek. De brief van Verbijsterd zou veilig zijn en die van Ontevreden ook.

Maar mijn hart ging nog steeds tekeer. Misschien was het geen slecht idee om een korte pauze in te lassen wat het plaatsen van nog meer brieven in het tijdschrift betrof, bedacht ik. En misschien ook in het schrijven aan de lezeressen. Tenslotte had ik de laatste tijd wel erg veel risico genomen. Het idee om me een tijdje gedeisd te houden trok me nogal aan.

Zenuwachtig keek ik naar de deur. Mevrouw Bird zat in haar kantoor en zou zich elk moment op ons kunnen storten. Ik kon het beste doen alsof alles volkomen normaal was. Ik zou haar post openmaken en dan acceptabele brieven en een exemplaar van het nieuwe nummer naar haar kantoor brengen.

Ik zei tegen mezelf dat alles helemaal goed zou komen en maakte de eerste brief open.

Beste mevr. Bird,

Zojuist heb ik een eindeloos anderhalf uur doorgebracht met het vasthouden van een streng wol terwijl mijn echtgenote die

ontwarde. Een door en door waardeloze toestand. Waarom wordt wol in vredesnaam niet in bollen verkocht?
Hoogachtend,
Weled. Hr. T. Leonard

Een vraag naar informatie over wol was een kolfje naar mevrouw Birds hand. Ik ontspande me enigszins en maakte de volgende brief open.

Beste mevr. Bird,
Ik ben verliefd op een jonge Poolse vliegenier die hier vlakbij gestationeerd is. We gaan al bijna een jaar met elkaar, en hij heeft me ten huwelijk gevraagd. Mijn moeder wil dat ik wacht tot na de oorlog, want ze denkt dat het niet blijvend is, maar ik houd van hem en ik weet dat hij van mij houdt. Hij heeft een goede opleiding gehad en is boordschutter, dus hij heeft een goede baan. Weet u wat het is? Als hij Engels was, zou moeder er in het minst geen probleem mee hebben, denk ik.
Vertel me alstublieft wat ik moet doen.
Verliefd

Arme Verliefd. Het was verschrikkelijk treurig en bovendien oneerlijk. Dit was ook niet de eerste brief die ik gezien had over dit onderwerp. Ik had al verscheidene van dit soort brieven gelezen: meisjes die geallieerde soldaten van overzee ontmoet hadden en verliefd geworden waren. Mevrouw Bird negeerde ze allemaal.

Vorige week had ik geprobeerd haar zover te krijgen dat ze er een beantwoordde, een brief van een leuk meisje dat heel erg verliefd was op een man die uit Tsjecho-Slowakije hierheen gekomen was om te strijden. 'Hij is een van de allerbeste mannen die u ooit zou kunnen ontmoeten,' had het meisje geschreven.

Ik had het erop gewaagd bij mevrouw Bird en bij wijze

van algemene vraag geïnformeerd of we brieven over 'buitenlandse vrijers' aannamen.

'Ik twijfel er geen moment aan dat hij een bijzonder dappere jongeman is,' antwoordde ze. 'We zijn de geallieerde soldaten allemaal buitengewoon dankbaar.' Daarna veranderde ze van toon. 'Maar zodra de oorlog voorbij is, wenst niemand hen meer hier en het is bijna zeker dat niemand haar dáár wenst. Trek niet zo'n gezicht, juffrouw Lake; zo zit de wereld nu eenmaal in elkaar. Dergelijke situaties kan men het beste op zijn beloop laten.'

Het had geen zin haar de brief van Verliefd te laten zien, maar ik vond het vreselijk om alweer een meisje dat het volste recht had om samen te zijn met wie ze maar wenste te negeren. Vooral nu niemand wist hoelang hij of zij nog te leven had, de vliegeniers nog het minst van allemaal. Waarom zouden ze niet gelukkig zijn? Het was al moeilijk genoeg om de liefde te bewaren te midden van de oorlog, ook zonder dat mensen die het niet begrepen het nog moeilijker maakten.

Ik dacht aan Edmund. Wij hadden elkaars familie al jaren gekend en toch had hij zich uiteindelijk absoluut beroerd tegenover me gedragen. En Charles? Ik wist niets over zijn achtergrond... behalve dat hij de halfbroer van meneer Collins was, en dat bracht niet bepaald veel helderheid. Maar ik wist in elk geval zeker dat, mocht ik hem aardig gaan vinden, het niemand uit mijn familie een lor zou kunnen schelen waar hij vandaan kwam, als hij maar een goede man was en mij fatsoenlijk behandelde. Ik begon te beseffen hoe ik geboft had, wat dat betrof.

Een indrukwekkend geruis op de gang luidde de dreigende verschijning van mevrouw Bird in.

'Bivakmutsen voor de manschappen,' verkondigde ze aan niemand en iedereen tegelijkertijd. 'Ik blijf anderhalf uur weg.'

'Ja, mevrouw Bird,' riep Kathleen, die de drukproef van een recept voor een met kerrie bereide gemengde-groenteschotel aan het corrigeren was.

'Juffrouw Knighton, ik wens niet dat er geschreeuwd wordt!' schreeuwde mevrouw Bird.

'Het spijt me, mevrouw Bird,' zei Kathleen.

'Wat zeg je?' schreeuwde mevrouw Bird en gaf het op. 'Die jongelui ook...'

En met een luid, afkeurend gepuf verdween ze naar buiten.

Terwijl Kathleen haar hoofd schudde en zich weer op het recept richtte – haar gezicht was een en al concentratie – keek ik naar het pak nieuwe tijdschriften op de vloer. De gedachte aan Edmund had me herinnerd aan mijn antwoord aan Verbijsterd, wier verloofde van de kook geraakt was. Hoe langer ik uitstelde om ernaar te kijken, hoe slechter ik me voelde. In mijn gedachten nam het inmiddels de helft van HENRIËTTA WEET RAAD in beslag. Een grote, dikke brief die mevrouw Bird niet eens gezien had, gevolgd door een advies dat zij beslist nooit gegeven zou hebben.

Met hetzelfde gevoel van angst en beven als tijdens het wachten op het voorlezen van de examenresultaten op school pakte ik de schaar van mijn bureau, knipte het touwtje door en pakte de stapel uit. Daar was het dan. Het nieuwe nummer van *Vrouw & Vriendin.*

Ik sloeg onmiddellijk de op twee na laatste pagina op, bijna verbaasd omdat ik de brief van Verbijsterd moest zóéken. Eigenlijk had ik verwacht dat die uit de pagina tevoorschijn zou springen met letters van minstens vijfentwintig centimeter hoog.

Ik ben heel erg verliefd op mijn verloofde, maar hij is opeens heel kil tegen me... Moet ik met hem trouwen en hopen dat hij bijdraait?

Het zag er precies zo uit als alle andere problemen. Een paar zinnen lang, met mijn antwoord er netjes onder.

'Wat een onfortuinlijke teleurstelling,' had ik geschreven – kordaat, zoals mevrouw Bird zou doen.

En treurig voor iedereen. Ik stel een hartig woordje met uw verloofde voor en als u er niet van overtuigd bent dat zijn hart erbij betrokken is, vrees ik dat het tijd is om alleen verder te gaan. Dat kan behoorlijk beroerd voelen, maar ik beloof u dat het beter zal gaan. Het huwelijk duurt heel lang en u verdient het samen te zijn met iemand die heel graag met u samen wil zijn. Ik hoop echt dat uw kerel alle zeilen bijzet, maar zo niet, dan zult u vast en zeker degene vinden die echt voor u bestemd is.

Daar stond het dus, zwart-op-wit.

Het was een heel vreemd gevoel. Deels voelde ik me een bedrieger. Wat wist ik tenslotte over het huwelijk? Maar toen ik het nog eens las, zag ik dat ik Verbijsterd wel enige hoop geboden had. Ze kon haar verloofde een kans geven, maar als hij niet beter zijn best deed, hoefde ze niet aan hem te blijven hangen. Al met al vond ik het geen slecht antwoord. Ik hoopte dat Verbijsterd het ermee eens zou zijn en hem op zijn falie zou geven of verder zou gaan en op een dag haar ware liefde zou vinden.

Ik moest een glimlach bedwingen voor het geval Kathleen me zou zien. Het was een fijn gevoel dat ik iets gedaan had. Ik kon het probleem niet oplossen voor Verbijsterd, maar ik had mijn best gedaan om een soort vriendin voor haar te zijn. En andere lezeressen zouden er misschien ook troost aan ontlenen.

Opgewekt dacht ik weer aan Verliefd. Zij verdiende het om gelukkig te zijn. Ze verdiende het om haar eigen keuze te mogen maken.

Mijn voornemen om me gedeisd te houden hield nog

geen drie minuten stand. Ik was te veel betrokken geraakt bij het leven van de lezeressen om de brief van Verliefd weg te gooien, of een van de andere brieven van lezeressen die ik misschien zou kunnen helpen. Hun brieven in het tijdschrift plaatsen was vreselijk riskant, maar ik schreef nu al meer dan een maand brieven terug en niemand had daar ook maar enig idee van. Dat deel van mijn plan was waterdicht, daar was ik absoluut van overtuigd.

Vannacht werkte ik niet in de brandweerkazerne en ik wist dat Bunty vanavond met William naar de bioscoop ging, dus ik zou alleen in het appartement zijn. Ik verstopte de brief van Verliefd onder een paar papieren tot Kathleen naar buiten ging en ik hem in mijn tas kon laten glijden. Daarna ging ik stilletjes door met het werk van de dag.

14

Op ons, Emmy Lake

Maandagmiddag na mijn werk belde kapitein Mayhew – of beter: Charles – me thuis op. Hij had een leuke telefoonstem en het ging heel goed allemaal. Charles zei dat hij zo blij was dat ik de luchtaanval van de afgelopen nacht zonder kleerscheuren doorgekomen was en ik zei dat het best meeviel allemaal en vertelde niet dat ik op een haartje na twee kinderen en een brandweerbrigade tot pulp verpletterd had zien worden op straat.

Het was nog wel even lastig om het onderwerp 'elkaar nog eens zien' aan te snijden, maar na een tijdje wederzijds gehannes – we zeiden telkens tegelijk allebei iets anders, door elkaar heen, en daarna dreigde het hele gesprek stil te vallen omdat we allebei niets meer durfden te zeggen – vatte Charles de koe bij de horens.

'Zeg Emmy, hou jij van dansen?'

'O ja. Kolossaal zelfs,' zei ik. 'Trouwens, Bunty en Bill zijn van plan overmorgen samen uit te gaan.' Ik hield op met praten en kromp ineen. Het klonk alsof ik viste naar een uitnodiging om ook mee te gaan. 'Niet dat ik vis naar een uitnodiging om ook mee te gaan,' zei ik er gauw achteraan.

Charles lachte. 'Dat zou ik helemaal niet erg vinden. Zou

jij het eigenlijk erg vinden als ik jou vroeg om samen met mij te gaan? Even voor de duidelijkheid.'

Ik lachte ook. 'Dat lijkt me heerlijk,' zei ik.

'Als Bunty en haar vriend het tenminste niet erg vinden.'

'Bunty zal dolgelukkig zijn,' zei ik, want daar was ik absoluut zeker van. 'En Bill ook.'

Daarna spraken we af hoe laat Charles bij het huis moest zijn en kletsten we nog een beetje door voordat we afscheid namen. Toen ik opgehangen had, bleef ik met een grijns van oor tot oor in de gang staan. Charles Mayhew wist me beslist op te kikkeren, dat moest ik toegeven.

Ook wat Bunty betreft, had ik gelijk. Toen ik haar over onze dansplannen vertelde, vond ze het het beste idee ter wereld, al was haar toevoeging 'En ik durf te wedden dat hij er niet bij het minste of geringste met de een of andere verpleegster vandoor gaat, zoals die Edmund' niet helemaal in de geest van 'vergeven en vergeten'. Zelf wist ik ook niet zeker of ik Edmund zou kunnen vergeven, maar ik deed wel mijn best om hem te vergeten.

Als Bunty hierdoor haar boosheid op die Edmund – zo noemde ze hem tegenwoordig altijd – achter zich kon laten, des te beter. En voor mij zou het ook een goede gelegenheid zijn om het goed te maken met Bill – al zei ik daar niets over tegen Bunty. Hoe langer ik erover nadacht, hoe meer het me speet dat ik hem zo'n uitbrander gegeven had terwijl hij in feite ongelooflijk dapper geweest was.

Op woensdagavond waren Bunty en ik al vroeg klaar. Zij had een lichtgroen jurkje aangetrokken dat ze op haar eenentwintigste verjaardag gedragen en zelf gemoderniseerd had met een laagje chiffon; dat stond vreselijk aardig en zweefde zo'n beetje om haar heen als ze danste. Ik had gekozen voor een nachtblauwe zijden japon die, hoewel hij al jaren oud was, mijn absolute lievelingsjurk was, het allermooiste kledingstuk uit mijn kast. En toen Bunts en ik bij wijze van oefening even snel het hele appartement door walsten, had ik alle hoop dat ik ermee door kon.

Omdat we tijd te veel hadden, volgde er een nogal slappe aanval van getob over de vraag waar we Charles en William zouden begroeten, want om ze alle trappen op te slepen naar ons appartement terwijl we op het punt stonden allemaal weer naar buiten te gaan leek een beetje dwaas. We overwogen een van de ontvangstkamers beneden te gebruiken, maar sinds Bunty's oma vorig jaar vertrokken was, was alles daar afgedekt met stoflakens. De ramen waren helemaal dichtgeplakt en de verduisteringsgordijnen zaten permanent dicht. De kamers waren nog muf ook en bovendien leken ze ons te voornaam en aandachttrekkerig vergeleken bij ons zolderappartement.

We besloten dat we de jongens boven zouden uitnodigen omdat we daar tenslotte woonden – en omdat William, die altijd het huis in- en uitliep om bij Bunty te zijn, zou denken dat we gek geworden waren als we iets anders deden. Bunty stelde voor dat we hun sherry zouden aanbieden als beloning en ik stelde voor dat we er zelf een zouden nemen om vast op gang te komen. Terwijl Bunty een grammofoonplaat van Joe Loss opzette en het volume omhoog draaide, gooide ik mijn sherry naar binnen en verplaatste zonder enige noodzaak een porseleinen eend op de schoorsteenmantel.

'Wees maar niet zenuwachtig,' zei Bunty beminnelijk toen de deurbel ging en ik de eend bijna te pletter liet vallen. 'We krijgen het vast knotsgezellig met ons vieren. Ga de deur maar opendoen.'

Het was negenentwintig minuten over zeven en nadat ik de drie trappen naar de voordeur af geroffeld was, bleef ik even staan om mijn zenuwen in bedwang te krijgen en mijn gezicht tot een uitnodigende glimlach te plooien.

'Oef,' zei ik hardop in de brede, ijskoude gang. Mijn mond was droog en mijn lippen bleven hardnekkig aan mijn tandvlees plakken. 'Goedenavond,' fluisterde ik tegen mezelf, precies op de toon die ik geoefend had. 'Goedenavond, Charles,' vervolgde ik iets bloemrijker tegen een grote Chinese vaas.

Die begroeting was niet al te moeilijk. Ik knipte het licht in de gang uit – zodat ik niet op mijn falie zou krijgen van een passerende Burgerwacht-opzichter – trok de zware tochtgordijnen opzij en maakte de voordeur open.

Charles stond in het donker op de drempel en glimlachte een beetje verlegen onder de rand van zijn legeruniformpet.

'Hallo, Emmy,' zei hij. 'Wat zie jij er leuk uit.'

Dat was reuze aardig, aangezien hij me niet echt kon zien met het licht uit.

'Goedenavond, Charles,' wist ik uit te brengen. Het kwam er ontzettend formeel uit; eigenlijk klonk het nogal alsof ik op het punt stond het nieuws voor te lezen op de radio. Even overwoog ik te zeggen dat hij er ook leuk uitzag, maar ik wist niet zeker of dat zo hoorde, dus klampte ik me aan de gordijnen vast tot ik de briljante ingeving kreeg hem te vragen of hij wilde binnenkomen. Zodra de deur veilig dicht was, knipte ik het licht aan en leidde hem de trappen op naar ons appartement.

Bunty – ik wist dat ze geoefend had om een nonchalante indruk te maken – stond in de woonkamer met haar ene hand op de schoorsteenmantel zo'n beetje in de verte te staren. Ze zag eruit als een mannequin die een japon showde voor *Vogue*.

Voordat ik hem kon aankondigen, kwam Bunty plotseling in actie en riep: 'Charles!' en Charles riep: 'Bunty!' – beiden op een toon alsof ze goud gevonden hadden. Daarna schudden ze elkaar de hand, opgelucht omdat ze elkaar weer bij de voornaam konden noemen en het lastige 'Zeg maar

Charles; noem mij dan toch Bunty'-gedoe hadden weten te vermijden. Daarna ging de voordeurbel weer.

'Alles goed?' vroeg Charles terwijl Bunty naar beneden holde.

'Nee hè,' zei ik zonder na te denken. 'Dat wou ik vragen. Wat een idioot. Ik. Jij niet, natuurlijk.' Ik grimaste. 'Ik vind het echt leuk om je te zien,' zei ik ten slotte maar, want zo was het.

Charles lachte. 'Ik vind het ook leuk om jou te zien,' zei hij. En toen pakte hij mijn handen beet. Dat was duizendmaal beter dan de handdruk die hij Bunty gegeven had, maar het betekende wel dat we midden in de woonkamer elkaars handen vast stonden te houden toen Bunty en William binnenkwamen.

'Goed zo,' zei Bunty, wat niet bepaald hielp.

Ik rukte mijn handen los en kreeg daar onmiddellijk spijt van. Helaas had ik geen idee hoe ik ze weer in Charles' handen zou kunnen duwen, dus gebruikte ik mijn rechterhand maar om William te begroeten. Dit was de eerste keer dat ik hem zag sinds de ruzie; daarom voelde ik me slecht op mijn gemak. Ik vroeg me af of hij daar misschien ook last van had. Hij leek me een beetje gespannen, maar dat kan ook verbeelding geweest zijn.

Net op tijd dacht ik aan mijn manieren en stelde de beide mannen aan elkaar voor; op de een of andere manier lukte dat me zonder over te komen alsof ik zojuist uit een gesticht vrijgelaten was.

Charles en William zagen er allebei schitterend uit in hun uniform en uitten onmiddellijk hun bewondering voor elkaars werk in 'de huidige situatie'.

'Ik weet niet hoe jullie dat klaarspelen,' zei Charles ernstig terwijl ze elkaar de handen schudden. 'Ik ben als de dood voor vuur. Ik heb de grootste bewondering voor jullie.'

Onwillekeurig herinnerde ik me dat Edmund tegen William nooit iets complimenteus over de brandweer gezegd had, en ik vond het ontzettend aardig dat Charles dat wel deed. Het was ook fijn om Bunty te zien stralen van trots.

Ik bood iedereen een glas sherry aan. Gelukkig had Bunts de tegenwoordigheid van geest gehad om de twee glazen die wij al gebruikt hadden te verstoppen, zodat niets wees op een onfortuinlijke verslaving. Aangezien het mijn tweede drankje in tien minuten was, was de kalmerende werking beter dan ik ooit meegemaakt had.

Nu iedereen zich ontspande, werd het gesprek uitbundig. We kletsten over het feit dat er niet genoeg jazz op de BBC-radio kwam, maar dat het super was als ze het een keertje wel draaiden, en dat Tommy Handley echt een heel rare snijboon was in het hoorspel *It's That Man Again*. Ik deed kolossaal mijn best om aardig te zijn tegen William, en hij deed evenveel zijn best om hoffelijk tegen mij te zijn, terwijl Charles grote belangstelling voor Bunty toonde en zij op haar beurt allerliefst tegen hem was. Op het laatst zou je haast denken dat we allemaal op het punt stonden met de verkeerde persoon te gaan dansen.

Het was een regenachtige avond, maar toen we op weg gingen naar West End, waren we allemaal in opperbeste stemming. Vooral William leek te snakken om te beginnen, en wij vieren arriveerden bij de danszaal toen de rijen voor de avondsessie begonnen aan te groeien. Het was een gemengd publiek: bendes soldaten, ook vrouwelijke militairen en mariniers, met een waar allegaartje aan accenten. Wij stonden in de motregen te wachten naast een paar vriendelijke Nieuw-Zeelanders die geestige commentaren gaven op de affiches met de kreet *Be Like Dad, Keep Mum*, en nog veel kleurrijker reageerden op de advertenties voor Land Girls. Charles trok zijn wenkbrauwen naar me op en ik lachte. Daar ging mijn plan om een carrièrevrouw te zijn die geen tijd voor mannen had.

Tegen de tijd dat we binnen waren, was de dansvloer stampvol. Aan het andere eind van de zaal speelde de band zich een slag in de rondte en als er niet zo'n zee aan uniformen geweest was en de meisjes in burger geen avondjaponnen, maar gewone jurken droegen, zou je gewoon vergeten dat er ook maar iets akeligs gebeurde in de wereld.

Vastberaden voerde William Bunty mee de dansvloer op, en Charles en ik bleven even naar hen staan kijken. Bunty zag er zo gelukkig uit toen ze begonnen te foxtrotten; het chiffon op haar jurk fladderde wijduit als de vleugels van een lieveheersbeestje dat elk moment kan gaan vliegen. Ik lachte hartelijk en wuifde naar hen.

'Volgens mij laten ze het verder aan ons over,' riep Charles boven het lawaai van de band en het geklets bij de bar uit. 'Wil je graag dansen, of zullen we eerst een drankje nemen om deze avond te vieren?'

'Een drankje klinkt heerlijk,' gilde ik. 'Hoewel, wat vieren we dan precies? Snel, daar is een tafel vrij.' Een stelletje verhuisde naar de dansvloer, dus ik greep Charles bij zijn arm en trok hem met me mee. Onbeleefd duwden we een kleine man die met een lang meisje stond te kletsen opzij, slingerden ons in het kleine fluwelen zithoekje dat zojuist vrijgekomen was en ploften zonder een zweem van decorum op het bankje neer.

Terwijl het andere stel verslagen toekeek, keken Charles en ik elkaar aan.

'Hoera!' zeiden we allebei tegelijk en daarna schoten we in de lach.

'Goed gedaan,' zei Charles en wuifde uitnodigend naar een kelner. 'Ik durf te wedden dat jij mieters kunt dansen. Zin in champagne?' Hij zweeg even en trok een gezicht. 'Sorry, hang ik erg de bink uit?'

'Welnee,' zei ik, alsof ik elke woensdagavond champagne dronk en uit dansen ging.

'Mooi zo,' zei Charles en bestelde een fles champagne. Hij wendde zich naar mij en glimlachte. 'Je beseft wel dat ik probeer eruit te zien alsof ik dit om de haverklap doe, hè? Vertel me alsjeblieft dat het me misschien een heel klein beetje lukt.'

Eigenlijk had ik het idee dat het hem bijzonder goed afging.

'Jazeker,' zei ik op aanmoedigende toon. 'Ik vind dat je het heel goed doet.'

'Gelukkig. Eerlijk gezegd weet ik niet precies wat me ineens bezielt. Ik ben me vreselijk aan het uitsloven. Als ik zo doorga, heb ik morgen een hekel aan mezelf.'

'Ach, maar we hebben iets te vieren,' schoot ik hem te hulp. 'Toch?'

Hij lachte. 'Zeg dat wel.'

'Alleen weet ik niet echt wat,' vervolgde ik. Het kan me ook eigenlijk niet schelen, dacht ik.

Charles zweeg even en leunde toen voorover om met me te praten. Zelfs in dit zithoekje werden we overspoeld door lawaai. 'Nou,' zei hij terwijl de kelner tweemaal zo snel als verwacht weer verscheen met een fles en twee glazen, 'ik vind dat we moeten vieren dat dit mijn prettigste verlof van mijn militaire carrière is, dankzij jou.'

Ik voelde mijn wangen rood worden.

'Eigenlijk heb ik daar niet zoveel voor gedaan,' zei ik. 'Alleen een keer naar de bioscoop en een telefoongesprek. O ja, en dit.'

De kelner liet Charles de fles zien en schonk, nadat Charles goedkeurend geknikt had, de champagne in.

Charles overhandigde me een glas. 'Het was me het jaartje wel,' zei hij met gefronste wenkbrauwen en de blik in zijn bruine ogen werd ineens bijzonder ernstig. 'Niet altijd dolle pret.'

Nu leek hij helemaal geen bink meer.

Hij schraapte zijn keel. 'Emmy, ik hoop niet dat je het erg vindt als ik zeg dat je me heel erg opgekikkerd hebt. Dat wilde ik even zeggen. Ik hoop dat je het niet erg vindt,' zei hij nogmaals.

Hij speelde met zijn glas en keek verlegen, maar tegelijk heel wilskrachtig.

Ik klampte me vast aan de steel van mijn champagneglas en dwong mezelf hem in de ogen te kijken. 'Ik heb het reusachtig naar mijn zin,' zei ik. Het kwam er zo zachtjes uit dat hij het vast niet hoorde. Zoiets wilde ik niet uitbrullen. 'Heel erg bedankt.'

Charles had de liefste ogen die ik ooit gezien had. Blijkbaar was er iets niet in de haak met de sherry die ik bij Bunty gedronken had, want ik kon nauwelijks ademhalen.

Hij hief zijn glas.

'Op ons, Emmy Lake,' zei hij terwijl we onze glazen lieten klinken en elkaar doordringend aankeken.

'Op ons,' zei ik en daarna zei ik, gewoon om het zeker te weten, zachtjes tegen mezelf: 'Goeie genade. Op ons.'

Daarna zeiden we geen van beiden iets en het was de gewoonste zaak van de wereld dat Charles zijn glas neerzette en over de tafel heen mijn hand pakte.

Zo troffen Bunty en William ons een paar minuten later aan, wat mij een luid 'O!' ontlokte; ik ging meteen rechtop zitten en rukte mijn hand weer los. Als Charles het al erg vond dat ik dat aan een stuk door leek te doen, of me onbeleefd vond, liet hij dat beslist niet merken. Hij trok alleen heimelijk zijn ene wenkbrauw op en glimlachte naar me.

Bij nader inzien bleek Bunty alleen oog voor William te hebben. We deden allemaal ons best, maar het gesprek kwam niet erg op gang met de muziek en het feestgedruis. Trouwens, William zat de hele tijd te wiebelen en zijn keel te schrapen. Hij leek nog nerveuzer dan eerder op de avond.

Maar zowel hij als Bunty bleef met alle plezier in het zithoekje achter toen Charles mij voorstelde om samen te gaan dansen.

De band was goed op dreef, en hoewel het stampvol was, liep niemand ons in de weg; het was alsof we de dansvloer voor onszelf hadden. Charles was een puike danser, ervaren en vol zelfvertrouwen. Bij hem kreeg je tenminste niet het gevoel dat je een zak steenkool was die op een kar gehesen werd, zoals weleens kon gebeuren als je een danspartner niet zo goed kende. Dansen met Charles was opwekkend en ik had het liefst de hele nacht door willen gaan. Zo had ik me bij Edmund – die trouwens niet van dansavondjes hield – nooit gevoeld.

We walsten en foxtrotten erop los en maakten volgens mij een behoorlijk wervelende indruk. Elke gedachte aan werk of kazerne, aan luchtaanvallen of andere zorgen, verdween als sneeuw voor de zon. Ik kon alleen maar dansen en lachen met een man die behoorlijk leuk was en die ik nog heel aantrekkelijk vond ook.

Toen de bandleider een korte pauze aankondigde, zetten wij koers naar onze tafel om weer op adem te komen. Williams nerveuze blik had plaatsgemaakt voor een grijns van oor tot oor en Bunty zat te sniffen en zag er gelukzaliger uit dan ik ooit gezien had.

Zo ongeveer ontploffend van geluk stak ze haar linkerhand omhoog.

'Kijk, Emmy! Kijk,' riep ze.

Mijn beste vriendin ter wereld was verloofd en ik hoefde maar naar haar gezicht te kijken om te snappen dat haar innigste wens vervuld was.

Meteen volgde een absolute chaos: Bunts en ik gilden als speenvarkens, vlogen elkaar om de hals en probeerden geen tranen te sproeien in het openbaar, en Charles zwengelde Williams hand op en neer en zei: 'Goed gedaan, ouwe jongen' alsof ze elkaar al eeuwen kenden. Daarna kwamen Bunty en ik tot onszelf en nu liet ze me de allerschitterendste ring met smaragd – die van Williams moeder geweest was – echt goed zien, en het was nog best moeilijk om niet opnieuw te gaan bulken.

Het was de allerleukste verrassing ooit.

'Bill zegt dat hij niet langer hoeft te wachten nu hij promotie gekregen heeft,' zei Bunty stralend. 'Suf hè. Ik zou toch wel met hem getrouwd zijn, wat hij ook doet.'

'Iemand moet jou van champagne voorzien,' grinnikte haar verloofde. 'We zouden allemaal wel 'ns gewend kunnen raken aan zo'n luxeleventje.'

Dat juichten we allemaal toe – letterlijk en figuurlijk – en toen keek Bunty mij aan. 'Emmy, ik moet één ding goed regelen,' zei ze en ze zette even een serieus gezicht. 'Jij wordt mijn hoofdbruidsmeisje, toch?'

Natuurlijk zei ik ja, en daarna bezweken we allebei zo'n beetje en uiteindelijk gaf Charles me zijn zakdoek. William had een tweede fles champagne besteld en we proostten allemaal op het gelukkige paar en de toekomst en de vrede en zelfs een keer op de koning en koningin.

William had zijn arm om Bunty heen geslagen en hield haar vast alsof hij haar nooit meer los wilde laten. Bunty keek hem telkens aanbiddend aan en hoewel ze Charles en mij deelgenoot gemaakt hadden van hun wonderbaarlijke nieuws, zag je zo dat er voor hen in de hele zaal niemand anders bestond. Uiteindelijk fluisterde Bunts in mijn oor of ik het erg zou vinden als ze weggingen, want ze wilde haar oma meteen opbellen. Natuurlijk zei ik dat ze dat moest doen; daarna galoppeerden ze de nacht in en lieten Charles en mij samen achterblijven om te dansen.

Hun gelukzaligheid was aanstekelijk. We bleven nog eeuwen dansen en hoewel we allebei zeiden dat onze voeten vreselijk zeer deden, liepen we zielstevreden, arm in arm, samen in het donker naar huis. Er waren luchtaanvallen boven het noorden van de stad, maar daar trokken we ons geen van beiden echt veel van aan.

Pas na middernacht arriveerden we bij het huis van Bunty's oma en toen bleven we nog een tijdje op de drempel staan fluisteren. Charles moest de volgende ochtend om vijf uur op de trein stappen om terug te gaan naar zijn regiment en we zouden elkaar voorlopig niet meer kunnen zien. Dat was een afschuwelijk idee en het was moeilijk om er niet ongelukkig van te worden, maar we kletsten zo opgewekt als we maar konden en waren het erover eens dat we het allebei erg leuk zouden vinden om elkaar te schrijven terwijl hij weg was.

'Ik ga niet somber worden,' zei hij. 'Want ik heb jouw brieven om naar uit te kijken, en je weet trouwens maar nooit wanneer ze weer verlof uitdelen.'

Dat vond ik een heerlijke leugen, dus speelde ik mee en zei dat ik hem – als hij dat wilde – afgrijselijk saaie brieven zou schrijven, zodat hij zich gelukkig kon prijzen dat hij weg was. Daarna hield ik mijn mond en we keken elkaar aan en hielden ons flink; want eigenlijk was het afschuwelijk om afscheid te moeten nemen nu we elkaar nog maar net ontmoet hadden, en ik dacht dat ik hem weleens heel erg aardig kon vinden.

'Jij bent grappig en leuk en je kúnt niet eens saai zijn, al zou je het proberen,' zei hij. 'Zelfs als je me elke dag schrijft, durf ik te wedden dat het je niet lukt. Ik zal jou natuurlijk ook schrijven.'

En voordat ik een grappig of leuk of niet-saai antwoord kon bedenken, boog kapitein Charles Mayhew zich voorover en kusten we elkaar, heel voorzichtig.

15

Ik weet wat ik doe

Charles hield woord wat zijn belofte om te schrijven betrof. Twee dagen later arriveerde er al een brief – die ik las terwijl Bunty door de woonkamer ijsbeerde en deed alsof ze er niet naar smachtte om te weten wat erin stond.

Beste Emmy,
Het is nog niet zo lang geleden dat we afscheid namen en terwijl ik het inpakken nog heel even uitstel, vraag ik me af of je me niet veel te enthousiast zult vinden als ik je vanavond schrijf.
Nou ja, die vraag heb ik de hele weg naar mijn appartement lopen herkauwen en ik heb besloten dat ik dat risico maar moet nemen!
Ik heb het zo reusachtig leuk gevonden om vanavond met jou uit te gaan. Ik wou dat ik langer in Londen kon blijven, maar wat een afscheidsfeest was het: lachen en praten, en dansen tot we geen voeten meer hadden! Ik kan me niet herinneren dat ik ooit eerder zo'n mieterse avond beleefd heb.
Emmy, ik ben buitensporig blij dat we elkaar ontmoet hebben. Ik zou het heel erg fijn vinden om je te leren kennen. Dit zal ik morgen op de post doen, als bewijs dat ik van plan ben zo vaak mogelijk te schrijven… en jou te houden aan je belofte mij ook te schrijven!

Nou, ik zei al dat dit maar een kattenbelletje zou worden en ik ben bang dat ik beter mijn plunjezak klaar kan gaan maken voor vertrek. Ik probeer nog een keer te schrijven voordat ik Engeland verlaat; daarna kan het wat meer bij vlagen komen, maar ze doen altijd wel hun best om de post bij ons te krijgen omdat dat altijd zo'n oppepper is.

Wil je Bunty en William nogmaals mijn oprechte gelukwensen overbrengen, alsjeblieft? Ik wens ze het grootst denkbare geluk.

Voor nu: tot ziens.

Groeten,

Charles x

Ik vond het een prachtige brief. Ik verloste Bunty uit haar lijden door hem aan haar voor te lezen en zij vond hem ook mieters. Daarna liet ik haar de brief zelf lezen en toen ze zag dat Charles ondertekend had met een kusje, raakte ze helemaal in hoger sferen.

Ook ik hield me aan de afspraak en begon Charles te schrijven; ik probeerde gezellige brieven te schrijven die hem aan het lachen zouden maken of op z'n minst zouden opvrolijken. Het zou ik-weet-niet-hoelang duren voordat hij weer op verlof kwam, en terwijl we reusachtig optimistisch deden over alles, koesterden we geen van beiden ook maar de minste illusie dat het karwei spoedig geklaard zou worden.

Het schrijven en verschillende keren herschrijven van mijn eerste brief totdat hij volkomen spontaan zou overkomen nam de hele avond in beslag. Ik begon reusachtig goed met 'Beste Charles', maar strandde daarna omdat ik in paniek raakte en helemaal niets wist te bedenken wat ook maar in de verste verte interessant was – en ik wist vrij zeker dat me dat ook nooit zou gaan lukken. Op de een of andere manier zette ik door en uiteindelijk had ik vier kantjes vol geklets, terwijl we nog maar twee dagen geleden afscheid genomen hadden.

Het vinden van een gepast einde van de brief was een

ware beproeving. Ik wilde hem niet zomaar napraten door 'Voor nu: tot ziens' te schrijven voordat ik ondertekende, en Bunty hielp me niet bepaald met de volslagen geschifte suggestie 'Voor altijd de jouwe', alsof het zo uit een van de romantische verhalen van meneer Collins kwam. Uiteindelijk vermande ik me en koos voor 'Groeten, Emmy' met een kusje, dus het paste toch nog bij zijn ondertekening.

We hadden elkaar nog maar een paar keer gezien, maar ik vond Charles erg aardig. Ik verwenste die stomme oorlog waardoor hij weg moest, al zou ik hem zonder die stomme oorlog waarschijnlijk nooit ontmoet hebben. En ik ging in elk geval niet met mijn ziel onder mijn arm naar hem lopen smachten alsof ik een zwijmelend schoolmeisje was. Dat was een van de weinige dingen waarover ik het absoluut met mevrouw Bird eens was: wij, vrouwen, mochten dan in Engeland zijn en niet echt vechten, maar we moesten ons steentje bijdragen. Ik had massa's te doen, zoals werken bij *Vrouw & Vriendin*, nachtdiensten draaien in de brandweerkazerne en Bunty helpen met het plannen van haar bruiloft.

Nog steeds beantwoordde ik zoveel lezeressen als ik maar kon. Ik las hun brieven altijd in de bus naar huis – doodsbenauwd dat ik er ongemerkt een zou laten vallen – en typte dan thuis als de wiedeweerga antwoorden uit terwijl Bunty nog aan het werk was op het ministerie van Oorlog. *Vrouw & Vriendin* werd nog steeds bepaald niet overspoeld met brieven aan mevrouw Bird, maar de laatste weken waren er wel een paar meer gekomen. Sommige briefschrijfsters zeiden dat ze van een vriendin over het tijdschrift gehoord hadden. Ik moest toegeven dat ik een of twee antwoorden van mevrouw Bird zo geredigeerd had dat ze een beetje minder nors klonken. Het advies was gelijk gebleven en daar ging het om.

Af en toe, als het rustig was in de kazerne, vroeg ik Thelma tussen neus en lippen door om haar mening, vooral over de problemen van oudere lezeressen. Eén dame had een gefrankeerde en aan zichzelf geadresseerde envelop ingesloten voor het antwoord, maar ik had geen flauw idee wat ik haar moest adviseren.

Beste mevr. Bird,
Mijn vriendinnen en ik zijn alle drie achter in de dertig en beginnen ons zorgen te maken over 'de overgang'. We hebben advertenties in uw tijdschrift gezien die zeggen dat een vrouw tussen de dertig en de veertig de moeilijkste tijd van haar leven doormaakt. Is dit een bakerpraatje? Onze vriendin Irene haalt Menopax bij de apotheek tegen opvliegers, maar ze ziet er niet anders uit en volgens mij voelt ze zich nog steeds de helft van de tijd vreselijk beroerd. Wat moeten we doen?
Hoogachtend,
Mevr. Winnie Plum

Ik had het eerst aan mevrouw Bird gevraagd – die minachtend gesnoven had en gezegd had dat Winnie Plum een bijzonder dwaze vrouw was – maar Thelma had veel sympathieker gereageerd. Zij zei dat de middelbare leeftijd volgens haar oudere zus niet bepaald een pretje was, maar ook weer niet het eind van de wereld, vooral niet als je zo nu en dan een gin-tonic nam en een paar Jimmy Stewart-films achter elkaar keek in de Odeon-bioscoop. En als dat niet genoeg was: Hare Majesteit de Koningin was veertig en zij zag er beeldschoon uit.

Dat was niet echt gepast om in een brief te zetten, maar ik vertaalde het in een bemoedigend antwoord aan mevrouw Plum, dat ik beëindigde met een optimistisch: 'Laat geen enkele levensfase u verhinderen alles te doen wat u wilt. Succes!'

Ik hoopte maar dat het zou helpen en dat het beter was dan niets. Wist ik maar meer over het leven! Mevrouw Bird ontving aardig wat brieven over 'de overgang' en hoewel het een van de weinige onderwerpen was die niet op de lijst met onacceptabele onderwerpen stond, kregen de lezeressen steevast te horen dat ze moesten ophouden met zeuren en gewoon moesten doorzetten.

Geen wonder dat de mensen liever een moderner tijdschrift lazen. Als je die een brief schreef en een postzegel insloot, stuurden ze je een folder over bijna ieder onderwerp waarover je vragen kon hebben. Kathleen kende iemand die voor een van de grootste tijdschriften werkte en die zei dat ze hele ploegen mensen in dienst hadden die de hele tijd informatie verstuurden.

Vaak had ik het gevoel dat ik mijn tijd verspilde. Daar zat ik weer heimelijk mijn best te doen om goede antwoorden te bedenken in de bus naar huis, terwijl andere tijdschriften datzelfde op industriële schaal deden. Informatiefabrieken. Dan zei ik streng tegen mezelf dat ik niet zo zwartgallig moest doen en gewoon moest doorgaan.

Er was tegenwoordig trouwens reusachtig veel om blij mee te zijn. De winter bleef weliswaar akelig streng en overheersend aanwezig, alsof hij niet van plan was te vertrekken, maar het vooruitzicht op de bruiloft van Bunty en William was het beste elixer aller tijden. Sinds de oorlog begonnen was, deed niemand meer aan lange verlovingen – wat best een hint voor mij had kunnen zijn met betrekking tot Edmund, nu ik erover nadenk – en omdat Bunty en William elkaar al eeuwen kenden, was er geen reden om te wachten. Ze hadden hun trouwdatum vastgesteld op woensdag 19 maart. Dat betekende dat we minder dan een maand hadden om alles voor elkaar te krijgen.

De bruiloft zou een rustige aangelegenheid zijn, in de dorpskerk van het dorp waar Bunty's oma woonde, gevolgd door een informele lunch bij mevrouw Tavistock thuis. Roy van de brandweerkazerne was er ondersteboven van dat hij Williams getuige mocht zijn, en mijn ouders zouden er natuurlijk zijn; alleen Jack zou waarschijnlijk geen verlof krijgen. Na de lunch zouden de kersverse meneer en mevrouw

Barnes vertrekken voor een huwelijksreis van twee nachten in de buurt van Andover; vrijdagmiddag moest William weer op zijn werk zijn. Er werd gefluisterd dat er tijdens de lunch een varkenslendestuk geserveerd zou worden.

Bij wijze van grap kocht ik *De gids voor de moderne bruid* als verlovingscadeau voor Bunty. Het boek was drie jaar oud en stond vol praktische adviezen en ideeën die nu, midden in de oorlog, hopeloos onhaalbaar waren.

'Geen huis is een thuis zonder piano,' las Bunty hardop voor en vervolgde somber: 'Dan zitten Bill en ik dus in de nesten.' Ze schaterde het uit.

'Ik vrees dat je dit niet serieus genoeg neemt,' zei ik en las over haar schouder mee terwijl ze de inhoudsopgave doorkeek. 'Zoek eens op hoe je de perfecte gastvrouw wordt door "spannend belegde boterhammen voor een informeel souper" te serveren.'

Bunty snoof.

'Gommie,' zei ze terwijl ze die pagina las. 'Geen idee dat je zoveel kon doen met een blik sardientjes. Ik moet nodig bijgespijkerd worden. Anders sla ik een modderfiguur.'

Daar moesten we nog harder om lachen. Alle ingrediënten waren nu onmogelijk te vinden, maar we bestudeerden het hoofdstuk 'Cocktailsuggesties' grondig, zodat we allebei vol zelfvertrouwen een bloody mary zouden kunnen mixen zodra de vrede uitgeroepen werd. De combinatie van wodka, tomatensap, citroensap en worcestersaus klonk nogal smerig, maar dat konden we niet weten voordat we het geprobeerd hadden.

Het was allemaal reusachtig grappig en al zou het fijn geweest zijn om maandenlang over een chique bruiloft-in-het-wit te praten – zoals we ergens anders of in een andere tijd hadden kunnen doen – Bunty was zo gelukkig en verliefd dat het niets uitmaakte. Ze wilde gewoon zo snel mogelijk mevrouw Barnes worden. Zodra William even bij het appartement aanwipte om haar te zien – telkens zodra hij even vrij had tussen zijn diensten door – zag je dat meneer Barnes het daar helemaal mee eens was.

Minder dan twee weken voor de grote dag was ik verwoed bezig Bunty's trouwjurk te maken van een bijzonder elegante groene floersstof – we hadden vreselijk geboft dat we die op de kop hadden kunnen tikken – die ze naderhand nog bij vele andere gelegenheden zou kunnen afdragen. Ik was geen al te beroerde naaister en tot dan toe ging het volgens plan. Bunty had de stof uitgezocht in warenhuis Army & Navy en moeder en ik hadden botje bij botje gelegd om hem te kunnen kopen. Bunty was verrukt. Mevrouw Tavistock verraste ons allemaal door een ongelooflijk charmant paar bruine suède pumps bij Lilley & Skinner te bestellen en een vriendin van Bunty's werk leende haar een schattig bruin hoedje met fluwelen lint, dat daar wonderbaarlijk goed bij paste. Weer of geen weer, Bunty zou er beeldig uitzien.

Op een avond kwam William onderweg naar de kazerne even bij ons appartement langs om een nieuwtje te vertellen. Ik had nog steeds geen gelegenheid gehad om met hem te praten over onze suffe ruzie. Thuis zat hij altijd aan Bunty vastgekleefd, en in de brandweerkazerne waren er altijd bendes mensen in de buurt of had hij het vreselijk druk. Zo druk eigenlijk dat ik me begon af te vragen of hij me wilde ontwijken.

Bunty liet hem binnen en samen renden ze naar de keuken; William leek wel een springveer ingeslikt te hebben en Bunty huppelde lachend achter hem aan de trap op, en zei dat hij stapelgek geworden was.

Ik stond een stuk haringpastei af te snijden om tijdens mijn nachtdienst te eten en keek op toen ze de keuken binnenkwamen.

'Avond, Bill,' zei ik hartelijk. 'Fijn om je te zien. Wil je een Jam Square? Bunty heeft ze gebakken.'

Met een vriendelijke glimlach gaf ik hem een van de gebakjes uit de broodtrommel.

'Mors nou geen jam op je uniform,' zei Bunty, die achter hem stond. 'Ik wil geen echtgenoot die zichzelf verslonst. En het is verspilling.'

William draaide zich om en sloeg zijn arm om haar heen. 'Ja, lieveling,' zei hij met een trots gezicht en op een toon alsof ze al honderd jaar getrouwd waren. 'Stel je voor. Over nog geen twee weken mag je me zoveel op mijn kop zitten als je maar wilt.'

'Nooit,' zei Bunty en we lachten allemaal.

'Trouwens,' zei Bill – hij presteerde het zowaar even op te houden met naar zijn verloofde grijnzen – 'ik kom een belangrijke sociale gelegenheid aankondigen.'

'Oeh,' zeiden Bunty en ik tegelijk.

'Ja,' zei hij. Hij was er allang aan gewend dat we als uit één mond spraken. Hij viste even in de zak van zijn uniform, haalde er een paar kaartjes uit en schraapte zijn keel. 'Ahum. Aanstaande zaterdagavond. Negen uur precies. Café de Paris. Dames, jullie zijn hartelijk uitgenodigd voor een aan de bruiloft voorafgaande viering ter ere van de beeldschone mejuffrouw Marigold Tavistock en haar grootste bewonderaar, meneer William Barnes.'

'Nee!' gilde Bunty.

'Goeie genade,' hijgde ik, diep onder de indruk. 'Nou ja, zeg!'

Bunty en ik keken elkaar met open mond aan. Café de Paris was geen gelegenheid waar we normaal gesproken ooit zouden komen. Het was het soort avondje uit waar rijke Londense types niet van opkeken, maar voor ons was het reusachtig chic. Bunty wilde er altijd al eens naartoe, wist ik, omdat de band het absolute einde zou zijn. En hoewel ze zei dat een meisje op haar werk beweerde dat het niet meer was wat het vóór de oorlog geweest was, was het mieters dat William dit georganiseerd had.

'Is dat dus wel goed genoeg?' vroeg William terwijl Bunty

bij zinnen kwam en hem omhelsde tot hij geen lucht meer kreeg.

'Ja, graag!' zei Bunty met haar gezicht in zijn jas. Toen liet ze hem even los en keek ineens treurig. 'O, maar ik wou dat Charles met Emmy kon gaan.'

'Doe niet zo gek,' zei ik bagatelliserend en duwde mijn avondeten in mijn tas. 'Ik heb hem nog maar twee keer gezien, en de eerste keer was jij erbij.'

'En hoe vaak heb je hem al geschreven?' plaagde Bunty. Ze kuste William op zijn wang en ging op zoek naar brood en boter voor hem om mee te nemen naar zijn werk. 'Ik heb nog nooit iemand zoveel brieven zien schrijven.'

'Bespottelijk,' zei ik terwijl ik de binnenkant van mijn tas aan een onnodige inspectie onderwierp.

'Jij bent de volgende,' lachte ze, wat een beetje al te enthousiast was.

'Eigenlijk heb ik al een vervanger geregeld,' sprong William voor me in de bres. 'Voor deze speciale gelegenheid leek het me gepast om mijn getuige uit te nodigen. Hopelijk vindt kapitein Mayhew het niet erg dat brandweerman Roy Hodges die avond met ons meegaat en juffrouw Lake vergezelt, als zij dat toestaat.'

'Natuurlijk,' zei ik, lichtelijk duizelig bij de gedachte aan de hysterische reacties die ik van de meisjes kon verwachten. 'Het zal me een eer zijn.' Toen herinnerde ik me iets. 'O nee,' zei ik. 'Ik moet zaterdagavond een dienst draaien.'

William grinnikte. 'Dat heb ik al geregeld,' zei hij. 'Vera wil wel voor je invallen, zei ze, als jij het niet erg vindt om een dubbele dienst voor haar te draaien.'

Dat overdonderde me. Ik moest toegeven dat het aardig van haar was.

'Hoera!' zei Bunty.

William kon niet ophouden met glimlachen.

'En Roy zal je nog verbazen. Hij mag dan tegen de veertig

zijn, maar ik heb gehoord dat hij behoorlijk de show steelt als het op dansen aankomt. En hij is al eerder in Café de Paris geweest, dus hij kan ons daar wegwijs maken.'

Dat was beslist een verrassing. Roy had een volkstuin en las graag detectives. Hij was absoluut een geschikte kerel.

'Pas maar op, kapitein Mayhew,' zei Bunty. 'Daar komt brandweerman Hodges, en hij is goed op de hoogte.'

Ik trok een gezicht naar haar en keek daarna op de keukenklok.

'Zeg' – ik wierp William een glimlach toe – 'vind je het erg als ik met jou meeloop naar de kazerne?'

'O, ik wilde vroeg binnen zijn,' zei William nogal kortaf.

De moed zonk me in de schoenen. William leek zo vrolijk; eigenlijk hoopte ik dat hij me vergeven had dat ik tegen hem tekeergegaan was. Ik ploeterde voort en probeerde de luchthartige toon vol te houden. 'Het is wel een beetje vroeg, maar nu Roy zo'n Fred Astaire blijkt, zullen de meisjes minstens twintig minuten nodig hebben om dat te verwerken voordat ze aan de slag kunnen.'

'Doe maar, lieveling,' zei Bunty. 'Maar je mag Emmy geen vragen stellen over mijn jurk. Die moet een verrassing blijven.'

William glimlachte sportief en kon geen nee meer zeggen. Ik pakte mijn tas en rende weg om mijn jas en pet te halen.

Goed ingepakt tegen de vochtige avondlucht begonnen William en ik aan de korte wandeling naar de kazerne.

'Ontzaglijk bedankt voor je uitnodiging voor volgende week,' zei ik terwijl we voorzichtig een weg zochten in het donker. 'Ik zie er zo reusachtig naar uit.'

'Bunty zou niet zonder je willen gaan. En, eh... ik natuurlijk ook niet.' Dat voegde hij er snel aan toe, maar hij bedoelde het vast goed. 'Kijk uit, daar zit een kuil.'

Ik manoeuvreerde om een groot gat in het plaveisel heen, waar een deel van een huis beland was toen het ongeveer een week geleden geraakt was tijdens een luchtaanval. Meneer Bone had me verteld dat er drie gezinnen dakloos geraakt waren en dat een van zijn *Daily Mirror*-lezers zijn onderbeen had moeten laten afzetten.

'Zware klap,' zei ik terwijl ik in het gat keek. 'Zei meneer Bone.'

'Geen idee,' antwoordde William. 'George en de jongens van de A-dienst hebben hier gewerkt. Dat is echt een goed team.'

'Absoluut,' zei ik met vuur. 'Dat geldt natuurlijk voor jullie allemaal.'

'Hm,' hoorde ik naast me in het donker, maar meer niet.

Ik kauwde op de binnenkant van mijn wang terwijl we verder liepen. Zodra ze getrouwd waren, zou William bij Bunty intrekken. Dan zouden ze samen in drie kamers op de begane grond gaan wonen. Bunty stond erop dat ik in het zolderappartement bleef wonen; dat was leuk, maar aan deze ongemakkelijke sfeer moest gewoon een eind komen. We mochten dan oude vrienden zijn, maar ik zou ook nog eens hun kamerbewoner worden. Bovenal wilde ik dat William wist dat ik verschrikkelijk blij was dat alles voor Bunty en hem zo goed uitpakte, en dat ik alleen boos geweest was omdat ik wilde dat hij veilig was. De lucht moest gewoon geklaard worden, zodat we verder konden.

Nu was het juiste moment. Ik zou het misverstand uit de weg ruimen, dan konden we daarna praten over de leuke dansavond en de bruiloft en weer normaal tegen elkaar doen.

'Lekker bewolkt, volgens mij gaat het...' zei William net op het moment dat ik losbarstte.

'Weet je,' interrumpeerde ik. Hij hield abrupt op met praten.

'Het spijt me. Ik, eh... nou ja, dat wilde ik alleen zeggen.'

William was een beetje sneller gaan lopen en ik moest draven om hem bij te houden – wat nog niet meeviel in het donker.

'Weet je, Bill,' zei ik half buiten adem. Ik raakte zijn arm even aan. Als hij weer wat langzamer ging lopen, kon ik fatsoenlijk mijn excuses aanbieden.

'We zijn al laat,' antwoordde hij, wat wel een heel duidelijke hint was dat ik mijn mond moest houden, maar hij hield tenminste wel op met grote stappen nemen.

'Ik wou alleen zeggen dat ik spijt heb dat we ruzie gemaakt hebben,' zei ik heel snel, voor het geval hij besloot weer in hoog tempo de benen te nemen. 'En ik ben echt ontzettend blij voor Bunts en jou.'

Hij knikte. 'Bedankt,' zei hij en zweeg even. 'Je weet hoeveel ik van haar hou, of niet soms? En ik ben geen idioot.'

'Absoluut niet,' zei ik.

'En Emmy, ik zou haar leven nooit willen verpesten. Dus om je de waarheid te zeggen: jij hoeft me niet te vertellen hoe ik mijn werk moet doen.'

'Ik weet het,' zei ik. 'Het spijt me echt.'

'Jij hoeft me niet aan mijn hoofd te zeuren over van alles.'

'Ja, ik begrijp het,' zei ik. Hij had het nu wel duidelijk gemaakt.

'Mooi,' zei William een beetje kortaf en begon weer door te lopen.

Ik bleef naast hem draven en probeerde me te herinneren waar de weg echt bijna onbegaanbaar was. Mijn zaklantaarn gaf zo weinig licht dat ik niet veel zag; ik stootte mijn voet tegen een steen en moest een sprongetje maken om er niet over te struikelen.

William was nog steeds aan het woord. 'Ik weet wat ik doe, Em. Jij niet. Terwijl jij in de kazerne zat, zijn wij al maanden elke nacht bezig dit te doen. Jij weet niet waar je het over hebt. Anders zou je weten dat het niet zo gevaarlijk is als het eruitziet.'

Dat vond ik nogal sterk. Ik wist wat ik bij de bominslag gezien had. Fred had tijdens die klauterpartij zijn arm gebroken zodat die onder een vreemde hoek uitstak, een aanblik waar de meeste mensen misselijk van zouden worden. En het platgebombardeerde huis was bijna ingestort terwijl iedereen daar bezig was. Je hoefde echt geen expert te zijn om te zien dat ze in gevaar verkeerden.

Nu waren we op de hoek van Bellamy Street, slechts twee minuten lopen van de kazerne. Ik had gehoopt dat we op dit punt al over Café de Paris zouden kletsen.

'Hoe dan ook,' zei ik in een poging positief te blijven, hoewel William me behandelde alsof ik zwakzinnig was, 'ik verheug me reusachtig op het Café de Paris.'

'... en in Church Street was alles in feite volkomen onder controle.'

Hij had mijn verontschuldiging nog steeds niet geaccepteerd en nu stak hij zowaar een preek tegen me af.

'Grote griebels, Bill, dat is larie,' zei ik, overmand door frustratie; mijn goede bedoelingen waren verdwenen als sneeuw voor de zon. 'Jij en de andere jongens werden zowat levend begraven.'

Hij stond stil.

'Niet te geloven, Emmeline,' snauwde hij. 'Kun je er nou niet 'ns over ophouden?'

Hij had me in geen jaren Emmeline genoemd. En ik wás erover opgehouden – in elk geval tot ik probeerde mijn excuses aan te bieden. Sinds de ochtend van het bombardement had ik Church Street niet eens meer genoemd en ik had er tegenover Bunty met geen woord over gerept. Door zijn reactie zou je haast denken dat ik het op een groot aanplakbiljet geschreven en in de kazerne opgehangen had.

'Nee, Bill,' zei ik. 'Dat kan ik niet. Niet als jij doet alsof het volkomen redelijk is om rond te ploeteren om een pop te redden, terwijl dat jou en de halve ploeg zowat het leven gekost heeft.'

Zodra die woorden uit mijn mond kwamen, had ik er spijt van. William bewonderde zijn ploegmaten en hield van hen alsof ze zijn eigen familie waren, dat wist iedereen. Dit had ik niet zo moeten zeggen. Ik had de anderen niet mogen noemen. Ik deed mijn mond open om me te verontschuldigen, maar hij was me voor.

'Dat is gemeen, Emmy,' zei hij. 'Dat is echt gemeen.'

Hij keerde me de rug toe en marcheerde met grote stappen weg in de richting van de kazerne.

'Bill,' riep ik, maar hij vertraagde zijn pas niet. 'Bill, alsjeblieft!'

Ik stond in mijn eentje midden in een gat in de weg het duister in te turen terwijl hij uit het zicht verdween.

'Hallo, ben jij dat, Emmy?' Voetstappen knarsten onregelmatig over de weg achter me. 'Wacht op mij, wil je? Mijn batterijen zijn leeg en ik zie geen klap.'

Het was Thelma. Wat een beroerde timing! Ik zei ook 'hallo' en probeerde mijn stem vrolijk te laten klinken.

'Gaat het een beetje, liefje?' vroeg Thelma, die een uitstekende radar had als iemand zich flink voordeed. 'Is onze William er in zijn eentje vandoor gegaan?'

'O, niks aan de hand,' loog ik. 'We zijn allebei een beetje laat, dus heb ik gezegd dat hij maar vooruit moest lopen.'

'De schat,' zei Thelma, waardoor ik me nog beroerder voelde. 'Hij is zo enthousiast over volgende week. Heeft hij jou al over zijn grote verrassing verteld?'

Thelma gaf me een arm en we liepen achter het flauwe schijnsel van mijn zaklantaarn verder de weg af.

'Café de Paris,' zei ze bewonderend, zonder te merken dat ik geen antwoord gegeven had. 'Vorige week vroeg hij mij of ik dacht dat Bunty en jij er blij mee zouden zijn en ik zei dat jullie helemaal hoteldebotel zouden zijn. Zijn jullie er enthousiast over?'

'Ja,' zei ik met een klein stemmetje. 'We kunnen niet wachten tot het zover is.'

'Snap ik,' zei Thelma en drukte mijn arm. 'En die goeie ouwe Roy kan zijn geluk niet op. Echt, die Bunty van jou boft maar. Is het niet mieters dat ze met zo'n leuke kerel trouwt?'

Ik knikte en voelde me waardeloos. Natuurlijk had Thelma gelijk. William was dol op zijn werk en overdreven fanatiek om te bewijzen dat hij zijn steentje bijdroeg. Maar ik wist heel goed dat hij meer van Bunty hield dan van zijn werk, dan van wat ook. Ik kon mezelf wel slaan omdat ik weer tegen hem gesnauwd had... We waren al jaren de beste maatjes en nu stond hij op het punt met mijn beste vriendin te trouwen.

Terwijl Thelma bleef babbelen, beet ik op mijn onderlip en liep zwijgend door. In de tien jaar dat William en ik elkaar kenden, waren we nog nooit chagrijnig tegen elkaar geweest, en nu dit. Ik voelde een golf van boosheid, maar niet op William... zelfs niet op mezelf. Het kwam door die stomme oorlog. Stomme, stomme, bloederige oorlog!

'Gaat het echt wel goed met je, Emmy?' vroeg Thelma in het donker.

'Ja, natuurlijk. Ik heb het alleen een beetje koud,' zei ik. Met mijn arm door de hare zette ik er de pas in naar de kazerne. Als ik snel was, kon ik William voor het begin van de nachtdienst te pakken krijgen en proberen alles eens en voorgoed recht te zetten.

16

Zich voordoen als een redactrice

Ik kreeg William niet te pakken. Ik negeerde het door Café de Paris teweeggebrachte enthousiasme van de meisjes van de B-dienst en ging naar hem op zoek, maar hij was diep in gesprek met kapitein Davies – over het materieel – dus moest ik wel terug naar mijn telefoon. Thelma en de andere meisjes volgden Bunty's plannen voor de bruiloft op de voet, alsof het een romantisch vervolgverhaal in *Vrouw & Vriendin* was. Iedereen vond het heerlijk zich op iets vrolijks te richten, vooral op kleding – tot in de kleinste details – en op geruchten over het soort eten, dat we nog maar zelden te zien kregen. Het plannen van een bruiloft voelde op de een of andere manier ook alsof je Hitler een oplawaai gaf. Hij kon zoveel Luftwaffe-vliegtuigen sturen als hij maar wilde, maar hij kon niet voorkomen dat mensen verliefd werden en dat iedereen daar enthousiast op reageerde.

Aan het eind van de nachtdienst wilde kapitein Davies het rooster met ons bespreken, dus uiteindelijk moest ik me haasten om nog op tijd thuis te komen. Daardoor liep ik William mis. Zoals gewoonlijk moest ik me snel omkleden voordat ik naar kantoor ging, en van slapen kwam het niet meer. Moeder liep er altijd over te tobben hoe we het volhielden. Ik had geen idee. We deden het gewoon.

Hoewel ik teleurgesteld was omdat ik William niet getroffen had – ik snakte er gewoon naar het hele het gedoe met hem uit te praten – verheugde ik me er echt op Kathleen alles te vertellen over Café de Paris.

Ik arriveerde al vroeg op kantoor en wrong me in ons kleine gezamenlijke kantoortje – de potplant had dringend water nodig, zag ik. Omdat ik alleen 's morgens werkte, had Kathleen de laatste post van gisteren op mijn bureau gelegd. Ik was blij te zien dat de stapel brieven voor mevrouw Bird ietsje hoger was dan gewoonlijk. Nadat ik mijn jas opgehangen had, ging ik achter mijn bureau zitten en begon het bergje post open te maken, vol hoop dat er genoeg zou zijn om door te geven. Ik had geluk: de eerste brief was een schot in de roos.

Beste mevr. Bird,
In uw tijdschrift hebben verschillende artikelen gestaan over het feit dat iets korter haar het veiligst is voor oorlogswerkzaamheden, maar mijn man wil het niet hebben. Als lang haar goed genoeg is voor Dorothy Lamour, dan moet het ook goed genoeg voor mij zijn, zegt hij. Hij zegt dat ik het niet naar achteren zou moeten spelden voor mijn werk.
Wat moet ik doen?
Getrouwd met een fan van juffrouw Lamour

Ik grinnikte. Na het lezen van dit soort brieven zat mevrouw Bird gewoonlijk meteen op de kast, maar volgens mij vond ze die heimelijk juist erg leuk. Ik wist vrij zeker dat zij geen idee had wie de Hollywoodactrice was – waarschijnlijk zou ze denken dat het een buurvrouw met slechte invloed was – maar ik wist ook zeker dat zij 'Getrouwd met een fan van juffrouw Lamour' zou opdragen voor de veiligheid een haarnetje te kopen.

Deze brief stopte ik meteen in de map voor mevrouw Bird.

En toen gebeurde het merkwaardigste wat ik tot nu toe meegemaakt had. Ik opende een brief van een lezeres die niet om advies vroeg, al kwam ze wel een beetje op stoom toen ze haar verhaal vertelde.

Beste mevr. Bird,
Hierbij wil ik u bedanken voor het afdrukken van de brief van het meisje dat zich Ontevreden noemt. Ik zou het lef niet gehad hebben om een brief te sturen, maar ik was reusachtig blij toen ik uw antwoord las.
Ziet u, ik was net als zij: ook mijn ouders zijn heel streng, terwijl ik deze zomer al twintig word. Ze wilden niet dat ik een vriendje had, vooral niet als hij bij het leger is of zo – zelfs niet degenen van wie iedereen zegt dat het aardige jongens zijn die je graag als schoonzoon zou willen hebben. Ik liep er echt over te tobben, want ik had een reusachtig aardige jongen ontmoet tijdens een dansavondje van de kerk, waar ik heen gegaan was zonder dat mijn ouders dat wisten. Ziet u, hij zit bij de marine en ik wist dat ze boos zouden zijn.
Ik liep me op te vreten bij de gedachte dat ze me konden betrappen met Leonard (zo heet hij), maar toen las ik dat u tegen Ontevreden zei dat ze flink moest zijn en met haar ouders moest praten en dat heb ik toen dus gedaan. En nu blijkt mijn moeders vriendin Edith een achternicht te zijn van Leonards moeder en zij heeft tegen mijn moeder gezegd dat je niemand een betere jongen zou toewensen en dat het bijna net zo goed is als met een predikant trouwen en zo.
In elk geval is mijn moeder er nu blij mee en Leonard is op de thee geweest zoals u zei dat hij moest doen en ze konden zo goed met elkaar opschieten dat mijn vader hem op het laatst 'jongen' noemde en nu gaan we echt samen uit en ik ben zo blij.
In elk geval wilde ik u heel hartelijk bedanken omdat u me de moed gegeven hebt om mijn mond open te doen.
Hoogachtend,

Mej. Lilian Banks

PS: Ik heb mijn vriendin Jennie aangeraden u te schrijven, want haar moeder behandelt haar echt vreselijk.

Het was een mieterse brief, maar ik was met stomheid geslagen. Dit was de eerste keer dat een echte, levende lezeres werkelijk zei dat ze mijn advies nuttig vond. En zij was niet eens degene wier brief ik beantwoord had. Tot nu toe waren de lezeressen van *Vrouw & Vriendin* een anonieme massa voor me geweest die door meneer Collins getroost en vermaakt werd en door mevrouw Bird als één groot, achterlijk kind behandeld werd. Ik had geweten dat ik met ze meeleefde en ze wilde helpen, maar dit was andere koek.

Ik zou het lef niet gehad hebben om een brief te sturen, maar ik was reusachtig blij toen ik uw antwoord las.

Daar had ik nog niet eens bij stilgestaan. Ik was bang geweest dat ik onderuit zou gaan door het verkeerde advies te geven aan degene die de brief geschreven had. Ik had niet verwacht dat honderden, misschien wel duizenden mensen mijn advies zouden lezen, en dat andere lezeressen die een beroerde tijd doormaakten er ook door bemoedigd konden worden. Wat was dit mieters. Ik voelde me de koning te rijk.

Al dat stiekeme gedoe, het op eieren lopen, zelfs de leugens tegen Bunty – door de brief van Lilian Banks leek het ineens allemaal de moeite waard. Ik vroeg me af hoeveel andere lezeressen hierdoor, net als zij, gerustgesteld waren.

Zodra ik de gangdeur hoorde opengaan, stopte ik Lilians brief terug in de envelop. Die zou ik vanmiddag, als ik weer thuis was, nog eens lezen. Intussen maakte ik de volgende brief open en las die vluchtig door.

'Morgen, Emmy,' riep Kathleen terwijl ze ons kantoortje binnenkwam. Zodra ze haar hoed afzette, danste haar haar los uit de speldjes. Ze trok haar jas uit en onthulde een felgeel vest met leren knopen die op miniatuurvoetballen leken.

'Morgen, Kath,' antwoordde ik. 'Wat een mieters wolletje. Fijn dat je de post op mijn bureau gelegd hebt; bedankt. En je raadt het nooit: ik ga naar Café de Paris.'

Ik babbelde verder, want ik smachtte gewoon om daarover te vertellen, maar Kathleen leek er met haar gedachten niet bij.

Nog voordat ze ging zitten, keek ze naar de brieven op mijn bureau en viel me in de rede. Haar stem klonk een beetje nerveus. 'Dat is een aardige stapel,' zei ze. 'Zitten er nog goede bij?'

'O, niks spannends,' antwoordde ik luchtig. 'Een over kapsels. Vast massa's onaangenaamheden die de prullenbak in moeten.'

Kathleen knikte. 'Ja, vast,' zei ze. Maar, eh... het valt me op dat mevrouw Bird de laatste tijd zo... nou ja, bijna áárdig wordt. Vind je niet? Ze was zo geduldig tegenover die lezeres die een moeilijke verloofde had. Ik dacht dat mevrouw Bird haar wel een idioot zou noemen, maar ze was eigenlijk heel vriendelijk.'

Kath glimlachte een beetje geforceerd. Haar stem klonk ook wat hoger dan gewoonlijk. Ik ging verzitten.

'O, ik weet niet,' zei ik. 'Dat kan ik me niet zo precies herinneren.'

'Deze week was er ook een,' vervolgde ze. 'Over een meisje dat achter de rug van haar ouders om met een soldaat omging. Het verbaasde me dat ze dat meisje geen uitbrander gaf.'

Ik kreeg het warm en begon mijn jasje uit te trekken.

'O, die? Zeg, het begint echt lente te worden, vind je ook niet?' vroeg ik. Mijn ene arm bleef in de mouw steken, achter mijn rug. 'Het is al zoveel warmer dan vorige week.'

Buiten stond een gure wind en gisteren was meneer Brand van de afdeling kunst weggegaan met winterhanden.

Kathleen ging door. 'Het is gewoon een beetje vreemd. Je weet dat ze altijd heel duidelijk is over dat soort zaken. Nogal een ommekeer. Vind je ook niet, Emmy?'

Mijn maag draaide om. Ik had altijd al gedacht dat als íémand me zou betrappen, dat waarschijnlijk Kathleen zou zijn. Zij las *Vrouw & Vriendin* van kaft tot kaft en ze was zo kien. Hoe had ik ooit kunnen denken dat ik haar voor de gek kon houden? Mijn hersens maakten overuren terwijl ik overwoog of ik haar in vertrouwen kon nemen. Het zou afschuwelijk zijn om niet de waarheid te vertellen. Eigenlijk snakte ik ernaar haar alles op te biechten; ik hoopte dat ik haar aan mijn kant kon krijgen, zodat we het samen zouden doen.

Maar dat kon echt niet. Kathleen was goudeerlijk, ze had een reusachtig sterke morele ruggengraat. En ik had me nota bene voorgedaan als de redactrice. Ik kon niet van Kath verwachten dat ze dit voor mevrouw Bird zou verzwijgen.

'Emmy?' herhaalde Kathleen. Intussen had ik het nog warmer gekregen en ik durfde haar niet aan te kijken. 'Ik wil echt niet vervelend doen. Maar je verzwijgt toch niks voor me, of wel?'

De gedachte haar hierin mee te slepen was vreselijk. Dat kon ik gewoon niet doen.

'Eigenlijk wel,' zei ik. 'Kath, kun je een geheim bewaren?'

Kathleen keek alsof ze daaronder zou kunnen bezwijken, maar knikte dapper.

Ik haalde diep adem.

'Zie je, ik heb… eh… ik heb verkering met Charles, de broer van meneer Collins.'

Het klonk nog overtuigend ook. Kathleen in vertrouwen nemen over iets wat wel spannend, maar niet vreselijk was, was de beste afleidingstactiek die ik had kunnen bedenken.

Al voelde ik me wel een mormel omdat ik Charles als dekmantel gebruikte.

Even aarzelde Kathleen; daarna werden haar ogen groter dan ooit en fluisterde ze: 'Nee!'

Ik knikte – met de schijnheiligste glimlach uit de geschiedenis. Gewoontegetrouw keken we allebei even naar de deur voor het geval mevrouw Bird uit het niets zou opdoemen. Toen dat niet gebeurde, drukte Kathleen met een uitdrukking van absolute verrukking en nog grotere opluchting haar handen tegen haar vest en zei een aantal keer achter elkaar: 'Gommie', 'de broer van meneer Collins' en: 'Stel je voor!'

De daaropvolgende tien minuten praatten Kathleen en ik honderduit. Ik vertelde haar het hele verhaal van Charles en zinspeelde op de mogelijkheid dat ik de laatste tijd misschien een beetje nerveus leek omdat ik een geheim had. Ik ging zelfs zover dat ik – met een zogenaamd onschuldig gezicht – vroeg waarom ze zich zorgen maakte over de brieven. Tot mijn opluchting wuifde ze het hele onderwerp weg en zei dat het aan haar lag en dat het niks was. Kathleen was zo goedhartig en zo hartgrondig blij voor me dat ze helemaal in de Charlessmoes trapte. Een kwartier geleden was ik nog in de wolken geweest over een bedankbrief van een onbekende. Nu werd ik behoorlijk misselijk van mezelf.

Terwijl ik probeerde te genieten van wat een leuk gesprek over romantiek had moeten zijn, deed ik mezelf een ernstige belofte: ik zou nooit, absoluut nooit meer brieven binnensmokkelen bij het tijdschrift.

Met al mijn goede bedoelingen had ik Kathleen bijna in een onmogelijke positie gebracht. Dat zette me aan het denken. Het was al erg genoeg dat ik Bunty niet verteld had dat ik de lezeressen terugschreef. Als mevrouw Bird de indruk kreeg dat Kathleen van mijn vervalsingen op de hoogte was, of zelfs als ze vermoedde dat Kathleen mij ervan verdacht en het háár niet vertelde, zou dat veel en veel ernstiger zijn. Dan leek het helemaal een samenzwering. Ik mocht gewoon niet riskeren dat Kathleen in de penarie kwam.

Ik zou voorzichtig doorgaan met het terugschrijven aan lezeressen, maar wat dingen afdrukken betrof moest het nu afgelopen zijn, ook al leken mensen als Lilian Banks erdoor geholpen te zijn.

Als om te bewijzen hoe riskant het allemaal was, vloog de deur van ons kantoor open en verscheen mevrouw Bird – met een vastberaden blik in haar ogen en van top tot teen in tweed gekleed – in de deuropening. 'Ik kan niet blijven,' kondigde ze aan. 'Er is een ongeluk gebeurd op een boerderij.'

'Dat spijt me echt,' zei ik terwijl Kathleen en ik tegelijk opstonden.

'Zijn eigen schuld,' antwoordde mevrouw Bird tamelijk opgewekt.

Daar viel niet veel tegen in te brengen; Kathleen en ik knikten en keken streng. Mevrouw Bird keek het kantoortje rond.

'Ik kom maandag terug naar de stad. Jullie hebben allebei wel genoeg te doen, neem ik aan? Hebt u acceptabele brieven voor me, juffrouw Lake?' Ze keek naar mijn bureau, waar Lilians bedankbrief lag – gelukkig in zijn envelop. Mijn hart begon sneller te kloppen. 'Vreselijk handschrift,' mompelde mevrouw Bird. 'Geen onaangenaamheden, mag ik hopen?'

'Absoluut niet,' zei ik met kolossale overtuigingskracht. 'Er zit zelfs een hele interessante brief bij van een dame die in verwarring gebracht is door een handlezeres,' voegde ik eraan toe – wat een bof dat ik die derde brief nog even ingekeken had. 'Ze verwacht veel van uw hulp.'

Mevrouw Bird fronste haar wenkbrauwen. 'Dat verbaast

me niets,' zei ze. 'Ik zal het maandag in overweging nemen. Weet u zeker dat jullie het allebei druk hebben? Ik meende geklets te horen.'

Op deze suggestie reageerden Kathleen en ik met gekwetste blikken en een verontwaardigde ontkenning.

'Goed,' zei mevrouw Bird. 'Ik moet gaan. Juffrouw Knighton, er ligt correspondentie in mijn uit-bakje. Zorg alstublieft dat deze afgehandeld wordt. Goedemorgen.'

En met die woorden zeilde ze het kantoor uit.

Ik had al de kriebels sinds ik op het nippertje aan Kathleens verdenking ontkomen was, en de verschijning van mevrouw Bird uit het niets – als een nogal stevige geest – had me een zenuwinstorting bezorgd. Met het argument dat ik meer ruimte nodig had om de post door te nemen wrong ik me langs mijn bureau, wierp Kathleen nog een laatste, waanzinnige glimlach toe en vluchtte de gang in.

Daar stond ik stil; ik leunde tegen de muur, deed mijn ogen dicht en klemde de brieven tegen mijn borst.

'Net ergens mee weggekomen?' vroeg meneer Collins, die bij de deur van zijn kantoor stond. Bij ieder ander zou ik dat beschreven hebben als 'op de loer liggen', maar meneer Collins kon altijd zomaar ergens staan zonder dat het verdacht leek. Hij had de journalistieke vaardigheid om zichzelf onzichtbaar te maken.

'O. Wie? Ik? O, gommie, nee,' zei ik, gevolgd door een ongeloofwaardig lachje. 'Het is alleen een beetje hectisch, dat is alles. Massa's te doen,' voegde ik eraan toe in de hoop een ijverige indruk te maken.

'Nou, dat is mooi,' zei meneer Collins. 'Misschien hebben we allemaal nog een week of twee werk als we het om de een of andere onbegrijpelijke reden druk hebben.' Hij lachte even, meer tegen zichzelf dan tegen mij. 'Je wilt me toch niet gaan vertellen dat er mensen zijn die het tijdschrift kopen?'

‘Nou ja, volgens mij wel,’ zei ik in de hoop een eventuele verdere ondervraging te voorkomen. ‘Waarschijnlijk ligt dat aan de zigeuners,’ voegde ik er in het wilde weg aan toe.

‘De zigeuners?’ Hij trok een wenkbrauw op en zuchtte diep. ‘Het is vrijwel onvermijdelijk dat ik er spijt van zal krijgen dat ik dit vraag, maar in vredesnaam, juffrouw Lake, welke zigeuners?’

Meneer Collins leek het altijd weer vermakelijk te vinden om mij ‘juffrouw Lake’ te noemen.

‘Die uit uw verhalen. Zigeuners. Die foerageren. In bossen en zo. De lezeressen zijn er dol op, meneer.’

Deze afleidingstactiek was bij lange na niet zo goed als mijn truc bij Kathleen, en tot overmaat van ramp had ik hem ‘meneer’ genoemd. Dat deed ik anders nooit.

Meneer Collins kwam een beetje dichterbij. ‘Alles goed, Emmy?’ vroeg hij.

‘Absoluut,’ zei ik. ‘Ik sta op het punt de post te sorteren. Die wilde ik net meenemen naar de oude journalistenkamer, als dat mag. Onze kamer is zo klein dat het raar is dat we die andere niet af en toe gebruiken. Ik wist niet of mevrouw Bird dat goed zou vinden.’

‘Ik zou niet weten waarom niet,’ zei hij. ‘Waarom richt je daar geen bureau in, als je meer ruimte nodig hebt? Zeg maar tegen Henriëtta dat ik daar opdracht toe gegeven heb, als je dat wilt.’ Hij glimlachte bij die gedachte.

Ik bedankte hem en zei dat ik zou vragen of Kathleen het geen probleem vond.

Kathleen vond het een puik plan. Zij zou het grotere kantoor ook wel willen gebruiken, zei ze, maar mevrouw Bird stormde nu eenmaal graag bij haar binnen en zou dat eind niet willen lopen. Kath kwam met me mee om de boel een beetje in te richten en nu mevrouw Bird weg was, lukte het me eindelijk haar over het avondje uit in Café de Paris te vertellen.

Mevrouw Bussell, de theedame, kwam zoals gewoonlijk precies op tijd. Ze wist warempel een zeldzaam Garibaldi-biscuitje te presenteren, waarvoor ze zich verontschuldigde 'omdat het bij die lammelingen van Italianen vandaan kwam'.

'Gelukkig heet het geen Mussolini-biscuitje,' zei ik behulpzaam. Terwijl ze het theewagentje weer naar de lift reed, hoorde ik haar iets zeggen wat niet voor publicatie geschikt was.

'Wat trek jij aan?' vroeg Kathleen, die de rozijnen – het waren er twee – uit haar biscuitje pulkte en heel langzaam opat. 'Wordt het een gelegenheid voor avondkleding?'

Ik knikte. 'Ik heb nog een zijden japon van toen ik eenentwintig werd.' Ik glimlachte. Wat leek dat nu lang geleden. 'Volgens mij is die wel goed genoeg.'

Ik verschoof een beetje op het lege bureau waarop ik zat. 'Het voelt wel een beetje overdreven, met alles wat er verder aan de hand is,' voegde ik eraan toe, slecht op mijn gemak.

'Welnee,' zei Kath. 'Het is juist mieters. En je moet van elke minuut genieten. Trouwens, het is onze plicht om dit soort dingen te vieren, of niet soms? Dat vinden de nazi's vreselijk.'

Ik lachte, blij dat we weer gewoon gezellig met elkaar aan het babbelen waren en dat ik geen vragen over de brieven hoefde te ontwijken.

'Ik weet niet zeker of Hitler zich zorgen maakt als ik naar een nachtclub ga,' zei ik. 'Maar ik snap wat je bedoelt. Zaterdag zet ik heel West End op stelten, dat beloof ik je.'

Zwierig hield ik mijn hand achter mijn hoofd en probeerde eruit te zien als een mannequin uit een modetijdschrift.

Er klonk een beleefd kuchje vanuit de deuropening.

'Henriëtta is nog afwezig, begrijp ik?' zei meneer Collins terwijl Kathleen en ik met schuldige gezichten van onze bureaus af sprongen. 'O, kom zeg! Jullie hoeven niet meteen in de houding te springen. Ik maak maar een grapje. Wat hoor ik allemaal over rondzwerven in West End?' Hij wierp me een zogenaamd strenge blik toe.

'O, ik ga niet echt rondzwerven,' zei ik. 'William, van Bunty, neemt ons zaterdag mee uit als een soort feestje vóór de bruiloft. Ze hebben geen verlovingsfeest gehouden.'

'Naar Café de Paris,' voegde Kathleen eraan toe – ze werd de laatste tijd dapperder wat het praten met meneer Collins betrof, en nu voelde ze zich bovendien geschraagd door haar enthousiasme over deze gebeurtenis.

Meneer Collins floot langdurig. 'Juffrouw Lake toch,' zei hij. 'Zeg, dat is me wat! Goede band. Overmatig dure champagne.'

Kathleen en ik keken hem verbijsterd aan. Had meneer Collins verstand van bands?

Meneer Collins rolde met zijn ogen. 'Ik ben nog niet helemaal antiek, weet je.'

'Natuurlijk niet,' hijgde ik en Kathleen knikte meevoelend.

'Eigenlijk nog best jong,' zette ik door, wat duidelijk weer te ver ging. Kathleen keek me waarschuwend aan.

'Al goed, Emmy,' zei meneer Collins, 'dat is weer te gek. Jong zijn is trouwens ook niet alles, neem dat van mij aan. Nou, je zult het daar vast reusachtig naar je zin hebben. En als er een luchtaanval is, zijn jullie daar vast even veilig als waar ook,' voegde hij eraan toe.

'Bent u weleens in Café de Paris geweest, meneer Collins?' vroeg Kathleen warempel.

Het was duidelijk dat ze in vervoering raakte bij het vooruitzicht van verhalen over dansen en muziek en avondjaponnen. In stilte wenste ik dat Kathleen met ons mee kon, want ze zou het vast mieters vinden. En ik beloofde mezelf dat ik in de toekomst niet zou wachten op gedenkwaardige redenen om uitbundig feest te vieren. Elke gewone verjaardag en elk tuinfeest zou genoeg aanleiding zijn.

Eigenlijk verwachtte ik dat meneer Collins nu een eind aan het gesprek zou maken, maar tot mijn verbazing glimlachte hij alleen maar, sloeg zijn armen over elkaar en leunde tegen de deurpost.

'Een paar keer, Kathleen,' antwoordde hij. 'Niet onlangs, moet ik toegeven. Aangezien ik zo verschrikkelijk oud ben.' Hij trok een wenkbrauw even op. 'Maar ja, ik ben er geweest, in de tijd dat Café de Paris net geopend was. Toen was ik beslist hipper.'

Kathleen en ik gaapten hem aan, vol verwachting. Meneer Collins – hip?

Dat was een verrassing! We hoopten op nog meer onthullingen, maar na een fractie van een seconde – waarin hij blijkbaar terugdacht aan een volkomen andere tijd – hield meneer Collins op met leunen, trok de onderkant van zijn vest naar beneden en humde.

'Lang geleden,' zei hij kortaf. 'Goed. Jullie kunnen beter aan de slag gaan, anders zwaait er wat voor ons allemaal.' Hij was weer helemaal in werkstemming. 'Emmeline, ik heb een hele stapel typewerk voor je als je daar tijd voor hebt. Een verhaal dat aan de kust speelt. Nogal saai, maar het loopt goed af. De komende uren zal ik niet op kantoor zijn, dus tot maandag. Veel plezier, zaterdag. Jou zie ik vanmiddag nog, Kathleen.'

Hij draaide zich om en wilde vertrekken, maar bedacht zich en kwam de journalistenkamer weer in.

'Wees voorzichtig, zaterdag. Het zou wel 'ns druk kunnen worden daar.' Hij keek even naar het plafond. Daarna knikte hij en vertrok.

Kathleen keek me aan. 'Gommie,' zei ze. 'Volgens mij vindt hij dat hij een beetje op je moet passen terwijl zijn broer weg is.' Ze giechelde en keek toen zenuwachtig de gang in.

'Sst,' zei ik. 'Hij wil gewoon aardig zijn. En jij vroeg hem nota bene of hij ooit in Café de Paris geweest was.'

'Ik weet niet wat me bezielde,' zei ze en greep naar haar voorhoofd. 'Echt niet.' Daarna keek ze me stralend aan. 'Maar o, het wordt vast mieters!'

Ik knikte, want daar was ik wel zeker van. En wat nu? Hier op het werk had ik het grootste probleem voorlopig opgelost, gelukkig. Nu gingen mijn gedachten terug naar Bunty… en William. Ik moest het eens en voorgoed uitpraten met William; pas dan zou echt alles tiptop in orde zijn.

17

Het veiligste en vrolijkste restaurant van de stad

Hoe slecht we ook met elkaar konden opschieten, ik was Vera kolossaal dankbaar voor het feit dat ze zaterdagavond voor me wilde invallen. Natuurlijk zou ik in ruil daarvoor haar dienst overnemen, zaterdag overdag. Hopelijk zou ik zelfs nog even een dutje kunnen doen, zodat ik fris en monter was voor Café de Paris. In de kazerne hadden de mannen natuurlijk hun eigen kamers met stapelbedden, maar er was ook een kleinere kamer waar wij, meisjes, zo nodig konden slapen, met twee stapelbedden en een paar muizen – die de chocoladereep die Joan heel onbezonnen 's nachts in de houten kledingkast had laten liggen opgegeten hadden.

Het plan was dat ik na mijn dienst zo snel mogelijk naar huis zou gaan. Daar zou ik proberen mezelf presentabel te maken. Dan konden we William en Roy thuis ontvangen met een drankje voordat we naar de nachtclub zouden gaan, waar we om negen uur moesten zijn. Het was krap allemaal, maar het kon net.

Zaterdagochtend marcheerde ik al vroeg naar de kazerne in de hoop William – hij had ook zijn dienst geruild, wist ik

– eerst nog te spreken. Ook Roy was al aan het werk toen ik arriveerde; hij zat met zijn hoofd in de motor van een van de pompwagens en floot er lustig op los.

'Morgen, Roy,' riep ik. 'Ben je onze wals al aan het oefenen?'

Roy ging rechtop staan, zodat hij weer van top tot teen te zien was, en begroette me vol enthousiasme. 'Dat was een quickstep, Ginger Rogers,' zei hij. Hij trok een gek gezicht.

Ik lachte. 'Geen paniek, meneer Astaire, dat wist ik wel.' Hij keek opgelucht. 'Helemaal klaar voor de grote avond?'

Roy keek naar zijn armen, die van de elleboog tot de nagels onder de smeer zaten. 'Over een paar uur herken je me niet meer,' zei hij en hij pakte zijn polshorloge, dat op de voorruit balanceerde. 'Griebels, ik kan maar beter gaan rijden!' Hij keek weer in de motor. 'Zo moet het maar goed genoeg zijn.'

'Is Bill al in de buurt?' vroeg ik.

Roy schudde zijn hoofd en deed de motorkap dicht. 'Nee, die werkt vandaag aan de overkant van de rivier. Daar hebben ze drie man tekort, dus vroegen ze of hij de leiding wilde nemen.' Hij zag mijn teleurgestelde gezicht. 'Geen zorgen, liefje; Arthur Purbridge valt vanavond gewoon voor hem in. Die zal wel blij zijn dat hij even weg is bij zijn Violet. Dat mens kletst je de oren van het hoofd.'

Ik speelde het klaar om zijn grap te lachen en daarna ging ik naar boven. Er zat niets anders op dan te wachten tot vanavond. Dan zou ik William in elk geval zien. De champagne zou me vast en zeker helpen om alles met hem uit te praten, zei ik tegen mezelf. Ik zou gewoon toegeven dat ik me als een idioot had gedragen, en daarna zou ik hem laten beloven dat we de rest van ons leven vrienden zouden blijven. Ondanks alles had ik er alle vertrouwen in. Bij zo'n speciale gelegenheid moest het toch een koud kunstje zijn om het goed te maken.

Het was rustig in de telefooncentrale, en kapitein Davies liet ons om beurten even rust nemen. Toch zou ik me pas echt op mijn gemak voelen als ik zeker wist dat ik op tijd weg kon. Het was een hele opluchting toen Mary voor de avonddienst binnenkwam, op de voet gevolgd door de jongens van de B-dienst – die vol grappen zaten en allerlei kleurrijke variaties bedachten op het thema 'put Roy niet te veel uit'.

Een halfjaar eerder zou ik hierom gebloosd hebben, maar inmiddels was ik wel wat van ze gewend. Dus liet ik de jongens nog even doorgaan en vroeg toen of ze soms wilden dat ik vergat thee voor hen te zetten. Iedereen was goed in vorm en pas na zes uur viel het me op dat Joan er nog helemaal niet was. Erger nog: Vera en haar vriendin Mo – zij had met Thelma geruild zodat Vera en zij dezelfde dienst zouden draaien – waren er ook niet. Kapitein Davies kwam uit zijn kantoor, keek snel de controlekamer rond en fronste zijn wenkbrauwen.

'Mevrouw North is ziek,' zei hij – dat was Joan. 'Dat hoor ik nu pas. Waar zijn de anderen?'

Het was al niet best om je dienst te missen, maar het was bijna onvergeeflijk als je de kazerne geen kans gaf om op tijd een vervangster te zoeken. Joan was er blijkbaar slecht aan toe.

'Zal ik de andere meisjes bellen, meneer?' vroeg ik. 'Om te kijken of iemand voor Joan kan invallen?'

'Graag, juffrouw Lake,' antwoordde de kapitein zonder enige opluchting te tonen. 'Nu meteen, alstublieft. En als het niet lukt, zeg het dan even. Dan zal ik koeriers naar ze toe moeten sturen. Het wordt een heldere nacht en we zullen het druk krijgen.'

'Ja, meneer,' zei ik en haalde de lijst met telefoonnummers – van iedereen die een telefoon thuis of in de buurt had – van het prikbord. Ik begon met Jocelyn Derrick, die altijd heel geschikt was en waarschijnlijk wel zou kunnen komen.

Terwijl ik haar nummer draaide, kwam Vera's vriendin Mo de controlekamer binnenstuiven. Toen ze kapitein Davies met zijn armen over elkaar naast haar lege stoel zag staan, stond ze abrupt stil.

'Het spijt me zo, kapitein, maar de bussen lieten het afweten,' kirde ze.

Bij Mo lieten de bussen het vrijwel voortdurend afweten, in ieder geval als het een rit naar de kazerne betrof.

'Vandaar,' zei kapitein Davies zonder enige emotie. 'En moeten we ervan uitgaan dat juffrouw Woods een soortgelijk probleem ondervindt?'

'O nee, meneer,' zei Mo, die aan amateurtoneel deed. 'Ik vrees dat Vera misschien een beetje te laat komt. Ze voelt zich niet lekker,' voegde ze eraan toe, iets zachter, om de ernst van de ziekte te benadrukken.

'Fijn dat u me dat even laat weten,' zei kapitein Davies droogjes.

'Ik zou haar moeder kunnen bellen,' zei Mo met een klein stemmetje – ze viel eindelijk uit haar rol.

'Dat zou ik maar doen,' zei de kapitein en na een laatste woedende blik op ons allen liep hij zijn kantoor weer in.

Jocelyn nam de telefoon niet op. Ik belde het volgende nummer op de lijst en luisterde intussen het telefoongesprek van Mo af.

'Goeie genade, Veer, hij is echt in een rotbui,' fluisterde ze. Haar gezicht betrok. 'O, je moet het zelf maar weten,' zei ze daarna en legde de hoorn nijdig op de haak.

'Ze zal haar uiterste best doen om hier zo snel mogelijk te zijn,' kondigde Mo in het algemeen aan en liep snuivend, maar met vorstelijke waardigheid, weg om dat nieuws aan kapitein Davies door te geven.

Zolang er maar twee meisjes bij de telefoons zaten, kon ik niet weg. Er zat niets anders op dan verder te zoeken naar een vervangster voor de afwezige Joan. Ik belde Bunty op om haar te vertellen hoe het zat.

'O lieve help, nee toch! Maar het geeft niet,' zei ze dapper, zoals een goed soldaat betaamt. Het lukte haar zelfs bijna om de teleurstelling niet in haar stem te laten doorklinken. 'Ik zal je spullen in een tas stoppen. Als het echt laat wordt, komt Roy die wel brengen en dan komen jullie gewoon rechtstreeks daarvandaan.'

'Ik zal er zijn, Bunty,' beloofde ik. 'Je weet dat ik dit voor geen goud zou willen missen.'

'Maak je geen zorgen, Em,' zei Bunty. 'Nu moet ik echt ophangen. Ik heb mijn krulspelden nog in – geen gezicht. Ik zie je wel verschijnen. En niks geks doen als er een luchtaanval komt, hè?'

'Nee,' zei ik, vastbesloten deze afspraak zo nodig te negeren. Nadat ik de verbinding verbroken had, keek ik op de klok en probeerde nogmaals Jocelyn te bellen.

Ditmaal had ik geluk. Hoewel ze nog maar net thuis was, zei ze meteen hartelijk dat ze zo snel mogelijk naar de kazerne zou komen. Dat was echt fideel van haar. Als Vera nou ook nog een beetje opschoot, zou ik vrij zijn.

Maar Vera schoot niet op. Eigenlijk wist ik wel zeker dat het Vera geen sikkepit kon schelen dat ze te laat kwam.

Om kwart voor acht was ze er nog niet. Jocelyn was wel bliksemsnel gekomen en even later kwam – na een machtig gejuich van de jongens beneden – mijn afspraakje voor vanavond binnen.

'Dames,' zei Roy, 'ik heb een modieus pakket voor juffrouw Lake.' Hij zwaaide met de weekendtas waarin Bunty mijn spullen ingepakt had.

'Nou ja, zeg,' zei Mary en we gaapten hem allemaal aan.

Roy maakte een vlotte buiging om onze aandacht in

ontvangst te nemen. Hij zag er piekfijn uit. Zijn uniform was zorgvuldig gestoomd en geperst – de knopen fonkelden warempel nog meer dan anders – en zo te zien had hij zijn gezicht aan barrels geschrobd met een Brillo-schuursponsje om te zorgen dat het brandschoon was. Bovendien had hij zoveel Brylcreem in zijn haar gesmeerd als menselijk mogelijk was; hij glinsterde aan alle kanten.

Jocelyn liet een luid, bewonderend gefluit horen – dat deed ze blijkbaar vaker. 'Gommie, hij heeft echt zijn best gedaan, hè?' grinnikte ze.

'Nou en of,' zei ik terwijl hij me de tas overhandigde. 'Hartstikke bedankt, Roy. Je ziet er echt mieters uit.'

Ik was geroerd omdat hij zoveel moeite gedaan had, al begreep ik best dat hij dat meer voor William en voor de brandweerbrigade deed dan voor mij. Vanavond zouden we veel mannen in militair uniform tegenkomen en ik wist dat Roy de brandweer niet voor schut wilde zetten.

'Schiet op, Assepoes,' zei Roy als – vrij ongeloofwaardige – goede fee. 'Doe je goeie goed aan, dan kunnen we weg.'

Ik glimlachte hem nog eens dankbaar toe en haastte me naar het damestoilet. Daar wurmde ik me zo snel mogelijk uit mijn uniform. Mijn haar zat van geen kanten, maar Bunty had een paar haarklemmen en een glitterhaarspeld in de tas gestopt, zodat ik het kon opsteken, wat me niet echt slecht afging.

Een snelle controle in het spiegeltje boven de wasbak wees uit dat ik vanavond niet zou kunnen rekenen op veel vleiende aandacht, maar toch maakte ik geen al te beroerde indruk. Snel poetste ik mijn tanden. Daarna verwisselde ik mijn dikke werkkousen voor een kostbaar paar kousen-ommee-uit-te-gaan, waarbij ik angstvallig zorgde dat ik er in de haast geen ladders in trok, en gooide mijn beste jurk over mijn hoofd. Avondschoenen dichtgespen – mijn handen trilden van spanning – een veeg lippenstift – als we daar eenmaal waren, zou ik het nog iets beter doen – en ik was klaar. Ik had er wel drie minuten over gedaan.

'Potjandorie, meisjes, wie is dat?' vroeg Roy toen ik de controlekamer weer inwandelde. Dat was reusachtig aardig van hem, en Mary en Jocelyn riepen: 'Oh' en: 'Ah'.

Ik viel behoorlijk uit de toon zoals ik daar naast mijn stoel stond, helemaal in het lang en met dansschoenen aan – terwijl alle andere meisjes in uniform waren – maar desondanks trilde ik van enthousiasme. In stilte wenste ik dat Charles daar stond – want ik durfde te wedden dat hij er in avondkleding of gala-uniform helemaal mieters zou uitzien – maar ik vond het een eer om door Roy vergezeld te worden. Nu wilde ik niets liever dan de stad in gaan, alles goedmaken met William en daarna volop genieten van de hele avond, samen met mijn beste vriendin en de jongens.

Toen begonnen de sirenes te loeien. Mijn hart maakte een duikvlucht.

'Maak je geen zorgen,' zei Jocelyn onverschrokken. 'Wij redden het hier wel. Vera kan hier over tien minuten zijn. Tot die tijd krijgen we het wel voor elkaar, toch, meisjes?'

Maar ik vertrouwde Vera voor geen cent. Nu er een luchtaanval was, wilde ik niet weggaan voordat zij arriveerde.

'Geen probleem,' zei ik. 'We wachten wel tot Vera er is. Vind je dat goed, Roy?'

Roy knikte en zei dat hij zou gaan kijken of hij intussen de jongens nog ergens mee kon helpen.

Binnen een paar minuten hoorden we het geronk van vijandelijke vliegtuigen. Met mijn helm over mijn haar – en de fraaie haarspeld – ging ik maar gewoon aan de slag; er kwam een telefoontje binnen over een brisantbom die er nogal een zootje van gemaakt had. Vlak boven ons was het afweergeschut ook begonnen.

Vera Woods slenterde uiteindelijk om vijf voor half tien de kazerne binnen, blakend van gezondheid – ondanks haar bewering dat ze waarschijnlijk pleuritis had. Ze was drieënhalf uur te laat.

Terwijl ik van mijn stoel sprong en mijn jas van de haak griste, verscheen kapitein Davies met een gezicht als een donderwolk.

'Juffrouw Lake, neem brandweerman Hodges mee en maak dat u wegkomt. Juffrouw Woods, ik wil u graag in mijn kantoor zien. Nu!'

Het kostte me beslist moeite om Vera niet verwijtend aan te kijken, maar ik had geen tijd voor flauwekul. Roy was klaar voor vertrek, en na een haastige afscheidsgroet aan de meisjes renden we de kazerne uit, de donkere straat op. Met het geronk van de vliegtuigen en het donderende afweergeschut boven ons hoofd gingen we op weg. Het bleek een bijzonder akelige luchtaanval te worden.

In het oosten werd de lucht al roze. Later, als de stad weer in brand stond, zou hij oranje en rood kleuren. Nu werd Londen nog verlicht door de maan, en daar maakte de Luftwaffe gretig misbruik van. Buiten de kazerne klonk het gebrom van de Duitse vliegtuigen veel zwaarder en overheersender, als een monster dat zijn vrienden roept. En dat was in feite ook zo.

Met mijn ene hand hield ik krampachtig mijn zaklantaarn vast, met de andere Roys arm. Het zou niet meevallen om een taxi te vinden, maar omdat die altijd bleven rijden – tenzij het in hun nabije omgeving vreselijk gevaarlijk werd – bleef ik hoop houden.

En ja, daar zagen we er een. De taxi kroop over de straat met een zielig klein lichtstraaltje bij wijze van koplampen.

'Taxi!' riepen Roy en ik tegelijkertijd. We holden achter de auto aan en juichten toen we zagen dat hij nog langzamer ging rijden.

'Zie je kans om naar Coventry Street te rijden, ouwe jongen?' vroeg Roy door het opengedraaide raampje.

De chauffeur grimaste. Het was een heftig kabaal in het midden van West End.

'Sorry, chef,' zei hij. 'Het is ronduit waardeloos vanavond. Als ik jullie was, zou ik de stad niet in gaan. Je kunt er beter thuis een gezellig avondje van maken.' Hij knipoogde naar Roy en schakelde over naar de eerste versnelling om weg te rijden.

Roy negeerde zijn dubbelzinnige grap en leunde verder naar binnen. 'Je zou ons er een enorme dienst mee bewijzen. We zijn van de brandweer,' voegde hij eraan toe – voor het geval dat de taxichauffeur zijn uniform niet gezien had.

De chauffeur rolde met zijn ogen, maar trok wel netjes de handrem aan voordat hij over Roys voet heen zou rijden. Roy bleef maar praten – die kon na de oorlog een fortuin verdienen door encyclopedieën aan de deur te verkopen, dacht ik onwillekeurig.

'Zie je, een van onze jongens gaat volgende week trouwen. Zij is het bruidsmeisje en ik ben zijn getuige. Normaal gesproken zou ik het niet vragen, maar...'

Net toen ik wilde zeggen dat we allemaal door een bom getroffen konden worden als hij niet snel besloot, zei de chauffeur dat hij het erop zou wagen en knikte dat we konden instappen. Hij stak van wal met een verhaal over zijn neef die brandweerman was in Limehouse, en dat het een ongelooflijk vuurwerk gaf als de havens rechtstreeks geraakt werden.

Terwijl Roy vol animo meedeed met sterke verhalen vertellen, ging ik wat gemakkelijker zitten. We hadden reusachtig geboft. Als het zo doorging, zouden we iets na tienen bij Bunty en William in Café de Paris kunnen zijn.

Voor de oorlog was het, als je wilde opscheppen door een taxi te nemen, nog niet eens zo duur om van Pimlico naar Piccadilly Circus te reizen. Maar de combinatie van wegblokkades, weggebombardeerde straten en de verduistering betekende dat elke reis driemaal zo lang kon duren als gewoonlijk, tenzij iemand een bom liet vallen op de door jou geplande route. Dan duurde het nog langer. Eenmaal onderweg kon je niets meer doen; het beste was buitensporig kalm blijven en hopen dat je op een gegeven moment wel zou aankomen. Londense taxichauffeurs waren kolossaal vastberaden: als er een ritprijs te verdienen viel, waagden ze het er altijd wel op, zelfs tijdens de luchtaanvallen. Elke taxichauffeur kon je vertellen dat ze de laatste tijd geen keus hadden. Of ze moesten eindeloos zitten theedrinken en met lege zakken naar huis gaan.

Vanavond ging het goed, ondanks het afschuwelijke kabaal overal om ons heen. Bommen explodeerden achter elkaar door, met reusachtige lichtflitsen die de straat een tel lang verlichtten, tot de volgende ontzettende dreun elders onze aandacht trok. Het joviale geklets van de mannen werd geforceerd opgewekt en stierf uiteindelijk helemaal weg terwijl we verder kropen, in files stonden en met horten en stoten door straten vol kraters reden. We namen sluiproutes die in de loop van het afgelopen jaar volslagen onherkenbaar geworden waren. Zo nu en dan moesten we rechtsomkeert maken vanwege een nieuwe wegblokkade als er na een explosie een halve winkel of een brok kantoor op straat terechtgekomen was.

Ik was in geen weken buiten geweest terwijl het zo erg was als nu. Dit was allemaal op veel grotere schaal dan tijdens die avond in de bioscoop met Bunty en Charles. Het was beslist geen goed idee om op een avond als deze West End in te rijden, maar deze afspraak wilde ik voor geen goud missen. Ik bleef dus stilletjes zitten en deed mijn best om niet ineen te krimpen bij al dat lawaai.

We kwamen tot Hyde Park Corner. Vanaf daar hadden we gehoopt Piccadilly te volgen en Coventry Street in te slaan naar Café de Paris. Maar hoezeer we ons ook gedroegen alsof alles prima in orde was, we konden geen van allen doen alsof we het gierende gejammer van vallende bommen niet hoorden. Een paar tellen later schudde de hele weg en de taxi verloor bijna zijn carrosserie.

Vlak voor Green Park kwamen we met knarsende remmen tot stilstand.

'Sorry, het wordt toch een beetje te lastig,' zei de taxichauffeur tegen Roy. 'Als ik u was, zou ik het er maar bij laten. Kan ik u op weg naar huis nog ergens anders afzetten?'

Ik schudde verwoed mijn hoofd, al werd mij niets gevraagd.

'Nee, wij komen er wel,' zei Roy terwijl hij zijn portefeuille uit zijn zak viste. 'Bedankt dat u ons tot hier hebt gebracht.'

Ook ik bedankte hem, klauterde de taxi uit en wenste de chauffeur een veilige reis terug.

Zodra ik het portier opendeed, rook ik brand. Een donderend geluid, een paar straten verderop, bevestigde mijn vermoeden: een voltreffer. Het lawaai van het afweergeschut was nu oorverdovend. Het gevecht vond pal boven ons hoofd plaats.

'Dat meisje van jou heeft wel lef,' hoorde ik de chauffeur tegen Roy schreeuwen, boven het lawaai uit. 'Pas maar goed op haar.'

Roy lachte, bedankte hem en schreeuwde terug dat hij dat zou doen. Daarna zwaaide hij en pakte mijn arm.

'Kom op, Emmy,' riep hij. Hij wist dat hij me niet hoefde te vragen of het wel ging. 'Zodra we daar zijn, zijn we zo veilig als wat.'

'Weet ik,' brulde ik terug. 'Het veiligste en vrolijkste restaurant van de stad.' Ik citeerde de advertentie voor Café de Paris, die in de Londense tijdschriften stond.

'Zelfs tijdens luchtaanvallen. Zes meter onder de grond!' vulde Roy aan. Maar daarna keek hij omhoog, waar een enorme vuurzuil de stad verlichtte. Hij zei iets buitengewoon onfatsoenlijks. 'Nu kunnen die ellendelingen echt zien wat ze doen.'

We hadden geen van beiden enige aanmoediging nodig om door te lopen. Je raakte eraan gewend om buiten te zijn tijdens een luchtaanval, maar dit was zenuwslopend. Bovendien waren avondschoenen niet het ideale schoeisel en ik had er heel wat voor overgehad om mijn wandelschoenen aan te hebben, maar ik tilde met mijn ene hand mijn lange rok op, pakte met mijn andere hand Roys arm stevig vast en liep op een draf mee toen hij met grotere stappen doorliep.

De Duitsers vermaakten zich prima, en hoewel we de Britse machinegeweren op volle kracht hoorden terugschieten, hield het afschuwelijke gejammer van de bommen niet op. We wisten allebei dat het erger werd. In het begin maakte Roy nog grappen terwijl we langs de winkels kwamen. 'Picknickmand voor Ascot?' riep hij toen we langs het luxueuze warenhuis Fortnum & Mason kwamen. 'Twee graag!' schreeuwde ik terug alsof we niets beters te doen hadden dan een lolletje maken. Maar het was moeilijk vol te houden. Tegen de tijd dat we op Piccadilly Circus beland waren, was ons komische nummer bijna uitgeput. Ondanks mijn hoge hakken renden we behoorlijk hard.

'Wil je een nieuwe cricketbat?' schreeuwde ik, opgelucht omdat we er bijna waren, toen we bij sportwinkel Lillywhites aankwamen. De ramen waren verduisterd, maar de reclameborden voor sportkleding – voor alle rangen en standen – hingen er nog.

Roy stond stil. Het oorverscheurende gefluit van een vallende bom klonk vlak boven ons hoofd. Het had geen zin meer om de realiteit te verdoezelen met grappen. Dit bombardement was verschrikkelijk dichtbij.

Roy trok me mee en duwde me met mijn rug tegen de afgesloten deuren van de winkel. We hielden ons aan elkaar vast en zetten ons schrap voor de komende schokgolf. Ik drukte mijn hoofd tegen Roys uniform, met mijn gezicht tegen een van de zilveren knopen die hij gepoetst en nog eens gepoetst had tot hij glansde. We waren zo dicht bij Coventry Street en bij het veilige Café de Paris.

Ik schaam me niet om toe te geven dat ik op het laatste moment mijn ogen dichtdeed, maar zelfs met mijn ogen stevig dichtgeknepen kon ik die ontzaglijke lichtflits niet buitensluiten.

Roy drukte me plat tegen de deur, gebruikte zijn eigen lijf als schild zonder aan het risico te denken, en ik trok hem nog dichter naar me toe en probeerde hem met louter wilskracht uit de baan van de komende luchtstroom te krijgen.

We klampten ons aan elkaar vast. Als ze een van ons te pakken kregen, zouden ze ons allebei te pakken krijgen, of ze wilden of niet.

En toen landden de bommen met een lawaai dat onze trommelvliezen dreigde te scheuren. Mijn ingewanden voelden aan alsof ze binnenstebuiten gekeerd werden. Alles om ons heen schudde op zijn grondvesten.

Maar ze kregen ons niet te pakken. Wij waren niet rechtstreeks getroffen.

Ik keek op. Terwijl hij zich nog altijd aan me vastklampte alsof zijn leven ervan afhing, keek Roy over zijn schouder naar de overkant van Piccadilly. Nu had hij dezelfde uitdrukking op zijn gezicht die ik in de kazerne zag als de ploegen opgeroepen werden voor iets afschuwelijks, bijvoorbeeld als een ziekenhuis of een school gebombardeerd was. Alleen was het ditmaal, in ieder geval voor ons, nog erger.

Ik wist waar hij naar keek. Coventry Street was getroffen.

Toen begonnen we te rennen.

18

Iemand richtte een zaklantaarn

Ondanks de verduistering konden we gemakkelijk zien waar we liepen, want alles werd verlicht door het luchtgevecht. Hand in hand renden we in volle vaart richting de bominslag. Roy sleepte me bijna achter zich aan, maar dat was niet nodig: ik was een goede hardloopster – op school al – en nu was ik me niet eens meer bewust van mijn hoge hakken of mijn dwaze, onpraktische jurk. Toen we dichter bij Café de Paris kwamen, kwamen we niet meer zo snel vooruit. Het werd moeilijk om ons een weg te banen tussen de massa's mensen die zich daar al begonnen te verzamelen. Vertwijfeld begonnen we ons tussen de mensen door te wringen, want we moesten de nachtclub in zien te komen.

Telkens weer zei ik tegen mezelf dat we het misschien mis hadden. Buiten het gebouw kon je niets met zekerheid zeggen. De straat lag vol glas omdat overal in de omtrek de ramen gesprongen waren, maar misschien was het niet wat we in onze ongerustheid vermoedden. Natuurlijk zou het voor andere mensen dan nog steeds afschuwelijk zijn, maar dan zouden we weten dat Bunty en Bill in veiligheid waren.

De wens was de vader van de gedachte.

Ik kon de hoofdingang van het café nog maar net zien. De dubbele deuren waren er niet meer. Iemand probeerde de restanten van de dikke verduisteringsgordijnen naar beneden te trekken, want die hingen in de weg. Geschokte, gewonde, gehavende mensen strompelden de straat op; ze hielpen elkaar of werden geholpen door de mensen die al buiten stonden.

'Brandweer,' riep Roy. 'Laat ons erdoor.' Hij duwde een dikke man die zich naar voren drong om alles beter te kunnen zien opzij en liet daarbij mijn hand los. Meteen keek hij achterom waar ik bleef.

'Loop door,' riep ik hem toe. 'Ik kom eraan.' Hij knikte en verdween de nachtclub in.

Ik probeerde hem te volgen en schreeuwde tegen de rug van de dikke man dat hij me moest doorlaten, maar de opening had zich gesloten en ik kwam er niet meer doorheen. Mensen die naar binnen probeerden te komen blokkeerden de weg voor mensen die naar buiten wilden. Iemand riep: 'Geef ze wat ruimte!' Boven ons brulden nog altijd de vliegtuigen en het afweergeschut bleef dreunen.

Even hield ik op met duwen en ging op mijn tenen staan. Een tenger gebouwde man in het grijs was bezig een dame uit het café mee te trekken, half slepend, half sjouwend. Ook zij was helemaal grijs. Maar het lag niet aan hun kleding; hun haar, hun gezicht en hun hele lichaam waren met stof overdekt, alsof ze in as ondergedompeld waren.

Iemand richtte een zaklantaarn op hen en de vrouw schreeuwde het uit, sloeg haar hand voor haar gezicht en kromp daarna ineen onder haar eigen aanraking. Bloed stroomde uit een reusachtige wond op haar voorhoofd; de rode vloeistof stak vreemd en schokkend af tegen het grijs.

Mijn vrienden waren daar binnen! Was Bunty net zo ernstig gewond als die vrouw?

'Laat me erdoor!' krijste ik met een stem die uit mijn

diepste binnenste kwam, en ik stompte uit alle macht tegen de dikke jassen die me de weg versperden. Roy was erdoor gekomen en nu kon ik dat niet. Alleen omdat hij groter en sterker was dan ik, en omdat hij een uniform droeg dat aantoonde dat hij goed getraind was en wist wat hij deed en echt kon helpen. Maar daar ging het niet om. In deze gruwelijke toestand werd ik razend van dit onrecht. Roy was Williams vriend. Bunty was mijn vriendin. Het was mijn taak om haar te vinden, om te zorgen dat ze veilig was. Ik vertikte het om aan de kant te blijven staan.

Ik bleef duwen en schreeuwde nogmaals, nu met meer gezag. Dat hielp nog steeds niet. Ik duwde nog harder.

Iemand greep mijn arm en zonder om te kijken probeerde ik me los te rukken. Maar een mannenstem die me vaag bekend voorkwam, bleef mijn naam noemen. 'Emmy. Emmeline. Emmeline... Juffrouw Lake.'

Ik draaide me om, helemaal gedesoriënteerd; in gedachten was ik al in het gebouw, op zoek naar Bunty.

'Emmy,' klonk de stem weer. 'Ik ben het.'

Meneer Collins pakte mijn schouders stevig vast en trok me weg van de plek waar ik naartoe moest.

'Lieve kind, God zij dank!' zei hij. 'Ik dacht dat jij daar binnen was. Ik was vanavond aan de beurt om de wacht te houden voor het geval er brand kwam. Bij het restaurant van mijn vriend.' Hij zweeg abrupt. 'Waar zijn jouw vrienden? Waar is juffrouw Tavistock?'

'Ik moet naar binnen,' zei ik, half tegen meneer Collins, half tegen mezelf, terwijl ik me lostrok uit zijn greep en weer probeerde door de mensenmassa heen te dringen. Het lukte me om een paar stappen dichter bij de deur te komen. Ik zag dat andere hulpvaardige mensen de nachtclub in wisten te komen; sommigen verdwenen in de diepte, anderen bleven bij de ingang staan en hielpen de volgende grijze mensen naar buiten.

'Komt goed, juf,' zei een opzichter van de Burgerwacht, die mij de weg versperde. 'Niet nodig om nu naar binnen te gaan.'

'Laat me erdoor,' zei ik en ik keek hem strak aan.

De opzichter keek naar mijn burgeroverjas, naar de zijden japon die eronderuit kwam en naar die stomme glitterspeld in mijn haar. Hij dacht waarschijnlijk dat ik dronken was, of dat ik een van de vrouwen was die altijd hier op straat rondhingen op zoek naar een kans om te plunderen.

'Doorlopen, liefje,' zei hij. Ik begon hem tegen te spreken, maar hij week geen duimbreed.

'Laat mijn vrouw erdoor, man.'

Meneer Collins stond weer naast me en blafte dit bevel met zijn meest heerszuchtige stem.

'Ze is verpleegster, idioot. Laat ons erdoor.'

Hij zwaaide met een identiteitskaart, zo snel dat de opzichter die niet echt kon zien.

'Dokter Richard Green,' zei hij, en duwde de kaart weer in zijn jaszak. 'Ga nu opzij, zodat we deze mensen kunnen helpen voordat ze nog meer bommen op ons laten vallen.'

Terwijl de opzichter aarzelde, zag ik mijn kans schoon. Met een gezicht waarbij het dominante gedrag van meneer Collins verbleekte, negeerde ik hem, balde mijn vuisten en baande me een weg naar binnen.

Telkens weer kwamen er geschokte en gewonde mensen uit de nachtclub naar buiten. Ik glipte langs hen heen, in tegengestelde richting. Pas later zou ik beseffen hoe egoïstisch ik bezig was geweest: ik koos zelf wie ik wilde redden. Maar op dat moment wilde ik niets anders dan Bunty vinden.

In het café was het pikkedonker en ik tastte in mijn jaszak naar mijn zaklantaarn. Nu ik eenmaal binnen was, verdween mijn woede. Het enige wat nog voor me bestond, was het vinden van Bunty en Bill. Mijn hart sloeg nog altijd razendsnel, maar nu had ik een doel, nu kon ik iets doen en voelde ik zelfs een soort kalmte.

De lucht bestond bijna geheel uit rook en stof en ik begon onmiddellijk te hoesten. Met mijn hand over mijn mond herinnerde ik me op de een of andere manier mijn brandweertraining – in de kazerne leerde zelfs het administratieve personeel wat te doen in geval van een voltreffer:

Er sterven meer mensen door verstikking dan door verbranding.

Blijf rustig.

Adem door je neus en hap niet naar lucht.

Op de tast liep ik een paar treden af, om puin heen stappend en geholpen door het licht van mijn zaklantaarn. De smalle lichtstraal viel op een rij van vier mensen die de trap op kwamen; ze hielden zich aan elkaar vast en vormden zo een menselijke trein naar de uitgang. Ze waren niet grijs, zoals de anderen, maar zwart van de ontploffing. Een man liep te huilen. Even dacht ik dat zijn smokingjasje misschien weggeblazen was, maar toen zag ik dat hij het om de schouders van de vrouw naast zich gelegd had; haar jurk was aan flarden. Niemand rende, niemand schreeuwde.

Meneer Collins bleef vlak achter me; hij hield zijn zaklantaarn boven mijn schouder en bewoog die heen en weer om te zien waar we waren.

'Emmy,' vroeg hij, 'waren ze aan het dansen, denk je? Waren ze beneden?'

Dat wist ik niet. Bunty en ik hadden het nog met elkaar gehad over de vraag of we een tafeltje bij de dansvloer of op het balkon moesten nemen. Waar zouden we het beste uitzicht op de band hebben? Dat frivole babbeltje was nu het belangrijkste ter wereld.

Volgens mij had ze gezegd dat ze beneden een tafeltje zou reserveren. Dat wist ik bijna helemaal zeker.

Ik richtte mijn zaklantaarn in de richting van het balkon, links van mij.

De balustrade die vanaf de trap omhoog liep, was gedraaid en verwrongen, als een reusachtige sliert drop. En daarachter… niets. Het balkon was er niet meer.

Ik knikte, meer tegen mezelf dan als antwoord op de vraag van meneer Collins, hield me stevig vast aan de trapleuning en klauterde voorzichtig de trap af; mijn schoenen knarsten op de vele glasscherven.

'Bunty!' riep ik. 'Bunty, ik ben het. We zijn er, lieverd. Het komt allemaal goed, we zijn er.'

Die toon gebruikte mijn moeder vroeger als ik een nachtmerrie had. Dan riep ik haar en zodra ik haar stem hoorde, wist ik – zelfs als de monsters nog in mijn kamer waren – dat ik dapper genoeg kon zijn om vol te houden. Dan hoorde ik terwijl ze door de gang liep haar stem, kalm en sussend, die me vertelde dat het allemaal goed kwam. Onophoudelijk, tot ze in mijn kamer was en het licht aandeed en de monsters weg waren.

'Bunty, we komen eraan!' riep ik weer. 'Vertel ons waar je bent, schat; we komen je helpen.'

Telkens weer riep ik haar en stond ik stil om te luisteren. Er kwam geen reactie. Ik hoorde gehuil en gekreun. Iemand riep om hulp, andere mensen riepen elkaars naam, iemand zei dat de ambulances onderweg waren.

Meneer Collins en ik stonden even stil bij wat tot voor kort de dansvloer geweest was. Nog steeds hield hij zijn hand op mijn schouder. Hij vroeg me wat Bunty droeg; ik herinnerde me dat het haar blauwe japon was en vertelde hem dat. Een blauwe avondjapon met ruches langs de zoom. Ik zei dat William zijn brandweeruniform aan zou hebben. Meneer Collins zei dat ik alleen aan Bunty moest denken, wat ik ook zag. Ik moest blijven roepen en luisteren, en aan niets anders denken. En hij zei dat hij vlak achter me aan kwam.

Ik richtte mijn zaklantaarn en bleef zoeken. Er lag puin

en glas en iets wat misschien ooit het balkon of het plafond geweest was, maar wat nu her en der verspreid lag over de vloer.

En er lagen lichamen. Ik hoorde mezelf 'O' zeggen en daarna nog eens: 'O.' Meneer Collins hield zijn hand op mijn schouder.

'Blijf haar roepen,' zei hij toen ik even ophield en mijn zaklantaarn ergens op richtte. Ik vermoedde dat het een mens was, maar ik wist het niet echt helemaal zeker.

'Dat is zij niet,' zei meneer Collins vreselijk zachtzinnig, en ik knikte.

Daarna bleef ik knikken, want hoe onvoorstelbaar afgrijselijk het ook was, het bericht dat deze arme ziel niet Bunty was, was het beste nieuws dat ik te horen kon krijgen. Ik begon haar opnieuw te roepen.

We liepen verder, klauterden over tafels heen, langs het lage podium rechts van ons, waar nog altijd mensen moesten zijn – de band, nam ik aan. Iemand riep: 'Het doet pijn, het doet pijn.'

Dat negeerde ik, wat afschuwelijk van me was. Ik negeerde mensen die aan het sterven waren. Op dat moment voelde het niet als een bewuste beslissing. Als Bunty nog leefde, zou ze hulp nodig hebben. Daarom liep ik door.

Er waren mensen en puin en stof en zo veel glas. We moesten bukken om bij ieder lichaam te kijken of het Bunty of Bill was. Telkens als dat niet het geval was, leek dit in ons voordeel te zijn, alsof de kans dat ze nog leefden daarmee groter werd. Niet iedereen kon dood zijn. Wat een verwrongen logica! Maanden later kon ik er nog van wakker liggen en me afvragen hoe ik van het ene moment op het andere iemand geworden was die zo kon denken.

Krankzinnig genoeg zaten, terwijl sommige mensen aan stukken gereten waren, anderen nog steeds op hun stoel aan tafel. Zwart van de springstof, dood, maar op het eerste gezicht ongedeerd. Een man hing over zijn tafel alsof hij dronken was. Zijn gezicht kon ik niet zien, maar ik zag wel dat zijn handen weg waren.

Ik keerde de man de rug toe en bleef Bunty roepen. Ik hoefde niet achterom te kijken waar meneer Collins bleef; ik wist dat hij bij me zou blijven. Terwijl alles om ons heen alleen maar erger en erger werd, stelde hij niet eenmaal voor terug te gaan. Daarvoor zou ik hem de rest van mijn leven dankbaar blijven, of hij nu mijn baas was of niet.

Er waren meer mensen binnengekomen om te helpen. Een man riep om een brancard. Een paar echte verpleegsters hielpen een met bloed bedekte dame en spraken met elkaar in medische termen. Ik hoorde Roys stem, iets verder achter in de zaal. Hij riep Bill en Bunty, keer op keer.

Toen we verder liepen, zag ik twee danseressen bij iemand neerknielen. De ene danseres scheurde een tafelkleed in stukken en de andere duwde de stof tegen het lichaam aan. Beide meisjes droegen danskleding met lovertjes en ze waren helemaal niet met stof bedekt of zwart geworden.

'Amy, vijf minuten later zouden *wij* daar gestaan hebben,' zei het ene meisje. 'Dat arme kind.'

Met ingehouden adem richtte ik mijn zaklantaarn op degene die ze probeerden te helpen. Ze was in haar onderkleding; haar jurk was weggeblazen door de ontploffing. Het was moeilijk te zien wie ze zou kunnen zijn. Maar ze had blond haar. Dit was Bunty niet. De danseressen waren blijkbaar in hun kleedkamers geweest toen het gebeurde.

Ik richtte mijn zaklantaarn achter hen. Kolossale brokken pleisterwerk waren vlak bij het podium op de grond gevallen.

Toen zag ik haar. Half begraven onder een van de brokken lag iemand met een lange japon aan. Je kon niet meer zien welke kleur de jurk had, maar wel dat het een lange jurk was, met ruches langs de onderkant.

‘Bunty!’ gilde ik.

Als een waanzinnige klauterde ik naar haar toe en viel naast haar op mijn knieën, zonder op het glas en de rommel om haar heen te letten. Een van haar benen zat klem en ze was bedekt met puin, maar ik wist dat zij het was.

Haar lippen weken uiteen en ze zei iets. Het was maar een klein geluidje en ik verstond niet wat ze probeerde te zeggen, maar het was genoeg om het zeker te weten: ze leefde nog!

‘Bunty, lieve schat, het komt goed,’ zei ik en ik raakte haar gezicht aan. ‘Het komt helemaal goed met je.’

Ik begon brokken pleisterwerk om haar heen weg te halen. Ook meneer Collins zat op zijn knieën puin te ruimen.

‘Je gaat niet dood,’ zei ik keer op keer. ‘We zullen hulp halen. Het komt helemaal goed met je.’

Bunty knipperde met haar ogen. Tweemaal. Haar ogen zaten vol stof en het kostte haar de grootste moeite om niet te hoesten. Maar ze keek me recht aan en het lukte haar met een zielig, schor stemmetje iets tegen me te zeggen.

‘Bill.’

19

Wij waren aan de beurt

Nadat de ambulances gekomen waren en Bunty meegenomen was, betaalde meneer Collins een taxichauffeur extra veel om ons ondanks de staat waarin we verkeerden mee te nemen en achter het lange grijze konvooi aan te rijden naar Charing Cross Hospital.

De rest van die nacht leek één lange, akelige droom, waarin ik moest uitzoeken waar Bunty precies was en erachter moest zien te komen of William al gevonden was. In het ziekenhuis leende ik muntjes van meneer Collins om mijn ouders op te bellen, maar ik kon alleen maar keer op keer zeggen: 'Bunty is gewond, pap. Bill wordt vermist en Bunty is gewond.'

Mijn ouders reden midden in de nacht naar ons huis. Bunty's oma kwam ook naar Londen, maar haar chauffeur bracht haar rechtstreeks naar het ziekenhuis. Meneer Collins en ik waren inmiddels naar huis gestuurd. Het ziekenhuispersoneel had per se mijn knieën – die ik aan het glas op de grond gesneden had – willen oplappen en weigerde halsstarrig mijn vragen over mijn vrienden te beantwoorden.

Zondag had de dag moeten zijn waarop Bunty en ik samen in ons appartement bleven om de betoverende opwinding van de vorige avond weer te beleven en te wachten op William – die zou komen lunchen – en dan zouden we alles samen met hem nog eens helemaal opnieuw beleven. Nu deed ik – terwijl mijn moeder eindeloos theezette en mijn vader per se het uitstekende werk van de verpleegster wilde overdoen – mijn uiterste best helemaal niets opnieuw te beleven.

Om tien voor elf ging de telefoon. Het was Bunty's oma. Mijn vader nam de telefoon op en zei verscheidene malen met zijn doktersstem: 'Ik begrijp het,' en: 'Mevrouw Tavistock, dat is een heel goed teken.' Daarna vroeg hij: 'En is er nog nieuws van William?' en na een korte pauze zei hij tamelijk opgewekt: 'Zodra ze meer weten, zullen ze het u vast en zeker vertellen.'

Daarna rondde mijn vader het gesprek af, kwam naast me zitten en pakte mijn beide handen beet.

'Ze is behoorlijk toegetakeld, lieve schat,' zei hij voorzichtig. 'En het zal aardig wat tijd kosten om te herstellen. Maar als ik het zo hoor, zal Bunty helemaal opknappen, dat beloof ik je. En we weten nog niet waar William is, maar mevrouw Tavistock zegt dat we dat vast snel te weten zullen komen. De gewonden zijn naar verscheidene ziekenhuizen gebracht, dus het duurt even om dat uit te zoeken.'

Na dat gesprek – in ieder geval het eerste uur daarna – leek alles er een beetje beter uit te zien.

Tegen twaalf uur ging de deurbel. Gesteund door het nieuws over Bunty en mijn geloof in de woorden van mijn vader ging ik naar beneden om de voordeur open te doen. Niet vrolijk, verre van dat, maar toch hoopvol.

Maar zodra ik de deur opendeed en Roy zag staan, wist ik het.

Hij had nog steeds zijn uniform aan, maar zonder pet en overjas. Dat hij ook nog stoffig en smerig was, viel me nauwelijks op. Ik zag alleen de blik op zijn gezicht.

'Emmy, liefje,' zei hij zacht terwijl hij op de brede drempel stond, 'mag ik binnenkomen?'

Ik verroerde geen vin.

'Heb jij hem gevonden?' vroeg ik fluisterend.

Roy knikte en glimlachte treurig, een flauw glimlachje waar zijn ogen niet aan meededen. Hij keek de gang in. 'We moeten gaan zitten.'

Ik voelde mijn adem in mijn keel stokken.

'Roy?'

'Hij is overleden, liefje,' zei hij zacht. 'Bill is dood.'

Als iemand in een film zoiets hoort, hapt ze naar adem of ze valt flauw of ze brengt op dramatische wijze de rug van haar hand naar haar mond. Maar ik deed niets van dat alles. Ik wilde nee zeggen, zeggen dat het niet waar kon zijn. Ik wilde tegen Roy zeggen dat hij het mis had. Ik wilde dat het tien seconden geleden was, toen ik het nog niet wist.

Ondanks alles bleef ik daar gewoon staan. Ik voelde me alsof iemand alle lucht uit me gezogen had. En toen begon mijn onderlip te trillen, zoals gebeurt als je klein bent en je het niet kunt tegenhouden.

Ik probeerde diep adem te halen en Brits en dapper te zijn, maar dat lukte niet, en toen kwamen de tranen. Massa's tranen. Waar kwamen dat soort tranen vandaan en hoe kwamen ze zo snel op?

Arme Roy! Voor hem was het ook afschuwelijk.

Hij stapte het huis binnen en nam me in zijn koude, stoffige armen en hield me stevig vast, precies zoals hij me vastgehouden had toen de bommen vielen, toen hij alles gedaan had wat hij kon om te zorgen dat ik niet gewond zou raken.

En ik omklemde hem net zo stevig, precies zoals toen, en probeerde Roy weg te trekken bij het gevaar.

Maar ditmaal konden we elkaar niet beschermen. Het was te laat. Alles was gewoon net te laat.

Ik kon niet ophouden met huilen. Roy liet me niet los.

Ik hoorde hem zeggen: 'Stil maar, liefje,' en zijn stem beefde. Ik wist dat hij zijn best deed om niet ook te huilen. Roy was een van de grootste helden van Londen. Een grote, stoere brandweerman. Maar Bill was zijn beste vriend.

Toen ik mijn ouders van de trap hoorde komen, liet ik hem voorzichtig los. Roys ogen stonden vol tranen. Ik snufte en probeerde op te houden met janken, want dat was niet eerlijk tegenover hem.

Mijn ouders hoefden niets te vragen. Moeder sloeg haar armen om me heen en zei: 'Ach, lieveling,' maar hoe graag ik me ook aan haar wilde vastklampen en wilde brullen van verdriet, ik wilde Roy daar niet alleen laten staan.

'Dit is Roy,' zei ik zielig. 'Bills vriend Roy. En *míjn* vriend.'

Roy schraapte zijn keel, ging rechtop staan, zei 'meneer' tegen mijn vader en stak zijn hand uit. Het moet vreselijk voor hem zijn geweest om ineens zo beleefd te moeten reageren. Mijn vader schudde hem de hand en pakte met zijn linkerhand Roys arm beet.

'Dank je wel,' zei hij dringend, en ik wist dat hij hem bedankte omdat hij voor mij gezorgd had. 'Dank je wel, Roy. Kom alsjeblieft binnen. We gaan een borrel voor je inschenken.'

Boven, in de woonkamer, liet mijn moeder Roy zijn uniformjasje uittrekken zodat zij een deken om zijn schouders kon slaan. Hij zei dat het niet nodig was – 'dank u' – maar zij hield vol en dus zat hij daar met een deken om zich heen, precies zoals de mensen die *híj* normaal gesproken hielp. Hij kreeg een groot glas whisky en hield dat stevig vast.

Ik ging op de sofa zitten, naast mijn moeder, die mijn hand bleef vasthouden. Ook ik kreeg whisky. Het smaakte even akelig als altijd. Dit was de laatste keer dat ik het ooit zou drinken.

'Weet je zeker dat het...?' vroeg ik.

Roy begon al te knikken voordat ik mijn zin kon afmaken.

'Het uniform,' zei hij en tuurde in zijn glas; daarna nam hij een grote slok. 'Hij was het.' Roy zag er nog beroerder uit dan zojuist in de gang.

Toen stelde ik de vraag waar ik het meest tegen opzag: 'Wie... wie vertelt het Bunty? Wanneer komt zij het te weten?'

'Dat weet ik niet, liefje,' zei Roy. 'Ik ben bij Bill gebleven tot...' Hij zweeg even. 'Tot ze hem afvoerden. Toen ging ik naar Charing Cross, maar daar verzuipen ze in het werk. Slechte nacht. Daarom kwam ik hierheen. Ik ga nu terug naar het ziekenhuis.'

Roy stond op. Hij zag er uitgeput uit.

'Helemaal niet,' zei mijn vader snel en hij stond ook op. Hij wierp mijn moeder een blik toe en zij knikte. Ik wist wat ze bedoelden. Het was niet eerlijk om Roy terug te sturen, en mevrouw Tavistock kon het beter van mijn vader horen dan van een politieagent of verpleegster.

'Mag ik mee?' vroeg ik. Ik wilde niet hier blijven zitten en nutteloos zijn. Ik wilde er voor Bunty zijn. 'Ik voel me prima. Echt,' voegde ik eraan toe. Dat was een leugen, maar daar ging het niet om.

Mijn vader schudde zijn hoofd. 'Nee,' zei hij ferm. 'Deze keer niet, engel. Roy en jij hebben allebei genoeg gedaan. Jullie moeten uitrusten. En ik ben arts.'

Hij keek ons allebei ernstig aan toen ik probeerde daartegenin te gaan en vervolgde: 'Echt, Emmy, ik heb veel meer kans om hen te spreken te krijgen als ik daarheen ga als Bunty's huisarts.'

Ik wist dat hij gelijk had. Ik zakte weer op de bank en gaf toe dat ik verslagen was.

Dit gebeurde elke dag met mensen in heel Londen, in

heel het land, in heel Europa. Overal kregen mensen het afschuwelijkste nieuws. Wij waren niet anders dan anderen. Nu waren onze vrienden aan de beurt. Wij waren aan de beurt. Maar dat maakte helemaal niet uit voor hoe we ons voelden.

Arme, arme Bill. En o, die arme Bunty. Alles waarvan ze ooit gedroomd had, alle plannen die ze samen gemaakt hadden... Alles waarop ze zich verheugd hadden...

De woonkamer zag er nog hetzelfde uit als de vorige dag om deze tijd. Er lagen ongeopende felicitatiekaarten en cadeaus en daar stonden de foto's met hun zilveren lijstjes: foto's van William en Bunty op een zomerse dag op de brink, een foto van een trotse William in zijn uniform toen hij net bij de brandweer gekomen was – Bunty was dol op die foto. Een klein blauw doosje op de koffietafel met de manchetknopen die ze voor hem gekocht had als bruiloftsgeschenk. En nu was alles voorbij.

Net toen ik dacht dat ik me niet ellendiger kon voelen, herinnerde ik me mijn dwaze, zinloze, sneue ruzies met Bill. Ik had beter mijn best moeten doen om hem mijn excuses aan te bieden. Ik had een manier moeten vinden om het eerder te zeggen. Ik had op tijd bij Café de Paris moeten zijn.

Vaag hoorde ik mijn moeder zeggen: 'Ga gerust, Alfred, wij redden ons hier wel.' En daarna kneep ze liefkozend in mijn hand zei: 'Ja toch, lieverd? Wij redden ons wel.'

Ik knikte. Maar er viel niets meer te redden. Dat kon ik haar niet vertellen, en ik had ook geen idee hoe ik het Bunty kon vertellen – dat ik ruzie geschopt had met Bill en Bunty teleurgesteld had. Dat een oude, dierbare vriend gestorven was terwijl hij een hekel aan me had. Dat kon ik niemand vertellen. Het was een gruwelijk geheim dat ik voor mezelf zou moeten houden.

Ik smachtte ernaar om Bunty te zien, maar alleen familie werd toegelaten en wij telden niet als zodanig. Moeder en ik vestigden onze hoop op het feit dat mevrouw Tavistock te oud en te hooggeplaatst was om te accepteren dat anderen zeiden wat ze wel en niet mocht doen. Als zij vond dat het goed voor Bunty zou zijn om ons te zien, zou ze er hoogstwaarschijnlijk voor zorgen dat we werden toegelaten.

Intussen zat ik die hele zondag in het appartement keer op keer te bedenken wat ik zou zeggen en hoe ik het zou zeggen. Hoe zwaar Bunty ook gewond was, ze zou blijven knokken, dat wist ik zeker. Maar hoe zou ze het nieuws van Bill opnemen? Hoe zou iemand daar ooit mee kunnen omgaan? En zeker nu het zo vlak voor de geplande bruiloft gebeurde… Ik wist niet hoe ik haar kon helpen, maar ik wilde alles voor haar doen wat nodig was.

Maandagochtend, voordat hij naar zijn patiënten terugkeerde, belde mijn vader meneer Collins op kantoor. Meneer Collins zei dat ik zoveel vrijaf moest nemen als ik nodig had, tot mijn vader zeker wist dat ik helemaal in orde was. Ik moest mevrouw Bird aan hem overlaten en zelfs niet aan *Vrouw & Vriendin* dénken. Meneer Collins wenste me het beste, zei mijn vader.

Daarna brachten moeder en ik nog een eindeloze dag door met wachten op nieuws uit het ziekenhuis. Eindelijk, aan het eind van de middag, belde mevrouw Tavistock om te vertellen dat Bunty bij bewustzijn was en dat ik haar wel een minuut of twee kon spreken als ik wilde. Binnen een paar tellen hadden moeder en ik onze jassen aan en waren we buiten. Het was geen bezoekuur, dus we wisten dat mevrouw Tavistock haar invloed had laten gelden.

In Charing Cross keek de zuster van dienst nogal vinnig, maar aangezien mevrouw Tavistock minstens een van de leden van het bestuur kende, moest ze wel een oogje toeknijpen – zij het met zichtbare tegenzin.

Mevrouw Tavistock kwam ons in de gang van het ziekenhuis tegemoet. Tenger gebouwd, maar recht van lijf en leden, en nog altijd met de elegantie van de opvallende schoonheid die ze vijftig jaar geleden was. Alleen zag ze er nu afgetobd uit, hoewel ze zoals altijd haar uiterste best deed een goede gastvrouw te zijn.

'Emmeline-lief,' zei ze met een hartelijke glimlach, en ze pakte mijn handen. 'Ik hoop dat je nog een beetje geslapen hebt.' Nu richtte ze zich tot mijn moeder. 'Elizabeth, wat vreselijk vriendelijk dat jullie hierheen gekomen zijn. Goed. Marigold... Bunty... is wakker. De artsen hebben alles gedaan wat ze op dit moment kunnen doen. Het beste nieuws is dat ze er alle vertrouwen in hebben dat het gelukt is om haar been te behouden.'

Ik probeerde niet geschokt te kijken. Mijn vader had niets gezegd over het kwijtraken van benen.

Mevrouw Tavistock schonk me een treurige, vriendelijke glimlach. 'Emmeline, ik ben bang dat Bunty er slecht aan toe is. Als jij haar liever nog niet wilt zien, begrijpt ze dat vast en zeker wel.'

Ik schudde snel mijn hoofd en mevrouw Tavistock ging door.

'Je moet weten dat Bunty nog geen woord heeft gezegd sinds ik haar het nieuws over William verteld heb.'

Mevrouw Tavistock hief haar kin een klein beetje op, alsof ze op die manier de reusachtige innerlijke inspanning om zich flink te houden kon ondersteunen.

'Ze denken dat ze in shock is, maar ik hoop dat ze misschien met jou wel wil praten, omdat jullie zulke goede vriendinnen zijn. Maar ik heb haar niet verteld dat je op bezoek kwam, voor het geval jij toch liever niet zou willen.'

Haar stem klonk dapper, maar ik hoorde toch dat ze diepbedroefd was.

'Ik wil haar heel graag zien, alstublieft, mevrouw Tavistock,' zei ik. Het maakte mij niet uit in welke toestand Bunty verkeerde. 'Mag ik nu misschien naar binnen?'

Na een instemmende knik wees de zuster van dienst me de weg – nog altijd tandenknarsend omdat Bunty's oma de ziekenhuisregels met voeten trad.

Ik was nog maar eenmaal eerder in een ziekenhuiszaal geweest, toen mijn broer Jack zijn blindedarm moest laten verwijderen. Dat was in het jaar voordat de oorlog begon. De lange ruimte die we nu binnenkwamen, was net zoiets; alleen waren alle ramen afgeplakt, vanwege de verplichte verduistering, en stonden de bedden een stuk dichter bij elkaar zodat er meer mensen in een zaal pasten. In het voorbijgaan zag ik niemand liggen met een blindedarmontsteking, geelzucht of een gebroken arm. Ze hadden vele verwondingen, zwartgeblakerde gezichten; bij sommigen was het hele lichaam ingezwachteld met kilometers onberispelijk wit verband.

Dit soort taferelen lieten de kranten niet zien.

De zuster van dienst liep kordaat voor ons uit.

'Uw vriendin zal het wel redden,' zei ze. 'Opgewekte glimlach, "kop op" zeggen en niet praten over wat er gebeurd is. Hier is het, rechts. U kunt op die stoel zitten. Ik kom over vijf minuten terug.'

Ze verhief haar stem, alsof Bunty doof was. 'Juffrouw Tavistock. U hebt bezoek. Vijf minuten,' zei ze, dat laatste weer tegen mij, en daarna beende ze resoluut weer weg.

Bunty's bed stond helemaal achter in de zaal, tegen de muur. Ik haalde zo diep mogelijk adem en probeerde – zoals geïnstrueerd – een opgewekte glimlach op te zetten. Het voelde helemaal niet als het juiste moment voor een opgewekte glimlach.

'Bunty?' zei ik zacht.

Ze lag bijna plat op haar rug, met haar rechterbeen opgehesen aan een soort katrol, en van de heup tot de voet in het verband. Haar linkerarm werd bij elkaar gehouden met spalken en nog meer verband. Overal waar geen verband zat, zag ik blauwe plekken en schrammen. Nu, bijna twee dagen na het bombardement, was haar gezicht vrijwel onherkenbaar. Een van haar ogen leek wel een reusachtige oesterschelp – zo ver opgezwollen als de geel en paars gekneusde huid maar kon rekken – alsof ze knock-out geslagen was door een beroepsbokser. Ik vocht tegen de neiging haar aan te gapen. Dat ik geen nepglimlach kon opzetten was tot daaraan toe, maar ik wilde Bunty beslist niet laten zien dat ik geschokt was.

Ik plofte nogal snel neer op de ijzeren stoel naast haar bed. Het liefst had ik haar omhelsd en haar verteld dat we allemaal wilden helpen om alles beter te maken, maar dat kon natuurlijk niet. Je kunt iemand die eruitziet alsof elke centimeter van haar lichaam pijn doet niet omhelzen. Ik wilde haar hand vasthouden, maar die ging schuil onder het verband. Daarom omklemde ik maar een stukje van het hagelwitte, gesteven laken, waarmee ik het effect van perfectie meteen bedierf.

Bunty had niet op mijn groet gereageerd en ik kon nergens uit opmaken of ze me eigenlijk wel gehoord had. Het oog dat niet toegetakeld en onbruikbaar was, bleef strak naar het plafond kijken.

'Bunty,' zei ik weer, zo zacht als ik kon, alsof het minste geluid haar nog meer pijn zou kunnen doen... alsof alles door de minste schok nóg erger zou kunnen worden. 'Ik ben het. Emmy.'

Haar borstkas rees en daalde met haar ademhaling en ik zag haar ene oog knipperen. Nu wist ik zeker dat ze wist dat ik er was.

'O, Bunts,' zei ik verbijsterd. Ik wilde zo dolgraag het juiste tegen haar zeggen. 'Ik vind het allemaal zo erg.'

Niets.

'We zijn er allemaal voor je. Iedereen is hier en we gaan je helpen om beter te worden. We zullen jou en je oma helpen, en mijn vader gaat met de dokters praten om te zorgen dat we precies weten wat we moeten doen om te zorgen dat je binnen de kortste keren weer op de been bent, en...'

Dit was ondraaglijk. Als ze me kon horen, hoe zou ze dan reageren? Misschien probeerde ze wel iets te zeggen, maar wist ze niet hoe.

'Eh... in elk geval, lieverd, hebben de dokters er alle vertrouwen in dat ze je been hersteld hebben en het doet vast vreselijk pijn allemaal, maar op een dag zul je je beter voelen, dat beloof ik.' Ik zweeg even. Wat wist ik er nou van? Wáárvan dan ook?

'O, Bunty,' fluisterde ik, hopend dat mijn stem het niet zou begeven, 'ik vind het zo erg van Bill.'

Bunty knipperde met haar ene oog, maar zei nog steeds niets. Haar gezicht was zo gehavend dat het onmogelijk was om welke uitdrukking ook te onderscheiden. Ik deed mijn mond open om verder te praten, maar voordat ik de woorden eruit kreeg, sprak Bunty.

'Hij heeft het me verteld.'

Het kostte haar moeite om te praten, maar het was een begin. Ik leunde naar haar toe en trok de metalen stoel naar voren om dichterbij te komen.

'Bunty, liefje,' zei ik en stak mijn hand uit om haar vingertoppen aan te raken, want ik móést haar laten weten dat ze er niet alleen voor stond. Als ik ook maar iets kon zeggen wat haar misschien kon helpen...

'Niet doen.'

Ik trok mijn hand terug, van het bed af.

'Hij heeft het me verteld,' zei Bunty weer. Haar stem klonk vlak, zonder enige emotie. Ze keek me nog steeds niet aan.

'Wat dan?' vroeg ik in een poging haar aan te moedigen.

'Rustig maar, ik weet dat het moeilijk is.'

'Dat je tegen hem tekeerging. Tegen hem schreeuwde.'

Dit overviel me. Tegen de gruwelijke achtergrond van Williams dood leken onze ruzies nog onzinniger dan tevoren. Snel probeerde ik alles recht te zetten.

'Goeie genade,' zei ik. 'Ja. We hadden inderdaad een onnozel verschil van mening.' Ik hield op. Het was niet mijn bedoeling geweest om het te bagatelliseren. 'Ik wilde alleen dat hij voorzichtig was,' zei ik ten slotte slapjes.

'Voor hem was het niet onnozel,' zei Bunty. 'Jij had het recht niet om dat te zeggen. Jij denkt dat je iedereen kunt opvoeden, maar dat kan echt niet. Je bent een bemoeial.'

De bitterheid in haar stem trof me diep.

'Bunty, het spijt me,' zei ik. 'Ik maakte me zorgen over hem. Ik dacht aan jou.'

Zodra ik dat uitsprak, besefte ik hoe stom het klonk.

'Echt niet.' Ondanks haar kwetsbaarheid klonk Bunty nu kwaad. 'En ik zou jouw beste vriendin zijn? Van je vrienden moet je het maar hebben. Jij denkt nooit aan anderen, je doet gewoon waar je zelf zin in hebt.'

'O, Bunts,' zei ik smekend. 'Het spijt me. Ik deed het niet expres.'

Bunty's stem klonk zwak, maar ze was nog niet klaar. 'Je doet het nooit expres. Maar je dringt anderen je mening op en daarmee maak je alles erger. Dat deed je ook bij Kitty. Jij zei dat ze voor haar kindje moest vechten. Dat hielp niet en ze werd er alleen maar verdrietiger van. Je dacht zelfs dat je wildvreemden bij het tijdschrift advies kon geven, maar dat kan echt niet. Jij had je er niet mee moeten bemoeien,' benadrukte ze weer.

Ik hield mijn handen zo krampachtig samengevouwen dat mijn knokkels eruitzagen alsof ze elk moment konden openbarsten. De paniek vloog me naar de keel. Bunty klonk alsof ze me haatte.

'Ik wilde niet dat jij wist dat Bill in gevaar geweest was,' zei ik. 'Ik heb hem verteld dat het me speet, en we hebben erover gepraat, en ik wilde weer sorry zeggen, maar ik kreeg de kans niet. Dat wilde ik doen zodra ik Café de Paris binnenkwam.'

Wat een armzalige waslijst van excuses. Bij elk woord verafschuwde ik mezelf meer.

'Je was er niet,' zei Bunty en eindelijk beefde haar stem een beetje. 'Hij maakte zich zorgen.'

'Dat spijt me heel erg,' zei ik, zoekend naar de juiste woorden. 'Ze hadden niet genoeg personeel in de kazerne. Ik vond niet dat ik weg kon.'

'Hij maakte zich zorgen over jou,' zei Bunty. 'Hij zei dat hij jou wilde zoeken voor het geval dat je nog steeds boos was.'

'Maar ik was niet boos,' zei ik ontzet, en bang voor wat ze hierna zou zeggen. 'Ik was niet boos.'

Langzaam draaide Bunty haar hoofd om en keek me eindelijk aan. Haar arme, gehavende gezicht stond ontzettend droevig.

'Bill wilde niet dat alles erdoor bedorven zou worden. Hij zei dat hij jou zou zoeken om alles uit te praten.'

Ze leek uitgeput, maar zette door.

'En toen stierf hij. Hij was op zoek naar jou.'

Ik dacht dat de wereld zaterdagavond ingestort was. Dat alles toen donker en vreselijk en op zijn allerergst was geweest. Blijkbaar had ik het mis gehad.

Zodra ik met mijn rug tegen de leuning van de stoel zat, kwamen de tranen.

Ik wist niet wat ik moest zeggen. Ik wist niets wat kon helpen, behalve dat het me speet, meer dan iets me ooit gespeten had. Dat wilde ik duizendmaal zeggen, net zo lang tot Bunty wist dat ik het meende. Maar zij wilde het niet horen. Zodra ik begon te praten, snoerde ze me de mond.

Haar stem klonk weer vlak, maar angstaanjagend duidelijk.

'Niet doen.'

De vastberaden voetstappen van de zuster van dienst klonken achter me.

'Ik kom nog wel een keer,' zei ik. 'Als jij je beter voelt. Dan kunnen we erover praten.'

Bunty keek me aan met al het verdriet van de wereld op haar gehavende gezicht.

'Je moet niet meer komen. Ik wil je niet meer zien.'

Toen draaide ze haar hoofd om.

De zuster van dienst begon iets kordaats te zeggen over vertrekken en ik stond langzaam op.

'Het spijt me,' fluisterde ik terwijl een reusachtige traan over de zijkant van Bunty's opgezwollen, onherkenbare gezicht naar beneden rolde.

De verpleegster zei dat ik moest opschieten.

Bunty zei niets meer.

20

Geloof me, schrijf!

Mevrouw Tavistock en mijn moeder stonden buiten de zaal op me te wachten. Natuurlijk zagen ze meteen dat ik zo wit als een doek was, maar ze dachten dat het door de schok kwam, omdat ik gezien had hoe slecht Bunty eraan toe was. Ik vertelde mevrouw Tavistock dat Bunty niet wilde praten – wat waar was, maar natuurlijk niet het hele verhaal. Daarna zei ik dat ik, als ze er geen probleem mee hadden, graag een luchtje wilde scheppen en daarom liever alleen naar huis wilde gaan. Moeder begon te protesteren en mevrouw Tavistock pakte mijn handen en zei dat ik zo'n lief meisje was omdat ik probeerde te helpen en dat ik me geen zorgen hoefde te maken en dat alles binnenkort weer helemaal in orde zou zijn.

Ik kon het nauwelijks verdragen.

Snel keerde ik hun de rug toe en maakte dat ik wegkwam uit het ziekenhuis. Ik holde de gang uit, roffelde de trap af en negeerde alle afkeurende ts-geluiden en uitroepen van 'rustig aan daar' en 'nou ja, zeg' terwijl ik me langs de receptie naar buiten haastte, de verduisterde stad in.

Mevrouw Tavistock was erg aardig, maar ze kende haar kleindochter niet zo goed als ik. Bunty wilde me niet meer zien. Ik zou het blijven proberen, maar ik wist dat ze het meende. Het was slechts een kwestie van tijd voordat haar oma me zou laten weten dat Bunty voorlopig niet in staat was om bezoek te ontvangen.

Het liefst wilde ik Bunty's verbod negeren en zo snel mogelijk weer bij haar op bezoek gaan. Ik moest uitleggen wat er met Bill gebeurd was en hopen dat ze het zou begrijpen. Het beeld van mijn vriendin in het ziekenhuis, vol pijn en diep verdriet, stond op mijn netvlies gegrift. Het ergste was nog dat mijn gedachten keer op keer bleven herhalen wat Bunty gezegd had: dat Bill naar mij op zoek geweest was toen hij stierf. Dat kon je zo mooi inkleden als je maar wilde, maar de boodschap was nogal duidelijk: het was mijn schuld dat hij dood was.

Naast het ziekenhuis was een klein café dat nog open was voor het personeel dat avonddienst draaide. Omdat ik nogal wankel op mijn benen stond, ging ik naar binnen voor een sterke kop thee. In het café was het warm en het rook er naar boterhamworst en carbolzeep, maar het was toch gezellig.

'Jongedame, voelt u zich niet goed?' vroeg de vriendelijke man achter de toonbank met een sterk accent. Hij was ergens in de vijftig en had een opvallende snor. 'U ziet wit. Ik ben Tsjecho-Slowaaks,' voegde hij eraan toe, blijkbaar gewend aan het feit dat iedereen met een buitenlands accent verdacht werd van sympathie voor de vijand.

'Het gaat prima, dank u,' zei ik, want ik wilde me niet laten kennen. Ik hoopte dat hij geen vragen meer zou stellen. Als hij nog vriendelijker tegen me deed, zou ik bezwijken. 'Zou ik een kop thee kunnen krijgen, alstublieft?'

'Natuurlijk,' antwoordde hij. 'Ga zitten. Ik zoek geheime suiker. Ssjt!' Hij knipoogde en wees naar een tafeltje in de hoek.

Ik knikte en probeerde 'Dank u' te zeggen, maar het kwam eruit als een soort hik, en hij wapperde me op een vaderlijke manier koelte toe met een theedoek. Ik vroeg me af hoeveel mensen hier elke dag vanuit het ziekenhuis binnenwankelden omdat hun leven op z'n kop gezet was.

Neuriënd brouwde hij de sterkste kop thee die ik sinds het uitbreken van de oorlog gezien had en serveerde die met een vijgenbroodje op het schoteltje en de duidelijke maar gebrekkig gesproken instructie: 'Eet, drink... van de zaak. Blijf tot rode wangen.'

Ik roerde mijn thee en bestudeerde de bemoedigende affiches die op de muren geplakt waren. Eén affiche beval de toeschouwers aan om aardappels te telen, terwijl een ander affiche hun voorstelde om in Spaarfondsen te investeren. Beide affiches suggereerden gegarandeerd succes, in elk geval wat betreft het leveren van een aandeel in de oorlogsinspanning. Een derde affiche toonde een heleboel vrouwen in de uniformen van verschillende legeronderdelen en diensten. 'Ze doen het grandioos!' verkondigde het onderschrift.

Ik bleef roeren. Ik deed het allesbehalve grandioos. Mijn aardige Tsjecho-Slowaakse vriend zong met een zachte bariton die in een andere tijd, in een andere wereld, in een goed koor op zijn plaats geweest zou zijn. Nu stond hij hier en zorgde voor een volkomen vreemde, gratis en voor niets, terwijl veel mensen hem als een bedreiging beschouwden als hij niet meteen zijn nationaliteit meldde.

De wereld was lelijk en krankzinnig geworden.

Met moeite hield ik me flink, dronk een slokje van mijn thee en werd onmiddellijk bijna duizelig van de hoeveelheid suiker – waaraan ik sinds lang niet meer gewend was.

Ik had geen idee wat ik nu moest beginnen. Bunty en ik zouden altijd met elkaar blijven kletsen, zelfs als we ruzie hadden, en dat kwam maar zelden voor. We waren al ons hele leven elkaars beste vriendin en hadden plechtig beloofd dat altijd te blijven. Alleen was het nu, volgens Bunty, mijn schuld dat haar verloofde dood was. Het was allemaal veel te groot en veel te akelig.

Op een tafel in de hoek tegenover mij had iemand de kranten van die dag en een paar beduimelde tijdschriften achtergelaten. *Vrouw & Vriendin* leek er niet tussen te liggen, maar ik moest wel meteen denken aan de ellendige ironie dat ik probeerde lezeressen advies te geven terwijl ik van mijn eigen leven een absolute puinhoop maakte. Mevrouw Bird zou gehakt van me maken als ik haar daar een brief over stuurde.

Ik bukte, deed mijn tas open en haalde het notitieboek tevoorschijn dat ik overal mee naartoe sleepte. Daar krabbelde ik altijd ideeën in voor antwoorden op de ingewikkelde problemen die mensen ingezonden hadden. Nu wilde ik op een rijtje krijgen wat ik Bunty moest vertellen, hoe ik alles voor haar zou kunnen verwoorden zodra ik weer een kans kreeg. Misschien kon ik het allemaal eens behoorlijk opschrijven en haar een brief sturen. Dan kon zij beslissen wanneer ze die wilde lezen.

Ik had niet echt een plan, maar beginnen met schrijven gaf me tenminste het gevoel dat ik iets deed. Ik wilde het beslist niet zomaar opgeven, net nu Bunty vriendschap harder nodig had dan ooit.

Liefste Bunty,

Ik weet niet waar ik moet beginnen of hoe ik het juiste kan zeggen, maar voor het geval het je te overstuur maakt als ik weer naar je toe kom, schrijf ik je in de hoop dat je mijn brief zult lezen. Wat ik boven alles wil, is dat jij weet hoeveel ik aan je denk en dat ik tegen beter weten in blijf hopen dat op een dag alles beter voor jou zal zijn.

Ik weet dat je vreselijk zwaar gewond bent, maar ik weet ook dat het verlies van Bill nog heel veel erger voor je is. Ik durf zijn naam nauwelijks te schrijven, want je moet nu wel zo'n vreselijke hekel aan me hebben. Woorden schieten tekort om te beschrijven hoe ontzaglijk het me spijt.

Bill had volkomen gelijk. Het was niet onnozel. We hebben ruzie gemaakt en ik heb een paar ellendige dingen tegen hem gezegd: dat hij te dapper wilde zijn op zijn werk en dat hij te veel risico's nam. Bunty, ik ben zo stom geweest. Het kwam er verkeerd uit en toen ik probeerde mijn excuses aan te bieden, ging dat ook helemaal verkeerd. Ik probeerde jou te beschermen en maakte me zorgen dat hij gewond zou raken, maar ik had niets moeten zeggen. Het was zijn baan en hij was een geweldige brandweerman. Dat wist iedereen. Wat een beroerde vriendin ben ik voor jullie allebei geweest.

De woorden rolden er in een waanzinnige stroom uit, maar ze leken niet veel te betekenen. Het was allemaal gewoon een berg smoezen. Als ik Bunty was, zou ik deze brief waarschijnlijk in stukken scheuren en nooit meer een brief van mij openmaken.

Ik voelde mijn schouders naar beneden zakken en leunde met mijn ellebogen op het tafeltje.

De bedrijfsleider veegde, nog altijd neuriënd, de vloer.

Hij hield even op en keek naar mij. 'Drink,' zei hij en knikte in de richting van mijn kop thee. 'Voordat koud is.'

Ik probeerde te glimlachen en hij keek me vriendelijk aan.

'En schrijf,' zei hij. 'Wie u ook schrijft, als ze van u houden, begrijpen ze.'

In stilte wenste ik dat hij gelijk had. Blijkbaar zag ik er net zo belabberd uit als ik me voelde, want hij zette zijn bezem tegen de muur en kwam naar me toe. Hij klopte me op mijn schouder.

'Geloof me,' zei hij. 'Ik heb veel klanten. Schrijf!'

Zijn vriendelijkheid ontroerde me. Hij probeerde me te helpen met thee en liedjes en geheime suiker.

'Dank u wel,' zei ik. 'Dat zal ik doen.'

Want hij had gelijk. Mijn woorden waren niet veel soeps – in feite wist ik niet eens of ze alles niet juist erger zouden maken – maar ik kon alleen maar mijn uiterste best doen om alles duidelijk te maken, zodat Bunty de waarheid wist. Ik kon geen vergeving van haar verwachten, maar ze moest weten hoezeer ik wenste dat ik kon veranderen wat er gebeurd was.

Ik nam een grote slok van de nog warme thee en pakte mijn pen weer op.

Bunty, ik dacht dat ik het zou kunnen goedmaken in Café de Paris. Ik dacht dat er tijd voor zou zijn. Dat had ik mis en daar zal ik voorgoed berouw van hebben.

Ik kan me niet voorstellen hoe afschuwelijk dit voor jou is en ik besef dat je me niet kunt vergeven. Ik zou er echt alles voor overhebben om alles te veranderen en met Bill te ruilen, dat kan ik je verzekeren. Ik meen het, geloof dat alsjeblieft.

Nu zal ik deze brief maar beëindigen. Wil je alsjeblieft je uiterste best doen om beter te worden en weer op de been te komen? We houden allemaal reusachtig van je en kunnen ons het leven niet voorstellen zonder dat jij weer helemaal gezond bent.

Bunty, weet alsjeblieft dat jij altijd mijn allerbeste vriendin in de wereld zult zijn en dat ik er altijd zal zijn voor het geval je me ooit nodig zou kunnen hebben.

Het spijt me zo erg.

Met heel veel liefs, voor altijd jouw

Emmy xx

Ik ging even met mijn rug tegen de leuning van de stoel zitten. Ik wist niet wat ik nog meer kon zeggen, maar ik wilde niet ophouden met schrijven. Het was alsof dit mijn laatste kans zou kunnen zijn om iets tegen haar te zeggen. Dat kon ik niet verdragen. Ik moest er nog één ding aan toevoegen.

PS: Ik zal je blijven schrijven, voor het geval je misschien voelt dat je mijn brieven kunt openmaken. Ik zal een aantekening op de voorkant van de envelop maken, zodat de verpleegsters weten dat ze van mij komen; dan kunnen zij die ook weggooien, als jij dat liever wilt. Em.

Ik zou blijven schrijven.

Voorzichtig sloeg ik mijn notitieboek dicht. Zodra ik thuiskwam, zou ik de brief overschrijven en opsturen.

Bunty mocht William verloren hebben en mij daarom hartstochtelijk haten – wat ik best begreep – maar ik wilde haar niet opgeven. Ik zou altijd haar vriendin blijven, of ze me wilde of niet.

21

De oorlog was smerig

Ik kreeg gelijk wat Bunty betrof. Later op die avond kwam mevrouw Tavistock naar het appartement en zei dat Bunty weliswaar ‘vreselijk goed opknapte’ en ‘binnen de kortste keren weer beter’ zou zijn – waar ik niets van geloofde – maar dat het waarschijnlijk beter was als ik voorlopig niet meer op bezoek kwam. Ik moest de artsen en verpleegsters de ruimte geven om alles te doen wat ze konden om haar te helpen.

Ik had geen idee hoeveel mevrouw Tavistock wist, maar ik zei: ‘Ja, natuurlijk’ en speelde het zelfs klaar nog iets te zeggen over hoe geweldig alle verpleegsters waren en hoe ontzettend knap de artsen geweest waren – wat klonk alsof ik een voorstelling in West End een goede recensie gaf.

Ik vond het niet meer dan correct om mevrouw Tavistock te vragen of ik Bunty mocht schrijven, waarbij ik mijn vingers achter mijn rug gekruist hield, want ik wist niet wat ik zou doen als ze nee zei. Heel even dacht ik dat ze aarzelde, maar toen herpakte ze zich en zei: ‘Natuurlijk.’ Wat een opluchting!

Ook wilde ze beslist dat ik in het zolderappartement zou blijven wonen, en daar was ik haar heel dankbaar voor. Al zou ik hier omringd zijn door voortdurende herinneringen aan Bunty en William – zodat ik elk moment dat ik thuis was door schuldgevoel overvallen kon worden – het betekende ook dat ik nog steeds deel uitmaakte van het leven van mijn beste vriendin. Bovendien hoopte ik dat dit inhield dat Bunty haar oma niet verteld had dat Williams dood mijn schuld was.

Er was echter wel een voorwaarde aan verbonden. Mijn ouders wilden per se dat ik Londen verliet en voorlopig bij hen kwam logeren om uit te rusten. Daar was ik vreselijk ongelukkig mee. Ik had geen rust nodig – tenslotte was ík niet gewond geraakt – en als ik naar het platteland afgevoerd werd, voelde ik me een bedrieger. Maar het was overduidelijk dat mijn ouders dit met mevrouw Tavistock hadden afgesproken, en ondanks een koppige woordenwisseling met mijn moeder had ik geen andere keuze dan toegeven. Anders zou mevrouw Tavistock haar huis in Londen afsluiten. Bunty's oma was altijd lief voor me geweest, maar ik wist wanneer ik verslagen was.

Roy had gezegd dat hij met kapitein Davies in de kazerne zou praten, en meneer Collins stond erop dat ik niet meteen weer aan het werk ging bij *Vrouw & Vriendin*, dus ik had geen reden om in Londen te blijven. Mij mankeerde niets, maar eerlijk gezegd vond ik het wel een opluchting dat ik iedereen nog niet meteen onder ogen hoefde te komen.

Meneer Collins wilde ik graag bedanken voor alles wat hij de nacht van de luchtaanval gedaan had, maar ik zou niet weten waar ik moest beginnen. Hij was buitengewoon vriendelijk geweest door in Café de Paris de hele tijd bij me te blijven en mee te zoeken naar Bunty. Ik wist niet of ik haar in mijn eentje wel gevonden zou hebben. Ik wist niet eens zeker of ik binnen had kunnen komen als hij niet tegen die opzichter gelogen had dat ik verpleegster was. En nu was hij alweer zo vriendelijk wat het werk betrof.

En dan was Charles er natuurlijk ook nog. Nog geen twee weken geleden hadden hij en ik samen gedanst en gelachen en beloofd elkaar te schrijven… tijdens een afscheidskus. Dat was destijds opwindend en leuk geweest, iets om naar uit te kijken. Wat moest ik hem nu schrijven? Hoe kon ik iemand die ik nauwelijks kende uitleggen wat er gebeurd was? Daar wilde ik niet over nadenken.

Dinsdagochtend stapten mijn moeder en ik op Waterloo Station in de trein. Terwijl de regen op het dak kletterde en mijn moeder uit beleefdheid een gesprek over voedseltekorten begon met een oudere dame die vlak bij ons zat, liet ik mijn hoofd tegen het raam van het tweedeklasrijtuig rusten en deed mijn ogen dicht.

Deze thuiskomst was volslagen anders dan mijn laatste logeerpartij. Toen hadden Bunty en ik een sneeuwgevecht met Jack gehouden. Iedereen was optimistisch geweest over mijn nieuwe baan, en luidruchtig woedend over Edmunds tekortkomingen. Nu was het huis in stilte gehuld. Little Whitfield was een klein dorp; iedereen kende William en Bunty en wist hoe dik we allemaal met elkaar bevriend waren. Bezorgde vrienden belden liever niet aan, maar klopten zacht op de deur. Zelfs vaders patiënten gingen bijna geruisloos naar zijn spreekkamer en weer naar buiten; alleen de gebruikelijke gesprekken over kinderen met de mazelen of opa met spit waren te horen.

Ik bivakkeerde in mijn oude slaapkamer, staarde naar het mooie bloemetjesbehang en ging alleen naar beneden voor maaltijden – die ik niet aanraakte – of om door de tuin te zwerven – waar ik niemand hoefde te spreken. Midden in de nacht, als mijn slaapkamer in duister gehuld was, keek ik door het raam naar buiten en naar boven en wenste dat er een vliegtuig zou verschijnen om me iets verschrikkelijks aan te doen. Anderen niet, natuurlijk, maar alleen mij.

Telkens weer vertelde ik mezelf dat ik mijn hoofd niet zo

moest laten hangen, maar ik kon niet anders. Het enige wat ik voor elkaar kreeg, was Bunty schrijven, zoals ik beloofd had. Korte, ingetogen, maar hoopvolle brieven, elke dag. Ik had geen idee of zij ze zou bekijken.

Ik dwong mezelf ook Charles te schrijven. Dat wilde ik niet, maar hij was zo vreselijk aardig geweest en aangezien hij Bunty en William ook ontmoet had, zou het ongelooflijk onbeleefd geweest zijn om het hem niet te vertellen. Ik kon hem niet vertellen dat het allemaal mijn schuld was, dus hield ik het zo kort mogelijk.

Beste Charles,
Ik hoop dat het heel goed met je gaat.
Ik weet niet of je broer hier misschien al over geschreven heeft, maar ik vrees dat ik nogal akelig nieuws te melden heb. Ik kan het nauwelijks verdragen om dit te schrijven, dus doe ik het maar snel.
Weet je, terwijl Bunty en William en ik uitgingen om hun verloving te vieren, kwam er een luchtaanval. Ze hebben Café de Paris gebombardeerd en Bill is omgekomen. Bunty is gewond en ze is er nogal slecht aan toe. Met mij gaat het prima, omdat ik te laat kwam en het bombardement misliep, en meneer Collins – sorry, ik kan hem geen Guy noemen – was er ook en hij heeft me geholpen om Bunty te vinden. Hij was zo aardig en je zou heel trots op hem geweest zijn als je hem gezien had.
Het spijt me dat ik je zulk afschuwelijk nieuws moet schrijven. Ik had beloofd dat ik je vrolijke brieven zou sturen.
Maak je alsjeblieft geen zorgen, want Bunty is wonderbaarlijk sterk en mijn vader zegt dat ze heel snel zal opknappen. Ik wilde dat ik haar kon helpen, maar mijn vader zegt dat de verpleegsters daar de allerbeste zijn. Ze is dus in goede handen.
Ik logeer een paar dagen bij mijn ouders, maar zal heel binnenkort weer in het appartement zitten.

Pas reusachtig goed op jezelf, wil je?
Groeten,
Emmy x

Meer wist ik hem niet te vertellen.

Mijn moeder deed de brief voor me op de post omdat ik het huis niet uit wilde. Het was gemakkelijk om thuis te zitten. Het enige wat ik hoefde te doen was een opgewekt gezicht opzetten voor mijn ouders en zeggen dat ik me elke dag beter voelde. Moeder probeerde me voor van alles te interesseren: dekens naaien voor de oorlogsinspanning of eieren verzamelen of zelfs gewoon even bij de buren op bezoek gaan om hun nieuwe hond te zien. Ze bedoelde het goed, maar het hielp niet echt. Ik was niet ziek of invalide en ik had veel te veel tijd om na te denken over alles wat er gebeurd was.

Een week na mijn thuiskomst zat ik op de vochtige oude houten schommel in de tuin en keek naar de eerste narcissen die hun kopjes naar boven staken, door het gras heen. Dat herinnerde me aan de eerste keer dat ik met Edmund uitgegaan was. We waren zeventien en we zouden gewoon gaan wandelen, maar hij stond op de stoep met een bos bloemen voor mij en keek verlegen. Bij die herinnering schudde ik mijn hoofd. In mijn o zo gemakkelijke, gelukkige leventje had zijn keus om er met een verpleegster vandoor te gaan aangevoeld als een klap in mijn gezicht. Nu leek het zo onbetekenend.

En wat had Bunty destijds gedaan? Een borrel voor me ingeschonken, me verteld dat Edmund een absolute sukkel was en dat hij het nooit beter zou treffen dan met mij. Ze stond onomstotelijk aan mijn kant, zonder een moment te aarzelen. Zoals altijd was ze de beste vriendin ter wereld.

'Idioot,' fluisterde ik tegen mezelf. Daarna zei ik wat harder: 'Stomme idioot die je bent.'

Als er prijzen voor zelfmedelijden uitgeloofd waren, zou ik de beste van de klas geweest zijn. Als Bunty hier was, als ze nog steeds mijn vriendin geweest was, zou zij, hoe beroerd alles ook was, nooit in zo'n neerwaartse spiraal van somberheid terechtgekomen zijn. Zij zou doorgeknokt hebben.

Ik moest nodig terug naar Londen en naar mijn werk. Dat was de enige manier om mezelf los te schudden uit deze wanhoop. Ik zou het mijn ouders duidelijk moeten maken, want tenslotte had ik het geluk dat ik gezond was.

Ik sprong van de schommel, liep het huis in en ging naar mijn kamer om mijn spullen te pakken.

●

Kon ik dit wel doorzetten? In mijn eentje terugkomen in het appartement was de eerste beproeving. Toen ik laat in de middag de deur opendeed en de muurlamp aanknipte, zag bijna alles er hetzelfde uit, maar toch was het volkomen anders dan voorheen. De koude woonkamer was stil en leeg. Moeder had de ongeopende felicitatiekaarten en huwelijkscadeaus weggehaald en verstopt. Nu was het ondraaglijk netjes, behalve mijn rommelige schrijfbakje naast de typemachine op de kleine teakhouten eettafel waaraan Bunts en ik samen aten – en waar ik stiekem mijn brieven voor *Vrouw & Vriendin* schreef als zij naar haar werk was. Er lag nog een stapel nieuwe brieven – die ik zo snel mogelijk had willen beantwoorden – verstopt in mijn slaapkamer. Ik wist niet wat ik er nu mee moest doen.

Voorheen had het beantwoorden van de brieven van lezeressen me het gevoel gegeven dat ik een doel had. Zelfs toen Kathleen me bijna betrapt had en ik besloten had geen brieven meer in het tijdschrift te plaatsen, had ik nog gedacht dat in het geheim brieven terug schrijven mensen zou kunnen helpen. Nu knaagden Bunty's woorden in het ziekenhuis aan me.

Jij dringt anderen je mening op en daarmee maak je alles erger. Je dacht zelfs dat je wildvreemden bij het tijdschrift advies kon geven, maar dat kan echt niet.

Ze had gelijk. Ik zou niet rond moeten rennen om brieven te posten, maar iets behoorlijks moeten doen voor de oorlogsinspanning. Terwijl ik de afgelopen week in het huis van mijn ouders zat, had ik bedacht dat ik me misschien maar moest aanmelden voor de training om fulltime motorkoerierster voor de brandweer te worden, in plaats van er alleen maar over te praten. Of misschien moest ik proberen bij een van de andere diensten te komen. Eerlijk gezegd maakte het me niet eens zoveel uit waar, als het maar betekende dat ik iets nuttigs deed.

Het zou in elk geval meer zijn dan ik nu deed. Ik wilde nooit meer hopeloos aan de kant van de straat staan terwijl brandweermannen andere mensen aan het redden waren. Nooit meer wilde ik iemand als meneer Collins nodig hebben om tijdens een noodsituatie bij iemand te komen. Ik besloot behoorlijk onderzoek te doen naar de verschillende diensten. Tenslotte kon ik me niet permitteren nogmaals een fout te maken en in het verkeerde baantje terecht te komen. Intussen zou ik me aanmelden voor meer diensten in de brandweerkazerne en me een slag in de rondte werken bij *Vrouw & Vriendin*. En ik zou me absoluut aan de regels houden. Geen geschrijf meer aan lezeressen. Geen bemoeienis meer met het leven van anderen.

Eindelijk had ik weer een plan – of in elk geval een beginnetje – en daar kikkerde ik van op.

Morgen zou ik weer naar kantoor gaan, maar eerst moest ik iets veel belangrijkers doen. Ik moest voor het eerst sinds de ramp bij Café de Paris terug naar de brandweerkazerne.

De moed zonk me in de schoenen.

Het globevormige drankkastje in de hoek lonkte naar me. Maar ik schudde mijn hoofd: mezelf moed indrinken zou niet helpen. Resoluut stond ik op van de bank en ging systematisch alle kamers door, knipte alle lampen aan en boende – louter en alleen om te vermijden dat ik over alles zou gaan zitten piekeren – elke vierkante centimeter van het vlekkeloze appartement nog eens grondig.

De volgende ochtend om half zes – ik had geen oog dichtgedaan – had ik me gewassen en mijn netste kantoorkleren aangetrokken. *Vrouw & Vriendin* durfde ik wel aan, maar Roy en de meisjes en alle vrienden van William onder ogen komen was beslist angstaanjagend. Hoe langer ik dat uitstelde, hoe erger het zou worden, dat wist ik wel. Terwijl de piloten van de Luftwaffe uit Londen vertrokken – en vast en zeker door onze jongens teruggejaagd werden naar Duitsland – trok ik mijn overjas aan, duwde mijn wollen baret tot over mijn oren en zette in het donker koers naar de brandweerkazerne.

De brandweerploegen van Carlton Street waren nog her en der aan het blussen, dus de binnenplaats was leeg toen ik aankwam. Aangezien ik de hele weg gerend had – het was gaan regenen – was ik blij met deze kans om op adem te komen en mezelf op orde te krijgen.

Ik zette mijn baret af en bleef hijgend op de lege binnenplaats staan. De B-dienst zou nu ongeveer klaar zijn: Thelma, Joan en Mary, en degene die voor mij inviel. Mijn keel kneep dicht. Hopelijk was het Vera niet.

Zelfs als zij er niet was, zou dit moeilijk worden. Mijn vriendinnen zouden lief voor me zijn, waardoor ik me een afschuwelijke hypocriet zou voelen, maar hun verdriet zien zou nog veel erger zijn. Tot nu toe had ik alleen maar aan Bunty en mevrouw Tavistock gedacht. En, egoïstisch genoeg, aan mezelf. Niet aan Williams vrienden en vriendinnen. Hij was reusachtig populair geweest in de kazerne, geliefd zelfs.

'Kom op, ertegenaan!' zei ik hardop tegen mezelf. Hoofd omhoog, schouders naar achteren. Als ze vragen hoe het met Bunty is, zeg dan: 'Het gaat vreselijk goed met haar.'

Ik deed de zijdeur open en liep naar binnen, langs de vochtige muur waar alle fietsen gestald werden, en de steile, donkere trap op. Nog eens diep ademhalen terwijl mijn hart bonkte van angstig voorgevoel.

Het sein 'alles veilig' was al meer dan een uur geleden gegaan. Terwijl buiten het eerste grauwe ochtendlicht langzaam in zicht schoof, waren binnen de meisjes van de nachtdienst nog steeds volop bezig met telefoontjes van inwoners van Pimlico, die zich naar buiten waagden om de schade van de afgelopen nacht op te nemen. Op dit tijdstip ging het meestal over mensen die klem zaten, gebouwen die konden instorten of die geniepige late branden die uit het niets oplaaiden als er lucht bij kwam, net als iedereen dacht dat het veilig was.

De telefooncentrale zag er precies uit zoals het hoorde: de telefoons stonden op de bureaus, het oproepbord aan de muur toonde welke ploeg waarheen ging, de grote klok bij de deur tikte de laatste minuten van de nachtdienst weg. Joan was aan het telefoneren, verwoed schrijvend, en Thelma en Mary schreven de aantekeningen van oproepen van de afgelopen nacht uit. Meer meisjes waren er niet. Thel en Mary keken op toen ik de kamer binnenkwam en stonden onmiddellijk op; hun stoelen krasten over de vloer. Mary keek even naar Thelma om te vragen wat ze nu moest doen, maar Thelma was al op weg naar mij. Ze vertrok haar gezicht in een vastberaden imitatie van een 'alles komt helemaal goed'-glimlach. Dat lukte mij ook nog net.

'Hallo,' zei ik en zweeg abrupt toen Thelma me omhelsde.

'O, liefje toch,' zei ze, en daarna nog eens: 'O, liefje toch,' met bevende stem in mijn haar, vlak bij mijn oor. Ze liet me niet los. 'Je bent een schat. Je bent een schat.'

Te veel van streek om te praten worstelde ik uit alle macht tegen de tranen die weer dreigden te stromen. Ik wilde de meisjes niet teleurstellen, dus knikte ik alleen maar en beantwoordde haar omhelzing.

'Ik vind het zo erg, Emmy,' zei Mary, die achter Thelma aan gelopen was. Ze klopte me een beetje verlegen op mijn schouder en toen ik opkeek, zag ik ook in haar ogen tranen. Thelma wist niets meer te zeggen, of, beter gezegd: zij kon ook niet meer praten. Ik hield mijn ene arm om haar heen geslagen en stak mijn andere arm naar Mary uit. Joan rondde haar telefoongesprek af, prikte haastig haar notitie op de pin met oproepen en kwam ook naar ons toe.

'O, Em,' zei ze en ik liet Thelma en Mary los om ook haar te omhelzen. Joan had altijd een zwak voor William gehad; ze zei altijd dat ze hoopte dat haar zoontjes later net zulke kerels zouden worden als hij was.

'Ik weet het,' zei ik in een poging troostend te klinken, niet hopeloos – zo voelde ik me wel.

Joans ogen stonden vol tranen. Ze hield mijn armen vast, net als Thelma, en probeerde dapper te glimlachen. 'Die arme jongen van ons,' zei ze hoofdschuddend.

Nu rolde, tegen mijn bevelen in, een dikke traan over mijn wang. Dit ging niet om ons. Het ging om het verlies van een sympathieke, dappere jonge man die nog niet eens begonnen was aan het leven dat hij verdiende. Mijn eigen schuldgevoelens hadden daar niets mee te maken. Bill was overleden. Het was niet te geloven.

Joan, Thelma en Mary – en nog duizenden anderen – gingen dag en nacht onder de meest angstaanjagende omstandigheden door met hun werk. Elke dag hielpen ze mensen die ze niet kenden en nooit meer zouden ontmoeten. Maar dit was hun vriend. Je flink houden en gewoon doorgaan was allemaal mooi en aardig, maar soms moest je wel toegeven dat het allemaal gewoon verschrikkelijk was. De oorlog was smerig en weerzinwekkend en oneerlijk.

Voor de verandering ging niet een van de telefoons over.

Even later liet ik Joan voorzichtig los, veegde mijn gezicht af en pakte haar hand en die van Mary. Zij staken allebei een hand uit naar Thelma en heel even stonden we daar met ons vieren midden in de telefooncentrale elkaars handen vast te houden alsof we een bijzonder geheim genootschap vormden.

Ik verbrak de stilte, want ik wilde niets liever dan zorgen dat ze zich – al was het maar een klein beetje – beter voelden of het – een heel klein beetje – gemakkelijker vonden om door te gaan.

'Kom op, meisjes,' zei ik, met beverige stem – maar ik deed mijn best. Ik keek Mary aan en voegde er heel vriendelijk aan toe: 'Kom, kop op.'

Nog maar vier maanden geleden was haar broer vermist geraakt in Afrika. Ik wist dat Mary's tranen voor William ook voor hém bedoeld waren. Ik kneep nog wat steviger in haar hand en hoopte dat ik keek als een geruststellende grote zus. Zij probeerde op haar beurt dapper te glimlachen.

'Goed zo,' zei ik. 'Grote meid.'

Thelma nam het stokje van me over.

'Moet je ons zien,' zei ze sniffend. 'Dat gaat zo toch niet? In uniform en zo.' Daarmee was ze uitgeput.

Joan probeerde manhaftig door te zetten. 'Wat zou Bill zeggen, hè?' zei ze in een poging grappig te zijn, maar haar stem trilde verdacht. 'Och heden,' zei ze tot slot. 'Och heden.'

Ze deden zo reusachtig hun best. Het was moeilijk te verdragen.

'Nou,' zei ik langzaam, 'volgens mij zou Bill echt verdrietig zijn omdat iedereen zo van streek is, maar ik denk dat hij het wel zou begrijpen. En waarschijnlijk zou hij proberen ons allemaal op te vrolijken.'

Het was min van me om namens hem te spreken, maar

iedereen leek ervan op te kikkeren. Ze knikten alle drie instemmend en deden hun uiterste best om te glimlachen.

Beneden klonk het geluid van een zware motor. De eerste ploeg was teruggekeerd.

Mary keek paniekerig en zocht snel een zakdoek. De andere twee volgden haar voorbeeld. Niemand wilde dat de jongens ons in tranen zagen.

'Het geeft niet,' zei ik. 'Ze zijn nog aan het parkeren. Ik ga zo wel naar beneden om hen te spreken.'

'Bedankt, liefje,' zei Thelma en snoot daarna kordaat haar neus. Ze leek zich even schrap te zetten voordat ze vroeg hoe het met Bunty ging.

'Het gaat ontzettend goed met haar,' zei ik mijn ingestudeerde antwoord op. 'Al zal het waarschijnlijk wel even duren voordat ze weer helemaal tiptop is.'

'Doe haar de groeten van ons, wil je?' vroeg Thel en ik knikte – met een misselijk gevoel.

Beneden hoorde ik het gebrom van meer pompwagens die de binnenplaats op reden, en de stemmen van een paar van de mannen. Er kon elk moment iemand de trap op rennen en om thee vragen.

'Ik moet naar beneden,' zei ik in de hoop dat ik kranig en optimistisch – en alles wat ik helemaal niet was – klonk.

'Zij willen jou natuurlijk graag spreken,' zei Joan.

Zou het? dacht ik. Ze moesten eens weten.

Met een laatste glimlach naar de meisjes ging ik naar beneden om Williams vrienden dapper tegemoet te treden.

22

Uw mevrouw Wardynski

Vanuit de kazerne liep ik, als een absolute lafaard, een heel eind om naar huis omdat ik niet langs de tijdschriftenkiosk van meneer Bone wilde komen. Hij zou vast al weten wat er gebeurd was en ik kon niet nog zo'n wanhopig treurig gesprek aan, vooral niet omdat ik wist dat hierdoor een oude wond – het verlies van zijn zoon – opengereten zou worden.

Op straat werd het steeds drukker omdat mensen naar hun werk gingen en ik keek naar beneden om oogcontact met eventuele bekenden te vermijden. Ik begon de eigenaardige uitdrukking die op hun gezicht kwam als ze me zagen al te herkennen. Een sprankje van nog net geen paniek, gevolgd door een vriendelijk bedoelde grimas terwijl de persoon in kwestie probeerde te bedenken wat hij zou zeggen, of – veel erger nog – probeerde zijn eigen verdriet te verbergen.

Zoals gewoonlijk passeerde ik de speeltuin en ik stond even stil om naar twee kinderen te kijken die met hun hond speelden. De kinderen gilden van plezier en de kleine terriër jankte van enthousiasme, zonder iets te merken van de kou, de regen en de reusachtige gapende kraters die de achtergrond vormden voor hun spelletjes. Het kleine meisje riep de hond en hij rende verwoed kwispelend naar haar toe. Ze tilde hem op en omhelsde hem stevig terwijl hij haar gezicht likte; zijn achterpoten hingen naar beneden – ze was te klein om hem goed vast te houden – en lieten vrolijke moddervegen achter op haar jas.

In stilte wenste ik dat ik in de speeltuin kon rondhollen, spelen en schreeuwen en lachen alsof alles koek en ei was. Heel even wenste ik dat Charles hier was. Hij zou mijn hand kunnen vasthouden en kunnen zeggen dat alles goed zou komen. Al was dat niet waar, toch zou ik het fijn vinden om het hem te horen zeggen. Hij kon zo zeker klinken, niet uit arrogantie, maar met een kalmte waardoor je je op de een of andere manier veilig voelde, alsof er geen probleem bestond dat niet opgelost kon worden.

Ik tikte mezelf op de vingers. Het had geen zin om nu sentimenteel over hem te gaan doen. De hemel mocht weten hoe hij over die hele treurige geschiedenis zou denken als hij eenmaal terugkwam. Ik kon niet blijven bluffen over Bunty's herstel. Wat zou hij dan van me denken? We kenden elkaar nog niet zo lang, en al schreef ik hem om de haverklap en had ik de eerste brieven van overzee al ontvangen, het was nog steeds zo pril allemaal.

Ik huiverde, sloeg mijn armen over elkaar om mezelf te beschermen tegen de regen en ging met flinke pas op weg. Thuis zou ik mijn gezicht wassen en mezelf toonbaar maken voor op kantoor. Dan kon ik beginnen aan mijn plan: zo druk mogelijk bezig blijven tot ik oorlogswerk kon krijgen en *Vrouw & Vriendin* de rug kon toekeren.

Op het werk reageerde iedereen, zonder uitzondering, heel lief op mijn terugkeer. Kathleen stond zelfs op de tweede verdieping bij de lift op me te wachten. Nadat ze me uitgebreid en bezorgd omhelsd had, liepen we samen de twee trappen naar het kantoor op. Kath had haar arm door de mijne gehaakt en vertelde me keer op keer hoe vreselijk ze het vond.

Nog voordat we bij ons eigen kleine kantoortje aankwamen, verschenen mevrouw Mahoney en meneer Brand in de gang en spraken me allerhartelijkst toe. Meneer Collins had blijkbaar verteld wat er gebeurd was; ze waren vreselijk aardig voor me.

Om de aandacht zo snel mogelijk van mezelf af te leiden, bedankte ik hen en verzekerde iedereen dat het puik ging en dat ik er echt helemaal aan toe was om weer aan de slag te gaan. Kath begreep de hint en joeg me snel naar mijn bureau.

Net toen ik mijn jas uittrok, verscheen mevrouw Bird in de deuropening. Ze was schitterend gekleed in een zwarte mantel met veren en een bijpassende hoed, als een bijzonder grote kraai die op het punt staat naar de kerk te gaan.

'Aha, Emmeline,' zei ze op zakelijke toon, maar op een aanvaardbaar volume, en ze gebruikte warempel mijn voornaam; dat was nog nooit gebeurd. 'Ik vond dat ik naar je toe moest komen.' Ze klemde haar lippen even op elkaar en keek plechtig. 'Ik hoor dat je het zwaar gehad hebt. Moeilijke tijd.'

Het was niets voor de waarnemend redactrice om Kathleens kantoor echt binnen te komen – gewoonlijk blafte ze ons van buitenaf haar bevelen toe. Het was een bijzonder verrassend en vriendelijk gebaar.

'Dank u wel, mevrouw Bird,' antwoordde ik, 'ook voor de week vrijaf.'

'Dat zit wel goed,' zei ze afwerend. 'Meneer Collins heeft me de details verteld. Beroerde toestand. Het zijn geen mensen, het is ongedierte. Goed dat u weer komt opdagen. Wiebelig?'

Ik schudde mijn hoofd. Ik was niet gewend aan mevrouw

Bird in meelevende toestand. Even keek ik naar Kathleen, die als aan de grond genageld stond toe te kijken.

'Dank u wel, mevrouw Bird,' zei ik nogmaals. 'Het gaat echt prima met me, dank u wel.'

'Goed zo,' antwoordde ze met een mengeling van geestdrift en – hoogstwaarschijnlijk – opluchting omdat ik niets afgrijselijks deed als in tranen uitbarsten. 'Het beste is om bezig te blijven. Stort u er helemaal op.'

Ik vroeg me af of dit het juiste moment was om haar te vertellen dat ik van plan was *Vrouw & Vriendin* te verlaten en te solliciteren naar een fulltime baan ten bate van de oorlogsinspanning, maar mevrouw Bird ploegde door.

'Meneer Collins zegt dat hij wel wat overwerk van u kan gebruiken. Perfecte manier om u weer in actie te krijgen.'

Ze was teruggevallen op haar gebruikelijke, veel beter te verteren benadering: de menselijke stoomwals.

'Eén extra middag per week en maandag de hele dag is besproken. Maar ik wil wel dat u de voorrang geeft aan mijn brieven. Juffrouw Knighton heeft genoeg werk aan de rest.'

Ik knikte dankbaar. Dat was precies wat ik op dit moment nodig had. Als ik ook nog meer diensten draaide in de kazerne, had ik geen tijd om overal over na te denken. Het enige wat ik zou moeten doen, was werken en slapen.

'Hoe dan ook, ik moet u waarschuwen,' zei mevrouw Bird en ze manoeuvreerde haar wenkbrauwen tot een frons waar melk ter plekke zuur van zou worden, 'dat we de laatste tijd bijzonder onverkwikkelijke correspondentie hebben gekregen. Buitengewoon onaangenaam.'

De brieven! Niet nu, dacht ik. Niet nu!

Mevrouw Bird keek dreigend. 'Smerigheid, juffrouw Lake. Ik weet niet wat onze lezeressen bezielt, maar ik vrees dat juffrouw Knighton tijdens uw afwezigheid verscheidene hoogst onacceptabele brieven in stukken heeft moeten knippen.'

Kathleen knikte en leek slecht op haar gemak. Met ingehouden adem wachtte ik af.

'Men mag natuurlijk hopen dat dit geen onsmakelijke nieuwe modegril is, maar ik zou u willen vragen buitengewoon waakzaam te zijn en alle onaangenaamheden aan mij te melden. Wij zullen in dit opzicht geen duimbreed wijken.'

'Uiteraard,' zei ik. 'Het gaat vast vanzelf weer over.' Ik beet op mijn tong. Wat suf om zo'n gemeenplaats te gebruiken, want dat irriteerde mevrouw Bird waarschijnlijk nog meer. Ik had beter moeten weten.

'Hm,' zei ze op dreigende toon en wendde zich daarna tot Kathleen. 'Ik ga naar de bestuurskamer om brandweeremmers te bespreken.'

En meteen was ze verdwenen.

Kath en ik keken elkaar aan terwijl de deuren naar het trappenhuis dichtknalden.

'Ze was heel aardig,' zei ik. 'Dat had ik eigenlijk niet verwacht.'

'Mevrouw Bird is echt niet gemeen,' zei Kathleen. 'Ze is alleen, eh...'

'Assertief,' zeiden we tegelijkertijd. Daar glimlachten we allebei een beetje om, ik voor de eerste keer in dagen. Het was niet veel, maar ik moest toegeven dat het een hele opluchting was om terug te zijn bij *Vrouw & Vriendin*. Hier kende bijna niemand William of Bunty en – ik weet het, het klinkt egoïstisch – alles was gemakkelijker als ik me geen zorgen hoefde te maken over het verdriet van anderen.

Ik ging op de rand van het bureau zitten en vroeg Kathleen of meneer Collins al aanwezig was.

'Die kan elk moment binnenkomen, denk ik,' zei ze. 'Hij is vreselijk bezorgd over je, Emmy,' voegde ze eraan toe. 'Hij is de hele tijd akelig stil en eerlijk gezegd nogal onuitstaanbaar.' Ze keek naar de deur. 'Hij zal vast heel blij zijn je weer te zien.'

Ik wist eigenlijk niet wat ik daarop moest zeggen; ik hoopte maar dat hij geen nodeloze drukte zou maken. Omdat ik over iets anders wilde praten, besloot ik het risico te nemen om naar de onsmakelijke nieuwe modegrillen van mevrouw Bird te vragen. Ik hoopte van harte dat Kath niet weer iets vermoedde.

'Dus er is weer wat kleurrijke correspondentie?' vroeg ik in de hoop dat het overkwam als niets meer dan belangstelling voor mijn werk.

Mijn hoofd deed pijn van de slapeloze nacht. Ik probeerde uit alle macht alles wat er gebeurd was uit mijn hoofd te zetten. Hopelijk zou Kath geen zedig bordje met 'Verboden Toegang' gebruiken, maar gewoon ingaan op mijn vragen.

Haar reactie viel me echt mee; ze plukte alleen even een paar pluisjes van haar wolletje en trok toen een lelijk gezicht.

'Ach, ja. Een paar brieven gingen wel een beetje ver, als je begrijpt wat ik bedoel. Omdat jij er niet was, moesten we hier alle zeilen bijzetten en zelfs mevrouw Bird heeft een paar brieven doorgenomen. Je weet dat we de laatste tijd wat meer binnenkrijgen dan gewoonlijk.' Kath zweeg even, keek achter zich en pakte een stapeltje brieven dat daar lag. 'Deze kwamen gisteren met de tweede post. Ik heb ze nog niet opengemaakt, maar mevrouw Bird heeft de andere helft persoonlijk geopend. Het bleken twee zwangerschappen te zijn en één lezeres die vroeg hoe je echtscheiding aanvraagt. Daar was ze niet bepaald over te spreken.'

Ik trok een meelevend gezicht.

'Mevrouw Bird zei dat als dit soort mensen ons tijdschrift wil lezen, we eerst maar eens goed moeten kijken waarover we schrijven, en vervolgens iets moeten doen om "het moreel te verhogen".'

Ik haalde mijn schouders op en keek neutraal, maar dat klonk niet best.

Kath praatte verder en bladerde intussen wat verstrooid de brieven door. 'Wat ik zo jammer vond: er was ook een alleraardigste brief van een dame die zei dat mevrouw Bird haar echt geholpen had. Die probeerde ik haar gisteren te laten zien, want ik dacht dat ze er blij mee zou zijn, maar ze zei dat ze er geen tijd voor had. Ik heb hem bewaard, want ik dacht dat jij er misschien van zou opkikkeren.' Kath keek me verontschuldigend aan. 'Het spijt me, dat kan natuurlijk niet. Maar jij bent altijd zo geïnteresseerd in de lezeressen, dus ik dacht... Nou ja... Hoe dan ook. Ik kan hem gewoon weggooien.'

'Nee, alsjeblieft niet,' zei ik. 'Ik wil hem dolgraag zien.'

Kathleen trok de onderste la van haar bureau open en overhandigde me een brief. Ik bedankte haar en legde hem op het stapeltje post van gisteren, zodat ik hem op mijn gemak zou kunnen lezen, zonder verdere discussie. Daarna vluchtte ik naar de andere kant van de gang om alle post open te maken en te wachten tot meneer Collins binnenkwam.

Vóór mijn week – onterecht – ziekteverlof had ik nog maar een paar uur in de oude journalistenkamer doorgebracht, maar ik was er nu al dol op. Nu was ik tenminste in een ruimte waar echte journalisten gewerkt hadden; dat gaf me het gevoel dat er toch iets terechtgekomen was van mijn oude droom om correspondente te worden. Ik had een romantisch beeld van hoe het hier geweest zou kunnen zijn toen *Vrouw & Vriendin* een succesvol tijdschrift was: vol schrijvers die met veel geroezemoes aan het werk waren en intussen ideeën, sigaretten en boterhammen met elkaar deelden. In stilte wenste ik dat het op een dag, na de oorlog, weer zo zou worden. Nu knipte ik het licht aan en deed een raam open, want de muffe lucht verzette zich koppig tegen elke verandering. Daarna ging ik achter het bureau zitten dat ik voor mezelf uitgekozen had. Het stond vlak bij de deur, zodat ik in de houding kon springen zodra meneer Collins me riep, maar het bood ook een aardig – zij het gedeeltelijk – uitzicht door het grotendeels afgeplakte raam over de daken van de gebouwen aan de overkant van de straat.

Het werd tijd om aan de slag te gaan. Ik maakte de brief open die Kathleen voor me bewaard had.

Beste mevr. Bird,
Ik wil u hartelijk bedanken voor het advies dat u me zo vriendelijk toegestuurd hebt in reactie op mijn brief van een paar weken geleden.
U kent mij als 'Verliefd', het meisje met de Poolse vliegenier, dat van haar moeder niet met hem mocht trouwen.

Mijn maag kwam in opstand. Dus deze brief had Kath aan mevrouw Bird willen laten zien. Over 'op het nippertje' gesproken…

Nou, mevrouw Bird, ik kan u vertellen dat mijn naam Dolly Wardynski is, of om precies te zijn: mevrouw Mieczslaw Wardynski. We zijn gisteren getrouwd!

'O,' hoorde ik mezelf zeggen en ik sloeg verrast mijn hand voor mijn mond. Wat heerlijk om dit te lezen na alle gruwelijke gebeurtenissen van de laatste tijd.

Ik heb uw advies wel honderd keer gelezen en overal heel goed over nagedacht, precies zoals u schreef. Daardoor wist ik zeker dat het me niet kan schelen of ik na de oorlog met Mieczslaw naar Europa moet verhuizen, of zelfs naar Amerika of nog ergens anders heen. Ik weet dat het moeilijk kan worden, maar zolang we samen zijn, vind ik het niet erg. Maar ik heb er ontzettend zorgvuldig over nagedacht, en mijn man – het is zo

heerlijk om dat op te schrijven! – en ik hebben het heel goed besproken en hij heeft me helemaal gerustgesteld.
Ik maakte me zorgen over moeder, maar u hebt me geholpen om dapper te zijn! Mijn ouders zijn er niet verschrikkelijk blij mee, maar uiteindelijk trekken ze vast wel bij.
Mevrouw Bird, ik kan u niet genoeg bedanken voor uw vriendelijkheid. Mijn man heeft een gevaarlijke baan en we weten geen van allen echt wat er allemaal kan gebeuren, maar nu ik zijn vrouw ben, ben ik het gelukkigste meisje ter wereld.
Uw
Mevrouw (Dolly) Mieczslaw Wardynski
Schotland

Verliefd had het doorgedreven!

Buiten probeerde een zwak, maar kranig zonnetje door de maartse wolken heen te dringen, en mijn enthousiasme voor Dolly werd slechts getemperd door het treurige feit dat ik dit aan niemand kon vertellen. Vooral niet op de redactie van *Vrouw & Vriendin*. Maar goeie genade, wat zou Bunty het heerlijk vinden om alles over deze heerlijke, goede afloop te horen… Even was ik in de wolken.

Meteen daarna stortte ik met een klap neer.

Natuurlijk kon ik het Bunty niet vertellen. Hoe kon ik dat ook maar een seconde gedacht hebben? Een brief van een vreemde die nu alles had wat Bunty verloren had – het kon gewoon niet erger. En trouwens, ik had haar niet eens de waarheid verteld: dat ik doorging met in het geheim brieven terugschrijven. Nee, als het erom ging hoe een beste vriendin zich behoorde te gedragen, bracht ik het er niet best van af.

Nu zat ik zo in de put dat ik nauwelijks hoorde dat meneer Collins de kamer binnenkwam. Pas toen hij een stoel bij een ander bureau vandaan haalde en naast me kwam zitten, keek ik op.

Hij zei niets, maar keek me bedachtzaam aan en boog zich naar me toe met zijn handen tussen zijn knieën. In het dagelijks leven was hij mijn baas, buiten het werk de broer van mijn kersverse vriend, en sinds vorige week iemand met wie ik de gruwelijkste ervaring van mijn leven deelde. Excentrieke, wispelturige, geestige en blijkbaar ook heldhaftige meneer Collins. Het tonen van emotie was niets voor hem, maar uit de blik op zijn gezicht maakte ik op dat hij worstelde met het vinden van de juiste woorden. Het zou volkomen ongepast, maar oneindig troostend geweest zijn als ik mijn armen om zijn hals had kunnen slaan en zijn jas kleddernat had kunnen bulken. Maar dat zou de hele maatschappij op zijn kop gezet hebben.

Uiteindelijk stak hij zijn hand uit en raakte mijn arm even aan, wat op zich al extreem was voor een kantoorsituatie.

'Gaat het een beetje met je?' vroeg hij zacht. 'Je hoeft hier niet per se te zijn, dat weet je.'

Ik knikte en gaf mijn inmiddels standaard reactie ten beste: het ging prima met me. Hij trok een van zijn wenkbrauwen op en gaf geen antwoord. Hij viel niet af te bluffen, dat had ik in de afgelopen weken wel geleerd.

'Ik neem ontslag,' gooide ik eruit. 'En dan meld ik me aan om fulltime bij de brandweer te gaan werken. Of bij een van de andere diensten.'

Meneer Collins knikte. 'Aha,' zei hij.

'Ik heb er de hele week over nagedacht. Ik wil iets nuttigs doen.' Met moeite probeerde ik het hem uit te leggen. 'Dit is niet genoeg. En trouwens, binnenkort zullen ze ook vrouwen gaan oproepen. Daarom neem ik ontslag.'

Ik zette me schrap voor een 'wees niet te impulsief'-toespraak.

'Gelijk heb je,' zei meneer Collins. 'Ik begrijp het wel. Is dat je ontslagbrief?'

Hij pakte Dolly's brief, die ik nog steeds vast had, uit

mijn hand en voordat ik hem kon tegenhouden, begon hij die te lezen.

'Goeie genade,' zei hij verrast. 'Henriëtta wist warempel raad. De wonderen zijn de wereld nog niet uit.'

'Soms helpt ze echt wel,' gooide ik er haastig tussendoor.

'Mooi zo,' zei meneer Collins en legde de brief op mijn bureau. Hij draaide zich half om en keek uit het raam. 'Heerlijk weer. De lente doet haar best.'

Hij keek me niet aan, maar bleef het uitzicht bewonderen terwijl hij verder praatte.

'Fijn om te weten dat die goeie ouwe *Vrouw & Vriendin* niet helemaal tijdverspilling is. Het is jammer dat je weggaat. Ik had een paar ideeën waarvan ik hoopte dat jij me ermee zou kunnen helpen.' Hij draaide zich weer om en glimlachte me vriendelijk toe. 'Maak je geen zorgen. Bunty heeft je vast hard nodig.'

Meneer Collins kon blijkbaar gedachten lezen. Ik wilde echt bij het leger, maar als ik helemaal eerlijk was, wilde ik – tot mijn eigen verbazing – eigenlijk nog niet weg bij hem en bij Kathleen.

'Misschien wil ik hier wel aanblijven tot ik daar echt aangenomen word,' zei ik.

Hij knikte verstrooid en keek naar een van de oude prikborden.

'Goed punt,' zei hij. 'Soms zijn ze vreselijk traag met benoemingen. Hé, dat artikel herinner ik me nog,' vervolgde hij en hij tuurde naar een vergeeld knipsel dat op de muur geprikt was, alsof al zijn aandacht daardoor in beslag genomen werd en het hem helemaal niet interesseerde of hij me kon overhalen om te blijven. 'Geschreven door een jonge vent. Lang niet slecht.'

Ik vroeg me af of de regering wel wist wat een aanwinst meneer Collins zou zijn als het erop aankwam van mensen gedaan te krijgen wat hij wilde. Ze zouden hem eens op een paar spionnen moeten loslaten.

Ik bezweek. 'Eh… mevrouw Bird zei dat u misschien wat meer hulp zou kunnen gebruiken. Het spijt me als ik niet zo enthousiast klonk.'

'De omstandigheden in aanmerking genomen vind ik je geweldig dapper,' zei meneer Collins en keek me – eindelijk – weer recht in de ogen. 'Goed, vertel me eens hoe het met Bunty gaat; dan zal ik daarna uitleggen wat ik nodig heb.'

23

Veel liefs, Emmy

Meneer Collins had plotseling een buitensporige hoeveelheid werk waarvoor mijn hulp noodzakelijk was. Hoe onwaarschijnlijk het ook leek dat hij met mevrouw Bird onder één hoedje speelde en een geheime missie had om mij bezig te houden, daar zorgde hij in elk geval wel voor. Hij wilde niet alleen dat ik zijn verhalen uittypte, maar ook dat ik ideeën aandroeg voor verhalen die mensen van mijn leeftijd leuk zouden vinden. En op een dag verraste hij me helemaal.

'Kun jij voor mij vijfhonderd woorden schrijven over het werken voor de brandweer?' vroeg hij. 'Dat zou interessant kunnen zijn voor onze lezeressen, vooral met de visie van een ingewijde.'

Eerst gaapte ik hem met uitpuilende ogen aan bij het idee dat iets wat ik geschreven had misschien echt – en nog legaal ook! – in *Vrouw & Vriend* afgedrukt zou kunnen worden, maar ik deed het wel. Hij zei dat het niet slecht was voor een eerste poging en vroeg of ik hem wilde helpen met een grappig stukje over 'de ideale secretaresse'. Daarna vroeg hij af en toe of ik research voor hem wilde doen, en brieven aan organisaties wilde schrijven om informatie te vragen. Hij vroeg om ideeën voor artikelen en ik kwam over de brug met lijsten vol suggesties. Het was interessant, en het hield mijn gedachten bezig. Ik voelde me zelfs een klein beetje een journaliste. Niet dat ik me nog altijd aan die droom vastklampte, maar toch genoot ik van dit werk en daar was ik meneer Collins dankbaar voor.

Ik werkte meer uren voor het tijdschrift en bleef vaak op kantoor tot lang nadat ik naar huis zou moeten, en in de kazerne draaide ik zoveel diensten als ze me toestonden. Ik ging naar het appartement om te slapen, te eten en brieven aan Bunty te schrijven – en ook een paar aan Charles – maar verder werkte ik aan een stuk door. Als ik ook maar even ophield, zou ik weer gaan nadenken over wat er gebeurd was.

Ik deed alles wat ik kon om mijn tijd te vullen, maar één ding deed ik beslist niet meer: brieven schrijven aan de lezeressen. Hoe hard ze hulp nodig hadden en hoe erg mevrouw Bird hen negeerde – het maakte niet uit: ik schreef niet terug.

Eindelijk deed ik precies wat Bunty gezegd had.

Het leek wel honderd jaar geleden dat ze me opgedragen had ermee te stoppen, maar hoe beroerd ik me daar destijds ook onder voelde, ik was gewoon doorgegaan. Nu kon ik het niet meer over mijn hart verkrijgen dat te doen.

Het was afschuwelijk de lezeressen in de steek te moeten laten, maar ik hield vol. Mevrouw Bird was nog altijd even onvermurwbaar; ze negeerde brieven of stuurde antwoorden die de meeste mensen de stuipen op het lijf zouden jagen, en zeker als je haar geschreven had omdat je een beetje in de put zat.

In één geval zwichtte ik bijna en beantwoordde ik de brief van een meisje met wie mevrouw Bird vast en zeker korte metten zou maken. Maar die brief verstuurde ik niet. Toen ik aan de ondertekening toekwam, hield ik op en ver-scheurde hem. Geen brievenschrijverij aan vreemden meer, geen gelieg meer!

Wel schreef ik elke dag aan Bunty, in de hoop dat sommige brieven gelezen zouden worden. Schrijven was zoiets als leven, maar dan op papier, en niet in de echte wereld. Eigenlijk beviel het me beter dan het echte leven. Als je op papier iets verkeerd gezegd had, kon je dat uitgummen of helemaal opnieuw beginnen. Bunty gaf echter geen antwoord.

Dus bleef ik gewoon schrijven. Soms over grote zaken, zoals de herdenkingsdienst die voor William gehouden werd, want hoewel ik in de kerk het gevoel had dat ik wel de laatste was die daar had mogen zitten, dacht ik dat Bunty op een dag misschien wel zou willen horen hoe mooi die dienst geweest was.

Vaak schreef ik over niets belangrijks, alleen over kleine dingen die zij misschien leuk zou vinden, en altijd als iemand naar haar gevraagd had of haar het allerbeste wilde wensen, schreef ik haar dat. Dat gebeurde eigenlijk om de haverklap. Iedereen wilde weten hoe het met haar was. Iedereen wilde dat ze beter werd.

Woensdag 19 maart 1941
Liefste Bunty,
Vandaag denken we allemaal aan jou.
Moeder belde om te vertellen dat dominee Wiffle vanmorgen een speciale dienst gehouden heeft voor Bill en jou.
Moeder heeft de bloemen in de kerk verzorgd. Ze heeft jouw lievelingsbloemen, narcissen, uit de tuin geplukt. Ze zei dat zowel de bloemen als de dienst prachtig waren. De bloemen zullen er vrijdag nog staan voor Bill.
Veel liefs,
Emmy x

Zaterdag 22 maart 1941
Liefste Bunty,
Ik weet dat het vreselijk zwaar voor je zal zijn om dit te lezen en het spijt me heel erg als het te veel is. Ik dacht dat je misschien op een dag alles zult willen weten over de herdenkingsdienst, dus hier komt het hele verhaal, voor het geval dat…
O, Bunts, je zou beslist apetrots geweest zijn als je er gisteren bij geweest was. Er waren bijna driehonderd mensen in de kerk. Bills vader was natuurlijk uit Cardiff gekomen, en het eerste wat hij deed, was vragen hoe het met jou ging.
Iedereen, echt iedereen uit het dorp was er. Massa's van Bills oude leraren; meneer Lewis deed de Schriftlezing en dat lukte hem heel goed.
Bijna alle jongens uit de kazerne aan Carlton Street – iedereen die kon – kwamen, en ook haast alle jongens van de plaatselijke brandweerbrigades. Kapitein Davies hield de prachtigste grafrede aller tijden. Hij zei dat Bill een van de allerbeste mannen was, absoluut de beste. Na de dienst gaf hij me de kaarten waarop hij zijn toespraak geschreven had. Ik heb ze bij deze brief gevoegd, voor jou.
Roy en Fred brachten een boek mee. Het staat vol berichten voor jou en dingen die de mensen over Bill wilden zeggen. Ik stop het ook in dit pakket en je oma zal het bij je komen brengen om te zorgen dat er niets kwijtraakt in de post.
We hebben 'I Vow To Thee, My Country' gezongen en daarna zong het brandweerkoor 'Oh Jesus, I Have Promised', zoals jij gevraagd had. Vader zei dat hij, toen ze 'Ik zal de strijd niet vrezen als Gij aan mijn zijde zijt' zongen, dacht dat het dak van de kerk geblazen werd. Ze zongen het met heel hun hart.
Hier laat ik het voorlopig bij, denk ik.
Ik denk aan jullie allebei.
Veel liefs,
Emmy x

Dinsdag 8 april 1941
Liefste Bunty,
Hoe gaat het met je? Ik weet niet zeker of je deze brieven leest, maar ik zeg tegen mezelf dat je dat doet en daardoor is het alsof ik met jou aan het kletsen ben.
Kathleen vroeg vandaag naar je. Ik heb haar verteld dat het ontzaglijk goed met je gaat. Ze vroeg me jou deze omslagdoek te sturen. Ze heeft weer last van haar tonsillen gehad en deze heeft ze in bed gebreid. Hij is voor als je weer naar buiten mag. Ze hoopt dat je hem leuk vindt.
Veel liefs
Emmy x
PS: Ik heb het aan mijn vader gevraagd en hij zegt dat het wel goed zit: je kunt niet met tonsillitis besmet raken door de wol.

Maandag 14 april 1941
Liefste Bunty,
Je oma zei dat je uit het ziekenhuis komt. Ik ben er helemaal hoteldebotel van, echt reusachtig blij.
Het zal heerlijk voor je zijn om weer op het platteland te zijn en iedereen zal vreselijk blij zijn je te zien. Londen zal vreemd zijn zonder jou. Ik weet wel dat we elkaar niet gesproken hebben, maar het is fijn om te weten dat je vlakbij bent.
Meneer Collins vroeg hoe het met je gaat. Ik zei dat het reusachtig goed met je gaat.
Goede reis,
Veel liefs
Emmy x
PS: Ik ben van plan het weekend na volgende week naar huis te gaan voor de verjaardag van mijn moeder. Dan weet je dat, voor het geval je nog iets uit het appartement nodig hebt.

Ik bleef elke dag schrijven.
Bunty gaf geen antwoord.

24

Beste mevr. Bird, weet u misschien raad?

In de brieven aan Bunty probeerde ik dingen te zetten die ze interessant zou kunnen vinden, of soms zelfs iets waar ze misschien om zou kunnen glimlachen. Ik schreef weinig over wat ik zelf deed of meemaakte. Vrolijke verhalen zouden klinken alsof ik lol trapte terwijl zij uitgeteld in bed lag. Treurige verhalen zouden klinken alsof ik liep te klagen.

Niets wat ik schreef, was echt goed genoeg, maar ik deed mijn best.

Ik schreef ook aan Charles: brieven die eigenlijk nergens over gingen, maar wel vermakelijk moesten zijn. Ik schreef over gewone, alledaagse dingen; hij schreef dat hij dat leuk vond omdat het een stukje van het normale leven was. Hij had het natuurlijk vreselijk gevonden wat ik over William geschreven had, en hij was reusachtig bezorgd over ons allemaal. Inmiddels ontving ik regelmatig brieven van hem en dat zou ik heerlijk moeten vinden, maar ik voelde me zo'n bedrieger omdat ik hem op de hoogte hield van Bunty's wonderbaarlijke welstand, terwijl ik haar al wekenlang niet gezien had.

Bijna een maand na het bombardement kon ik er niet meer tegen. Hoewel ik besefte dat hij me waarschijnlijk nooit meer zou willen zien zodra hij dit wist, schreef ik hem de waarheid.

Lieve Charles,

Heel erg bedankt voor je laatste brieven; gisteren kwamen er twee tegelijk, mieters.

Het spijt me dat ik je deze week niet geschreven heb. Ik zit het uit te stellen omdat ik je iets heel ernstigs moet vertellen over Café de Paris. Dat had ik je al weken geleden moeten vertellen, meteen nadat het gebeurde, maar ik ben een lafaard.

Weet je, vlak voor die avond hadden William en ik ruzie gemaakt: een afschuwelijke ruzie, want ik ben heel stom geweest en heb hem ervan beschuldigd dat hij te veel risico's nam tijdens zijn werk. Het is allemaal te beroerd om er verder op in te gaan, maar ik heb dingen gezegd die volkomen onterecht waren en het is me nooit gelukt behoorlijk mijn excuses aan te bieden. Toen ik bij Bunty op ziekenhuisbezoek kwam, vertelde ze me dat Bill zich daar vreselijk druk om maakte en dat hij, toen ik te laat kwam voor die dansavond, naar me op zoek ging om het goed te maken. En toen kwam hij om. Er was nog meer aan de hand, maar in feite is het mijn schuld.

Bunty is vreselijk boos op me en dat kan ik haar niet kwalijk nemen. Als ik schrijf dat het goed met haar gaat, vertel ik eigenlijk alleen wat ik van haar oma gehoord heb.

Charles, ik ben een waardeloze vriendin voor haar geweest en daar heb ik geen excuus voor. Het spijt me heel erg dat ik je zo'n afschuwelijk verhaal moet vertellen, maar ik kan niet meer tegen je liegen. Als jij me niet meer wilt schrijven, begrijp ik dat natuurlijk volkomen.

Blijf alsjeblieft reusachtig voorzichtig en zorg goed voor jezelf, wil je?

Je eigen
Emmy xx
PS: Ik heb niemand op het werk hier iets over verteld, maar als jij vindt dat je dit aan je broer moet vertellen, begrijp ik dat natuurlijk.

Met lood in mijn schoenen deed ik de brief op de post en ik verwachtte niet ooit nog iets van hem te horen.

Toen zijn volgende brief arriveerde, durfde ik die nauwelijks open te maken.

Mijn liefste Emmy,
Dit schrijf ik in haast, want vanavond moeten we weer opbreken, maar ik moest je meteen terugschrijven. Ik heb je brief (nr. 14) net gelezen en ik zou niets liever willen dan dat ik nu bij je kon zijn. Ik zou mijn armen om je heen willen slaan en je willen vertellen dat ik vind dat je ontzaglijk dapper bent wat de gebeurtenis in Café de Paris betreft. Nu ga ik ook even heel streng voor je zijn, want je moet me iets beloven: je mag jezelf niet de schuld geven! Geen moment. Luister je, lieveling?
We mogen elkaar dan nog niet zo lang kennen, maar volgens mij weet ik zeker dat jij nooit iets zou doen om William of Bunty te kwetsen. Ik weet dat je heel veel om hen geeft. Ik hoop dat het niet ongepast is als ik zeg dat ik William een bijzonder geschikte man vond, een prima kerel, en daarom zou hij vast begrijpen dat jij het alleen maar goed bedoelde.
Het moet vreselijk voor je zijn om je zoveel zorgen over Bunty te maken. Ze zal te zijner tijd vast en zeker wel bijtrekken.
Ga door, lieveling, schrijf me wanneer je kunt – je brieven vrolijken me echt op – maar als je verdrietig of bezorgd bent, kun je het me ook vertellen, en ik beloof je dat ik dat niet erg vind.
Met veel liefs,
Charles xxx
PS: Ik zal dit niet aan Guy vertellen. x

Hij had nog nooit 'met veel liefs' geschreven!

Ik las deze brief tientallen keren. Het was zo'n opluchting en hij reageerde liever dan ik ooit had kunnen hopen. Dat was een lichtstraaltje en daardoor kon ik het ook op de moeilijkste dagen volhouden, al geloofde ik niet dat Bunty uiteindelijk zou bijdraaien.

Toch bleef ik ook haar schrijven. Elke keer dat ik een brief postte, duimde ik dat ze terug zou schrijven, maar dat hielp niet. Mevrouw Tavistock hield mijn ouders op de hoogte en op hun beurt belden ze mij als er nieuws was. Er was altijd 'heel veel vooruitgang', maar dat hoopvolle bericht werd altijd getemperd met 'maar Bunty is nog vreselijk moe' en 'de artsen zeggen dat ze echt rust moet houden'. Zelfs mijn vader wist nu geen details omdat mevrouw Tavistock een privéverpleegster ingehuurd had om voor haar te zorgen en een of andere chique arts die verschrikkelijk goed scheen te zijn.

Ik miste mijn beste vriendin ontzettend. En ik miste mijn vriend William ook. Hoewel iedereen in de kazerne zich vreselijk flink hield, wisten we allemaal dat hij een reusachtig gat achtergelaten had. Ik had er nog steeds grote moeite mee om te accepteren dat we hem nooit meer zouden zien.

Nadat Bunty uit Londen naar het platteland overgebracht was, had ik minder kans dan ooit om haar te spreken, maar ik moest toegeven dat ik aan de andere kant blij was dat ze nu minder gevaar liep. Hitler, die tot dan toe gefaald had, besloot nog eens een heel forse poging te doen ons allemaal om zeep te brengen en hoe beter het weer werd, hoe vrolijker de Luftwaffe tekeerging. De luchtaanvallen kwamen weliswaar met tussenpozen, maar ze waren weer zwaarder geworden. Dit was bijna nog erger dan toen het elke nacht raak was. Je wist nooit precies of Londen de klos zou zijn, of de bocht van Bristol, of Sunderland of Cardiff.

Je kon nauwelijks opgelucht zijn terwijl je wist dat iemand anders ergens anders het zwaar te verduren had. Hitler schoot er natuurlijk geen klap mee op, maar zelfs Joan, die de veerkracht van een gladiator bezat, vroeg somber of 'die vuile smeerlap' er ooit nog mee zou kappen.

Door extra diensten in de kazerne en meer uren bij *Vrouw & Vriendin* had ik het voortdurend druk en daar was ik dankbaar voor. Ik had er een hekel aan om alleen te zijn, maar ik had de moed niet om met de meisjes op stap te gaan, al bleven ze het proberen en lukte het hun soms om me mee te krijgen.

Het was bijna twee maanden na de ramp in Café de Paris en ondanks de bemoedigende lentezon voelde het soms alsof ik een soort robot geworden was en voortploeterde met meer fut dan ik eigenlijk kon opbrengen. Toch wist ik dat ik niet zo defaitistisch moest zijn. Op een stralende ochtend – zo'n ochtend waarop de lente de zomer leek op te roepen eindelijk eens aan het werk te gaan – marcheerde ik door de grote hal, op weg naar *Vrouw & Vriend*, en wuifde in het voorbijgaan naar de receptioniste.

Toen ik in de lift stapte, vroeg ik me af of ik op weg naar boven nog even snel een dutje zou kunnen doen. Twee journalisten van *The Evening Chronicle* stonden een belangrijke primeur te bespreken, zonder namen te noemen. Een paar maanden geleden zou ik enthousiast afgeluisterd hebben in de hoop iets van een exclusief verhaal op te vangen. Nu deed ik mijn ogen dicht en wenste dat de lift klem zou komen te zitten; dan kon ik me op de vloer laten zakken en indommelen.

'Morgen, Kath,' riep ik terwijl ik de deuren naar de lange, donkere gang van *Vrouw & Vriendin* openduwde. Onderweg naar het grotere kantoor waar ik nu bijna permanent woonde, keek ik even om de hoek Kathleens kamer in. Meestal zat ze net zo om een praatje te springen als ik, maar vandaag was haar stoel leeg en hing er geen jas aan de kapstok.

Mevrouw Bird doemde dreigend op uit haar kantoor met een gezicht als een donderwolk en het nieuws dat Kathleens moeder had gebeld: Kathleen had een akelige aanval van tonsillitis en haar tonsillen moesten eruit, oorlog of geen oorlog. Een verbijsterend vertoon van zwakheid, als je het mevrouw Bird vroeg.

'Had ze als kind al moeten laten doen,' zei ze. 'Juffrouw Lake, u zult een handje moeten helpen. Meneer Collins zal het zonder u moeten doen.'

Meteen werd ik weer in Kathleens kamer geïnstalleerd en ik kreeg een berg typewerk te doen. Daarna werd ik naar het noorden van Londen gestuurd voor een boodschap waar bijtende woorden en een pakje – dat sterk naar boerderijen rook – aan te pas kwamen.

Voordat de dag om was, had ik het grootste respect voor Kathleen. Voor iemand die niet veel op kantoor was, leverde mevrouw Bird een reusachtige hoeveelheid werk op. Je kon het niet bepaald een ontspannen baantje noemen. Alle patronen op juistheid controleren, waar Kathleen zo'n tien minuten voor nodig had, kostte mij uren. Kath wist altijd waar alles was, kende alle telefoonnummers en adressen van de medewerkers uit haar hoofd en wist, zonder ook maar de minste trammelant te maken, altijd alles op te lossen.

Ik werd ook nog op ontelbare missies gestuurd, steevast om 'belangrijke pakketten' af te leveren bij de 'goede werken' van mevrouw Bird of om in de rij te staan voor levensbelangrijke voorraden die ze onmogelijk kon missen.

Tegen het eind van die week kon je gerust zeggen dat onze hele redactie niet kon wachten tot Kathleen terug was. Ik deed mijn best, maar verstond de geschreeuwde, gecodeerde instructies van mevrouw Bird vaak niet. Meneer Collins moest aanpoten om zijn eigen administratie bij te houden en meneer Newton van de afdeling advertenties moest vaker binnenkomen. Mevrouw Bird klaagde voortdurend dat alles zo'n gezeur was. Niemand had het hart haar tegen te spreken.

Het betekende ook dat ik heel weinig tijd gehad had om de brieven van de lezeressen te sorteren, dus de maandag daarop kwam ik vroeg binnen om mijn achterstand met de post in te halen. Het was een behoorlijk opgewekt stapeltje correspondentie, te beginnen met een brief aan de filmrubriek van meneer Collins, waarin om een gesigneerde foto werd gevraagd; daar kikkerde ik echt van op. Ik kon niet wachten om het gezicht van meneer Collins te zien als hij dit las. Hij zou er een rolberoerte van kunnen krijgen.

Ik ging door en maakte een envelop open die geadresseerd was aan HENRIËTTA WEET RAAD. De brief kwam van een lezeres die op haar vijfenveertigste worstelde met 'een lastige kin'. Precies het soort brief waar mevrouw Bird plezier in had, al had ik bij voorbaat medelijden met Lastige Kin, die waarschijnlijk op haar kop zou krijgen voor een weerzinwekkende hoeveelheid ijdelheid 'op haar leeftijd'.

De volgende brief was nogal eigenaardig. Getypt, niet handgeschreven, en zonder postzegel of adres van de afzendster, gericht aan mevrouw Bird en ondertekend met 'Angstig'.

Ik draaide het papier om en begon het begin te lezen.

Beste mevr. Bird,

Weet u misschien raad?

Ik schaam me om u te schrijven, maar ik weet niet wat ik anders moet doen. Weet u, ik stel iedereen teleur. Eerder dit jaar was ik betrokken bij een luchtaanval en daarbij ben ik gewond geraakt, en nu denk ik dat ik de moed verloren heb. Zodra ik afweergeschut of andere harde geluiden hoor, schrik ik me een ongeluk.

Ik vind het niet fijn om naar buiten te gaan, zelfs niet de tuin in, en ik maak me zorgen dat ik nooit meer de oude zal worden.

Nu hield ik even op met lezen. Ik had al vaker dit soort brieven gelezen. Lezeressen die het zwaar te verduren gehad hadden, echt verschrikkelijk, maar die zich nu schaamden omdat ze het gevoel hadden dat ze niet langer hun steentje bijdroegen.

Natuurlijk zouden ze zich niet zo moeten voelen. Je kon van geen enkele vrouw verwachten dat ze gewoon doorzette na het meemaken van zoiets vreselijks. Dat realiseerde ik me nu meer dan ooit. Zelfs vóór de bom op Café de Paris had ik vreselijk te doen gehad met de vrouwen die schreven dat ze angstig waren of ineens merkten dat ze bang waren voor klappen en botsingen of zelfs gewoon bang in het donker, terwijl ze daar nooit eerder last van gehad hadden. Ik had verschillende vrouwen een vriendelijke brief teruggeschreven, en had mevrouw Bird gesmeekt een van die brieven in het tijdschrift te beantwoorden, maar ze was genadeloos geweest.

'Ruggengraat, juffrouw Lake,' zei ze. 'Dát hebben deze vrouwen nodig. Met zenuwen winnen we de oorlog niet. Ze moeten zich vermannen en doorzetten.'

Dat was mevrouw Bird op haar ergst: ze wees alles wat zij als zwak beschouwde af. Ze verwachtte van iedereen grenzeloze veerkracht en gestage taaiheid. Geen wonder dat mensen zich vreselijk voelden als ze hiertegen op moesten boksen.

Volgens mij was het volkomen redelijk om bang te zijn dat iemand een bom op je zou laten vallen. Niemand die ook maar een beetje normaal was, zou er ooit aan gewend raken. Dat betekende nog niet dat je zwak was of dat je niet wilde volhouden.

Ik beet op mijn onderlip. Misschien was ik gewoon bevooroordeeld.

Maar nee, dat was het niet. Deze lezeres had – net als alle andere lezeressen die mevrouw Bird hierover geschreven hadden; in feite net als iedereen, als het erop aankwam – wel degelijk reden om zich wiebelig te voelen. Ik wist absoluut zeker dat ze geen preek over ruggengraatloosheid nodig had, maar een beetje vriendelijke steun.

Ik richtte mijn aandacht weer op de brief.

Ik verzeker u dat ik het absoluut niet zal opgeven. Ik ga weer aan het werk zodra ze me dat toestaan en ik me een beetje beter kan bewegen. Maar ik maak me zorgen omdat ik weet dat ik zenuwachtig zal zijn, wat onvaderlandslievend en verkeerd is, en ik voel me zo n lafaard omdat ik zo diep gezonken ben.

Ik heb onlangs mijn verloofde verloren en sinds hij omgekomen is, denk ik niet dat ik ooit nog van iemand wil gaan houden.

Ik ging op het puntje van mijn stoel zitten om de woorden beter te kunnen lezen. *Ik wil niet eens met iemand praten, zelfs niet met mijn beste vrienden…* Was het mogelijk dat deze brief van Bunty kwam?

Ik mis hem verschrikkelijk, ik kan niet eens vertellen hoeveel ik hem mis, maar ik weet dat een heleboel mensen veel slechter af zijn dan ik en dat ik mijn hoofd niet zo moet laten hangen. Er zijn honderden meisjes van mijn leeftijd die oorlogswerk doen, voor hun familie zorgen en hun steentje bijdragen, en ik schaam me om toe te geven dat ik bang word, vooral als ik de sirene of vliegtuigen hoor.

Ik verwacht niet anders dan dat u me ontzettend

zwak vindt, maar ik maak me zorgen dat er weer vreselijke dingen zullen gebeuren. In uw tijdschrift schrijft u veel over wat we moeten doen voor de oorlogsinspanning. Wat moet ik doen als ik me alleen maar nutteloos en alleen voel?
Hoogachtend,
Angstig

Ik legde de brief op mijn bureau, leunde tegen mijn rugleuning en keek de kamer rond, alsof het antwoord daar misschien ergens te vinden was.

Daarna klakte ik gefrustreerd met mijn tong en keek naar de envelop. Het poststempel was Cheltenham. Dat was helemaal niet bij Bunty in de buurt en ik wist zeker dat ze daar niemand kende.

Maar toch…

Ik leek wel gek om te denken dat deze brief van haar zou kunnen komen. Wat een dwaasheid. Als Bunty wilde praten, zou ze mij geschreven hebben en zeker mevrouw Bird niet. Ik zuchtte diep en voelde me afschuwelijk.

Arme Angstig. Ik las haar brief nog eens door en voelde vreselijk mee met dit meisje op het dieptepunt van haar leven. En als Bunty zich nu ook eens zo voelde? Precies zo somber en niet eens in staat haar beste vriendin in vertrouwen te nemen?

Eigenlijk zou ik Bunty hierover moeten schrijven. Over dit andere meisje. Misschien zou ze daardoor geholpen zijn, of misschien zou dit zelfs alles wel veranderen.

Lieve Bunty,
Een van de brieven aan mevrouw Bird was van een meisje dat bang was en zich daar vreselijk over voelde en niemand onder ogen wilde komen en zich schaamde omdat ze bang was.
En dat deed me aan jou denken…

O ja, dat was precies de brief die je zou willen ontvangen nadat je half kapot geperst was en je verloofde verloren had vanwege de vrouw die nu schreef om je te vertellen hoe ongelukkig en beschaamd je wel moest zijn.

Ik schudde de gedachte aan mijn beste vriendin van me af. Eigenlijk maakte het niet uit dat deze brief niet van Bunty kwam, want het bleef ontzettend treurig. Een lezeres die bijna alles verloren had, maar ernaar snakte om op te staan en meer te kunnen doen, te reageren op de oproep om mee te helpen.

Nu besefte ik dat ik niet alleen medelijden met dit meisje had, ik was ook trots op haar. Reusachtig trots, omdat ze dapper genoeg was om toe te geven dat ze bang was.

Waren we uiteindelijk niet allemaal af en toe bang – stiekem? Al zouden we dat alleen maar aan onszelf toegeven, omdat we niemand anders teleur wilden stellen...

Ik herinnerde me hoe ik toegekeken had terwijl William en de jongens die kinderen uit dat platgebombardeerde huis probeerden te krijgen. Wat had ik me nutteloos gevoeld. Gek van angst had ik op de stoep gestaan, doodsbang dat een van hen – of het hele groepje – verpletterd zou worden. En later was ik bang geweest toen ik naar Coventry Street rende, vrezend voor wat ik zou kunnen aantreffen toen de bommen op Café de Paris vielen. En hoe vaak was ik niet geschrokken als de telefoon te vroeg in de ochtend overging, of heel laat in de avond, omdat het slecht nieuws zou kunnen zijn?

Dat had ik nooit aan iemand verteld, want dat deed je niet. De kranten en de radio en zelfs tijdschriften als *Vrouw & Vriendin* hamerden op lef en dapperheid en karakter. Ze hadden het over veldslagen die gevochten werden, vooruitgang die geboekt werd. Ze zeiden dat we allemaal ons mannetje moesten staan, onze gezinnen draaiende moesten houden, zorgen dat alles hetzelfde bleef voor als de mannen thuiskwamen, want daar streden ze tenslotte voor. Zorg ervoor dat je er nog steeds aardig uitziet, met een pittig kapsel, verwaarloos jezelf niet. Dan zou Hitler zien dat hij ons er nooit onder zou kunnen krijgen. En ook na een half jaar bombardementen moest het thuisfront draaiende gehouden worden, en daarbovenop verwachtten we van onze lezeressen dat ze een leuke blouse en het laatste beetje rouge apart hielden voor bijzondere afspraakjes en romantiek als hun mannen met verlof thuiskwamen.

Hoe vaak zeiden we ‘Goed zo’ tegen onze lezeressen? Hoe vaak kregen vrouwen van wie dan ook te horen dat ze het kolossaal deden? Dat ze niet de hele tijd van staal hoefden te zijn? Dat het niet erg was om je een beetje beroerd te voelen?

Ik wist hoe Angstig zich voelde. Ik wist dat ze een vriendin nodig had.

Het was weken geleden dat ik voor het laatst een lezeres teruggeschreven had, want ik hield me trouw aan mijn belofte – aan mezelf – om niet in de problemen te komen en Bunty niet teleur te stellen. Geen brieven meer, niets meer het tijdschrift binnensmokkelen. Negeer ze gewoon – hoezeer ik ook dacht dat ik had kunnen helpen. Maar dit was anders. Deze lezeres moest ik antwoorden en proberen te helpen.

Ik trok de bovenste la van mijn bureau open, haalde er een nieuw vel papier uit en draaide het in mijn typemachine.

Beste Angstig,
Hartelijk bedankt voor uw brief. Het spijt me echt te horen dat u het zo zwaar gehad hebt. We hopen allemaal dat u heel snel weer beter zult worden en we willen ons oprechte medeleven uitspreken voor het verlies van uw verloofde.

Zonder erbij na te denken schakelde ik over op de 'grote zus'-stijl die ik altijd probeerde te gebruiken in brieven aan lezeressen. Ik probeerde te klinken als iemand die je kon vertrouwen, die jou begreep en die je vriendin wilde zijn als het allemaal vreselijk was.

> Goed dan. Misschien vindt u dit verrassend, maar ik wil 'Goed zo' tegen u zeggen omdat u me deze brief geschreven hebt. Ik zal heel duidelijk zijn en u moet goed naar mijn advies luisteren. U bent geen lafaard, u stelt niemand teleur en in feite zou u heel trots op uzelf moeten zijn omdat u uw best doet onder de slechtste omstandigheden.
>
> U bent gewond geraakt en u hebt iemand verloren van wie u heel veel hield. Denk geen moment dat het laf of verkeerd is als u somber of bang bent. Ik weet zeker dat onze andere lezeressen het niet erg zullen vinden als ik zeg dat velen van ons precies weten hoe u zich voelt.
>
> We doen allemaal ons uiterste best om te zorgen dat we deze oorlog winnen, en dankzij meisjes zoals u zullen we die ook winnen. Somber zijn nadat er iets vreselijks gebeurd is, laat zien dat u een normaal en bijzonder fatsoenlijk mens bent. Iedereen die bij zijn gezonde verstand is, zou zich somber voelen na het verlies van een geliefde.
>
> Dat gezonde verstand is precies hetgeen waarvoor we strijden en juist daarom zal een zekere krankzinnige nooit winnen.

Ik hield even op. Ik wist dat ik gelijk had, en ik wilde dat Angstig dat ook wist. Sneller typte ik verder, zo snel dat de typemachine ratelde en de hamertjes bijna achter elkaar bleven hangen.

Overal in de beschaafde wereld zijn vrouwen zoals u, die veel om hun geliefden geven en doorzetten in bijzonder moeilijke tijden. Als Hitler zijn zin kreeg, zou niemand ooit nog om iemand anders of iets anders geven dan om hem en zijn weerzinwekkende ideeën.
Beste Angstig, u moet weten dat dat fascisme is en dat Hitler een dwaas is.
Als we op een dag ophouden met om anderen te geven en te laten zien dat we mensen zijn, kunnen we ons beter overgeven. Dus maakt u zich geen zorgen omdat uw tranen momenteel wat hoog zitten. Misschien beseft u het niet, maar waarschijnlijk hebt u gewoon een beetje te veel uw best gedaan om dapper te zijn. Wees niet te verlegen om hier met uw vriendinnen over te praten. Het is niet onvaderlandslievend om je zorgen te delen met een goede kameraad en misschien kunnen jullie elkaar zelfs helpen.

Voordat ik het laatste gedeelte van mijn brief probeerde te schrijven, aarzelde ik. Kon ik iets zeggen wat haar misschien zou helpen?

Tot slot: ik vrees dat er geen gemakkelijk antwoord bestaat als het erom gaat of u ooit weer van iemand zult kunnen houden. Geef uzelf de tijd. U zult uw eerste liefde nooit hoeven vergeten en u hoeft niet meteen een nieuwe liefde te vinden. Ik zou willen dat ik met een toverstaf kon zwaaien om u te helpen Helaas kan ik

dat niet. Maar u moet weten dat u er niet alleen voor staat.
Iedereen hier bij *Vrouw & Vriendin* weet dat u ontzaglijk uw best doet en buitengewoon dapper bent – evenals heel veel lezeressen.
We zijn buitensporig trots op het feit dat we aan jullie kant staan.

Weer stopte ik. Gewoonlijk zou ik de brief ondertekenen met 'Hoogachtend, mevr. H. Bird', en vervolgens netjes in de bijgevoegde geadresseerde en gefrankeerde envelop opsturen, maar deze brief bevatte geen envelop en zelfs geen naam en adres van de afzender.

Ik maakte de klem los, trok het vel papier uit de typemachine en legde het op mijn bureau. Daarna leunde ik op mijn ellebogen en zat met de handen in het haar – letterlijk en figuurlijk.

Mevrouw Bird zou niet eens overwegen deze brief in haar rubriek te beantwoorden. Als ik alle voorzichtigheid overboord gooide en hem in Henriëtta weet raad probeerde te smokkelen, kon ik niet hopen dat het niemand zou opvallen. Hij was veel te lang om tussen de andere brieven te verstoppen. Deze brief zou, samen met mijn antwoord, het grootste deel van de adviesrubriek in beslag nemen. Er zat niets anders op dan ze allebei in de prullenbak te gooien.

Door het open raam kwam een felle windvlaag naar binnen en de vellen papier op mijn bureau begonnen te fladderen. Snel sloeg ik er met mijn hand boven op, een beschermend gebaar.

Dat kón gewoon niet. Ik wilde niet dat deze brief verloren ging! Dit meisje mocht niet genegeerd worden; ze verdiende beter. Onze lezeressen verdienden beter. Bunty verdiende beter.

Ik stond op en deed het raam dicht. Daarna liep ik naar de andere kant van de kamer en weer terug. Mevrouw Bird kon nu elk moment binnenkomen en bevelen schreeuwen voordat ze het kantoor verliet voor een van haar 'goede werken' en de rest van het werk aan ons overliet. Wat misten we Kathleen! Sinds zij met ziekteverlof was, was er vaker trammelant geweest dan ik tijdens al mijn voorgaande weken bij *Vrouw & Vriendin* meegemaakt had.

Wie had er eigenlijk nog tijd om HENRIËTTA WEET RAAD te controleren? Wie zou het, nu Kathleen weg was, zien als de adviesrubriek er een beetje anders uitzag dan gewoonlijk? Zou het ook maar iemand opvallen als die uit niet meer dan één brief en één reactie bestond?

Het was een krankzinnig idee.

Terwijl mijn hart als een razende tekeerging, stopte ik de brief, samen met mijn antwoord, in een grote vaalgele envelop en schreef met de hand 'Mevr. Mahoney – HENRIËTTA WEET RAAD, special – voor de zetter!' op de voorkant.

Ergens in de gang bulderde een bekende stem: 'JUFFROUW LAKE? IS DAAR IEMAND?'

Zoals altijd klonk het alsof iemand een misthoorn gebruikte tijdens een seance.

'Ik kom eraan, mevrouw Bird,' riep ik terwijl ik opstond en me schrap zette voor nog meer geschreeuw.

'WAT ZEG JE?' antwoordde ze.

Ik legde de envelop voor mevrouw Mahoney in het uitlaatje op mijn bureau, zei tegen mezelf dat het allemaal goed zou aflopen en haastte me de gang op om haar oproep te beantwoorden.

25

Mijn naam is Eileen Tredmore

De vaalgele envelop ging naar mevrouw Mahoney en naar de zetter. Als ik me had willen bedenken – wat ik midden in de nacht, élke nacht, beslist wilde – was het nu te laat. De brief van Angstig en mijn antwoord zouden in het tijdschrift terechtkomen. En ze zouden bijna de hele halve pagina van HENRIËTTA WEET RAAD in beslag nemen. Zoiets riskants had ik nog nooit gedaan.

Ik probeerde het uit mijn gedachten te zetten en me op andere dingen te concentreren.

Kort daarna was het 'hang de vlag uit' geblazen voor iedereen op kantoor, want een week later kwam Kathleen terug. Ik was net op weg naar haar kamer met een voorraad kantoorbenodigdheden toen haar glimlachende gezicht verscheen bij de toegangsdeuren naar de gang van *Vrouw & Vriendin*. Ze wuifde enthousiast met beide handen, op een jazz-achtige manier, en fluisterde: 'Hallo.' Haar keel deed nog zeer, maar ze was er.

'O Kath, wat heerlijk om je te zien,' zei ik en omhelsde haar. Ik was echt dolblij dat ik mijn vriendin terug had, en dat was niet eens omdat zij het volle gewicht van mevrouw Bird op haar schouders zou nemen. Het kantoor was zoveel somberder geweest zonder haar.

'Mevrouw Bird was zo chagrijnig als een beer met hoofdpijn toen je weg was,' zei ik. 'En ze heeft aardige dingen over je gezegd.'

Dat laatste bedoelde ik als een compliment, maar Kathleen keek gealarmeerd.

'Nee, dat is juist goed,' zei ik snel. 'Ze zegt dat jij weet hoe het zit, wat ze van ons niet kan zeggen.'

'Gommie,' kraste Kathleen. We wisten allebei dat dit zo'n beetje het hoogst haalbare was.

'Ze zal echt blij zijn dat je terug bent,' zei ik, in de wetenschap dat mevrouw Bird zich nog liever voor een bus zou gooien dan dit toe te geven.

Kathleen keek verrukt en daar ging het om. Ze verdiende het ook dubbel en dwars. Het was heerlijk om haar weer terug op kantoor te hebben en mijn humeur werd meteen beter dan het in weken geweest was.

We bleven in de gang staan en ondanks het feit dat Kathleen geen kik zou mogen geven, raakten we gezellig aan de praat. De vorige dag was ik weer eens op een missie voor mevrouw Bird gestuurd, wat inhield dat ik bij warenhuis Fortnum and Mason op zoek moest naar boter in blik. Dat was werelddelen verwijderd van mijn eerdere dromen van een carrière als oorlogscorrespondente; nu maakte ik er een grappig verhaal van, zodat Kath zou denken dat alles helemaal tiptop ging.

Ik speelde net een spectaculair gedeelte van de anekdote uit – waarbij ik de rollen van twee verkoopsters, een man met een parkiet en mezelf op me nam – toen meneer Collins arriveerde – voor de verandering redelijk op tijd – en Kath erop stond dat ik het hele verhaal nog eens vanaf het begin vertelde. Ik overdreef het nog een beetje meer en voor het eerst in eeuwen werd de gang gevuld met gelach. Met een nietmachine in de lucht zwaaiend voor het effect kwam ik tot de clou van mijn verhaal.

'En hij zei: "Dat denk ik niet. Wat jij, Gladys?"' eindigde ik zwierig, en mijn collega's lachten nog uitbundiger.

Op dat moment arriveerde mevrouw Bird.

Zodra ik haar zag, wist ik dat er iets heel erg mis was.

Mevrouw Bird zweeg als het graf. Ze was geruisloos de gang binnengegleden, bijna alsof ze wieltjes gebruikte, zonder trammelant of luidkeelse aankondigingen. Haar gezicht stond niet alleen strak – dat was ik wel gewend – maar uitgesproken boosaardig.

Kathleen en meneer Collins stonden met hun rug naar haar toe, maar toen mijn glimlach verdween, keken ze allebei om en gingen snel aan de kant voor het geval ze erlangs wilde. Mevrouw Bird negeerde hen. Ze bleef mij strak aankijken.

Meneer Collins keek eerst naar haar en daarna naar mij.

'Goedemorgen, mevrouw Bird,' zei hij volkomen gepast.

Mevrouw Bird gaf geen antwoord.

'Goedemorgen, mevrouw Bird,' herhaalden Kathleen en ik als uit één mond.

Mevrouw Bird bleef mij doordringend aankijken. Ik had nog nooit iemand zo ijzig zien kijken. Niemand verroerde een vin. Toen pakte mevrouw Bird – nog altijd zonder haar blik van mijn gezicht af te wenden – een stuk papier uit haar reusachtige zwarte tas.

'Dit,' zei ze met onheilspellende stem, 'is een brief.'

Ooit had ik haar geschreeuw aan de angstaanjagende kant gevonden, maar dat was nog niets vergeleken met nu. Haar gezicht was bleek en ze zag eruit alsof ze elk moment kon ontploffen.

'Dit is een brief die aan mij geadresseerd is,' zei ze tussen haar opeengeklemde tanden door. 'Een brief die ik, bij gebrek aan voldoende personeel, gisteren zelf geopend heb. Juffrouw Lake, wilt u misschien weten wat erin staat?'

Ik speelde het klaar om te knikken.

Terwijl ze mij nog altijd woedend aankeek, gaf mevrouw

Bird het stuk papier aan meneer Collins. 'Meneer Collins. Als u zo vriendelijk zou willen zijn...'

Meneer Collins nam het zwijgend van haar aan. Ik hoopte – maar dat durfde ik niet te verwachten – dat hij een opmerking zou maken, iets zou zeggen om de stemming te verlichten – wat hij soms voor elkaar kreeg. Nu deed hij echter alleen wat hem opgedragen werd.

> *'Beste mevrouw Bird, mijn naam is Eileen Tredmole. Ik geloof dat u persoonlijk contact hebt met mijn dochter, die u waarschijnlijk kent als mevrouw Mieczslaw Wardynski.'*

Meneer Collins keek op, eerst naar mevrouw Bird en daarna naar mij. Ik was waarschijnlijk nog bleker geworden dan mevrouw Bird. Er was zoveel bloed weggetrokken uit mijn hoofd dat ik diep moest ademhalen om te zorgen dat ik niet flauwviel. Zodra ik de naam hoorde, wist ik dat ik eindelijk betrapt was.

'Lees verder, meneer Collins,' zei mevrouw Bird.

Meneer Collins schraapte voorzichtig zijn keel en vervolgde:

> *'Mevrouw Wardynski is mijn dochter. Ze heet Dolly Tredmore en ze is zeventien jaar oud. Tot vorige maand woonde ze bij mijn man en mij thuis in Uxbridge, Middlesex.'*

Ik slikte. Mijn keel voelde zo droog als een woestijn. Zeventien was verschrikkelijk jong om te trouwen, zelfs in oorlogstijd. Ik had niet gedacht dat Dolly echt zo jong was. Ze had de toestemming van haar ouders moeten hebben om te trouwen. *Ik maakte me zorgen over moeder,* had ze geschreven. *Maar u hebt me geholpen om dapper te zijn...* Daaruit had ik opgemaakt dat ze haar ouders had kunnen overhalen.

'U moet weten,' las meneer Collins, *'dat mijn dochter een paar weken geleden de benen heeft genomen naar Schotland om daar te trouwen met een eenentwintigjarige man op wie ze verliefd denkt te zijn. Tegen onze wensen in, zonder onze toestemming en – zoals ik onlangs ontdekt heb – gebaseerd op uw advies.'*

Hij hield op met lezen, haalde zijn linkerhand door zijn haar en keek mevrouw Bird aan. 'Mijn excuses, mevrouw Bird, maar ik begrijp het niet helemaal.'

Eindelijk rukte mevrouw Bird haar ijskoude, woedende blik los van mijn gezicht.

'Meneer Collins,' zei ze, 'u zult ontdekken dat juffrouw Lake een spelletje met ons gespeeld heeft.'

Ik begon verwoed na te denken. Hoe had mevrouw Bird in vredesnaam begrepen dat het bij mij vandaan kwam, en – wat er meer toe deed – wat kon ik ter verdediging zeggen?

'Ik heb…'

'… mijn handtekening vervalst. En slecht ook,' siste mevrouw Bird, wier kille kalmte zichtbaar aan een zijden draadje hing. 'Mevrouw Tredmore was zo goed om de brief in te sluiten die haar dochter ontvangen heeft, op briefpapier van *Vrouw & Vriendin*, in blauwzwarte inkt ondertekend door ene mevrouw Henriëtta Bird. Een weerzinwekkende boodschap die ik beslist niet geschreven heb, met een handtekening in een kleur die ik nooit gebruik. Een kleur waaraan naar mijn overtuiging juffrouw Lake wel de voorkeur geeft. Om nog maar te zwijgen over het feit dat u, juffrouw Lake, de enige bent die toegang heeft tot de correspondentie van mijn lezeressen.'

Ze boog zich dreigend over me heen.

'Werkelijk, juffrouw Lake,' zei mevrouw Bird, 'dit is nauwelijks een zaak die Agatha Christie waardig is, vindt u wel? Tenzij u wenst te suggereren dat iemand anders hierbij betrokken is?'

Er was geen alternatief. Ik moest het eerlijk bekennen.

'Het spijt me,' zei ik met een heel klein stemmetje. 'Ik heb het gedaan. Ik wilde helpen.'

Als ik dacht dat opbiechten een goed idee was, had ik het volkomen bij het verkeerde eind. Meneer Collins en Kathleen draaiden zich snel om en keken me aan met hun mond open van verbazing. Kathleens afgrijzen was al erg genoeg, maar meneer Collins was veel erger; hij keek absoluut ontzet.

'Het spijt me echt heel erg, mevrouw Bird,' zei ik weer. 'Het was niet mijn bedoeling om te doen alsof ik u was.'

Mijn eigen woorden klonken me steeds zwakker in de oren. Hoe kun je een hele brief schrijven, die ondertekenen met een andere naam en verzenden, en dan nog niet de bedoeling hebben te doen alsof je iemand anders bent?

Ik was er te veel aan gewend geraakt. Hoewel ik onder mevrouw Birds naam schreef, was ik degene die meeleefde en advies gaf. Dat had ik volkomen logisch gevonden. Mevrouw Bird wilde niet eens naar deze brieven kijken en ik viel alleen in om de lezeressen te helpen.

Nu klonk dat bespottelijk.

Ik omklemde nog steeds de nietmachine waarmee ik vijf minuten geleden in het rond gezwaaid had om anderen aan het lachen te maken – uitslover die ik was! Nu waren mijn handen zo klam van het zweet dat ik hem nauwelijks kon vasthouden. Ik had me vaak afgevraagd wat er zou gebeuren als ik door de mand viel, maar ik had me nooit echt voorgesteld welk effect het op mijn vrienden zou hebben.

Kathleen verdiende eeuwige roem en deed veel, veel meer dan haar plicht toen ze het woord nam.

'Mevrouw Bird,' fluisterde ze, 'misschien was het gewoon een domme fout? Emmeline bedoelde het vast niet...'

Ik kon Kathleen niet in vlammen laten opgaan omwille van mij. Het was al volkomen zeker dat ik de zak zou krijgen.

Het zou nog erger zijn als ik op de koop toe mijn vriendin meesleurde in mijn ondergang.

'Het zit wel goed, Kathleen,' viel ik haar in de rede. 'Dank je wel, maar het zit wel goed. Dit is helemaal mijn fout. Het spijt me echt verschrikkelijk, mevrouw Bird. Ik zal meteen mijn spullen gaan pakken.'

Ik schoof in de richting van de kamer om mijn jas en hoed te halen. Eigenlijk wist ik niet of ze op het punt stond de beveiliging te bellen of me zelf op straat te gooien.

Maar mevrouw Bird wilde daar niets van weten. 'Wat denkt u wel dat u doet?' riep ze, eindelijk over de rooie. 'U denkt toch niet echt dat u hier zomaar naar buiten kunt wandelen? Juffrouw Lake, bent u krankzinnig geworden?' Haar gezicht was paars van woede.

'Hoeveel?' siste ze. 'Hoeveel hebt u er geschreven?'

Kathleen keek me wanhopig aan en probeerde me overduidelijk over te halen 'alleen deze' te zeggen.

'Dat weet ik niet precies,' zei ik naar waarheid. Ik probeerde het uit te rekenen. Het was eigenlijk nogal een heleboel als je ze allemaal bij elkaar optelde. 'Eh… ongeveer… misschien… dertig? Of nog wat meer?'

Ik voelde dat ik bloosde. Als de anderen dachten dat dit was omdat ik me schuldig voelde, hadden ze het bij het verkeerde eind. Ik bloosde omdat ik de tel kwijtgeraakt was.

Aan de brieven die ik het tijdschrift binnengesmokkeld had, durfde ik niet eens te dénken. Ik wilde niet weten wat mevrouw Bird zou doen als ze dat ontdekte.

'Dertig?' Kathleen hapte naar adem, met ogen als schoteltjes – nee, als soepborden. Zelfs mevrouw Bird was verrast.

Meneer Collins mompelde een lelijk woord en mevrouw Bird keek hem vernietigend aan.

Ik durfde nauwelijks zijn kant op te kijken. Hij had zijn hoofd gebogen en wilde me niet aankijken. Zijn blik bleef strak op de vloer gericht.

Ik moest toegeven dat dertig als een reusachtige hoeveelheid klonk. Dit viel niet meer weg te redeneren als een vergissing-met-de-beste-bedoelingen. Ik had iedereen ontzaglijk misleid.

Mevrouw Bird wist zichzelf nog net in de hand te houden. 'Aha,' zei ze. 'Allemaal in mijn naam geschreven?'

Ik knikte, diep ongelukkig. Eigenlijk wilde ik zeggen dat ze allemaal aan mensen gericht waren die wij, *Vrouw & Vriendin*, hadden geholpen – hoopte ik. Dat verscheidenen van hen teruggeschreven hadden om te bedanken, onder wie lezeressen die de twee problemen die ik in het tijdschrift gezet had gelezen hadden en zich gesteund voelden door mijn antwoord. En dat Dolly Wardynski, wat haar moeder er ook van vond, getrouwd was met de man van wie ze hield en dat ze wonderbaarlijk gelukkig was. Maar ik zei niets van dit alles. Want gezien in het bijzonder kille licht van de gang van *Vrouw & Vriendin* was het schrijven van brieven onder een andere naam, om welke reden ook, gewoon helemaal verkeerd.

'Juffrouw Lake,' zei mevrouw Bird, 'beseft u wel hoe ernstig dit is? Ik weet nauwelijks waar ik moet beginnen. Bedrog, smaad, eerroof... De politie zal dit buitengewoon ernstig opvatten.'

'De politie?' Het kwam uit mijn mond als gepiep.

'Uiteraard.'

Mevrouw Bird zweeg even en voordat ze verder kon praten, greep meneer Collins plotseling in.

'Laten we ons nu inhouden, mensen. Laten we allemaal heel, heel kalm blijven,' zei hij terwijl mevrouw Bird hem ziedend aankeek. 'Henri... Mevrouw Bird, alstublieft.' Hij worstelde om de juiste woorden te vinden. 'Juffrouw Lake is bijzonder stom geweest.' Hij keek me bijna even kwaad aan als zij. 'Maar ik weet zeker dat we deze moeilijke kwestie kunnen regelen zonder hulp van de politie.'

Aan zijn gezicht zag ik dat hij razendsnel dacht. 'Tenslotte zou daar, eh... ruchtbaarheid aan gegeven kunnen worden. Ja. En dat zou zelfs nóg schadelijker kunnen zijn voor Launceston Press.'

Dat was een zeldzaam geïnspireerd argument; ik had me het liefst op hem gestort om hem honderdduizend maal te bedanken.

'Ik weet zeker,' zei hij tot slot, 'dat dit op gepaste wijze afgehandeld kan worden binnen de muren van Launceston.'

'Ik heb Lord Overton al op de hoogte gebracht,' zei mevrouw Bird.

Lord Overton. Nu voelde ik me echt misselijk. De man die overal de leiding over had. De man op wie ik koste wat kost indruk had willen maken.

Het werd echt, helemaal menens.

Meneer Collins gaf het echter nog niet op. 'En terecht,' zei hij op een toon waarin hij op heroïsche wijze respect, charme en bezorgdheid – allemaal tegelijk – wist te combineren. 'Lord Overton zal ongetwijfeld precies weten wat we het beste kunnen doen. Volledig in overleg met u, uiteraard.'

Mevrouw Bird tuitte haar lippen en dacht tamelijk lang na. Ze mocht dan buiten zichzelf van woede geweest zijn en bijna op het punt gestaan hebben de politie te bellen, maar ze was ook ontzaglijk loyaal aan de reputatie van Launceston en van Lord Overton.

'Hm,' zei ze. 'Dat zullen we zien.' En daarna strekte ze zich in haar volle, formidabele lengte uit en zei, met een gezicht alsof het de onsmakelijkste taak van haar leven was om mij te moeten toespreken: 'Juffrouw Lake, u hebt mij, mijn tijdschrift, uw werkgevers en uw collega's, die u misschien als vriendin beschouwden, in een verkeerd daglicht gesteld. Als u het geluk hebt dat ik geen aanklacht indien – en dat kan ik niet garanderen – besef dan dat uw ontslag en de referentie die ik zal schrijven een einde zullen maken aan elke carrière die u misschien had willen volgen. U wordt geschorst zonder salaris, met onmiddellijke ingang. Meneer Collins, de bestuurskamer.'

Meteen draaide ze zich op haar hakken om en stevende de deur uit.

Er viel een afschuwelijke stilte. Kathleen keek alsof ze overal op aarde liever zou willen zijn dan daar en meneer Collins keek alsof hij met zichzelf worstelde en niet wist wat hij moest zeggen.

Mevrouw Bird had gelijk. Ik had mijn vrienden verschrikkelijk teleurgesteld.

Het was vreselijk om hun gezichten te zien.

'Kathleen, meneer Collins,' begon ik. 'Het spijt me zo ontzettend. Ik probeerde te helpen. Ik dacht niet dat het...'

Meneer Collins stak zijn hand op om me het zwijgen op te leggen. 'Emmy,' zei hij, me eindelijk aankijkend, 'wat heb je in vredesnaam uitgespookt?'

Kathleen leek nog verontruster dan tevoren. Als meneer Cóllins niet wist wat hij moest doen, was alle hoop verloren.

Ik deed mijn mond open om nogmaals mijn excuses aan te bieden, maar meneer Collins viel me in de rede. 'Nee,' zei hij, 'ik wil het eigenlijk niet weten. Blijf hier wachten tot ik terug ben. En probeer in vredesnaam intussen niet nog meer te verwoesten.'

En toen vertrok hij.

Even bleven Kathleen en ik allebei stilletjes staan. Ik had geen idee wat zij dacht, maar ik probeerde verwoed iets te bedenken om haar ervan te overtuigen dat ik het alleen maar goed bedoeld had. Het was reusachtig belangrijk voor me wat zij ervan vond.

Eindelijk zei ze iets. Ze leek nog steeds vreselijk van streek en je kon zien dat ze over ieder woord goed nadacht.

'Het komt wel goed,' zei ze langzaam. 'Meneer Collins zal het wel oplossen. Het komt allemaal goed.'

Lieve Kathleen. Lieve, goedhartige Kathleen die altijd op zoek was naar de zonnige kant van alles.

'Dat denk ik niet, Kath,' zei ik. 'Ditmaal heb ik het echt verbruid.'

Op dat moment gingen de toegangsdeuren van *Vrouw & Vriendin* weer open en ik sprong een meter in de lucht van schrik, want ik verwachtte mevrouw Bird te zien, geflankeerd door de politie, maar tot mijn grenzeloze opluchting was het Clarence met een pakket exemplaren van de oplage van deze week.

'Goedemorgen,' zei hij enigszins onzeker. Het was ook voor hem duidelijk dat er iets aan de hand was. 'Ik heb jullie exemplaren van het huis.'

'Dank je wel, Clarence,' zei Kathleen en voor de verandering werd Clarence niet rood en raakte hij niet in paniek van haar stem. Hij overhandigde mij het pakket alsof het een onontplofte bom was en haastte zich zo snel mogelijk weer de deuren uit.

'Nou,' zei Kath met een dappere glimlach, 'we hebben tenminste iets te lezen tijdens het wachten.'

Ik kon het niet opbrengen om haar glimlach te beantwoorden; ik liep achter haar aan het kleine kantoortje in.

'Aan jou mag ik het toch wel uitleggen, Kath?' vroeg ik.

'Natuurlijk,' antwoordde ze; haar stem klonk hees. 'Eigenlijk mag ik niet eens praten, dus ik luister wel.'

Ze zette haar hoed af, trok haar jas uit en rekte zich uit om die op te hangen.

Ik zette het pakket op haar bureau neer. Zoals gewoonlijk hadden de drukkers de exemplaren ingepakt in een groot vel niet-doorgesneden pagina's. De vertrouwde kop van de rubriek HENRIËTTA WEET RAAD gaapte me aan.

Daar stond het. Zwart-op-wit. Onontkoombaar. De brief van Angstig, die ik in het tijdschrift geplaatst had.

26

Absoluut niets meer te verliezen

Zodra meneer Collins uit de bestuurskamer kwam, vertelde ik hem dat ik de brief in het tijdschrift geplaatst had. De brief en mijn antwoord namen het grootste gedeelte van de rubriek in beslag. Eindelijk drong de realiteit tot me door en zelfs ik vroeg me af wat me in vredesnaam bezield had.

Ik was ervan uitgegaan dat meneer Collins razend zou worden. Maar nee, na een moment van ongeloof keek hij totaal verslagen, wat eigenlijk nog veel erger was. Eerst zei hij iets lelijks – twee keer; vervolgens zweeg hij een hele tijd en toen gaf hij eindelijk antwoord.

'Het spijt me echt, Emmy,' zei hij, 'maar ik weet niet hoe ik dit nog kan oplossen.'

En toen werd ik naar huis gestuurd.

Ik wist niet wat ik moest doen.

Versuft liep ik terug naar het appartement. Ik merkte mijn omgeving nauwelijks op en deed er veel langer over dan een uur – wat normaal gesproken genoeg was. Gewoonlijk speelde ik, als ik naar huis wandelde, vanaf het kantoor van *Vrouw & Vriendin* tot het eind van de Fleet Street mijn lievelingsspelletje: raden wie van de voorbijgangers journalist was. Wie haastte zich terug naar zijn kantoor met een 'primeur van de eerste orde'? Nog maar een paar maanden geleden had ik gedacht dat ik mezelf ooit als een van hen zou kunnen beschouwen. Vandaag hield ik mijn hoofd gebogen. Nu had ik niets meer met journalistiek te maken.

Vluchtig keek ik of er een bus aankwam, maar ik wilde eigenlijk helemaal niet zitten of stilstaan. Als ik in de bus ging zitten, zou ik waarschijnlijk helemaal de moed opgeven en het uitbulken. Nu probeerde ik wanhopig bij zinnen te komen. Wat een ellendig misbaksel was ik!

Voor alle andere mensen was het een gewone werkochtend en terwijl ik langs het Victoria Embankment liep, vroeg ik me af of iemand zou vermoeden dat het in alle opzichten met mij gedaan was. Iedereen leek ergens heen te kunnen en iets belangrijks te doen te hebben. Postjongens renden langs met pakjes, gewichtig uitziende ambtenarentypes beenden in de richting van het ministerie van Bevoorrading, vrouwen uit de voorsteden knipperden met hun ogen tegen het felle zonlicht terwijl ze zich om de zandzakken heen een weg baanden vanuit de metro.

Ik wilde vluchten, me verstoppen of gewoon even helemaal niet bestaan. Hoe kon ik alles ooit nog rechtzetten?

Ik had geen idee hoelang het zou duren voordat ik iets van meneer Collins of mevrouw Bird zou horen. De gedachte dat ik in het stille appartement, omringd door herinneringen aan Bunty en Bill, zou moeten wachten, werd me te veel. Waarschijnlijk zou ik wel bij mijn ouders terechtkunnen, maar het leek me verschrikkelijk het hun te moeten vertellen.

Ik nam een flinke omweg naar huis, slenterde opzettelijk traag langs de Milbank en staarde in het water van de Thames. Vanavond zou ik met een opgewekte glimlach in de kazerne moeten verschijnen en iedereen recht in de ogen moeten kijken. Wat zou Thelma van mij vinden? En van onze heimelijke, bedachtzame gesprekken over de lezeressen? Zou ze nu denken dat ik haar alleen maar gebruikt had vanwege haar adviezen?

En Charles... Ik kreunde hardop en een dame achter een kinderwagen keek gealarmeerd naar mijn gezicht.

Zou meneer Collins het hem vertellen? Ik zou het hem niet eens kwalijk nemen als hij onmiddellijk zijn broer schreef om hem te vertellen met welk misdadig type hij zich bijna ingelaten had. Die gedachte kon ik niet verdragen. Charles had me zo lief geschreven, hij was zo bezorgd geweest na Café de Paris. Hij was altijd optimistisch en probeerde altijd te klinken alsof er van zijn kant geen vuiltje aan de lucht was, en hij had echt buitengewoon geschikt gereageerd toen ik hem over William geschreven had. Maar dit zou vast en zeker ook voor hem te ver gaan. Of hij het nu via zijn broer ontdekte of van mij hoorde, volgens mij zou hij nooit meer iets van me willen weten zodra hij de waarheid wist.

Bij elke stap voelde ik me ellendiger. Ik had zoveel mensen teleurgesteld. Maar het allerergste was dat ik mijn gedrag zou moeten verklaren tegenover mijn beste vriendin.

Lieve, lieve Bunty! Nu wenste ik meer dan ooit dat we nog vriendinnen waren. Bunty zou weten wat we moesten doen. Natuurlijk zou ik het haar niet kwalijk nemen als ze woedend op me zou zijn omdat ik er op mijn werk zo'n vreselijke puinhoop van gemaakt had. Maar ik wist dat zij me niet in de steek gelaten zou hebben.

Toen ik eindelijk bij het appartement aankwam, had ik mijn besluit genomen. Ik had absoluut niets te verliezen.

Voordat het officieel werd en mijn hele familie en al mijn vrienden de waarheid ontdekten, zou ik nog één poging wagen Bunty te spreken. Nog één keer proberen om haar persoonlijk te vertellen hoezeer het me speet.

De telefoon stond in de gang op de begane grond. Hij was jadegroen – wat zowel ongewoon als reusachtig opzichtig was – en Bunty had haar oma twee jaar geleden overgehaald hem te kopen. Mevrouw Tavistock vond hem vreselijk en zei dat het echt een telefoon voor acteurs en maîtresses was, maar ze had hem toch gekocht. Die herinnering riep een treurige glimlach bij me op.

Ik ging bij het rozenhouten wandtafeltje zitten en voordat ik van gedachten kon veranderen, belde ik de telefooncentrale en vroeg de telefoniste om de interlokale verbinding tot stand te brengen.

'Hallo, mevrouw Vincent,' zei ik tegen de huishoudster van mevrouw Tavistock toen ik doorverbonden was. 'U spreekt met Emmeline Lake. Zou ik mevrouw Tavistock mogen spreken, alstublieft?'

Mevrouw Vincent aarzelde en zei toen dat ze zou kijken of Bunty's oma thuis was. Ik wachtte, stond zenuwachtig op en vlocht het groene snoer van de telefoon tussen mijn vingers. Na verscheidene minuten hoorde ik dat de telefoon aan de andere kant opgenomen werd.

'Emmeline,' zei Bunty's oma. 'Wat aardig. Gaat het goed met je?'

'Ja, dank u wel, mevrouw Tavistock,' loog ik glashard. 'Met u gaat het ook goed, hoop ik?'

Mevrouw Tavistock bevestigde dat en vroeg naar het weer in Londen. Ik bevestigde dat het uitstekend weer was en vroeg naar het weer in Little Whitfield, wat eveneens uitstekend bleek te zijn.

Alles leek op alle fronten helemaal eersteklas te zijn.

Eindelijk, nadat ik een martelend beleefd gesprekje over de laatste lentebloemen in de tuinen van mevrouw Tavistock doorstaan had, raapte ik mijn moed bij elkaar.

'Mevrouw Tavistock,' begon ik, 'zou ik Bunty misschien even mogen spreken, alstublieft? Tenminste, als zij zich daar goed genoeg voor voelt? Ik wil haar alleen even gedag zeggen.'

Dit was de eerste keer sinds onze ontmoeting in het ziekenhuis dat ik het had durven vragen. Nog steeds draaide ik aan het telefoonsnoer – dat inmiddels ernstig gevaar liep inwendige breuken op te lopen.

Ik hield mijn adem in. Zelfs nu verder alles zo ontzettend vreselijk en hopeloos was, zou het, als ik Bunty alleen maar even gedag mocht zeggen, als ik alleen maar even mocht vragen hoe het met haar ging, allemaal niet meer zo belangrijk zijn.

Mevrouw Tavistock gaf niet meteen antwoord. Eindelijk schraapte ze haar keel en zei, heel vriendelijk: 'Het spijt me, Emmeline. Bunty voelt zich niet goed genoeg om aan de telefoon te komen.'

Er viel een korte stilte. Ik zocht naar een goed antwoord. Ik had een Plan B waarmee ik mevrouw Tavistock misschien om de tuin zou kunnen leiden.

'Puik,' zei ik en probeerde opgewekt te klinken. 'Mag ik dan misschien even aan komen waaien om haar te spreken? Een minuutje maar. Dan hoeft ze niet op te staan om aan de telefoon te komen of andere vermoeiende dingen te doen. Gewoon even bij haar zitten. Een minuutje maar.'

Mevrouw Tavistock was echter niet gemakkelijk te overtuigen. 'Het spijt me echt, Emmeline,' zei ze. 'Maar Bunty ontvangt niemand. En ze woont hier inmiddels niet meer. Het spijt me, Emmy,' herhaalde ze. 'Bunty wil niemand spreken.'

Mevrouw Tavistock mocht me niet vertellen waar Bunty precies was, maar zei wel dat ze haar de hartelijke groeten van me zou doen. Daarna gaf ik de hoop op.

27

Lord Overton zelve

De daaropvolgende dagen wist ik door te komen met lange wandelingen langs de rivier en ik probeerde niet aan de toekomst te denken. Eigenlijk probeerde ik nergens aan te denken.

Een week later was het bijna een opluchting om op Launceston House ontboden te worden, zelfs al was dit omdat ik Lord Overton zelve onder ogen moest komen. Volgens mevrouw Bird was mij op staande voet ontslaan nog een gemakkelijke uitweg. Nu de brief van Angstig in het tijdschrift afgedrukt was, leek het bijna onvermijdelijk dat ze haar dreigement om een aanklacht in te dienen zou uitvoeren. Ik had geen idee wat ik dan zou doen.

Om halfeen, vlak voordat ik bij een van de invloedrijkste mannen in de wereld van uitgeverijen op het matje moest komen tijdens een tuchthoorzitting, was meneer Collins nergens te bekennen. Ik had gedacht dat hij erbij zou zijn, maar ik was alleen. Ik kon hem niet kwalijk nemen dat hij me liet zitten. Het was nog de vraag of ik hem, of zijn broer, ooit nog te zien zou krijgen.

Ik had de eigenaar en voorzitter van Launceston Press nog nooit in levenden lijve gezien, maar toen ik, met mijn allerbeste mantelpakje aan, in het kantoor van Lord Overton stond – ik vroeg me af hoe boos hij precies zou zijn – herkende ik hem onmiddellijk. Het levensgrote geschilderde portret in de marmeren entreehal leek precies, en bovendien hing op elke verdieping van het gebouw een grote foto van hem, waarop hij eruitzag als een staatsman, streng en onverbiddelijk. Nu was hij hier: een indrukwekkende gestalte met kolossale witte wenkbrauwen, kaarsrecht achter een gigantisch teakhouten bureau – precies het soort bureau dat de waarnemend directrice van *Vrouw & Vriendin* in mijn fantasie moest hebben.

Naast zijn bureau zat mevrouw Bird, met een onvermurwbaar gezicht en stijf van sluimerende woede, in haar kolossale, zwarte, bevederde mantel.

'Zo, juffrouw Lake,' zei Lord Overton, door halvemaanvormige brillenglazen turend naar een document waarin, naar ik aannam, mijn overtredingen opgesomd werden. 'Moet ik hieruit opmaken dat u de lezeressen van *Vrouw & Vriendin* opzettelijk geadviseerd hebt met gebruik van de naam van mevrouw Bird?'

Nu hij het zo stelde, leek het zelfs nog erger.

Lord Overton klonk alsof hij iemand toesprak die dermate niet goed snik was dat ze opgeborgen zou moeten worden.

'Ja, meneer,' zei ik. 'Ik vrees dat ik dat gedaan heb. Hoewel eigenlijk niet echt expres,' voegde ik eraan toe, waardoor mevrouw Bird bijna van haar stoel viel.

De voorzitter trok een wenkbrauw op.

'Lord Overton,' zei mevrouw Bird, terwijl ze ritselend ging verzitten op haar stoel, 'niet alleen met gebruik van mijn naam, maar met mísbruik van mijn naam, waarbij de naam van *Vrouw & Vriendin* en die van Launceston Publishing in verband gebracht worden met uitermate slecht geïnformeerde, gevaarlijke nonsens. Ik huiver bij de gedachte aan wat ze andere lezeressen verteld heeft. En daarbij,' vervolgde ze toen Lord Overton keek alsof hij wellicht zou proberen te spreken, 'gedraagt ze zich zonder enige moraal door zich bij het hogere personeel naar binnen te wurmen om haar carrière te bevorderen. Het tart werkelijk iedere beschrijving. Ongelooflijk.'

Lord Overton keek me over zijn brillenglazen heen doordringend aan, zei 'Hm' en keek weer naar het verslag.

'Juffrouw Lake,' zei hij, 'dit laat zich lezen als een tamelijk buitengewone opsomming van misleidende activiteiten. Buitengewoon! Hebt u iets ter verdediging aan te voeren?'

Mevrouw Bird was altijd zo kwaad over alles dat ik er al bijna aan gewend geraakt was. Vandaag was ze buiten zichzelf van woede, maar dat had ik verwacht en ik was er beslist niet door geschokt. Maar Lord Overton was een heel ander verhaal. Een paar maanden geleden was ik nog zo hoteldebotel geweest bij de gedachte een baan in zijn bedrijf te krijgen dat ik tijdens mijn sollicitatiegesprek niet eens goed geluisterd had. Wat híj van me vond, was ontzaglijk belangrijk voor me, maar alles wat hij over me wist, stond in het vernietigende verslag op zijn bureau. *Een opsomming van misleidende activiteiten.* Geen wonder dat hij me bekeek alsof ik een vreselijke idioot was, een smet op het blazoen van zijn uitgeversimperium.

Hij mocht niet zo slecht over me denken! Ik kon de beschuldigingen niet ontkennen, maar ik kon wel proberen strijdend ten onder te gaan.

Lord Overton wachtte op mijn antwoord.

Ik haalde diep adem. 'Meneer,' zei ik, 'ik wil graag zeggen dat ik ontzettend spijt heb van de problemen die ik veroorzaakt heb. Ik heb mevrouw Bird onvoorwaardelijk mijn verontschuldigingen aangeboden en ik besef dat mijn daden onverdedigbaar zijn.'

Bijna zonder ademhalen ging ik door, want hij mocht

niet denken dat dit alles was. 'Maar, Lord Overton, in feite probeerde ik niet te doen alsof ik mevrouw Bird was, en ik wilde zeker niets doen wat haar een slechte naam zou bezorgen. Ik schreef alleen de lezeressen terug als mevrouw Bird hun geen antwoord wilde geven omdat hun problemen onacceptabel waren – er is een lange lijst van onderwerpen die we moeten negeren.' Dat laatste zei ik er terloops even bij. 'Hoe dan ook, massa's brieven klonken zo treurig en bezorgd en ellendig. In sommige gevallen was het schrijven van de brief de laatste strohalm. En sommige problemen zijn gewoon vreselijk. De vrouwen doen allemaal zo hun best met alles en hun mannen zijn weg of ze hebben hun kinderen niet bij zich. Of juist wel, maar daar voelen ze zich ook beroerd onder omdat ze gebombardeerd zouden kunnen worden, en bij sommigen is dat ook echt gebeurd. En ze zijn moe en... en soms gewoon eenzaam, en soms worden ze verliefd op de verkeerde man en –'

'JUFFROUW LAKE!'

Mevrouw Bird schreeuwde harder dan ooit. Ze was vrij lenig overeind gesprongen en zag er beslist uit alsof ze me elk moment een dreun zou kunnen geven.

'DIT IS WERKELIJK ONACCEPTABEL!'

Ik had niets meer te verliezen.

'Nee, mevrouw Bird,' zei ik met stemverheffing. 'Dat is niet eerlijk van u.'

Mevrouw Bird greep naar haar hart en haar mond viel open.

'Het spijt me echt heel, heel erg,' zei ik snel tegen Lord Overton. Ik praatte weer zachter en probeerde uit alle macht niet over te komen als een nukkig kind, maar als een verstandige volwassene. 'Maar eerlijk gezegd, meneer, wilde ik alleen maar helpen. Misschien weet ik niet veel, maar ik weet wel hoe het is om jong te zijn en een beetje de kluts kwijt te zijn. En ik weet wat alle andere tijdschriften schrijven en voor hun lezeressen doen,' zei ik bijna smekend. 'Zij geven wel antwoord op hedendaagse problemen. En ze verkopen ook ontzettend goed,' voegde ik eraan toe.

Nu was ik uitgeput en ik voelde me ten einde raad. Thuis had ik geoefend op een weldoordachte, waardige verdediging – hoopte ik – maar ik had er niets van gebruikt. Dit moest wel het einde betekenen.

Er werd op de deur geklopt, en nog voordat Lord Overton de kans had om 'Binnen' te snauwen, vloog de deur open en haastte meneer Collins zich de kamer in. Hij zag er nog slordiger uit dan gewoonlijk, met ongewassen haar en zijn stropdas halfstok. Het was beslist niet gepast om zo op een hoorzitting te verschijnen, maar dat kon me niet schelen. Ik was ontzaglijk blij hem te zien.

'Goedemiddag,' zei hij. 'Lord Overton, mevrouw Bird. Mijn excuses dat ik zo laat ben.'

Op mevrouw Birds gezicht stond overduidelijk verontwaardiging over zijn toestand te lezen, maar ze bleef zwijgen terwijl Lord Overton meneer Collins begroette en zijn verontschuldiging hartelijk accepteerde. Het viel me op dat ze op vertrouwelijke – zij het niet echt gelijke – voet met elkaar leken om te gaan.

'Goed, Collins,' zei de voorzitter. 'Dit is nogal een puinhoop, vindt u niet? Een akelige toestand. Mevrouw Bird vertelde dat juffrouw Lake feitelijk door u in dienst genomen is?'

'Dat is juist, meneer,' antwoordde meneer Collins.

'Zonder mij te raadplegen,' viel mevrouw Bird hem in de rede.

'Mevrouw Bird,' zei meneer Collins beleefd, 'ik meen dat u in die periode niet op kantoor was en het druk had met andere zaken.'

'Belangrijk oorlogswerk,' snauwde mevrouw Bird en ze zag haar kans schoon om het gesprek naar zich toe te trekken.

'Lord Overton, ik moet opmerken dat meneer Collins in dit geval niet in staat is onbevooroordeeld te spreken. Ik vrees dat hij een persoonlijke relatie met de beschuldigde heeft.'

De wenkbrauwen van Lord Overton schoten omhoog tot onder zijn haar.

'Grote goedheid,' zei hij. 'Werkelijk?'

Ik keek naar de grond. Ik wist niet waarover ik me het meest opgelaten moest voelen: over het feit dat ik 'de beschuldigde' genoemd werd – wat klonk alsof ik een moordenaar was – of omdat mevrouw Bird zojuist een nogal buitensporige suggestie gedaan had.

'Volgens mij verwijst mevrouw Bird hier naar mijn jongere broer,' zei meneer Collins kalm. 'Juffrouw Lake heeft Charles ontmoet en schrijft met hem terwijl hij overzee is, in dienst van het leger. Dat is geen geheim. Ik vind het eigenlijk behoorlijk geschikt van haar. Het is daar verrekte zwaar. Sorry, meneer… eh… tamelijk zwaar.'

Zelfs meneer Collins besefte dat je vandaag beter geen grove taal kon gebruiken.

'Eerlijk is eerlijk. Hij doet vast en zeker geweldig werk,' zei Lord Overton. 'Niet relevant voor dit gesprek.' Mevrouw Bird bromde en werd genegeerd. 'Zo,' zei Lord Overton nu rechtstreeks tegen mij. 'Juffrouw Lake, hoewel ik de geestdrift waarmee u over onze lezeressen spreekt prijzenswaardig vind…'

Mijn hart maakte een sprongetje. Mevrouw Bird probeerde hem in de rede te vallen, maar Lord Overton stak zijn hand op om haar het zwijgen op te leggen. Mijn hoop steeg tijdelijk tot grote hoogte – en stortte toen snel ter aarde.

'Het blijft een feit dat u het op u genomen hebt om zonder toestemming te corresponderen onder de naam van mevrouw Bird. U moet begrijpen dat dit volkomen onacceptabel is. Hoe goed uw bedoelingen ook waren, u hebt de reputatie van zowel uw waarnemend redactrice als van *Vrouw & Vriendin* geschaad. Ik kan werkelijk niet...'

'Ontsla me alstublieft niet, Lord Overton,' smeekte ik vertwijfeld.

'Meneer, zou ik u even mogen onderbreken?' vroeg meneer Collins tegelijkertijd.

'Wat?' vroeg Lord Overton, wiens geduld opraakte. 'Ik heb nog een vergadering. O, vooruit dan maar, Collins, maar blijf alstublieft bij het onderwerp.'

'Dank u wel, meneer. Dat zal ik doen.' Meneer Collins knikte. 'Ik kom net van de afdeling advertenties. Ik heb informatie die u volgens mij misschien wel wilt horen.' Hij haalde zijn notitieboekje uit zijn zak, sloeg het ergens achterin open en zocht al pratend naar de juiste pagina. 'Weet u, het heeft er alle schijn van dat *Vrouw & Vriendin* nieuwe levenskansen krijgt.'

Lord Overton zei: 'Hm' en: 'Ga door.'

'Volgens meneer Newton – hij is onze inkomstenman – is het aantal abonnementen de laatste twee maanden opvallend toegenomen en lezeressen hebben een aantal artikelen waar juffrouw Lake rechtstreeks bij betrokken was hun goedkeuring gegeven. Verscheidene nieuwe artikelen van mijn hand waren volledig haar idee, en ze heeft me ook gestimuleerd beter mijn best te doen op het terrein van de fictie. Daar zal ik u niet mee vervelen,' zei hij haastig toen Lord Overton zijn hand weer ophief. 'En bovendien –'

'Goed, Collins, zo is het wel genoeg,' zei Lord Overton.

'DIT IS SCHANDELIJK!' bulderde mevrouw Bird zo hard dat iedereen schrok. 'Meneer Collins is volledig bevooroordeeld. Moet ik u herinneren aan de weerzinwekkende, onvaderlandslievende brief die vorige week achter mijn rug afgedrukt is? Een zenuwachtige lezeres die bijna een halve pagina vol sympathie kreeg? Het zag eruit alsof wij voor Hitler werken. Lord Overton, luister niet naar hem.'

‘Dat is er per ongeluk in gekomen,’ loog meneer Collins met een uitgestreken gezicht. ‘De inkomsten uit advertenties zijn met negentien procent gestegen,’ vervolgde hij zijn eigen verhaal.

‘Werkelijk?’ vroeg Lord Overton met een geïnteresseerde uitdrukking op zijn gezicht. ‘In welke periode?’

‘De laatste vier weken,’ zei meneer Collins luchtig. ‘Misschien moeten we nog een pagina extra gaan drukken als we voldoende papier kunnen bemachtigen. Meneer Newton denkt dat we goede kans maken om er weer helemaal bovenop te komen.’

‘Lord Overton, ik moet echt –’

‘Dank je wel, Henriëtta!’ snauwde Lord Overton terug. ‘Ik hoor het echt wel. Goed. Onvaderlandslievend? Ik denk niet dat ik zo ver zou willen gaan. Ik heb de brief in kwestie aan mijn vrouw laten lezen en zij vond het antwoord buitengewoon vriendelijk. Zelf vond ik het gedeelte waarin Hitler een dwaas genoemd werd, erg aardig.’

‘POLI-tiek, Lord Overton,’ snauwde mevrouw Bird – halverwege het eerste woord herinnerde ze zich dat ze niet moest schreeuwen en dempte ze haar stem tot halve sterkte. ‘In *Vrouw & Vriendin*. Waar gaat dat heen? Bolsjewisme. Let op mijn woorden.’

‘Slecht nieuws voor WAT DE POT SCHAFT,’ zei meneer Collins zachtjes. ‘Kool en nog eens kool, volgens mij.’

‘Bolsjewisme? Welnee,’ zei Lord Overton. Hij begon verveeld te klinken. ‘Ik vond dat die krankzinnige goed op zijn nummer gezet werd. Zou iedereen nu zijn mond willen houden?’

Mevrouw Bird keek alsof ze ter plekke een hartverlamming zou kunnen krijgen.

We hielden allemaal onze mond terwijl Lord Overton, klakkend met zijn tong, alles grondig overpeinsde.

Eindelijk sprak hij weer. ‘Het spijt me,’ zei hij. ‘Maar het blijft een feit, juffrouw Lake... O, in vredesnaam. Is dat mijn secretaresse? Wat nu weer?'

We keken allemaal naar de deur. Daarachter hoorden we de secretaresse van Lord Overton iemand streng vertellen dat hij of zij hem nu niet kon spreken.

'Absoluut niet,' hoorden we haar stellig zeggen.

'Het spijt me verschrikkelijk,' klonk een vrouwenstem. 'Maar we moeten hem echt...'

De deur vloog open.

'Wie is dat?' vroeg Lord Overton, tot het uiterste getergd.

'Wacht!' hoorde ik mezelf roepen. En daarna veel zachter: 'Wacht.'

Daar, in de deuropening, stond – manhaftig worstelend om de deur open te houden en de kolossale, overvolle postzak die hij torste niet te laten vallen – Clarence. En bij hem stond – bleek, broodmager, met een vuurrood litteken op haar voorhoofd en steunend op een wandelstok – Bunty.

Meneer Collins liep met grote stappen de kamer door en bood haar zijn arm. Bunty nam die aan en gearmd kwamen ze langzaam samen de kamer binnen.

Bunty was hier...

Ik maakte een onherkenbaar, waanzinnig geluid – half snik, half lach.

Ik had geen flauw idee waarom ze hier was, maar dat maakte niets uit. Het maakte niets uit dat ik elk moment de laan uit gestuurd kon worden en dat alles één grote ramp was. Bunty was beter – of ten minste hard op weg beter te worden – en ze was hier, en ik zou haar eindelijk kunnen spreken.

Plotseling werd ik bang. Ik had zoveel uit te leggen. Ik kon niet gewoon naar haar toe hollen en zeggen hoeveel spijt ik had. Als ze nu eens voor iets heel anders kwam, iets waaraan ik niet gedacht had, en helemaal niet om mij te zien? Wat moest ik beginnen als ze me nog altijd haatte?

'Hallo, Em,' zei Bunty met de dapperste glimlach ter wereld – haar magere gezicht lichtte helemaal op.

Ondanks het feit dat ze er verschrikkelijk breekbaar uitzag, duwde ik Lord Overton bijna opzij om bij haar te komen en vloog haar om de hals.

'Het spijt me zo,' zei ik. Onder haar mantel was ze vel over been, voelde ik. 'Het spijt me zo vreselijk.'

'Het is goed,' zei Bunty. 'Heus. Het is echt goed.'

'Zou iemand me alstublieft willen vertellen wat er allemaal gebeurt?'

Bunty trok zich los en stelde zich voor, met haar charmantste glimlach. 'Lord Overton, het spijt me dat ik zo kom binnenvallen. Mijn naam is Marigold Tavistock. Ik heb de brief geschreven die vorige week in het tijdschrift afgedrukt werd. De brief die Emmeline beantwoord heeft. En dit is Clarence, die ik beneden tegengekomen ben.'

Lord Overtons gezicht sprak boekdelen. 'Ik heb geen idee wie deze mensen zijn.'

Ik keek Bunty met open mond aan terwijl zij verder sprak.

'Clarence had deze zak net afgeleverd. Hij is vol brieven, meneer. Aan *Vrouw & Vriendin*. Van mensen die blij waren met wat Emmy geschreven heeft. En, eh... ze waren ook blij met mijn brief.'

'Meneer,' zei Clarence. Tot algemene verbazing – ook van hemzelf – kwam dit eruit in een schitterende bariton, alsof hij in een mannenkoor uit Wales zong. Verbijsterd liet hij het hierbij en concentreerde zich op het peinzend voor zich uit kijken met een nobel gezicht dat bij zijn nieuwe stem paste.

Lord Overton had nu de blik van iemand die per ongeluk op een tentoonstelling van moderne kunst terechtgekomen is en niet de moeite wil nemen te doen alsof hij er ook maar iets van begrijpt. Hij kneep zijn ogen tot spleetjes en keek achterdochtig.

Mevrouw Bird was tijdelijk met stomheid geslagen geweest, maar werd nu echt indrukwekkend rood en bewoog onrustig in haar zwarte, met veren bedekte mantel; al met al zag ze eruit alsof ze elk moment een kolossaal ei kon gaan leggen.

'Hoe hebben zoveel mensen het kunnen zien?' vroeg Lord Overton. '*Vrouw & Vriendin* heeft een oplage van niets. Ja, ja, ik weet dat er meer abonnementen zijn, maar toch niet zoveel?'

Meneer Collins leek slecht op zijn gemak. 'Ik, eh… Nou ja.'

'Wat is er, Collins? Wat hebt u nu gedaan?'

'Nou ja, meneer, ik heb het over de brief van juffrouw Tavistock gehad met een bevriende journalist bij de Press Association,' zei Collins. 'Zij vonden het nogal een interessante invalshoek – jonge vrouwen aan het thuisfront – en telegrafeerden het verhaal door… Eerlijkheid en lef en zo. Het heeft nogal wat publiciteit gekregen. In feite maakten we er een behoorlijk goede indruk mee.'

'Lord Overton, ik dacht dat u wel een paar van die brieven zou willen zien,' zei Bunty. 'Daarom heb ik Clarence gevraagd ze allemaal mee naar boven te nemen.'

Ik had geen idee hoe Bunty dit wist. Ik was bijna even verbijsterd als Lord Overton.

'Er zullen nog wel meer brieven komen, lijkt me,' zei Bunty. 'Lord Overton, wilt u Emmeline alstublieft niet ontslaan of de politie bellen? Ze is ontzettend stom geweest, maar ze heeft het niet zo bedoeld en ze zal het echt nooit meer doen, eerlijk niet.'

Bunty keek de voorzitter aan met zo'n treurige glimlach dat ik bijna in de lach schoot. Ook ik had nu de moed hem te verzekeren dat ik van nu af aan alles zou doen wat me gezegd werd, door wie dan ook.

'Ik vrees, dames,' zei Lord Overton onaangedaan, 'dat dit

een zakelijke kwestie is en dat uw betraande ogen en treurige gezichten, hoe aandoenlijk ook, geen indruk maken. Hoe dan ook, niemand zal de politie bellen. Henriëtta, voordat je iets zegt: ik begrijp precies wat je hiervan vindt en dat kan ik je niet kwalijk nemen. De hele toestand is een schande. Maar ik wens niet dat mijn organisatie bespottelijk gemaakt wordt.' Hij wierp een blik op een fraaie klok op de schoorsteenmantel en keek ongeduldig. 'Een gearresteerde assistente zou een buitenkansje voor de concurrentie zijn. En wat de roddelbladen aangaat –'

'Lord Overton,' viel een verstikte stem naast me in, 'ik moet hiertegen protesteren. Dit is een grof schandaal. Ik zal mijn ontslag moeten nemen. Deze hele affaire,' zei mevrouw Bird, die weer op stoom kwam, 'is nonsens. Ik zal juridisch advies inwinnen.'

Lord Overton zuchtte diep. 'Henriëtta,' zei hij bijna terloops tegen haar, 'sinds je terug bent, dreig je vrijwel wekelijks ontslag te nemen.'

'Ik kan u voor het gerecht dagen,' zei mevrouw Bird.

'Doe dat alsjeblieft niet,' zei Lord Overton bijna vriendelijk. 'Dat is zo akelig modern.'

Even vreesde ik dat meneer Collins in de lach zou schieten, maar het lukte hem om er een hoestje van te maken. Lord Overton had mevrouw Bird nauwelijks kwader kunnen maken als hij haar mantel in brand gestoken had.

'Juist,' zei ze, al haar waardigheid bijeenrapend. 'In dat geval...'

Met een majestueus geruis van veren en floers stevende mevrouw Bird langs ons allen de kamer uit.

Lord Overton zuchtte opnieuw, ditmaal vrij opgewekt.

'Goed,' zei hij toen de deur dichtgeslagen werd. 'Hoe vermakelijk deze episode ook is – ik heb niet meer zoveel plezier gehad sinds 1889, toen mijn grootvader me een week in de postkamer liet werken; ja, jongeman, gaap me maar aan' – Clarence vergat nobel te kijken en viel bijna flauw – 'dit heeft veel te veel van mijn tijd in beslag genomen. Juffrouw Lake, ik vat dit niet licht op. Mevrouw Bird heeft absoluut gelijk. Uw gedrag is niet te tolereren. Aan de post te zien is het geen complete ramp, maar daar gaat het niet om. U mag niet doen waar u zin in hebt, tegen alle regels in.'

'Nee, Lord Overton,' zei ik en sprong in de houding. 'Nooit.'

'U hebt duidelijke leiding nodig, en iemand die u nauwlettend in de gaten houdt.'

'Ja, meneer.'

'Maar u lijkt wel een bepaald soort begrip voor jonge mensen te hebben.'

Hij keek me bedachtzaam aan.

'En als we op deze respons kunnen afgaan, zou u weleens iets op het spoor kunnen zijn. *Vrouw & Vriendin* maakt al decennia lang deel uit van onze familie, al moet ik toegeven dat we het blad misschien enigszins verwaarloosd hebben. Ik heb liever dat het geen schipbreuk lijdt. Ik zal dit verder bespreken met meneer Collins. Vertrek nu alstublieft uit mijn kantoor, juffrouw Lake, en neem uw vrienden mee.'

Ik verroerde geen vin. Meneer Collins keek me dreigend aan.

'U raakt uw baan nog niet kwijt,' zei Lord Overton langzaam en duidelijk, omdat ik hem onnozel aankeek. 'Blijf maar thuis tot maandag.'

Daarna wendde hij zich tot meneer Collins.

'Collins,' zei de voorzitter, 'u zult haar in de hand moeten houden. En om te bewijzen dat ze het serieus neemt, wil ik dat het aantal abonnementen in de komende drie maanden verdubbelt. Als jullie dat samen voor elkaar krijgen, zal ik juffrouw Lake misschien laten blijven.'

'Komt voor elkaar, meneer,' zei meneer Collins opgewekt.

Lord Overton keek mij weer aan en fronste zijn wenkbrauwen.

'Jongedame, u hebt verrekte veel geluk gehad. Verrekte veel. Ga nu weg en laat me met rust.' Hij zweeg even en ik wist zeker dat ik hem een glimlach zag bedwingen. 'En vertel Henriëtta in vredesnaam niet dat ik "Verrekte" gezegd heb.'

28

Je gaf de moed nooit op

Ik begon Lord Overton uitbundig te bedanken, maar hij had me de rug al toegekeerd en liep naar een dienblad met kristallen karaffen – precies zulke karaffen als ik in de kamer van mevrouw Bird verwacht had aan te treffen. Meneer Collins gebaarde dat ik moest maken dat ik wegkwam voordat de voorzitter van gedachten veranderde. Clarence sjouwde de volle postzak de kamer uit; Bunty en ik gingen voorzichtig achter hem aan.

Zodra we de deur achter ons dichtgetrokken hadden, haastte Clarence zich naar beneden. Ik begeleidde Bunty naar een grote chesterfield in de wachtkamer van Lord Overtons kantoor. Ze zag er uitgeput en echt afschuwelijk kwetsbaar uit.

Juffrouw Jackson, de secretaresse van Lord Overton, keek op van achter haar bureau, waar ze haar bewakersfunctie weer vervulde. Ik ging ervan uit dat ze zou zeggen dat we moesten doorlopen, maar ik had het mis.

'Dat is goed,' zei ze en stond op. 'U mag daar zitten. We willen niet dat hier iemand flauwvalt, dat geeft zo'n rommel.' Ze glimlachte naar Bunty. 'Ik heb uw brief aan *Vrouw & Vriendin* net gelezen. Maakt u zich vooral geen zorgen. U bent heel dapper geweest. Goed gedaan.'

Bunty leek aangenaam verrast.

'Goed,' vervolgde juffrouw Jackson. 'U kunt hier gerust vijf minuten blijven terwijl ik theezet voor Lord Overton.'

'Ik denk dat Mylord misschien al overgegaan is op iets sterkers,' suggereerde ik.

Juffrouw Jackson keek me aan. 'Hm. U hebt wel indruk gemaakt, hè?' zei ze en richtte zich daarna weer tot Bunty. 'Ik zal u ook een kopje thee brengen. Ga daar maar zitten en als u zich zo beroerd voelt als u eruitziet, doe uw hoofd dan tussen uw knieën. Niet kwaad bedoeld.'

En daarna liet ze Bunty en mij alleen.

Even zwegen we allebei. Er was zoveel gebeurd en nu het drama van vandaag voorbij was, was Bunty zichtbaar uitgeput. Ik wist niet waar ik moest beginnen.

'Jij hebt Lord Overton definitief aan de drank gebracht,' zei Bunty grinnikend. Daarna wist zij ook niets meer te zeggen en keek zwijgend naar haar schoenen.

Bemoedigd door het feit dat het echt iets voor de oude Bunty was om dit te zeggen, probeerde ik te beginnen.

'Dank je wel, eh... dat je vandaag gekomen bent.' Ik aarzelde even. 'Hoe wist je dat eigenlijk?'

'Ik zag mijn brief staan,' antwoordde Bunty. 'In *Vrouw & Vriendin*. En jouw antwoord. Ik wist dat jij het geschreven moest hebben, maar ik kon bijna niet geloven dat het er echt in stond. Uit wat jij verteld had, begreep ik dat mevrouw Bird daar nooit toestemming voor zou geven. Dus heb ik meneer Collins te pakken weten te krijgen en hij heeft me alles verteld. Hij zei dat hij probeerde alles op te lossen, maar dat het er niet best uitzag.' Ze zweeg even. 'Eigenlijk was het allemaal mijn schuld, vond ik. Als ik die brief niet gestuurd had, zou jij die niet in het tijdschrift beantwoord hebben. Ik had hem geschreven toen ik bij een specialist was, in de hoop dat jij misschien zou raden dat ik het was.'

Haar stem stokte en aan haar gezicht zag ik dat ze overspoeld werd door pijn. Daarna probeerde ze het weer.

'Dat was stom, ik weet het,' zei ze. 'Ik had je persoonlijk moeten schrijven. Maar dat durfde ik niet. Nadat ik jou al die weken zonder antwoord had laten zitten.'

Daarna keek ze ontzettend treurig. 'Het spijt me zo, Em. Ik had eerder met je moeten praten. Ik heb je vreselijk behandeld.'

Verbijsterd gaapte ik haar aan.

'Jíj hebt míj vreselijk behandeld?' vroeg ik en ik plofte op een andere – bijpassende – stoel neer. 'Maar Bunts, het is allemaal mijn schuld.'

In gedachten had ik miljoen keer geoefend wat ik zou zeggen als ik de kans kreeg, maar nu ze hier, in de wachtkamer van Lord Overton zelve nota bene, tegenover me zat, was het moeilijk om de juiste woorden te vinden. Ik was nog steeds doodsbenauwd om echt te praten over wat er gebeurd was.

'Ik heb overal een zootje van gemaakt,' zei ik eindelijk. 'Ik heb het nu niet over *Vrouw & Vriendin*, al weet ik best dat het een idioot idee was om lezeressen te gaan schrijven. Maar dat maakt niet uit.'

Ik haalde maar eens diep adem.

'Ik heb het verknald met Bill,' zei ik. 'Je had gelijk. Het is mijn schuld dat hij gestorven is.'

Bunty begon iets te zeggen, maar ik schudde mijn hoofd en ze liet me uitpraten.

'Je had gelijk over die stomme ruzies. Het waren mijn zaken helemaal niet en ik had me er niet tegenaan moeten bemoeien.' Mijn stem werd schor. 'Ik had niet te laat moeten zijn in het...' Eigenlijk wilde ik die naam nooit meer noemen. 'In Café de Paris. Het was allemaal mijn schuld. Het spijt me zo, Bunty. Echt waar.'

Bunty pakte mijn hand en hield die stevig vast.

'Nee, Em,' zei ze. 'Het was jouw schuld niet. Niemand kon er iets aan doen.' Ze beet op haar lip en concentreerde zich op wat ze wilde zeggen. 'Dat meen ik. Bill vertelde dat jullie ruzie gemaakt hadden. Hij zei dat jij geprobeerd had het goed te maken, maar dat hij je de kans niet gegeven had.'

Ze keek me recht in de ogen. 'Emmy, het kwam niet door jou. Dat mag je nooit meer denken. Als hij jou niet was gaan zoeken en ik niet op zoek was gegaan naar een telefoon om je te bellen, zouden we allebei naar onze zitplaatsen gegaan zijn.'

Haar stem beefde, maar ze wendde haar blik niet af.

'Em,' fluisterde ze, 'alle mensen in dat gedeelte zijn gestorven. Die zijn allemaal dood.'

Ze slikte moeizaam.

'Ik gaf jou de schuld, Em, terwijl jij er niks aan kon doen. Ik was zo kwaad omdat ik hem verloren had. Volgens mij wilde ik gewoon iemand kwetsen. Ik ben degene die excuses moet aanbieden. En weet je wat eigenlijk nog het ergste was?'

Ik schudde mijn hoofd. Bunty's ogen stonden vol tranen.

'Het ergste was de gedachte dat ik jou ook verloren was. Het was al erg genoeg dat hij doodging. Maar zonder jou was het alsof er helemaal niemand meer over was. Ik weet zelf ook niet wat me bezielde.'

'Onvoorstelbaar,' zei ik.

'Ik ging er niet bepaald goed mee om,' zei Bunty. 'En wat in die brief stond, meende ik ook. Ik voel me zo'n klungel. Kijk jou eens, jij zet door. Jij zou het niet opgeven.'

'Echt wel,' zei ik snel. 'Griebels, als dat mij overkomen was, zou ik de hele boel bij elkaar bulken. En trouwens, kijk maar wat een puinhoop ik er hier van gemaakt heb. Ik ben zelf hartstikke waardeloos, potjandosie.'

Bunty veegde haar ogen af en wist een glimlach op te brengen. 'Is iedereen in de journalistiek zo grof gebekt?' vroeg ze.

Ik grijnsde terug. 'Daar lijkt het wel op. Niet dat ik echt in de journalistiek ben. En tot een kwartier geleden werkte ik helemaal nergens meer. Jij kwam met Clarence en al die post aanzetten, en dat was mijn redding. Jij, en meneer Collins met zijn inkomstenpraatje.'

'Nee,' zei Bunty. 'Jouw brieven waren míjn redding, Em. Elke dag opnieuw. Ik heb elke brief die je me stuurde gelezen. Zelfs toen ik niet wist hoe ik terug kon schrijven. Je gaf de moed nooit op. En hoe erg alles ook werd, hoe wanhopig ik me ook voelde, ik wist altijd dat er een brief zou komen. Je hebt me nooit opgegeven. Daarom wist ik uiteindelijk dat ook ík de moed niet op hoefde te geven.'

Ik wist niet wat ik moest zeggen. Er was een redelijk grote kans dat ik in tranen zou uitbarsten, precies op het moment dat juffrouw Jackson terug zou komen. Ik probeerde me niet op het verleden, maar op vandaag te richten.

'Ik kan nog steeds amper geloven dat je hier naar het kantoor kwam, Bunts,' zei ik. 'En dat je bij Lord Overton naar binnen stormde. Het leek wel iets uit een film. Reusachtig heroïsch.'

'Dat was ik niet van plan,' zei Bunty met een blik alsof ze versteld stond van zichzelf. 'Ik zou alleen naar Londen gaan om te kijken of ik terug wil naar het appartement. Daar maakt oma zich een beetje zorgen over. Zij zit daar nu op mij te wachten. Eigenlijk,' vervolgde Bunty, 'maak ik me daar ook een beetje zorgen over. Alleen al, eh… al die bruiloftsdingen zien, weet je.'

'Moeder en ik hebben het een beetje opgeruimd,' zei ik zacht. 'We zijn heel voorzichtig geweest.'

Bunty keek dankbaar, maar bezorgd. 'Echt waar? Bedankt.'

'Het is er allemaal nog steeds, natuurlijk. Voor wanneer je er wel naar wilt kijken.'

Bunty beet weer op haar lip.

Ik ploeterde voort. 'En,' waagde ik, 'ben je van plan om terug te komen?'

Bunty knikte. 'Tenzij jij een nieuwe huisgenoot gevonden hebt,' grapte ze dapper.

'Nou ja, Clarence is te jong,' zei ik.

'En meneer Collins is te oud,' zei Bunty expres, en toen ik opgelaten bloosde, voegde ze eraan toe: 'Wat jammer dat hij geen jongere broer heeft.'

We lachten allebei.

'Je hebt nooit iets over Charles geschreven,' vervolgde Bunty. 'Gaat het wel goed?'

Ik knikte. 'Dat hoop ik wel. Ik dacht dat jij het niet zou willen weten.'

'Idioot! Natuurlijk wil ik het weten,' zei Bunty. 'Ik wil alles weten wat er gebeurd is. Ik heb je ontzettend gemist, Em.'

Achter de zware eikenhouten deur van Lord Overtons kantoor barstte een diep, bulderend gelach los.

Bunty en ik keken elkaar aan.

'Dat is een goed teken,' fluisterde Bunty.

'Duimen maar,' zei ik. 'Jij komt toch echt weer in Londen wonen, Bunts?'

Ze knikte. 'Als jij het tenminste niet erg vindt dat ik hiermee achter je aan stommel,' zei ze met een blik op haar wandelstok, en bonsde ermee op de vloer.

'Doe niet zo suf,' zei ik. 'En trouwens, binnenkort zoef je me weer voorbij.'

'Nou ja, ik ga er eeuwen over doen om de trappen naar het appartement op te komen,' zei Bunty. 'Ik heb oma gevraagd of ze het goedvindt als we een paar van de andere kamers in gebruik nemen. Eerlijk gezegd is ze niet bepaald dolblij dat ik weer terugga, maar als we dat willen, vindt ze het wel goed.'

Bunty hoefde het niet voor me uit te spellen. Ik wist dat het niet om het traplopen ging; het appartement was voor haar nog te vol met herinneringen.

'We zouden een kostganger kunnen nemen,' stelde ik opgewekt voor.

'Zie je oma's gezicht al voor je?' lachte Bunty. 'Die wordt gek als we dat doen!'

'Iemand die haar goedkeuring kan wegdragen,' stelde ik voor, ook lachend. 'Een behoeftige, adellijke persoon. Of iemand uit de Eerste Wereldoorlog.'

'Of van het werk?' deed Bunty, nu echt geïnteresseerd, mee. 'Op het ministerie van Oorlog zijn bendes mensen die een kamer nodig hebben.'

'Strikt geheime mensen,' zei ik. 'Of zelfs...'

'Spionnen!' riepen we tegelijkertijd.

'We zouden de kelder ook kunnen verhuren,' voegde ik eraan toe.

'O ja,' zei Bunty, warmlopend voor een nieuw plan. 'Dat zou reusachtig zijn. Mevrouw Harewood, de buurvrouw, kent bendes interessante types. Ontheemde Europeanen, vrije Fransen –'

'Die allemaal undercover moeten blijven,' viel ik haar in de rede, met een gezicht alsof ik het weten kon. 'Onze kant, uiteraard.'

'Uiteraard,' zei Bunty. 'Echt, Em, ik vind dit een super idee. We kunnen allerlei spannende mensen te logeren hebben.' Het magere gezicht van mijn beste vriendin lichtte op. 'O, Emmy,' zei ze. 'Ik ben zo blij dat ik terug ben.'

'Ik ook,' zei ik met een brede grijns. 'Kom op, Bunts.' Terwijl ze zwaar leunend op haar stok overeind kwam, gaf ik haar een arm. 'Laten we naar huis gaan en nieuwe plannen beramen.'

Dank jullie wel

Dank aan de beste mensen ooit, die *Beste mevr. Bird* onderweg geholpen, gesteund en aangemoedigd hebben tot het een boek werd. Zonder jullie zou ik nog steeds ergens op een kantoor uit het raam zitten kijken en me afvragen of ik ooit zelf een boek zou kunnen schrijven.

Tijdens het schrijven van deze roman heb ik veel gelezen: boeken en artikelen natuurlijk, en honderden tijdschriften uit die periode. Ik bedank iedereen die naar mijn vragen over het leven in de oorlog geluisterd heeft, vooral mijn ouders, die tijdens eindeloze bezoeken, telefoontjes en e-mails uitgehoord werden over hun kindertijd, en mevrouw Brenda Evans, die zich minzaam door mij liet overvallen terwijl ze van familiehoogtijdagen had kunnen genieten. Mijn bijzondere dank aan mevrouw Joyce Powell, die samen met haar dochter Jane James zo vriendelijk was mijn vragen over het werken voor de vrijwillige brandweer te beantwoorden. Mevrouw Powell, u was mijn inspiratie voor het lef van Emmy, Bunty en de meisjes van de B-dienst tijdens de luchtaanvallen. Ik hoop dat ik u en uw vriendinnen recht gedaan heb, en dat u me wilt vergeven waar ik me dichterlijke vrijheid veroorloofd heb. Als er feitelijke fouten in dit boek staan, is dat uiteraard helemaal mijn schuld.

Dank je wel, Jo Unwin, mijn kranige agent, die vriendelijk en pienter en onbevreesd en geestig is, de ultieme strijder voor een tobber als ik. Door jou is dit hele proces dikke pret geworden. Saba Ahmed, Isabel Adomakoh Young en

Milly Reilly, bedankt voor het feit dat jullie me altijd het gevoel geven dat ik een echte schrijver ben.

Aan iedereen bij Picador en Pan Macmillan: dank dat jullie vanaf het begin zo bemoedigend en enthousiast waren over *Beste mevr. Bird*, in het bijzonder Paul Baggaley, Anna Bond, Katie Tooke, Kish Widyaratna, Camilla Elworhy en Nicholas Blake. En natuurlijk vooral ontzaglijke dank aan Francesca Main voor haar bedachtzaamheid, vriendelijkheid en louter redactionele verbazingwekkendheid. Het is echt een eer om met jullie samen te werken.

Deborah Schneider van Gelfman Schneider, de vervulling van mijn droom om een uitgever in de VS te hebben, ik ben jou en iedereen bij Scribner zo dankbaar, in het bijzonder Nan Graham, Emily Greenwald en Kara Watson, die de aankomst van manuscripten volgepropt met tachtig-jaar-oude Brits-ismes zo wonderbaarlijk gracieus weten te slikken.

Alexandra McNicoll, Alexander Cochran en Jake Smith-Bosanquet van C+W, bedankt voor het rondom de planeet verzenden van Emmy en Bunty en het dagelijks riskeren van internationale betrekkingen door mevrouw Bird met hen mee te zenden. Ik hoop echt nog steeds dat jullie een grote wereldkaart hebben, en bendes houten boekjes die daar met een stok overheen geduwd worden!

Al mijn briljante vrienden en vriendinnen – in het bijzonder Katie Fforde, Jo Thomas, Penny Parkes, Judy Astley en Clare Mackintosh – dank voor jullie bemoediging en geloof vanaf het begin en omdat jullie zeiden dat ik moest doorzetten. Katie, jij bent mijn held, en dat zul je altijd blijven! Julie Cohen, dank je dat je de geduldigste, meest inspirerende mentor bent, met het meeste inzicht: een schrijvende *wing commander* van de hoogste, vriendelijkste orde. En Shelley Harris, dank voor het lezen van een eerste, onsamenhangende half-kladversie en de generositeit om mij te laten geloven dat er op een dag een echte agent zou zijn die het misschien wel zou willen lezen.

Janice Withey en Inca, die honderden kilometers met me meegelopen hebben terwijl ik alsmaar over mijn droom doorzaagde: jullie lieten me praten en hebben niet een keer gezegd dat ik mijn mond moest houden... Jullie verdienen een gouden plak voor deze zware marathon! Gail Cheetham, die luisterde, en begreep waar ik het meest om geef. En Rachel en Chris Bird, die dit allemaal zo'n beetje vanaf de eerste dag meegemaakt hebben en er altijd waren, wat er ook gebeurde. Mevrouw Bird zou trots zijn jullie naam te mogen delen, zij het uiteraard hartgrondig ontzet bij de gedachte aan wijn en hapjes die over de schutting doorgegeven worden.

En Brin Greenman, Nicki Pettit, Mary Ford, Sue Thearle en Ginetta George: voor miljoen dingen sta ik bij jullie in het krijt, maar ik koester het absoluut dat jullie als vanzelfsprekend aannamen dat ik in staat zou zijn een boek te schrijven. Met jullie als vriendinnen zou het weleens mogelijk kunnen zijn om bijna alles te bereiken, denk ik zo.

Ten slotte mam, pap, Toby en Lori: dank voor alles. We mogen dan niet talrijk zijn, maar er is geen familie ter wereld die zo hecht is. Dank jullie wel!

AJ Pearce is opgegroeid in Hampshire, Engeland, en studeerde aan de Universiteit van Sussex. De toevallige ontdekking van een damesblad uit 1939 inspireerde haar tot een nog altijd groeiende verzameling. Tegenwoordig woont ze in het zuiden van Engeland en werkt ze freelance. *Beste mevr. Bird* is haar eerste roman.